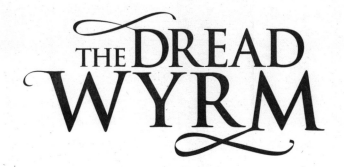

THE DREAD
WYRM

Also by Miles Cameron from Gollancz:

The Red Knight
The Fell Sword

THE DREAD WYRM

MILES CAMERON

GOLLANCZ

LONDON

Copyright © Miles Cameron 2015
Maps copyright © Steven Sandford 2013
All rights reserved

The right of Miles Cameron to be identified as the author
of this work has been asserted by him in accordance with the
Copyright, Designs and Patents Act 1988.

First published in Great Britain in 2015 by Gollancz
An imprint of the Orion Publishing Group
Carmelite House, 50 Victoria Embankment, London EC4Y 0DZ
An Hachette UK Company

A CIP catalogue record for this book is available
from the British Library

ISBN 978 0 575 11337 4

1 3 5 7 9 10 8 6 4 2

Printed in Great Britain by
CPI Group (UK) Ltd, Croydon, CRO 4YY

www.traitorson.com
www.orionbooks.co.uk
www.gollancz.co.uk

To the members of the Compagnia della Rose nel Sole

NOR...
HURAN

Squash Country

N'Pano

Thorn

INNER
SEA

Nigara

ADNACR

Ruin

La Tour

Alli
Lissen
Carak
Hawks

Cohocton R.

Hawthorne R.

The Stones

South Cohoton

The ALBIN

HARD FELLS

N

ALBA
ENCIRCLED by the WILD

SOUTH HURAN
The Great River
THRAKE
Green Hills
Middleburg
Lonika
Amfipolis
THRAKE B
To Alba
MOREA
LIVIAPOLIS
MOREA BAY
NORTH

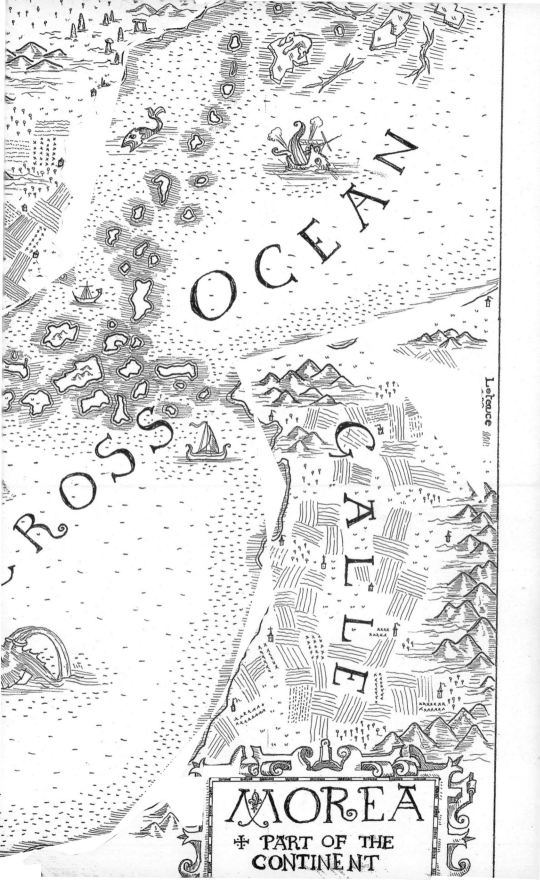

OCEAN

CROSS

GALLE

Lefeuce

MOREA

✠ PART OF THE
CONTINENT

Prologue

Across the north of the Nova Terra and the Antica Terra, spring came. It came, too, in Galle and Etrusca, in Arelat Arelat, where men had begun to learn to fear the night again, and in Iberia, where it came early. But it came first in the fields of Occitan, where husbandmen and goodwives got down to the serious work of manuring and planting fields as soon as the ice in the old furrows was thawed and the ground began to soften. Depending on the wealth of the farmer, from yeomen with stone houses and two ploughs' worth of oxen or big horse teams, to tiny huts on the edge of the debatable lands, where a young couple would harness themselves—together—to a homemade plough and the biggest child would drive it, furrows were cut in the cold ground, and every day those furrows crept north, from Occitan's early sun to the borders, and in some cases fire-blackened fields of Jarsay, and then north again to the Albin and the Brogat, where there were fewer peasants and more yeomen, but also more farm labourers with no land at all; where big iron ploughs cut the earth deeper to make up for the later sun.

South to north, then, the earth was turned wherever the hand of man reached.

And the same sun that warmed the fields warmed the tiltyards. In the castle courtyards, or by the stables, or under the outermost walls, or in the old castle ditch were the fields of Mars, the hard places where young men and a few women learned to be hard. Older men stretched aching muscles and warmed winter-stiffened joints and cursed their fading youth or their blossoming age. Men who lived by war looked at the increase of their waists and worked harder during the abstention of Lent, and their strokes at pell and quintain were quickened by war and the rumour of war. In the west of Occitan and Jarsay and the Brogat, spring brought raids from the Wild; hungry men and worse things dared the fickle weather to strike at isolated holds and forest homes, and some knights had more than practice by the first Sunday in Lent. The same dragon's-eye view that might have shown the peasants turning the earth would have shown smoke rising from burned steads all along Man's western frontier with the Wild.

In safe places farther from the threat of irks and boglins, the fighting professionals heard of the King's tournament in Harndon, and dreamed about it. New harnesses were made or fitted; mail was repaired, older harness polished and mended and polished again as warriors prepared to join the retinues of the great lords who would fight before the King of Alba himself. Words of the preparations for the tournament were spread by jongleurs and troubadours and singers and whores, tinkers and mercenaries and sheriffs and monks and any other man or woman who travelled the hideous mud of the thawing roads.

And, from Occitan to the Brogat, rumour said that in Morea, the Red Knight had won another surprising victory before the ground thawed and made himself master of the whole country. In Occitan, men sang a new troubadour song about him and his Red Company, and when a troubadour sang that he was recruiting, twenty younger sons hugged their mothers and donned their armour and rode north to a far-off place called the Inn of Dorling.

It was spring, and young men's fancy turned to war.

Chapter One

The Inn of Dorling—The Company

Sauce was standing on a table in a red kirtle that laced up under her left arm—laces that showed she wore no linen under it. She was singing.

There's a palm bush in the garden where the lads and lassies meet,
For it would not do to do the do they're doing in the street,
And the very first time he saw it he was very much impressed,
For to have a jolly rattle at my cuckoo's nest.

Aye the cuckoo, oh the cuckoo, aye the cuckoo's nest,
Aye the cuckoo, oh the cuckoo, aye the cuckoo's nest,
I'll give any man a shilling and a bottle of the best,
If he ruffles up the feathers on my cuckoo's nest.

Well some likes the lassies that are gay well dressed,
And some likes the lassies that are tight about the waist,
But it's in between the blankets, that they all likes the best,
For to have a jolly rattle at my cuckoo's nest.

I met him in the morning and he had me in the night,
I'd never been that way before and wished to do it right,
But he never would have found it, and he never would have guessed,
If I had not shown him where to find the cuckoo's nest.

I showed him where to find it and I showed him where to go,
In amongst the stickers, where the young cuckoos grow,
And ever since he found it, he will never let me rest,
'Til he ruffles up the feathers on my cuckoo's nest.

It's thorny and it's sprinkled and it's compassed all around,
It's tucked into a corner where it isn't easy found,
I said, "Young man you blunder..." and he said, "It isn't true!"
And he left me with the makings of a young cuckoo.

Her voice wasn't beautiful—it had a bit of a squawk to it, more like a parrot than a nightingale, as Wilful Murder said to his cronies. But she was loud, and raucous, and everyone knew the tune and the chorus.

Everyone, in this case, being everyone in the common room of the great stone inn under the Ings of Dorling, widely reputed to be the largest inn on the whole of the world. The common room had arches and bays, like a church, and massive pillars set straight onto stone piers that went down into the cellars below—cellars that were themselves famous. The walls were twice the height of a man, and more, hung with tapestries so old and so caked in old soot and ash and six hundred years of smoke as to be nearly indecipherable, although there appeared to be a great dragon on the longest wall, the back wall, against which ran the Keeper's long counter where the staff, and a few favoured customers, took refuge from the army of customers out on the floor.

Because on this, the coldest spring night of Martius yet, with snow outside on their tents, the Company of the Red Knight—that is, that part of the company not snug in barracks back in Liviapolis—packed the inn and its barns to the rafters, along with several hundred Moreans, some Hillmen from the drove, and a startling assortment of sell-swords and mercenaries, whores, travelling players, and foolish young men and women in search of what they no doubt hoped would be "adventure," including twenty hot-headed young Occitan knights, their pet troubadour and their squires, all armed to the teeth and eager to be tested.

The crowd standing packed on the two-inch-thick oak boards of the common room floor was so dense that the smallest and most attractive of the Keeper's daughters had trouble making her way to the rooms behind the common. Men tried to make way for her, with her wooden tray full of leather jacks, and could not.

The Keeper had four great bonfires roaring in the yard and trestle tables there; he was serving ale in his cavernous stone barn, but everyone wanted to be in the inn itself, and the cold snap that froze the water in the puddles and drove the beasts of the drove to huddle close in the great pens and folds on the Ings above the inn was also forcing the greatest rush of customers he'd ever experienced to pack his common room so tightly that he was afraid men would die or, worse, buy no ale.

The Keeper turned to the young man who stood with him on the staff side of the bar. The young man had dark hair and green eyes and wore red. He was watching the common room with the satisfaction that an angel might show for the good works of the pious.

"Your blighted company and the drove at the same time? Couldn't you have come a week apart? There won't be enough forage for you in the hills." The Keeper sounded shrill, even to his own ears.

Gabriel Muriens, the Red Knight, the Captain, the Megas Dukas, the Duke of Thrake, and possessor of another dozen titles heaped on him by a grateful Emperor, took a long pull from his own jack of black, sweet winter ale and beamed. "We'll have forage," he said. "It's been warmer in the Brogat. It's spring on the Albin." He smiled. "And this is only a tithe of my company." The smile grew warmer as he watched the recruiting table set against the wall. The adventurous young of six counties and three nations were cued up. "But it's growing," he added.

Forty of the Keeper's people, most in his livery and all his kin, stood like soldiers at the long counter and served ale at an astounding rate. Gabriel watched them with the pleasure that a professional receives in watching others practise their craft—he enjoyed the smooth efficiency with which the Keeper's wife kept her tallies, the speed with which money was collected or tally sticks were notched, and the ready ease with which casks were broached, emptied into pitchers, the said pitchers filled flagons or jacks or battered mugs and cans, all the while the staff moving up to the counter and then back to the broached kegs with the steady regularity of a company of crossbowmen loosing bolts by rotation and volley.

"They all seem to have coin to spend," the Keeper admitted grudgingly. His elder daughter Sarah—a beautiful girl with red hair, married and widowed and now with a bairn, currently held by a cousin—stood where Sauce had been and sang an old song—a very old song. It had no chorus, and the Hillmen began to make sounds—like a low polyphonic hum—to accompany her singing. When one of the Morean musicians began to pluck the tune on his mandolin, a rough hand closed on his shoulder and he ceased.

The Keeper watched his daughter for long enough that his wife stopped taking money and looked at *him*. But then he shrugged. "They have money, as I say. You had some adventures out east, I hear?"

The Red Knight settled his shoulder comfortably into the corner between a low shelf and a heavy oak cupboard behind the bar. "We did," he said.

The Keeper met his eye. "I've heard all the news, and none of it makes much sense. Tell it me, if you'd be so kind."

Gabriel paused to finish his ale and look at the bottom of his silver cup. Then he gave the Keeper a wry smile. "It's not a brief story," he said.

The Keeper raised an eyebrow and glanced out at the sea of men. Ser Alcaeus was being called for by the crowd, and his name was chanted. "I couldn't leave you even if I wanted," the Keeper said. "They'd lynch me."

Gabriel shrugged. "So. Where do you want me to begin?"

Sarah, flushed from the effort of singing, came under the bar and took her baby back from her cousin. She grinned at the Red Knight. "You're going to tell a story?" she said. "Christ on the cross, Da! Everyone will want to hear!"

Gabriel nodded. Ale had magicked its way into his silver cup. The magick had been performed by a muscular young woman with a fine lace cap. She smiled at him.

"It's not an easy story to start, sweeting." He returned the serving girl's smile with genteel interest.

Sarah wasn't old enough to take much ambiguity. "Start at the beginning!" she said.

Gabriel made an odd motion with his mouth, almost like a rabbit moving its nose. "There is no beginning," he said. "It just goes on and on into the past—an endless tale of motion and stillness."

The Keeper rolled his eyes.

Gabriel realized he'd had too much to drink. "Fine. You recall the fight at Lissen Carak."

Just behind the Red Knight, Tom Lachlan roared his dangerous laugh. Gabriel Muriens snapped his head around, and Lachlan—the Drover, now, almost seven feet of tartan- and grey-clad muscle, with a broad, silver-mounted belt and a sword as long as a shepherd's crook—flipped the gate back on the bar and stepped through. "Boyo, we all remember the fight at Lissen Carak. That was a fight."

Gabriel shrugged. "The magister who now styles himself Thorn—" He smiled grimly, paused, and pointed at a glass-shielded candle on the cupboard. A dozen moths of various sizes flitted about it.

Across the press of the crowd, Mag felt the pull of *ops*. She tensed.

He stood on the bright new mosaic floor of his memory. Prudentia stood once more on her plinth, and her statue was now a warm ivory rather than a cold marble, the features more mobile than they had been in his adolescence and her hair the same grey-black he remembered from his youth.

He knew in his heart that she was now a simulacrum not an embodied spirit, but she was the last gift that Harmodius the magister had left him, and he loved having her back.

"Immolate tinea consecutio aedificium," he said.

Prudentia frowned. "Isn't that a bit…dramatic?" she asked.

He shrugged. "I'm renowned for my arrogance and my dramatic flair," he

6

said. "He'll be blind and with a little luck, he'll attribute it to the said arrogance. Consider it a smokescreen for our visitor. If he's coming."

She didn't shrug. But somehow she conveyed a shrug, perhaps a sniff of disapproval, without moving an ivory muscle.

"Katherine! Thales! Iskander!" he said softly, and his memory palace began to spin.

The main room—the casting chamber—of his palace was constructed, or remembered, as a dome held aloft with three separate sets of arches. In among the arches were nooks containing statues of worthies; his last year as a practitioner had clarified and enhanced his skills to add another row.

On the bottom row were the bases of his power—represented by thirteen saints of the church, six men, six women, and an androgynous Saint Michael standing between them. Above the saints stood another tier, this one of the philosophers who had informed his youth—ancients of one sect or another from various of the Archaic eras. But now, above them stood a new tier; twelve worthies of a more modern age; six women and six men and one cloaked figure. Harmodius had installed them, and Gabriel had some reservations about what they might mean—but he knew Saint Aetius, who killed his emperor's family; he knew King Jean le Preux, who stopped the Irk Conquest of Etrusca after the catastrophic collapse of the Archaic world; he knew Livia the empress and Argentia the great war queen of Iberia.

As he called the names, the statues he indicated moved—indeed, the whole tier on which they stood moved until all three tiers of statues had moved the figures he named to the correct position over the great talismanic symbol that guarded the green door at the end of the chamber. Recently, there had appeared another door, exactly opposite the green door—a small red door with a grille. He knew what lay there, but he went out of his way not to go too close to it. And set in the floor by Prudentia's plinth was a bronze disc with silver letters and a small lever. Gabriel had designed it himself. He hoped never to use it.

"Pisces," he said.

Immediately under the lowest tier of statues there was a band. The band looked like bronze, and on it were repoussé—apparently—and engraved and decorated in gold and silver and enamel a set of thirteen zodiacal symbols. This band also rotated, although it did so in the opposite direction to the statues.

Clear golden sunlight fell through the great carved crystal that was the dome above them, and it struck the fish of pisces and coalesced into a golden beam.

The great green door opened. Beyond it was a sparkling grate, as if someone had built a portcullis of white-hot iron. Through its grid came a green radiance that suffused the casting chamber and yet was somehow defined by the golden light of the dome.

He grinned in satisfaction and snapped his fingers. Every moth in the great inn fell to the floor, dead.

Sarah laughed. "Now that's a trick," she said. "How about mice?"

Her son, just four months old, looked at her with goobering love and tried to find her nipple with his mouth.

Gabriel laughed. "As I was saying, the magister who now styles himself Thorn, once known as Richard Plangere, led an army of the Wild against Lissen Carak. He enlisted all the usual allies: Western boglins, stone trolls, some Golden Bears of the mountain tribes and some disaffected irks from the Lakes; wyverns and wardens. All of the Wild that's easy to seduce, he took for his own. He also managed to sway the Sossag of the Great House, those who live in the Squash Country north of the inland sea."

"And they killed Hector! God's curse on them." Sarah's hate for Hector's killer was as bright as her hair.

The Red Knight looked at the young woman and shook his head. "I can't join you in the curse, sweeting. They have Thorn as a houseguest, now. They left him, you know. And—" He looked at the Drover. "The Sossag and the Huran would see *us* as the murdering savages who stole their land."

"A thousand years ago!" Bad Tom spat.

Gabriel shrugged. At his back, Ser Alcaeus was playing a kithara from the ancient world and singing an ancient song in a strange, eerie voice. Because every word he sang was in the true Archaic, the air shimmered with *ops* and *potentia*.

Ser Michael slipped under the gate of the bar and found space to lean. Kaitlin, his wife, now so heavily pregnant that she waddled instead of walking, was already snug in one of the inn's better beds. Behind him, Sauce—Ser Alison—glared at a Hillman until he pushed more strongly against his mates and made room for her slight form to ease by him.

He made a natural, but ill-judged, decision to run his hand over her body as she passed, and found himself wheezing on the hard oak boards. Her paramour, Count Zac, stepped on the fallen Hillman and vaulted *over* the bar.

The Hillman rose, his face a study in rage, to find Bad Tom's snout within a hand's breadth of his own. He flinched.

Tom handed the man—one of his own—a full flagon of ale. "Go drink it off," he said.

The Keeper glared at the incursion of Albans now encroaching on the smooth delivery of ale. "Didn't I rent you a private room?" he asked the captain.

"Do you want to hear this tale, or not?" the captain said.

The Keeper grunted.

"So Thorn—" Every man and woman in earshot was aware that the captain or the duke—or whatever tomfool title he went by these days—had just said Thorn's name three times.

Three hundred Albin leagues north and west, Thorn stood in a late-winter snow shower. He stood on the easternmost point of the island he had made his own, his place of power, and great breakers of the salt-less inner sea slammed against the rock of the island's coast and rose ten times the height of a man into the air, driven by the strong east wind.

Out in the bay, the ice was breaking.

Thorn had come to this exposed place to prepare a working—a set of workings, a nest of workings—against his target: Ghause, wife of the Earl of Westwall. He felt his name—like the whisper of a moth's wings in the air close to a man's face on a hot summer night. But many said his name aloud, in whispers, often enough that he didn't always pay heed. But in this case, the naming was accompanied by a burst of power that even across the circle of the world made itself felt in the *aethereal.*

The second calling was softer. But such things run in threes, and no user of the art could ever be so ignorant as to attract his attention and leave the third naming incomplete.

The third use was casual—contemptuous. Thorn's sticklike, bony hands flinched.

But the Dark Sun was no casual enemy, and he stood in a place of power surrounded by friends. And he had made Thorn blind, as he did on a regular basis. Carefully, with the forced calm that, in a mere man, would have involved the gritting of teeth, Thorn mended the small gap in the *aether* made by the calling of his name, and went back to crafting his working.

But his patience had been interrupted and his rage—Thorn thought dimly around the black hole in his memory that once he had been *against* rage—flowed out. Some of the rage he funnelled into his working against Ghause—what better revenge? But still he felt that the Dark Sun made him small, and he hated.

And so, without further thought, he acted. A raid was redirected. A sentry was killed. A warden—a daemon lord, as men would call him—was suborned, his sense of reality undermined and conquered.

Try that, mortal man, Thorn thought, and went back to his casting.

In doing so, like a bird disturbed in making a spring nest, he dropped a twig. But consumed by rage and hate, he didn't notice.

"Attacked Lissen Carak, and we beat him. He made a dozen mistakes to every one we made—eh, Tom?" Gabriel smiled.

The giant Hillman shrugged. "Never heard you admit we made any mistakes at all."

Ser Gavin chose to lean against the bar on the other side. "Imagine how Jehan would tell this tale if he was here," he said.

"Then it would be nothing *but* my mistakes," Gabriel said, but with every other man and woman in red, he raised his cup and drank.

"Any road, we beat him," Tom said. "But it wasn't no Chaluns, was it? Nor a Battle of Chevin." Both battles—a thousand years and more apart—had been glorious and costly victories of the forces of men over the Wild.

Gabriel shrugged. "No—it was more like a skirmish. We won a fight in the woods, and then another around the fortress. But we didn't kill enough boglins to change anything." He shrugged. "We didn't kill Plangere or change his mind." He looked around. "Still—we're not dead. Round one to us. Eh?"

Bad Tom raised his mug and drank.

"In summer we rode east to the Empire. To Morea."

"That's more like it," said the Keeper.

"It's a tangled thread. The Emperor wanted to hire us, but we never knew what for, because by the time we heard, he'd been taken captive and his daughter Irene was on the throne. And Duke Andronicus was trying to take the city."

"By which our duke means Liviapolis," Wilful Murder said to his awe-struck new apprentice archer, Diccon, a boy so thin and yet so muscular that most of the women in the common room had noticed him. "Biggest fewkin' city in the world." Wilful knew what it meant when all the officers gathered, and he'd wormed his way patiently into the story circle.

The Keeper raised an eyebrow. His daughter laughed. "Way I hear it, she had 'im taken so she could have the power."

"Nah, that's just rumour," her father said.

The Red Knight's companions didn't say a thing. They didn't even exchange looks.

"We arrived," the captain said with relish, "in the very nick of time. We routed the usurper—"

Tom snorted. Michael looked away, and Sauce made a rude gesture. "We almost got our arses handed to us," she said.

The captain raised an eyebrow. "And after a brief winter campaign—"

"Jesu!" spat Sauce. "You're leaving out the whole story!"

"By Tar's tits!" Bad Tom said.

Just for a moment, at his oath, a tiny flawed silence fell so that his words seemed to carry.

"What did you just say?" Gabriel asked, and his brother Gavin looked as if one of Tom's big fists had struck him.

Bad Tom frowned. "It's a Hillman's oath," he said.

Gabriel was staring at him. "Really?" he asked. He sighed. "At any rate, after a brief but very successful winter campaign, we destroyed the duke's baggage and left his army helpless in the snow and then made forced marches—"

"In fewkin' winter!" Bad Tom interjected.

"Across the Green Hills to Osawa to retrieve the Emperor's share of the fur trade." The captain smiled. "Which paid off our bets, so to speak."

"You ain't telling any part of this right," Sauce said.

Gabriel glared at her—she couldn't tell, despite knowing him many years, whether this was his instant anger or a mock-glare. "Why don't you tell it, then," he said.

She raised and lowered her eyebrows very rapidly. "All right then." She looked to the Keeper. "So we—" She paused. "Got very lucky and—" She thought of the security ramifications and realized she couldn't actually name Kronmir, the spy, who had left the enemy and joined them and even now was making his way to Harndon with Gelfred and the green banda. "And...we...er..."

Gabriel met her eye and they both laughed.

"As I was saying," he went on. "A month ago and more, we found through treason in the former duke's court in Lonika the location of the Emperor, and we staged a daring rescue, met his army in the field and beat it, and killed his son Demetrius."

"Who had already murdered his father," Ser Alcaeus muttered, joining the circle.

"So we returned the Emperor to his loving daughter and grateful city, took our rewards, and came straight here to spend them," the Red Knight said. "Leaving, as you don't seem to notice, more than half our company to guard the Emperor."

"His mouth is moving and I can't understand a word he says." Bad Tom laughed. "Except that we're all still being paid."

Ser Michael joined the giant. "You told what happened without any part of the story," he said.

"That's generally what happens," Gabriel agreed. "We call the process 'History.' Anyway, we've been busy, we have silver, and we're all on our way south. We'll help Tom get his beeves to market and then most of us will go to the king's tournament at Harndon at Pentecost."

"With a stop in Albinkirk," Ser Michael said.

Gabriel glared at his protégé, who was unbowed.

"To see a nun," Michael added, greatly daring.

But the captain's temper was well in check. He merely shrugged. "To negotiate a council of the north country," Gabriel corrected him. "Ser John Crayford has invited a good many of the powers. It'll run alongside the market at Lissen Carak."

The Keeper nodded. "Aye—I've had my herald. I'll be sending one o' my brats wi' Bad Tom. It's a poor time to go, for mysel." He wrinkled his nose. "And ye—pardon me. But you may be the king o' sell-swords, but what ha' ye to do wi' the north country?"

Gabriel Muriens smiled. For a moment, he looked rather more like his mother than he would have liked. "I'm the Duke of Thrake," he said. "My writ runs from the Great Sea to the shores at Ticondaga."

"Sweet Christ and all the saints," the Keeper said. "So the Muriens now hold the whole of the wall."

Gabriel nodded. "The Abbess has some of it, out west. But yes, Keeper."

The Keeper shook his head. "The Emperor *gave* you the wall?"

Sauce had a look on her face as if she'd never considered the implications of her captain being the Lord of the Wall. Bad Tom looked as if an axe had hit him between the eyes. Gavin was looking at his brother with something like suspicion.

Only Ser Michael looked unfazed. "The Emperor," he said lightly, "is very unworldly." He scratched his beard. "Unlike our esteemed lord and master."

Whatever reaction this comment might have received was lost when a slim man with jet-black hair emerged from the dumbwaiter that brought kegs from the deep cellars. The Keeper's folk rode the man-powered elevator from time to time, usually for a prank or when ale was needed very quickly; but most of the folk standing on the staff side of the bar had never seen the black-haired man before. He wore a well cut, very short black doublet and matching hose and had pale, almost translucent skin, like depictions of particularly ascetic saints.

"Master Smythe," Gabriel said, with a bow.

The Keeper puffed his cheeks. "Could we," he said carefully, "move this to another room?"

One by one they passed under the bar into the outer common room and then forced their way to the end of the great hall and out into a private solar under the eaves. It was chilly, and the young woman who had so carefully given the captain the eye knelt gracefully and began to make up a fire. She lit it with a taper and then curtsied—but this time her bright eyes were for Master Smythe.

Master Smythe surprised them all by watching her as she left for wine and ale, and a tiny wisp of smoke came from one nostril. "Ah, the children of men," he said. He raised an eyebrow at Gabriel. "What curious animals you are. You don't want her, but you resent her wanting me."

Gabriel's head snapped back as if he'd been struck and, behind him, Father Arnaud choked on his ale and hid his face.

"Must you *always* say what other people are thinking?" asked the Red Knight. "It would be a bad enough habit with your own thoughts. Please don't do it with mine."

Master Smythe smiled politely. "But why resent me?"

Gabriel exhaled for so long that it wasn't a sigh. It was like a physical release of tension. His eyes moved—

He shrugged. "I miss the company of women in my bed," he said with flat honesty. "And I like to be desired."

Master Smythe nodded. "As do I. Do you perceive me as a rival?"

Sauce stepped in. "Given that you're some sort of god and we're not, I'm sure he does." She smiled at the black-haired man. "But he'll get over it."

"I can fight my own fights," the Red Knight said, putting a hand on

Sauce's shoulder. He nodded graciously to Master Smythe. "We are allies. Allies are—often—potential rivals. But I think you put too much on my surface thoughts and my animal reactions. I like a wench, and sometimes," he smiled, "I do things from habit."

Master Smythe nodded. "For my part, I am a surly companion, my *allies*. Do you know that before this little matter of the sorcerer in the north, I was quite happy to lie on my mountain and think? I retreated from this world for reasons. And as I play this game, the reasons seem to me ever more valid." He looked around. "I am not filled with a sense of ambition or challenge, but just a vague fatigue. Facing our shared foe—" He paused. "I'd really rather that he just went off to another plot, another world."

The serving girl returned. She had broad shoulders—extraordinarily broad. She had a peculiar grace, as if life in a big body had forced her to some extraordinary exercises.

The Red Knight leaned over. "You're a dancer!" he said, delighted.

She bobbed her head. "Yes, m'lord," she said.

"A Hillman!" Gabriel said.

Master Smythe laughed. "Surely—surely we call her a Hillwoman."

She blushed and looked at the ground and then raised her eyes—to Master Smythe.

Gabriel took a sip of ale. "I think I've lost this round," he said. Sauce rolled her eyes and leaned against the table.

The fire roared to life, the kindling bursting into an almost hermetical fire so that the small room was instantly warmer.

Father Arnaud whispered something as Bad Tom pushed in, and Sauce roared. "It's like watching two lions with a bunny," she said.

Father Arnaud was less than amused.

Master Smythe took his ale and sat in the chair at the end of the table, and the rest of them made do with two benches and a collection of stools brought by a trio of boys. There wasn't really room for everyone—Ser Michael was filling out rapidly and bid fair to reach Bad Tom's size; Bad Tom folded himself into a nook by the chimney, as if storing heat for his future of sleeping out on the moors with his flocks. Sauce hooked a stool across from the captain. Mag came in and settled on the bench next to the captain, and Gavin took the other side. The Keeper took a stool at the far end of the table from Master Smythe. Ser Alcaeus stood behind the captain, leaning with his shoulders wedged into the oak panels. Wilful Murder stood in the doorway for as long as a nun might say a prayer, and the captain made a sign with his hand and the old archer slipped away.

"Where is the remarkable young man?" Master Smythe asked.

"We have a whole company of remarkable young men." Gabriel nodded. "You mean Ser Morgon?"

Master Smythe nodded and blinked. "Ah—I expected him here. He is in Morea."

"Where he belongs, at school." Ser Gabriel leaned forward.

"You have left half your company in Morea?" Master Smythe asked.

"Ser Milus deserved an independent command. Now he has it. He has almost all the archers and—" The Red Knight paused.

Ser Michael laughed. "And all the knights we trust."

Master Smythe nodded. "Hence your escort of Thrakian ... gentlemen."

Ser Gabriel nodded. "I don't think any of them plan to put a knife in my ribs, but I think it's better for everyone that they aren't in Thrake for a year or two."

Count Zac came in and, at a sign from Sauce, closed the door with his hip. He had a tray full of bread and olive oil. He went and balanced with Sauce on a small stool.

"And we have Count Zacuijah to keep the rest of us in line," Ser Gabriel said.

"And the magister you carried in your head?" asked Master Smythe.

There were some blank looks and, again, Sauce made a face that indicated a connection made. She bit her lip and looked at her lover. He shrugged.

Most of the men and women present had never seen the captain so at a loss—so hesitant. But he mustered his wits. "All my secrets revealed. Well. Maestro Harmodius has re-established his place in the ... um ... corporeal world."

Master Smythe nodded. His gaze rested on Count Zac. "And you just happen to have joined our little cabal?" Master Smythe asked.

"I want to see a tournament," the easterner said. "Besides, nothing exciting will happen in Morea now."

Alcaeus grunted. "Your mouth to God's ear," he said.

Count Zac shrugged. "Yes—unless *someone* poisons the Emperor."

Alcaeus put a hand on his dagger.

Master Smythe allowed a wisp of smoke to escape his nose. He pulled a pipe from his pocket—an amazing affectation, an Outwaller habit almost never seen in civilized lands—and began to pack it full of red-brown leaf mould. "Could we begin?" he asked mildly.

Gabriel spread his hands. "I have very little to report. And little to say beyond—thanks. We really could not have accomplished anything without you. It pains me to say it, but without your hand on the delicate balances of power and *logistika,* we'd have failed last winter."

Master Smythe bowed his head in gracious assent. "How was the petard? The explosive device?"

Ser Michael barked a laugh. "Loud," he said. "My ears still ring sometimes."

Master Smythe played with his beard as if he'd never noticed he had one before. "Splendid. There will be more toys of a similar nature coming along in the next months. Indeed, I have arranged—or I will—that you can collect them in Harndon." He looked around. "We are coming ... to the difficult part."

Sauce allowed her nostrils to flare. "That was the easy part?"

Master Smythe sighed. He put his pipe to his lips—a very long-stemmed Outwaller pipe decorated in an extravagant excess of porcupine quill work—and inhaled, and the pipe lit itself. "Yes," he said. "In the next phase, almost whatever we do, we will be noticed. Even now, our adversary must be wondering if there is another player in the game. Or if the dice are rigged. He has made two attempts to put his pawn on the throne of Alba. He has made a half-hearted attempt to bring about the collapse of Morea. I think he believes that his adversary is Harmodius. So far." Master Smythe smiled with prim satisfaction. "Now—" He exhaled smoke. "Now he is bending his schemes to Ticondaga and Dorling. My own backyard."

Ser Gavin stiffened.

"Down, boy," Ser Gabriel said. "I'm sure that Mater can overcome anything we face."

Master Smythe shook his head. "Ghause is the victim of her own vanity," he said.

Gabriel nodded. "I've always thought so."

Father Arnaud laughed, and so did Sauce. Bad Tom allowed a snort to escape him. "Comes by it honestly," he said.

Gabriel pretended to fan himself with his hand. "If you are all quite finished," he said.

"They love you," Master Smythe said. "Laughing at you helps them deal with your tiresome arrogance."

"You do just keep saying these things. You must be very difficult at parties." Ser Gabriel nodded. "Can I try that thing?"

"He just wants to learn to blow smoke," Sauce said.

Ser Gavin was unhappy and it showed on his face. He pulled on his own beard and then shook his head. "He's going for Ticondaga? What are we doing to counter him?"

Master Smythe handed his pipe to the captain. "We're trying not to be deceived. We're trying not to tip our hand. He—you know who I mean—does not care a whit for Ticondaga. He wants Lissen Carak and what lies beneath it. But—but. Do you know how my experience of your reality functions?"

Silence fell.

"You can imagine from the intensity of our stares how much we'd *like* to know," Ser Gabriel said. He coughed and handed the long pipe to Master Smythe.

Master Smythe laughed. "I had that coming. Very well. If I play no part in your affairs, I find it fairly simple to observe them in a general way. In fact, it is as easy as breathing for me to regard the general flow of your reality, past, present and, as you see it, future. Or, as I might put it in your excellent language, in your infinity of presents."

He looked around. "But once I reach out to interfere—" He adjusted a cuff. He seemed to notice the back of his hand for the first time—stared at it, and as he stared it became less smooth, more like the back of a mature man's hand. He raised his eyebrows as if surprised. "Hmm. At any rate, once I poke about, I change everything. As do all my kin. As do you, for that matter—heh, heh."

He laughed for a moment. No one joined him.

"Bother. What I mean is that the closer I am to the action, the less I see. The fewer infinities of the present are eventuated." He paused. "Understand?"

Sauce sighed.

Mag smiled. "Because you have chosen to interfere, you are in this sequence of events with us, and you can't see much else."

"Well said. Yes. But the delicate bit is that my presence here modifies the...the...the everything. It is a different everything than if I were not here. With our adversary and others also—I like the word interfere, it's absolutely correct—with all this interference from my kind, none of us can see anything. It is possible that we're drawing everything into a single thread."

Mag spoke like a character in a passion play. "Fate," she said. "Fate is when several of you all interfere together."

"As perceived by you," Master Smythe said. He raised his eyebrows. "At any rate, I know depressingly little about the next few months. But enough of us are now interfering that our adversary has to notice. Further, he's pouring power into several of his shadows and his puppets and his tools, and the results will be...cataclysmic."

"Couldn't you do the same?" Tom asked. "I mean—if the bastard cheats, cheat back."

Master Smythe nodded. "I already have. The sword by your side, Ser Thomas—the black powder that burns." He put a hand to his chin. There was something wrong with the gesture, as if his arm joints had a little too much free play. "But if there are sides in this game, I represent a side that wishes for—the most powerful entities to play by the rules. I would hesitate to describe my side as *good*. I would merely emphasize that my side has a smaller body count and tends to minimize—" He glanced away. "Negative outcomes," he muttered.

"That's heartening," Gabriel said. "We're on the side with fewer negative outcomes. We could embroider that on the company flag." He took a long pull at his ale. "I appreciate that you are not *trying* to be mysterious and difficult, but you are succeeding magnificently. May I try returning your words? You are saying that the more you help us, the less you can see of what's actually happening. You are saying that there are several of you, which I guessed but I don't think we've ever heard said plainly before. You'll help us to a point, but to do more would jeopardize—" Here Ser Gabriel laughed. "Your moral convictions as a deity. Or a dragon."

"Or whatever the fuck you are," said Sauce.

"Yes," Master Smythe said. "You are an apt pupil."

"Can I ask you some questions?" Ser Gabriel asked.

Master Smythe drank. "Of course. But you understand that this is about entanglement with your...event sequence. The more questions I answer, the more entangled I am, even if I take no action."

"Bless you," Ser Gabriel said. "But that's your trouble, not ours."

"I agree," said the dragon.

"Will Harmodius now change sides?" Gabriel snapped.

A pained look crossed Master Smythe's usually immobile face. "Master Harmodius is far along the road," he said. "So far that he may decide to be a side, rather than adopt one. It heartens me that he was so conservative with his powers in the recent contest. I cannot go beyond that."

"Will de Vrailly kill the King?" Gabriel asked.

There was the sound of a dozen breaths all sucked in together.

Master Smythe let a trickle of smoke—artificial smoke, not his own—come out of his mouth. "The sequence, as it applies to the King of Alba, is now completely opaque to me," he said. "I can't see a thing." He sighed. "But I do not see anything happening to the king except his becoming more of a tool."

Ser Gabriel sat back. "Damn. How about this spring? Right now? The drove and the fairs?"

Master Smythe nodded. "Again, I am too close to all of these. My adversary must be very close to exposing me. But I see this much; Thorn has made alliance with the entity who calls himself 'the Black Knight.' They have both slaves and allies in the north—and elsewhere—and they are preparing a major effort. Their scouts have already entered the Adnacrags—indeed, a few foolish creatures attempted to pass my Circle and a dozen raids are aimed into the valley of the Cohocton even now. So yes—yes, I expect that you will be attacked on the road, and that efforts will be made to disrupt trade. My adversary understands trade."

They all sat, digesting this packet of information.

"Will there be another attempt on the Emperor?" Ser Alcaeus asked.

"I'm not a prophet," Master Smythe said with visible irritation. "And given your own hand in these events, you are perilously close to annoying me."

Every head turned.

Alcaeus flushed. "I have chosen my side. I'm here."

Master Smythe shrugged. "Any road, I'm too close to it. But I will say that any event that threatens the stability of the city is a threat to... everything."

"How very enigmatic and helpful," Father Arnaud said. "Will you attend the Council of the North? You are one of the important landowners."

This sally caused Master Smythe to smile. "By your God, Father, that was witty." He looked around. "No, I will not attend. We are, as I have tried to say, too close to the tipping point where our adversary detects my interference pattern. That would be very difficult for me. I cannot be seen to directly aid you or I am revealed. And then—then, we fail." He shrugged. "Even this is an evasion. I can take certain actions—others are too revealing."

"Because he is stronger than you?" Ser Gabriel asked.

Master Smythe frowned. "Yes."

"Drat," Ser Gabriel said.

"Is there a God?" asked Sauce.

"You don't mince about, do you?" Master Smythe asked. "Child of man, I have no more idea than do you." He took a long pull on his pipe. "I will say that as my kind is to your kinds, then it would not surprise me to find an order of beings that were to us as we to you, and so on. And perhaps, above us all, there is one. And perhaps that one caring and omnipotent, rather than uncaring, manipulative, and predatory." He shrugged. "May I share a hard truth?"

"Do you do anything else?" the captain snapped back.

"All practitioners of the art—of whatever race—reach a point of practice where they ask: *what is real?*" He looked around. Mag shrugged, as if the question was unimportant, and Gabriel flinched.

"Yes," he said.

"If you can manipulate the *aethereal* by the power of your will alone, and shape it to the image you hold only in your head," Master Smythe said softly, "then it behooves all of us to ask what the act of belief actually contains. Does it not?"

Sauce shook that remark off the way she'd shake off an opponent's inept blow. "But you don't know, yerself," she said. "One way or another."

Gabriel suddenly had the same almost feral look of understanding that Sauce had worn when she understood that the Muriens family now controlled the whole length of the wall. "You mean that—my whole life"—he took a breath as if it hurt—"is not by God's will or his curse, but by an interference pattern of your kind creating my *fate?*"

"Ah!" said Master Smythe. "That is, in fact, exactly what I mean." He paused. "But not just my kind, children of men. All kinds. Your reality is the very result of the interference pattern of an infinite maze of wills. What else could it be?" He smiled, the smile of the cat about to eat the mouse. "Your kind twist the skein of fate, too. You yourself, ser knight. Mag, here. Tom Lachlan. Sauce. Alcaeus. All of you."

Gabriel drained all the ale in his cup.

"Fuck you all, then," he muttered.

Mag glanced at him. "I have a question, too," she said quietly.

Master Smythe's eyes rested on her. She met his squarely. And smiled. He had beautiful eyes, she thought.

"The Patriarch," she began.

"A very worthy man," Master Smythe said.

"He suggested—mm—that living on the frontier—with the Wild—had some effect on our powers." Once she began to speak, it appeared that Mag wasn't sure what she was asking.

Master Smythe pursed his lips. "An astute observation to which I will add one of my own. When two cultures face off in a war, do you know what the most common result is?"

Mag swallowed. "One is destroyed?" she asked, her voice suddenly husky.

Master Smythe shook his head as if she was an inept student. "No, no," he said. "That scarcely ever happens. They come to resemble one another. War does that."

"So you're sayin'—" Mag paused. "That we are coming to resemble the Wild?"

"Mag, the Wild is a term of art used by men to describe all of us who are *not* men." Master Smythe smiled wickedly. "Women might do well to join us, but I digress." He seemed to find himself very funny, and he gasped silently for a moment. When no one joined him, he sighed. "The Wild is not a conspiracy. It's a way of life. But the longer you are in contact with us, the more like us you'll become. In fact—" He shrugged. "In fact, those with the long view would say that men—and women—are more adaptable than any of the other interlopers here, and are learning the Wild all too well." Master Smythe spread his fingers on the table and looked at them with real curiosity. "You know that all the other races fear you. And that you are the—is there a nice way of putting this? The favourite tools of all the Powers. Inventive, endlessly violent, not terribly bright." He smiled to take away the sting.

"Weapons?" Gabriel asked, his head coming up. "Tools?" He thought for a moment. "Defenders?"

"Goodness, ser knight, you don't imagine you are *from here*, do you?" asked the dragon.

"Stop!" Bad Tom said. He got to his feet. "Stop. I've had eno'. Ma' head hurts. I don' need to know the secrets of the universe. I'm not altogether sure you aren't talking out o' your smoky wee arse."

Father Arnaud got to his feet. He'd never agreed with Tom before, but it seemed a good place to start. "I'm not sure that they can handle any more, Master Smythe. The reality men build is more fragile than they know."

"You are wise," Master Smythe said. "Would you like to have back your power to heal?"

Father Arnaud reacted as if he had been struck.

Ser Gabriel rose and stood by him. "That was cruel," Gabriel said.

Master Smythe looked puzzled. "In truth, I mean no cruelty. The good father—a worthy man, I suspect—has lost his powers due to the workings of a tiny creature...bah, it's almost impossible to explain. But he thinks it is mysterious, perhaps mystically tied to his sin." Master Smythe shrugged.

"I understand feeling of sin. I believe in the pursuit of excellence, and I have failed myself. Too often." He smiled like a man who grins through pain. "Perhaps this is why I fancy humans so much. Here." He slapped Father Arnaud on the back and turned, just as the young woman with the broad shoulders entered with two foaming pitchers of ale.

She curtsied without spilling a drop.

"Do you like trout fishing?" Master Smythe asked.

The young woman lit up like a newly lit lantern. "I love the little ones in the high mountain streams, my lord," she said.

"Yes," he said. "They're beautiful when they are young." He placed the tray on the table and turned back to the room full of knights. "Good evening, allies. Or friends—I'd rather have some friends. The worst is coming. But as I said before: what we do is worth the doing. That's all the reward we get." He raised a mug.

All of the people in the room raised theirs. "To victory," he said.

"To victory," they all repeated. Master Smythe bowed. Then he took the young woman's hand. "And the avoidance of negative outcomes."

"Sir?" she asked.

"We're going fishing," Master Smythe said.

The door closed behind them.

Mag shrugged. "The girl wasn't protesting," she said.

"Oh, my God," Father Arnaud said aloud.

Gabriel released a long breath, as if he'd been holding his for a long time. "Just so," he said.

Morning came—earlier for some and later for others, and for a few, lucky or terribly unlucky as the case might be, there had been no sleep and now there was work.

For Nell, there were six horses to prepare. There was the captain's magnificent eighteen-hand stallion, Ataelus, a new acquisition from Count Zac, a black demon with a changeable temper and a vicious bite. But on this crisp early day in Marius, Ataelus behaved himself with decorum. His only sign of equine restlessness was engendered by a mare—every few minutes, he'd raise his great head and pull his lips back over his teeth. But he was too well-bred to give voice to his thoughts.

Nell liked him. She put a lot of effort into his glossy black hide. He had four white stockings, which was judged unlucky by Albans and lucky by the steppe nomads of the east. Nell worked her way through her wallet of curry combs, coarse to fine, working at the horse with careful sweeps, wary of the places where his coat changed directions. She hummed as she worked.

She had every reason to be happy. Yesterday, the captain had praised her—by name—for her work. The wound on her face was healing nicely, with a little help from Mag, and would not leave a scar. Best of all, the new archer with all the muscles had made his views clear last night by running his tongue over her cheek.

Eventually she'd had to put a thumb in his side to curb his enthusiasm a little. What he had in mind led to babies, and she had other plans, but it had been delightful nonetheless.

She hummed Sauce's song. No young cuckoos for her.

When she had three horses done, she went and woke him up. Once she'd made her views on intercourse plain, he'd become a fine companion and a source of warmth. And of fun.

Boys were like horses, Nell had found. A firm hand on the reins, and never a sign of fear, and all went jogging along. "Hey! Sleepy head!" she said, and gave him a loving kick in the ribs.

He mumbled, threw an arm out and got a mouthful of straw.

"Drums will beat any minute now, boyo. Get your muscular arse out of the straw. Ser Bescanon loveth not his defaulters. Hey!" He rolled over to avoid her, and she jabbed calloused thumbs into both his sides.

He exploded out of the straw like something out of the Wild.

She dissolved into giggles.

He tried to kiss her, and she reached into her belt pouch and handed him a five-inch length of liquorice root. "Your mouth smells like the jakes," she said. "We have standards here, boyo. You took the captain's silver—get moving."

He rolled over, his dirty-blond-brown hair full of straw. "What do I do with it?" he asked.

"Farm boys," she said, rolling her eyes. She was exactly one year from being a farm girl herself. "Captain says that cleanliness keeps you alive and that dirty soldiers die." She spoke with the conviction of the convert. She knew damn well that the company were cleaner than any enemy they'd met except the Morean guards.

"Do I have to wash?" he asked, as if asking if he had to be turned into a snake by a sorcerer.

"Wednesdays and Sundays when you ain't fighting," she said. "Wash and clipped and shaved. When you been wi' us a year, you can have a beard, but only if the *primus pilus* says so."

"By Saint Maurzio!" the boy said. "You have a rule for everything."

"Yep!" Nell said. "Now get your arse moving. I've been working an hour already."

Out in the inn yard—as big as the drill field of many a castle—the Keeper had allowed four bonfires to burn all night. A hundred men and women were gathered around the four fires, all working—men brought wood, or arranged straight-sided kettles, or stirred them.

Nell took the boy by the hand and walked him across the yard to Ser Michael's mess. The great knight himself was nowhere to be seen—no one expected knights to cook and clean unless they were in the shit. But his new squire, Robin, was sitting in his pourpoint with his master's golden knight's belt of heavy plaques across his knees. He and a pixy-faced Morean girl were polishing the plaques with rags dipped in ash.

Robin, who was a good sort and widely popular, was also a lord in his own right. Nell liked him because he kept order well, was polite to young girls and worked all the time. Nell mostly rated people by the amount of work they did.

She bent her knee. "My lord?" she said.

"Morning, Nell," Robin said, still polishing. "Who's he?"

"Took the silver penny last night. Hight Diccon Twig."

Robin nodded to the new boy. "Welcome to the company, young Diccon."

Robin was perhaps three years older than Diccon, but no one made any comment. Robin had fought well at the big battle outside Lonika—he was no longer "young Robin." Soon he would be "Ser Robin." Everyone knew it.

"My da—" Diccon looked at the ground. "...my da calls me 'Bent.'"

Robin smiled. "No. Sorry, Diccon. It's a good name, but a master archer had it and it died with him. Got another?"

"My mother calls me a God-Damned Fool," Diccon said with a smile.

"Good, you'll fit right in. Don't worry about a nickname, Diccon. You'll get one when it comes and not before." Robin looked at Nell.

Nell said, "I think he's to be your archer."

Robin raised an eyebrow. "Well—we can certainly use the help. Diccon, get me four armloads of firewood and talk to that woman in the blue kirtle and the soldier's cloak for further orders."

"Who's she?" Diccon asked.

Robin's face became a shade less friendly. "Diccon, in the normal run of things, you don't speak to me at all and you don't ever ask me a question. Eventually—" He smiled at Nell. "Eventually you'll be welcome to say what you please and ask all the questions you like. But just now, I gave you an order—to do work that will benefit everyone in our mess group. Don't give me any shit. Go do your work."

Nell stood with crossed arms and didn't do anything to support the boy. He flushed with anger, but he swallowed it and went to get wood. Nell followed him. "She's Lady Kaitlin's maid, and she's sort of the head noncombatant in your mess group. She and Robin give the orders."

"What's a fewkin' mess group?" Diccon asked.

She looked at him, as if enjoying his confusion because it reminded her how far she'd come. "Do you know what a lance is?"

He didn't stay in an ill-humour long. He grabbed a good armload of wood—nice dry maple—and started back to the fires. Just to be supportive, Nell took an armload, too.

"A spear about ten feet long?" he said.

"It's a knight, a squire, an archer or two and a page," she said. "Two lances make a mess group, with their lemans and their—"

"What's a leman?" he asked.

"Lover. Whore. Partner. Wife. Husband. Whatever." Nell laughed. "You only get to have one permanent-like with the captain's permission."

"Christ, it's worse than being a monk!" Diccon said. He dropped his wood on the right pile and then stooped to stack it before going back for another load. Six pairs of watching eyes noted him stack the wood he'd just dumped with approval.

Nell shrugged. "Lemans cost money for food and bedding and everything. Any road, we don't leave ours behind. So the veterans have lemans and they bring up the numbers of a mess group to ten or twelve. Everyone in that group eats together, sleeps together, and works together. Most of us fight together." She grunted as she lifted a big chunk of oak.

He took it from her and held out his arms to be loaded up. "You in my group?" he asked.

"No, sweet. If I were, I wouldn't buss you or allow any liberties. Got that? It's a rule, too." She smiled. "I'm the captain's page. I'm in the command lance."

"Is that special?" Diccon asked. His eyes were brimful of questions.

"It'll be more than a mite special if I don't have the horses ready for inspection. We move in two hours." She dropped her load on the pile. "Stack mine, will ye?" she asked. "I'll come see you later. Anything you fuck up, just say you're sorry. Don't cross the captain or the *primus pilus*. That's all the advice I have."

She went back to where Robin was sitting. He had a cup of hippocras in his hand and he was looking at Ser Michael's sabatons, which had somehow started to rust overnight.

"I'm a dead man," he said.

Nell thought that was probably true, but felt no pity. She bobbed her head. Squires got one bended knee first thing and then they were pretty much just folk. "I don't think the new boy has anything," she said. "Not even a blanket, and certes no horse or arms."

Lord Robin sighed. "I'm going to catch it. Nell, can you ask Toby to help me?"

"If'n you'll see to it that the new boy gets sorted," Nell said. She smiled to show she wasn't entirely serious.

Robin looked pained. "You like him," he said.

Nell shrugged. "Yes, sir."

Robin nodded. "Please find Toby," he said.

Toby was attending the captain, and Nell didn't even try and find him until all the horses were done. The sun was well up by the time she found them both, out behind the inn's barns.

"Toby, Toby," the captain said. "Again."

Toby was stripped to hose and a doublet and both men were covered in sweat. They both had arming swords in their hands and, after the captain spoke, Toby cut hard at the captain's head.

The captain retreated his front foot to his back foot so that he stood in a narrow stance and his forward leg was pulled out of an adversary's range, standing straighter as he slipped the front foot back and covered his head with his sword. *Garda di testa*. Nell knew all the guards, now.

Then he uncoiled like a viper striking and Toby got his sword up. But his slip wasn't deep enough—he didn't pull back his front foot enough. Still, he covered his head well, and he countered—the same cut.

The captain pulled back his front foot and covered his head. And cut— Toby raised his sword without retreating.

The captain's sword moved so fast that it was like watching a hummingbird strike. It came to rest against Toby's outthrust thigh.

Ser Gabriel frowned. "You're tired. We'll call it for today, Toby. But you have to learn to move your legs."

Toby looked frustrated and angry.

The captain's eye caught Nell. "Good morning, young lady. How is my beautiful new horse?"

"Eating, my lord," Nell answered. "It's all he does. He'll need exercise today."

The captain smiled. "If I don't get on him today, you take him tonight. Yes?"

"Of course, my lord."

He looked at her and raised an eyebrow. "Do you need something, Nell?"

"No, my lord. But I need Toby, if he's at leisure." She hoped that Robin appreciated how well she was keeping her end of the bargain, because this was leading with her chin. The captain could be savage, especially early in the morning after he'd been drinking.

Toby sheathed his arming sword after looking at the blade for nicks. "I'm with you, Nell," he said.

The captain made a sign that they could talk. He was examining his own blade, the new red-gripped arming sword that matched his long sword for war—gilt-steel guard and round pommel, and two newfangled finger rings on the guard.

"What do you need?" Toby asked. He was breathing hard.

"Robin needs you. He's hard pressed for time and water got at Ser Michael's armour."

"Sweet Jesu and all the saints!" Toby shook his head. "If a man will spend all night in the arms of a—" He looked at Nell. "I'll go."

"Feel free to give him some shit," Nell said. "But I promised to fetch you." Whatever Toby lacked in fighting skills—he was late to the life of arms and a slow physical learner—he was the best metal polisher in the company.

The captain had not sheathed his sword. "Nell—do I gather that you are at leisure?"

Nell's heart did a back-flip. "Er...yes?" she said.

The captain nodded. "I don't think I've paid enough attention to your training, lass. Have you been practising?"

"Yes, my lord. Sword and poleaxe. Ser Bescanon and Ser Alison. And gymnastika with Ser Alcaeus and swimming with—" She flushed. "With the women."

The captain nodded. "You relieve my mind, Nell. But I know you took a wound in Morea and I have a mind to be a little more attentive to your life of arms. Draw."

She had her arming sword on her hip and she took her sword carefully from her scabbard.

She was afraid of the captain at the best of times. She admired him, but he was older, bigger, and he had a temper. And his eyes glowed red when she made him angry or frustrated him.

Standing across the grass from her, he was as tall as Ataelus and his sword seemed huge, but the worst of it was that his eyes weren't red. They were reptilian.

"I'm going to make some simple attacks," he said. "Try not to die." He smiled. "It would take me years to find another page as good as you."

That cheered her up.

He struck.

She'd gotten into a guard—Ser Alison said always do what you know, and she knew that she liked having her sword out in front of her. In a world where everyone was bigger, stronger and longer limbed than she, Nell had learned that basic centreline guards were for her.

She flicked her blade into *frontale*, crossing the captain's blade. His wrist was like iron, but she'd swaggered blades with Wilful Murder and Long Paw and even Ranald Lachlan in the practice yards of Morea.

He bounced back and cut again. She made sure to slip her front foot and sure enough, he cut at her leg.

He saluted her. "It's such a pleasure to find that someone is paying attention." He cut at her head—left/right in two tempi.

She covered and covered, but the second was sloppy and late.

He did it again, faster. But she was ready and made both covers.

He thrust.

He left the needle sharp point of his arming sword at the laces of her pourpoint. "Up until that point, you were positively excellent, except your sloppy draw."

All she could think was, *How can anyone be that fast?*

From that point until they were summoned to breakfast, he made her draw her sword and return it without looking at her scabbard. She put the point of her sword through the web of her left thumb and cursed. He made her continue, and she hated him.

Father Arnaud came out in his black pourpoint. It was a handsome garment for a priest sworn to poverty—black wool velvet, closely embroidered in organic curves that emphasized his physique, which was excellent even by the company's standards.

"You're my third customer this morning," the captain joked, waving his sword at his confessor. "Nell, don't be angry. You are coming along nicely. But if you fumble your draw you never get to test your swordsmanship, because you're dead. And if you can't sheath your sword while you watch your opponent—" He shrugged. "You might still be dead."

Nell bent her knee to the captain. "Thank you, my lord, for the lesson."

Ser Gabriel nodded his head. "Every morning, now, I think—you and Toby."

She had moved from anger to floating on a cloud. Praise? For her use of arms? Training with Ser Gabriel his self?

Nell wanted to be a knight. So badly she could taste it. And she knew she'd just moved a rung up that ladder.

"She pricked her hand," Ser Gabriel said to Father Arnaud.

The priest smiled. It was a happy smile, a joyous smile. "May I see?" he asked.

She held out her hand.

He made a face and said, "*In nomine patris*," and her hand was whole. Just like that. It didn't even hurt.

"My God!" she said, shocked.

"Yes," said Father Arnaud. He beamed.

Breakfast had been called twice, but one of the advantages of being the captain of a rich company of mercenaries is that you know someone will keep your food hot.

"He doesn't threaten your beliefs?" the captain asked as he stepped to the right, trying to baffle his adversary's patient attempts to change the tempo.

Father Arnaud smiled. "Not in the least," he said. "If belief were easy, everyone would do it."

The captain's sword flicked out. The two men were wearing steel gauntlets as a concession to the sheer danger of sparring with sharps. Father Arnaud twisted and flicked the captain's blade up and to his own right but his counter-cut found the captain out of distance.

"He scares the crap out of me," the captain said. He cut down from a high inside guard—*sopra di braccio*—but it was a feint. Father Arnaud pulled his hand back but the captain's blade wasn't there anymore, but describing the almost-lazy arc of an envelopment. Father Arnaud slipped it with a wrist-flick to find that it, too, had been a feint.

"That's it," he said with the captain's sword at his chest. "Now I know you are the spawn of Satan. No mortal man can use a double envelopment with a war sword."

The captain laughed so hard he had to go down on one knee. "You should fight my brother," he said, breathing like a smith's bellows. "They must have searched your entire order for a man so good with both weapons and flattery," he wheezed. "Hah!" He laughed again. "It was pretty good. I was afraid...I don't know."

"You are a curious man," Father Arnaud said. "You were afraid that I would be hurt by your friend the dragon. Instead, he healed me, and in more than just my own powers."

Gabriel sat back on his heels. "I'm glad. Let's eat."

They walked companionably into the common room. There were boards laid on a trestles and long benches and boxes, and grey-clad drovers sat intermixed with the knights and archers of the company. It was warm, and there was food—piles of cut bacon in big, deep wooden bowls cut from tree burls, and bread fried in fat with egg on it; good maple syrup in pitchers, buttermilk and hot wine and sassafras tea. Again, the inn staff moved like the professionals they were—huge wooden platters of food emerged from the kitchens to replace those emptied by guests—hot wine was produced, and honey.

There was a hush when the captain came into the hall, and then everyone went back to eating. The captain sat at a table with Father Arnaud, Sauce, and Ser Alcaeus. Bad Tom paused to talk to a drover and then came and settled next to Sauce, making the bench creak.

"Well?" Tom asked.

Gabriel shook his head. "We have to be very careful about our talking," he said.

"Do you trust him?" Sauce asked with a head jerk to indicate the absent Wyrm.

Gabriel wrinkled his nose as if he smelled something bad and shook his head rapidly. He pulled a knife and a pricker from his baselard sheath and began to eat.

Tom nodded. "I need to move while the weather holds," he said. "My lads will be that sorry to miss another night here, but I have—" He shrugged. "Three thousand head or more for Harndon. Last year the whole herd went to Lissen Carak. And the army."

Gabriel didn't quite look up, but their eyes met. "You're going to Lissen Carak and then to Harndon? Yes?"

Tom frowned. "If I can find a buyer at Southford, I'm of a mind to sell him part of the herd for Lissen Carak—for the fair."

"I need you at Ser James's council," the captain said.

Tom was entirely reasonable. "I wouldn't miss it. But that's Albinkirk, and I don' need to risk me beasties one league west o' the fords." He leaned forward. "Keeper says there's daemons in the woods and the Huran are moving."

Ser Gabriel's smile was thin. "Then we should probably stop talking and get a move on. Corporals and above, outside in the yard. Then we move."

His authority was so palpable that Ser Gavin almost saluted his brother.

Armoured and ready to ride, Sauce stood by her horse in her ancient arming jacket, the one she'd stopped wearing almost a year before. She'd been forced into it this morning because her new, beautiful scarlet arming coat with its finely worked grommets and fancy quilting had torn—two grommets ripped clean through by the lace that held her right arm harness. The old one was smelly and too tight and crisp with old sweat on old leather and linen so filthy it felt like felt.

She mused on the feeling. Considering, as she munched an apple still hale after a winter in the inn's cellars, that she'd once been used to clothes this filthy; she'd once been quite a tough thing, and now she chafed, her shoulders unused to the rough fabric.

"I'm getting soft," she said.

Mag was already up in her wagon seat, high above Sauce. "Don't you believe it, my sweet," Mag muttered. "What you are getting is *older*."

Sauce winced.

Mag was sewing away at her nice arming coat, and Sauce, who was virtually blind to both *ops* and *potentia* was still able to feel the strength of the older woman's working, the way a blindfolded prisoner might feel the kiss of the sun.

Around them, one by one, the knights and men-at-arms of the company came out of the common room, paid their tabs and tallies at a long table set in the yard for the purpose and went to get the last points tied on their harnesses, or to get a strap or buckle looked at.

Ser Dagon La Forêt paused by Sauce's horse. He was shifting uncomfortably inside his new six-piece breastplate. He settled it on his hips and winced. He gave Sauce a rueful smile. "Must we ride in harness every day? Couldn't we let some of the bruises heal?"

Sauce was pleased at some remove to know that she wasn't the only one bitching.

Ser George sighed. "If there's a safer place in all Nova Terra than the country around the Inn of Dorling," he said.

Mag laughed and nodded her agreement. "Only a fool would come inside the Circle of the Wyrm," she said.

The Wyrm of Ercch—sometimes known as Master Smythe—held a territory many leagues across, centred on the white-topped Mons Draconis. The drovers and the inn lived within the Wyrm's claim, and prospered. Travellers were seldom disturbed, although a few faint-hearted souls claimed to have seen a flying creature as big as a ship and refused to pass that way again. Merchants, on the other hand, always travelled across the Wyrm's dominion.

Sauce handed her apple core to her riding horse. "By all accounts, the Outwallers came right up the stream and hit the drovers—inside the circle," she said.

Ser Dagon grimaced.

"Company's never been ambushed," said an archer, the master tailor, Hans Gropf. He was standing with his palfrey to hand and two small boys waxing his leather gear at his feet.

Ser Dagon nodded his acknowledgement.

"Company's only four years old," Wilful Murder muttered. He stood in the middle of the yard, watching everyone with his mad eyes. He was holding all the horses—Nell's job, but he liked the chit and she'd run off to get her boy onto the right pony, or somesuch. "Lots o' time to get bounced and massacred. When we get soft. Mark my words."

Ser Dagon shook his head. "Well—I'll just suffer in silence, then."

"If'n we start any later, we might as well wait 'til tomorrow," Wilful Murder muttered, loudly enough to wake the dead.

Sauce saw the captain, standing in the inn door. Bad Tom came out and embraced the innkeeper's eldest, Sarah, his dead brother's wife. It was quite an embrace. Some of the pages looked away, and some whooped.

Mag's head turned, and Sauce saw her searching the baggage train—all apparently a chaos of horses and wagons and donkeys and wicker baskets. Looking for her daughter Sukey. Who had been Tom's lover for a year and more, and now was publicly displaced.

The captain—Gabriel, as he now was called—materialized at her elbow, as the bastard had the habit of doing, with Ser Michael and Ser Bescanon at his heels. Just looking at him made her smile.

"Where's the good count?" Ser Gabriel asked.

"We had a trifling disagreement," Sauce said in a put-on version of the genteel accent. "He's off grooming his vanity."

Ser Gabriel's face twitched but gave no more away. "Sauce, will you take your banda and cover the baggage train?"

Sauce nodded.

Ser Gavin walked up. Apples were the fashion of the day, and he tossed one to his brother. "Can we get moving?" he said impatiently.

Tom appeared. If he was concerned that he had just publicly humiliated the daughter of the most powerful sorceress in a hundred leagues, he gave no sign. "You called?" he asked.

The captain nodded. "You're not my *primus pilus*," he said. "You're the Drover. I can't order you into my line of march."

Tom laughed. "Nah—never think it. I'll follow you. The fewkin' sheep are so slow I'd just as soon butcher the lot."

The captain nodded sharply, all business. "Right, then." He looked around for Count Zac, found him, and beckoned him. When the short easterner rode up, the captain bowed, since, technically, he and Zac were peers. Zac returned the bow. He glared at Sauce.

Mag narrowed her eyes at Tom.

Ser Dagon smiled innocently at Ser Gavin. Ser Gavin, who was particularly eager to reach his lady love at Lissen Carak, shifted uncomfortably, as if by moving his hips he could get the column moving.

The captain sounded remarkably like himself. "Friends," he said, "I begin to suspect that if I don't offer you a constant diet of danger and drama, you go and manufacture it for yourselves." He looked around. "Very well—Count Zac, if you will be pleased to lead the way. Ser Michael with me, then Gavin, and then Ser Dagon followed by Ser Bescanon. Baggage last, covered by Ser Alison. The drove brings up the rear. They'll raise a lot of dust, and we don't want to be the drag."

"You are taking the precautions of war," Count Zac said, somewhere between a protest and a query.

"Master Smythe made his views plain," he said. "There's a big force north of us, forming at the edge of the Adnacrags. We're leaving the Empire and entering Alba. The sun has been warm long enough for every Outwaller in the world to have slipped south past Ticondaga. Right? We're at war. When someone like Master Smythe gives you a warning, you're a fool not to heed it."

Their nods were uniform.

"Good. Let's ride," the captain said in his captain voice.

That voice relieved Sauce. The more he was Gabriel, the less she felt she knew him. She preferred the captain, with his steady arrogance and his adamantine self-assurance. Gabriel had entangling alliances that the captain didn't have—a mother, a family, a set of alien obligations.

Sauce got her steel-clad leg over her riding saddle and waved at her squire, who had both her chargers. "Keep close," she said. If the captain said war, it paid to listen.

The new trumpeter sounded a long call—the last summons. Ser Alison trotted her horse along the restless ranks of her ten lances, arrayed just outside the inn's gates. Then she placed herself at their head and saluted the captain as he rode out with Ser Michael and the banner—three *lacs d'amour* in gold on black. Father Arnaud carried the banner today. The company was split into three, Sauce knew, and had new recruits in every lance, so that discipline had to be fiercer than usual and little things like saluting were suddenly important. The company's gonfalonier, Ser Bescanon, was now the *primus pilus*, and few of the oldsters took well to his taking Bad Tom's role. No new banner bearers had been appointed, and the company's well-loved Saint Catherine was in Liviapolis with Ser Milus and the White Banda.

Behind the captain's own extended lance—banner, trumpeter, his own squire, Toby Pardieu, and his page, Nell, and his archer, Cully—came the lances of his household; Father Arnaud had acquired his own lance, with two squires and two pages—a popular man, for all that Sauce found him hard to talk to. Then Ser Francis Atcourt, with his squire, page, and pair of veteran archers. Then Angelo di Laternum, once Ser Jehan's squire, now leading his own lance. The last two knights were magnificent in new armour that flashed in the sun; Chris Foliak, always a popinjay, and Ser Phillipe de Beause, who was a famous enough jouster to have his own invitation to the royal tournament. Behind them came the newest recruits—two gentlemen of Occitan, Ser Danved Lanval and Ser Bertran Stofal and their squires, pages and archers. Ser Danved was almost as wide as Ser Bertran was tall, but they were veteran lances from the south, and they were accounted fine jousters. Ser Danved had a loud voice that was almost always on offer—a contrast to his brother-in-arms, who was almost always silent.

The command lances were all in scarlet and gold, even the pages. The pages wore eastern turbans with plumes over their helmets, and had curved sabres, Etruscan steel breastplates, and hornbows. They rode fine eastern mares, small horses with elegant heads and endless enthusiasm.

The command lances reeked of opulence and military power. Sauce knew it was advertising, but in war, advertising paid off as well as it did in prostitution, and she laughed to think about the similarities between her first profession and her second.

The command lances turned sharply off the road after trotting out of the gate and formed from column into line facing her across the road. The captain caught her eye and smiled. She saluted again with her sword.

Count Zac cantered across her vision, beautifully intercepting his troop of Vardariotes, two dozen steppe nomads who were at least two thousand leagues from home and two hundred from their barracks at Liviapolis. Sauce had no idea what bargain the captain had struck with the Emperor, but it had included the loan of her lover, and she thanked him silently, even if the man was being an arse this morning.

Zac looked at her, horse perfectly collected under him as he passed as if in review in front of the captain. He had the golden mace of his imperial authority in his fist, and he used it to salute the captain, and then he turned and flashed her one of his wide-open grins.

She relaxed. She hadn't realized how much their spat had put her on edge, but as soon as she relaxed, she mocked herself inwardly for allowing a man—any man—to dictate anything to her.

Count Zac and his troop wore the scarlet and gold of the imperial livery. For the first time, Sauce noted that, since the captain had added gold to his own livery, his command lances matched the imperial livery.

She frowned.

Ser Michael's lances—he commanded eight of them, this trip—appeared next. He had the bulk of the new recruits, and some men, even men-at-arms and knights, didn't have their scarlet yet. They were out of scarlet cloth, and only the fair at Lissen Carak or the shops of Harndon would improve their lot. But they still made a brave sight—twenty men-at-arms and as many archers and pages, although Sauce could see some awkward young men and a shockingly slim young woman who lacked a saddle, an arming coat, or even a sword. She had a bow over her shoulder and she rode barefoot.

"Who's the trull?" Sauce asked without turning her head.

Ser Christos—a Morean veteran with enough experience to lead an army, who'd been assigned to her, a man who'd actually wounded Bad Tom in single combat—grunted. "You should see her shoot," he said. "I didn't catch her name." His Alban was halting but coming along, and his tone was confiding but respectful. He'd given her no trouble and in fact, despite his odd accent and weird views on religion, was like an old veteran and not a new recruit, so she turned in her saddle and gave him a gap-toothed smile. "Someone should get her some kit," she said.

Mag had rolled her slab-sided wagon to the edge of the road, at the head of twenty such. She leaned down. "We're out of everything," she said. "And I mean, everything."

Sauce was watching Ser Gavin's lances pass by. They were well-ordered. Ser Gavin had mostly Albans, and he'd picked up four new lances at the inn, young men in search of "adventure." So his troop also looked like a patchwork quilt of unmatched horses and mixed armour.

Ser Dagon had veterans, too, and his men looked worn and able, at least to a professional eye. Not a buckle out of place, and most of the brass and bronze polished, after a night of heavy drinking. For Sauce's money, the apparently indolent Ser Dagon was a more natural choice for *primus pilus* and she was still puzzled that the captain had given Bad Tom's job to the former captain of the Emperor's mercenaries, an Occitan knight who hadn't had any great reputation in the Emperor's service and whose company Bad Tom had wrecked in a single charge. But as the Occitan knight's lances came down the road, Sauce had to admit they looked good, and the man knew all the Archaic war manuals that the captain worshipped as other men worshipped...well, the Bible. The Occitan knight's men rode matched bays, every one of them, knight, page or archer. Almost all of them had scarlet arming coats or at least temporary surcoats, and their metal was all well-polished.

Ser Alison looked back at her own. She had a mixed bag. The Moreans liked her—they'd nicknamed her "Minerva" and none of them gave her any crap, and her Morean Archaic was native. So she had more men-at-arms with worse equipment but excellent drill. She needed to come up with a great deal of gold to pay for a hell of a lot of new harness.

But they were good men and women, and they were hers. The last fight had promoted her to sub-contractor—she now hired her own lances and took a bigger cut, instead of merely working for the captain as a junior officer. Short of having her own company, she had arrived.

She grinned. The sun was shining, and she was a knight. She still had her sword in her hand from saluting the captain and the banner, and she turned her riding horse and waved her sword like some knight of romance. "On me!" she called.

Her knights and their lances filed off from the right, enveloping Mag's wagons between two long files of fighters. As soon as they were clear of the stone-wall-lined roads through the endless sheep and cattle pens—all full of the drove—she raised one gauntleted hand over her head and moved it in a circle, and her pages left the column to rove over the countryside alongside the column, east and west.

That always gave her joy—a mere hand motion, and thirty people sprang into action.

Sauce herself trotted alongside Mag's wagon. Her riding horse didn't quite bring her level with the head woman.

"All done," Mag said, biting off her thread with sharp teeth. "And now I don't have any more scarlet silk twist, either."

Sauce smiled. "Thanks, Mag. It's beautiful. Your work is always beautiful." She handed her coat back to Robin, who turned his horse and went back along the column to put the precious garment safely in a pannier.

Mag smiled, looking both tired and old. "Thanks, dear." She shrugged. "I was making something, and now—"

Sauce knew that she'd lost her man—Ser John le Baillie. One of the best of the men. Only a middling warrior, but patient and good at almost everything. She'd liked John, who'd never given her any shit. Unlike many men.

"Have you misplaced it?" Sauce asked.

Mag shook her head. "I've lost interest in it," she said. "I was making John a nice pourpoint. Like yours."

"Oh," said Sauce. She felt foolish. Mag was as well armoured as the captain, in her own way. She never gave out much of her feelings, which Sauce rather liked.

Sauce tried to change the subject. "Have you noticed the captain's got his household in the imperial colours?" she asked.

Mag laughed. "Noticed? I cut the cloth, Sauce." She smiled. "Cloth of gold. Sometimes I find all this a little hard to believe."

"Me, too," Sauce allowed.

They rattled along for half a league. For all their late start, it was a beautiful day. Behind them, the Green Hills rolled away to the north, with Mons Draconis rising to the north-east, its volcanic cone appearing soft in the middle distance and out of proportion to the rolling downs on either hand.

But ahead, like a wall across their path, stood the forest. It didn't mark the edge of the Wyrm's circle, which was a good deal farther on, but it did mark the border of the Wild. Morea was old, and settled, and the hand of man lay heavily there, but to the west of the vales of the Green Hills the woods grew tall and old, and despite the royal roads, a squirrel could leap from tree to tree from the wood line ahead all the way to the northern end of the Adnacrags or west to well past the wall where it came south of the inner sea.

"Hard to think that all this was ours once," Sauce said.

Mag was coming home to her own country, but she nodded. "Certes," she said. "When I was a girl, we used to play knights and monsters in the old shielings behind our house. A travelling friar told me they were part of a town—a really big town. All this was farms, once. Men lived here."

The trees ahead were as tall as church spires. "That was a long time ago," Sauce said.

"Aye," Mag admitted. "Two hundred years and more before Chevin was fought."

"There's now as much Wild inside the wall as outside," Sauce went on.

Mag nodded. "I heard there's as many folk living in the Wild as in the civilized lands," she said. "The Wyrm—Master Smythe as is—said something to the point." She smiled at Sauce. "So what's the Wild? If'n folk live there? And what's civilized?"

Sauce, who'd grown up as a whore, didn't need that comment explained at all.

Because it was early spring, many of the trees were still bare, although there was a sort of green haze over the distant woods that suggested growth and budding. And there was no dust. The royal road under their hooves and wheels was stone. Sometimes it washed out and had to be repaired, and some of the patches could crumble but mostly it was hundreds of leagues of flat, straight road, wide enough for two wagons abreast.

Behind them on the road came the Drover's household, a dozen mounted carls with heavy axes on their shoulders. Thanks to Tom, they rode instead of walked. They wore full mail and gleaming helmets, some of apparently eldritch design with tall peaks and long bills and scallops and whorls. Hillmen were much given to display. Gold glinted from their belts and harnesses.

Bad Tom made no move to ride up and join either Sauce or Mag.

"You going to speak to Tom about your Sukey?" Sauce asked.

"No," Mag said, in a tone that suggested that no further discussion needed to be had on that subject.

Sauce considered riding out and inspecting her outriders.

She tried a different approach. "You ever consider what the captain's actually after?" she asked Mag.

Mag smiled. It was her warmest smile of the day so far. "Yes," she said softly. "All the time."

Sauce shook her head ruefully. "I just want it to go on and on. Adventure after adventure. But he's after somewhat, ain't he?"

Mag nodded. "Yes, dear."

Sauce turned and looked at the older woman. "Don't patronize me," she spat.

Mag rolled her eyes. "No. Sorry, sweet. But none of you think about it much. You just swing your swords and ride on, don't you?" She looked north. "He's made himself the Duke of Thrake."

"But that's not for real." Sauce looked up at the older woman. "He's not going to sit at Lonika and administer justice and be a great lord, is he?" In fact, she realized, she'd watched him do so for five days after the battle at the crossroads. As if he'd been born to it.

Which, of course, he had.

"Shit," she said aloud.

"I think it is for real," Mag said. "I think he's made two fortunes in three years, and then he's added a great principality which will, at least for a few years, pay his taxes—a steady income so great I can't really imagine how much money he'll have. And he sank his claws into the fur trade. He's getting a tithe on the imperial tax on furs. He and his father now—literally—own the entire border with the Wild."

"He hates his father," Sauce said.

Mag looked interested. Everyone in the company knew that Sauce went way back with the captain, but few had the spirit to question her.

"Hate's too strong," Sauce admitted. "But his father and mother did something—awful. Rotten. An' he ran away." She looked at Mag. "He's not just going to share the wall with them."

Mag looked ahead at the line of trees. "Never is a long time," she said slowly. "And power is even thicker than blood. Ser Gavin is in contact with Gabriel's mother. I *know*." She smiled fastidiously. "Gabriel's mother is the most powerful of her kind I've ever encountered." She frowned. "Except the former Richard Plangere. As great as Harmodius, but all green."

Sauce frowned. "You mean all this—riding on errantry and rescuing princesses and getting contracts—it's all just another play at power?" She spat. "Fuck. I don't believe it."

Mag laughed. "For the life you've led, child, you can be naive. What else is it all for, to the likes of them?"

"He's not one of them!" Sauce said.

Mag sighed. "I suspect I like him as much as you do, sweet," she said, as she might to a child who'd just had her first courses. "But this is what they do. They are not like you and me. They're like animals in the Wild. They play for power."

Towards evening, the pace picked up, and they moved quickly. Sauce knew from her outriders that they were passing through the battlefield where the drove had been massacred by Outwallers last year, and that no one wanted to camp among the bones and the ghosts. The column began to string out, and a mist rose out of the deep valley of the stream.

Sauce left the column to check her outriders. Many of her Moreans had never seen woods like this—great beeches and oaks seventy feet high, with a few birches interspersed, the boles so big that two men couldn't pass their hands around them and the undergrowth almost non-existent, especially under the oaks, although there could be tangles of blown-down limbs or even whole trees uprooted. Maple trees like green cathedrals rose above the beeches. It was beautiful, if you let yourself look.

Besides the woods, she was still grimly pleased with what she found. The Morean stradiotes knew their business, and their pages were mostly tenants and what an Alban would have called sergeants and what they lacked in experience they made up for in caution. Sauce moved along their line, pleased that each man—no women—kept his partners in sight. Evening made the woods noisy, and there were enough large animals moving to keep the vedettes awake.

Sauce wished for Gelfred, but the green-clad huntsmen were away. On another mission. Not to be discussed.

He was playing for power. She saw it now, and it pissed her off. He was doing something he knew the rest of them wouldn't approve of—which was why he'd split the company. She knew that Ranald and Gelfred and the loathsome Kronmir had all gone somewhere. She had her suspicions that they'd gone south to Harndon.

These were surface thoughts, because the caution her outriders were showing was infectious, and because she had enough experience of the Wild to know that something was wrong.

She cantered up behind a pair of her men, Spiro and Stavros, both watching the woods across a glade to the south. Both had their bows in their hands.

Sauce reined in. "Stavros, back to the wagons, tell Mag we have something—not an alarm, but time to be careful. Then up the column, find the captain and get his arse out here. With my compliments."

The man snapped a crisp salute, turned his horse on its hindquarters and raced away.

Spiro frowned. "Could be a deer," he admitted.

Sauce nodded. She was still on her riding horse and sorry for it. "No self-respecting deer would be this close to a moving column," she said.

She felt foolish, having ridden out of the column without a heavy lance or her fighting helmet. She loosened her sword in its sheath.

Something moved across the clearing.

And the mist was rising. The sun was just on the point of going down to the west—they were late on the road.

About another hour of light.

"We're too exposed here," she said calmly. "Back away."

Spiro was delighted to concur, and they backed their horses among the trees—from copse to copse, one turning and then the other, covering each other.

Her opinion of Spiro went up and up. She'd barely met him, but he was solid and dependable and his head was everywhere. He was clearly shit-scared, and equally clearly good at dealing with it.

She saw movement to the west, and then a flash of reassuring scarlet. At the same time she saw her next pair of outriders waving, and she and Spiro bore west and north through a tangled thicket and emerged into another glade. Count Zac was there with four of his men.

She was so glad to see him that she felt a moment's disorientation, and then she realized how much terror she'd felt—

"Ware!" she shouted. Its approach had been gradual, but now she knew the feeling. She'd felt it at Lissen Carak. Some of the creatures of the Wild *exuded* terror.

Spiro looked over his shoulder—raised his bow—

Sauce dragged her sword clear and cut—

The thing leapt. Sauce smelled the burned soap smell and saw the bright red crest. Her blow was parried with the bronze haft of a heavy stone axe—a magnificent weapon of polished lapis that came back at her like a nightmare.

The daemon sprouted a feathered shaft. She got her sword on the haft and let the weight of the blow slide off her like water off a roof as her riding horse panicked between her legs—and bolted.

The daemon—twelve feet of muscled armour and blood-red webbed crest and gills—slammed his lapis axe into Spiro, killing him instantly, crushing his ribs into his heart. Then it rotated its hips, pointed the elegant bronze staff of his axe and a beam of coherent light blew Count Zac out of his saddle. The little man landed like a sack of wheat.

Sauce was wrestling with her reins. When her palfrey stopped and reared, Sauce rolled over the horse's rump—in armour—and landed on her feet. She turned.

The *adversarius* was forty feet away, twice her height, and glowed with arcane power.

Sauce had a fortune in wards on her harness—one from Mag and one from the Red Knight himself.

His blue-white fire struck her in the chest.

And dispersed.

"Fuck me," Sauce said, and charged.

The daemon shaman hesitated, obviously disconcerted by her attack and the failure of his sorcery. It gathered power—Sauce saw that much.

A gob of white fire travelled across the shaded glade like a ball thrown by a grown man. It struck the daemon low, on the hip, and the daemon's belt of what appeared to be emeralds burst into fire.

The thing stumbled, looked wildly around, and another ball of white fire struck it in the torso just as Sauce's sword cut at the thing's outthrust, scaled leg. Blood and fire sprayed in every direction, the axe flashed at Sauce and she slipped her lead foot and made a two-handed cover. The axe slammed into her blade and snapped it, and the point of her own sword cut into her left hand right through a heavy gauntlet.

But she was otherwise uninjured, and when a third gout of fire struck the daemon, it shuddered and said one word, and was—

—gone.

Count Zac was not badly hurt. Spiro, on the other hand, was messily dead. The captain's post-mortem that night was highly complimentary to Sauce. He ended by saying, "Let's try not to lose any more." He shook his head and looked at Mag.

"I hit the damned thing three times," Mag said. "It had a layered protection and some serious skills."

The captain had a cup of watered wine in his fist and he was sitting in a camp chair with most of his officers. Zac was still in Father Arnaud's hands.

"What was it doing out there, alone?" the captain asked. He looked around. "We're still in the circle."

Tom, who was grumpy because he'd missed a fight and grumpier because everyone was praising Sauce, spat. "Wild's got to have young fools as much as folk," he said.

"You'd know," Sauce said.

The captain laughed. "I thought you two were sick, or something. I suspect that we are watched. My sense of the arcane in the air is that our daemon came the way he went. That's why it was so clever of Sauce to understand." He looked at Mag.

Mag nodded. "That's consistent with what I felt—pulses of *potentia*. If it was powerful enough, it came—and then went."

"The outriders surprised it," Sauce said. "It didn't expect resistance so far out from the column."

Ser George rolled his eyes. "Once again, the omnipotent captain reads the enemy perfectly."

Ser Danved laughed and pounded his saddle. "He does posture on and on..." He looked around.

Ser Francis Atcourt slapped him on the back. "Don't worry, he loves being told when he's posturing," he said.

Instead of rising to the quip, Ser Gabriel smiled. "In fact, Master Smythe warned me pretty carefully. I cannot claim this one, and thus I'll try not to be insufferably glad that a powerful mage-warrior couldn't even get a view of our column." He was silent a moment. "We'll bury Spiro in the morning, and then, I'm afraid, we'll march the whole company over his grave."

Ser Bescanon had fought the Wild most of his youth, but he was shocked. "That's desecration!" he said.

The captain shrugged. "Less a desecration than having something dig his corpse up and eat it," he said. "We're in the Wild. Let's keep that in mind."

"I miss Morea already," Ser Michael said. "Everyone remember how we said fighting in Morea was dull? We were fools."

The next morning arrived earlier than anyone wanted. And Sauce began to see that Ser Bescanon might have talents in Bad Tom's direction after all. He had the entire quarter guard out and moving through camp, waking everyone. The captain's trumpeter sounded the call every minute for ten minutes, and the woods rang with his trumpet. It was freezing cold; wooden buckets had a rime of frost, and the horse lines were horse-huddles.

It was not their first day on the road, but it was the earliest start with all the new recruits. Tents were slow coming down. Ser Gavin, temporarily in charge of his brother's household, had trouble finding enough spare bodies to get his brother's great pavilion packed, and Mag had to shriek like a hen wife to get *her* wagons packed. The sun climbed in the sky, and Count Zac emerged from Father Arnaud's tent pale and shaken.

Sauce threw her arms around him. "I thought you were fucking *dead*," she said.

"Me, too," Zac admitted. "I owe Kostas the shaman. Big time."

Father Arnaud smiled at them both. And then they sensed his attention leaving them, and they both turned.

A flight of faeries emerged out of the morning mist. They flitted about the clearing, moving rapidly from point to point like cats sniffing out a new house.

Eventually they gathered into a cloud of colours, a ball of darting and moving shapes. The ball moved cohesively across the clearing.

No one moved.

Bad Tom was standing while his squire—Danald Beartooth—laced his byrnie.

The faerie swarm floated to a stop in front of Bad Tom.

"*We were Hector,*" they said. "*We remember. We do not forget.*"

Tom flinched. "Hector?" he asked.

Just for a moment, the swarm took the shape of the dead Drover, Hector Lachlan. "*We remember,*" they said.

Bad Tom watched them. "I remember, too," he said.

"*We wait for you,*" they said. "*We remember. You are the sword.*"

Tom drew the great sword by his side with a ferocious fluidity, but as quick as he was, the whole cloud of faerie folk was faster.

His sword glowed in red and green and blue like the shimmer of a peacock. "I'll be right here waiting for you," he said. "Come and try me."

The faeries seemed to sigh. "*The day cometh, man. You are the sword. We remember.*"

And then they flitted away, each one going in a different direction, exploding outwards into the new day.

One faery, bolder than the others, circled close. But, alone, its voice was so quiet that only Tom could hear it.

"*We will be there for you,*" he said, and flitted away.

Mag looked at Sauce. "I used to love them, as a child. I cried when I realized what they are."

Sauce was still locked in an embrace with her lover. "What, then?" she asked.

"The soul vultures," Mag said grimly.

The captain had to ride out and direct the turn-over of the camp-guards to the outriders himself—too many new officers and too many new people. He, too, missed Gelfred.

A league farther on the road, they passed Gilson's Hole, a break in the road. The road here had once crossed the wetlands of a large marsh on a causeway, with the upper waters of the Albin to the east, out of sight and farther down. Years and years ago, something had blown a forty-foot hole in the fabric of the road, and a combination of ill luck and botched maintenance attempts had created a hole that filled with water and wouldn't drain, surrounded by forty bad paths around it through what was increasingly a rank and fetid swamp, not a freshwater marsh—and a settlement had grown on the high ground just to the west and south, where a low ridge offered good air and good grazing, and a higher ridge offered safety. The settlers had specialized in getting cargoes across the hole. There'd been talk of building a bridge. They'd built a small fort on the higher ridge.

Last year, the Sossag had come and burned the settlement and killed most of the folk. The fort had held through the troubles and some families had survived, but only one family had returned. The goodwife came out of her little stockade to watch the first outriders negotiate the paths around the hole, and she'd sent her eldest boy to guide them. The captain spoke to the boy and gave him six golden ducats to guide the whole column, and it still took them almost the rest of the day to get all the wagons and the drove around it.

They camped in the clearing, and because they'd had a short day, the captain ordered Oak Pew to gather a work party and clear the burned steads. A hundred men and women made short work of it, stacking the un-ruined boards and heavy house timbers and building bonfires of the rest.

The goodwife curtsied her thanks. "It's hard to look at," she said. "We got away, but others didn't. And with the—wreck—gone, mayhap other folk'll settle back."

"Do you have a man, Goodwife Gilson?" the captain asked. He was sitting on her firewood porch, drinking his own wine. He'd brought her some. She had twelve children, the oldest daughter old enough and more to be wed, and the youngest son barely out of diapers.

"He's hunting," she said. Only her eyes betrayed her worry. "He'll be back. Winter was hard." She eyed the six gold ducats—two years' income. "I reckon you saved us."

The captain waved off her thanks, and after hearing everything she knew about traffic on the road and creatures in the woods, he went back to his own pavilion. The quarter guard was forming, and there were six great bonfires burning, fed from the remnants of twenty houses and twenty fire-wood piles.

His brother was sharing his pavilion, and he was standing in front of it in conversation with Ser Danved, who was in full harness, leading the night watch. The captain came up and nodded, intent on his bed.

Gavin pointed out over the swamp. "This position is nigh impregnable from the north and east," he said. Out in the swamp, faeries flitted and smaller night insects pulsed with colour. The swamp spread almost a mile north and south, which was why no one had driven a new road around it.

The sky in the west was still coloured rose, and silhouetted the stockade of the small fort behind them—currently sheltering the baggage and part of the quarter guard, on alert.

Gabriel looked around in the dusk light, as if seeing it for the first time.

Ser Danved, who always had a comment for every situation, laughed. "It's fine if you don't mind having both of your flanks in the air," he said. Indeed, at their feet, a small stream—the captain had stepped over it on his way to his tent—ran down from the higher ridge into the swamp, and provided the only cover for the ridge's northward face on its burbling way to the Albin, miles to the east. "Jesus saviour, this must be the only place in the world with a swamp halfway up a mountain."

Bored and tired, the captain shrugged. "If I ever have to fight Morea, I'll keep it in mind," he said. He passed into his tent, and caught Danved and Gavin exchanging a look of amusement.

He ignored them, intent on bed.

They had two alarms in the night. Both found the captain fully armoured and ready, but there were no attacks and no engagements.

In the morning, the captain found a splay-footed track just south of the horse lines, and a heavy war arrow. He brought it to Cully, who eyed it and nodded.

"Canny said he hit something. Even a broken clock is right twice a day, it seems." Canny was a barracks lawyer and a liar and scarcely the best archer, but the bloody fletches told their own story.

The captain tossed the arrow in the air and snapped his fingers. The arrow paused—and hung there. The captain passed his hand over the length of the broken arrow and the head flared green.

Slowly, as if a vat filling with water, something began to form in glittering green and gold, starting from the ground. Soldiers began to gather in the dawn, and there was muttering. The captain seldom used his hermetics in public.

Mag came and watched him work.

He was in deep concentration, so she

found him in his palace. As they had once been bonded—however briefly— she could enter his palace at will. He smiled to see her.

"A pretty working," Mag said.

"Gelfred's," he said. "A sort of forensic spell. All the huntsmen have variants of it."

She watched him as he manipulated his ops in four dimensions and cast, his use of power sparing and efficient.

The thing continued to fill with light.

"What is it?" she asked.

"I have no idea," he said.

It had an elongated head and far too many teeth. The head seemed to speak more of fish than of animal—streamlined and armoured. The neck was draconian—long and flexible. The body seemed armoured in heavy shell, at odds with the elegant neck.

It crouched, ready to attack, back bent at an unnatural angle, at least to a man, with back-hinged arms and legs.

They both emerged from their palaces together to look at what he had wrought.

"What is that thing?" Ser Gavin asked. "I thought I'd seen—everything."

Ser Gabriel shrugged. "I suspect that the Wild is much bigger than our notions of *everything*," he said. "What is it? It's the thing that came for our horses last night. Good shooting, Canny. Next time, kill it."

He clapped his hands and the sparkling monster vanished and the arrow fell into his hands. He handed it to Wilful Murder. "Put that head on a shaft," he said. "And keep it to hand."

"An' I know why," Wilful said. He was pleased to have been picked—it showed.

The captain got on his riding horse, the last fires were put out, and the column began to ride. Wilful was one of the last men at the fires, and then he used the goodwife's breakfast fire to get his resin soft. He didn't leave the clearing until the sheep herd was moving, and he waved to Tom as he cantered past, leaving a mother and twelve scared-looking children alone with the Wild.

He handed the completed arrow to the captain, and Ser Gabriel took it, said a few terse words in Archaic, and handed it back to Wilful, who put it head up through his belt.

Six miles on, where the old West Road—really just a trail, and scarcely that—branched towards the tiny settlement at Wilmurt and the Great

Rock Lake before plunging north into the High Adnacrags and eventually reaching Ticondaga, the scouts found a man, or the ruins of one. He'd been skinned and put on the trail, a stake through his rectum and emerging from his mouth. His arms and legs were gone.

Count Zac frowned. "I'll have the poor bastard cut down and buried," he said.

The captain shook his head. "Not until after the column rides past," he said. "I want them all to see."

Ser Michael caught his eye. "The hunter?" he asked quietly.

Ser Gabriel sighed. "Hell. I didn't even think. Oh, the poor woman."

Ser Michael nodded.

"I'll go," Father Arnaud said. He snapped his fingers and Lord Wimarc, who had joined them with word of the council at the Inn of Dorling, brought him his great helm.

The captain thought a moment. "Yes. Take Wilful. Get the body down and decently shrouded. Father, offer to take the family with you. Best take a wagon. Drat. This will cost me the day."

"It might save your soul," Father Arnaud said.

Their gazes crossed.

"I have to consider the greater good of the greater number," the captain said calmly.

"Really?" asked Father Arnaud. "Am I addressing the Red Knight or the Duke of Thrake?"

The two men sat on their horses, eyes locked.

"Michael, can you think of a way I can tell the good father that he's right and still appear all powerful?" He laughed. "Very well, Father. I am suitably chastened. War horse and helmet. Ser Michael, you have the command. If my memory serves there's a wagon circle about half a league on, just after crossing good water. Give me one of the empty wagons and I'll take Zac and half his lads."

"And me," Ser Gavin said.

The captain smiled impishly. "Knights errant," he said. "Mercy mild. Father Arnaud, Gavin, our lances, and Zac." He put a hand up. "No more!"

Other knights volunteered, and Sauce thought they were a pack of tomfools. So did Bad Tom when he came up.

The "empty" wagons proved to be full to bursting with the loot of southern Thrake, and some very red-faced archers—and men-at-arms—watched their belongings unloaded onto the wet stone road.

The captain was scathing. "A fine thing if they were to hit us right now," he said. "Ripped to pieces because we had too much loot. Get it put away, gentlemen. Or dump it in the ditch." He saluted Ser Michael.

Ser Michael did not sound like the nice young man they all knew. He sounded like the son of a great noble.

"Well, gentlemen?" they heard him say. "Time's passing. I'll just say a prayer for the captain's success. And when I'm done, I'll ask Mag to set fire to anything left on the road. Understand?"

Mag smiled.

Sauce laughed. Ten minutes later, moving again, she looked up at the wise woman. "Would you have burned it?" she asked.

Mag laughed. "With pleasure," she said.

Sauce swore. "He sounds like the captain," she said, waving at Ser Michael.

Mag laughed again. "He went to all the best schools," she said.

The captain took his command lances; Atcourt, Foliak, de Beause and Laternum, as well as the new Occitan knights, Danved Lanval and Bertran Stofal. With Father Arnaud's lance and Ser Gavin's and his own, he had a powerful force, and the spring sun glittered on their red and gold as they rode back down the road towards the Hole. Count Zac rode ahead, the red foxtail of his personal standard shining in the sun, and half a dozen of his steppe riders spread through the trees on either side.

The company archers rode on either side of the wagon. They were all veterans, and Cully, the captain's archer, was the company master archer. He rode a fine steppe horse and his eyes were everywhere. All of the archers had their bows strung and in their hands. Ricard Lantorn, despite being mounted, had an arrow on the string of his war bow.

The pages brought up the rear. In the captain's household, even the pages had bows and light armour, and they, too, were strung and ready. The captain's caution had communicated itself fully.

The spring day was pleasant. The sun was high, and the world and the woods seemed at peace. Robins sang in the high branches of the beech wood through which the Royal Road ran. A woodpecker began his endless hammering, searching for early bugs on a tall dead tree. A few early insects droned along the column. The weather was cool enough to make an arming coat and a few pounds of mail and plate seem comfortable. At the clearing, they could see the loom of the Adnacrags in the north—low hills, dark with trees, in the foreground, and farther, the sharper shapes of the high peaks—snow capped, streaked in the dark lines of distant streams.

The captain rode with his senses stretched.

His brother glanced over at him.

"Asleep?" he asked with a smile.

Gabriel shrugged. "Something is troubling me."

"Beyond that we are riding into an ambush?" Ser Gavin asked.

"That thing—whatever the hell it was," Gabriel said. "I wish I'd had a corpse. But it's not *from here*." He struggled for words. "And when I think about the things Master Smythe said—I wonder what that means."

Gavin gave him a look that suggested that his brother thought that watching the woods for ambush might be more productive.

"I need to—never mind. I'm not going to be very communicative for a few minutes." Gabriel shrugged his shoulders, moving the weight of his harness off his hips for a moment.

"Should we change horses?" Gavin asked.

Gabriel looked around. "Not yet. I want my charger fresh."

All around him were excellent knights who had killed very powerful things. He

turned inside himself and went into his palace. Everything was there, and he bowed to Prudentia, who smiled.

"Watch for me, Pru," he said. "I need to go in there."

She turned her ivory head and glanced at the door. "On your head be it," she said. "It should be safe enough."

Very cautiously, like a man approaching a sleeping tiger, Gabriel walked over to the red door. With a deep breath that had no real meaning in the aethe-real, *he put his hand on the knob and pushed it open.*

Instantly he was in Harmodius's memory palace. But nothing was crisp and clear except the golden door at his back and Harmodius's mirror, a device he'd used. It was an internal artefact that allowed the user to "see" any potentia— *any workings—cast directly on his person. Harmodius had spent too long imprisoned in another's false reality to allow himself to ever be fooled in such a way again. Gabriel was briefly surprised that the old man hadn't taken the artefact with him, but he smiled at the thought—of course, it was a memory artefact.*

Harmodius's abandoned memory palace stretched away from the centre checkerboard and the free standing mirror to a distant and dusty obscurity, like a summer house infrequently used. Gabriel moved cautiously across the parquetry floor and then—very carefully—began to examine some of the old man's memories.

It was very dark, and he could only see things dimly. He was rarely frightened in his memory palace; casting in combat would have been too difficult otherwise, and the lack of time inside the palace usually gave a caster time to be calm and thorough, but here, in this unlit shadow realm of another man's mind, Gabriel was scared almost to panic. He had no idea what rules guided his passage through Harmodius's mind or memories. He only knew that as the man had occupied his head for almost a year, the red door must lead here. Harmodius had entered his own memory palace often enough, but this was only the third or fourth time that Gabriel had gone the other way, and the first time since it was—unoccupied.

And of course, with the guiding light of the other essence gone, it was dark.

"Summoning," Gabriel said aloud.

It grew lighter. And he watched a memory flit across the floor in wisps, like a marred projection or a magic lantern slide with honey on it. It was an interesting memory; Harmodius was sitting with Queen Desiderata in a room and casting. She provided the ops.

Gabriel watched the summoning. Because it had involved the casting of a form, the memory was very clear, and he could follow the shadows of its casting around the chamber of Harmodius's mind.

But the experience began to leach at him somehow. He couldn't put a finger on the experience to name it, but he felt as if—as if he was Harmodius—so he was not Gabriel. And it was almost physically painful, almost like dreams of leprosy or watching another man get kicked hard in the groin.

There was more light.

He stepped towards the golden door, which seemed farther away.

The lights grew brighter.

Gabriel moved—decisively. He ran across the tiles, past the mirror and, to his immense relief, the door did not flee before him and he grasped the golden handle. He pulled the door open and found Prudentia standing at the other side with an arm outstretched to him and he stumbled through.

He stood in his own palace and breathed deep. The sun fell like golden fire from the dome overhead and outside his green door, great gouts of green potentia rolled and seethed like the sea in a storm.

"Something is coming," Prudentia said.

Gabriel patted her ivory hand.

"Was it bad?" she asked.

"Whatever that was, it misses its master," Gabriel said. "I don't think I could face it again."

He surfaced into the real and looked around. It was still a brilliant spring day. Squirrels were running along branches that overhung the road.

"Stay sharp," the captain yelled.

After the captain's shout, every man looked around carefully, and for fifty jingling strides, the only sounds were those of horse hooves on stone, the woodpecker in the distance and the rattle of armour and horse harness.

The captain pushed his *aethereal* sense out as far as he could. He was surprised how far that was. He was not broadcasting—to do so would be to announce his presence as far away as the villages of the Huran. Instead, he listened passively. He was able to detect a strong presence well to the east; another enormous presence the same distance and more to the north that almost had to be his mother.

The Wyrm was a dull warmth from over the *aethereal* horizon—a line that had almost nothing to do with the actual horizon. It had never occurred to the captain before that moment to ask why distances and horizons were different in the *aethereal*, but in that moment, he thought of how he might hide—if he could map the gradients of power.

Distraction is one of the most dangerous failings in a hermeticist. He was building a mapping process in his memory palace when he realized that his horse had stopped moving.

Ser Gavin gave him a look left over from childhood. "Fat lot of good you are, my overmighty brother," he said. "Asleep?"

Gabriel looked round, disconcerted. The wagon was rolling to a stop in front of the goodwife's house. The older girl had just run inside, calling for her mother, and the archers were leering. The girl had been on the porch, spinning, wearing only a shift.

Francis Atcourt was leering, too. Gabriel raised an eyebrow and the dapper knight raised his and grinned.

"Not something I expect to see in the woods every day—a girl that pretty," he said.

Chris Foliak, Atcourt's usual partner in crime, grunted. "And she's coming with us," he said.

"And we're *protecting* her from the *monsters*," Ser Gabriel said slowly. "Not, gentlemen, being the monsters ourselves."

"I won't hurt her at all!" Foliak said, grinning. But when he met the captain's eye, his smile vanished. "Only having a joke, my lord."

Gabriel reached out again. There was something—

Father Arnaud emerged with the goodwife.

"How can you be sure it was my man?" she asked on the porch.

"We can't. But having seen the signs, the captain feels you're better in the walls of Albinkirk." Father Arnaud glanced at Ser Gabriel.

"Shall I describe him for you? The old da, he was not a tall man—"

Father Arnaud shook his head.

"But what if there's some mistake, and I pack and leave?" she asked. "And he comes back looking for his bairns and a spot o' supper?"

"Mama," the older girl said carefully. She had a low voice and she was still wearing only a shift. "Mama, these gentlemen think there's somewhat unnatural, right here. They want to go. They ain't stayin'. If'n we want to be with them, we need to go."

The goodwife looked around. "It's me home," she said quietly.

"And I hope that in a month you can return to it," Gabriel said. "But for the moment, ma'am, I'd request you and your oldsters get everything you can into that wagon."

The goodwife wrung her hands for as long as a child might take to count ten.

"Yes," she said. "But what if it were'n my old man?"

"We'll leave a note," Ser Gabriel said.

"Ee can't read," the goodwife answered. "You take the kiddies and I'll stay."

"I'd rather you came, ma'am," Ser Gabriel said.

She went in, and her two eldest, a boy and a girl, went to help. When the girl emerged with the first armload, she was fully dressed in a kirtle and a gown of good wool, which showed that she had some sense, or quick ears.

The boys began to move wooden crates and trunks into the wagon, and before the sun had sunk a finger's width, the children—all twelve of them—were up on top of the load.

"By Saint Eustachios," the woman said. "It's lucky we'd scarce unpacked. I hate to leave my good spinning wheel. There it is. And my baskets. Good boy."

"You're coming, then?" asked the captain.

She looked down. "Children need me," she said. "The priest says...he says—" She put her head down.

Father Arnaud looked hurt.

"War horses," the captain called. "Three leagues to go and three hours of good light. Let's move."

Cully shook his head. He took a heavy horse-dropper out of his quiver and tucked it through his belt. He exchanged a long look with flap-eared Cuddy, his best mate.

"Fuck me," Cuddy said.

The captain rode with his head down, concentrating. He was nearly sure he'd caught something, or someone, breaking cover—a hermetical power trying to conceal itself.

Count Zac's horsemen moved back and forth at the forest edge, winnowing the ground like a team of hayers with scythes. They now rode with arrows on their bows, and once, when a deer broke cover, they all shot before they fully identified the threat, or lack thereof. The deer was butchered on the spot—intestines removed, and the rest hung between two of the spare horses.

"That will attract anything we haven't already attracted," Gavin muttered. He scratched his shoulder. Then he reached back under his harness to scratch.

The captain looked up into the branches and saw the edge of a wing—a flash of a talon.

"Wyvern!" he called.

In an instant, every weapon was drawn. Eyes strained towards the sky.

The Red Knight backed his horse a few steps. "I think it wanted to be seen. And we're still in the Wyrm's circle. Someone's either cocky or insane."

Gavin frowned. "Or trying to make our friend show his hand." His voice was muffled by the pig snout on his bascinet.

"Move!" called the captain. "Eyes on the woods. Only men on the road watch the sky. Keep moving. Let's not be out here after dark, eh?"

"Didn't Alcaeus get ambushed right here?" Gavin asked.

"Further east—four hours' ride from Albinkirk," Ser Gabriel said. "Drat."

"Drat?"

"I have a flickering contact. There's something out there, trying not to be seen, but using power. Only a little. It has some sort of ward." He frowned.

Ser Gavin rose in his stirrups and looked around.

Ser Gabriel's horse plunged forward. "Faster," he said.

The wagon team began to canter, and the wagon jolted along the ancient stone road. The horses began to go faster.

"No bird song," Ser Gabriel shouted. "Ware!"

Off to their right, one of Count Zac's men drew to his cheek, his body arched in his light saddle, and loosed as he rose in his stirrups. He loosed *down* as if shooting at the ground, and his horse sprang away.

Something as fast as a rabbit and ten times as large appeared and struck the archer's horse.

He loosed his second arrow, point blank, into the thing's back from above.

His mare stumbled, and four more of the things hit her, tearing chunks off her haunches. She screamed but lacked the muscles to kick or even stand, and she slumped, and her rider somersaulted clear, drew his sabre and died valiantly, ripped to pieces by a wave of the things—ten or more, as fast as greyhounds but ten times as ferocious.

Zac's other horsemen were already raining arrows on the pack, and it took hits.

"Hold!" called the captain. "On me," he said to the knights. "Squires— charge."

Behind him, Toby led the squires in a charge at the rest of the pack. The war horses were a different proposition from the riding horses, and whatever the things were, they died under the big steel-shod hooves. Bone cracked and chipped.

Shrill eerie screams ripped across the road to echo off the far trees.

Cully had all the archers together around the wagon. Francis Atcourt's young page, Bobby, had all the archers' horses in his fist and looked ready to cry.

The horses began to panic, and the boy lost them, the reins ripped from his hands.

"Wyvern!" Cully said.

In fact, there were two wyverns—or even three. One scooped up a horse—Count Zac's much beloved spare pony—and with one enormous beat of its sixty-foot wingspan was gone.

The other went for the wagon. It took Cully's horse-dropper in the neck and flinched, but a flailing fore-talon ripped a small boy in two, covering his siblings with his gore. Ricard Lantorn put a needlepoint bodkin deep into the thing's left haunch and Cuddy's horse-dropper, released from a range of twelve feet, went in high on the thing's sinuous neck just below its skull.

The wagon was an organ playing a discordant wail of terror. Its team bolted down the road.

The wyvern baulked, turned on the archers.

Father Arnaud's heavy lance struck it under its great, taloned left arm and went in almost as far as his hand and the great thing reared back, took

49

two more arrows and failed to land a claw before Chris Foliak's lance spitted it.

Ser Francis Atcourt's lance was the *coup de grâce*, striking it in the head as its neck began to sink and its eyes filmed. It fell.

The archers whooped.

Atcourt put up his visor. "Well," he said to Father Arnaud, "I—"

A gout of blue-white fire struck Father Arnaud. It lifted him from the saddle and slammed him to the ground.

Atcourt pulled his visor down.

Ser Gavin galloped by. "Save the children," he roared. The first wyvern was coasting along, skimming the trees above the runaway wagon.

The captain rose in his stirrups and pointed a gauntleted fist. A beam of red light travelled an arrow's flight into the woods and something there was briefly outlined in red.

"Damn," the captain said.

His attack and the counter-spell were almost simultaneous. There was a detonation in front of him and his horse shied—and subsided.

He backed the horse. He had a great many tricks since the last time he'd been in a fight like this, and he cast, and cast, and cast.

A bowshot away, his opponent was silhouetted against the foliage by a matt-black wall. The creature itself—a daemon—was lit from beneath by a simple light spell cast at the ground before it and thus not susceptible to a counter.

The tree beside it exploded, wicked shards of oak as sharp as spears whipping through the air.

The adversary struck him with a gout of white fire and then another. He took both on his shields and lost both shields in the process.

"*Fiat lux,*" he said aloud, and loosed his own bolt of lightning.

But the adversary was gone, skipping across reality.

Down the road, the second wyvern stooped, trading altitude for airspeed and calculating nicely with the ease born of long and predatory success, passing just over the last overhanging tree branches before a long stretch with no cover on either side of the road for half a bowshot—a short causeway over a marsh. It plucked one of the goodwife's children from the wagon, decapitated one of her daughters with a talon flick, took a raking blow from the oldest daughter with a scythe and banked hard, skimming low over the reeds and the beaver house and rising neatly over the trees on the north side of the road.

The panicked horses took the wagon off the causeway, and the wagon stopped, the horse team mired immediately and screaming and neighing their panic as the wave-front of the wyvern's terror passed over them again.

Ser Gavin and young Angelo di Laternum cantered up. The run along the road was already tiring their war horses.

The wyvern consumed its prey—a simple flip of the child into the air and a spray of blood visible two hundred yards away. Cully's long shot from the end of the causeway fell away short.

"Under the wagon!" Gavin shouted at the goodwife and her brood. "Into the water. Under the wagon!"

The goodwife understood, or had the same notion herself. Grabbing her youngest, she leaped into the icy water. It was only thigh deep.

"Dismount," Gavin snapped at the young Etruscan man-at-arms. Both of them swung heavily to the ground and pulled heavy poleaxes off the cruppers of their saddles. Angelo had a long axe with a fine blade. Ser Gavin had a war hammer—a single piece of steel that was deceptively small.

Cuddy and Flarch ran along the causeway like athletes in a race. Flarch—one of the company's handsomest men—never took his eyes off the banking wyvern.

Cully loosed another light arrow and scored against the wyvern, who was too low and slow to manoeuvre.

"Ware!" Cully called. He'd picked up *another* wyvern coming in from the setting sun in the west, right down the road. Four of them, now.

The squires' charge was more successful than any of them would have hoped.

The daemon's ambush—it certainly appeared to be an ambush—had been sprung from too close. There were three daemon warriors behind the first creatures, but they were so close behind that Toby's charge first trampled the imps—Toby's immediate name for the toothy monsters which had attacked the mare—but then crashed into the first of the adversaries. The beaked creature was as shocked as Toby, but his axe was faster than the daemon's and he landed a hasty blow on the thing's brow-ridge, cutting away a section of its engorged crest. Blood—red, too red—erupted as if under enormous pressure.

By sheer good fortune, Toby's mate, Adrian Goldsmith, was right behind Toby, his horse on exactly the same line, and Adrian's unbroken lance took the stunned daemon squarely in the mouth—entered, tore a furrow along its tongue and severed its spine. The lance broke under the weight of Goldsmith's charge.

Marcus, once Ser Jehan's page, an older man and not the best jouster, missed his strike and died, as a great stone-headed axe caved in his helmet and pulled him from his horse, but the horse, forced to turn, put both metal-shod forefeet into its master's killer. Neither blow was mortal for a daemon, but the two knocked the big saurian back a yard or more and cost it its balance as it fell over its dead kin. It never got to rise, as Toby pulled his horse around. The horse did the work and Toby rode out its panicked rage.

The third daemon warrior broke to the left, its heavy haunches powering it as fast as a war horse through the undergrowth. It ran for its life.

And its allies.

Gabriel Muriens slipped off his horse neatly and quickly, freeing his feet from the big iron stirrups, getting his left leg over the high war saddle and putting his breastplate against the saddle's padded seat as he slid to the ground.

Nell—scared beyond rational thought and yet ready—took the great horse's reins. She'd just seen more power at closer range than she'd ever seen in her life—six exchanges of levin and fire, whirling shields of pure *ops* and a sword of light.

Without comment she handed her master his *ghiavarina*. He began to walk into the woods. Nell thought he looked like a predator stalking prey.

He spared one thought for the fights further down the road, turning his entire armoured body to look into the distance, but he didn't raise his visor, and then the point of his heavy spear and the beak of his visor rotated back into the deep woods and he went forward.

Nell took the war horse and led it back down the road towards the archers. There was fighting in the woods to the north—the squires. And the archers had all followed the wagon, while the pages had followed Count Zac somewhere.

Nell was all by herself. And there were things moving in the woods south of the road.

After a moment of panicked *lèse-majesté*, she vaulted into Ataelus's war saddle. The great horse tolerated her, even sidled to allow her to settle her weight. Horses liked her, and Ataelus knew her well enough.

She moved her weight to bring him to a trot.

The thing—she had no words for it—exploded out of the brush to her left, but she had a heartbeat of warning and Ataelus was ready, weight on his rear haunches, and he sent the thing flying with a right-left hoof combination. The dead thing lay like a sack full of raw meat and teeth.

"Good boy. Pretty boy." Nell soothed the horse, showing as little fear as she could. Ataelus was quivering and Nell quivered with him. A few yards away, Lord Wimarc stood over the prone priest, and farther along the road, two of the knights were spurring their mounts back—towards Wimarc and the captain.

There was a flash behind her. For an instant, her shadow and that of the horse were cast, black as pitch, on the trees to the south of the road. Even at the edge of her vision, the sheer whiteness left spots.

Without volition, she turned her head after flinching.

Fifty paces away, the captain stood between two great trees. Five paces away was a daemon, his red crest fully erect, his grey-green skin glowing with power, his beak a magnificent mosaic of inlays—gold and silver, bronze and bone. He was taller than a war horse and wore a loose cloak of feathers that sparkled with fire—and which seemed to have been torn.

He also had a large splinter of wood through one shoulder and bright red blood leaked around it.

He had an axe of bronze and lapis. He pointed the haft at the Red Knight and a gout of raw power, unformed *ops*, crossed the space.

The Red Knight stood in a guard as if facing a more prosaic opponent. His spearhead was down on his left side, and the haft passed across his hip—*dente di cinghiare*. His spear rose and he seemed—as far as Nell could tell—to catch the unseemly gout of raw power and toss it aside. He stepped forward with a double pass.

The daemon cast again—the same gout of power, this time tinged with green.

The captain didn't falter. He caught the attack high and flung it down where it burst in a shower of burned leaves and exploding frozen ground.

The lapis axe whirled and a great green shield appeared, heart shaped, traced magnificently in the air by the bronze shaft of the monstrous axe.

The captain closed another pace, spearhead low and haft now high, and as the third attack—three spheres of green-white fire at pin-point intervals—left the axe shaft, the captain's spear turned a half circle on his forward hand, and the spearhead, glowing a magnificent blue, collected all three spheres in its sweep, and they hurtled into the woods. One blew a head-sized fragment out of an ancient oak tree, one passed all the way through the grove and crossed the road within a few feet of Nell's head to explode in the thicket behind her, and the third vanished into the sky.

Nell watched her captain close the last pace into engagement range and saw his spear lick out. It passed effortlessly through the daemon's glowing shield, which vanished with the shriek of an iron gate torn from its hinges. The great saurian, driven to extremes, used his bronze axe-haft to parry the blow.

The *ghiavarina* passed through the axe haft like a cold knife through water. An incredible amount of hoarded *ops* exploded into non-*aethereal* reality.

The storm of power seemed to consume the daemon. It passed the captain the way the sea passes the prow of a ship, and even as the shaman slumped, the captain—subsumed him. The great creature began to unmake from the head down, his very essence leached and his corporeal form un-knitting even as the storm of his own power made his skin boil and explode outward in superheated destruction.

Nell retched.

The nearby oak tree, already damaged by the sorcerous overspill, gave a desperate crack.

The tree fell.

Toby watched the last daemon warrior run. He'd seen enough fights to know a healthy fear—*what if he has friends?*

He reined in. "Hold hard," he called.

Adrian was still trying to draw his sword, which, in the hurry of combat, had rotated too far on his hips and was now almost lost behind him.

"Marcus is dead," he said. "Father Arnaud's still down on the road. Lord Wimarc's standing over him."

Toby got his horse around and reached behind his friend and drew his sword. He put it in Goldsmith's hand. The artist was shaking like a beech tree in a wind.

"You got it, Adrian," Toby said. "That was a preux stroke."

Adrian gave him an uneven smile. "It was, wasn't it? Christ—all the saints. Thanks."

There was a flash of light so bright that both squires were stunned for a moment.

"Captain's doing something," Toby said, turning his horse to face the empty woods.

Adrian was looking at the ground. "Daemons, Toby."

"I know!" The older boy looked around, completely at a loss. To the east, the captain was in some sort of sorcerous duel—there were pulses of power so rapid he couldn't follow them.

To the north there was a flash of red, and then another.

"More daemons?" Adrian said. His voice was high and wild, but his sword was steady enough.

"Back to the road," Toby decided.

"What about Marcus?" Adrian asked.

"He's dead and we aren't," Toby said. "We'll come back for him."

He backed his horse to get clear of the brush and turned. Adrian followed him.

There was an explosion to the north, not far away. It was so great that both men and their horses were covered in gravel and sticks and a hurricane of leaf mould. The horses bolted.

Neither man was thrown. The company stressed riding skills for its squires, and they'd spent almost a year training with the steppe nomads of the Vardariotes.

Toby's masterless horse burst onto the road a few horse-lengths from Nell, mounted on Ataelus. She was paper white. The horse half-reared then neighed at the familiar horses, who both slowed to see their herd leader so calm.

Something horrible was a tangled mass of blood and broken teeth between the huge war horse's feet.

"There he is," Toby said. Lord Wimarc was ten horse-lengths away, standing with a spear over the prone form of Father Arnaud. There was blood dripping from his spear. He was watching the ground south of the road. Francis Atcourt was just dismounting by his side and Phillipe de Beause was still mounted, watching the sky. Two hundred paces to the west, the sun was setting in splendour and a knot of archers could be seen, all drawing and loosing as fast as if repelling the charge of a thousand Morean knights. They had Ser Danved and Ser Bertran covering them. Both had swords well-bloodied.

Something passed overhead and darkened the sun. The shadow went on forever, and Toby raised his head in despair—

The great oak tree fell. Gravity was faster than the captain's best reactions and stronger than all the daemons in the Wild and the oak tree's top smashed him to the ground and he thought—

Cuddy drew and loosed, grunting as his shaft leapt into the air, and without pausing or following its flight he bent, took his next shaft, sliding the bow down over it and lifting it already nocked.

Needlepoint bodkin.

Needlepoint bodkin.

Broadhead.

Broadhead.

Beside him, Flarch's elbow shot up in his exaggerated draw posture—he was a thin man and he pulled a heavy bow and his body contorted with every full draw, his back curved like a dancer's.

As he released, he took his next arrow from his belt. "Two," he spat.

He meant he had two shafts left.

Both wyverns had chosen to turn in place, gaining altitude and timing their strike so that they could envelop the desperate stand of the knights and archers, splitting the archers' efforts and the knights' attention.

But it had cost them. All the archers were hitting at this range.

Gavin stood in *coda longa* with his war hammer stretched out behind him, prepared to deliver an enormous blow. Di Laternum had his spiked axe up in front of him.

The wyverns finished their turn and their sinuous necks flashed as one as their heads locked on to their shared prey. Both monsters screeched together.

The wave fronts of their conjoined terror struck. Di Laternum fell to one knee. Gavin's shoulder flared in icy pain and his mind seemed to go blank.

Flarch lost the arrow in his fingers.

Cuddy loosed and missed.

The smaller wyvern was the size of a small ship, its body forty feet long top to tail and its wingspan sixty feet or more. Its underside was oddly flecked with the fletchings of a dozen quarter-pound arrows.

Its mate—if the mighty monster had a mate—was bigger. Its wings seemed to block the sun, and its body was a mottled green and brown and white like old marble. Its wave of terror was far more subtle than its younger partner's—its terror promised freedom through submission.

The children under the wagon all screamed together.

And then a taloned claw the size of the wagon took the greater of the two wyverns and ripped one of its wings from its still-living body.

Darkness blotted out the sun. Night fell.

The dragon was so huge that no mere human mind could encompass it. Its taloned feet were themselves almost as large as the wyvern's body. The mortally-stricken wyvern wheeled into a catastrophic crash with a scream of rage and humiliation.

The younger monster turned on a wing tip. It was cunning enough to pass *under* its titanic adversary, rushing for open sky and rising on a lucky thermal even as the dragon turned in the sky, so close to the ground that the vortices at its sweeping wing tips a thousand feet apart launched small spouts of leaves and the rush of its passage knocked men flat.

The wyvern rose and turned, going north. The thermal lifted it—

Ser Gavin watched with savage satisfaction as the thing was chased down. The dragon—incredible as it was—was faster.

The wyvern made two attempts. Because of the altitude, both were visible. First it dived for speed, and then it tried to fly very low, turning under its mammoth adversary again.

The dragon pivoted in mid-air. It was too far away for its size to register—far enough that the whole of the incredible monster was visible, top to toe, a bowshot or more long, with a neck as long as a road and a noble head with nostrils as big as caves and teeth as tall as a man on a horse.

The great mouth opened, and all the men on the road gave a shout.

Silence fell.

And then all hell was given voice in the woods north of the road.

When the ambush was sprung, Count Zac's first thought was to envelop the northern arm of the ambush. It was bred in him, not a conscious decision. He gathered every man on every pony, all the pages and his own survivors, and they rode into the deep woods north of the road, sweeping wide around his best guess of where the enemy might lie.

The great wardens were no aliens to the easterners. The lightning-fast carrion dogs were a terrible surprise, but he'd seen them now.

Like the veteran hunters they were, the Vardariotes spread as they rode, casting a net as wide as they could. The pages tended to clump up. Zac ignored them as amateurs.

His own boys and girls trotted—and then when his sweep turned in a neat buttonhook south, and he raised his arm, they reined in.

Every man and woman with him drew their sabre and placed it over their right arm, so that the gentle curve nestled in the archer's elbow, sword drawn and ready.

In his own language, Zac called, "Ready, my children. Be the wind!"

The pages followed, screeching.

Zac was confident of his location and his array. He cantered back south, his skirmish line flashing red behind him.

And, as he expected, the enemy had forgotten him. They had formed up to converge on another target, perhaps never having noticed his envelopment. His satisfaction was marred by how many of them there were. Twenty daemons were not going to be swept away in a charge.

He had two calm heartbeats to take it in—three great wardens struggling with the branches of a downed tree. Another raising a stone axe and striking—what, the tree?

Perhaps Zac caught a glimpse of red and gold surcoat. Perhaps he did indeed have a spirit to advise him. Perhaps his instincts for war were so finely honed that he guessed.

"Through them!" he called. He loosed his first arrow, leaned over his horse's mane, and began to kill.

Gabriel lay, trapped in the weight of his armour, pinned to the ground by an oak branch that lay across his torso and had crumpled his left greave and broken the leg inside it.

He tried to use *potentia* to move the tree. The pain from his leg was so distracting that he hadn't even managed to open his visor when the first daemon appeared, sprinting in heavy-footed majesty, leaping through the branches.

Gabriel watched it come. He stretched out his right hand for his *ghiavarina*.

It was too far.

He worked to summon it. He *couldn't* even *get* into *his palace. He reached for Prudentia* and a wave of pain thrust him back into bloody reality.

The daemon's stone axe swept up. He saw its open beak, heard its scream of triumph.

He thought quite a few things—about Amicia, and Irene, and Master Smythe.

And then, despite the last efforts of his straining right hand to grab the *ghiavarina*, the axe fell.

The daemon's weapon seemed to slide around his head. It *missed*.

Gabriel didn't pause to consider the ramifications, although he was fully aware that he should be dead. He got his right hand on his baselard and drew it. Its effect was tonic—he steadied. The baselard itself held power—

The daemon—so close as to be like a lover and smelling of burned soap and flowers and spring hay—cursed. Even in the alien language, his curse was obvious—the great axe flew up again—

Gabriel *dived into his place of power. He leaped onto the bronze disc set in the floor and pulled the lever. This simple symbol governed a nested set of pre-prepared workings, each cascading into the next.*

Gold and white and green light flared in a set of nested hemispheres over his prone body.

Zac saw the fireworks and drew the correct conclusion—loosed a shaft with the daemon nearly at the point of his arrow, whirled and loosed again over his shoulder even as his magnificent pony leapt the downed tree and then he was turning.

But the wardens were running. One of their number lay with his feet drumming in the final dance and one of his best warriors, Lonox, was down, cut from the saddle for being too daring, but the wardens wanted no more of the fight.

Kriax, a woman with a face so tanned it seemed made of leather, reined up. "We have them!" she shouted and gave a whoop of pure delight.

Zac pursed his lips. "If I set this ambush..." he said, and waved.

She turned and looked at him. Her eyes were slightly mad with unexpressed violence.

"...I'd have a covering force," he said. "Back to the road and break contact."

She saluted with her sabre as her left hand flicked her bow back into the case at her hip. She gave a specific scream—an ululating yell.

Like a flock of starlings, the whole line of Vardariotes turned all together and rode away, leaving the pages—exhilarated and terrified—to follow. Zac bellowed for them in his version of Morean.

He rode over to the tree. The Megas Dukas was no doubt under the brightly coloured shields. Another warden lay there, too, his body sliced neatly in half by sorcery and both sides cauterized. A third lay pinned, badly wounded, under the branches of the trees. Some sand and a gilded beak suggested the ruin of a fourth.

"Hey! Captain!" Zac called. "Hey! We're here!" He edged closer to the tree.

Eerily, like something really bad on the steppes, the voice came straight into his head.

Be sure, Zac. When I drop these wards, I'm going to have nothing left.

Zac didn't like the voice in his head at all. "Can we leave you? To make sure? No fucking idea what happened to the east."

Hurry, said the voice.

Ser Gavin had scarcely been engaged in the fighting, but he was sorely tested in the aftermath. Aware—as they were all aware—that the captain was down and so was the chaplain, Ser Gavin had to comprehend the scale of the fight, covering as it had, three different venues spread over almost half a league of ground, and then isolate and secure his three widely spread parties.

He insisted that they be secured first, before any acts of mercy or rescue began. The downed captain, surrounded in his *aethereal* shells, he left to Count Zac. The chaplain's body—dead or dying—he put in the charge of Ser Francis Atcourt and the squires, and the drowned wagon and the family he left to young di Laternum, who was suddenly thrust into command, with the sun setting in the west and children sinking in the mud and an unknown enemy moving in the woods to the west. Cully stepped up to the young man-at-arm's shoulder and whispered in his ear.

Ser Gavin rode briskly up and down the road in the fading light. His second time past the squires, he took Toby off the watch and ordered him to take his riding horse, ride his charger, and try to fetch help.

Toby glanced west, gulped, and nodded.

No questions were asked. Every man and woman present knew how dangerous their situation was.

Ser Gavin knew what his brother would do next. The immediate crisis was past. It was time to plan.

He ticked off the points on his armoured gauntlets.

First, gather all his people in one place. Nothing along the road was particularly defensible. But in one place, with a couple of fires and a deception or two, they'd have a chance.

Horses. The horses would have to be picketed. There was no forage and none closer than the swamp.

He rode back to di Laternum, who had the goodwife out of the water and had, himself, waded into the mud and retrieved the mangled corpse of one of her children. The other was, of course, gone. Cully had an arrow on every string—and had the wagon out of the water, for which incredible engineering feat No Head received Gavin's terse and hurried thanks. Two horses from the wagon team were coyote food, and two were exhausted but alive.

The goodwife, a solid woman who had seen many defeats, was sunk in her grief. Ser Gavin rode up to her—at a loss. She knelt in the road next to the appallingly small bundle that was her dead second daughter.

"I made her," she said. "I made 'em all, and I sweated blood, and I love 'em. Oh, blessed Virgin, why?" She looked up at the knight. "You came to *rescue* us?"

Ser Gavin had seen enough grief to know the anger was a part of it.

"Into the wagon," he said gruffly. "We'll mourn tomorrow. Tonight, we live."

"I'm not—" the woman said, but whatever she was not, her eldest daughter took her elbow and moved her to the wagon.

"But Jenna! We can't leave Jenna to get ate!" she wailed.

Her eldest son, without even a flirtation with hesitation, scooped up the bloody linen shawl that held his sister's corporeal remains and carried it—tenderly—to the wagon.

Cuddy had the heads of both horses. They were weak and twitchy and deeply scared.

Ser Gavin reined in.

Cuddy waved him off. "I'm gonna walk with 'em."

"We're going back," Ser Gavin said. "For the captain."

"Course we are," Cuddy said.

"Amen to that," No Head agreed.

Gavin wanted to gallop down the road. There were ten minutes of useful light left, and something was making noise north of the marsh.

It made him want to cry, deep inside, that he was learning to lead men from his brother—the brother whose effeminacy he'd mocked throughout his youth. But he took the time to turn his horse and clap a hand on di Laternum's arm as the wagon began to move. "Well done," he said.

The Etruscan boy—he looked like a boy now, with dark circles under haunted eyes—shrugged. "I scarcely did a thing, my lord," he said. "Cully…"

Ser Gavin managed a hard smile. "Listen to Cully. But think for yourself, too." He gave the boy a crisp and very real salute, hand to his visor, and cantered off east to find his brother. He still didn't know if his wonderful, terrible brother was alive or dead.

And only now could he let himself wonder.

Zac had a cordon around the tree, and he'd found the shaman's feather cloak and the pieces of his axe.

Feeling almost foolish, he said aloud, "Darkness is close. You're safe for the moment. I have people all around you." He shrugged, talking to a rainbow. "Your brother has taken command."

Good. When I let go, the pain may knock me out. There's some better than remote chance I'll just die. I've made a stupid mistake and I'm out of ops.

Count Zac crossed himself and touched an amulet.

The rainbow of light shimmered and went out. The woods were suddenly darker.

The captain screamed.

When Gavin had the archers—when the knights and squires were together, and the wagon was parked over Father Arnaud, who hadn't moved—he led every spare man to try and save his brother.

Who was still alive, as could be told from his screams.

It took an hour of torch-lit axe-work to clear enough of the trunk to allow them to make the right effort, and the constant movement of large animals or enemies out in the darkness did nothing to improve Ser Gavin's sense of urgency.

But he pretended to be calm, and twice, he told archers to take their time.

The steppe woman, Kriax, volunteered to go into the darkness and watch. She slipped from her pony and vanished into the haze at the edge of the torchlight.

"She has cut many throats at home," Zac said with a shrug. "That's why she's here."

It took ten men and a woman to move the tree. By the time they levered the section of trunk off his brother's legs, the stars were out in the sky above.

Ser Gavin calculated constantly. *Assume that the company is camped a league from where we left them. That's four leagues from here. An hour for Toby to find them, if something doesn't eat him. An hour back, and half an hour to raise the force to get it done right.*

I should never have sent him alone. I should have gone myself. Or sent Nell and Cully with him to get the message through.

But a wyvern would eat all three of them.

I've heard wyverns are blind at night. And that they can see in the dark.

I hate this. Is this what he does every day? What Pater does? Decide people's lives?

Ser Gavin sat on his war horse, still in full harness, his shoulders straight, and pretended to be a tower of strength and leadership. Like all commanders, everywhere.

When the pole star rose, the archers sung a quiet night prayer and everyone joined in, even Cuddy, who was notorious for his blasphemy. When the prayer was done, Kriax slipped into the fire circle and tossed a toothy head on the fire. She had a grim smile, and Zac had to bandage both her arms, which had been savaged. She never so much as grunted. The squires watched her with something very like worship.

Adrian Goldsmith volunteered to crawl out into the darkness.

Gavin let him go.

They built a second fire—a decoy. They put it up the road, and then they built a third down the road.

The third watch came. Ser Gavin began to despair that he would have to add Toby to his butcher's bill. His brother wasn't moving, and neither was Father Arnaud.

Ser Gavin started to pray.

Gabriel was not so much unconscious as deep in his palace—by far pleasanter than screaming his lungs out at the pain from his crushed and mangled right leg. Even as it was, a tidal wave of pain would, from time to time, push him out of the aethereal *and into the* real. *Where he would be painfully aware of his loss of blood, of how cold he was, and how little time he had left to live.*

He tried to sort the shaman's memories—those he'd managed to take. His sublimation of his opponent had been too fast and too thorough. And he'd spent the power foolishly. His shields—his emergency spells—had been far too powerful. He could see, now—too late—the error in design that allowed them to seize every scrap of his power, like a tax collector seizing a poor man's assets.

He replayed the other daemon's cut at his head. His unprotected head.

I should have died. But I didn't.

And now—even now—I should probably be dead.

It occurred to him to work out why he was alive. There was a small, constant feed of *potentia* coming from outside. He could feel it.

It occurred to him—time was a problem in the palaces—that he should try to find Father Arnaud.

To think was to act.

He stepped across into the chaplain's memory palace and found himself in a darkened chapel. It was beautiful—the lectern was a magnificent bronze of a pregnant Madonna with her hands crossed over her stomach, standing quietly. A magnificent stained-glass rose window rode over him, set—in the freedom of the memory palace—as a three-dimensional rose roof that rose like a cupola of glass. On the window were portrayed scenes from the life of the saviour, but it was too dark to determine what, exactly, they were.

Indeed, it was very dark, and very cold, and Gabriel's first thought was that the light behind the window was fading.

"Arnaud!" he called.

To think was to find.

Father Arnaud lay in the midst of his place of power, arms out-flung. He smiled at Ser Gabriel.

"Welcome," he said. "It might have been better if we had been this way when I was alive."

"Alive?" Gabriel asked.

"My body is passing," Arnaud said with some humour. "In the *real*, I have perhaps twenty heartbeats left."

Gabriel reached for his link, checking, like any veteran magister, for enough ops to heal.

Arnaud smiled. "No. I will heal you. I will give you this last gift. And as I cross the wall and go into the far country, I leave you this. Save them, save them all. In doing so, brother, you will save yourself." He smiled, again with pure good humour, and Gabriel could see what a handsome young man he had been. "Please accept these gifts."

Arnaud's body gave a convulsion, and light flared, and for a moment—an eternal moment—the chapel was bathed in light. The figures of the rose window leapt into life, and a leper was cured, a blind man given his sight, a dead man raised, and a centurion's servant saved.

"Arnaud!" Gabriel shouted.

But the miracle of light was declining, and in its wake the cold of absolute void, and the dark.

Gabriel wrenched himself clear of the dying man's palace and woke.

The pain was gone. Around the fire stood a dozen men and women and every head was turned to him, and they all looked stunned.

His leg was healed.

Gabriel burst into tears. "I don't want this!" he shrieked.

And then rolled over and put his hands on either side of his chaplain's helmeted head. But Father Arnaud was a corpse, and wherever he had gone, his face was calm and wore the gentle smile of absolute victory.

When the flare of power lit the *aethereal* worlds, Thorn was hovering, torn by indecision, balanced on the knife edge between aggression and caution. He'd followed some of the combat; he sensed the Dark Sun's injury and depletion but he had a healthy fear of the Dark Sun's reserves and talent. To project himself across the *aethereal* could be done but was, itself, fraught with peril. And it would expose him, like an army too far from its supplies, to envelopment. It was too new a talent to be trusted. And his dark master was not available for advice or encouragement.

Something passed across the divide between life and death—something mighty.

Is he dead? Thorn whispered into the darkness. Suddenly bold, he cast himself across the abyss.

Gavin was kneeling by his brother. He had not seen his brother cry—not openly—since the other man had been a boy, and it made him feel sick with old feelings of rage and weakness and bullying strength.

But Gabriel's tears were quick. Almost like a mummer or a vagabond actor at a fair, he raised his head, eyes still full of tears that glittered in the firelight, but his voice was suddenly steady.

"Everyone run," he said. "Now."

"Incoming!" shouted Adrian Goldsmith. The squire didn't sound terrified—he sounded relieved. "It's Ser Michael!"

Ser Gavin froze.

Something began to form at the edge of the firelight.

"Run," Gabriel said.

He meant it. Perhaps he leaked *ops* into his command. But every man and woman at the fire broke and ran into the dark.

Gabriel tried to rise. But he had nothing left—except the trickle of *ops* that had, against all odds, preserved him.

He sighed. He heard horses on the road, heard voices.

He got to one elbow.

The heavy black shadow became material.

Thorn emerged from the *aethereal* with a hiss of lost air and bite of incredible cold. He was no longer like a tree. He was now more like a shadow or a pillar of smoke, lit from behind by a red fire. Two eyes glowed high above the captain.

A horse bellowed its fear.

"Ahh!" Thorn intoned. The syllable was full of surprise and satisfaction.

Gabriel lay and swallowed bile.

Then Mag was there. She was a woman of middle height, wearing the cowled hood of a woman pilgrim. She didn't even have a staff.

In the *aethereal*, she wielded a pair of scissors made of light, and she reached to cut Thorn's links to his home and his base of power. Her strike was faster than the flicker of summer lightning, and she did not guard herself, so decisive was she.

Gabriel had time to register the shriek of Thorn's disappointed rage, and the un-human magister was—*gone*.

Just for a moment, Mag seemed to tower over the fire like an avenging angel, and then she was just an aging woman in a cowled hood.

She leaned over the captain, who managed a very shaky grin. "I'm not having a good day," he said.

Mag kissed his cheek. "Stay with us, my dear."

"That was—" Gabriel struggled for words.

Mag laughed. "I've been wondering when he might try a straight-up kill," she said. "I've been working on that for months." She was brimful of power—and pride. Until she saw Arnaud.

She bent over him, but he was dead.

Gabriel reached up and put a hand on her skirts. "Did you—hit him?"

"No. He bolted at my first twitch." She smiled. "I knew he had to." Her smile grew shakier. "That is, I hoped he had to."

She sat suddenly. And then she put a hand on the dead priest's hands, and cried.

Chapter Two

Albinkirk

The company that rode into Albinkirk was sober, watchful, and grief-stricken. The company flags were furled, and the lead wagon held corpses—any observer could see as much.

Ser John Crayford watched them come through the gate and rode immediately to the head of the column, instead of reviewing and saluting the entire company.

The young sprig of last year was older. Much older. He wore a small pointed beard and his eyes were tired. His face was an expressionless mask of fatigue and unexpressed grief.

"How can I help?" Ser John asked.

Ser Gabriel took his offered hand. "Today, barracks. Tomorrow..." His eyes flickered aside. "Tomorrow, a priest you like and a church. We have a dozen dead." His eyes held grief—actual grief.

Welcome to growing up, laddie, Ser John thought. But he had kindness in him, too, and in fifty heartbeats his squire was riding for the bishop while his valet led the outriders to the barracks. The castle was still half-empty. With the company at a little over a third of its strength, he could put every man and woman in a bed, or at least on a straw pallet.

Ser John got the tale of the ambush from Kit Foliak, who he knew from his younger days, as the tired squires and pages began to sort the packs and the leather bags and the wagons and the horses in the citadel's courtyard, paved with uneven stones five centuries old.

When he'd seen to the company's basic comforts, he went with Ser

Ricar Fitzalan—a thinner and fitter version of the King's captain—into his hall and sent a boy for the Red Knight. The man came with his famous brother, and sat in a tall chair piled with cushions while his valet raised one of his legs, elevated it, and put it on a stool. The slip of a girl was quick, efficient, and apparently unconcerned by her master's vague nastiness.

"Stop that—fuck, you're hurting me," the captain spat. "Damn it, girl. Stop fussing. No, I do not want water. Get your hands off me."

Nell ignored him resolutely, following Mag's orders.

Ser Gabriel was out of his harness, and his fine velvet arming coat was filthy.

The man seemed to come to himself. He sighed and looked at Ser John.

"I beg your pardon," he said. "I'm not myself."

Ser Gavin shrugged and accepted a cup of wine. "You seem exactly like yourself to me," he said. "I'm not sure we've been introduced. I'm Ser Gavin Muriens. This is my brother, Ser Gabriel."

Ser John rose and bowed. "Ser John Crayford. I know your brother, from the siege and all that followed." He looked at the surly captain. "And for lifting my two best men-at-arms when he went past last time."

Ser Ricar laughed aloud. "Well, I don't know either of you, but I'm Ser Ricar Fitzalan. The old king's bastard. And captain of the bodyguard."

Ser Gavin bowed. "I saw you after Lissen Carak. Indeed, we were within a few beds in the dispensary of the sisters."

Ser Ricar bowed from his seat. "Of course. My apologies."

"Hah! One linen-wrapped body looks much like the rest," Gavin said. "But Sister Amicia pointed you out."

Ser John leaned forward. "Kit Foliak says you were ambushed—beat the ambush—and that a certain former king's sorcerer tried to clinch the bargain."

Gabriel played with his untrimmed beard. "Master Foliak is very free with his information. But yes."

Ser John shook his head. "I mean no harm and, by God, sirs, I believe we are of the same metal. If there need be factions, surely we are all King's men? And all of us foes of Plangere and his ilk."

Gabriel's smile was not friendly. But he sighed—a long exhalation. He looked at his brother, who twitched an eyebrow.

"Ser John, I'm a churl today. I'm not at my best, and I beg your pardon." He bowed slightly in his chair.

Ser John reflected the bow exactly.

Ser Gabriel looked out the window at the spring rain. They'd lost a day crossing the last stream before Albinkirk, the north branch of the West Kanatha. It was flooded to a roaring torrent by the spring melt. It had taken too long for tired men to get the wagons across.

The captain's tongue had been too active and too biting.

He regretted it. He stared out the window and no one spoke. Finally he said, "I lost too many men. And a—a friend."

Ser John thought *ahhh*.

Less intuitive, or simply blunter, Ser Ricar held out his cup for more wine and asked, "What hit you?"

Ser Gavin's voice was not much less strained than his brother's. "Four wyverns," he said. "Twenty daemons and a shaman. Something we've never seen before." Gavin gestured vaguely over his shoulder. "We brought two corpses to show you. We call them imps." He looked away. "We lost three men to them."

Ser John shook his head. "I am sorry for your losses, Captain. And sorry you were attacked; I try to patrol my lands. Where were you?"

"The Hole," Ser Gabriel said. "Not in any way your fault."

Ser Ricar and Ser John exchanged a look. "So far south and east!" Ser Ricar said.

"Thorn's coming," Gabriel said, and the name was like a curse. "You know, until now, I have not taken him seriously. Like a fool. Like a fool. I gave him a year to recover, and now look." Gabriel's face wore the same anger that the goodwife had worn. "He's back."

"Brother—" Gavin said with a cautioning hand.

Gabriel shook it off. "You have called a council," he said to Ser John. "I'd like to attend with my brother. With Tom Lachlan, who is now the Drover."

Ser John nodded. "We'd be proud to have you, sir knight. The Abbess will be here, and most of our northern gentry will be here or be represented."

"I can represent the Emperor," Gabriel said.

Ser John's eyebrows shot up, but he had heard the rumours.

"And as Duke of Thrake, I think I deserve a seat at the table," he added.

"Or the whole table," Ser Gavin muttered.

Ser John frowned. "Well—you gentlemen will dominate my council, then, with your mother. She's expected tomorrow from Ticondaga."

A difficult silence fell.

Ser John wondered what he'd said.

Finally, Ser Gabriel gave a laugh that had a sob in it. "Am I safe in assuming that the Abbess will bring Sister Amicia?" he asked.

Ser John smiled. "Of course. She's essential to our defences."

Gabriel nodded. "Perfect," he said. He held out his cup. "I'll need some more wine."

An hour later, Ser Gavin had his brother in a bed, in a clean nightshirt, and lightly drunken on wine and lots of water. "Brother," he said.

Gabriel smiled ruefully. "I'm well. Well enough. You go."

Gavin shook his head. "I'll stay."

Gabriel raised his head. "I'm not a fucking weakling, brother. Trust me, I'll weather this. And you've waited almost a year to see her. Go! At the very least, she needs to know that Mater might be here, and what that will mean."

"Sweet Christ, I hadn't even thought—" Gavin smacked his head. "Oh, dear God."

"Exactly," Gabriel said. "You must go. And I will stay here, and play the role. Come back—but don't despair. The worst is over."

Gavin looked at his brother with too much understanding. "No, it isn't."

Gabriel frowned. "I didn't know how much I liked him," he said. "I didn't..."

Gavin sighed. "I did. Ever since Kaitlin's wedding. He was one of us as much as if he'd ridden with us for years. Christ, listen to me. I've only ridden with you a year."

"I have that effect on people," Gabriel said. But he managed a smile. "I mean it. Go kiss the Lady Mary from me, too. Bring her if you think she'll survive Mater. And don't, if you don't. We'll ride south in five days."

"You still mean to go to the tournament," Gavin said.

Gabriel nodded. "Gavin, I've made plans and I've made other plans. Nell!" he shouted, and Nell appeared.

"Nell, I would like to formally apologize for my behaviour."

"Apology accepted," Nell snapped.

Gavin laughed outright. "Just what you deserve."

Gabriel shook his head. "Nell, I need the scroll tube. You know it, the ivory one."

Wordlessly, Nell went back to the outer room. And returned with a scroll tube.

"If I die—this is the plan." Gabriel shrugged. "Master Smythe told me that if we missed the tournament, we'd probably rue it. He's so helpful that way. For what it's worth—and my credibility is a little singed, I admit—Plangere just lost a powerful controlled mage and the daemon warband took heavy losses. I intend to advertise that he came—and he ran." Gabriel's smile had nothing of pleasure in it, and everything of predatory anticipation. "He lost four wyverns, too. That will hurt his credibility with them."

"So?" Gavin asked, holding the tube.

"So I do not want to speak my plans aloud, brother. For various *reasons*." He pursed his lips. "Read the scroll and give it to Tom and Michael, and then bring it back here so I can make it ash."

Drawn like a moth to a flame, Gavin was already reading. He whistled, and raised his head. "Holy Mary mother of God," he said in shock. "Who else knows this?"

"Gelfred. Ranald. Kronmir." Gabriel shrugged. "To be honest, none of you know everything I know."

"You are so trusting," Gavin said.

"If I go down, it's yours," Gabriel said.

"You almost died, didn't you?" Gavin said.

"I should be dead, right now," Gabriel said.

Bad Tom, missing his cousin's calm efficiency, divided his herds in the fields south of Albinkirk. A flurry of messengers found him an Etruscan factor and one of Ser Gerald Random's company clerks, and between them they took financial responsibility for a third of the herd and hired, on the spot, twenty of the captain's men-at-arms, hurriedly placed under Sauce and Ser Gavin, and rode away west to the fair at Lissen Carak.

Bad Tom fretted at the delay, but he had no choice. So he read the scroll that Ser Michael handed him, grinned at the captain's former squire, and handed it back. He drank off a stiff cup of wine and looked at Ser Michael.

"I'm sending Kaitlin to Lissen Carak," Ser Michael said.

Bad Tom poured a second cup. "He almost died, and I wasn't there," he said suddenly.

Ser Michael nodded. "Me, either."

Tom met the other knight's eye. They were suddenly within a finger's breadth of being of a height. "I don't want to be somewhere else when he goes down. I want to be in the shield ring. I want to swing the last blow over his corpse. I want the sword women to take me with him when they go."

"You're not exactly a Christian, are you, Tom?" Michael asked.

Tom gulped wine. Very quietly, he said, "Have you read yon?"

Michael nodded.

"Tar's tits," Tom said.

Michael considered that for a long time. Then he smiled. "Yes," he said, and went to spend a few last hours with his wife.

Kaitlin was her usual self—buoyant and undemanding and centred on the needs of others. She wanted Michael to take her to the captain, but Michael was against it and, besides, he knew that Ser Gavin was riding in the morning. "Let the captain sleep," he said. "You can see him in the morning, when we bury the priest and the children." His voice was rough with forced nonchalance.

Kaitlin, who had a clearer idea of what the chaplain might have meant to the captain than most of her husband's peers, let it go, and spent the night curled in her husband's arms. In the morning—well rested—she levered her growing bulk off the bed. "No longer the prettiest maid in the valley," she said.

Ser Michael knelt and kissed her hands.

"He was a good priest," she said. "He married us."

Michael smiled. "Cully says he died healing the captain. That—" He paused.

Kaitlin frowned. "What?"

"Cully—this is Cully, sweetie, not some pious croaker—Cully says a man in a ragged robe came and knelt by the captain, and he woke up."

Kaitlin crossed herself. "A saint?" she asked.

Ser Michael frowned. "I'd hate to think so," he said. "I enjoyed jousting with him too much."

The whole town came out in the spring rain. The rain fell in sheets, and made the turf—still frozen deep under—springy and squishy like a huge pile of wet wool.

Every man-at-arms in the town came in his harness, and squires cursed them.

And the Bishop of Albinkirk stood in the rain. The coffins were plain boards. One was empty, for the lost child, and there were only red scraps in poor Robin's coffin, rushed and overwhelmed and devoured by imps after he lost control of the horses. The goodwife stood by the coffins of her dead children, and her eldest daughter stood with her, but now wore the scarlet tabard of the company, and even through the rain a distance could be seen between them.

The priest's coffin had the banner of the Order of Saint Thomas over it, and no other marking but the dead priest's crucifix, helm, and gauntlets.

Like every man present, the bishop was soaked to the skin, and cold.

He raised his arms.

"What words can I say that will equal the deeds of these people?" he asked. "How can I express a mother's grief? Or a knight's impotence in the face of death?"

The only sound was the rain. Gabriel flinched.

"In the beginning was the *word*," the bishop said. "Word" echoed. "Only the true word, the *Logos*, could speak for these. As the Logos was, in the beginning, so he will wait until the end, alpha and omega. And, we can only hope, wait patiently for all of us to come to him." He stood, arms wide, his soaking vestments hanging from him and his face raised to the sky.

Perhaps they expected a flash of lightning, or the acknowledgement of the heavens, but there was only an icy wind.

Six knights—Ser Gabriel, Ser Thomas, Ser Gavin, Ser Michael, Lord Wimarc and Ser Alison—lowered Father Arnaud into the muddy hole prepared for him. Toby had a pile of earth covered carefully with oil cloth, and he'd done the same for every dead archer and page and squire and child. One by one, the soaked knights lowered their dead into the embrace of the mud, and then put fresh earth atop them.

The goodwife stood and wept. When the last coffin passed her, she reached out to touch it, and then turned away.

Ser Gabriel stood with the bishop. "You are a man of power," he said.

The bishop shrugged. "Today I am a man with no power to make a mother feel the love of God," he said. "And no interest in pious mouthings."

Ser Gabriel nodded. There was cold water running down his spine. His arming coat had soaked through.

"He was a great man." Ser Gabriel surprised himself to say it.

"You loved him, then?" the bishop asked.

Ser Gabriel turned away. Then, very slowly, he shrugged. "He was a fine man-at-arms and my people loved him."

"And you?" asked the bishop.

"Why must you ask?" Gabriel said. His shields were back up—a smile twisted his mouth. "I have some pious mouthings of my own to deliver, my lord bishop."

He walked over to the company. They were as still as if on parade—a rank of knights and men-at-arms, and then a rank of squires, a rank of archers, and finally a rank of pages. Ready to receive a wyvern or a cavalry charge. Or bad news.

The captain stood in the rain. He raised his head and looked at them. "When we make mistakes, people die," he said. "When we do our jobs well, other people die. Death is part of our trade—always there. And, like wages, it's not fair. Why the baby? Why not someone old, like Cuddy?"

A few daring souls tittered.

The captain looked around. "I don't know. I don't know why Arnaud died, instead of me. But at another level, I know *exactly* why Arnaud died, and why Robin died and why we're standing here in the rain. We're here because we chose—we chose to fight. Some of you joined the company to fight for something you liked. Some of you fight for each other. Some for gold coins and a precious few fight because mayhap we'll do some good, whatever good is." He looked around. "The baby didn't choose to fight, though. Nor the mother."

He shrugged. "My point is, we *know* who killed them. We're in the middle of a fight. The bishop reminds you of God's mercy. I will only say this: I will not forget why they died, and when the moment comes..." He took a deep breath, and the men and women in the front row could see the red clash of his eyes. "If I am spared to that moment, *my sword will not sleep.*"

A sigh escaped the company, as if the whole body were a single person.

The Bishop of Albinkirk turned away in anger.

The captain squared his shoulders. "Company!" he called, as if his voice had never trembled with emotion.

They snapped to attention.

"Take your proper," he called, "distance."

The corporals slipped out of the front line and went forward three paces.

The three red lines turned about, and walked off—three paces for the second line, six for the third, nine for the fourth.

He signalled Ser Bescanon, who walked out from the officers' rank and unsheathed his sword. He saluted with it, and the Red Knight returned his salute and walked off into the rain.

Ser Bescanon's high cheekbones and long Occitan nose were dripping under his faceless cervelleur. "Have a care for your armour!" he bellowed. "Company—dismiss!"

They ran for shelter. Squires and pages cursed.

The bishop went and stood beside the captain under one of the eaves of the stable. "Revenge?" he asked. "Is that how you motivate them?" His voice was flat with anger.

The captain's slightly reptilian green eyes seemed to sparkle. "My lord bishop, today—for the first time in a long time, let me add—revenge is what motivates *me*. They will follow."

"You spurn everything for which that gentle man stood," the bishop said.

The captain stood for a moment, tapping his riding gloves impatiently on his armoured thigh. He seemed on the edge of saying something but, instead, he held his peace, and his face became a smooth mask.

Then the mask failed him. The captain leaned close, his eyes very slightly tinged with red, and the bishop had to force himself to stand his ground. "You know," he said softly, "that gentle man was killed by a shaman—a creature who had been bound. Magisters call it *turning*. You know it? A creature's own will is stripped away, and replaced by the control of another. I killed the shaman, my lord bishop, but he was as helpless and as guiltless as your Jesus as a babe. He was a tool. I'm sick of it. I'm sick of *being* a tool and of using others as tools and the whole bloody game."

This was so far from what the bishop had expected that he had readied a very different argument. So he had to fold away his text, and take a deep breath.

"Then don't play," he said.

The captain's eyes were a calm green again and the threat of emotional violence seemed to have subsided. He shrugged. "Do you know the questions that are asked of a knight at his making, my lord?"

The bishop nodded.

"I believe in those questions," the captain said. "Who will protect the weak? Who will defy the enemy? Who will defend the widow and the orphan, the king, and the queen? Even, when forced to it, Holy Mother Church?"

The bishop blinked. "Jesus said we should turn the other cheek. Jesus said *nothing* of a triumph by violence."

"Yes, well." The captain smiled. "I think Jesus would have had a hard time with Bad Tom." His riding gloves struck the steel of his cuisses with a snap.

"For now, though, the answer to those questions is—I will. I will defy the enemy. I've finished sacrificing my pieces one at a time." He shook himself.

The bishop smiled. "You aren't even talking to me, are you?"

The captain shrugged.

"I'm going to send you a new chaplain," the bishop said.

Snap went the gloves.

"Make sure he's a good jouster," the captain said.

Ser Alcaeus was drawn to the walls. In his life, he had known much sweetness and much horror, but no experience had equalled the intensity—and the terror—of the minutes after the walls were breached in the siege of Albinkirk. He went to the stretch of northern walls that he had held, and met there—to his stupefaction—a young crossbowman he had known during the siege.

"By Saint George," Ser Alcaeus said. He embraced the man. "Stefan?"

"Mark, and it please my lord," the young man said.

"I thought you were dead," Ser Alcaeus said.

Mark shrugged. "I thought so, too. I fell from the wall." He shrugged. "I woke up hungry and with two broken legs." He shrugged again. "Nothing found me to eat me, I guess." He barked an uncomfortable laugh. "Now I guard the same stretch of wall."

They looked out over the north and west together.

To the north, the Wild stretched on like a dark carpet, the great trees in the middle distance fading into the tall mountains of the Adnacrags and their white-clad peaks. A single road, wide enough for one wagon, wound out of the wooded hills at the edge of sight along the stable banks of the Canata river that came, cold and black, out of the mountains and descended into the valley through abandoned farmsteads and newly colonized steads and a handful of tilled fields from families that had survived the siege and planted last season.

There was a convoy on the road, glittering with spear points. It was still a good league from the walls, and yet it seemed to flare with colour.

To the south-west, the Royal Road ran up from the great ford at Southford and up to the south gate of Albinkirk, and then west out the west gate and on the north bank of the Cohocton. The north road—often a pair of wagon ruts—joined the Royal Road almost a half a league out from Albinkirk's walls, where the flooded waters of the Canata ran south from the mountains and poured under the three stone arches of the ancient bridge, which the prosaic inhabitants called Troy, a hamlet of nine houses and a fortified tower.

Out on the Royal Road beyond Troy, a party of three people on horses— or perhaps donkeys—ambled in the clear spring air. The downpour had swept the sky clear and the wind had driven the clouds south. The heavy downpour had flooded the streams, but it had stripped the last ice out of the shaded corners of the fields.

"They must be damp," Alcaeus said. He turned to young Mark, who shrugged.

"Sometimes I think of killing myself," Mark said suddenly. His voice was flat.

Alcaeus looked at him carefully. He had things to do, and plots to weave. But this was a man who'd faced the wave of monsters with him.

So Alcaeus leaned casually back against the cold merlons of the curtain wall and tried to look nonchalant. "Why?" he asked quietly.

The young man looked out over the fields. "It's all I think about." He shrugged. "There's no time before it. The attack. It is just...dark."

Alcaeus nodded. "You think that perhaps this is not the best job for you?" he asked. "The same piece of wall?"

"They all died," Mark said. "Everyone I knew. Everyone but me." He turned and looked out over the fields. "I think that I died, too. Sometimes that's how I make sense of it. I'm dead, and that's why—" His voice had begun to rise in pitch.

Alcaeus had seen all the signs before.

"That's why you should be dead, too, but you aren't—" Young Mark stepped in close and went for the baselard at his waist, but Alcaeus, who had seen men broken by war and terror since he was a child, stripped the weapon from him and put the man down on the catwalk as gently as he could.

"Guard!" he called a few times.

The two roads met by the inn at Troy. The inn was small, nothing like the fortified edifice at Dorling, but the King's Arms at Troy was a pleasant building with six mullioned windows newly replaced by the innkeeper, a tall, thin man whose Etruscan parentage showed in his straight black hair and aquiline nose. Sheer luck had preserved his roof and his floors from the forces of the Wild; he'd helped hold the walls of Albinkirk and done his best to fight fires. He'd poured his fortune into restoring his inn, preparing for what he hoped might be better times, and he'd watched with sickened apprehension as more and more reports came into his common room of raids on the frontier, of monsters and death.

The morning rain had been so heavy on the frozen ground that his lower basement had flooded, and he was down there, bailing with a bucket with all four of his scullery maids and both of his grooms, when his wife's shrill voice summoned him to the common room. He pounded up the steps with the grooms at his heels and he took the long Etruscan halberd off its pegs behind the great fireplace as he passed and turned into the great low common room that was the centre of his inn—and his village.

There were neither irks nor boglins in the courtyard. Instead, framed in the doorway was a knight in the richest armour Giancarlo Grimaldo had ever seen. He bowed.

The young knight returned his bow. "You are the keeper?" the young man asked.

"My lord, I have that honour," Giancarlo said, setting his halberd into the angle that the mantelpiece made with the wall.

"I am Ser Aneas Muriens, and my mother, the Green Lady of the North, wishes to take her midday meal in your establishment." He inclined his head slightly. "We are wet, and my mother is chilled."

"I will make up the fire and serve you only the best." The yard outside was filled with men-at-arms and servants, and they would all need to be fed. It was two months' business in a single convoy, and all he had to do was survive it.

He turned to Nob, his best groom. "Run along to Master Jean's and ask for both his daughters. Quick as you can."

His wife leaned forward and hissed, "And send Jean's son Robbie to Lady Helewise at the manor house and see if you can get her girl and Jenny to serve the duchess. Fetch Lady Helewise herself if she can come."

Nob was out the kitchen and running in heartbeats, spraying new mud as he went.

But the great Duchess of Westwall was not coming in. She was out in the stone-flagged street—stone flagged only to the limits of the village, and with the sewer running down the middle in stone-slabbed confines cleaned by an old stream—sitting on a magnificent, high-blooded eastern riding horse. Chatting with a nun on a donkey.

"Let her through!" Ghause snapped at her men-at-arms. Her tone of command gave way to the dulcet accents of seduction as she leaned down. "My gossip, the saintly Amicia. Give an old woman your blessing, my sweet."

Amicia had had several minutes to recognize the banner, and the men-at-arms. She knew Ghause's youngest son and her captain. She still found the impact of the woman enough to rob her of words.

Ghause Muriens, mother of the Red Knight and of Ser Gavin, wife of the Earl of Westwall, was not a tall woman, although few people remembered her as small. She was, in fact, just five feet tall in her stockings; though not so small when booted and spurred atop a tall horse. Her honey-blond hair was as unmarked by time as her face or the skin of her neck or the tops of her breasts, and she wore the very latest in Etruscan fashion, a long pointed hat with a great spray of ostrich plumes held in an heraldic brooch, a perfectly dry cloak in her own colours of green and sable, lined entirely in sable so black it looked hermetical and trimmed in royal ermine to which she had every right as the king's sister. She wore gloves of dark green and two matching emerald rings in red gold, and her waist was clasped with a heavy knight's belt of cockle shells in the matching gold, and a similar chain—the shells full size—lay over her shoulders and breasts under her cloak. Her spurs were gold like a knight's, and she wore a great sword of war—an uncommon accoutrement for a woman even in Alba—the scabbard green and all its fittings gold.

Just behind her in the crowded street was a great bird, too big to be a hawk and possibly large even for an eagle, on a perch and jessed and belled and hooded. It was huge. The size of a big dog. It gave a mad screech that made horses shy.

The duchess glanced at it and turned back. She wore the value of the whole village on her back. The people came to their doors or lined the street to see her, and she waved politely and smiled.

Amicia took a deep breath, dismounted, and curtsied.

The duchess smiled. "You are really such a pretty thing. Don't you think those breasts and those legs are wasted on God? He doesn't care. Let him have the ugly old maids. Those legs were made for sport, sweeting."

Ghause's men-at-arms were used to her. No one leered. No one commented.

Amicia rose from her curtsey. "No one could be immune to your grace's flattery, or fail to perceive your meaning," the nun said.

Ghause smiled. "I like you, my little witch. Come and share a meal with an old woman. You know my son is, by all report, in yonder fortress."

Amicia smiled. "So I have heard."

"You look tired," Ghause said. "Too much prayer?"

Amicia was tempted to say that she'd been drained of her *ops* for two days and nights, but chose not to share that. She made herself smile. "Too many young lovers," she said.

Ghause's beautiful blue eyes almost bulged. There was a long silence, and then she snorted so hard that her horse started and she had to curb the animal. Then she laughed and laughed.

Amicia was not used to the level of service that the duchess provided. The duchess retired and changed into a yet more splendid dress of green velvet that left no man present in any doubt as to the shape—and tone—of her body. Her hair was brushed until it shone like the red gold of her jewels.

It came to Amicia that the great duchess was nervous.

The innkeeper and his staff were as courteous as the strain of twenty men-at-arms and forty more servants on a country inn could leave them, and she chose a strong red wine to steady her nerves, but the best tonic was the sight of Helewise—Lady Helewise to the older locals. She was the lady of a manor just to the south, and she came in quietly, wearing a good wool gown and an apron, with her daughter Phillippa and another girl the same age, Jenny, both pretty and blond and capable of being gentlewomen when called on to do so. After a whispered conversation with the innkeeper, Helewise went out into the yard and spoke to the captain of the duchess's men-at-arms and took wine to Ser Aneas in person.

Ser Aneas gave her a deep bow. "You are no inn servant," he said.

She smiled at him. "Nor I am, ser knight, but in a village, we all help each other. Especially in these times, mm?"

The men-at-arms were all gentlemen, and they had dismounted, and stood in knots in the yard. The inn was too small for them to all go in at once.

Through the windows, Helewise could see the keeper's wife bustling to make the two common room long tables fit for gentry.

"We will have two tables ready for you in a moment," Helewise said. "If you gentlemen would be kind enough to enter in files, and file to your seat, that would allow the duchess some privacy. And allow us to get you fed efficiently."

Ser Aneas bowed.

Phillippa and Jenny came into the yard with silver trays—her own—full of good Venike glasses, each filled with the best Occitan, a sweet wine that travelled well. They served like ladies, and the gentlemen appraised them with the glass and the silver.

Helewise took Ser Aneas's glass. The duchess's captain bowed. "I am Ser Henri," he said with an accent as Venike as the glass.

Helewise dropped him a straight-backed curtsey without tilting her tray. "My lord does us honour."

Ser Henri laughed. "By God, I've seen more courtesy in this inn yard than in a year at Ticondaga."

Helewise nodded. "You'll find that the keeper is your countryman, if I read your accent aright, my lord."

"By the cross of Christ!" Ser Henri said. "Mayhap he has some of the wine of home, then. Goodwife? My lady?"

Helewise nodded. "Folk hereabouts call me a lady, ser knight. But my husband, while a good man-at-arms, was never a knight."

She went in with her tray—but not before her eyes summoned her daughter and Jenny, who were basking too long in the admiration of twenty young men.

"What brings you to Albinkirk?" the duchess asked. She had a healthy appetite—she wolfed down half a rabbit, all of a capon, and moved on to a dish of greens in the new fashion, apparently oblivious to the miracle of the innkeeper having greens in late Martius.

Amicia ate more sparingly due to her Lenten vows, but the food was good and the wine better. She sat with the duchess, curtained off from the men-at-arms who were now seated and loud, ensconced at the two long tables nearest the door.

"My Abbess does not feel that she can travel just now," Amicia said. "I will represent the Order at Ser John's council."

The duchess met her eye. "You are *full* of surprises, my love. Will you sit in Sophie's chair and be the Abbess? By God, that might be enough power to turn my head away from marriage. Who wants men anyway?" She laughed, swallowed a morsel of truffle and sat back to sip wine. "Outside of the one thing they do well."

"War?" Amicia asked.

"An excellent point. War and sex." Ghause smiled. "I am just a crude old woman."

"So you insist," Amicia said.

Ghause raised a hand and one of her own ladies came.

"Fetch me the keeper," Ghause said. "So—you feel you might have to spurn my son's advances to make yourself the most powerful woman in the north?"

Amicia felt that she was getting better at dealing with Ghause. "No, I don't feel that way at all," she said.

The innkeeper came through the curtain and bowed deeply.

"Keeper—your food is wonderful. I am *most pleased*." The duchess held out her hand, and the keeper bowed and kissed it—an almost unheard of honour given their relative stations. "And these dumplings—what are they?"

The keeper bowed. "In Etrusca, they are called *gnocchi*."

"Made with truffles," the duchess said.

"Your grace has all my secrets," the keeper replied gallantly. "But I will tell my wife. She made them."

Ghause nodded. Her green eyes were smiling. "I feel these dumplings might threaten the shape of my thighs but, by the crucified Christ, they make me want to eat all day." She sparkled at him.

He bowed, clearly overwhelmed.

She dismissed him with a wave. "I will tell every gentle I meet to visit you," she said. "Please feel free to display my arms in your window."

The keeper bowed and retired, the colour of his spring business altered for the better. Amicia had a glimpse of Lady Helewise—a good friend—and the two women shared a glance, and the curtain closed.

"So you won't change your mind," Ghause snapped at Amicia, the moment that the keeper was gone, as if the interruption had never taken place.

Amicia was tempted, to her own surprise, to confide in this terrible woman, but she held her peace. "No, your grace."

"Damn you, then. You'd have made me some fine, sly, long-legged grandchildren with powers." She leaned in. "If you won't have him for yourself, will you help me find him a mate?"

Amicia gave a small cry.

Ghause laughed grimly. "Just as I thought."

"But of course I'll help," Amicia said. She was surprised at herself—at the speed of her reaction and its intensity. She'd had a year to adjust. She was in charge of her own destiny.

Ghause smiled. "You are very brave. Good. Come, travel with me, and we'll hold each other up, as women must in this world."

In two hours, the inn had fed and wined the duchess, all her staff, twenty men-at-arms and their squires and pages, the bird's handlers, two huntsmen in charge of a pair of dead aurochs in a wagon, and a hundred horses had been fed and watered. Every man and woman in the village had been involved at some level, from the making of winter sausage last autumn to the desperate plea for grooms and maids.

Ser Henri tossed a purse to the keeper as the great hooded bird cleared the yard in its green and gold wagon. "I will not forget this inn," he said. "My thanks, and those of every one of my knights."

He trotted his great war horse—all the knights had mounted their heavy horses for the entry into Albinkirk—and rode out after his convoy.

The keeper went wearily into his common room, where half the village was being served a pint of ale. He upended half a year's profits on the serving counter in front of his wife, who hugged him.

He turned to Helewise. "Gold, or ale?" he asked.

She smiled. "That was not enough of a favour to need repayment," she said. She enjoyed her pint of ale, collected her daughters, and walked them home across the muddy fields along the still-frozen margins.

The Duchess of Westwall's entry into Albinkirk was anything but spontaneous. Her men-at-arms glittered and any sign of travel stain or mud had been erased at the inn, and the whole column swept into town like an avenging army. Her men-at-arms wore matching green and gold; her wagons were gold and green, and the enormous bird, a tame monster of some sort, was itself badged in gold and green, like the duchess herself in her emeralds. Most of the population of Albinkirk was in the streets, and Captain Henri distributed largesse to the poor from his saddlebow.

The duchess rode in the middle of her column. She was greeted at the gate in blazing sunshine by Ser John, and escorted up through the narrow and winding streets to the citadel, where she and her immediate staff were to be housed.

She stood in the great hall under the timbered roof and smiled at Ser John, who felt the power of her like a stallion smelling a mare, and the bishop, who treated her more as a forbidden text, and saved his warmth for Sister Amicia, with whom he shared a chaste embrace.

"But where are my sons?" the duchess asked.

Ser John bowed. "Ser Gabriel and Ser Gavin are hard at work in my tiltyard," he said.

"Send them to me when they are presentable," Ghause said. She offered her hand to the Captain of Albinkirk. Over her shoulder, she said to Ser Henri, "Feel free to take Ser Aneas to his brothers."

She put her arm through Amicia's. "Come," she said.

Amicia knew that she was being used for something. But she had little enough choice, and she went willingly with the duchess.

Four huntsmen brought the bird.

If the morning had been wet and filled with mourning, midday had been dryer and had been as physically hard as the morning had been on the spirit. The captain had seemed determined to unhorse every member of his company, and he rode his great war horse Ataelus on course after course. He'd stretched Ser John over his crupper early, as Ser John had to greet the man's infernal mother. The Captain of Albinkirk knew his lower back would feel the force of the blow for days—but when the duchess swept regally to her rooms, Ser John led her household knights back into the yard, mounted with them, and rode to the tiltyard under the walls, facing south.

As he arrived, Ser Alcaeus unhorsed a young Occitan spectacularly, dropping the man without appearing to alter his own seat. He swept down the list with his unbroken lance tip high.

There were twenty women and a hundred men watching. They applauded.

Ser Michael entered the lists at the eastern end, and Bad Tom entered from the west. They were plainly armoured, without surcoats or fancy harness, and both wore great helms for jousting instead of their bascinets.

They flicked salutes at each other and the horses moved.

Ser Henri nodded approval. "These are very good," he said.

They met—and passed. Both lances broke in a spray of ash splinters. Both men were as erect as equestrian statues.

Ser John smiled grimly. "They are very good," he said. "If you'd care to play, just take a place in the line down there." Below them was a chute, with a line of mounted men on war horses. War horses that fidgeted, farted, and threatened to kick or bite.

Ser Henri rode down into the chute, and so did Ser Aneas. A few of the other men-at-arms joined in. Others dismounted, gave their horses to grooms, and began to spar with swords or wooden wasters—or just to stop at the barriers and watch.

Ser Gavin broke a lance on Ser Bescanon, who got his lance tip on Ser Gavin's helmet but failed to strike the crest.

Ser Phillipe caught a young knight from Jarsay in the shoulder, and his strike destroyed the other man's pauldron and injured his shoulder. A dozen men took the injured knight away, and Ser Phillipe, visibly shaken, had his shield dismounted and withdrew.

Two unremarkable courses were run, and Ser Henri rode forward. He took a lance from Toby, who was serving every man-at-arms on that side of the lists.

Ser Gabriel was seen to move his horse forward, past Ser Francis Atcourt, who raised his visor and said something in derision.

Ser Henri saluted, and charged. Seconds later, he was lying unconscious on the sand, and the Red Knight all but rode over him returning. Ser Gavin was seen to speak sharply to his brother.

Ser Aneas, one of the youngest men to joust that day, readied himself to meet Ser Gavin, his brother. He conceded nothing; his horse rode at the very edge of the barrier, and he put his lance into his older brother's visor.

Both spears exploded—and *both* men lost their helms, split by the blows, and rode bareheaded in opposite directions. They were wildly applauded.

Ser Henri was quick to recover, and insisted he'd never been fully unconscious.

Ser Gavin had an odd look when Ser John approached him. "That looked—rough," Ser John said.

Ser Gavin looked away. "He was our jousting instructor. From boyhood."

Ser John laughed. "A case of the biter bit?" he asked.

Ser Gavin met his eye. "Don't let my brother face him again," he said.

Ser John nodded. "I have run lists afore. But I'll bear that in mind. Your lady mother wishes to see you both."

Ser Gavin nodded. "So I gather from the string of pages we've had. But our mater wants to see Gabriel first, so I'll cool my heels."

Ser John scratched under his aventail. "In that case, I wonder if we might gather all the captains for a brief—mmm. A meeting before the council."

Ser Gavin looked at Ser Henri, helmet off and a pair of pages serving him water. "That might be a fine notion," he said.

Before three more courses had been run, a table was waiting in the outer yard and wine was served. Ser Gabriel sat in harness with Ser Gavin, Ser Michael and Ser Thomas. Ser Henri sat with Ser Aneas. Ser John sat with Ser Ricar Fitzalan. Ser Alcaeus joined them after a final course with Count Zac, who was perhaps the most unconventional jouster anyone had ever seen.

Ser John got straight to the point. "Gentles all—my thanks. The council is for politics. But it seems to me—with so many puissant gentlemen all gathered together—that we could send a small army into the field right now, and perhaps put the Wild back on its haunches."

Ser Gabriel drank off his wine. "That's blunt. You'd like to use my lances—my professionals—for free."

Ser John nodded. "Yes."

Ser Thomas the Drover raised an eyebrow. "And all my cousins, too? Who'll command 'em? Hillmen don't take orders from everyone."

Gabriel laughed. "In my experience, from anyone."

Bad Tom grinned.

Ser John looked at Ser Ricar. "The Captain of the King's Guard will take the field."

Ser Ricar rose. "If you gentlemen agree, I'll call a muster. I'll pay king's wages for ten days. We'll sweep the north bank of the Cohocton and cover the fair. With a hundred lances and the support of the sisters of the Order there's not likely to be anything we can't handle."

"Ten days!" Ser Thomas shook his head. "The forage by Southford won't feed my beasts ten days."

"If we don't cover the fair…" Ser John shrugged. "The convoys are just coming in from the south," he said. "I'm trying to keep the roads clear, but—"

Ser Gabriel—the mercenary—surprised them all. He stood. "I'm for it. Tom, let's give them a week and then see where we all are. Ser Ricar, can you make do with a week, and an option for a few more days if required?"

Ser Henri raised an eyebrow. "It is not my choice but my lady's," he said. "But it sounds worthy, and certes, Ticondaga would be better knowing the south was safe."

Zac raised two bushy eyebrows at Ser Gabriel. He gave a slight nod.

"Count Zac is an officer of the Emperor," he said. "He serves with me in my person as the Megas Dukas of the Empire. He will join you for your spring hunt."

Ser Ricar clanked over to the dapper easterner and shook his hand. Ser Alcaeus took out a wax tablet and began to write at his captain's elbow. "We have forty lances and another twenty *stradiotes*," he said. "Ser Henri?"

The Etruscan rubbed his head. "If the duchess agrees," he said carefully, "I have twenty lances. And four huntsmen who know the enemy intimately."

Ser Ricar nodded. "I also have forty lances, though eight of them are on patrol even now."

"So—with the count's imperial troops, we can muster as many as six hundred men," Ser Ricar said with relish. "By God, gentlemen."

Bad Tom sighed. "Well, I can gi' ye another hundred who'll face anything in the Wild."

"I count this a favourable sign, gentlemen," Ser John said. "The council has not even begun, and we have an army in the field." He turned to Ser Ricar. "When will you march?"

"Dawn," Ser Ricar said. "I'll open the ball with a sweep along the west road. I know our fathers all taught us not to split a force, but I'll send half north of the Cohocton and half south, and we'll clear the whole convoy route on both banks."

Ser Gabriel rose. "Then, if you gentlemen will settle the minutiae of what you have clearly planned, I will release my soldiers under Ser Bescanon. I must visit my mother."

He bowed to all—even Ser Henri—and walked across the springy turf to where his squire waited.

"Why does he set my teeth on edge?" asked Ser Ricar.

"He was not like this as a boy," Ser Henri said. "He was a most unmanly boy, much given to—"

Ser Gavin appeared between them, and there was no more reminiscence.

Ser Gabriel unarmed carefully, and went to his room to bathe. In his room, alone with Toby, Nell, and two of his Thrakian servants, he drank two cups of malmsey and put on a suit of red wool worked with his arms, a golden spur rowel of six points that might have been mistaken for an hermetical symbol. He put on his gold belt of knighthood. He didn't wear a sword, but he didn't disdain his ivory-gripped baselard.

Nell and Toby had some idea what he was going to. They both tried to smile.

He had time to wish he had Tom, or Alison. Or Arnaud.

He walked to the small balcony his room had, high above the valley. He took one breath, drank off the last of his wine, and set the cup down a little too hard.

"No," he said, when Toby, dressed in his best, presented himself as an escort. He motioned instead to Ser Christos's son, Giorgos, a tall Thrakian with a beak of a nose and no Alban whatsoever. "Please come with me," he said in High Archaic. He smiled at Toby to indicate that there was no slight intended, but he didn't need to have his mother's words repeated.

And then he went out into the hall. Giorgos knew the way—it was his duty—and led him to the south tower. They climbed two dozen steps in a tight stairway and emerged onto a platform with two doors. Giorgos knocked and they waited.

A demure young woman with red hair and bronze eyes opened the door and curtsied. She led them into the outer solar, almost identical to the same chambers that Ser Gabriel had in the north tower.

"Is that my prodigal son?" Ghause called. "I have a present for you, my darling. Come in."

The bronze-eyed young vixen opened the door to the inner solar, and Gabriel, after a deep breath, and ignoring the trembling of his hands, walked in.

Amicia sat in the sunlight, doing embroidery. The winter had sufficed for her to learn some of the tricks of it, and she'd learned to make letters with a prick stitch and to cut them out and overcast stitch them to an altar cloth before couching them in silk thread. She was slowly working the paschal cloth of her chapel at Southford, the linen and silk going everywhere with her, packed in oiled silk and canvas. Helewise had taught her—a lady's pastime, and not usually one for nuns. Her I H S was crisp, the gothic letters elegant and almost even.

She was working on the last I in domini when Ghause joined her in the inner solar and began to fuss with the great bird on the perch.

Amicia realized she was casting.

Ghause finished with some tuneless, throaty sounds that made Amicia blush.

Ghause laughed. "Ah, my pretty, I usually work alone. And naked."

Amicia laughed. "As did I, once."

"We are not so different," Ghause said.

Amicia put her head down and went back to her stitches. "What is it?" she asked.

"A gift for Gabriel. No, don't get up. That will be him now." She put one hand on the inner solar door and called, "Is that my prodigal son? I have a present for you, my darling. Come in."

Then she flung the door wide. As she did, with her right hand, she removed the cover on the great bird.

It was bigger than Amicia had imagined, but her shock was completely overwhelmed by the reality of Gabriel Muriens.

It was not that he had changed.

It was merely that he was.

Gabriel lost control of his face and his heart, like an untried army in an ambush. He was blind with the sight of Amicia, and unwarned, unprepared—a grin covered his face, and he stepped forward and took her hand and kissed it.

And she flushed.

And his mother laughed.

And the young griffon on the perch, a true monster of the Wild, was subsumed in a wave of *love.* It gazed on Gabriel, raised its great wings, and poured its own love back. It gave a great cry as if its heart had been pierced.

Ghause's laughter rose. "Oh! Brilliant!" she said. She stepped forward like a victor delivering the *coup de grâce*, and kissed her son on the cheek. "Two presents, then."

Amicia, moved beyond endurance, rose too quickly and stepped on her altar cloth. But she set her face, and pushed past him, and walked, head high, out of the room.

"She'll come back," Ghause said. "She wants you more than she wants her anaemic vows."

Gabriel was trembling.

"I have brought you a mighty gift," Ghause said. "And where are my thanks? Hello, my son."

"You used her to bait the impressment of a griffon?" Gabriel asked.

"Of course! What better love bait than your leman? As good as anything in a romance. And look, it's done! Your own griffon, which cost me a lot of effort, too." Ghause was not a woman given to prattle, but the rage on her son's face scared her. "Oh, my dear. Griffons need to be greeted with love. That's all that holds them. You cannot *turn* a griffon. They're too stupid. And too smart. Now he's all yours." She smiled. "All's well that ends well."

"You have not changed much," Gabriel said. He did smile at the griffon. He walked to the perch and cooed at it. Him.

"How old?" he asked.

Ghause smiled inwardly, knowing she had indeed impressed him. "He's about two months old and he eats like ten wolves. He'll be four times that size in six months. His mother was big enough for a grown man to ride."

"You killed her," Gabriel said.

Ghause sputtered with indignation. "She was wild! And dangerous!"

"The same might be said of you, Mater." Gabriel was gazing into the eyes of the monster. It looked back at him like a great daft cat.

"You have changed, my son," Ghause said. "Look at you. A Power."

"This is the wrong day for you to say that, Mother." Gabriel stumbled to the window and looked out. Then he turned, unable to stop himself, and went back to the bird.

"But you are a Power, now," she purred. "I made you to be one, and look at you. They worship you. They all worship you."

"Stop it!" he said.

"When you take the kingdom, they will—"

He met the griffon's wide, mad, delighted eyes.

"He'll need constant attention, of course," she said. "You wouldn't believe how much effort I put into this, child. I—"

"Mother," Gabriel said. "Please stop."

He turned and they were eye to eye.

"You always were a stiff-necked boy," she said with a sniff.

"You killed my tutor and my master-at-arms," he said.

She frowned. "I most certainly did not. Henri killed your so-called master-at-arms, and Prudentia—" She shrugged. "I don't honestly know what happened."

"You ordered them killed," he insisted.

"How tiresome. Stop changing your ground. Killed, ordered killed? What boots it, my child? They were nothing. They were leading you astray and, let us admit it, you needed to be a little tougher. Didn't you?" She put a hand on his chest, fingers splayed.

He left it there.

Ghause looked up into his face. When last she'd seen him, he'd been a little taller than she, and now he towered over her. Suddenly her pupils widened.

"Where is Ser Henri?" she asked.

Gabriel laughed. "I am not you, Mother. I did not kill him. Only his amour propre took any injury."

Ghause stamped her foot. "Let us not waste our time together, love. I have many things to share with you—workings to share, plans to make." She smiled. "You are Duke of Thrake now!"

He responded to her smile and her tone of pleasure. She was his mother. "I am, indeed," he said.

She laughed, a throaty, rich laugh. "Oh, my dear heart! Every inch of ground along the wall is ours. The earl and I—and you—what a kingdom we will make!"

Gabriel ran his fingers gently through the great griffon's feathers. "No," he said.

She frowned. "What do you mean 'no'?"

Gabriel shrugged. "I mean, I have no intention of taking any lessons from you in diplomacy. Whatever you intend, I am not party to it. While we are on this uncomfortable ground, you may add the hermetical arts. I suspect you have nothing to teach me, and anyway, I wouldn't trust you in my head."

"Nothing to teach you!" Ghause replied, now stung to her core. "You are my child. I *made* you."

Gabriel gave her a little bow with an ease that made him proud of himself. His mother terrified him, but by God, he was keeping it in. He clasped his hands together to hide their trembling.

"I had Harmodius in my head for a year," he said, every syllable like the blow of a trebuchet.

"You work the *gold*?" she asked.

In the *aethereal*, in her other sight, *she watched as he plucked a ray of sunshine from the gold and her own breath from the green and bound them into an amulet.* He handed her a little Herakles knot of rose stems.

She accepted it.

It burst—a little explosion of rose petals and incense.

"I have my own plans. They do not include you." Gabriel bowed. "I admit I do want the griffon."

Ghause bent her head. She backed away a step, in defeat. "As you will, my puissant son," she said, and with the ease of years of practice, kept the ring of triumph from her voice.

My son! Together, we will rule everything. After I take you back.

An hour later, Gavin found his brother alone in his own outer solar. He'd been warned by Nell.

He found Gabriel feeding a dead chicken, feathers and all, to a griffon that seemed to grow before his very eyes. The very air was tainted with the thing's smell, like a musky eroticism flavoured with blood.

"You alive?" Gavin asked. "What the hell is that?"

Gabriel sighed. "Very much alive. That is, sorry, hurting, anxious, and in a black mood. It's like being fucking fifteen all over again." He smiled bleakly. "But she gave me a griffon! He's lovely, ain't he?"

Gavin laughed and poured wine. "I'd like a griffon, too. I see I don't rate one." He shook his head. "Is my sudden desire to rut with any servant girl I find willing—"

Gabriel winced. "That may just be me. No, it's the griffon. He can't help it. They all emit love, and drink love, and... think love."

Gavin laughed. "Blessed Virgin, it's like being fifteen. Make it stop!"

"You mean the sudden peaks of desire, or the effect Mother has on us? Just like being fifteen," Gabriel said. He tossed the chicken's head into the air, and a great talon caught it and the eagle-beak crunched it. Gabriel stepped away, and Gavin, as if engaged in wrestling, tricked his weight and forced him into an embrace.

"No," Gavin said. "We're not children, and we won't take sides. When we were young, she divided us and conquered us."

Gabriel hugged him a moment and then stepped back. "She used Amicia against me."

Gavin laughed bitterly. "You should have heard her advice about Lady Mary!" He blushed even to think of it. "I don't feel I can just wander off to Lissen Carak and leave you." He shrugged. "You know she has Aneas with her."

"I know," Gabriel said. He put his hand on his brother's shoulder. "You know—sometimes, you really are the best brother," he said. "Go and be with your lady love. I'll stay home with our mother." He sighed. "And Aneas."

"And your lover, the nun," Gavin said.

Gabriel sat down and put his head in his hands. "Exactly."

"No one can say we aren't an entertaining family." Gavin sat opposite his brother. "Why the nun, brother? She's pretty enough, I admit. I rather fancied her myself." He shrugged. "But..."

Gabriel sat back. "How very often I've wondered, brother. I think I'm a bear-hunter caught helplessly in my own bear trap."

"You worked something on her?" Gavin asked.

"Something like that," Gabriel answered. He smiled wryly. "Whenever you think you are very clever, that's when you are getting ready to be awesomely stupid."

"Based on your own experience?" Gavin asked. "I should stop drinking if you're serious about letting me go."

"The fewer witnesses the better," Gabriel said.

"And her notion of making Pater the King of the North?" Gavin asked, his hand on the door latch.

Gabriel smiled grimly. "The frosting on the bun, dear brother. She thinks I made myself Duke of Thrake to secure her borders."

Ser Gavin turned, hand still on the door. "Did you?" he asked.

The silence stretched.

Ser Gabriel came and put his hands on his brother's shoulders. "Gavin, once upon a time, I had plans. Now, they have changed." He looked away. "So the answer is not simple."

Gavin nodded. Then gave up on annoyance and embraced his brother again. "You are the king of ambiguity," he said.

"Send Lady Mary my best regards," Ser Gabriel said.

The Council of the North started with little fanfare and less ceremony than anyone expected. The next morning, all the principals gathered in the great hall of the citadel. No trumpets sounded, and even the duchess seemed subdued.

Ser John Crayford sat at the head of the table. He was wearing a good green pourpoint and matching hose, and his businesslike attire was reflected on every participant except the duchess. She faced him down the length of the table, enthroned in a tall wooden chair her people had brought and surrounded by her maids. She wore figured velvet shot with gold thread—embroidered griffons.

On the right side of the table sat Amicia, for the abbey at Lissen Carak, and Lord Wayland—hardly a famous name, but Gregario, Lord Wayland, was the chief of the small lords of the northern Brogat, the Hills, and the lands just south of Albinkirk. He was himself a famous swordsman, and he wore the latest Harndoner fashions. By his side was his ally and lifelong friend, the Grand Squire, a dapper, handsome man of fifty in a green pourpoint cunningly embroidered—another of the north country's famous swordsmen, and one of the north's richest landowners. Closest to the duchess sat the Keeper of Dorling's son. He was a tall, hard-faced youth, called Allan. In the Keeper's own country, they called him Master of Dorling.

Across the table from them sat Ser Gabriel in his person as the Duke of Thrake, and Ser Thomas as the Drover, and Ser Alcaeus, representing the Emperor as Ser John represented the King. By courtesy—there had been other Councils of the North—a seat was left empty for the Wyrm. There were no Orleys left to take the seat by Lord Wayland. Instead, Lord Matteo Corner sat with Peter Falconer—the first the chief of the Etruscan merchants then in the north, and the other an officer of Ser Gerald Random. Between them, they knew, and might speak for, the mercantile interests. Across from them, the council was balanced by the interests of the Church in the person of Albinkirk's bishop. It was an august gathering, and aside from the duchess's ladies, Ser Gregario's wife Natalia in the most fashionable dress in the hall, and Toby and Jamie, the squire of Ser John, the hall was empty of servants—and moths.

No one was late. When everyone was seated, Ser John rose.

"My lady duchess—my lord Duke of Thrake, my lord bishop, Master, ladies and gentlemen," he said. "I am a mere soldier. But I have summoned this council in the name of the king, and I'm most grateful—in his name—that the king's own sister and the rest of you have found time and means to come.

"My intention is simple. I want to create a unified plan to defend the north country this summer—yes, and for many summers to come. Thanks to your efforts, we have already put a small army in the field at no cost to the people of this district and, if God will grace our efforts, that's a fine opening to our discussions."

He looked over the table. "My scouts, and those of the Emperor and the duke, have provided us with reports that the bishop's scribes have copied for all of you," he said. "In brief, Plangere is coming. He has an army of the Wild and another of Outwallers, and he has new allies—Galles, who have a flood of reinforcements from home." Ser John looked around.

Ghause looked bored. "So?" she asked.

"So, my lady duchess, he has the force to take Albinkirk. Or Ticondaga. Or Middleburg. Or Lissen Carak. Or even Lonika. But not any of them, if we all field an army together." He was going to go on, but Ghause interrupted.

"Fiddlesticks," she said. "Poppycock. I can see straight through him and he's as impotent as—" She gave a wicked smile. "Never mind. He failed to defeat Ser Gabriel the other day—and he failed to take Lissen Carak a year ago."

Ser Gabriel pursed his lips. "I don't agree," he said.

Ghause looked at him as if he was a mythical being. "I'm sorry, my child. Did I mishear you?"

Gabriel shook his head slightly. "I had a chance to learn from one of his officers."

Ghause raised a perfect eyebrow. "You tortured him?"

"I subsumed him and took his memories," Gabriel said.

A near perfect silence fell over the table.

"Ah," Ghause said, with a smile that could only be described as motherly. "Please go on."

"I have the impression, first, that the attempt on me was put together with clay and spit, and was not a serious effort. Despite which"—he looked away—"it was very nearly successful."

"Perhaps," Ghause said.

"And I also received the impression that Plangere is well-prepared. That the extent of his own preparations left him unwilling to take any risks." Gabriel shrugged. "Why should he?"

"I don't believe there's enough men and power in the world to take Ticondaga," Ghause said.

"No fortress is stronger than the men on its walls," Ser John said. "And no fortress can stand a year of siege. Starvation can take any stronghold."

Ghause sighed. "So much drama. Very well, what do you want?"

"I want to appoint a Captain of the North. And I want to have him muster an army."

"This captain is to be you?" Ghause asked.

Ser John shrugged. "I was thinking of your son, Gabriel."

Gabriel looked surprised. "I am going to the tournament at Harndon."

Ser John nodded. "Harndon is five days' ride for a single determined man and his escort. Faster if there's a change of horses." He looked over the table. "Wherever he strikes, we'll be able to combine our forces. While I have greater fears for our ancient fortresses than the duchess, I agree that none of them will fall quickly. We will have a month or more to raise our armies if we are prepared."

"My husband is ready to lead an army straight at the sorcerer, if that's what you want," Ghause said. She sat up, like a fierce hawk disturbed at her rest. "Why wait for him? Why not strike him first?"

Ser Gabriel frowned. "By water, your grace?" he asked.

Ghause smiled. "Yes, my child. By water."

"You are a puissant magistra, Mother. Would you allow an attack on Ticondaga by water?" Ser Gabriel's tone was quiet and respectful.

Ghause laughed. "I agree that water is a wonderful element to manipulate," she said.

"And every step he takes south of the inner sea stretches his resources," Ser John said. "Why should we go there and stretch ours?"

Lord Corner put his hands flat on the table. "Not all of us are men of war," he said. "I see no reason to risk an army in the Wild."

Ghause laughed—a genuine laugh, not her laugh of derision. "You are in the Wild right now, my lord," she said. "Or perhaps I should say, there is no Wild. Irks and boglins—men and priests. And little to tell between them."

Lord Wayland was a careful man. He leaned back, one finger against his chin. "It is always easier to rally men to defend their homes than to invade someone else's."

Now Ghause snorted her derision.

Amicia looked up and down the table. "My lords—how will we know when the sorcerer launches his true effort? Will he not attempt to deceive us?"

Ser John smiled at her. "An excellent point. No army will march and denude any district. We must have an arrière-ban ready to stand on the defence."

Ser Gabriel met Amicia's eyes. "It is an excellent point, Amicia. But I think that we can build a mobile army that will move faster than Thorn can."

A frisson of power passed through the air.

Ghause threw back her head and laughed. "Bless you, my child," she said. "You amuse me. Taunt him!" She smiled. "Thorn," she said, seductively.

The air darkened a moment.

Eyes were wide.

"Leave it there," Ser Gabriel snapped. "If we say a third, the die is cast. As it is, it will stay in the air." He smiled. "I see all sorts of things that can go wrong, Ser John. But Alcaeus and I have a chrysobul from the Emperor authorizing us to call on the field army, which will, by the first of April or so, be at Middleburg."

Ser John looked up in surprise. "My pardon, my lord duke, but the chatter in the market is that the Emperor is bankrupt and cannot field an army."

The Duke of Thrake smiled mirthlessly. "What do you think we were doing last year?" he asked. "Dancing? The Empire has a field army. It will be at Middleburg."

Ser Thomas slammed a fist on the great table. "I like what I'm hearing," he said. "I like the notion of the fight this season and not next. But I have my herds to move, and most of the tail of my best men is with me. I can send a man home to muster levies, but until the drove is over—"

"I mislike the idea of keeping an army in the field all summer," Lord Wayland said. "We're not the Emperor with an army all the year. Fields must be ploughed. My archers are my yeomen. My spearmen are my herds-men." He shrugged.

Next to him, the Grand Squire grinned and nodded. "I wouldn't mind a season of campaigning," he quipped. "But my people would. And my wife, come to think of it."

"A shirt of mail is a year's lost herds." The Bishop of Albinkirk spoke seldom, but he spoke well.

Ser John looked at Ser Gabriel. "Can you command the Emperor's army?" he asked.

Ser Gabriel looked at his hands. "Yes," he said.

Ser Alcaeus was seen to smile.

"Then let us build a force here, based on your company and Ser Ricar's. I'm sure we can pay your wages." He looked at the merchants, who flinched.

Ser Gabriel shook his head. "I'll pay my own," he said. "I'm the Duke of

91

Thrake. I had other plans, but I'll put them aside for the summer. We can keep the northern levies and the Hill clans as our reserve."

"But what of the Royal Army?" Ghause asked, too sweetly.

Ser John frowned. "I do not think we can rely on the Royal Army this summer," he said primly. "I don't think we will see them north of Harndon." He sighed. "Or if we do, we may rue it." He looked around. "I would rather not speak all my thoughts than lie. But unless I am mistaken, the Royal Army will not save us this year."

"Because of raids in the south?" the Etruscan merchant asked.

"Because Alba is on the brink of a civil war," the bishop said quietly.

Ser John leaned back. "We are all king's men here," he said. "We will *be* the Royal Army."

Ser Alcaeus looked as if he was going to choke.

Ser Gabriel frowned. "We will be an allied army of the north. If the Emperor contributes troops, he will not want to be seen as a vassal of the King of Alba."

The Duchess of Westwall nodded. "Well said, my son. We are allies, not feudatories. Let that be clear." She looked around—more like the griffon than was quite right. "Consider this, gentles—if the Royal Army cannot help us, and if we must raise our own army to hold back this petty sorcerer, what will we do when a serious threat comes? Why pay our taxes to a distant king who cannot defend us? Why not have *our own king*?"

Ser John sat up straighter, and looked at the duchess. "I beg your pardon, your grace, but are you contending that the Earl of Westwall is *not* the vassal of the King? Are you suggesting..."

The duchess smiled. It was the sort of smile one might imagine on a particularly subtle fox just before he eats the chicken. "I am a poor weak woman with no great head for politics, Ser John. I speak no treason when I say that my brother cannot defend us. His writ does not run here." She smiled, and her smile narrowed. "I merely tell you, brave knights, that neither my husband, nor I, will be bound by a document or an agreement that decribes us as the king's vassals or *requires* our knight service. On the other hand, if such an agreement is worded as an alliance, we will eagerly contribute to both the field army and to the total effort and the costs."

The Bishop of Albinkirk narrowed his eyes. "You see the Adnacrags as a sovereign county?" he asked.

The smile that the duchess wore grew, if anything, a little wider. "I have said no such thing," she said. "Yet, I imagine that were we to make ourselves sovereign, we would only aid our own defence."

"This is treason," the bishop said.

"Make the most of it," the duchess snapped.

"We owe our service to the king—" Ser John began.

"Why?" Ghause asked. "He's just a man—and a feckless one. The way I hear it, my son and Sophie saved you all last spring. The way I hear it, the King almost lost his army in the woods and had to be saved by his slut of a Queen and the river fleet. And now he's let in an army of Galles who are running rough-shod over the south. I'm here to tell you that we will not allow them into the north." She sat back.

Lord Wayland's eye went to hers. He said nothing, but his cautious expression betrayed his interest.

The young Master of Dorling shook his head like a man shaking off sleep. "My da holds our place from the Wyrm," he said. "I am not the king's man, and saving your grace, I'm not your man, either." He looked around. "I like the notion of alliance, but I have nothing to say about any new kingdom except a word of advice: only a fool changes horses in mid-stream."

The duchess's head went back like that of an angry horse.

Ser Alcaeus nodded. "I think I might speak," he said quietly, "for all of us who are not Albans—and say that this talk of a kingdom in the north is immoderate. I think that if it continues, my Emperor would require that I withdraw. I must say on his behalf that Thrake is a province in the Empire, and that Ser Gabriel's possession of it is at the Emperor's pleasure. The Empire does not function as a set of infeudations, nor are our lands inheritable without the Emperor's permission, my lords. The Emperor owns *everything.* He can grant or remove any title at any time."

Ghause smiled poisonously. "Does that include the Emperor's throne, ser knight? Is it not held by right of inheritance?"

Ser Alcaeus looked surprised. "The Emperor is chosen by God," he said.

"Usually after a lot of poisoning and knife fights," Ser Gabriel said. He shook his head. "I'm sorry, *your grace,* but the north is not ready to have a sovereign kingdom."

"Then the north is full of fools," Ghause said. "Ask your imperial riding officers—ask anyone who lives on the wall! There's as many people north of the wall as south. There's *towns* north of the wall. All of them could be ours!"

Her son shook his head. "Yours, you mean. I'm sorry, *your grace,* but our intention is the protection of our estates—not the raising of a new banner in the Game of Kings."

Ghause sat back and sniffed. "Well," she said. She smiled. "We'll see, then, won't we?"

While every leader present was willing enough in principle, every side room in the citadel seemed to have two or three great lords discussing, debating, and often enough, shouting. If Ghause had intended to divide the council of the northern lords, she had succeeded to perfection.

"Your lady mother cannot imagine that we'd sign away the king's rights to the whole of the north country!" Ser John said to the Red Knight. Now that he knew the boy was the Earl of Westwall's son, he found his infernal arrogance easier to stomach—the more because the boy seemed to have grown a little more human in the past year.

The new Duke of Thrake sat with his back against the oak panelling of Ser John's private study. "Neither the earl nor the duchess has ever had much time for the king," he said slowly. "And it hasn't troubled you before. Or has it?"

Ser John was pacing up and down. "I will share my thoughts, my lord. Last year—during the siege—we received no succor but yours and, in the end, the Royal Army. We had no help of your parents. I confess I am less than pleased—indeed, I'm bitter." He pointed at the great hall. "At least the King came. The earl was five days away, and he never twitched."

Ser Gabriel rolled some good Etruscan wine over his tongue and looked out the window, where sheets of rain were filling the creeks and making the task of the field army more difficult and vastly more uncomfortable.

"But you have asked me to command," Ser Gabriel said.

"You are the most famous commander in Nova Terra just now," Ser John said.

"And the Westwall heir," Ser Gabriel added, a nasty note in his voice.

Ser John swirled wine in his silver cup and then turned to face the younger knight. "Yes. Why hide it? Surely your mother will sign and your father will commit if you are to have the command?"

Ser Gabriel shook his head. "I truly doubt it. I'm sorry, Ser John. I'm still under contract to the Emperor. As the Emperor's man—I have no feudal obligations at all in Alba—I would be willing to command your field force after I return from the tournament, but it is not vital to me. In fact, to me it looks like a summer of brutally hard work for no money and little thanks."

Ser John managed a smile. "You describe my whole tenure as Captain of Albinkirk."

Gabriel rose. "Ser John, I agree that having a mobile force to face the Wild is a necessary evil. I will command it for a summer—and pay my own wages from my tithe as Duke of Thrake. I will do this whatever the Earl of Westwall chooses to do. I will leave most of my people here with you. But I will not make the least effort to convince the earl or my mother to join this alliance, and can offer you no counsel about them."

Ser John stood, too.

"Where do you think Thorn will strike?" he asked.

Ser Gabriel shook his head. "Middleburg would have been weak had I lost in the east. But I didn't, and now it is very strong. Albinkirk—let us be realistic. Albinkirk has a solid captain and a small army—and is close to Lissen Carak and a magnificent array of magisters who have, since last spring's near disaster, come into their own."

"The nuns?" Ser John asked.

"Yes. I'd be very surprised indeed if Thorn tried again there. Were he to re-invest Albinkirk and Lissen Carak he would have to do both together, would he not?"

Ser John had not considered this. "Ah—yes. Because leaving either one would leave a force operating behind his siege lines. Bah—you are the right man to command."

"I have read some very good books. The Archaics thought deeply about war, Ser John. At any rate, he would have to divide his efforts, whatever solution he chose, and the morale consequence of a second failure in the same place would probably be disastrous for his forces."

Ser John smiled. "I just make war. I see you think about it."

Ser Gabriel shrugged. "That leaves Ticondaga—it's the most exposed. Or he might strike west, into the upper lakes country, and spend the summer gathering allies. There is a rumour that he and the Faery Knight quarrelled over the winter. Do not imagine that the Wild is a unified force. And luckily for us, the more puissant he grows, the more likely it is that other Powers in the Wild will try to drag him down."

"Try to drag him down?" John said. "You are leaving something unsaid, I think."

Ser Gabriel leaned close. "I think perhaps he has...help."

"Saints alive!" Ser John said. "Saint Maurice and Saint George, my lord. You speak of the Enemy?"

Somehow, that old name for Satan made Ser Gabriel smile. "Perhaps I do. The sorcerer is, at least, more dangerous than the sum of his parts." He leaned back. "This is not something to be discussed aloud."

Ser John nodded. "I thank you for your confidence," he growled.

"His help will not keep other Powers in the Wild from contesting with him," Ser Gabriel said.

"So you think we might get through this summer untouched!" Ser John said.

Ser Gabriel gave a thin smile with no mirth whatsoever. "If we do, it will only be because he has chosen to make himself far more powerful for *next* spring. And if he does, I have no idea where he might strike." Gabriel settled back against the wood panelling. If he had intended to leave, he had changed his mind.

"You think Ticondaga then?" Ser John asked.

"I think it is the most exposed fortress we have; its lord and lady do not really desire to cooperate with the rest of us, it is the strategic key to the lakes and the inner sea, and despite its reputation for invulnerability, it is overlooked by Mount Grace." Ser Gabriel shrugged. "And—do you really want to face an army of the Wild in the deep woods?"

Ser John nodded. "You are very persuasive. And the Galles?"

Ser Gabriel frowned. "I confess I cannot fathom what they are about.

But with a Galle knight at the king's court and another leading an army in the far north—" he waved a hand. "Jean de Vrailly is..."

"Insane?" Ser John asked.

The Red Knight raised an eyebrow. "Your words, my lord captain."

Ser John nodded emphatically. "I mislike the man, and Ser Ricar detests him."

Ser Gabriel nodded. "You understand that if Alba is indeed tipped towards civil war, Thorn"—he seemed to savour the name—"might be our salvation."

It was Ser John's turn to frown. "Why?"

"Because if he strikes into a civil war, every baron will unite against him under the king, and that will be the end of it." Ser Gabriel spoke with all the arrogant satisfaction that made him so easy to loathe. He made it sound as if he'd planned the whole thing.

Ser John put his wine cup down.

"Come, Ser John," Ser Gabriel said. "Let's put our crooked dice away and speak like honest men. It is civil war that you fear, and not the sorcerer in the north. And you want to know where I stand, where the Westwalls stand, where the Brogat barons stand."

Ser John's eyes narrowed. "If the King were to send de Vrailly north to collect taxes as he did in Jarsay last summer, we'd have a war right here." He frowned. "Your lady mother said as much."

Ser Gabriel nodded. "I thought that's what you feared. It is certainly what the duchess fears—she's more interested in laying the claims to her own sovereignty than in facing the sorcerer."

"Where do *you* stand?" Ser John asked.

Ser Gabriel met his eyes. "As the Duke of Thrake? Or as a sell-sword?" He smiled. "Nay—I'll answer honestly. I despise de Vrailly. But there's no reason behind it. I met him, and I know him." The Red Knight leaned back and sipped wine. "So are you really assembling a northern army to face de Vrailly?"

"God between us and evil!" Ser John spat. "I would never fight against the king, no matter how misguided he might be. But if I can build a force in the north, I'll tell the King that the northern army is his taxes 'in kind' and give de Vrailly no excuse to march here."

The Red Knight raised his goblet and toasted his companion. "Well thought out. I missed it—a fine gambit." He sat back, savouring the wine and the idea together. "On that understanding, perhaps I'll modify my course and approach my mother." He smiled, clearly pleased. "For everyone's benefit."

"I can see through a brick wall in time," Ser John grumbled, but he was pleased. "Now—when you go south, will you take my writ and gain the king's appointment? And you see why I must have your lady mother's agreement as a vassal and not as an ally?"

Ser Gabriel closed his eyes and frowned. "Damn," he said. "I'll do my best."

A day later—the hour after dawn, and the spring sun was the warm, golden colour that men remembered in mid-winter. It sparkled on the muddy puddles that lay at the corners of fields, where snow had lain just a few days before. Ser Ricar's messengers brought word—a day of constant fighting, but no organized foe, and the roads both north and south of the fords were clear.

For an entire day, the duchess hinted that sovereignty was her price for alliance, and most of the other lords refused to discuss what was to some treason, and to others irrelevant.

In the great hall, for the Red Knight a day that had begun well with Ser John proved trying. His mother refused to discuss vassalage; she was using the council to press her claims to a kingdom, and her pretensions were scaring the Brogat barons. By dinner, she was flirting outrageously with Lord Wayland, whose slow and cautious politics were in danger of being overwhelmed by the main force of a low-cut gown and a pair of flashing eyes.

After dinner, Ser Gabriel sent a note by means of Nell, and then went in person to his mother's door. The bronze-eyed girl opened it and bade him welcome, her cool, demure voice oddly at odds with her body and eyes.

"Your lady mother bids you wait, sir knight," she said.

Ser Gabriel bowed distantly and sat in a chair in the solar. He leafed through an illustrated breviary; he picked up a very prettily inlaid lute and started to play an old troubadour song, and found it wildly out of tune.

He began to tune it.

Time passed.

A string broke and Ser Gabriel cursed.

Bronze-eyes smiled prettily.

There were noises on the other side of his mother's door, but none that made any sense, and eventually, having found a set of strings inside the belly of the instrument, having stripped the offending string, which had been the wrong-sized gut all along, having replaced the string and then tuned the instrument to its intended range and not the very odd tuning that his mother had arranged, he played *Prende I Garde.*

"You are splendid!" Bronze-eyes said, enthusiastically. She clapped her hands together.

Ser Gabriel rose. "Please tell my mother I was most pleased to have this opportunity to tune her instrument, and she may call on me at any time." He handed the lute to the servant girl. She dropped a beautiful curtsey.

"If there is anything I might do to help you pass the time," she whispered.

He paused. And sighed. "Have a pleasant eve," he bade her, and passed the door.

He considered going to the great hall and joining the men there. He considered inflicting his anger and his annoyance on strangers.

He even paused outside the chapel, where he saw a straight-backed nun in the gown of the Order kneeling at the altar. He stood and watched her.

She didn't turn her head.

Eventually, he took his irritation to his own rooms. Toby and Nell stayed out of arm's reach, and with the assistance of two cups of wine, he managed to get to bed.

To the ceiling over his bed, he said, "I prefer fighting."

Then he lay and felt the fracture in his leg throb. He lay there with the pain, and thought about life and death and Father Arnaud. And Thorn, and his master, and where it all had to end. He was beginning to see the end. He lay, and imagined it.

Eventually he began to consider his miraculous survival of the recent ambush. That gave him the opportunity to savour each error he had made in the course of the fight—committing the knights too early, overpowering his emergency shields so that they drained him of power. Allowing an oak tree to fall on him.

He shook his head in the darkness.

At some point in the night he began to consider the constant flow of *ops* that had trickled to him while he lay awaiting death.

He heard Toby toss on the straw pallet at his feet.

Ser Gabriel considered many things, and eventually, his annoyance increased by each new thought, he *entered into his memory palace and walked along the floor.*

Prudentia nodded coolly. "You remind me of an unruly boy I knew once," she said.

"Are you simply magicked to say these things? Did he invest you with some particular ability to assess my thoughts and make suitable witticisms?"

Prudentia's blank ivory eyes seemed to glance at him. "I believe my re-creator discovered that a great many of my habits of thought were overlaid on your memories and he retrieved them."

"Well," the Red Knight said. "Well." He went to the door to Harmodius's palace. "I need to see something from another angle." He opened the door and went in.

It was dustier than before. Now that he thought about it, he realized what the old man must have done. Because somewhere in his memories, he must hold Prudentia's palace. And that suggested that if he spent too much time here, in Harmodius's memories, he might—just possibly—be in danger of either becoming the old man or empowering some sort of simulacrum of him.

"Not what I'm here for," he said.

He went and stood in front of the mirror.

In the reflection, he seemed to be wearing a ring of fire, and around his right ankle was a golden band. The band was joined to a chain.

"Son of a bitch," he said.

Eventually, he must have slept, because he awoke, his eyes feeling as if they were made of parchment and his mouth dry and his head throbbing. He lay, listening to Toby lay things out on the chest at the foot of the bed, and then the scale of his disaster and the throbbing of his right leg coincided, and he rose into the chilly air, his mood already savage.

He dressed quickly, and Toby kept his head averted. The boy's fear of him angered him further. He could sense his own failure to modify his temper.

At some remove, he didn't care.

"Where's Nell?" he asked.

"Stables, your grace." Toby was not usually so formal. "Shall I send for her?"

"No," the captain said. He sat and stewed. He knew what he had around his ankle, in the *aethereal*. He knew it was very powerful, and he suspected he knew where it came from.

Nell came in.

"Message for you, your grace," she said.

Nell brought him a note, and he read it at his own table. His colour heightened and his face went blank.

"Wine," he said.

It was early morning, and Toby frowned.

"I'm sorry, Toby, is there a problem?" Ser Gabriel asked in his most poisonous voice.

Toby glanced at Nell, who, having handed over the note, was busy sorting clean laundry in the press. Toby stood up straight. "I have hippocras," he said, and went to the fire.

"I asked for wine," the captain said. "Hippocras has all the spirit boiled out."

"May I say—" Toby began with all the dignity a seventeen-year-old can muster.

Ser Gabriel raised an eyebrow. "No," he said. "Your opinion is not required."

Toby reached for a wine bottle, but Nell reached out and tipped it on the floor.

It smashed.

Before the pieces were done moving, the captain was out of his chair and had Nell by the throat. "I asked for wine," he hissed. "Not adolescent criticism."

She looked at him, eyes wide.

He let her go slowly.

Nell shook herself and glanced at Toby, who had his hand on his dagger.

The captain sighed—a long sigh, like the air hissing out of a dead man's lungs. Without apology, he stepped out into the hall.

He didn't slam the door.

He didn't get a cup of wine, either.

Gabriel was almost insensible to the world around him as he stalked along the tower's outer hall and down the winding stairs, so angry at himself that he could barely breathe. He walked through the great hall without acknowledging anyone, and brushed past his mother without a word.

She smiled.

He paid her no heed, but walked out into the muddy yard and collected his riding horse, saddled by a pair of frightened grooms, and mounted. His anger communicated itself instantly to the horse, who began to fidget.

"Perhaps if you were to hit it *very* hard," came a soft voice from the gloom of the stable.

At the sound of her voice, his rage drained away, leaving him merely—deflated.

He turned the horse. The yard was almost empty, and his Morean page, Giorgos, was the only one of his own people in the stable.

"I got your note," he said.

"And it lightened your mood?" Amicia said, emerging from the shadows with a palfrey's reins in her right hand. "Shall we delight your lady mother by riding out into the spring sun?"

"Only if we come back with our clothes all muddy," Ser Gabriel said. His breathing was coming short, as if he'd been in a fight. "I'm sorry that she used you for the griffon." That wasn't what he'd meant to say.

Amicia mounted, throwing her leg over the saddle like a man. It was neither ladylike nor elegant, although it did show a fine flash of leg. It reminded Ser Gabriel that Sister Amicia had not been raised a gentle, and was largely self-taught. At everything. Including the casting of complex sorceries.

"People will talk," he said, trying to find a light-hearted note. "If we ride without an escort."

"*Honi soit qui mal y pense,*" she said in passable Gallish.

They rode out into a brisk day, with a hint of old winter in every shadow and a kiss of spring in the bright sunshine. She wore her hood up until they were clear of the gates of the town, and then she threw it back, and her rich brown hair was blown free of her wimple in seconds by the stiff north wind. She caught the wimple before it whipped free, like a flag in a storm, and tucked it into her bosom.

She smiled. "Do you know how long those things take to sew?" she asked. "I can't lose one."

Ser Gabriel could not fail to meet her smile. "I see you are learning to embroider," he said. "*La Belle Soeur de Forêt Sauvage.* Doesn't it bore you?"

"Oh, no!" she said, with delight. "No, I relish it. It is like going to mass. So—calming. Time to think. I have done a great deal of thinking this winter—since I met your mother."

Gabriel sighed. "Yes?" he asked. He noted, at some remove, that his hands were shaking.

She looked at him. "And you?"

He pursed his lips. "I have thought a great deal," he said.

She laughed. "It is easy to plot and devise other people's lives, is it not? So much easier than working on your own." She turned her horse at a side road short of the bridge. "Come, Gabriel. We are going to talk about the rest of our lives."

Gabriel reined in his horse. "Amicia," he said. His voice rose in pitch.

She looked back. "Gabriel. Let us get this done."

He sat, his horse unmoving. He was silent for so long that she had to wonder where his head was, and then he said, his voice strained, "I think you should just say it. I don't need to ride off into the copse of woods to hear it."

"On the highway?" she asked.

"Amicia," he said, and he paused. He looked away.

She turned her horse back. "I don't want to be interrupted," she said.

Slowly, as if against his will, his horse followed hers.

They rode another league, until they came to a small chapel. It was not quite a ruin—the stones were green with moss, the roof of slate was still supported by its ancient wooden beams, but it sagged in the middle. The altar stone was still solid, and there were bunches of snowdrops on it. Inside, it was pleasant enough—brisk, but not wintry, and the odour of incense mixed with a flat mossy smell.

Gabriel saw to their horses and followed the nun into the chapel. At the door, he paused.

"I'm gathering that you are not bringing me here to succumb to my worldly advances," he said.

"That sounds more like the man I knew at the siege," she said. She went to the altar and kindled a small fire, lit two candles and placed them on the altar. Almost instantly, the candles made the small space seem dryer and more homey.

Then she drew a stool from behind the altar and sat. "I come here often," she said. "The light is good."

"And it is full of power," he said.

"And God's light," she said.

Their eyes met. Hers were brown, and his were green, and each looked far too long, so that the silence grew uncomfortable, and then stretched to a flinching unease and through it.

In the aethereal, *they stood on her bridge, with the clear waters of the Wild flowing under it and the golden light of the sun pouring down through a clearing in the trees. In her palace, the trees had the full and dusty green leaves of late summer.*

"We didn't need to ride out of the fortress to do this," he said.

Amicia did not wear a robe and gown in the palace, but a tight green kirtle. "I wanted you to have time," she said. "Everyone has ambushed you this week. I was not going to be one of them."

Gabriel was in red; he leaned on her bridge. "I think you have brought me here to break off," he said. "And I think the ambush is of some duration."

She smiled. "Love—love, what break can there be between two sorcerous mortals who can walk in and out of each other's minds?"

Gabriel smiled as if she'd said something very different. "So linked that their ops pass back and forth without volition?" He didn't look at her. "Why didn't you come with me, Amicia?"

"I had other duties. I made a different decision." Her ambiguity was redoubled in the aethereal.

"Amicia." He turned and met her look—in the aethereal. *"I'm pretty sure that you agreed to come with me and be my wife."*

She shrugged. "I did. And I was wrong to, and I wronged you. But in taking my vows, I was true to myself. And I do not regret my vows." She smiled sadly. "I will never be your wife. Nor your leman. There, it is said. Again."

"Did I have to come here to have you say it?" he asked. "Or are you just one of those people who needs to be convinced?"

He stepped forward, his eyes hungry, and she stopped him. His reaching arms caught nothing.

"In the real," she said, "you can overcome both my body and my will. Here, I am your peer."

Baulked, his eyes flashed red and his rage was writ plain.

And then he stepped back and all but hissed.

"Love," she said. "Do you need my body? Is this a matter of love, or mastery? Is it that my Jesus blocks your mighty will? Why can you not be satisfied with this? How many mighty powers stand in each other's heads and talk? It is more intimate than any lovemaking."

Gabriel leaned back against the railing of the bridge.

"I wondered if you would allow me into your palace," he said.

"Why would I not?" she asked.

"Because of what you would hide from me," he said. "It's obvious here, is it not?" As he spoke, he pointed to his feet.

A tiny tendril, like a wisp of hair, tailed away from his right heel and fell away into the rushing water below.

Amicia put a hand to her neck.

Gabriel nodded. "At least twice, when I should have died—should absolutely, unequivocally have been dead—I have not died. The most recent occasion was so obvious that I had to know the cause." He smiled. *"I knew we were linked by the ring. But the ring merely covers something, doesn't it?"*

Amicia found it difficult to avoid his eyes. In fact, no matter where she turned, he seemed to be standing with his arms crossed.

"Why have you ensorcelled me?" he asked.

Amicia raised her head. "I cannot speak of it. What is done, is done."

"There speaks the language of love." He snorted.

She coloured.

He left her for the real.

"I brought you here," she said icily, "to tell you some things."

He smiled at her. Even in his current state, just to look at her warmed him. But he held up his hand. "I don't think I want to hear them. Amicia—for whatever reason we are joined—you know me better than many. Or at least, I imagine you know me well. And I have to tell you that just now, I'm at my limit. I don't need to know any more. I need to deal with my mother, and go to Harndon. In a week, or a month, or a year, if we are both alive, I would ask that we have this conversation again. And that you release me from your spell. But not, I hope, your love." He smiled. "You needed no spell to hold me."

"Hold you? Damn you and your arrogance," she said. "I have made my vows."

"My dear, girls leave convents every day. What kind of God would demand your chastity like a jealous lover? If you wish to commit to your God, be my guest, but don't hide behind your vows." He smiled. "There. I, too, have thought and thought. And those are the words I say to you." He took his gloves out of his belt. "I love you, Amicia. But..." He paused, and bit his lip.

Amicia shrugged. "My answer will be the same. You should marry the Morean princess."

He stopped moving.

"Irene. We all expected you to marry her. Even your own people expected it. Did she have warts or something? I understand that she's the most beautiful woman in the world—at least, I've heard it said." Amicia smiled. "I really just want you to be happy."

"So you have placed a mighty working on me?" Gabriel said.

Amicia shrugged.

"Can you remove it?" he asked. "I tried last night and failed."

"Let me set this out for you," she said like a schoolmistress for a not-very-bright pupil. "You accuse me of casting some *praxis* that is protecting you from death. And you'd like it removed." Her arch tone was almost contemptuous.

His anger flared. "No one else can do this to me," he spat. "Damn you. But yes. Take it away."

"Your mother can do this to you," Amicia said. "I spent a day with her and you know what? I liked her. I found that we agreed on some surprising things. For example, we both agreed that you needed to be protected." Amicia took a deep breath. "And for this I'm to be damned?"

Gabriel paused.

"You still have a healthy element of small boy in you, shouting *I can do it myself.* And in many ways you can. But—"

He shook his head. "I'm sorry, Amicia, but you have no idea what you're talking about. My mother is not—anyone's friend. Even her own. She is a *Power.*"

Amicia nodded, lips pursed and eyes narrowed almost to slits. "Gabriel Muriens, *I am a Power.*" She stood. "Just when you begin to woo me successfully—and you do, the mere sight and sound of you, as God is my witness—your overbearing—" She stopped. "You do yourself no favours. I am not a girl. I am not witless. I can, in fact, heal the sick, and make fire rain from the sky."

He looked away. "I am not the only arrogant fool here," he said. He went to the doorway. "I thought we'd go for a ride. And perhaps kiss. And maybe you'd tell me why you've placed a working on me. And I'd forgive you." He shook his head. "Instead, I have to at least consider that you and my mother are working together on whatever fool scheme she's devised for my future as the messiah of the Wild. I find that hard to credit, but if it is the case—"

"Forgive me?" she asked. Despite her best efforts, tears burst from her eyes. "You would *forgive me* for *saving your life?*" She looked at him, shaking her head. "And you think I'm plotting with the *Wild?*"

"Yes," he said.

"You idiot," she said.

He took a trembling breath and stepped forward.

She straight-armed his advance. "Go," she said.

She heard him mount his horse. And she heard him say, "Fuck," quite loudly and distinctly, and then he rode away, and she gave vent to a year's worth of frustrated tears.

Ser Gabriel appeared in the great hall just before noon. He was a trifle muddy and more reserved than usual, and Ser John beat him at chess so easily he felt the other man must be distracted.

"I'm not myself," the Red Knight said, although the acerbity with which he said it made him seem very much himself. "I intend to take my household and depart in the morning."

Ser John started. "By God, Ser Gabriel," he said. "I had counted on you for the rest of the council."

Ser Gabriel shook his head. "I need to get to Harndon. The tournament is what—nineteen days away? I'd like to have a rest and a chance to do a little politicking before I cross lances with anyone. You can plan the logistics of the mobile force as well as I—better for knowing the suppliers. I need to be anywhere but here."

Ser John raised both eyebrows. "I am sorry. Has my hospitality gone awry?"

Ser Gabriel managed a good smile. "Nothing of the sort. You are a fine host. I brought my own black mood with me." He frowned. "I still need to discuss the agreement with the duchess."

He sent young Giorgos, who went and returned.

In his flawless High Archaic, the young man said, "The *despoina* is closeted with the good sister," he said. "The duchess is no doubt making her confession."

"No doubt," the Red Knight said. He rose, bowed and went out into the yard.

Bad Tom was cutting at a pell.

Ser Gabriel sent Giorgos for his war sword and went to the next pell, displacing a dozen other men who, in one look, decided to do their training elsewhere. He attacked the pell ferociously, and then, with a poleaxe, more pragmatically, raising splinters and then cutting them away.

Tom redoubled his efforts for a while, perfectly willing to compete at pell destruction.

But wood chips were not particularly satisfying, and Bad Tom grinned. "Care for a dust-up?" he asked.

The Red Knight tossed his weapon to Giorgos. Without further words, he stripped his doublet, opening the lacings as fast as his fingers would go.

Ser Michael came out of the back of the stables.

"Cap'n's going to wrestle with Bad Tom," Cully said. "Household's marching tomorrow." He raised an eyebrow. "His leg still hurt?"

Ser Michael nodded. "Not all that's hurting, by all accounts," he said. "We can't leave tomorrow," he said.

Out on the sand, Tom and Gabriel, naked to the waist, were circling.

They came together. The captain took one of Tom's arms, and Tom wrapped him in a tight embrace and held him tenderly.

"You good?" he asked. He hadn't even bothered to throw the smaller man.

Ser Gabriel leaped away. Then he attacked.

He landed a fist, and Bad Tom bent lower, and the expression of mild pleasure on his face changed to one of joyous ferocity.

"Uh-oh," Ser Michael said to Toby.

Toby, who was packing armour, sighed.

Tom threw the captain, face first. Ser Gabriel rolled, but Tom was atop him, and caught an arm and forced him to the ground. "Yield," Tom said.

But he was a second too soon. Ser Gabriel turned inside the grab and spun under Tom's arm, avoiding the dislocation of his shoulder.

Tom locked his arms around the captain's head and rocked him back and forth gently. He took a step back. "Yield," he said again.

Ser Gabriel swung his feet forward in a way that made his friends wince for his neck, got a purchase, and tried to free his head.

Tom let him go.

Quick as a viper, the captain got an arm under Tom's left arm, passed his head through, and went for the throw.

Bad Tom bellowed in real rage and hooked Ser Gabriel's foot, kneed him ungently in the balls and dropped him on the ground. In the process he put his knee behind the captain's knee.

"You stupid fuck," Bad Tom bellowed, sweat and spittle dripping off him. "I could ha' maimed you for life. I had your fewkin' head in a lock. I might hae snapped your fewkin' neck. And you would na' yield. What sport is that?"

Ser Gabriel lay on the sand, face up, his hands clasped between his legs, panting. His right leg lay at an odd angle.

"Damn me. I didna' mean to hurt you, you loon." Tom reached down and grabbed the captain's hand.

Ser Gabriel allowed the Hillman to drag him to his feet, and then he screamed and fell.

He came to almost immediately.

Gabriel gave Tom a shaky smile. "Oh, yes. Let the punishment fit the crime."

Ser Michael brought him cold water, and he drank.

He met Michael's eyes.

"You had that coming," Michael said.

"What's the matter?" Bad Tom asked. "The little nun? She's coming."

Before he was done speaking, Sister Amicia bustled into the yard, her wimple flapping like the wings of a sea bird. She had two other sisters at her shoulders.

She glared about her with disapproval. Bad Tom shrank away. Ser Michael stood his ground.

"Ser Gabriel has re-broken his leg," he said.

Amicia knelt by the Red Knight, who lay on his back. She ran her hands over his leg and leaned down.

"I must have your word that you will not endanger my healing or refuse God's gift," she said, quite clearly. "For a week."

Gabriel's face worked, and no sound emerged.

Ser Michael leaned in. "He agrees," Michael said.

She joined hands with the other nuns, and the three of them sang—a polyphony. And Amicia's voice soared over their quieter, lower voices, up and on.

When she was done, every man in the yard was on his knees. She smiled. "Don't let him break it again," she said.

She rose. Gabriel watched her silently.

In his memory palace, she stood by Prudentia. "I have healed you. But you can't be so foolish."

He nodded.

"I'm sorry, Gabriel. I—"

He raised a hand. "I'm sorry, too. But I'm not ready to talk more."

Her head snapped back. But she continued to smile at him. And slipped away with her two serving sisters.

With Bad Tom on one side and Ser Michael on the other, Gabriel made it to his feet and hobbled to the bench.

"She's a force," Bad Tom said, placing his charge on the bench.

"She's not so little," Gabriel said. He felt better—for no reason.

Tom laughed. "Not where it matters, anyway. If you'd taken my advice during the siege—"

"The advice that I *rape* her?" the captain asked. Ser Michael caught his breath.

"Rape is a strong word," Bad Tom said. He scratched his beard. "Some ladies like a little persuading. Like horses."

Ser Gabriel drank a dipper full of cold water and spat a little blood. "I don't think that would have worked," he said.

Bad Tom looked out over the great north woods. "Aye. It doesn't always work." He grinned. "But it can save a mort of time."

Ser Gabriel looked at his friend. "Tom, what would you do if a lady pushed you to the ground and stuck her tongue in your mouth?"

Ser Michael snorted.

Tom snorted. "Is this something philosophical? Because by our lady, I promise you that will never happen here in the world." More soberly, he sighed. "But I take your point."

They sat in silence for a moment. Michael took Toby by the elbow and hauled him out of the small side-yard where the pells stood.

"She said no," Tom said, with a glance at Michael's retreating back.

"She's working with my mother," Gabriel said.

Tom shrugged. "Who cares? You love her?"

Gabriel nodded.

"Well, then, bide your time."

Gabriel laughed. "I'm getting advice on love from a Hillman."

Tom raised an eyebrow. "Well, laddy, I might point out that I have a fearsome record of lovers and you, as far as I know, seem to miss more than you make. You might do better than take my advice." He looked at the smaller man. "I reckon there's been mayhap twenty nights in the last hundred I haven't had a woman to warm my bed. Most of them would do't again. Hae you done as well?"

Gabriel shook his head. "I'm not sure this is a matter where a high score indicates victory, but very well. Your advice is?"

"This castle is full of lasses who would jump in the blankets with ye for a song. For a look and a smile. The bronze-eyed vixen as waits on your lady mother..."

"Your advice is that I can win the love of a nun by fornicating with my mother's maid?" Gabriel asked.

Tom smiled lazily. "Aye. That sums it up nicely."

Gabriel shook his head. "I need to talk to my mother. I'm just avoiding my duty." He got up. "Thanks for the fight. I'm sorry I cheated. I'm angry."

"Oh, aye," Tom said. "I'd never hae guessed." He put an arm around the younger man. "Best rid yourself o'it."

"Of what?" Gabriel asked.

"Father Arnaud's death," Tom said. "He's dead. He died well. All glory to him. And you know what's wrong wi' you? You want to be God. You want to hae saved him. An' you did not. He died."

Gabriel sighed.

"Let him go. And while yer at it, stop trying to be God." Tom smiled. "I confess ye do it better than many. But Arnaud went his own road. He's gone." Very softly, he said, "You want me to find you a willing lass?"

Gabriel laughed. He wheezed a little, and finally rose to his feet. "Is that your cure for everything?" he asked.

Tom nodded. "Pretty much. Sometimes..." He shook his head. "Sometimes ale helps. But not as much as a wench who wants ye."

Gabriel got a step away when Tom rose. Gabriel turned.

"I read your plan," Tom said.

"And?" Gabriel asked.

"I'm in. I don't think I want to be Drover, anyway. I think that should be for Ranald." He nodded. "I'll sell the herd in Harndon. And then I want my job back. Do I need to kill Bescanon?"

Gabriel smiled. "No," he said. "No, but Tom, sometimes I find it awfully refreshing to see the world from your eyes."

"Aye," Tom said. He grinned. "I like to keep things simple."

He found his mother in her solar. She made him wait again, but she was alone.

"The nun won't have you," his mother said. "And you've ruined my lute. It was tuned to a casting pattern and now it is banal."

Gabriel smiled and kissed his mother on the cheek. "The sele of the day to you, too, Mother."

The bronze-eyed maid came in with wine and curtsied. Gabriel watched her with an appreciation whetted by Tom's comments. She was remarkable. Gabriel had a suspicion that she had been *prepared* for him.

She blushed when her lowered eyes happened to intersect with Ser Gabriel's.

"She won't give up her vows. She's after Sophie's title." Ghause laughed.

"What, to be the king's mistress?" Gabriel asked. "I'm surprised. She's never mentioned it."

Ghause glared at her son, her eyes slightly mad, like the griffon's. "She intends to be Abbess."

"She told you this?" Gabriel asked. He was fascinated—mostly because his theory that Amicia was working with his mother was being shredded. By his mother. She could be a fine actress, but he didn't think she could pull this off.

"Not in so many words," his mother said, pouting.

Gabriel sat back. "You mean, Mother, that if you were in Amicia's place, the only reason you would stay out of my bed would be to acquire more power."

Ghause snarled, but her snarl became a laugh. "Fair eno', my son. Now—you never came here of your own will."

Gabriel nodded. "I want you to agree to the alliance—as vassals of the king."

Ghause swore and stood. "Christ's bloody crown of thorns, boy. I will not be my brother's vassal for *anything*."

"Even if doing so would avert civil war?" Gabriel asked.

"Better and better," Ghause said. "Let him rot. Let him *die*."

Gabriel sat back and crossed his legs. "I told him," he said simply.

Ghause paused. She looked at her son for a long time, and then said slowly, "You told him—what?"

"I told him that I was your son. By him." He put his hands behind his head and looked at the ceiling.

Ghause rose slowly. "You what?"

Gabriel sighed. "I told him. I felt he needed to know."

Ghause's mouth moved, but no words came out.

Gabriel watched her. "I could go to court and present myself as the king's bastard by his sister," he said. "I suspect that would have an effect. I might even prevent the civil war. Perhaps he'd make me his heir!"

"You wouldn't dare! I don't want anything *given* by that bastard! I want him brought low!" Ghause was on her feet, her voice rising.

"You know, Mother, those may be things you want, but they are not things I want. If you want to destroy the king, you need to affect that on your own. I will not be your tool. And in the meantime, if you would like to please me, sign this agreement as the king's vassal. In my turn, I'll promise you—and your mate—my support as Duke of Thrake."

Ghause pursed her lips. "No. I don't give a fuck if you want to lie naked at his feet. Go—lick his arse for all I care." She put a hand on the treaty, written out fine. "I will sign it, though. I'll be a lickspittle and sign it as a vassal. I can repudiate it any time I like. Only make me one promise, and I'll comply."

Gabriel braced himself. "Does it involve murder?"

"No, marriage." She sat again. "Marry the girl of my choice. I promise she'll be handsome and have a good dowry and power. Give your word to marry her at my whim and I'll sign your paper."

Gabriel drew breath.

Ghause leaned towards him. "Forget your little nun. Or tumble her to your heart's content when you've got your bride in kindle. I admit, for all her low birth, I like the nun. I think I could fancy her for myself." She licked her lips. "What was wrong with the princess Irene?"

"You are the second person to ask me that today," Gabriel said, a little wildly.

"Well?" his mother insisted.

"She tried to kill her father?" Gabriel said. "She poisons people?"

Ghause shrugged.

Gabriel sat back and laughed. "I confess, you'd like her, and you two would have *so much* to talk about over your sewing."

Ghause met his eye. "You think I'm crude and vicious," she said. "But yon princess is what she is. She is what her court has made her, and if you were a good knight and a good husband, she'd ha' no need to poison you, would she?"

Gabriel put his face in his hands. "Is that the measure of wedded bliss?" he asked.

"Pretty much," Ghause said. "I've been with the Earl of Westwall for twenty years and more. And we ha' not killed each other." She snapped her fingers, and her maid returned and poured more wine. "Did the princess offer?"

Gabriel thought a moment. "No. Although I suspect that she will be offered—by her father. Soon."

Ghause smiled. "And you have not said no?"

Gabriel thought again. "No."

Ghause nodded. "You could be Emperor," she said.

Gabriel nodded. "Yes. But no. The Empire does not transfer power by blood, and when the Emperor dies. Has it occurred to you that I don't share your ambitions?"

She ignored him. "I'll sign your paper, and you'll take the bride I assign you. And no quibbles—I know you."

Gabriel stood. "I'm tempted just to lie and agree. I think maybe I could save hundreds of lives by agreement. But you know, Mother, tonight I'm at my limit of being *used* by the powers of the world. So—no." He picked up the parchment. "Won't you just sign because you *are* the king's vassal?"

She frowned. "It is nothing to you that he forced me—a chit of a girl, his own sister?"

Gabriel nodded. "Yes, Mother. For all that stands between us, I agree. I hate him, I think he's false as a caitiff and that everything he's ever done is poisoned by what he did to you." He shrugged. "But—if all of us cling to our hates, we'll never move forward. If that fool de Vrailly marches north this summer..."

"The earl will destroy him," Ghause said with satisfaction.

Gabriel looked at her. Then he shrugged. "Very well, Mother. I think that you have chosen your road. And I have chosen mine."

She frowned. "So you will not marry a girl for me?"

"Nor be party to any plot or plan of yours," he said. "More, I'm going to go tell Ser John that I cannot accept command of the northern army. Given your stance, and the earl's, the King would never agree to it."

"Fine," she said. "You won't help me? Your own mother? Then go to hell, my son." She blew him a kiss.

He went out through her solar with her curses ringing in his ears.

He went straight back to Ser John and dropped the parchment on his desk. "My apologies, Ser John. I cocked that up."

The Captain of Albinkirk sighed. "She won't sign?"

"She consigned me to hell." Gabriel raised his hands.

"Damn. Your own mother." Ser John shook his head.

Ser Gabriel spread his hands. "I must decline to be your commander, Ser John. I'll leave you to puzzle out why."

"Christ on the cross, your mother *wants* war with the king?" Ser John sat in shock.

Ser Gabriel said nothing. After a pause, he said, "As soon as the tournament is over, I'll return to Morea. I promise you that if you call, the Emperor will send a force. I will probably not accompany it."

"Damn. Damn and damn. Can you tell me why the duchess hates the king?"

Gabriel shook his head. "No, Ser John." He paused. "It's not my story to tell." He shook his head. "But she will not change her mind."

Dinner in the great hall was a desperate affair. Sister Amicia sat silently, and her eyes never touched Ser Gabriel's. The Duchess of Westwall alternated between crass and arch, and neither note struck home on her target, her son, who sat as isolated as a priest might be by an altar screen, alone with his thoughts. Ser John tried, and failed, to create a conversation. His efforts made it as far as the venison pie and then died, and the rest of the dinner passed in silence, punctuated by the duchess's pro forma flirting with the now receptive Lord Wayland and her wilful ignoring of the Keeper's son.

A pair of messengers arrived, both from Ser Ricar. Ser John went out to hear them, and the dinner broke up.

Gabriel watched Amicia for any sign he might speak to her. She chatted with the Drover as if she had no other need for company, and then she sat and played chess with her friend, the bishop.

His mother watched him with an intensity equal to the chess players.

Finally, Gabriel went to his room.

His leg hurt, and he hated everyone.

In the midst of undressing, he put a hand on Toby's arm, and the young man mostly fought the urge to flinch.

"I'm sorry, Toby," he said.

Toby flushed. And said nothing.

Morning—a cold, wet day that didn't so much promise spring as hint vaguely at it. The rain seemed colder than snow, and the air was wet, and the wind bit through a wool cloak.

The Duke of Thrake rose early. He appeared in the great hall wearing a miniver riding gown that was worth a fortune—white wool embroidered in his arms on the outside and three hundred matched squirrel skins on the inside. He wore it over his harness.

Ser John's squire, young Jamie, a Hoek boy, intercepted him. "Your grace," he said with a bow. "The Captain of Albinkirk requests that you attend him. There is news."

The Red Knight's anger had leached away in a good night's sleep and left him only throbbing pain and a nagging sense of loss. He bowed in return. "Lead me," he said. He turned to Ser Michael. "Making my farewells won't be quick. You might as well grab a sausage in the kitchen."

Michael nodded, collected the Drover's son, who wore his regalia over his harness, and found a side table covered in dishes.

Ser Gabriel followed Jamie out of the hall and into the barracks tower where the Captain of Albinkirk had his office.

Ser John was sitting in an old, black robe and was wearing spectacles. He had a bag on his desk, and opposite him sat a very young man wearing the golden belt of a knight.

The Red Knight smiled. "Ser Galahad!" he said. Galahad D'Acon had been one of the heroes of the fight at Lissen Carak.

"So kind of you to remember me, your grace," the younger man said, rising so suddenly that his spurs tangled.

"Young Galahad comes as a royal messenger," Ser John said. "He brought us several writs." Ser John scratched his beard and straightened the spectacles on his nose.

"And to save my life," Galahad said. He shook his head. "The queen's knights…" He looked at Ser John. "She sent me herself. The Galles are killing our people, and the King does nothing to prevent it." He clenched his fists. "They talk of arresting Lady Almspend."

Ser John nodded. "You've had a difficult journey," he said to the young knight. "Go get some food."

As soon as Galahad was out the door and Jamie Le Hoek had closed it, Ser John turned, tapping a scroll on his teeth. "He was on the road for nine days. Bad weather and mud and too many convoys to pass."

Ser Gabriel settled into the chair, still warm from the messenger's heat.

"De Vrailly is going to formally accuse the queen of adultery," he said. "As the king's champion, he'll accuse her."

Ser Gabriel turned this piece of information over. And over. "I see," he said.

"I doubt you do," Ser John said. "This'll be the war."

"The queen is that popular?" Ser Gabriel asked, rhetorically.

"The King must have lost his wits," Ser John said. "T'other scroll is a tax demand on the Earl of Westwall."

Ser Gabriel smiled. "I see," he said. Because he did.

"There's more. The Archbishop of Lorica has called a council to investigate..." He looked down. "A range of charges of heresy," he quoted. "Against the Order of St. Thomas." He met the Red Knight's eyes. "I have to tell you, your grace, that the nun's preaching is listed on the charges."

"Sister Amicia?" Gabriel asked.

"She's virtually a saint, to the people hereabouts," Ser John said. "There isn't a man-at-arms in Albinkirk who hasn't felt her healing. Or her wisdom."

Ser Gabriel flushed.

Ser John frowned. "It's as if the King is working to destroy the kingdom." He shook his head. "De Vrailly's accusation will no doubt take place at the tourney."

"And de Vrailly will be the accuser," Ser Gabriel said.

"Can you take him?" Ser John asked.

Ser Gabriel sighed. "Mayhap," he said. "I hesitate to stake the future of Alba on it."

Ser John shrugged. "They say he's the best knight in the world."

The Red Knight smiled. "Ah, well. They say I'm the spawn of Satan." He laughed. "Tourney is eighteen days away."

The two men sat in a companionable silence. Finally Gabriel rose. "I need to say farewell to my lady mother."

Ser John nodded. "You won't change your mind?" he asked.

"I may yet, Ser John. In a way—an odd way—the King has just played into the duchess's hands." He rose.

Ser John shook his head. "I still can't believe he'd take such foolish counsel."

Ser Gabriel nodded. "Ser John—I suggest to you that the Galles at court do not have the king's best interests at heart."

Ser John nodded.

Gabriel went out, with the sound of his armour ratcheting along the corridor.

Gabriel knocked at his mother's outer door, and then, after some time had passed, he worked a *praxis* and opened it.

"Don't you dare!" his mother shrieked.

Gabriel opened the inner door. The bronze-eyed girl slipped from the bed, her body blushing her embarrassment from nose to navel, and passed behind the hanging that concealed the garde de robe.

"I need to speak to you, Mother," Gabriel said. His voice was cheerful. He was fully in command of himself. "I see we really do share some tastes."

His mother sat up, her body barely concealed by a shift. "You always were an impetuous lout," she said.

"The King has sent you a summons, ordering you to pay twenty years of back taxes. And threatening war if you don't." Gabriel leaned back and settled his right pauldron into a dent in the stone of the wall.

"The fool," Ghause spat.

"In more ways than one, Mother. I've changed my mind. I'll accept a bride, in exchange for your seal on this alliance." He handed his mother the scroll. "How do you manage to stay so young?" he asked.

"Murdered virgin's blood," she said, her eyes on the document. "Powdered unicorn horn." She looked up. "Poppycock. It's just exercise, my dear, and good breeding, and a little sorcery." Without any fuss, she slipped out of the bed and lit a taper by *ops*. She took sealing wax and affixed her personal seal. "You won't regret this."

"I suspect I will, Mother. But it occurred to me that I didn't actually think a thousand lives were a fair trade for my connubial bliss. I reserve only your maid. I won't marry her." He smiled. "Though I might want her after I have my new bride in kindle."

His mother smiled and then bit her lip. "You're hiding something," she said. "I know you."

"I am," he said. "But if we're both lucky, you'll never know what. I'm off for Harndon." He bent, and quite formally kissed her hand.

She laughed. "You are being foolish, my boy. But I am glad to have you back at my side."

He nodded. But in his new-found wisdom, he chose not to answer her.

The southbound convoy formed by the outer gates of the town. The Red Knight was leaving many of his best men and women behind, and taking only his household. Ser Michael rode at the head, carrying the new banner—the banner of Thrake, a golden eagle on a ground of dark red. Ser Phillipe de Beause, Ser Francis Atcourt and the young Etruscan, Angelo di Laternum, and Chris Foliak were resplendent even in the rain. Behind them came their squires and pages, and two wagons of baggage and harness, under Sadie Lantorn, whose career as a woman of the company was apparently unaffected by her sister's marriage into the highest ranks of the gentry. Sukey had other duties for a few days.

As a rearguard, the Duke of Thrake had six Morean lances under Ser Christos—his first command in the company, although he had once been the *strategos* for the former duke. With him were five other magnates of Thrake, and if they objected to having to ride into the frigid delights of an Alban spring, they kept their views to themselves. Ser Alcaeus, who might have been expected to stay with his banda, was instead riding with them.

Out on the plain that stretched to the river, the Hillmen could be seen forming their flocks and herds and moving them across the water at Southford. The process had been going on for two days.

The Red Knight looked around for the one face he missed, and gave up. He drew his sword and flicked a salute at the gate guard, who returned it more formally, and Ser John, mounted on a pretty bay, came out and locked hands with the Red Knight.

"I'll do my best," Ser Gabriel said.

"I still can't believe she agreed. What did she ask for?" Ser John asked.

Ser Gabriel smiled. "A life of chastity," Ser Gabriel said. He left the older knight speechless and led his household and their baggage south, to the ford.

At the ford, he found the woman he'd missed. Sister Amicia sat on her little horse with her two attendants, Sisters Mary and Katherine.

"May we accompany you on the road?" she asked.

The Red Knight used his knees to press his riding horse close to hers. Her smile was brave. He hoped his was as good.

"You mean you wish to spend ten days on the road to Harndon with us?" he asked.

"I've been accused of heresy," she said, her back straight and her head high. "I intend to meet it in person, and not cower here. I gather you have similar plans."

He thought of various quips, but it had always been her courage he loved best. He bowed. "I'd be delighted to have your company, Sister."

Horse by horse and wagon by wagon, the ferry took them across. In each ferry load, the weight was made up by sheep or cattle—enormous cattle with vicious horns. The lowing of the herds, the belches and farts, the sound of chewing, the hollow tread of their hooves, went on and on.

Bad Tom met the Red Knight on the south side. The road up from the ferry to the high bank was solid mud, and the younger nun's palfrey almost lost its rider going up.

"You brought her," Tom said with real approval.

"It's not what you think," Ser Gabriel said.

Bad Tom laughed. "Sometimes I think you're the smartest loon I've ever known," Tom said. "And other times the greatest fool."

Amicia rode up in the last sentence. She laughed.

Ser Gabriel laughed. "Ten days on the road with you lot?" He smiled. "Let's go to Harndon," he said.

Two hundred leagues to the north, Thorn stood in his place of power, staff in left hand, but this time he cast no power. He was in his new form of stone and wood, tall and impregnable. He held the results of a year of breeding a careful, dreadful nurture.

At a distance, his right arm would have seemed to be sheathed in fur. Closer examination would indicate a dozen giant purple-black moths, each as big as a heavy bird of prey.

He reached through the *aethereal* until he made contact with the aura of power that was his Dark Sun. He showed the aura to his moths, and he flung his arm up, like a falconer sending his bird after prey.

And they flew.

Chapter Three

Harndon—The Queen

Spring was a season made for joys, but Desiderata had few enough of them. She sat in her solar with Diota brushing her hair.

"Never you fuss, lass," Diota prattled. "Soon enough he'll come back to his duty."

"Duty?" Desiderata asked.

"Don't snap at me, you minx," Diota said. "You know what I mean."

"You mean, when I've had my baby, my body will be desirable again, and my lover will return?" the queen asked, mildly enough. "You mean that this is the role of women, and I should abide it?"

"If you must," Diota said. "That's men."

"He is the king," Desiderata said.

"He's ill-advised," Diota said, patiently. "That Rohan all but pushed the red-headed vixen into the king's arms. The chit never had a chance."

"I agree that she's little to blame," Desiderata said. She enjoyed the kiss of the sun on her bare shoulders and her hair, and listened to the sounds her baby made—increasingly strident and yet beloved sounds.

She was contemplating her unborn child when a bell rang and the outer door opened.

"Fuss, it's the witch," Diota spat, and moved protectively to her mistress's other side.

Outside, a young woman said, "And where is the royal lady this morning?" in a Jarsay accent.

Lady Genevieve was the plainest—and eldest—of the queen's ladies, a good ten years older than the queen. She wore a cross big enough to hang on a wall and her dress was plain to the point of being frumpish. She wore dark colours and sometimes even wore a wimple, although today she wore her hair in an Alban fashion—each plait was wound in the shape of a turret, making her head look like a fortress gate, which the queen found particularly apt.

"Welcome, Lady Genevieve," the queen said.

"All this hair brushing is mere vanity," Lady Genevieve said. She sat without asking permission. "I have brought you some religious instruction." She looked at Diota. "You may go."

The queen frowned. "My lady, it is for me to welcome or dismiss my servants. Of whom you yourself are one. I have never been much for formality, but you may stand until I ask you to sit."

"Do not give yourself airs," Lady Genevieve said. "You are a wife taken in adultery, bearing another man's bastard, and the sign of your shame is on you every instant." She remained seated. "My lord de Vrailly has sent me to attend you, and I shall. But do not pretend with me."

Desiderata nodded slowly. "So you refuse my command," she said.

Lady Genevieve was the widow of a southern lord. She knew how to make herself obeyed. "I will accept any reasonable command," she said sweetly. "Let me read to you from the Life of Saint Catherine."

"What if I do not wish you to read?" the Queen asked, already weary.

"You are unwomanly in your striving," Lady Genevieve said. "A woman's role is passive acceptance, as I told my husband on many occasions. Indeed, I was a byword for passive acceptance." She snapped her fingers. "If your woman is to remain, she may as well be useful. I'll have a cup of sweet cider, Diota." She turned back to the queen. "Where was I? Ah yes— passive acceptance."

Diota slipped out and found Blanche, one of the queen's laundry maids, in the outer solar.

The nurse took a cup and poured cider from a jug, and then, catching Blanche's eye, she reached under her skirts and wiped her hand there and then used it to stir the cider.

Blanche stifled a cackle and handed the nurse a slip of parchment that had been pinned to a shift.

Another of the queen's "new ladies" came in the outer door without knocking, but by the time she came in, Blanche was folding shifts and putting them into the press.

Lady Agnes Wilkes, twenty-nine, unmarried, and with a face capable of curdling milk, stalked in and looked sullenly at the serving girl. "What are you about, slut?" she asked.

Blanche kept working. "Folding, milady."

Lady Agnes frowned. "Do this sort of thing at night," she said. "I don't need to see your kind in these rooms by day, and neither does the queen. What if the King were to come?"

Diota slipped away with her cup of cider and gave it with a sketchy curtsy to Lady Genevieve, who didn't acknowledge her at all. She took the cup and drank from it. "Tart and sweet," she said.

Diota smiled happily. "A pleasure to serve you, my lady," she said.

"Well," Lady Genevieve said. "A change for the better, then. I see Lady Agnes has come in and I'll exchange a word with her." The older woman rose and set her cup down with a click.

She went out, and they could hear her in the outer chamber.

Diota handed the Queen the slip of parchment. The Queen seized it, read it—and then put it in her mouth and began to chew.

Diota collected cups and a shift and began to tidy the queen's private chamber.

The two ladies came in. "Your Lady Rebecca has deserted you," Lady Agnes said with real satisfaction. "Lord de Rohan sent for her this morning, but she's fled. Many things are missing—she was a thief as well as a heretic. I am here to make an inventory."

"Lady Rebecca had no need to steal," the Queen said. "She was the lord chancellor for half a year."

Lady Agnes made a face, and Lady Genevieve made a rude noise. "Perhaps the King pretended that she was the chancellor," she said. "No woman could ever hold such an office." She spoke as if she relished the low estate of women. "What foolishness. Women have no aptitude for such things. When I was with my husband, I cultivated a becoming passivity. I *never* put myself forward."

"What happened after?" the queen asked sweetly.

"After what, my dear?" Lady Genevieve asked.

"After your husband died?" the Queen asked.

Diota almost choked, but Lady Genevieve frowned. "I have no idea what you are about, madame."

The queen rose.

"You need to dress," Lady Agnes said. The Queen was wearing only a shift, and her belly was magnificent—and very visible.

"I am more comfortable like this," the queen said.

"You are lewd. Indecent." Lady Agnes began to seize clothes from a cabinet.

"In my private solar?" the queen asked. "I think not."

"I do not wish to gaze on your body," Lady Agnes said. At odds with her words, her eyes were on the queen's belly.

"You are very wanton," Lady Genevieve said. "We will dress you. It is time you had the becoming clothes of a matron, and shed all this vanity."

The queen smiled. Her smile was lazy and slow, and took its time, and in the end, she shocked Diota.

"You know, my ladies," she said. "I think perhaps you have the right of it, and my baby has addled my wits. I will, indeed, cultivate a becoming passivity."

Blanche took her laundry basket and went into the corridors below the Queen's Tower, moving briskly. No one particularly wanted to see servants in the formal areas of the palace, not even trusted servants like Blanche, who wore the crisp red and blue livery of the winter. It had only changed ten days ago, and her sideless surcoat and matching kirtle marked her as "belonging."

Of course, few were quite so rude about their wishes as the queen's new "ladies."

Ladies, Blanche thought to herself, and crossed the corridor that led to the King's Tower after a careful glance in either direction. The Galles who now inundated the court like crabs at high tide were often present here, gathered in little knots with their cousins and brothers, looking for offices and sinecures.

They were the most determined rascals she'd ever known. None of them had tried outright rape—not yet—but she'd been offered every insult short, and various grasping hands and sweaty palms and scratchy moustaches had tried her virtue over the last few months.

Blanche's contempt—the contempt of an attractive young woman—was absolute. She loathed them for their obvious contempt for women, she thought them weak for their ceaseless striving, and she cursed them with the worst derision she could offer because they appeared desperate. None of them had any idea how to approach a woman—all the servants said so. They were as aggressive—and mindless—as hungry wolves.

Blanche passed the king's corridor with a feeling of relief, her mission nearly complete, and descended two winding stone staircases—servants' stairs, and thus almost unfailingly safe. She passed one of the upper palace male servants—Robin le Grant, wine steward—who gave her a bow and a smile.

The servants were developing a whole language for the situation. That smile meant the stairs were clear.

Blanche slowed her pace and breathed a little easier. Her contempt for the Galles was not unmixed with fear.

She passed the kitchen corridor with a nod to three kitchen girls she knew.

"Laundress was askin' for you," said the nearest. She flashed a smile.

Blanche suspected that all three of them were malingering—loitering in corridors was not encouraged by the Butler, who was both a gentleman and a senior servant and ruled with a rod of iron. But she returned their smiles. "Stairs is clear," she said as she swept past and turned again, walking down the familiar short flight of steps. To the right was the river gate, or at least the portions of the old fortifications and the corridors that led there. To the left lay the laundry, a kingdom—or rather, a queendom—entirely populated by women. There were laundresses who actually washed, and laundresses who only ironed, and laundresses who were really fine seamstresses for everything from repair to marking—every garment in the palace was marked with the owner's initials in fine, neat cross-stitching. All in all, from twelve-year-old Celia who washed the dirtiest linens to ninety-year-old Mother Henk who could barely work but still had the finest embroidery stitches in Harndon, the laundry employed forty-five women all day, every day. The Laundress—Goodwife Ross—wore upper palace livery but never left her domain.

She was standing by the door to her alcove when Blanche came by. Blanche curtsied—the laundry was formal enough.

"I worry for you, lass," Dame Ross said. She looked in the basket.

Blanche shook her head. "No mending for the queen."

"Any trouble?" the Laundress asked.

"No Galles in the corridors. The queen's new *ladies* were a treat though." No palace servant ever spoke slightingly of any member of the upper classes—not directly. It was all tone and eye contact, nothing that could be reported or punished.

Goodwife Ross narrowed her eyes. "Anything I should know?"

"Lady Agnes suggested that I had no business in the queen's chambers. And me in my livery!" Blanche spat her words with more vehemence than she'd intended.

The Laundress pursed her lips. "I see," she said.

Blanche dropped a short curtsey—the bob of the working woman. "I'll be about it then, ma'am," she said.

Goodwife Ross dismissed her with a wave. The goodwife was aware—in the vaguest way—that Blanche "did something" for the queen. That was sufficient for her.

Blanche took her basket into the steamy main laundry. The moment she upended it on the sorting table, her life as the queen's messenger vanished to be replaced by her usual life.

"Blanche! There you are! Be a sweet and fetch us a cup of water?" asked rheumy old Mother Henk.

"Blanche, you promised to teach me stem stitch!" begged young Alice.

"Blanche, there's a mort of fine sewing waiting in your basket and I've all I can do keeping the King in braes," snapped Ellen. Ellen was the other upper palace laundress who wore livery and was allowed to collect laundry in the public rooms of the palace. Like Blanche, she was young, pretty, and had worked in the palace since she'd been a young child.

By that point in her work day, Blanche was delighted to collapse onto one of the backed chairs that the fine sewers used while mending. From the pockets under her kirtle, Blanche fetched out her prize possession—her sewing kit, with a pair of steel scissors made by Master Pye himself, a pair of silver thimbles, a dozen fine horn thread winders full of threads—white linen, white silk, black linen, black silk, and this season, red and blue for the livery.

Ellen was putting thread on her winders. Thread came from the dyers in skeins, and sewing women and tailors had to wind it onto something of their own. Blanche owned two beautiful thread winders—a tiny one of ivory that had been her mother's and another of mother of pearl from far off Ifriquy'a. Both were at home.

"If the King wears his hose any tighter," Ellen said and shook her head. Laid across her lap were a fanciful pair of hose, one leg alternating diagonals of red and blue, the other leg solid scarlet with a patch of superb gold embroidery. The hose were in the latest style that joined at the top, and they had torn in the crotch.

"He's too old for these tight things," Ellen said. A year ago, open criticism of the king's taste in clothes would never have been uttered. Blanche felt disloyal just listening.

Ellen frowned, aware of her transgression. "I only mean..." She paused. And looked down at her scarlet thread winder. She finished it off and then loaded her blue.

Her thought was unspoken, but they didn't need to share it. Blanche knew that Ellen's criticism was not for the King, but for his new lover, a red-headed girl of seventeen. Lady Jane Sable. Her name was never mentioned in the servants' halls below. She seemed to inspire in the King a sort of ferocity to pretend he was young, and his pursuit of youth—hers, his own—had led to a loss of royal dignity that all the servants felt reflected on them.

Lady Jane was herself not so bad. She was well-bred enough to be careful; she was cautious about the king's reputation, and she was polite to the servants. But she had her own waiting woman, Sarah, and her laundry never came to the laundry. Sarah ate in her mistress's rooms and never came into the great hall below stairs where the servants dined and many slept. The lady's father was already the leader of the pro-Galle faction of Albans.

Blanche began to repair the queen's shifts. She had patiently run up half a dozen new ones that suited the queen's changed shape, working at home with her mother, and now even the new shifts were having their carefully felled side-seams pulled.

Blanche pulled a small seam-ripper—a razor sharp knife with a rebated point, just a few inches long, and another product of Master Pye's superb eye and hand—from her basket and began to open a side seam.

"Blanche!" called Goodwife Ross. Blanche rose to her feet, dropped her sewing into the basket beside the chair and rushed to the Laundress, whose commands were not to be ignored. She still had her little knife in her hand—it was precious, five days' wages' worth of steel and it would slice through her pockets in a heartbeat. She tucked it behind her ear.

"Blanche, I need you to run a message to Master Cord's down Cheapside. And ask where our spring linen order is. I'm that vexed and I misremembered this morning."

Indeed, the whole establishment ate fine white linen the way a newborn suckled milk, and Master Cord's later delivery was playing merry hell with the laundry.

Blanche bobbed a curtsey.

"I'll have Ellen finish the shifts," Goodwife Ross said.

Blanche shook her head—one tiny sideways motion to indicate disagreement was allowed in senior staff. "I'll take it home, if'n it please you, ma'am."

Goodwife Ross nodded her strong approval. "Good. Ellen has her hands full. Fetch your basket and skip along."

Blanche stepped back into the seamstress's room and re-packed her basket.

Ellen sighed. "A nice spring day? I'd like to be sent with the errands."

Blanche frowned. "Goodwife worries about ye, Ellen."

"I can handle myself," the young woman said. But where Blanche was tall and broad shouldered, Ellen was doll-like and slim as a reed. The strength of Blanche's arms and hands was legendary among the pages and squires to whom she'd taught a few manners—even before the Galles came.

"None of us can handle the Galles," Blanche said. "Are you careful when you walk out? Never the same route twice?"

"Yes, Mother," Ellen said, and laughed. "May I please have another cup of milk?" Both girls laughed. "But Blanche, ain't *you* a Galle?"

Blanche nodded. "My pater was, sure enough." Blanche de Roeun, a town in Galle, once. Now she was Blanche Gold.

Ellen shrugged. "So there are some good Galles."

Blanche frowned. "Some? These are a blight. Galles is lovely folk, Ellen. Think of the Count D'Eu!"

Ellen smiled. Both girls admired him. "Well, if you'll not tell me how to walk and suck eggs, I'll not twit you with your Galles."

Blanche grinned. "Sorry, sweet."

"*You* be careful," Ellen said.

Blanche kissed her on the cheek. "Always careful, my honey."

She was out the door of the laundry, under full sail as Ellen, a shipwright's daughter, liked to say. Blanche did not generally enter or leave the palace in broad daylight. She came so early in the morning that the squires weren't up, and she left when they started drinking. But she'd hurt one of the Galles—and she knew that they had her marked.

Past the water-gate corridor.

But the main hall corridor up the stairs was crowded with gentles. She knew from the bottom of the steps, just from their shoes—mostly long-toed poulains—that she was looking at Rohan's crowd; a dozen Gallish knights and squires. The worst.

She froze, her foot on the third step.

"There's a pretty slut," someone said above her.

"Thighs as white as her name, I'll bet," said another.

She knew them all, even if they didn't know her. Rohan was the very worst—the centre of the poison, so to speak. His eyes crossed hers.

She dropped her eyes and passed back a step.

"The king!" someone shouted, and all the courtiers stiffened. That would mean that the King was passing from his apartments to the great hall. Courtiers lined the corridor, hoping to be recognized and spoken to.

"Jeffries! Malquil!" Rohan said quietly, his voice calm and even. "See the bitch on the steps? She's the queen's lap-dog. Maybe her she-whore. Take her and give her a dose of manhood, eh bien?"

The two men he'd named turned and started down the steps. Neither was a Galle. Both were Alban squires dressed as Galles, in skin-tight hose and very short doublets. The taller of the two came down two steps at a time and cut her off from the right hand turn.

Blanche didn't panic, although two strong men scared her. She turned left, into the water-gate corridor, hoping for some loitering staff, but the corridor was empty.

She moved.

They were almost at her shoulders. She screamed—loud and long—hoisted her skirts and *ran*.

Everyone north of Cheapside knew how fast Blanche Gold was. Her legs were very long, and she knew how to use them, and the straight corridor offered no hindrance. It was almost completely dark, but she knew it intimately, at least for the first twenty yards.

She side-stepped the old fountain base. One of the squires didn't. She was five paces ahead of them now. Their long-toed shoes and skin-tight woollen hose laced to their doublets were *not* made for running, and her palace shoes and bare legs were.

A childhood of playing in these corridors, and Blanche had options.

She went left, towards the water gate. Now she was against the outer walls, and shafts of light crossed the corridor. She took the turn at speed and allowed herself to strike the outer wall lightly with her shoulder.

She could hear their poulains slapping on the floor.

She hadn't dropped her basket, and as she slowed for the gate, she used it to cushion her impact with the far wall. Then she went down the sharply angled steps, worn by two thousand years of use, and she was already surrounded by the strong, muddy river smell.

She moved as fast as she could on the slippery steps, praying that there were guards at the bottom and that the gate was open.

The Virgin was with her as she prayed, and there, on the narrow dock, were two of her least favourite guardsmen, both portly and both known for their roving hands and shifty eyes. She'd never been so happy to see them.

"Eh, Blanche!" said the nearer.

She smiled. "Ned!" she said.

The first of the two squires emerged onto the dock.

Blanche flicked her eyes at the squire. He was already hesitating. His friend emerged from the water gate, rubbing his thigh.

Ned wasn't slow. He grunted and shifted his weight—just a half step. But his obvious intention was to block access to the dock.

"No one but livery on the dock, less'an you have a king's writ," Ned said.

His partner grunted. They both had good brown poleaxes that shone in the spring sun, a rich ruddy brown. They were both in the new livery, and the squires were not.

The nearer squire drew himself up. "I mean to have a word with that slut," he said. "I think that she . . . stole from me."

He stepped forward, and Ned placed the point of his poleaxe at the squire's nose. "Best take that up with the Laundress. That's Goody Ross, last corridor but one."

"Do you know who I am?" the man asked.

"Can't say I do," Ned said, managing to side-smile at his partner. "But I know I'm a King's Guardsman and you ain't."

A water taxi—a small boat poled by a grown man—saw Blanche and began to pole up the side channel to the water gate, eyes hopeful.

Blanche shot the squire a reproachful glare. "Which the Laundress sends me to Cheapside," she said. She spat into the dirty water. "I don' steal." She locked eyes with the man. "I'm the queen's laundress, sir."

He shocked all of them by grabbing for her.

Ned tipped him in the water.

Blanche didn't stay to see the end. She skipped into the approaching boat as two more foppishly dressed men appeared on the dock.

"Take her!" yelled the other squire, the one rubbing his thigh.

The man in the water surfaced. "You're dead!" he shrieked.

Blanche settled into the stern of the boat. The waterman's expression showed nothing. "Where bound, mistress?" he asked.

She couldn't afford to be taken all the way to Cheapside—it would cost a full day's wages.

They were already clear of the walls of the palace, and she could see four big round ships anchored to the river bank on their side.

"Venike," the waterman said. "All the way from Ifriquy'a, if you will believe it." He sighed. "Now that's navigation, mistress."

There were big crowds there—small boats all around the tall Venike ships, and then crowds on the shore and an impromptu market.

"Boat following us, mistress," the waterman said. "He has oars and I don't. He's going to overtake us."

Blanche looked back into the sun-dazzle of the water. She could just see a boat, its oars whipping furiously. In it were two men—maybe three.

"Can you land me by the docks?" she said.

"No place for a decent woman," the waterman said. "You in trouble?"

Blanche nodded.

The waterman looked back. "I'll slow 'em for ye." He smiled. "For a kiss."

Blanche looked at him and smiled.

The waterman poled furiously, and the two craft passed downstream. Blanche couldn't tell which was faster.

The waterman passed under the great stern of the Venike flagship, towering above them like a church, with windows and windows like a great house. In the stern gallery, a Venike man-at-arms in full harness pointed a warning finger at them, but Blanche waved and he waved back.

The waterman put the prow of his little boat ashore so that Blanche had only to give a brave leap and she'd be on the port stairs, where the poor came to wash.

He stepped nimbly over the centre seat. "Kiss!" he said.

She handed him a silver farthing, and then, an honest maid, leaned up and kissed him lightly on the lips.

He smiled. "Honest coin, fair maid."

She grinned and leapt over the bow, made the steps without slipping, and ran up the steps.

At the top, she turned—deliberately—into the thickest part of the crowd. The Venike had a special privilege, and were allowed to set up a market wherever they pleased. The tables they had laid over barrels were covered in goods worth a fortune—worth ten fortunes. She caught the flash of ivory—whole tusks, and the dead white tusks of the unnatural Ummaroth. She saw silk and inlaid wood and silver.

She passed along the back of the packed crowd of nobles and merchants at the tables. She wore royal livery, she was pretty, and she had a lifetime experience of moving through crowds.

She was also becoming aware that the portside market was *full* of Galles. For the first time—as she saw heads turn—she began to be truly afraid. It was all a game until they caught her, and if they did it would be horrible. Ruin, damnation, pain and humiliation and outrage.

And always the girl's fault.

She never let herself think about it, but now, in broad daylight in the king's capital surrounded by predators, Blanche found herself *angry*.

But her choices were narrowing. She cursed her own courage, that had led her to turn *away* from the laundry and head for the water gate. She was about to reach Waterside, the slum of warehouses and brothels and sailor's taverns just north of Cheapside. A place she would never, ordinarily, have gone, day or night.

She looked back one more time, eyes searching for one familiar livery, one friendly face—one of the Queen's knights or squires. There were few enough left, but even a King's Guardsman might help now.

No one. Not even a clerk in the Random livery. The Randoms were known to be loyal and discreet . . .

Her royal livery made her too obvious. She could see the heads turning, could feel the intensity of their regard. Gallish voices called back and forth.

Blanche turned into the mouth of an alley. She walked past the body of a dead cat and hoped it wasn't an omen. Garbage—mostly vegetable matter—lay in heaps, and her good palace shoes squelched through it.

Her anger grew.

"Voisi! Voisi!" voices shouted at the mouth of the alley.

She ran.

Ten yards in front of her, the alley split, running to either side of a brothel that stood like the prow of a ship, called, with devastating originality, the "Oar House." From the very point of the corner hung the sign, a pair of oars crossed with an erect penis thrust suggestively between them, in case anyone missed the sign's meaning.

Blanche knew where she was. She turned left and continued to run. Any of the pimps hereabouts would trip her up just to see what happened—so she was careful and kept to the middle of the street.

Catcalls and whistles followed her.

She turned at Sail Maker's Lane. She was tending towards Ellen's father's shop—and at the same time wondering how much these men would dare.

Ellen's father was not the man to save her.

But deliberation takes time, and she heard pounding feet.

She turned again, into the alley that ran parallel to the sail lofts where big ships paid to dry and mend their canvas.

An arm barred her progress—she slammed full tilt into it and fell, basket flying.

Panic bubbled close.

"What's your hurry, my pretty?" said a lout. He wore old parti-colour in a southern livery and had a club in his belt. He squinted at her.

She rolled, fouling the whole of her best livery in the watery slime of human and animal excrement of the alley. But she got a hand on the handle of her basket—

A hand grabbed her left arm in a vise of iron.

She screamed. Knowing it was probably the wrong thing to do—that it might attract more predators. But her courage was cracking, and she knew what was coming.

"Look what I have!" said an Alban voice. But as she turned her head and her right hand came up, she saw it was another Alban boy aping the Galles in his tight hose, his arse hanging out in the breeze. Something pricked her right arm as she tried to fight him...

He put his hands around her waist from behind and tried to nuzzle her neck.

She raised herself on her toes, her hands on his, and as the master-at-arms taught the maids, she broke his grip and slammed her basket at him. With her right hand she pulled the offending object from her hair—her thread knife.

She slammed it into his reaching hand and it went all the way in and ripped out again, sharp as any razor. Blood fountained, and the man stumbled back.

He couldn't take his eyes off it. "I'll do you, you bitch!" he shouted.

The southerner tried to grab her. With the grace of desperation, she pivoted and slammed her skirted knee into his balls—hard enough contact to make him mew like a kitten, although his backhand almost knocked her down. She scraped her thread knife over his face and backed into the alley.

She backed three steps. It looked like a dead end—she prayed, and prayed, her mind running too fast, and she saw the dead man's feet—a corpse—and thought of how soon she'd join it. And how odd that the dead man's boots had curly toes like a Moor's.

She toyed with using the little knife on her own wrist. It was a mortal sin. Eternity in hell.

She wished that she was a little luckier, but the dead end was resolutely dead.

The little knot of men were playing with her now. They knew she had nowhere to go, and they were laughing. The bleeding man laid claim to be first on her body.

She looked for a weapon.

"Look out! She bites," laughed one of the Albans. He had a big dagger in his fist, and he thrust it into the southerner as he passed, and stepped aside as the blood flowed. The southerner looked stunned by his own death, and the squire laughed.

He looked at Blanche. "Come out, you little slut, and take what you get. If I have to dirty myself dragging you out, I'll slit your nose when I'm done fucking you." He smiled, raised his hand, and beckoned.

She shrank back.

"Last chance," he said.

The alley ended where four ramshackle buildings came together, and two of them shared an ancient set of roof trees. Blanche had seen the gap—at her head height—the smell of piss told her that men and animals stood here to urinate, especially when it was raining. The gap was too high for her.

She whimpered.

"Stupid slut," the man said.

"Four men on one poor girl!" she managed. "You cowards!"

He shrugged. But he respected her enough to keep his knife well forward, and he pushed in.

She decided to make him kill her, and she attacked.

He passed the dagger effortlessly under her hand and broke her right wrist in the twinkle of an eye. Her beautiful sewing knife fell in the piss.

He kneed her in the gut so hard that she threw up as she fell to her knees.

"Now," he said, with grim humour, "I think I've earned the right to be first. I—"

She didn't really see what happened, because her head was down, but suddenly there was an apparition out of hell in the alley—a big man, black as night, in outlandish foreign clothes.

The black man had come out of the gap above her. The dead man's boots—the man wasn't dead. Her disoriented senses allowed her that much.

"Who the *fuck* are you?" the squire said. He backed up a step and went for his sword.

The blackamoor stood easily, legs slightly apart. He wore a curved sword, sheathed.

The squire's friends shouted from the mouth of the alley.

Blanche pushed a vomit-soaked strand of hair out of her mouth and tried to think.

The squire drew, and as his hand moved, the black man drew, and cut—one incredibly beautiful motion—a minute pivot of the hips and the squire's sword—and hand, still attached—fell to the earth.

The squire shrieked. It was the sound of a man having the soul ripped from his body, and like Blanche, he fell to his knees. Blood fountained.

He seemed unable to understand what had happened. He leaned forward, and his searching left hand found his severed right and tried to pull it to him.

The black man snapped his sword in a short arc, and the very tip passed across the wounded man's eyes and through the bridge of his nose, killing him instantly with an economy of effort that was wasted on the onlookers. The squire fell forward over his own lap, still kneeling.

The blackamoor stepped forward. Blanche got her hand on her sewing knife—like her clothes and her skin, it would wash. Her right wrist was broken or sprained. It would mend. She pushed her back against the filthy wall behind her and levered herself up.

Her linen basket had not spilled. She dropped the knife into it and picked it up left handed. She wasn't thinking well. She needed the knife.

The black figure was not a daemon. He was an infidel—she'd seen his kind a few times. Black men were part of her life—Joe Green was the king's greengrocer, and Miles Greathorn was black as pitch and in the King's Guard. But this man's blackness was almost blue, and he was taller and thinner than the others she'd seen.

And very still. He was at the mouth of the alley, now, and yet it was as if he'd never moved. His sword appeared almost small in his hands, held out behind him like a tail.

She watched the Galles hesitate.

The paynim didn't hesitate. When the other men paused, he leaned and his blade snapped in a short arc, and blood fountained.

"Go for the watch!" shouted the wounded man.

The infidel moved his sword into a new guard, held economically in front above his hips, the curving point aimed at the Galles. The biggest of them drew—and attacked.

The black man spun and spun again.

The biggest Galle fell like a tree, and the paynim's blade flicked back to kill the man he'd wounded.

There were now five corpses cooling, counting the southerner.

The Galles and their friends backed away. "You can't do this," one said, over and over.

Another began screaming for the watch.

Blanche's head began to work again. However black the man might be, and dressed like a foreign unbeliever, he'd saved more than her life. And the watch, whatever she might say, would side with upper class men over a dirty woman and a foreigner. Unless they were very lucky and got someone she knew, like Edmund.

Very carefully—he was unbelievably lethal, and his stillness was as terrifying as his colour—she moved behind him. She talked to him as if he was a horse, sure that he couldn't speak her language.

"If you come with me—just come. I'm not going to hurt you—passing behind you, kind sir. Come along with me." She passed behind him, well within the lethal range of his curved blade. Her knees were watery and her hands shook and her wrist throbbed with a sick kind of pain, but she bit down on the urge to be weak.

Like a skittish horse, she knew she had his attention by the tilt of his head.

She passed behind him, out of the mouth of the alley, stepped past the dead man who lay there and heard people coming.

"Come!" she said.

In the far distance, she heard "Watch, watch!" bellowed.

"Come!" she shouted. He was not moving.

She turned. She'd tried. Down the hill lay Cheapside and safety.

"Come on!" she called. She extended a hand—a damaged, blood-soaked hand. It was swelling already.

He flicked her a glance—and moved. He stooped over one of his victims and picked up the man's hat, and in two strides, he'd cleaned his sword with the hat, tossed it aside and returned the curved blade to his scabbard without looking.

She began to run.

He followed her.

Her wrist began to throb, and every long stride hurt it more, and she tried to catch it in her left, and that hurt—she screamed. She hadn't meant to, but her scream came out with the pain and she was kneeling in the street. Now one of her knees hurt, too.

Another armed man had appeared.

He had a naked sword in his hand, and he was as tall as a tree and almost as wide as a house.

She shuddered in relief, because everyone in her part of Harndon knew Ser Ricar Orcsbane, Knight of the Order.

But even as her vision tunnelled, she knew she could not let go.

She got her head up.

"Ser Ricar!" she said. "Oh, Christ—he saved me, ser knight."

Ser Ricar was under a vow of silence. He looked at the paynim. He kept his long sword between them.

"He saved me, you hear me, ser? Galles attacked me—Sweet Virgin, mother of God—" She was babbling, and somehow, she was listening to herself babble from a great distance and the pain was ebbing and flowing like a tide.

She moaned, and tried to sit up.

They were of a height, the two men—one pale and red haired, with freckles across his enormous nose, and the other black as pitch with indigo added. The Ifriquy'an's nose was smaller and finer, but otherwise, they were a measure of wide shoulders and narrow waists. Their swords were a match, too.

Both looked at the girl who had fallen forward over her knees. Both kept their swords up, between them, with the ease of long familiarity.

And neither spoke.

In the near distance, voices cried for the watch.

Ser Ricar gave the very slightest bow. Then, like an uncoiling spring, he sheathed his sword and bent, lifting the fallen woman as if she was made of feathers.

She stiff-armed him with her uninjured left hand. "Don't touch me!" she spat, though she heard herself say it from a distance. "I can walk!"

The infidel allowed himself a smile. He inclined his head, and his sword vanished into the mouth of its scabbard.

The Knight of the Order released Blanche and stepped back, hands held up.

Blanche got to her feet. "I'll get myself there," she said grimly.

The Knight of the Order gave her a bow—respect, admonition, concurrence—it was a very expressive bow. And then he turned and ran down the hill toward Cheapside, Blanche trailing, stumbling, but managing her legs the way a mother might manage wayward children, and, last, the infidel.

Albans, like many folk, have never been fond of what they don't know. Hence, the new Archbishop of Lorica was almost always referred to as the "new bishop" as if newness itself was something disgraceful.

The new bishop, Bohemund de Foi, was a Galle. This, too, led to an illogical prejudice. Most of the population of Harndon had names that indicated a Gallish origin; merchants and apprentices and nobles, too. Under the Semples lay Saint Pols. Under the Dentermints lay D'Entre Deux Monts. Six hundred years of prosperous trade between Harndoners and their Gallish cousins should have built trust and love, but it hadn't, and despite Gallish fashions, Gallish swords, and Gallish Bible covers in every home, Galles were often the subject of biting witticisms or even riots, and the new bishop's origins would have told against him had he been of saintly and humble demeanour.

In fact, the opinion of the people kept the young Archbishop of Lorica in a state of constant ferment. He was booed in the street, he had clods of earth thrown at his palanquin, and when one of his priests was accused of some very venal flirtation with one of the boys in the ritual choir of the cathedral, the man was badly beaten by apprentices.

So it was in no humble or contrite mood that the most powerful cleric in Alba met with his political ally and cousin, Jean de Vrailly, and his household. Present at de Vrailly's table was his other cousin, the Count D'Eu; the Sieur de Rohan, whose power at court was beginning to eclipse de Vrailly's own; and Ser Eustace l'Isle d'Adam, a rising star among de Vrailly's knights.

De Rohan was the last to arrive and the first to speak. "I have under my hand the good squire Maurice d'Evereoux," he said, indicating a young man standing in the doorway. "He is prepared to report on the latest outrage perpetrated by the Queen's people. I am very sorry to tell you gentlemen that four of our people have been killed."

The Archbishop's hand went to his throat—the other men present touched their swords.

"What killed them?" de Vrailly spat.

"A woman—one of the Queen's tire women—summoned a daemon on a public street. The daemon killed four of our noble squires. When our people attempted to pursue the thing, a knight of the so-called 'Order of Saint Thomas' was seen, sword in hand, defending the thing."

The Count D'Eu leaned back, an enigmatic smile on his face. "If it killed four of our squires, messieurs, why did it need defence?"

De Rohan shot him a look full of scorn. "My lord, why ask such a thing? I merely relate the events as they happen."

D'Eu laughed softly. "Do you know Blanche Gold?" he asked. "I do not think that the notion that she conjured a daemon is going to play especially well." He looked around. "Not least as it's a fairly obvious lie."

De Rohan shot to his feet. "Do you, monsieur, give *me* the lie?"

D'Eu didn't stir. "Yes," he said. "I say you lie." He nodded to his cousin. "He is lying on purpose, to make trouble."

De Rohan's face carried honest, blank amazement.

De Vrailly frowned in distaste. "I wish you would not speak so of the good de Rohan in public; he seeks only to serve."

"Does he indeed, cousin?" D'Eu rose. "I offer to fight you, de Rohan— right now. By the Law of War."

D'Eu was in his harness. De Rohan wore the long pointed shoes and short gown of a courtier.

Jean de Vrailly nodded, jaw outthrust. "I take your point, fair cousin. Monsieur de Rohan, you will kindly return to wearing your armour on all but formal occasions. We must remind the court at all times what we represent—the manly virtues that their effeminacy has forgotten."

D'Eu shook his head. "Nay, cousin, I mean it. This gossipy viper has nothing in his head but the destruction of the Queen and the smearing of her reputation. I say he lies. I offer to prove it on him, with my sword." D'Eu leaned back. "Par Dieu, I'll even let him put on his harness—if he can find it."

Silence fell.

De Rohan was white as parchment. "You— You traitor!"

D'Eu frowned. "My pardon, Monsieur, but detesting you is not treason."

"You are the one who shields the Queen and warns her!" he began.

Jean de Vrailly stood. "As master of this household, I must require you, cousin, to withdraw your challenge."

Gaston D'Eu also stood. "On what grounds?" he asked.

Jean de Vrailly's eyes all but begged him to withdraw. "By my will," he said.

"You mean, when you killed Towbray's cousin and I begged you to withdraw—that was different?"

"He challenged my honour," Ser Jean said patiently.

"De Rohan has just pronounced me a traitor," D'Eu said reasonably.

"He will retract it," de Vrailly said.

D'Eu nodded, pursed his lips, and sat. "I will consider," he said.

De Rohan frowned. He whispered a few words to his squire, D'Alace, and looked at l'Isle d'Adam. "If I am to be given the lie, perhaps I should not continue," he said.

"I will continue," the Archbishop of Lorica said. "And perhaps no lout will give *me* the lie. These people hate us. They are nothing but a nest of heretics and rebels. And the so-called 'Order of Saint Thomas' is nothing less than a heretical cult. They harbour witches and Satan-workers, and they have never been approved by the scholastica."

Patiently, as if dealing with a fool, D'Eu said, "Cousin, you must have been here long enough to know that the Albans follow the Patriarch in Liviapolis and not the Patriarch of Rhum. They care nothing for our scholastica or the theology of the bishop or the University of Lucrece."

"Heretics," Bohemund de Foi insisted. "The Patriarch of Rhum has never approved of them. And he, not the upstart infidel in Liviapolis, is the primarch of the world."

D'Eu made a motion of his hand. The motion suggested that he wiped his arse with the bishop's argument.

The bishop turned bright red. "You dare!"

D'Eu set his jaw. "What I see, *gentlemen*, is a small set of my country-men determined to stop at nothing to create a civil war here. I will be kind and suggest that it is ignorance and not malfeasance that leads you, my lord archbishop, to say these things."

De Vrailly tapped a thumb on his teeth. "The Order of Saint Thomas were, my lords, fine knights and good men-at-arms when fighting the Wild."

"Oh, the Wild!" the archbishop all but spat. "All day I listen to this prattle. Weak minds deluded by satanic manifestations! The Wild is nothing but a snare of this world, like women's wiles and gluttony."

De Vrailly combed his twin-pointed beard with his fingers. "In this, my lord archbishop, I cannot agree. The Wild is—quite palpable. My angel says—"

The archbishop held up his hand. "Please, Monsieur de Vrailly."

Silence fell for a moment as the two men glared at each other.

"I propose we move against this Order and suppress them," the bishop continued. "I have recorded enough of their use of satanic powers to burn every one of them. They brag of their powers." The archbishop turned on his cousin. "And you threaten your immortal soul every time you consort with them. Or the Queen and her witches."

De Vrailly was not a man who enjoyed being spited, especially not at his own table and in front of his own squires. "You speak too forcefully for me, my lord archbishop," de Vrailly said.

"I speak for the good of your soul," de Foi replied. "The Queen is a witch and must die. The Order are her minions. Everyone in this room knows that what I say is true. If we are to save the souls of these Albans, we must begin by ridding ourselves of these two forces for evil."

Gaston D'Eu snorted his derision. "I don't know any such thing," he said. "And I recommend that my lord archbishop take a dozen of his priests and some animals and ride west into the mountains. I would strongly suggest that what he experiences there may change his mind. If he survives the experience at all." D'Eu tapped his dagger on the table.

His lieutenant, D'Herblay, laughed with him. Even de Vrailly nodded.

The King's Champion frowned. "As is often the way, there is merit in what my cousin the count says."

De Rohan shook his head. "Do you deny that the Queen has committed adultery? We have shown you proof often enough. Are you suddenly a convert to her party?"

De Vrailly shook his head. "I am saddened that we are so divided on these matters. No—I know in my heart she is an evil woman. My angel has told me."

At the word "angel" the archbishop slapped his hand to his forehead, as if in pain.

"I would at least like to order—in the King's name—the arrest of this woman, Blanche Gold." De Rohan took a scroll and handed it to de Vrailly. "She has consistently been one of the Queen's go-betweens with her lovers. We have witnesses," he said in a low voice.

Gaston D'Eu watched his cousin accept the scroll and he rose. "I cannot be party to this," he said.

De Rohan shrugged. "Then take your divisive accusations and your treasonous talk and go, my lord."

D'Eu shrugged. "I have already challenged you. I cannot do so again. That you ignore my summons to combat says all that needs to be said."

De Rohan didn't meet his eye.

"Coward," D'Eu said.

De Rohan grew red.

"Caitiff. Poltroon. False knight." D'Eu shrugged. "I see that my words cannot move you. I pity you." D'Eu turned. "My dearest lord, I take my leave."

"Wait!" de Vrailly said. "Ah, sweet cousin. Please await my pleasure."

D'Eu bowed and left with D'Herblay at his shoulder.

"He will ruin everything we seek to build here," de Rohan said, pleading with de Vrailly.

The King's Champion looked at him with surprise. "How can you not respond to his challenge?" he asked.

De Rohan drew himself erect. "I serve a higher cause. I can ignore a private quarrel, no matter how unfair it is."

De Vrailly pursed his lips. "I think you should fight him," he said. "You are a great knight. I trained you myself. You are the match for any man but me." He raised an eyebrow. "Otherwise, I have to wonder if he is right. Don't I? And my lord archbishop, I can't support arresting the Order of Saint Thomas. We'd have riots. And they help us hold the frontiers."

The archbishop looked pleadingly at de Rohan.

De Rohan sighed. "If you have lost confidence in me, my lord, perhaps I should withdraw to the King's court at Lucrece." He bowed to the archbishop. "I agree that they are a nest of heretics. A woman saying mass? It's an abomination."

The bishop raised his eyes to heaven.

De Vrailly looked at them both for a long time, his expressive, wide blue eyes going back and forth between them. "Archbishop, I have every respect for the cloth, but I have difficulty separating your rank from your youth. De Rohan, if you do not feel that you can respond to my cousin's challenge then you have my permission to withdraw to your estates in Galle." He rose, his armoured legs making a slight *clack* as his legs went straight.

When he and his men-at-arms were gone, the archbishop put a hand on de Rohan's arm. "I'll deal with it," he said. "I have a man."

De Rohan shook his head. His hand on the table was shaking. "That he would dare!" he hissed.

The archbishop put a hand over de Rohan's. "In a week—less, if the winds are fair—we'll have three hundred lances, fresh from Galle. We will own this city, and we will have the whip hand we need."

"He exiled me!" de Rohan said.

The archbishop shrugged. "Wait and see," he said with a smile.

When the impromptu council broke up, de Rohan and his people went back to court, where the Count of Hoek's new ambassador was due to be received by the King. Jean de Vrailly listened to his squire for a moment and followed the younger man into his private study, where D'Eu stood quietly.

"Cousin," he said.

"I'm going back to Galle," D'Eu said. "I'm sorry, cousin. These men are disgusting. I will not be linked to them. And there is word that..." He sighed. "There is word that the Wild is attacking Arelat. Even Galle."

De Vrailly nodded. "I, too, have heard this. Bohemund and his people are full of it—because they have this foolish belief that there is no Wild but only the forces of Satan." De Vrailly shrugged. "Perhaps they are correct."

"I have lands in Arelat," D'Eu said. "I am no good to you here, and I have knight service to perform at home. Please let me go."

De Vrailly paced. "We are close, I think. When I have brought the Queen to trial—"

"An innocent woman," D'Eu said flatly.

"And when the rest of my knights arrive—"

"A foreign army to cow the Harndoners," D'Eu said.

"Cousin, my angel has told me—directly—that I must become King to save this realm." Jean de Vrailly crossed his arms.

D'Eu came and embraced him. "You know I love you," he said. "But I will not be party to this anymore. I wash my hands of it. I think you are wrong—you *and* your angel. And I say that, in your delusion, you have unsavoury allies and you ignore your own beliefs."

De Vrailly's nostrils flared. "Name one!" he said.

"You preach the Rule of War. But you forbade me to kill that poisonous viper de Rohan." D'Eu all but spat. "The Rule of War was made for this—when I know in my heart a man is false as black pitch, I kill him. Yet you—*you* have forbidden me to kill him."

De Vrailly ran his fingers through his beard and turned away in frustration. "I was surprised," he said. "But—my angel has told me—"

"Your angel may be a devil!" D'Eu said.

De Vrailly put a hand on his sword.

They faced each other. "Go," de Vrailly said.

D'Eu bowed deeply. "I will be gone on the first ship of spring, my lord cousin," he said.

An hour later, Jean de Vrailly was on his knees before his magnificent triptych of Saint Michael, Saint George, and Saint Maurice. He was in his full harness, and the lames around the kneecaps cut into his knees, even though he wore padded hose—bit into them savagely.

He mastered the pain, and remained kneeling.

And he prayed.

His cousin's stinging words had hurt him. The more so as, in the privacy of his own chamber, he had doubts—severe doubts.

So he knelt, punishing himself for his doubt, and begging his angel for an appearance.

An hour passed, and then another. The pain in his knees was now such as to make it past the guards of his experience and his immunity to the minor pains of wearing his harness. Now he had to admit to a niggle of fear for his knees—how long could mere flesh stand to be tormented by steel?

And his hips—the weight of his mail, of his breast and back, ground into the top of his hips as if he was being pressed to death. If he was standing or riding, the straps on his shoulders would have distributed the weight.

A theologian would have told him that he was committing sin. That by forcing himself to the point of injury, he was testing his angel, and hence, God.

De Vrailly was untroubled by such thoughts.

And eventually, his angel came.

"Ah, my true knight," the angel said, his voice like the bells of high mass and the trumpets of the King's court, all together.

De Vrailly bowed his head. The angel was so *bright*.

"My child, you must want something," the angel said sweetly.

De Vrailly's head remained down.

"You have doubts," the angel said, amused. "Even you."

"My lord," de Vrailly said.

"The Queen is most certainly a witch," the angel said. "She uses the powers of darkness to entrap men." The angel's voice was the very essence of reason.

"My lord—"

"You, de Vrailly, must be King here. Only you." The angel spoke the words softly, but with great force.

De Vrailly sighed. "I like the King." He shook his head. "And I am not sure that the Queen..."

The angel smiled. "Your conscience does you credit, good knight. And de Rohan surely rivals Judas as a scheming betrayer."

De Vrailly's head shot up. "Yes! To think that work was one of mine—"

"The King of Kings must use the tools that come into his hand," the angel said. "Even de Rohan."

De Vrailly sighed. "As always, Puissant Lord, you put my mind at rest." De Vrailly paused. "But I loathe de Rohan."

The angel nodded. "So does God. Imagine how He felt about Judas."

The angel put an insubstantial hand on de Vrailly's head, and his power flowed through that hand and over de Vrailly, so that for a moment he was suffused in rich, golden light. "You will have much sorrow in the coming days," the angel said. "This is no easy task I have set you. Beware the snares. When the King is gone—"

"Where will he go?" de Vrailly asked.

"When the King is gone to death, then you will know what to do," the angel said.

The appearance of an Ifriquy'an in the yard was made even more exotic by his being with Ser Ricar and the beautiful Blanche, whose tall, wide-shouldered good looks were admired—from afar—by every apprentice at Master Pye's. More boys had been injured swashbuckling to win her attention than any other girl's in the square.

Edmund, who had charge of the yard for most purposes these days, had the gates opened to admit them and never gave it a thought. Ser Ricar had saved almost every one of them from the increasingly violent attacks of the King's enemies. His sister Mary had been attacked, knocked down, and kicked—and then saved by Ser Ricar. Nancy had been forced to decline service in the palace—the dream of her youth—because their mother would not allow her to walk unaccompanied through the increasingly dangerous streets.

There was a rumour that Jack Drake was back.

Spring was bringing more ills than reliefs, except for frozen young men whose numb fingers caused accidents during the winter. And as the tournament was coming apace, the yard was overflowing with work.

Blanche was taken into Master Pye's house, where his wife put her in a small room with its own fire and waited on her as if she was the Queen in person.

In the kitchen, Ser Ricar drank mulled ale against the cold rain.

The black man drank only water.

Up close, Edmund found him handsome in a disconcerting and alien way. His features were regular, his eyes large and well spaced and deeply intelligent.

Nor did he appear to be under a vow of silence. At the table, when he broke bread, he inclined his head and spoke—some foreign words that sounded like a prayer.

Master Pye came in with his spectacles dangling around his neck. He glanced at the black man as if he saw such in his wife's kitchen every day and poured himself a cup of the warmed ale.

"Aethiope?" he asked the black man.

The man rose and bowed, his hands together as if praying. "Dar as Salaam," he replied.

Master Pye nodded. "Allah Ak'bhar," he said.

The infidel nodded.

"You speak the pagan tongue?" Edmund asked his master.

"Pagan? Not so fast, young Edmund. Heretical, perhaps." He shrugged. "Dar as Salaam—the greatest city in the world." He smiled. "Fine swords." He shrugged. "Not really the best armourers."

"You went there?" Edmund asked.

Master Pye frowned. "I was on a ship in the harbour eight days, wind bound. Went ashore and didn't get made a slave." He shrugged. "When I was young and foolish."

The black man had a habit of sitting perfectly still.

"This man is someone important. What happened?" Master Pye was in a hurry.

Edmund shook his head. "Ser Ricar was there."

The Order knight shook his head. He wrote on a wax tablet and Master Pye looked at it.

"Random has a clerk who speaks Ifriquy'a. Or Wahele or Bemba, I forget which." Master Pye took his own wax tablet, wrote a note and put his ring on it to seal it. "Take this to Ser Gerald."

Edmund took the tablet.

Master Pye gestured with his hand. "I think you should run."

Ser Gerald Random came in person, stumping along with his master clerk who handled all his foreign shipments.

His clerk wore a gold ring and black cloak like a man of property. He bowed with his hands together.

The black man returned the bow most courteously.

The clerk spoke.

The black man answered.

After two exchanges, the black man spoke at some length.

On the fourth exchange, he smiled. It transformed his face.

The clerk looked up. "He's a messenger. He's looking for—for Magister Harmodius."

"He's a little late," Ser Gerald said.

"He says he came ashore from the Venike ships; that the Golden Leopard refused to serve or house him, and he intended to leave Harndon at first light." The man spread his hands and smiled. "He *apologized* for killing four men, but said that they attacked a woman, and he cannot allow such a thing."

Two hours had passed since the two matched giants in ebony and ivory had stumbled into the yard. They'd had enough reports of the carnage in Palm Alley to know who had attacked Blanche and who had died.

"He seems unconcerned," Ser Gerald growled.

His clerk shook his head. "Boss, I was there a year. I met men like this. They have a saying, 'That which is, is.' And they say, *Inshallah*, which means, 'Let it be as God wills.' "

"Deus Veult!" Ser Gerald said. He nodded.

Ser Ricar nodded.

"No wonder they get along," Edmund said, not very loud.

Master Pye leaned in. "I have a shop to run. We have a hundred items to deliver in fifteen days. And my gut feeling is that this is going to make a storm of shit." He looked at Ser Ricar. "Can you hide him?"

Ser Ricar nodded.

The clerk spoke to the infidel, and he shook his head vehemently.

"He says he has a mission and he must go. He says that if we'll hide him for one night, he'll be gone by daybreak." The clerk smiled. "He says if we'd retrieve his horse, he'd be eternally grateful."

Ser Gerald rolled his eyes.

"Grateful enough for me to get a long look at his sword?" Master Pye asked.

An hour later, while Ser Gerald dickered with a bored Venike factor for a sea-sick stallion, all the apprentices and journeymen gathered in the Master's shop around the clean table he kept there. Nothing went on that table but finished metal and parchment; today he laid his wife's third best linen table cloth atop it after sweeping it, and the infidel knight—all the apprentices agreed he must be a knight—drew his sword and laid it on the table.

The strong daylight from the gable overhead made the blade seem to ripple and move.

Every metalworker in the room sighed.

The sword was a hand longer than the longest sword the shop had ever made, and swept in a gradual curve from the long, two-hand hilt all the way to the clipped point with its rebated false edge. The grip was white ivory from the undead mammoths of the deep south, and the crossguard was plain steel. Set into the blade—a masterpiece of pattern welding— were runes.

"Are the runes silver, Master?" Edmund asked. The colour of the runes was just barely perceptible as different from the rest of the blade.

Master Pye shook his head. "Oh, mercy no, Edmund. They are steel. Steel set into the steel."

"Look at the finish," murmured Duke. He had become the shop's expert of finishing, and he now had a dozen boys working for him.

Sam Vintner, the most junior man present, was trying not to breathe, but he sighed. "So beautiful!" he said.

Tom leaned very close. "Magicked," he said.

The infidel was on his toes, watching them very carefully. He was very tense.

The clerk made reassuring noises.

"He says—he says that in his own country, he would never allow any but his master or the Sultan to touch his sword. He says his master has filled it with power."

Master Pye nodded. "Aye, lads. It's full of power." He went to a cabinet in the wall behind his prie-dieu and opened it with a word. The journey-men all knew what it was—a secret cabinet with a hermetical lock. Only the older boys knew how to open it—it was where the precious metals were kept.

Master Pye took out a set of spectacles that appeared to have lenses of faceted jewels. He leaned over the sword and put the jewels over his eyes.

"Sweet Mary, Queen of the heavens and mother of God," he said.

He took them off and handed them to Edmund, who had never used them before. In fact, Edmund, now the senior journeyman in a shop big enough to be called a factory, was learning that Master Pye had more secrets than a necromancer.

Edmund put them on. The cabinet shone with energy in mage light.

The sword lit the room.

"What do you see, lad?" Master Pye asked him.

"The sword!" Edmund said.

"Aye," Master Pye said. "It is a sword in the *aethereal*, too." He pointed at the cabinet, which was merely a point source in mage light. "Things that are magicked are like shadows, and the hermetical *praxis* burns like a flame in the *aethereal*."

"But this is a sword," Edmund said. He took off the glasses and handed them to Tom, who was bouncing impatiently.

The infidel was still nervous. He spoke.

The clerk translated, after a long pause. "He asks if any of us know Harmodius."

Tom put a hand on his master's arm. "He's got a magick ring," he said, looking through the jewels at the paynim.

"Aye. He's trouble, and no mistake. What do you boys reckon, when you see a sword that's a sword in both the real and the *aethereal*?" Master Pye was pedantic, because he was *always* teaching.

They all looked at each other.

Edmund said slowly, "That it will function as a sword. In the *aethereal*, too."

Master Pye gave him the glance of approval that they all treasured. He was not big on praise, was Master Pye. But he was more than fair. "Indeed, boys. That's what is called a Fell Sword. Except that that's a Fell Sword that will cut in the real *or* in the *aethereal*." He bent over it and fitted a very pragmatic and ordinary loupe in his eye.

"I wonder who made it?" he asked.

The clerk repeated the question, and the infidel knight began to answer. He spoke for some time, and long before he was done, the clerk began writing.

"He says his master re-made it. But he says that it was made more than a thousand years ago."

Edmund all but choked.

Master Pye nodded. "Ahh!" he said, with utter delight. "It is one of the six!" He lifted the sword from the table, and in that gesture, he was transformed from a tall, ungainly man with bulgy eyes and bad breath to a hero of legend whose shadow fell over the table like a figure of menace.

"Who is your master, my lord?" he asked.

The clerk repeated the words.

The infidel spoke. *"Abū l-Walīd Muḥammad bin 'Aḥmad bin Rušd."* He bowed. His eyes were on the sword.

Master Pye smiled. "I confess to a very boyish inclination to try and cut something with it." He carefully put it on the table, and returned to being a bent-shouldered man in late middle-age with a fringe of hair and bulging eyes. "His master is Al Rashidi."

The journeymen all breathed in together.

"The Magus!" Edmund said.

Master Pye pointed at the tiny sign of an eye emerging from the sun. "The very same." He offered his right hand to the infidel.

The black man took his hand.

Master Pye did something with his hand—changed grip somehow.

The infidel knight grinned. "Ah—*rafiki!*" he said.

"He says, 'Oh, friend!'" said the clerk.

Master Pye nodded. He turned.

"Boys, that's one of the six—on a table in our shop. I expect that in the next quarter hour, we'll have the most complete set of weights, measures and dimensions for that sword as exist in all the world. Eh?"

He took the clerk by the shoulder and led him—and the infidel, who didn't want to leave his weapon—out of the shop.

"Six?" Duke asked.

Tom whistled. "Don't you know anything?"

Duke gave him a look that promised bruised knuckles. Duke had made journeyman on pure talent, and lacked the book learning of the other journeymen.

"Hieronimus Magister was the greatest magus of the Archaics," Edmund said. "You should read his essay on the property of metals. It is the origin of proper study." He shrugged. "At any rate, he was the greatest of mages. In their world, he is treated as a prophet." He pointed out the door, where the black man had gone. "When the Umroth attacked, he made a hundred swords for the Emperor's guard to use against the not-dead."

Tom was measuring and Sam was writing everything in his neat hand on wax.

"At the end of the last Umroth war, only six remained. They kill—both here and in the *aethereal*. But strange events follow them—weather, monsters, the Wild, assassins." Edmund shrugged. "I thought they were a myth."

Duke reached out—always the boldest of them—and picked up the great curved sword.

"Holy Mother of God," he said.

He, too, seemed to grow in stature and dignity.

"Oh," he breathed. He put the sword down, carefully. "Oh—my God."

As Duke was never impressed by anything, Edmund couldn't stop himself. He plucked up the sword.

Once, as a child, Edmund had gone with his mother and sisters to the cathedral and there, by chance, he had been standing in the nave when the sun emerged from the clouds and shone directly through the great central rose window of the cathedral. All around him, light exploded into bloom and in that moment, he had felt the touch of God—the direct, intangible presence of the universe and all wisdom, and everything: his sister's laughter, his mother's whisper, the priest's hands, the passage of the smoking censor through the perfumed air, the perfection of its arc and the gleam of its silver shell; and every dust mote and every hint of the last chord of the last hymn and the whispers of the nuns and the gleam of a rich woman's buttoned sleeve—everything made *sense*.

Edmund had never forgotten that moment. It was at the heart of his craftsmanship.

And now he relived it in half the beat of his heart. He was the sword. The sword was in him and over him. And everything, everywhere, made sense.

He regained control of himself—aware of a nearly overpowering urge to use the blade on something—anything—to feel its perfection in culmination, almost exactly the feeling he had when he lay beside Anne and kissed her and wanted more. To finish.

To be complete.

Instead, he laid the sword gradually down on the table.

"Be careful," he said to Sam. "But you must try it."

"Can you imagine wearing that every day?" Edmund asked Duke.

Duke sighed. "Oh—aye. I can imagine." He smiled weakly. "I wanted to cut you in half, just to see if I could."

Neither laughed.

An hour later, a boy came from Prior Wishart with a note for Ser Ricar. By then the sword was returned to its owner, who seemed profoundly more at ease to have it at his side. He was seated at a table in the yard, writing out words in his odd flowing runes at the dictation of Ser Gerald's clerk.

The clerk made an odd gesture. "He speaks Etruscan well eno'," he said. "I'm trying to give him a few words in Alban."

"Etruscan?" Master Pye asked. He shook his head.

Ser Ricar appeared at his elbow and handed him a note.

Master Pye took the note and read it.

"Christ on the cross," he snapped. "Boys! On me!"

Long before the King's Guardsmen came, Blanche was gone, and her bed was stripped and the maids were washing in the yard. The black man vanished as if he had never been, and Ser Ricar vanished with him.

The guardsmen searched in a desultory way. Blanche had friends throughout the palace. The guardsmen were not very interested in finding her, but they had a warrant for her arrest.

When they were gone, Mistress Pye put her arms around her husband. "Bradley Pye," she said. "I think it is time to get out of this town."

He was watching the last two guardsmen as they went through his gate.

"Worse 'n you think," he muttered. "They're going to suppress the Order."

His wife crossed herself. "Blessed Saint Thomas," she said.

Master Pye had tears in his eyes. "My life's work is here," he said. "But our secret guards will be gone, now. The prior's calling his knights away before the King can get to them."

"So?" his wife asked.

"So we're naked," Master Pye said. "And an army of Galles will land in the next day or two. Gerry says the Venike know they're coming."

"Gerald Random won't let us down." Deirdre Pye shook her head.

"I'd be happy if you were gone," Master Pye said. "You an' the maids."

"Bradley Pye, when will you learn that we're not hostages? We're willing hands." His wife crossed her arms.

Pye pursed his lips. "We'll see," he said.

No Galles came the next day, or the next.

Outside the southern walls of the city, the bleachers rose for the tournament, and lists were built. There were lists for foot combat, with oak beams four fingers square that rested on oak posts, so that a knight in full armour, thrown by another, wouldn't budge the fence. Four feet high, eighteen feet on a side—a bear pit for armoured fighters.

The mounted lists were more complicated; a central barricade the height of a horse's haunches, walled in oak boards, the whole length of the course, with another oak fence all the way around the outside, a hundred and fifty feet long and forty feet wide.

Both lists were nearly complete. At the foot lists, a dozen pargeters and painters had begun hanging painted canvas and leather decorations that looked, for all the world, like solid gold and silver pedestals holding magnificently decorated shields.

The Master Pargeter already had a master roll of every knight and squire expected to fight. On the ninth and tenth pages, shields had been added to indicate the late entries—Galles who had not yet arrived, and Occitans who were rumoured, even now, to be en route.

The royal arms decorated the royal pavilion—the King was a noted jouster and had every intention to participate—and the stands.

The Master Pargeter had narrow red lines through a number of coats of arms, as well, from the original roll. The Earl of Towbray was no longer included. The Count of the Borders had been ordered to take a force of Royal Foresters into the west country in response to raids from the Wild. Edward Daispansay—the Lord of Bain—had taken his retainers and left the court a month before. Only his son Thomas remained, and the difference on his arms—an eight-pointed star—was, thankfully, an easy correction to paint.

The Count D'Eu, the Champion's cousin and a famous lance, had just withdrawn that morning.

But the biggest change was that the Queen's arms had been ordered stricken from the record. Desiderata's arms—the Royal Arms of Occitan, quartered with Galle and Alba and supported by a unicorn and a Green Man, were well known throughout the kingdom, and her knights had, on other occasions, been the most cohesive team after the King's. Now her arms were banned, which led to a great deal of speculation among the workmen, and not a single one of her knights was to break a lance or swing a sword in the lists.

Ser Gerald Random, the King's "merchant knight," stood on his wooden foot, supported by a thick ebony cane with a head of solid gold, watching the workmen. Around him stood most of his officers for the tournament, and with him was the new Lord Mayor of Harndon, Ailwin Darkwood, and the past mayor, Ser Richard Smythe.

A dozen sailors were rigging an enormous awning over the bleachers.

"I saw 'em do it in Liviapolis," Ser Gerald said. "Mind you, they had a magister to seal it."

The Lord Mayor made a hasty wave of his hand. "God between us and evil. Until we're rid of the new bishop, don't even speak of such things."

Random spat in annoyance. "Gentles," he said, "among us, we control most of the flow of capital in this city." He looked around. "Are we going to stand for this?" He pointed his elegant cane at the two pargeter's apprentices who were carefully taking *down* the Queen's arms from the central viewing stand over the mounted lists.

"What choice do we have?" Ser Richard asked. "I don't have an army. Nor am I much of a jouster."

Ser Gerald looked around carefully. "There's Jacks moving into the city," he said. "And there's Galles coming. And a tithe of fools who ape the Galles."

Darkwood spoke very quietly. "And Occitans. The Queen's brother won't just stand by and let her be arrested."

Ser Gerald looked around. "Let's speak frankly, gentles, as it becomes merchants. Leave lying to the lords. The King's champion and his cronies are leading us into a civil war, as sure as the wind blows."

The other two men shifted uncomfortably.

"And if they fight here, in our streets—" Ser Gerald narrowed his eyes. "Imagine fire in our houses. And soldiers. Looting."

"Sweet Christ, we'd all be ruined." Ser Richard shook his head. "It would never happen here."

Ser Gerald looked around again. "Since my adventure last year among the Moreans," he said with some authority, "I have friends among the Etruscans."

"So I've noted, to my discontent," admitted Darkwood. "There were Venike and Fiorian merchants who got their furs before I did!"

Ser Gerald raised an eyebrow. "There was fur eno' for every house," he said. "And one of my principal backers asked that I make sure the Etruscans weren't cut out. Any road—the Venike captain, Ser Giancarlo, what docked Thursday last—he's brought me news." He looked around again. "He says the King of Galle has ordered all this. That it is a plot—that de Vrailly works for the King of Galle. That he will seize the kingdom and hold it for his master."

Ailwin Darkwood tugged his beard. "I've always thought so. Since the assault on our coinage started."

Ser Gerald was surprised. "But—"

Darkwood shrugged. "I take my own precautions. What do you suggest we do?"

Ser Gerald raised an eyebrow. "Nothing against the King," he said.

Ser Richard looked furtive. "This is treason."

Ser Gerald shook his head vehemently. "Nothing against the King, I said."

Master Ailwin and Ser Gerald both glared at Ser Richard. "What do you have planned?" Ser Richard asked, but his body language clearly said that he was not with them.

An hour later he was sharing wine with the Archbishop of Lorica, who affected unconcern.

"Fear nothing, good Ser Richard. Some of your countrymen are traitors, but the King is safe. Indeed, I think I can tell you that in the next few hours, a plot will be revealed that will do much to allay your fears."

Ser Richard rose. "Random and Darkwood and Pye, between them, control most of the militia—the Trained Band. They will use it."

The archbishop laughed. "Peasants with pitchforks? Against belted knights?" He laughed heartily. "I hope they try. In Galle, we encourage them—it thins the herd."

Ser Richard knew little about war, but he tugged his beard in agitation. "I think your knights may find them formidable, ser. At any rate, I must away. I cannot have my hand in this. After this unpleasantness is over, I'll need to do business with these men."

The archbishop escorted him personally to the door of his chamber, saw him handed out the door, and returned to his desk. To his secretary, Maître Gris, a priest and doctor of theology, he said, "That man imagines that when we are done, he can go back to his business." He shook his head. "Usury and luxury and gluttony."

His secretary nodded, eyes gleaming.

"We will have the richest church in all the see of Rhum," the archbishop said.

"And you will be Patriarch," his secretary said.

They shared a glance. Then the archbishop shook himself free of his dreams and leaned back.

"Fetch me my Archaic scribe," he said.

The secretary frowned, but he went out, his black robes like a storm cloud.

The archbishop concentrated on a letter explaining—in measured tones—that no priest of the church was subject to any civil or royal law, and that the Manor Court of Lewes had no jurisdiction nor right to hear any case against their reverend father in Christ.

His secretary returned. In tones of quiet disapproval, the man said, "*Maître* Villon."

A thin figure in the threadbare scarlet of a lower caste doctor of law bowed deeply.

The archbishop could smell the wine on him. "Maître," he said sharply.

The red man stood solidly enough. "Your eminence," he said.

The archbishop gestured sharply at his secretary. "I will handle this," he said.

His secretary nodded sharply.

The archbishop sat back. "Maître Villon, you understand, I think, why I brought you to Alba."

Maître Villon's bloodshot eyes met his and then the doctor of law looked at the parquetry floor in front of him. "I am at your eminence's will," he said softly.

"Very much so, I think," the archbishop said. "Need I go into particulars?"

Maître Villon didn't raise his eyes. "No, Eminence."

"Very well. I wish a certain set of events to come to pass. Can you make them happen?"

The man in red nodded. "Yes, Eminence."

"I wish a man to die." The archbishop winced at his own words.

"By what means?" the doctor of law asked.

"By *your* means, Maître Villon." The archbishop spoke sharply, his voice rising, like a mother speaking to a particularly stupid child.

"By the hermetical arts," the doctor of law said softly.

The archbishop half rose. "I have not said so!" he said. "And you will keep a civil tongue in your head. Or you will have no tongue at all."

The red-clad man kept looking at the floor.

"Can you effect this?" the archbishop asked.

The red-clad man shrugged. "Possibly. All things are possible."

"Today." The archbishop leaned forward.

The man in red sighed. "Very well," he said. "Can you have someone get me something he wears? Something he wears often?"

The archbishop seemed about to expostulate, but then paused. "Yes."

The man in red nodded. "If, perhaps, someone could steal his gloves? I assume he is a gentleman."

The archbishop was looking elsewhere. *"Pfft,"* he said.

The man in red ignored him. "And then, later today, we could return his gloves, as if they were found in the street."

"And you can work your hideous perversion in that little time?"

The man in red bowed. "In your eminence's service."

"You try me, Maître Villon. Yet I hold you and all you think dear in my hand." The archbishop fingered the amulet he wore with his cross.

The man in red shrugged. "It is as you say, Eminence." He sounded tired, or hopeless, or perhaps both.

As he went out, the secretary glared at him with unconcealed hate.

"How can you allow such a man to live?" he asked.

"Tush, Gilles. That is not your place to ask." The archbishop frowned. "Have you not asked yourself whether Judas was evil, or whether he was bound to deliver our lord to the cross? And thus merely a tool of God?"

The secretary shrugged. "The scholastica tells me that it was a matter of God using Judas's evil for His own purposes."

The archbishop sat back. "If God is free to use evil to further His ends, so then am I." He looked over his steepled hands. "What of the Almspend woman?"

The secretary shook his head. "She went to a house she has in the country. I sent men. They did not return." He shrugged. "It has become difficult to hire sell-swords, Eminence. The King's Guard has hired every armed thug in the city."

"That's de Vrailly, preparing for a fight with the commons," the archbishop said. "We need our own swords. Some swords that don't wear our livery."

The secretary nodded. "A man was recommended to me, Eminence. A foreigner, from the far north."

"Well?" The archbishop was not renowned for his patience.

"I will see if I can contact him. He is very—careful." The secretary shrugged.

The archbishop smiled. "He sounds Etruscan. Etruscans are the only professionals in these matters. I wish I'd brought a team from Rhum. If he seems suitable, retain him."

The secretary bowed.

The Count D'Eu was moving briskly about Harndon, paying his debts. Tailors and grocers and leatherworkers and all the trades who supported his household, he visited in person and paid in silver.

Many a Harndoner who cursed Galles every day had reason to bless him, and Gerald Random shared an embrace. "It'll turn," he said, somewhat daring. "You should stay."

The count met his eye. "No," he said. "It will not turn. Ward the Queen. They mean her harm. And the King, in time, I think."

"And you will just leave?" Ser Gerald said. He held up a hand. "I know—"

The Galle shook his head. "No, Monsieur. I know you are a good homme d'armes and an honest merchant. So I will only say this: the rumour from my home is that the Wild is coming to my doorstep. I wish to go home and do the work for which God has chosen me."

Ser Random bowed. "Can't say fairer than that," he said.

At the door, the Count D'Eu slapped his magnificent gold plaque belt and turned to his squire, Robert. "Young man, what have I done with my gloves?"

Robert looked around wildly. "You had them, my lord. You wore them when we were in the tailor's. With the bishop's men."

The count frowned. "Eh bien," he said.

The sun was setting over the distant mountains when the Gallish ships appeared in the firth. Word spread up through the town—almost every man from the corner beggars by the Order of Saint John's almost empty hostel to the Royal Guards on the walls knew what the ships contained. Men and women went to evening mass with their eyes on the firth.

They made the riverside docks only at first light—the packed men onboard had had to endure one more damp, cold night. But in the bright sunshine of a spring morning, the first day of Holy Week, the ships unloaded onto the same quays where the Venike round ships had unloaded and marketed their wares. But whereas the Venike brought silk and satin and samite and spices, the Galles brought more than three hundred lances of Gallish chivalry—big, tall, strong men. Each Gallish lance contained a knight and his squire, also armoured, and a rabble of servants and pages, in numbers that varied according to the social status of the knight.

The Sieur Du Corse, a famous routier, led the Galles down the gangplanks, and then stood, a baton in his hand, as the ships disgorged his men, their armour, their weapons, and all their horses. The horses were not in good shape, and some were unable to stand.

The King's Champion, Jean de Vrailly, came in person, mounted and in a glittering new harness, the one of blued steel he would wear for the tourney. He was cheered in some streets.

He dismounted easily and embraced Du Corse, and they mimicked friendship with the slippery grabs of men covered in butter—steel arms grappled steel breasts. But the display seemed genuine enough.

"I asked for a company of Genuans. For some bowmen—or Ifriquy'ans like the King of Sichilia uses." De Vrailly pursed his lips. "But your lances look fine, Blaise. Magnificent."

Blaise Du Corse was as tall as de Vrailly, with hair as black as de Vrailly's was white-gold. He was from the southern mountains of Galle, where the Kingdom of Arelat and the Kingdom of Galle and the Etruscan states all came together in a region of poverty and war and uncivil society. A region famous for soldiers.

"Ah, my lord. Truly, I meant to bring you more, but our liege the King has forbidden it. And more particularly, your friend the Senechal de Abblemont has forbidden it." Du Corse shrugged. "I almost didn't come. And Jean." He put a hand on de Vrailly's arm. "We have to go back. As soon as we've done the King's work here."

"Back?" de Vrailly said.

"There's an army of the Wild in Arelat," Du Corse said. "No—spare me, sweet friend. I've seen some heads. No fearmonger could create such a thing. They say that the Nordikaans have war on their very borders. They say that the Kingdom of Dalmatis is already fallen."

"Blessed sacrament!" De Vrailly took a deep breath. "And the King? And the seneschal?"

"Are raising the whole of the *Arrièrre Ban*. Every knight in Galle will go east before midsummer." Du Corse raised both eyebrows. "So I am told to say, privately, *hurry*."

They watched a dozen sailors and longshoremen winching a heavy war horse up out of the belly of the largest round ship.

"Abblemont wished to point out to you," Du Corse continued, "that you have almost a *thousand* of our kingdom's lances. A tithe of our total strength, and in many cases"—Du Corse grinned—"the best men." His eyes went to a young woman on a balcony, waving. "What a pretty girl. Is Alba full of pretty women?"

De Vrailly frowned. "Perhaps. Midsummer? Bah. Well—we will see."

Du Corse frowned, but it was more a comic face than an angry one. "I cannot see anything here that can stand against a thousand of our kind," he said. He winked at someone over de Vrailly's shoulder.

A full bowshot away, the archbishop turned from the windowed balcony of his Harndon episcopal palace. He smiled easily to his secretary. "So— we have enough iron to hold the streets. Please tell Maître Villon to see that it is done."

"See that what is done?" asked his secretary.

The archbishop smiled. "Best you not know, my son," he said.

He sat at his desk and reviewed a set of documents he had had prepared. Each of them bore the bold signature and seal of the Count D'Eu.

He sighed, and inserted them, one by one, with his own hands into a small leather trunk—the sort of box lawyers used for scrolls and wills.

He locked the trunk, and threw the key into his fireplace. Then he rose. "I will be attending the King," he told his chamberlain, who bowed.

Desiderata had spent three whole days in prayer, most of it on her knees. She was a strong, fit woman and by her arts had more knowledge of the babe within her than most midwives might have managed, so her piety no more affected her than to make her wish for better cushions on her private prie-dieu, where she knelt in front of a magnificent picture of the Virgin in a rose garden.

She spent a day perfecting her ability to read aloud from her *Lives of the Female Saints* and *Legends of Good Women* while moving about inside her inner palace. It was far more difficult than she had originally expected— reading aloud clearly occupied more of the waking mind than she had thought.

Despite which, by midday on the second day, knees aching like fire and her back near to separating from her breastbones with the pain of kneel- ing, she had it. She needed the outward show of piety to cow her new "ladies," all of whom were spies, and none of whom had the brains of a newborn kitten.

The Queen knew she was in difficulty. The world around her had moved from long shadows to open war; her people were all gone except Diota, and she knew that an open, legal charge of adultery was in the works.

They had even stooped to attack her laundrywoman. The charge—of sorcery—was absurd. But it had effectively isolated her. Without knights or squires or any ladies she could trust, she had no word from the outside.

The archbishop might have been shocked to know that the Queen scarcely troubled herself about any of that. She allowed herself to worry that Diota might be killed, or Blanche taken. Beyond that, she expended not a whit of her powers or her thoughts.

Instead, she bent most of her conscious thought to the dark thing that dwelt in the palace foundations. Or perhaps merely visited them.

Somehow, it was her enemy. She had known this the moment she touched it, deep in the old corridors where Becca Almspend had taken her. Its enmity was as familiar as the touch of a lover. She wondered if she had awakened it with her touch, or Becca with her hermetical studies. Or whether it was always there. Some days it seemed completely to be absent.

She bit her lip. Her outward self almost lost the thread of the passage she was reading aloud—she fought down a wave of petty pains—her breasts, her hips, her back, her knees.

Any thought of her husband hurt her to her core.

Almost, she could accept the charge of adultery. Because in one short year, she had come from love to something very like hate. A cold, menacing hate. A hate that chewed at the edge of her waking mind and threatened her powers and her confidence and her very awareness of herself as herself.

And again, as surely as old Harmodius had banished the daemon, she banished her thoughts of her husband and locked them away.

And followed the thread of black that ran from her rooms down into the depths of the palace.

No one had ever taught the Queen to walk free of her body, but it had seemed perfectly reasonable to her, since she was very young, that if one could invert the normal, ordering one's palace, one could walk free through a door in that palace and out into the waking world. And as was often the case for Desiderata, the thought was the action, and she had attempted it.

Now she walked the winds almost at will. And hence this gentle and pious deception—the ladies all watching her in amazement as she spent her days in prayer. Her careful practice—it could be quite painful to be interrupted when walking abroad.

With a last, inward check and a mental sigh, she released her hold on her temporal body and drifted clear.

Lady Agnes was kneeling with her ample behind firmly seated on a stool hidden in her skirts. This did not amuse or disturb the Queen—she merely noted it. She had noted before that the world of colour and high emotion that was her life in the real was muted when she let her spirit walk the winds.

She allowed herself to sink through the floor.

She knew from experience that many parts of the palace were warded—indeed, almost every home, even the lowliest peasant's cot, had wards to protect the inhabitants against ghosts, not-dead and wind-walkers.

Oddly, many such wards were placed on doors but not walls, on windows and not on floor joists. She knew—with some bitterness—that she could not escape the bounds of the palace. It was a warded fortress, and what was in would stay in just as surely as that without would stay out.

But inside much of its confines she could move at will, if she kept her concentration pure. She felt the extreme cold of stone that never saw the sun, and then she was warmed—a floor below, the Royal Chamberlain saw to the King's chamber as his clean sheets were set to his bed.

She did not linger to see what sign there might be of other women. She needed no further proof of who the King was. Or what he had done.

Almost, that scrap of thought was enough to destroy her concentration. But Desiderata's will was a pure, hard thing like eastern steel, and she went down, and down again, bands of light alternating with darkness as she went into the old halls below the palace, always following the black thread that she had found in her own fireplace.

But when she entered the deep corridor—the old path, or road, that Lady Almspend had first showed them—it was like returning to a house from a trip to find that mould and rot had set in. The corridor was so full of the black ropes of the twisted thing's sorcery that she was almost entangled.

She was not quiet enough.

The blackness was everywhere—and she hovered above it, unwilling to touch it even in incorporeal form. But she could *see* it with a true sight, and see how much of it there was—enough thread to make a hundred carpets, piled in loops and whorls throughout the deepest corridor, and there, where she had stopped it with Almspend and Lady Mary, stood a wall of black.

Twice before, Desiderata had come here and driven the walls back to their origin, the stone set in the oldest wall of the castle.

Now it knew her.

The threads came at her, all at once—an infinity of black silk flying through black air like a dark net.

Desiderata set her *aethereal* form on the level with the floor and allowed the silk threads to permeate her non-being.

Whatever had prepared this trap had expected a more solid body.

She felt its hate.

She took in a great breath, and as she exhaled, she made her breath the very spirit of spring, filled with sun and light, love and laughter, green leaves and new flowers and the smell of grass in the sunshine and lilacs in the dark.

Her conjuring drove back the threads as easily as a good sword would cut through snow—more, as the threads melted as they contacted her force, withering, retreating and unmaking as she advanced.

She spread her incorporeal hands.

Between them a great globe of glowing gold began to form.

"Give us the babe!" whispered the ribbons of black.

She gave them the globe, instead. And it floated forward, like a sun, a veritable sun, burning and lighting with a brilliance that no mortal eye could tolerate.

It passed the wall of black—and illuminated it.

A mighty pulse of power struck at her, like a child swatting a fly, and she rose on the energy and retreated before it, her own casting burrowing like a woodworm into the coils of her adversary.

Once more it struck, this time with a ravening dog of many heads and teeth—a slavering horror that emerged from the wreckage of the black *aethereal* curtain—to savage nothing but a ghost.

She *felt* the entity respond—and understand.

It lashed at her with pure *ops*.

The ramifications of the blow flung her out of the corridor and almost as far as the living world.

Only then did Desiderata begin to know fear.

But fear usually made her stronger. She controlled the flight of her incorporeal form and steadied it—laid a trap in the *aethereal* for any immediate pursuit and saw with savage satisfaction that her guess was correct.

And still the entity was incapable of quenching her initial casting.

She fled to the real, hoping that her work was done.

In the real, her aching body was still kneeling, and her lips still moved. Saint Ursula. She knew the tale all too well. Her consciousness snapped back into the body in time to prevent a collapse.

She could not prevent her head from falling forward over the book.

Far beneath her, she could *feel* her great *praxis* moving, like a living thing, into the very heart of her adversary's darkness.

"If your grace is done praying," Lady Agnes said, her voice a whine of accusation, "I'm sure we have tasks before us!"

Whatever else might have been said was interrupted by the chamber doors being flung wide.

There, framed in the doorway, was the Archbishop of Lorica. At his shoulder was the King's new chancellor, the Sieur de Rohan, and behind them—almost in shadow—the King.

She started to rise, and her knees and back protested so that she almost fell. She—the most graceful of women—pinned by her pregnancy. She fought the urge to whimper, gritted her teeth, and forced herself to her feet. The archbishop's every sinew expressed his excitement. Never before had Desiderata so completely seen expressed the phrase *trembling with excitement.* It was as if the man had a fever.

De Rohan, de Vrailly's former standard bearer and most dangerous minion, was, by contrast, almost bored. Merely fulfilling the function to which he'd been appointed.

And the King—his face was almost slack. His eyes flickered.

Oh, my love. When did you become so weak? Or were you always so?

"Your grace!" said the archbishop. His voice, always high, was shrill. He calmed himself. "Your grace. I come before you with a writ signed by the King."

"Yes?" she said. While she knew what it must be, she had, in her heart, expected the King to refuse to sign it.

The archbishop produced a writ. She could see the King's seal.

"I arrest you for the treason of murder with sorcery," he said, his voice loud and piercing.

She was taken by surprise. "Murder? With sorcery?" she asked, as if struck by lightning.

"That you did work the death of your lover, the Count D'Eu, by the arts of Satan, when he renounced you as a lover and threatened to leave the court and reveal you!" said the archbishop.

Her so-called ladies hastened from the room, leaving her alone.

"Search her room," muttered de Rohan. He had with him a dozen Royal officers—all recent appointees, and no members of the Royal Guard at all.

"This is infamous," the Queen said. "Untrue, foolish, and pernicious." She paused. "The Count D'Eu is dead?" she asked. She remembered his hard arm under hers at the Christmas revel on the ice.

The King stepped forward from his place behind his officers. "Madame," he said gravely, "I'll do you the honour of pretending that you do not already know."

Desiderata didn't back a step. "Tell me, then," she said flatly.

"We have all your letters to him," the King said, the ire in his voice now openly menacing.

A royal sheriff handed a leather trunk to the archbishop. He tried to open it, found it locked, and handed it back to the sheriff.

"That's none of mine," said the Queen. "That is not mine, and not—"

"Silence, woman!" said the King.

"Your grace, you *know* where I keep my letters!" the Queen said.

The King looked away. "I do not know you at all," he said sadly.

With a snap, the little leather trunk opened, and a dozen parchments fell to the floor. The sheriff put his baselard back into its sheath.

From where she stood, the Queen could see that every letter held the Count D'Eu's seal.

"Do you think he would seal his love letters?" muttered the Queen.

"Who knows what traitors and heretics think?" spat the archbishop. "Confess, and avoid the stake, your grace."

"Confess what?" Desiderata asked. "I am guiltless. I carry the King's son. I have never ceased to strive for this kingdom, and the Count D'Eu was never even my friend, much less my lover. This is all absurd."

The King was reading one of the letters, his face a flaming red. "That you would dare!" he shouted, and threw it in her face.

"Confess to the murder of D'Eu, and the King, in his mercy, will spare your life." The Sieur de Rohan stood easily, his voice bored. "See to his majesty. He is over-wrought."

The King was reading another letter.

Desiderata was closer to panic than the old horror under the palace had moved her, but she held her ground. "Your grace, those letters are palpable forgeries. Your grace. *You know my hand!*"

The King whirled on her, and raised his fist. But he lowered it, his lips quivering with rage, his jowls—had he long had jowls?—making him look more sad than angry. "I thought that I knew you," he said. "But de Vrailly was right. Take her from my sight."

"Where, your grace?" asked de Rohan.

"The deepest pit of hell, for all I care," said the King. He seemed to have aged ten years before their eyes.

The Queen drew herself to her full stature—not just in the real, but in the *aethereal*.

The archbishop clasped the talisman at his breast. "Do your worst, whore of Satan!" he said. "I am protected against all of your kind."

Desiderata smiled with all the scorn she could muster. "The difference between you and I," she said, "is that I would not stoop to destroy you if doing so would save my soul. I make and heal. I bring light to the dark. And when I do, your kind scuttle for the narrow places the light will not reach."

She took a single step forward, and the archbishop stepped back unconsciously.

She tossed her head. "Where are you taking me?"

As the door closed behind her, she heard de Rohan's oily voice say, "But your grace, now we must take thought for her brother."

The Queen whirled. "Your grace!" she shouted.

The sheriff—cowed by her rank and her condition—let go her elbow.

The door opened. Again, the King was framed in it.

The Queen raised her chin. "I demand a trial," she said.

Her husband paused. Their eyes met.

"I am absolutely guiltless, my lord. No man has known this body save you." The Queen did not plead. Her anger was plain—and to most men, proved her innocence. No one could act such a part.

"Take her away," whispered de Rohan.

"This is Alba, not Galle," said the Queen. "I demand a trial, by my peers, in public."

Wat Tyler slipped into Harndon amidst the chaos of the arrival of the Galles. His clothes were ruined, and his face wore the marks of heavy weather and constant strain. A gate guard might have questioned him for the great bow on his back alone, but the movement of a thousand armed Galles through the streets had stripped the gates of all but a token force, and those men still on the gates cared for nothing but what was going on inside their city.

As his new ally had promised him.

He crossed the First Bridge with the flood of morning market customers and farmers, and helped unload a wagon in East Cheaping before he walked uphill into the stews behind the docks. He saw more poverty than he remembered from his last visit, and more beggars.

He exchanged a sign with a beggar-master.

The man nodded at his bow. "That won't win you no friends with the magistrates," he said. "Only a citizen of Harndon—"

"I know the law," Tyler said.

"You look like you've been in some hard places, brother," muttered the beggar-master. In fact, he was more than a little afraid of Tyler, who smelled like the wilderness.

Tyler shrugged.

The beggar-master took him to chapter, a gathering of beggars—sanctioned since Archaic times by dukes and kings, and now held in the old agora by the Tower of Winds. The Beggar King sat on the steps of the old Temple of Ios. There, three Archaic stele formed a natural throne of incredibly ancient white marble.

The Beggar King wore a crown of leather. Unlike most kings, he sat alone. He had no court. Nor was he big, nor ferocious-looking. In fact, he was so nondescript in his dirty leathers and old wool, his lanky brown hair shot with grey and his long beard, that he might have been any peasant or out-of-work farmer on the streets.

"Wat Tyler," he said. "Last I saw you, you was off to win a great victory against the King."

Tyler shrugged. "We lost."

The Beggar King nodded. "Well. And now you're back."

"Not for long. Does my place still hold?" Tyler asked.

The Beggar King looked around. The senior beggars and beggar-masters grinned.

"Aye, Wat. Your place still holds." The King laughed.

Tyler took his great bow off his back and leaned on it. "I've walked from N'gara," he said. "I'd be right thankful for a jack of ale and a bowl of something."

"N'gara?" the Beggar King said. Silence had fallen. "Next you'll be telling us you met the Faery Knight."

"Somewhat like that," Tyler answered.

A fat woman put a jack in his hand.

He raised it in thanks and drank deep. "Comrades," he said. "That's the first ale I've had in many a month."

"You were far off in the Wild," the Beggar King said. "And now you've come back—a hard road. You never was a real beggar, Wat. What are you here for this time?"

Tyler shrugged. "I'll hide a month or two. Pick up some lads as want to fight. And be away before summer comes."

"Same as always," the Beggar King said.

"Aye," Tyler said.

"And you aren't just here because the tournament is upon us, and there's money to be gained everywhere?" the Beggar King asked.

"Tournament?" Wat asked.

"Christ and his saints, man—you must have been in the land of the faeries. There's a great tourney to be fought, a million sculls to pick the pockets of and a thousand shills to fleece." He grinned. "If we're not killed by Galle routiers first."

"Routiers?" Tyler asked.

"Killing always did get your attention, Wat. The King's champion, de Vrailly—"

"May he rot in hell," Tyler said.

"Ah—sometimes we even agree. May he rot in hell—he sent to Galle for a fresh army. And they sent him one, but they ha' troubles of their own, seemingly, and we get the tall knights and the scrapings of their jails. They kept all their proper soldiers home to fight boglins." He laughed.

Tyler nodded. "Don't talk to me about boglins," he said. "I've had a bellyful."

The younger of the female beggar-masters cackled. "You home to stay, then?"

Tyler shook his head. "No, Lise. I ain't, like I said. I'll be gone afore midsummer."

"You'll help us kill some Galles?" the Beggar King asked.

Tyler nodded. "You know me, King."

"We know you," the Beggar King said. "Lucky you came," he admitted. "We don't have the muscle we'll need for these Galle bastards."

Tyler nodded. "They die, pretty much as easy as any other man," he said, his thumbs rubbing the beeswaxed wood of his great bow.

Lise stepped forward—a big, handsome ruin of a woman with a red nose and lank black hair. "One o' my girls—robbed, throat cut. Scale Alley." She folded her arms. "Three Galles, all new off the boat. Crack says he'd know 'em again."

The Beggar King rubbed his hands together and looked at Wat.

Wat sighed. "You making me pay dues, King?" he asked.

"No," the King said slowly. "No. You can walk away. You earned it a hundred times. But—if'n you want *help*, well, we want help, too."

Tyler frowned, thinking of his task.

But some ties were thicker than blood or water. He turned his eyes to Lise without moving his head. "You tell me where to find 'em. Livery, lodging. All the usual."

She came up and kissed him. "Some o' we missed you, Wat."

"I'll bet you say that to all the hired killers," Tyler said, with a spark of his ancient self.

The sway of her hips held no promise for him, though, and the spark died.

He was given a space on a floor under a tavern. And he began to eat, and enjoy being warm—the two greatest pleasures left him.

The Queen's arrest was a wonder—an expected shock, but still a shock when it happened. The sheer number of Galles in the street was another shock to every Harndoner, and the sheer criminality of their servants and spearmen was beyond anything the people of Harndon had ever seen.

Thirty men and a dozen women died the first night. Twenty Gallish spearmen burned down an inn when they were thrown out—for theft. They killed every man who came through the door out of the smoke.

The High Sheriff went to the palace for soldiers with whom to make arrests, and never returned.

In broad daylight, a party of routiers stormed a jeweller's booth in the market by Cheapside. They killed the man and his daughter and took all their gold, silver, and copper—including some fine enamels.

And then they swaggered through the rapidly closing stalls, picking valuables off other shop tables. A merchant who protested was stabbed and left kneeling in the muck, his guts spilling around his hands.

They sacked a dozen more shops, gathering adherents as they went, and then went down to the riverbank as if they owned the place, and laid their loot on blankets to divide it—exactly as if they were in a city taken by storm.

It was there that the Trained Band found them.

The Trained Band was a muster of all the very best trained and armed citizens of Harndon. Any man or woman who was formally signed as an apprentice to one of the seventy-three recognized guilds or trades was automatically made a citizen, with freedom of the city and the right to bear arms and travel, but many other people had the same rights; most householders who held in freehold, and most servants of the two great priories, and the King's household and the Queen's, and hundreds of others—fencing masters, for example, and school teachers. And a variety of men and women who'd been granted the status and cherished it—including some knights and nobles.

The muster of the city was the assembly of every man or strong woman who owned and could carry weapons. The Trained Band was the pick of the whole. The elite of the Trained Band tended to be from the guilds that made and used weapons; the bowyers, the fletchers, the butchers, the armourers and the sword smiths.

The Trained Band was ready at a minute's notice to be the armoured fist of the city, but they generally worked at the behest of the Sheriff and the Lord Mayor, and they tended to obey the niceties of the law.

Michael de Burgh was a fencing master and owned a prosperous tavern. He had been a soldier, and it was rumoured that he ran a string of brothels. But he was one of the eight captains of the Trained Band, and he was the man on duty. The routiers on the riverbank gathered in knots, weapons in hand, as the Trained Band marched up to the edge of Cheaping Street.

De Burgh stepped out of the ranks of his spearmen.

"Throw down your weapons," he shouted in a voice fit to wake the dead and make them do drill. "Throw them down and lie down. You are all—"

He looked down in surprise at the heavy arbalest bolt that had punched through his heavy coat of plates and the mail beneath it. He was not a slim man, and the bolt went into him up to the fletchings.

A shocked screech.

But he knew his duty. "Under—arrest..." he managed before he pitched over.

The men behind him in the Band knew their duty, too.

Battles are generally the result of someone making a serious mistake. The Battle of Cheaping Street was the result of two sets of mistakes. On the one hand, the routiers had never encountered resistance from townspeople or peasants. Their experience in Galle was that the only men who would face them were knights. All other resistance would melt away before their ferocity and superior equipment and skill.

The men of the Trained Band were used to facing opponents who were better trained—or monstrous. They made up for their disparity in fine equipment and discipline. But they had never experienced a hard fight in their own city. Out in the Wild—yes. Not in the streets around the market.

The routiers charged with a yell of fury that shook the windows around the market.

The left end of the Band's line didn't loose a single bolt, as they were unready for immediate violence. They hadn't seen Captain de Burgh get hit, and they had no idea what was going on. Many men at the left of the line were still shrugging into hauberks and buckling their breast-and-backs. Men had sausages dangling out of their mouths.

At their end, the routiers struck like wolves at a flock of sheep, and men—especially the rear rankers—broke, ran and were cut down. Most of the routiers had bills or poleaxes, and they used them cruelly, killing the wounded on the ground, hacking militiamen down as they turned to run. A generation of fletchers' apprentices died in seconds. The Butcher's Guild lost a master, four journeymen and a dozen apprentices as the line caved in.

At the other end of the line, the result was utterly different. The armourers had been right behind the captain. They had been the first men called, and the first in armour.

The Captain of the Crossbows—a stepping stone to the command of the whole Band—ordered his men to loose their bolts.

Sixty arbalest bolts struck the front rank of the charging routiers. The volley was sufficiently crisp that the bolts striking home sounded like a wooden mallet striking meat.

The armourers, on the word of command, levelled their heavy spears and charged.

Edmund—front rank, right marker, corporal—was calm enough to spare a glance at the crispness of his front rank before he caught a screaming Galle under the chin with his heavy spear. The blow almost tore the man's head from his body, and Edmund shortened his grip, pulled the weapon clear of the corpse and stepped forward so as not to impede the men in his file behind him.

Thirty routiers went down in a few seconds. Their ferocity was flayed by the crossbowmen—when they hesitated, the young, strong, and extremely well-armoured apprentices and journeymen of the Armourer's Guild reaped them like ripe wheat.

The fight turned like a pinwheel, and a full minute had not yet passed.

But as most such fights do, the result rested on spirit. The routiers had no reason to stay, beyond loot and pride. The Band were protecting their homes and livelihoods. They held.

The routiers broke. They ran into the market—overturning tables and slaughtering anyone who stood near enough to be reached with a blade.

The Band—that part of it that had held together—gave chase.

The market became a scene from hell.

As the butchers—who had broken and now reformed—turned on their tormenters for revenge, the massacre began to spread down Cheaping Street in both directions.

Captain de Burgh was down. In fact, his life was gurgling out of him. There was no one to give orders.

The whole of the "Battle of Cheaping Street" lasted less than two minutes. But the massacre that followed went on for hours, as a mob of apprentices and militia began to hunt and kill every Galle—or anyone who looked to them like Galles. The rumour spread that the Galles had seized the Queen and that added a new fuel to the fighting.

By the time Holy Thursday dawned, five hundred Harndoners were dead and as many Galles, most of them servants, grooms, whores, and other relative innocents. Much of the dockside north of the Cheaping was on fire—the slums around the Angel Inn. Men said the Galles had set the fires to cover their retreat, and the Band—now out in force with their six surviving captains—stood guard while the guilds and the poor fought the fires. Sluice Alley was ditched across to make a fire brake.

The last fires didn't go out until noon, at which point the whole city, Harndoner and Galle, subsided into surly exhaustion.

De Vrailly stood in an embrasure of the palace, looking out over the rising smoke by the river—smoke so thick it mostly obscured First Bridge and the areas across the river. Only the masts of the great Venike cogs—all of which had slipped their cables and re-anchored in midstream—could be seen above it.

"This is the Queen's doing," de Vrailly told the King.

The King nodded.

"Her partisans were primed for this rebellion." De Vrailly shook his head. "I have lost good men—loyal men—to the canaille of this accursed town." He was so angry he could barely speak. "I would like to strike back at these mutineers."

De Rohan handed him a set of scrolls. "Your grace, these are orders for the arrests of the ring leaders," he said. "They are exhausted—sated with their depravity. We can strike now, with our retainers and the Royal Guard."

The King appeared confused. He had chosen to read the arrest documents. The scroll he'd opened bore the name Gerald Random.

"Ser Gerald is one of my most loyal knights," the King said.

De Rohan shook his head vehemently. "Not at all, sire. He's a renegade—a traitor in service to the Queen."

The King made a face. "Rohan, you have the oddest notions. He is the *master of the tournament.* A Royal officer—"

"He was in the streets all night in armour, leading the town's rabble of a militia against *my men,*" said de Vrailly.

"There is some mistake," the King said. He crossed his arms. "I will not sign an arrest warrant for Ser Gerald Random."

De Rohan looked at de Vrailly.

The King leaned out over the wall. "How many men do you have?" the King asked.

"All of Du Corse's men and all of my own," de Vrailly said. "And the Royal Guard," he added quickly.

The King looked at him as if seeing him for the first time. "Almost three thousand men," he said.

De Vrailly smiled grimly. "Yes, your grace."

"And you plan to use them against the Trained Band of Harndon." The King shook his head. "Made up of the best men of this city—the masters and journeymen."

"We will destroy them," de Vrailly said happily enough.

"You will destroy my city!" the King said suddenly. "You will behead the trades. You will leave me a burned-out shell."

De Vrailly's head snapped back as if he'd been struck. "I will expurgate treason!"

The King shook his head. "No, de Vrailly. You are *creating* treason. And you don't have enough men, even with Du Corse, to take Harndon against the will of the whole population."

De Rohan, misunderstanding, made a face. "We have hired every sell-sword and every mercenary in the city or passing nearby. We have all the soldiers."

The King looked out over his city. He turned back to de Vrailly. "No. I will not have it." He opened his mouth to say more—to speak his will.

De Rohan stepped boldly in front of de Vrailly. De Vrailly looked at him, appalled, but the King's eyes were on de Rohan.

"Your grace's feelings for your subjects do you credit," he murmured. "But you squander your fine feelings on the very men who helped the Queen make you a figure of fun."

The King paused. His colour rose—a sudden flush.

"We have tracked the woman who carried the Queen's messages," de Rohan said. "She went straight to the house of your armourer, Master Pye, from the Queen. Master Pye then summoned Ser Gerald Random." De Rohan had it pat. It was his business—to know, and where he could not know, to create. "Men—good men—died to bring us this information."

The King stood, balanced on some sort of edge. He was searching for something; his mouth moved. "If the Queen," he said, hesitantly. "If the Queen was not..."

De Rohan spoke over him—an unheard of piece of lese-majeste. "But the Queen is an adulteress."

The King swung on de Rohan. "That is *not* proven."

De Vrailly was not pleased. His colour was high. He stepped away from de Rohan as if the man carried leprosy. Nonetheless, he said, "I will prove it on any man's body," he said. "We will give her a public trial. Trial by combat."

The King looked at them both. He seemed, in that moment, to shrink. He turned his back on them. "You may not arrest Ser Gerald," he said.

De Rohan—delighted by the idea of a trial by combat with de Vrailly as the accuser—stepped closer to the King. "We can invite him to the palace. With the other ring leaders."

De Vrailly smiled mirthlessly.

"You will hear his treason from his own lips," de Rohan said.

The King looked at both of them with weary distaste. "Everything was better before you came," he managed. Then he looked at the ground.

"When we are done, we will leave your kingdom stronger, and your rule on surer ground," de Vrailly said. "No king should have to be beholden to a rabble of fishmongers and labourers for his crown."

De Rohan winced.

The King sighed. "Leave me," he said.

"We shouldn't go," Master Pye said. "I know Ser Jean, and I know the King."

Darkwood looked at Master Pye. "That's close to treason."

Master Pye looked bored. "I count the King as a friend. I ha' known him since I fitted him for rings when he was going boar hunting—I don't know. Thirty years? He's a fine lance. The best, they say, in the west." Master Pye leaned back—in full harness—and rested his lower back on the edge of his low chair. "He's not so deft in counsel, and I speak no treason when I say he's always had a tendency to do what the last loud voice bid him."

"Which did us well eno' when the Queen was the voice at his pillow," Ailwin Darkwood said, fingering the massive chain of office he was wearing over his tightly fitted coat of plates.

"An' now he's being led by a pack of foreigners," muttered Jasop Gross, alderman, under-sheriff, and Master Butcher. In despite of his name, he was thin and handsome for his fifty years. "Sweet Jesu, friends, we're in a pickle."

"There's Jacks at work in the streets," Ser Gerald said. "And where's Tom Willoughby?"

"Where's the Sheriff?" Master Gross asked. "They say he arrested the Queen and now he's locked in with her."

"I always said Tom Willoughby was a fool," Ailwin Darkwood said. "And you gentlemen wouldn't hear me."

"I heard you," said the only woman present. Anne Bates was the only woman in Alba to be head of a guild. She was the Master Silversmith for Harndon; she was an alderman. She was forty-five and iron-haired. The joints on her fingers were already heavy with arthritis, but her long nose and pointed chin and the perfection of the white linen of her wimple were more than just concessions to femininity. She raised her chin. "I heard you every time. He's a fool. And now, instead of standing on custom, he's arrested the Queen. Do you lot know where this Gold girl is?" She looked around. "The Galles want her badly."

No one would meet her eye.

She snorted. "You're keeping it secret? What a pack of fools. We hang together, *friends*, or we'll all hang separately. I'm too old to plead my belly. Ser Gerald, what would you?"

Ser Gerald nodded. "I'd go. With Ailwin. And Master Pye."

Pye shook his head. "My sense is that de Vrailly—or if he can't stomach it, that oily rat de Rohan—will have our heads on spikes before we even see the King."

Ser Gerald shook his head. "I can't imagine the King—"

"He allowed his God-damned *wife* to be taken for adultery," Master Pye said with emphasis that was reinforced by the fact that no man present had ever heard him use an oath before. "We're nothing. Think on it, Gerald! Desiderata is in irons. That's the power that de Vrailly and de Rohan wield."

Anne Bates made a face. "I say it's the new bishop."

Pye shrugged. "Last fall—when they started coming after my yard—a Hoek merchant came to see me. He made threats. When he left, the Order had him followed. He went straight to de Rohan." He looked around.

Random sat suddenly, as if his harness weighed too much. "What do we do?" he asked. "Turn Jack? Down with the King?"

Master Pye shook his head. "I don't know what to do."

Anne Bates looked at Ser Gerald. "I'll go with you, Ser Gerald. A knight and a lady—hard cheese if the Galles are so dead to honour that they'll put our heads on spikes after promising us a safe pass."

Ser Gerald looked at the rest of them. "You say the King always goes with the last voice," he said. "Let it be ours, then. I can shout pretty loud. Better than a Galle, I reckon."

"You lose your temper, Gerald," Master Pye said. "And if you do, you're cooked. One word they can take as treason—remember that. In their eyes, the Queen's a traitor. Anything you say about her is reversed for them."

Random shrugged.

An hour later, having kissed his wife, he followed a dozen King's Guardsmen into the mouth of Gold Square, which was lined with the richest men and women in the city.

Ser Gerald had no eyes for them. His eyes were on his escort of Royal Guardsmen. None of them wore the golden leopards on their shoulders—and three of them wore scarlet surcoats so ill fitting that they flapped in the breeze. The leader looked familiar.

He smiled at Ser Gerald.

Ser Gerald gave him a nervous smile back. He'd changed out of his harness and wore a fine black gown, proper attire for a man of his age, and good black hose; a chain, and his plaque belt and sword. "How long have you been in the Guard?" he asked the man.

The man was quite young. He shrugged. "Two days," he allowed.

"You from Harndon?" Ser Gerald asked.

"No, ser knight," the young guardsman said. "I'm from Hawkshead, west of Albinkirk."

Ser Gerald stopped, struck by the coincidence. "I fought there last year, at Lissen Carak," he said.

All three Guardsmen nodded. "We know," said another, quietly.

"I'm not a rebel," Ser Gerald said.

The leader of the Guardsmen spread his hands. He really looked familiar, but Ser Gerald couldn't place him. "We know, Ser Gerald," he said. "I have your safe conduct in my purse. We'll take you to the King, and bring you back." He looked around at the crowd of aldermen and senior masters who stood in Gold Square. "You have my word."

His steady voice and the King's livery did much to sway the crowd, and Ser Gerald walked up the hill—wearing a sword, and clearly not a prisoner. At the top of Cheapside, he met Anne Bates, wearing enough fur and gold to look like a duchess. He bowed, and she took his hand. Her escort was the same size as his own. All the Guardsmen seemed to know each other.

He kept trying to place the officer, who seemed very young for his role.

Nothing came to him as they walked through the quiet streets. Everything still reeked of smoke. All the bodies were gone, but there were buildings missing like rotted teeth in a beggar's mouth, and people missing, too.

Random's father-in-law, a past Master Stonemason, was dead, his head caved in by a poleaxe. So were many other men—and women—who counted for something in the squares of the city.

Past the scorched buildings and the scrubbed cobbles, he could see movements in the next street—Fleet Street. A heavy patrol of the Trained Band was moving parallel to the Royal Guard.

He couldn't imagine Edmund and his mates attacking the Royal Guard, but their armoured presence made him feel calmer.

They went under the first portcullis of the outer ward, and left Edmund's men behind.

The portcullis closed.

Even his Guardsmen looked startled.

Anne Bates, who was no kind of a flirt, clasped his hand.

Ser Gerald raised his chin, and walked on.

"Who's the old woman pretending to be a lady?" de Rohan asked one of his men.

"No idea, my lord," the man said.

"Find out," de Rohan hissed.

No one came back to tell him, and the pair moved into the corridors of the palace.

De Rohan moved ahead of them, and arranged for the doors of the Royal Chamber to be closed.

He turned to de Vrailly. "The canaille sent Ser Gerald Random."

De Vrailly looked at him with indifference. "So?" de Vrailly asked.

De Rohan forced himself to speak slowly. "I do not think Ser Gerald should be allowed to speak to the King."

"Because in fact he is not guilty of treason?" de Vrailly snapped. "Because you are afraid of him?"

The word "afraid" was fraught with peril for a Galle. De Rohan flushed.

"It would be better if he did not reach the King," de Rohan said.

De Vrailly shrugged. "Better for you, perhaps," he said.

He motioned at the soldiers at the doors. The chamber was opened, and Ser Gerald Random and Mistress Anne Bates announced. They walked—fearlessly, or so they appeared—down the long silk carpet to the throne, where they bowed.

The King sat alone. Even the Queen's throne had been removed.

"Ser Gerald," the King said. He looked tired, and sad. "What is this I hear, that you bore arms against me today?"

Ser Gerald shook his head. "It's not my place to disagree with your grace," he said. "But I would never take up arms against my sovereign."

"That's what I told de Rohan. But he says..." the King said.

De Rohan stepped forward out of the ranks of courtiers. Most of the courtiers were nobles of the southern Albin—the men and women who lived in Harndon. But almost a third of the men present wore the tighter, brighter fashions that marked them as Galles.

"I say you are a traitor," de Rohan said.

Random frowned. "It's difficult for me to understand you, sir. Your accent is too thick."

A few brave souls tittered. In fact, de Rohan had a scarcely noticeable accent unless he was flustered.

"Be silent!" de Rohan spat.

Ser Gerald bowed. "I cannot remain silent while you slander me, my lord. And I am here, I think, to speak, not to be silent."

De Rohan pointed at Random. "He has coached the go-between—the girl who takes the notes to the Queen's lovers." De Rohan looked apologetically at the King. "I would rather say no more in public. It is too—disgraceful."

Random shook his head. "What a foolish accusation. My lord, I do not even live in the palace."

Mistress Anne curtsied. "Your grace, I beg leave to speak."

The King waved a hand. "Please."

"Your grace, I believe we were invited here to speak to your grace, and not to this foreign lord." She managed half a smile. "Your grace, I'm a woman of business, not a courtier. If this were a business meeting, I would say that this man is trying to keep us from speaking our piece."

The King looked at de Rohan. Then back at Mistress Anne.

"Speak, and be assured of my patience," he said.

She curtsied again. "Your grace. The people of the city were attacked without provocation by the men-at-arms these Galles brought into our midst. Men and women of worth have been killed—"

"Men of worth?" de Rohan asked, his sneer palpable. "Some beggars?"

"My father-in-law," Ser Gerald said.

"My nephew," Mistress Anne said.

The silence was as palpable as the sneer had been.

"They looted and stole and raped, and when we called out the watch, they were beaten." Mistress Anne paused. "And when we called for the Trained Band, they *killed the captain*."

"Lies," de Rohan said.

De Vrailly shrugged. "In Galle—" he began.

"You are not in Galle!" Mistress Anne snapped.

"No one was fighting *against the King*," Ser Gerald said carefully. "We were protecting our homes. From thieves and murderers."

"A fine tale of lies," de Rohan said. "You and your rebels massacred our people. You killed our servants—unarmed boys and girls."

The King looked at Ser Gerald.

He looked down. Then he looked up. "After they killed men of the Trained Band, we broke them. And we chased them, and as God is my judge, we were as bad as they."

The King winced. "Damn," he said. "Do you want a civil war, Random? Killing Galles in our streets—is that the rule of law?"

Stung, Ser Gerald stepped back. "Christ on the cross, your grace! They killed upwards of a hundred of your *citizens*. And in the eyes of many people, *your grace*, the Galles are coming to represent *you*."

"Ah," said de Rohan. He pointed at Ser Gerald. "Ah—now we see it."

"Represent me how?" the King asked carefully.

"Your grace, you brought them here. You should send them away." Ser Gerald set his foot and leaned on his cane. His missing foot was troubling him.

Very carefully, de Rohan said, "And what of the Queen?"

Ser Gerald drew a breath. He looked at Mistress Anne.

Mistress Anne curtsied again. "Your grace, we're here to speak to you. Not this creature."

The King exploded in impatience. "As God is my witness, woman! This man is not a 'creature' but a lord of Galle and one of my ministers and you will treat him with respect."

Mistress Anne stepped back a pace.

De Rohan allowed himself a small smile. "What of the Queen, Master Random?"

Random looked at de Rohan. "Your grace, could you see to it that this Lord of Galle uses my proper title?"

De Rohan shrugged. "Merely an oversight, Ser."

Random met his eye. "Ser Gerald."

De Rohan shrugged. "As you say."

"Get to the point!" spat the King.

"What of the Queen?" asked de Rohan for the third time. "How do the commons view the arrest of the Queen?"

Ser Gerald exchanged a look with Mistress Anne. "There's not one man nor woman in the city that believes the Queen to be guilty of ought save love for your grace," said Ser Gerald.

De Vrailly had remained silent until that moment. He was not in armour—a rare moment for him—but wore a mi-parti pourpoint; the left side was of purple and white brocade, and the right of yellow silk. He wore his sword, the sword of the King's Champion; he was almost the only man in the hall to wear a weapon, besides the King and Ser Gerald.

"She is an adulteress and a witch and a murderer," de Vrailly said. "I will prove it."

"You will prove it?" Ser Random asked, somewhat taken aback by the ferocity of the charges.

"I have challenged for trial by combat. The so-called Queen murdered my cousin D'Eu, and I will kill her champion and prove her guilt." De Vrailly glared at Ser Gerald. "Will you champion her cause, Ser Gerald?"

De Rohan was seen to smile.

Gerald Random had not risen to his current level without knowing when a negotiation had sprung a hidden trap. He counted to five—a tactic that had served him well in other negotiations. He ignored the panic that the trap, now revealed, caused in his throat.

If he declined, then he appeared to agree to the guilt of the Queen, and de Rohan could ask a series of questions about the riots and the support for the Queen in the streets that would quickly go awry.

If he agreed, he was a dead man.

"When, my lord, do you plan to try this case?" Random asked.

"In the lists, on the first day of the tournament," the King said.

Random bowed. "If your grace will relieve me of the duties of Master of the Tourney," he said. "And if your grace feels that a man with no right foot, no formal training at arms, and fifty years of age is the man to defend his wife in the lists—" Ser Gerald extended his wooden foot so all present could see it, and bowed over it—a move he'd practised many times with his wife, hoping for a happier occasion as Master of the Tourney. "If that is the case," Ser Gerald said without a touch of the derision he might have used, "then I would be honoured to risk my life for her grace, who I see as blameless."

Even de Vrailly caught the clear implication. For de Vrailly to fight Ser Gerald would make a laughing stock of the whole matter. And would be tantamount to the King declaring himself on the side of the accuser.

It was a calculated risk. And while the King's face clouded over, and his temper boiled, Ser Gerald's knees shivered, and he had trouble keeping his feet, or keeping the bland indifference that would be most hurtful to the King's Galles on his face.

But Gerald Random had been scared many times. And he reminded himself that if he died in the lists defending the Queen, nothing about it would touch the horror of Lissen Carak and the things trying to eat him while he was alive.

He crossed himself.

De Rohan shrugged. "Of course, if you are afraid," he said, but the words fell flat. Even de Vrailly looked at him as if he was some sort of worm.

Mistress Anne nodded. "And you have a licence? From the church?" she asked in a low voice.

The King's face was bright red. "What licence do I need, sirrah?" His voice implied that she was a fool.

Mistress Anne curtsied. "Saving your grace's pardon," she said. "My husband is a clerk."

The King looked at the Archbishop of Lorica.

He glanced at his secretary. The man writhed a moment. And then whispered in his master's ear.

"This council is dismissed," the archbishop said after a long look from the King.

Strong hands gripped Random's arms. He didn't struggle—he knew he'd failed. Even if they didn't send him to fight for the Queen.

"Your grace!" he called. "These men are trying to bring down your kingdom!"

"Silence!" shouted de Rohan. "Your audience is at an end."

"They lie, your grace!" Random shouted. He had a loud voice. "A fabric of lies. They have sent all your good men from court and now they ride you like a horse!"

By his left side, one of de Rohan's men said to the guardsmen, "Take them somewhere they can enjoy his grace's hospitality."

"We are here under your grace's safe conduct!" Random bellowed. But the King had left the chamber, and de Rohan stood by the throne.

"Enjoy the next few hours," de Rohan said with an easy smile. "They are my gift to you."

Hard hands dragged Random and Mistress Anne from the chamber, and down the first steps—past the laundry, and towards the dungeons.

The archbishop's secretary was always on a tight schedule, and he left the palace late, wearing a plain brown robe like a mendicant friar, and went down into the town with two of his master's guards.

Outside the gate was a large crowd of Harndoners.

"Master," whined one of his guards. "We can't go out in that. They'll rip us apart."

The learned doctor looked from one scared face to another. Since he knew—few better—what excesses these men were capable of, he was always surprised at the extremity of their cowardice.

Nor was Maître Gris without resources of his own. He puffed out his cheeks. "Very well," he said. "You may bravely guard the palace. I'll go have a cup of wine." He shoved one of them in the chest.

The man, startled, backed up. "What the hell!"

"Now knock me down," Maître Gris said. "And then go back inside."

The man gave him a gap-toothed grin that lacked any pleasure—and hit him quite hard.

Maître Gris lay on the cobbles until the throbbing subsided, and picked himself up. An old woman—a crone, really—used her cane to help him up, and he blessed her automatically.

"God's curse on them Galles," she said.

Maître Gris joined the crowd. He moved with it for a while, gathering comments that his master might use, and then slipped away into the city.

The Angel Inn sat behind Sail Maker's Lane in Waterside, just a few big buildings away from the Oar House. The inn was a fortress in miniature, with four linked buildings around a central court; balconied and walled in wood facing inward. In high summer, troops of players, minstrels, vagabonds, troubadours, mimes and acrobats would perform in the courtyard, and the inn, despite the unsavoury reputation of the neighborhood, had a fine reputation for food and for drink. Sailors and their officers frequented the place, and so did soldiers.

Maître Gris was the only monk. But he had nowhere to change into another disguise, nor were itinerant friars so very rare in taverns. He sat at a common table for a while, listening.

Buildings had been burned in the neighbourhood. The local men were outraged, and Maître Gris knew in half an hour that his life would be forfeit if they knew he was a Galle. He began to regret coming; their hatred was so inveterate that it sickened him, and he had to listen to an endless litany of hate.

He was a thoughtful man. He considered the hate that his master was brewing. The wine was terrible, the beer excellent.

"Are you by any chance looking to hire a scribe?" said a man.

He was tall, had grey-brown hair and wore a good green wool pourpoint and a brown and green cloak. He wore an elegant black wool hood trimmed in miniver and he threw it back as he sat.

He was not at all what Maître Gris had expected. He did not have missing teeth, nor scars, nor a squint.

"You are...?" Maître Gris began.

The man also wore a fine black-hilted baselard long enough to serve as a sword. "At liberty," he said pleasantly.

With the Oar House so close, the Angel did not run to slatterns or whores, and the man who waited on them was short, pudgy, and might have been cheerful if he had not just lost his older brother to the Galles.

"Yer foreign," he spat accusingly at the well-dressed newcomer.

"I am from the Empire," said the man. He bowed.

"Not a fuckin' Galle?" the boy said.

The newcomer's pronunciation and accent could not be hidden. "No," he said pleasantly. "I am from the Empire."

The serving boy jutted his jaw. "Say somethin' in Archaic."

The man spread his hands. "*Kyrie Eleison*," he said. "*Christos Aneste*."

The boy made a face. "Right enough, I suppose. What can I fetch you, Master?"

"Dark ale," said the man in the fur-trimmed hood. He looked across the table. When the potboy was gone, he said, "You are very brave, or very stupid. Or just desperate."

Maître Gris frowned. "I understand that you are available," he said.

The man in the black hood bowed his head in assent.

"My master," Maître Gris said.

"The Archbishop of Lorica," said the other man.

The friar rose. "I do not think..." he said.

The other man waved at him. "You want to hire an intelligencer," he said. "Please—I only meant to offer you my bona fides. What kind of man would I be if I did *not* know who you were?"

Maître Gris regarded the man. "As a foreigner, you will not know any more than I know, here." He leaned forward. "What is your name?"

The imperial shook his head. "Names will not help anyone here. In a few days—a week—given some money, I can have a network of informers who can supply almost anything." He shrugged. "It is a craft, like any other. Some men work gold. I work people."

The ale arrived. The imperial took a deep draught of his and smiled. "That's a fine ale," he said.

"You cannot expect me to hand you money and trust you to do your work," Maître Gris said.

The other man gave a lopsided smile. "And yet, everything would proceed so much better if you did," he said. "Mistrust is inefficient."

Maître Gris shook his head. "I want information about Lady Rebecca Almspend," he said. "She has disappeared."

The man opposite him pursed his lips. "I have heard that name," he admitted. "She was sent into voluntary exile, was she not?"

Maître Gris nodded. "Good, I'm glad you know of her. Find her, and we will talk about money and networks of informers."

He rose. The other man took another sip of his ale and shook his head. "No," he said.

"What, no?" the friar asked.

"I'm sorry, but I do not work for free. Ever. I'm quite well known, in my way. I do not work for employers who distrust me, and I do not work for free." The other man shrugged. "I will not wander the city looking for a missing noblewoman. That would be very dangerous, just now. I work through others, and that costs money."

Maître Gris was shocked. "And how do I know you would act properly?"

The other man shrugged. "How do you know that a servant will light your fires every morning? Or fetch a chalice when you want to say mass? You see, I assume that you are a cleric of some sort. What possible benefit would I accrue by taking your money and running?" He shrugged. "The sum isn't big enough for me to steal," he said.

"How much?" Maître Gris asked, sitting again.

The imperial allowed himself a very small smile. "Ten ducats a week for every informer I recruit and pay. A hundred ducats a week for me. If any other services are required, I have…friends…to whom they can be contracted." He spread his hands. "They are efficient, trustworthy, and always clean up after themselves. They are very expensive, and yet many clients find that they are much cheaper than amateurs."

Maître Gris shook his head. "I cannot agree to any of this."

The other man finished his ale and rose. "I suspected as much. I will meet you one more time—that is all. I do not make multiple meetings. It is unhealthy. If you wish to reach me again, please leave a slip of parchment with no marking on it pinned with a tack to the water gate of the palace. Do this in the morning, and I will meet you—at this very table—that night." He shrugged. "Or someone representing me will meet you." He frowned. "You are foolish to be out in the streets and I, frankly, do not fancy being hanged beside you."

Maître Gris rose again. "But—" he said.

The other man simply walked away. He paused by the innkeeper's bar, and said a few words—the innkeeper growled at him, that much was visible.

The foreigner spread his hands, as if showing he was harmless. Then he sang something.

Nothing could have been more incongruous. He sang a short song in Archaic—his voice was beautiful. Some of the men in the tavern fell silent.

Then he went out.

The Angel being the Angel, and the man being so well-dressed—and foreign—a pair of men with clubs followed him into the dark alley.

He moved very quickly. They had to run to keep up with him, and when he turned into Sail Maker's Lane, they were both breathing hard.

And he was gone.

Both men cursed and went back to the inn.

Jules Kronmir jumped lightly to the ground and shook his head before walking down the hill, towards Master Pye's yard by a circuitous route that took him the better part of the evening.

Good Friday dawned in heavy rain and cold, as if spring was unwilling to come. The tournament was five days away, and there was a rumour in the streets of Harndon that the Prince of Occitan was a day's ride away—indeed, that he'd halted at Bergon, the country town of North Jarsay, to spend the day on his knees.

The same rumour said that he had a hundred lances with him. And that he'd have more, but his army was fighting the Wild in the mountains. Without him.

"He's comin' for his sister," people said.

The King's Guard—or rather, the sell-swords and thugs making up the King's Guard—were seen in the markets. With most of the citizens in church, they moved to take possession of the market squares and rally points, and no one stopped them. Families leaving church, tired and sad at the end of a day of the Passion, found Guardsmen and Galles at every street corner. There were a few incidents, but even the Galles seemed quiet in the face of the day of fasting, the end of Lent, and the violence of two days before.

Just before darkness fell, the King's Champion rode through the streets with a hundred Gallish lances. There were Albans among them—local knights who'd seen which way the wind was blowing, and devoted King's men. They marched a relief through the streets and changed the guards at each market square. Everywhere they went, they posted a proclamation.

It announced the Queen's Trial by Combat on Tuesday next.

It attainted Ser Gerald Random for treason, and Mistress Anne Bates, and a woman called Blanche Gold, as well as Lady Rebecca Almspend and Ser Gareth Montroy, the Count of the Borders, along with Ser John Wishart, the Prior of the Order of Saint Thomas.

And it forbade all assembly by more than four persons of either sex, for any reason, or the public bearing of arms.

Master Pye sat in his private workroom with his lead journeymen. Duke had pulled a copy down from the market cross in the square where they had their Maypole.

"Probably a crime to take it down," Sam Vintner said.

Master Pye glared. "No time for foolishness," he said.

The journeymen sat and fretted.

"What do we do, Master?" Edmund asked.

Master Pye blew out his cheeks, took off his spectacles, rubbed them on his shirt, and put them back on his nose. He stared into the darkness of Friday evening.

"How did they do it so fast?" he asked the darkness.

Duke raised his head. "You..." and he paused.

They all looked at Duke. He was the only boy born in the streets. The others came from guild houses. Duke thought about things differently.

Duke shrugged.

Master Pye cleared his throat. "Favour us with your views, lad," he said, and his voice was not unkind.

Duke shrugged again. "You take it all for granted," he said. He sounded as if he was angry—or if he might weep. "It's bloody good, this thing we have. But you forget it's not natural. You expect everyone to cooperate with the law. To make the law work." Duke took a deep breath. "But all you have to do is lie. If enough people lie, all the time, then there isn't enough truth for law to work. That's how I see it." He looked at his feet. "If enough men are greedy, and willing to lie to get what they want?" He raised his head and faced them. "Then it's easy. Their way is easy. And you lot will sit here and debate. When the only real answer is to arm, go out in the streets, and fucking kill every Guardsman and every Galle on every corner until we hold the city."

Edmund drew in a breath in horror. He had had a bad week; the man he'd killed haunted him. It had been—so easy. Like fencing in the yard. But the real man had fallen like a carcass cut down by a butcher. But worse—bloodier...

"See?" Duke said. "You all still think that if you do nothing, maybe it will go away."

"We fought!" Sam Vintner said.

Duke jutted out his jaw. "You know, I'm not a nice boy like you. My experience is—you *always* have to fight. Fighting is the normal way."

Master Pye chewed his lip. "Duke, there's merit in what you say. And mayhap we need a little more fire under us—by all the saints, people have been placid these few months. Wealth and good food and safety make men and women like cattle, right eno'." He looked around at all his senior men. "But Duke—if we kill the Galles and the King's men then we're rebels."

"That's just a word," said Duke.

"Not when the Galle knights come through our squares, killing our people," Master Pye said.

"We need the Order," Edmund said.

All the men there knew that the Order's knights were somewhere. Ser Ricar no longer wore the black and pointed cross, and he'd been seen twice—once after he escorted the black man out of the city, and another time Edmund had seen him talking to a tall man in a fine black hood.

Master Pye surprised them by shaking his head. "We can't count on the Order to do our fighting for us," he said. "Duke's right, and he's wrong." He chewed on his lips a little while. "I'm sending all o' you north, to Albin-kirk. It's too late for the fair, but there's an empty smithy there and Ser John Crayford offered it to us. You can't stay here. You'll fight—and die." He shook his head. "It's going to be awful."

Duke glared. "Just run away?" he asked. "And what of all the orders for the tourney?"

Master Pye nodded. "I'll be on the next attainder list," he said. "And we don't have the swords—not if every man in the whole City Muster stood against them. Three thousand Galles? Christ, boys, think on what the routiers was like."

"We can fight," Edmund said. He looked at Duke, who nodded.

"Can Ann fight? How about your sisters? Eh? Blanche? Want her to fight?" Master Pye shook his head. "Lads—either you are or you ain't my people. You wear my livery, you eat my food. Now I'm giving an order. You pack the mint and all the armoury. And tomorrow, when I give you the word, you ride out into the city and over First Bridge." He looked at Duke. "More than half the goods we're working so hard to complete are for men now attainted as traitors." He shrugged. "I'm not minded to complete the King's harness, either."

Edmund wanted to cry. "But—how? I mean—won't they stop us?"

Master Pye shook his head. "You worry about moving four wagons over muddy roads. I'll worry about getting you out of the city." He waved them out in dismissal.

In the dungeons, the Queen sat in near perfect darkness. She had one window, high in the wall of her cell, and it allowed in some light during the day. She had a bed, and wall hangings and clean linen, and excellent food.

And very careful guards. She didn't know any of them, despite their red surcoats. But they were cautious and courteous.

It might have been restful, except that de Rohan came every day to examine her. He brought a dozen monks and other creatures, and they filled her cell while he asked her, unblushing, to tell her the dates her courses had run, the names of her lovers, the date on which she had lost her virginity, and a thousand other little humiliations.

She ignored him, and eventually, each day, he went away.

It was easier to ignore him because she was, already and perpetually, under attack. His voice wasn't even a pinprick compared to the assault of her real enemy, and the black serpent—that's how she had begun to think of Ash, her foe—never ceased to press against the walls of her memory palace. There were no overt attacks.

Just a constant, deadly pressure on her mind.

He was insidious, too. Twice, defending the sanctity of her memory palace, Desiderata found false memories trying to leach through her walls. The memory of lying with Gaston D'Eu was laughable—her new enemy clearly had no notion of how a woman perceived the act of love. But the memory of giving Blanche a letter—a sealed letter—was almost tangible, and terrifyingly like a genuine memory.

And he gloated. That's the reason she knew his name. Ash. So...fitting.

She began to grow scared. Desiderata was not easily made afraid, but here, in the constant darkness, with no sun and no friend, no Diota, no guardsman she could trust, without even a dog or a cat, she was oppressed by a power far beyond her own.

After a day of near defeat—by which time she had begun, like a mad person, to doubt her own thoughts—she turned to prayer. And not simple prayer, but sung prayer.

She sang. And while she sang, having practised this, she began to weave herself some protections, spending carefully some hoarded *ops*. She was shocked—almost shocked out of her palace—to find how little *ops* she had.

But she worked. She stayed on her knees for most of Good Friday, allowing the pale light of the rainy spring sun to fall on her face, replenishing what little power she could muster, making *ops* into *potentia* and then to *praxis*.

Singing hymns of praise to the Virgin, and all the while, holding back the night in the fortress of her mind.

The sun went down.

Why do you do this to me? she asked the blackness outside her memory palace.

The blackness made no answer. It was not even green—just black.

Slowly, she worked. And with her will along, she reinforced her hope. To Desiderata, the loss of hope would be the loss of everything.

But she had doubts, and they were like stealthy miners working under the walls of her fortress.

Why has the King deserted me?
Why does he believe them?
Why did he rape his sister?
Who is this man to whom I am married?
Did I ever know him at all?
Why is my palace built atop this evil thing?

The last question seemed to bear the weight of many meanings.

The guards changed outside her door. She heard the stamp of feet, the whisper of sandals, and knew that de Rohan was back with his minions. She kept her head bowed, her now-lank hair hanging over her face. She continued to sing—her six hundred and seventieth Ave Maria. As she completed it, she went straight into her favourite Benedictus.

And in her mind, she placed another small, carefully wrought brick of power in the growing citadel she was creating.

Her perception of the world was imprecise. She had very little aware-ness to spare for de Rohan, but she noted that he was alone, except for two guardsmen.

He began to speak.

She paid him no heed.

He went on, and on, hectoring, bullying.

She managed another brick. It glowed in soft gold, and she loved it, cherished it and the work she was doing, like fine embroidery done in *potentia*.

She felt his hand on her neck.

"Stand away from the Queen, my lord," said the guard.

She was shocked—so shocked that in a single beat of her heart she almost let it all slide away. The pressure pushed in—she lost an outer room of her memory and Occitan and her childhood slipped away.

But she could hear.

"You may leave now," de Rohan said. "I am safe enough with her. I am protected against her witchcraft."

The guard did not move. "Orders," he said. "Step away from the Queen, my lord."

"I order you out," de Rohan said. "There, nothing easier."

His hand on her neck tightened slightly. His other hand at her head was possessive—and horrible.

She drove her elbow into his thigh and rolled onto the floor—simultaneously using all her power to fight the rising tide of attack in her head.

De Rohan was unprepared for her physical resistance and stumbled. The guard caught his elbow—and moved him across the room while he was off balance. "Stay away from the Queen's person," said the guard. He had almost no inflection in his voice. Just a man doing his job.

"I *order* you to let go of me and to leave me to this. Do you understand me?" de Rohan asked. "Do you know who I am?"

The guardsman rattled his spear against the bars on the door.

"Eh, Corporal. This gentleman is ordering me to leave the room," he said.

De Rohan frowned.

The corporal addressed was in a long mail coat over a clean jack and his scarlet surcoat fitted well. "He cannot leave, my lord." His accent was northern.

De Rohan smiled and tilted his head. "Very well, then," he said. "I will leave, and I will inform the King that you obstructed my investigations." He drew himself up. He was a big man—as big as his distant cousin de Vrailly.

The corporal nodded. "You'll do what you think's best, of course," he said.

"He meant her harm," the first guard said. "Had his hand on her throat."

The corporal frowned.

"You're a fool," de Rohan said. He walked out of the cell and went quickly up the steps, past the guardroom and up into the palace.

"Not as big a fool as some," muttered the corporal.

"What do we do if they come to kill her?" asked the guard.

"Grow wings and fly," said the corporal, a little pettishly.

Desiderata heard the entire exchange. She was so deep in the defences of her mind that she wasn't sure she had it right, but she shook off the looming shadows.

"You saved my life," she breathed.

The guardsman was just leaving the cell. He smiled at her.

"We're here for you, your grace," he said.

It was almost as shocking as de Rohan's touch. "Who sent you?" she asked.

The corporal made a sign. The guardsman gave a wry smile. He pointed at the walls and then at his ear.

"Best get back to praying, your grace," he said.

De Rohan was beside himself with anger. He turned to his senior officer Ser Eustace De l'Isle d'Adam.

"Where are they?" he asked.

L'Isle d'Adam shook his head. "No one can tell me," he said.

"Fetch the captain of the King's Guard," de Rohan snapped.

L'Isle d'Adam shook his head again. "Fitzroy is in the north, fighting the Wild," he said.

"Who is the Lieutenant of the Guard?" de Rohan asked.

"Montjoy's son, Ser Guiscard," l'Isle d'Adam said slowly. "Of course, with the arrest of his father—"

"Bon Dieu! Do you mean to say that the officer in charge of the King's household is Gareth Montjoy's son?" De Rohan had never troubled to learn the intricacies of the court—he'd become master of it so quickly he hadn't needed to.

"I fear so," l'Isle d'Adam said.

"Ventre Saint Gris! You try me, l'Isle d'Adam! So that when I ordered that peasant Random and his trull to the dungeons...?"

"They never made it there," said l'Isle d'Adam with some amusement. "Calm yourself, my lord."

"Do you mean to tell me that he recruited all the new guards?" De Rohan put a hand to his chin. "Damn me. The two on duty in the dungeon—" He paused. "So the palace could be riddled with traitors."

L'Isle d'Adam raised an eyebrow. "Pardon me, my lord, but I think that you are being too dramatic. He hired the sell-swords we sent him. Perhaps there are Queen's men among them—a few." He shrugged. "What of it? Two days past Easter, and we are done with all that."

"Who commands the King's Guard now?" de Rohan demanded. "Are there other officers?"

L'Isle d'Adam, in no way the other man's social inferior, rolled his eyes. "How would I know? Do I look like a beef-eating Alban?" He shrugged. "Tell the King to appoint a new captain."

"Fitzroy is his half-brother." De Rohan shrugged.

"You got him to arrest his own wife," l'Isle d'Adam said with some asperity.

"She is a witch and a murderess," de Rohan said primly.

L'Isle d'Adam sneered. "Keep it for the commons," he said. "Handsome piece like that—Christ, did you visit her alone?" He leered. "Did she ensorcel you? With her wiles?" He laughed coarsely.

De Rohan shook his head so hard spittle flew. "Leave me."

The archbishop spent a bad night. Twice, crowds attacked his episcopal palace, and in the morning, six hundred men-at-arms had to march through the streets to rescue him. He went to the great cathedral and found it locked; he ordered it opened and found that every altar had been stripped and washed, and not a relic or chalice was to be seen.

In a fury, he went to the Royal Palace. After a stormy interview with the King, he said a private mass in the Royal Chapel—stung by the King's assertion that in Alba, no mass was celebrated on Holy Saturday until the midnight of Easter. His mass was well-attended by some elements of court. Then he moved into new apartments, proclaiming that he could not trust his person in the streets.

Just after the bell rang for two o'clock, sentries on the wall called "Fire" and men ran to the walls to see.

The great episcopal palace was afire.

In an incredibly short time, the training and discipline of the Gallish knights was proven. Most of them were in full harness. Their war horses were saddled and ready, and they rode down into the town, a mighty armoured column. Even in the narrow streets of Waterside they were unstoppable, and no one tried.

The episcopal palace was surrounded by four wide streets. It sat alone above Cheapside, and now it burned, and threatened no other building. The knights dispersed a crowd by killing some looters and anyone else caught loitering near the fire, but their very violence discouraged any who might have helped them fight it.

So, like soldiers the world over, they sat on their horses and watched it burn, and made jokes about sending for sausages.

The whole situation might have been comic, but just before darkness fully descended, three of the squires at the end of the long line of armoured men saw a pretty young girl look winsomely around a corner. They followed her on horseback. The knights laughed to watch them go.

It was ten minutes before their knight found them—all three lying face up, with heavy arrows in their faces or throats. All had had their throats slit for good measure.

More was slit than just their throats.

The Galles exploded in rage.

Harndoners began to die.

An hour later, the archbishop sent Maître Gris to pin a scrap of parchment to the water gate.

Edmund, the journeyman, led six badly loaded wagons out of the city. They passed the gate at First Bridge, where two bored sell-swords in royal livery passed them with nothing more than a wink. On the wagons, or mounted on twenty horses and ponies, were the whole of Master Pye's establishment; his best anvils, and his treasure. As well as half the pretty young maids of Southend—Edmund's sisters and his Ann and both her parents. They were hardly alone. The road across the bridge was thick with people, all dressed as if for pilgrimage and carrying a few treasures, water bottles and food.

After a long and very loud fight with his wife, Master Pye had eschewed martyrdom and rode with them.

The only one of their people missing was Blanche. Ann said that she had gone to the Queen. Edmund thought her very brave, but he had other concerns. Like the guards at the gates.

The Royal Guards seemed to take no notice of them. They allowed thousands of people out through the gates, and then, an hour later, an officer came with horses, and they rode away with him, leaving the gates unguarded.

Easter Sunday dawned. Lord Mayor Ailwin Darkwood's head adorned the great gate of the palace. Alongside it hung a dozen others of less repute, supporters of the city and the Queen—Diota's head was there, as well, a warning to all the Queen's loyal people.

Curiously, as his name was first on the execution list, Ser Gerald Random's head was nowhere to be seen.

The archbishop, architect of the executions, celebrated high mass in the cathedral. His people had to supply every vessel and every vestment. The cannons had emptied the cathedral on Holy Saturday, and in the chaos of the burning of the episcopal palace, all of the riches of Saint Thomas had vanished. But whole neighbourhoods had burned. Some blamed the Jacks, others the Galles.

When he emerged from the first mass of Easter the sun was brilliant in the sky above him. It shone on the blood in the streets, and on the armour of the Occitan men-at-arms who were making camp beyond Southgate.

Occitans and Galles had little to say to each other at the best of times. By noon there was a rumour that there had been a fight in the streets behind Southgate.

Suddenly, the streets were full of Galles and Royal Guardsmen. As on Good Friday, every square was occupied, and every tower manned.

The same sun shone like a torch through the high window of the Queen's cell. It was the first direct sunlight, clear and golden, to touch her skin in four days. It was like a lover's kiss—like a moment of salvation.

Her hair hung like the mane of a wild horse. She hadn't changed her garments in three days, afraid that she might be attacked while changing—afraid that any complex physical activity would distract her from the fight in her head.

She had not eaten in two days, and the child within her protested by kicking and kicking. Her sides hurt—her back burned like fire. The new milk in her full breasts soaked against her shift and smelled. Her swollen breasts hurt her—too sensitive, too full. The weight of her belly was like that of a sinner's chains in hell.

But the sun—the sun's touch—was pure. And the guardsmen had preserved her hope, even if she did not understand why. And then on Saturday night, in the utter dark, Blanche had come—a girl she'd seldom noticed. Blanche had combed out her hair, and prayed with her.

Guardsmen had let her in, and then let her out.

On Easter morning, the oldest guard put a tray of bread and cheese on the floor and made a point of eating a nibble of each.

"No need to starve yourself, your grace," he said. "Your brother's on his way. And we won't let anything happen to you."

He seemed disappointed when she didn't respond, but the pressure did not become less with the advent of the day. If Easter had any magic, it was only in her heart. She dared not pause to eat.

She could only drink in the golden light like a newborn suckling at the breast. Food, her brother, her failure of a husband...

That was all for another world.

In the darkness of last night, she had worked out what *it* wanted.

It wanted her baby.

She could feel *it* now, looking to enter into her, and through her, her son.

She drank the golden light. Her world was reduced, in four straight days, to this—*resistance*.

Working swiftly, she embroidered the new rays of *ops* into refined *potentia* and built the resulting material into her wall.

Her body was far away. She loved it, but there was little she could do for it.

She wanted to weep for the pain that hunger and deprivation were causing her baby.

She could smell the cheese. She wanted a moment to eat and drink the clean, cool water.

She did none of these things. Instead, she drank the pure golden light and waited.

And prayed.

On Easter eve, Prince Raymond of Occitan sent a herald to the King of Alba.

The King met the herald in the great chamber. It was hung with garlands—a veteran of the Alban court would have found them thin. The Queen was in prison; her ladies were all exiled, and the female servants of the palace had, in a body, stayed at home. Rumours of rape and assault by the Galles on the maids were rife; no girl wanted to admit to being attacked but mothers, angry or in mourning from the violence in the city, kept their girls home, and in many cases their boys as well.

The King's eyes wandered over the flowers—too few—and the ribbons, which were sparse and, in at least one case, dirty.

Jean de Vrailly stood by the throne. He, too, saw the frayed and dirty ribbon.

"Your grace, if I may, should never have put himself in a position to be so embarrassed by common people." He walked across the near-empty hall and pulled down the offending ribbon.

The King had his chin in his hand. He was not well-dressed—in fact, clean against the spirit of the day, he wore black. "What?" he asked.

"In Galle these things are better ordered," de Vrailly said. "And the lower people would never dare this sullen revolt."

The King stretched his feet out. "You mean, stay at home. On a feast day."

De Vrailly looked at the King. "What ill-humour is this, your grace?"

At the far end of the hall, Royal Guards in brilliant scarlet escorted a tall young man whose honey-blond hair and elegant features might have been irkish. Indeed, many troubadours claimed irk blood flowed among the people of Occitan. They spoke a different form of Gallish, and they sang songs from Iberia and Ifriquy'a as well as from Alba and Galle. In the coastal towns, there were even mosques, tolerated by the princes. Occitan was a land of song, and oranges.

And very skilled knights.

The herald wore the full costume of his trade—a tabard of golden silk checked in azure, with the imperial eagle spreading his mighty wings over all, worked in silk couching so accurately that it looked like a real predator ready to leap—very much at odds with the Alban and Gallish heraldry of formalized, ritual beasts and heads.

The herald moved with the grace of a dancer. He was as tall as de Rohan or de Vrailly, and he bowed deeply before the King, his right knee firmly on the floor. His hose were silk—the best hose in the room.

De Rohan entered from the King's rooms, late, flustered, and moving quickly. Behind him came a dozen well-dressed men in silk and wool and fur, adding to the lustre about the King. A full half of them were Albans. The events of Holy Week had polarized opinion throughout the Brogat, Jarsay and the Albin, and many men—King's men—had swallowed their dislike of the Galles in the face of violence. Every action by the re-born Jacks in the countryside recruited yeomen and knights for the King—and de Rohan.

De Rohan's latecomers took a moment to settle, and were joined by a dozen priests and monks and the Archbishop of Lorica, also late.

The herald waited patiently, his face expressionless. His eyes never shifted from the King's.

The King nodded to the herald.

He raised his staff. "Your grace, my lords and ladies of Alba, the Prince of Occitan sends his greetings," he said. "My lord has come to settle any issue of accusation between the King of Alba and his wife, my sister, the Lady of Occitan."

De Rohan did not even wait for the King to reply. "This is a matter affecting only the sovereignty of the Kingdom of Alba, and is, we regret—"

The herald quite clearly ignored him. He had a rich voice—he almost sung his words. "Upon arrival in this land, my master has had neither greeting nor guesting from his cousin the King of Alba. And upon approach, he has received threats—"

De Rohan opened his mouth and the King of Alba made a sudden movement. Even de Rohan had to be silent in the face of the King's direct order.

"—and now discovers that the Queen of Alba, his sister, has been accused of witchcraft, of murder, of treason and of adultery," the man's beautiful voice went on. "Which accusations, my master finds abhorrent, and the more so as they are to be tried by combat, a barbaric practice antithetical to the teachings of the Holy Church—"

The archbishop shouted. His voice was a trifle high—he was young. "Absurd! Who is this boasting coxcomb to tell me what the Holy Church—"

Maître Gris leaned over to say something in his ear.

"Shut up!" he told his secretary, still too loud and too shrill.

"—but a convenient fiction to cover a crime," the herald finished. He neither smiled nor frowned.

"You dare?" de Rohan said.

"My master demands the immediate release of the Queen into his custody. He is not interested in honeyed words and delay. Give him the Queen his sister tonight."

"These are not the words of negotiation," the King said wearily.

The herald took a glove from his belt. "If my master's most reasonable demand is not satisfied," he said. "This glove will guide his next action."

"Are you threatening *war*?" de Vrailly asked. "You cannot be serious."

"We will not release the Queen, who is a criminal and a witch," de Rohan said. "*Thou shalt not suffer a witch to live.*"

The King looked at de Rohan and rose to his feet. "Master Herald, I need a moment to confer with my officers of state. Please be kind enough to—to wait."

The herald bowed.

At the King's rising, everyone had bowed. Now they formed a corridor, and he walked down it, from his throne's dais, off to the right, and through the great oak doors to his tower and the royal apartments.

The archbishop caught de Vrailly's arm. "You must stay here and watch this so-called herald."

De Vrailly looked at the archbishop. "You think...?"

The archbishop frowned. "I merely guess that he, too, is a sorcerer. Watch him."

The archbishop hurried away, leaving de Vrailly poised in a rare moment of indecision. But he did not think that the King faced any threat from his cousin, and he had just been threatened with war by the King of Occitan. A thought that made him smile with something like glee.

He turned, his armour clacking softly, and went to stand in front of the throne, his sword drawn.

In the King's inner council chamber, the King sat at the head of the table, flanked by the archbishop, as chancellor, and de Rohan, as first privy council. Next at the table sat Du Corse, now Marshal of Alba, and across from him, l'Isle d'Adam, second privy council.

De Rohan began talking before the King was seated. He was excited.

"Your grace, my lords, we have a golden opportunity here if only we can grasp it." He smiled at the King. "The Occitans are neighbours—and foreigners. We can unite the support of the people who matter to us—the knights and the gentry—to fight them. Their coast is rich. The campaign will pay for itself."

Du Corse was cautious. "We have very little time," he said. "And for myself, I have heard that the men of Occitan know how to wield a lance, and I have never trusted armchair generals who tell me wars will be over by midsummer."

The King raised his head. "Why do we have very little time?" he asked.

Du Corse froze. It was perceptible. Then he shrugged. "Your grace must know that our Kingdom of Galle is also threatened by the Wild," he said.

The King's eyes went to those of the archbishop. "You maintain, I think, that the Wild is a fable," he said. "A snare of the enemy."

Du Corse looked away.

De Rohan frowned. "We must discuss what answer to make to this coxcomb." He nodded to the archbishop. "I like the word."

The King sat back, and scratched his beard. "No. I want to hear the archbishop tell me his views on the Wild. In light of there being an attack in Galle."

"Fleeing men report ten where there is only one," the archbishop said. "It is all exaggeration and fable."

Du Corse frowned.

The King looked around as if for wine. He shrugged. "But Monsieur Du Corse will take his lances home to fight it," he said slowly. "What is your departure date, Du Corse?"

Du Corse too obviously looked at de Rohan.

When the King had moments like this, the Galles were used to de Vrailly smoothing things over with his absolute certainty. The archbishop regretted leaving him behind—but only until he saw de Rohan pour wine at the sideboard, and then he knew he'd guessed correctly.

"That date is of little moment compared to the presence of a foreign army on our doorstep," de Rohan said, setting the King's golden cup at his elbow. It was small personal services like this that had won the King's esteem when de Rohan was only de Vrailly's standard bearer. The King, despite the vector of the conversation, smiled warmly at de Rohan.

The King liked to like people. But he shook his head. "It is not an army. One of my guardsmen says it is fewer than three hundred knights, no archers, and no spearmen. They came for the tournament, gentles."

De Rohan grinned. He couldn't help himself. "Better and better," he said.

The King looked down the table, took a long draught of wine, and then shrugged. "I don't see where you want to go with this, de Rohan."

The first privy council smiled. "Only three hundred knights?" he said. "It could be the shortest war in history."

At that, the King's head snapped around.

But de Rohan was only just warming to his idea. "A complete victory— it will take the wind out of the sails of the Queen's supporters, it will deflate the commons and show our power and unite the gentles against the foreigner." He raised his eyebrows at Du Corse. "And pay the routiers in loot."

Du Corse frowned.

But anything he might have said was interrupted by the King, who shot to his feet. "That's it, then," he said. His open palm slapped the table so loudly that the archbishop jumped. "I have had time to think of many things, *gentlemen*. And it occurs to me—I have begun to think—that you—do not..."

Suddenly he slumped. His knees relaxed, and he went down into his chair. Only the immediate presence of de Rohan and two large servants kept the King from falling to the floor.

"A surfeit of wine," de Rohan said with a soft smile. "You heard him, my friends. '*That's it.*' He agreed."

Du Corse narrowed his eyes. "That's how it is going to be, is it?" he asked.

De Rohan pursed his lips and wiped his hands fastidiously on the King's cloth napkin. "On Tuesday, de Vrailly will kill the Queen's champion. We'll burn her as a witch, and the rest will follow easily enough."

L'Isle d'Adam shook his head. "He'll never stomach it." He looked at de Rohan. "Grande Dieu, de Rohan, I do not think I can stomach it."

"You do not think she is guilty?" de Rohan asked.

L'Isle d'Adam shook his head. "I do not think there's a man present who could stomach burning the Queen."

"She's a heretic—a temptress—a seducer and a murderer," the archbishop spat.

"As I said, I do not think there is a *man* present who could stomach it," l'Isle d'Adam said. "May I suggest—very strongly, Monsieur de Rohan— that the Queen suffer an accident after her trial by combat?"

"Perhaps trying to escape?" Du Corse said. "For the love of God, de Rohan—we don't have ice water in our veins like you. And the commons…"

De Rohan snapped his fingers. "That, for them," he said.

Du Corse nodded very slightly. "What a fine time you will have ruling this fair country when I take my lances back to the King."

De Rohan turned to the two big servants. "Take him to bed," he said.

They bowed.

"Do you have any news of our army in the north?" de Rohan asked.

Du Corse sighed. "Army is far too strong a word. Ser Hartmut has a fine siege train and about a hundred lances—and some sailors."

"Too far away to be any use," de Rohan said.

Du Corse looked at l'Isle d'Adam and shrugged again. "Monsieur d'Abblemont had a plan for the union of our forces," he admitted. "And he was intending to reinforce the so-called Black Knight with two hundred more lances this spring." He looked at de Rohan, his face wrinkling with suppressed displeasure. "But I suspect the troops were never sent. The King and council in Lutrece are adamant about the summer campaign. The reports from Arelat are very serious."

"Shall we go back and inform the herald of the King's decision?" de Rohan asked. He seemed uninterested in the events in Arelat.

"What do you perceive was the King's decision?" Du Corse asked.

"Why, war, of course!" de Rohan said. "In the morning, at dawn, the King asks that you attack their camp."

Du Corse nodded again, very slightly. "We are very chivalrous, are we not?" he asked.

By the time the first market carts rolled into the squares of Cheapside on Easter Monday, the boys who spread news knew there had been a battle.

Most of the Royal Guard, and all the lances that the Conte Du Corse had brought from Galle, rode through the town before first light. They passed without challenge through Southgate.

They formed, four deep, across the front of the Occitan camp, where sleepy sentries watched.

One of the sentries blew his horn.

The "Alban" army charged the camp.

It should have been a massacre. The Galles were in full harness, and so were the men of the Royal Guard. Most of the Occitan knights, stumbling from their decorative pavilions, should have been unarmed and unprepared.

They were not. They were fully armed, cap-à-pied.

There were also surprisingly few of them—only a hundred or so, led by a knight in the blue and gold chequey of the royal house. There were no squires and no pages.

The Occitans gathered together in the tight wedge and charged the "Alban Army" that outnumbered it ten to one.

The fighting was brutal. And very skilled. The Galles suffered because their horses were not yet recovered from the sea voyage. The Occitan horses were superb.

But no knight can triumph at odds of ten to one.

Du Corse eventually unhorsed the blue and gold knight, after they had gone lance to lance and sword to sword. And finally, dagger to dagger. Du Corse got his arm in front of the other man's neck and his dagger pommel past his head, hooked him and threw him to the ground.

Even then, the blue and gold knight would not relent. He found a sword on the ground and fought back—even as a dozen Gallish and Alban knights cut at him. He killed a horse, dismounting an Alban midlands knight named Ser Gilles. He cut the Conte Du Corse's reins.

He was like a madman, and the other Occitan knights were as bad. Each one seemed to require a siege. The sun rose, and they were still fighting. The surviving Occitans drew into a ring in the middle of their camp—about twenty of them. They were surrounded by tent stakes and ropes and fallen tents, and the Galles and Albans had to dismount to face them. The blue and gold knight was still on his feet, although blood was seeping through some of the joints in his harness.

Du Corse, bleeding from a smart thrust to the inside of his left elbow, sent them a herald.

He came back. "They call us all cowards and caitiffs. They say there is no parley with evil."

"Christ, what fools," muttered Du Corse. "Bring up crossbowmen and shoot them down, then."

Forty feet away, de Vrailly led a fourth charge at the tight circle of Occitan knights. Again, as in his first three attacks, he put one down with a great blow of his poleaxe—his almost inhuman speed at the moment of contact, his size and his deceptively long reach made him lethal. His axe slammed, almost unimpeded, into an Occitan knight's faceplate—the visor crumpled backwards, destroying the man's face.

But the circle closed, and the Occitans were too well-trained to lose another man. De Vrailly took a blow and then another, and had to stumble back, baulked of his prey—the Occitan banner.

De Vrailly saw the red-and-blue liveried crossbowmen moving at the edge of his vision, limited as it was by his own visor. He gritted his teeth and turned and clanked back to where Du Corse sat on a fresh horse.

"You cannot do this," he said.

Du Corse spat. "I can, my lord, and I will. I need lose no more knights."

"We are the better men." De Vrailly was enraged. "By God, ser knights, do you doubt this?"

Du Corse shook his head. "Not in the least, my good de Vrailly. But in this case—these men are like assassins. They have drunk wine or taken opium or something like it. They intend to fight to the death. I see no reason to give them any more of my knights."

De Vrailly looked up at the new marshal. "I was against this surprise attack. And look, *Marshal.* It was no surprise. The Occitan prince was warned, and he has slipped away—leaving a handful of very brave men to die."

"A foolish choice." Du Corse was resentful. He might have said, *amateurish.*

De Vrailly spat. "As God is my witness, my lord, you have erred grievously in this. And the Prince of Occitan left these men to lure us to shame. Shame! I say, he left a few good knights to prove that we were base. And par Dieu, monsieur, so we have proved ourselves to be."

"The Occitan prince's cause has been found wanting on the field of battle," Du Corse said. "That is all."

"Let me take my squires," de Vrailly pleaded. "Let me fight them. Man to man. One to one. Until we have killed or taken them. We will—*Deus Veult.* I know it."

Du Corse motioned at the captain of his crossbowmen. "Monsieur de Vrailly, *you* may have a very different fight tomorrow." He nodded. "We cannot have you exhausted for the Queen's trial." He pointed at de Vrailly's foot. "You are wounded. I insist you retire."

The crossbowmen were just thirty yards from the tight circle of Occitan knights. The Occitans saw them, but at first refused to believe it.

As the crossbowmen—most of them Albans—spanned their heavy arbalests, the Occitans called insults.

Clear in the cool spring air, one accented jibe carried to Du Corse. "These are the Gallish knights of whom our fathers told us?"

One of the Occitans had a wine cup from somewhere. He held it aloft, his visor up, and he laughed and drank.

The Occitans began to sing. They were big men, but men who trained in singing as well as in fighting, and their voices rose in a polyphony.

De Vrailly's face darkened and grew mottled with rage. Occitan and Gallish were different enough in pronunciation—but the words were clear enough.

The crossbowmen leaned their spanned weapons on the tops of their great pavises to steady them.

"No!" bellowed de Vrailly.

"You can send your squires to fight the survivors, if you insist," Du Corse said. He turned in his saddle. "Loose!"

Desiderata was very far gone when the woman came.

She was scarcely able to distinguish between the real and the *aethereal* anymore. At first she thought the woman was Blanche, come to help her. Reality and the *aethereal* had all but merged to her sight, and she had begun to overlay the *aethereal* version of the world on the real, so that the shadows were darker where the thing called Ash seemed to pool, and the bright green coils that some other power was laying, hideously, about her and what bloomed inside her showed stark against the walls of her cell.

But despite the crisis in her sanity—and her outward attempts to repel her enemies, if they were not creations of her mind—she was also aware that it was Easter—the greatest festival of the Christian year. And the moment of rebirth in all the old ways. The moment when young spring killed old winter.

In between her prayers to the Virgin—a ceaseless litany—she thought of her springs. Of her riding out in spring with fifty knights to make the May come in. Of the fecund earth, and the dances. The green of the grass.

It was with these two thoughts in her head—the green of the leaves of spring and the Virgin—that she first saw the woman come through the door of her cell.

The closed door.

She did not shine. In the *aethereal*, she appeared solid, and in the real, she appeared insubstantial. There was no outward sign of power about her—a tall, grave woman who wore a simple kirtle of rich brown.

But as Desiderata looked at the brown, she thought it was perhaps a foreign textile, some wonderous silk of Morea or farther afield. The brown was itself made up of a thousand tiny patterns—there, of flowers, a riot of colour covering whole fields, if only for a few days, and then another portion with a border of birds so cunningly wrought that they appeared to move and sing, and another, a lady on horseback, riding with a hawk on her wrist...

The lady had a dignified face. The face of mature wisdom, and fecund strength. Motherhood and virginity, or perhaps something older and better than mere virginity—a serenity of strength.

Desiderata was on her knees, and her mouth was already saying the Ave Maria.

She raised her hands to the woman.

Who smiled.

"Oh, my child," she said sadly. "Would that I might tell you *they know not what they do.*"

Her voice was low and clear, vibrant with energy. Just to hear her made Desiderata straighten her back.

The woman bent, a hand on Desiderata's head and another on her back.

All of Desiderata's pains fell away, leaving her only the ache of knowing how near to term her pregnancy was.

The pools of black became palpable, and manifested.

"Tar, you hypocrite!" said the dark voice.

"Ash, you try me." The woman moved a hand.

"You interfere as freely as I do," Ash said.

The woman interposed herself between Desiderata and the pool of darkness. "No," she said. "I obey the ancient law, and you break it."

Ash laughed, and nothing about the laugh was like a laugh save the outward sound. "The law is for the weak, and I am strong."

The woman raised her arms. "I, too, am strong. But I obey the law. If you flout it, it will punish you. Stronger immortals than you—"

"Spare me your mythology," Ash said. "I will have the child. Now you have interfered directly, breaking the compact. Now you are as much a law-breaker as I."

"Spare me your immaturity. I did not strike the first blow, or the tenth. And you know—you must know—how tangled has become this skein." She brought her arms together.

"So tangled that only I can follow it. Come, entangle yourself, and I will destroy you, too." Ash's voice grew in strength.

"Can you?" Tar asked.

"Enough that I know that this one will die by *your* hand." Ash's laughter was like the cries of souls in torment. "And the child either will never be born, or will be mine from birth, by the actions of *your people.*"

Even as he spoke, he grew, and as he grew, his assault on Desiderata's mind became more intense, until it was like a barrage of trebuchets.

Had she not prepared...

But she had. Her golden wall of power accepted blow after blow.

The woman spoke again, even though by now she was surrounded by darkness.

"If you continue to waste your strength on mortals, you will in time teach them to fight you. Look—even now, this daughter of mine has built a wall you cannot easily breach. What if she teaches it to others?" She sighed. "Are you so sure that you can survive what is to come?"

"Survive?" Ash asked. "I will triumph."

The blackness filled the room.

His power in the real was something against which Desiderata had no defence, and she was losing the will to breathe.

The woman was no longer visible. Desiderata had time to wonder what she was hearing—whether this apparent conversation between Satan and the Virgin was occurring in the real or in the *aethereal*. Or somewhere else.

Or just inside her head.

One of the golden bricks in her wall of solitude shifted. The shift was minute, but terrifying.

Ash chuckled, like blood running over a stone.

"You were a fool, woman, for coming to *my* place of power." Satan's voice was strong and level.

"Really?" the woman asked. "My power thrives equally in light and darkness." She seemed to sigh. "Does yours?"

The progress of time outside in the room was glacial. Seas rose and fell. Lands shifted—mountains grew and then stone cracked and they eroded away. Erosion changed the shape of worlds hanging in the infinite universe of hermetical spheres.

Or so it seemed to Desiderata.

And then something in the cell was different.

The air smelled of decay. And mould.

But also of new life.

"Many things grow in the darkness," the Virgin said. "And *you cannot stop them.*"

The choking blackness gave way to a thicker darkness and a wider range of smells. Earth. Old basements. A wine cellar and the wine. Old cheese.

"You!" Ash said.

"Of course," the other voice said. "Many beautiful things grow in the darkness. But I am not restricted by the darkness, and you have made an error."

Suddenly, light flooded the room.

The floor of the room was gone—the cold stones, the hole in the corner, the recess where plates were left.

All gone.

The floor was a hand's breadth deep in rich loam. And now, in between beats of Desiderata's rapidly beating heart, something sprouted in the soil, and strands of green—not the virulent green of the Wild, but the natural green of the wilderness—leapt from the rich soil and began to grow. It grew straight into the pools of darkness, piercing the darkness the way the light could not. Even as the green spikes grew, they developed barbs.

The Virgin allowed herself to sink onto a bench that had appeared.

The sound of a choir began—

A shriek began—

And both were buried under the voices of a hundred thousand angels—or perhaps faeries. The briars leapt to the ceiling, which was now a luminous gold. The briars gave forth blossoms, a profusion of them so rich as to beggar thought, and they burst into flower—red and white and pink roses, and the smell of roses swept the cell like a cleansing tonic and routed the darkness like an avenging army.

And then every blossom began to move—the petals began to fall and the legions of faery angels seized on each falling petal and carried them to the figure of the woman seated in the middle of the rose garden.

Desiderata sighed. For the first time in as long as she could remember, the black assault on her wall had ceased. "Oh, Blessed Virgin! You have saved me," Desiderata said.

The woman turned slightly, and raised a corner of the wimple that hid her face. "This is not victory, my child," she said. "Nor is this even the turning point. I have only restored equilibrium."

"Liar!" shouted Ash. "Hypocrite!"

But he was very far away.

The first day of the tournament—the day of the Queen's trial by combat—dawned grey and foggy.

The guards found the Queen asleep in her cell—a cell, they said, that had become a rose garden overnight. Many men—hard men—fell to their knees as the Queen emerged from the cell. She was dressed in a plain brown gown, and her pregnancy was so pronounced as to make her ungainly—yet she was not. She was calm, and beautiful.

They put her in a wagon. They did so with surpassing gentleness.

She was taken through the streets of the city, and she could see how few people there were. She knew nothing of what had passed, but she could guess much from the burned buildings and the silence.

But what men and women there were bent their knees as her cart passed. And many, many men, and not a few women, buttoned their hoods against the unseasonable cold and damp and followed the cart out to the tourney grounds.

The gates of the city were open and, outside the city, the lists and the stands and all the pavilions for a great tournament were prepared.

And mostly empty. Thousands had left the city.

They took her from the wagon and set her on a chair—not in the stands, the formal stands, to be above the lists, but at eye level with the men who would fight.

Only then, quite late in the proceedings, did she fully understand. Her understanding came from seeing the pole of iron, with a huge pile of wood already piled about it.

She did not avert her eyes. She looked at it.

She turned to one of the men guarding her. "Is that for me?" she asked. Her voice sounded deeper than she had expected.

"Your grace, I…" He swallowed.

"It is, if my champion fails," she insisted.

Her guard nodded.

"Is my brother here?" she asked calmly.

Her guard would not meet her eye. "No," he admitted.

In the middle-distance, emerging from the fog of early morning, she could see a great column of richly clad nobles and ladies approaching. At its head she saw the King, attired in his usual red. He appeared listless, puffy-eyed and absent as he approached.

By him was Jean de Vrailly, in armour, cap-à-pied. And around him were half a hundred other Galles, all fully armoured, even de Rohan. There was no shortage either of Alban nobles, men and women. Many of the Alban knights wore harness, too.

The King was directed by a sergeant-at-arms to the pavilion where he would await the events, but he rode past the gesticulating man, and his horse's hooves rang on the ground as he approached like a bell tolling her doom.

But his face was working like an infant in the moment that the pain hits, just as it opens its mouth to cry.

One of the Galles—de Rohan—tried to take the King's reins. "You must not speak to her," de Rohan insisted. "She is a criminal and a heretic."

The King jerked his reins expertly from the other man's grasp, and just for a moment the Queen was reminded of who he truly was—or had been. The best knight.

The Queen rose, made a curtsey. "A boon, your grace!" she called. Again, her voice was as clear as a perfect spring day.

He nodded. He closed his eyes—as if he had to concentrate to hear her.

It came to her that he was drugged. Or crazed.

"Save our son," she said.

The archbishop laughed mockingly. "Save your bastard?" He shook his head. "You—"

The King raised a hand for silence.

But the archbishop leaned down from his horse. "Shut her up," he said. "Your bastard goes to the fire with you."

"This is your God of mercy, my lord?" Desiderata asked, her voice gentle. "To kill the child with the mother? The innocent child? *The heir of Alba*?"

"God will know his own," the archbishop spat.

The King was having trouble remaining mounted. A pair of guardsmen came and supported him. He tried to speak, but de Rohan waved, and the men-at-arms led his horse towards the Royal Pavilion.

De Rohan lingered. "Count your remaining breaths," he said. He smiled.

Desiderata felt liberated. She'd seldom been so calm—so strong. "You enjoy making hell come to earth, do you not?"

De Rohan's smile, if anything, grew. "It is all shit," he said. "Don't blame me for it." He breathed on his vambrace and polished it on his white surcoat.

She met his smile with one of her own. "It must be terrible," she said with the clarity of the edge of death. "To be both selfish and impotent. How I pity you." She reached out a hand—not in anger, but in sorrow.

He flinched. "Don't touch me, witch!"

She sighed. "I could heal you, if you gave me the time."

"There's nothing to heal!" he spat. "I see through the lies to the truth. It is all shit."

"And yet from your shit grow roses," she said. "Burn me, and see what grows."

Now he backed his horse away. "No one will save you," he said.

She smiled. Her smile was steady and strong, and utterly belied the fatigue graven into her face. "I am already saved," she said.

Chapter Four

The Wild

Nita Qwan and his two companions, Gas-a-ho, the shaman's apprentice, and Ta-se-ho, the old hunter, spent one of the most comfortable winters of their lives—even a life as long as Ta-se-ho's—in the halls of N'gara. Food and warmth were plentiful. So was companionship. Gas-a-ho passed in one winter from a gawky boy with aspirations to the rank of shaman to a serious young man with dignity and a surprising turn of mind. Tamsin, the Lady of N'gara, had passed much time with him, and he had benefited from it.

Ta-se-ho had also benefited. He looked younger and stronger, and when the sap began to move in the trees, and when the preparations for war began to grow serious, it was he, despite his age, who sat down in the great hall and suggested that they leave.

"I have heard matrons and shamans agree that the early spring is the most dangerous time to travel," Nita Qwan said. In fact, he sought nothing but reassurance. His wife would bear their first baby soon, and he wanted to be home.

He also wanted to be away from the endless temptations of the hall—flashing eyes and willing companions and the new seduction of fame. Nita Qwan the warrior. Nita Qwan, the Faery Knight's friend.

Nita Qwan, Duchess Mogon's ally.

Ta-se-ho nodded as he did when someone younger made an excellent point. "This is true. The soft snow of spring is the most dangerous snow. Heavy rain on snow is when those walking in the Wild die. Nonetheless—"

The old hunter sat back. "It came to me in a dream—that the sorcerer's people would have an even harder time. The Rukh? They would die faster than we, as the ice breaks and the waters move. His men? His allies? Without raquettes, they are dead. Even with them—this is a time of year when the People can travel. Not safely, but safer than our enemies. We know the ground and the snow and the little streams under the rotting snow."

Unannounced, Tapio, the Faery Knight, appeared and sat. His recovery from his duel with Thorn had been rapid, but it had left its mark—his face was thinner and one shoulder sat higher than the other.

"Your people, oh man. They will need to move quickly. Sssilently." He flashed a fanged smile. "Before Thorn can ssseize them." He nodded to Ta-se-ho. "You think well, old hunter."

"I had a dream," Ta-se-ho said with a slight inclination of his head. "I was reminded by ancestors that we used the snow of spring to escape *you*."

Tapio showed his fangs mirthlessly. "Perhapsss. Timesss change. Enemiesss change."

"You killed many of the People, Tapio," Ta-se-ho said.

Tapio raised a hand and moved it back and forth as if it was a balance point. "And now I will sssave many." He looked around.

Duchess Mogon, utterly graceful despite the bulk of her big reptilian body, came and squatted down. Lady Tamsin was with her.

She waved a hand, casually, and a glowing curtain of purple fire descended on them.

Mogon gurgled. "It is time," she said, as if she was answering a question someone had put to her.

"I had a dream," Ta-se-ho said.

Mogon nodded. "My hearing is not limited to the tiny fraction of the world humans hear," she said. "Nor am I so very old. You wish to move across the spring snow."

Nita Qwan thought of his pregnant wife. "He proposes that we move the Sossag people *now*."

Mogon shook her head. "My people are all but useless at this time. Until the sun warms the hillside, we have only our human allies to protect our fields." She showed all her teeth. "Not that we are impotent. Merely that we do not go far abroad."

Tapio looked at Nita Qwan. "Can you do it?" he asked.

Nita Qwan shrugged, his hands in the air. "Ta-se-ho says we can do it," he said. "I am not really a great warrior and I know almost nothing about moving at this time of year, except that it will be brutally hard and very cold and wet."

Ta-se-ho laughed. "When has the Wild been anything but cold and wet for our kind?"

Tapio nodded. "I will prepare you sssome toysss, that may make your journey easssier."

Nita Qwan bowed. "The Sossag people thank you."

Mogon snorted. "I will go home in a week or two, when the lake begins to break up," she said. "Bring the People to me. We will be strong friends."

"But not your warriors," Tapio said.

Nita Qwan and Ta-se-ho nodded. "We know what to do."

The journey around the inland sea was hard. It was so hard that, later, Nita Qwan thought that all his life as a slave had been nothing but a test for the trek.

There were only the three of them and three toboggans. Tapio and Tamsin gave them several wondrous artifacts; a clay pot that was always warm, day and night, and whose warmth seemed to expand or contract depending on where it was—on the toboggans, it was merely warm enough to warm hands, but in a small cave, it was like a large fire. Each of them had mittens, made of a light silky stuff by the lady Tamsin and her maidens, and the mittens were always dry and always warm. Gas-a-ho had a small staff with which he could make fire.

"I made it with Tapio's help," he said modestly. "He and the Lady taught me so much."

Even with these items and several more; even with the best and warmest clothes made by all the Outwaller women at N'gara and with blankets provided by the Jacks and the good wishes of every man, woman, and creature in the fortress—even then, the trip was horrible.

Each day, they walked across soft snow. Their snow shoes plunged into the snow as far as their ankles and sometimes as deep as their knees, so that half an hour into the day, walking was already a nightmare and after eight hours, it was like walking in deep mud. Every stream crossing was treacherous, and required the careful, patient removal of the raquettes, the plunge up to the groin in deep old snow so that each man could cross, rock to rock, on now-exposed streams. Toboggans had to be carried across, and every day the streams rose. Ponds and small lakes were still highways for rapid movement on the ice, but the ice would break soon.

They went as fast as their muscles would allow.

Camps were made in places no sane man would camp in summer—on exposed rocks, in the snow cave created by two downed evergreens, under looming rock faces and in the middle of stands of birch. Fires sank into the snow and vanished unless supported by a lattice of sodden logs. They slept on their toboggans. No one bathed or changed clothes.

Ta-se-ho smoked constantly. But he would not let them give in to fatigue, and when they had turned the corner on the endless swamps and soft snow of the N'gara peninsula, he led them along the edge of the inland sea, where for two days they made rapid time, all but running on the ice.

Until the ice broke and Nita Qwan went in.

They were close to shore, near the end of a day of cutting across a big bay, so far from land that they had passed terrifyingly close to the ice edge and the water. And late in the day, safe, apparently, Nita Qwan had turned aside to piss in the virgin snow, taken a few steps off the beaten snow where their toboggans had passed . . .

He felt the ice give, saw the snow darken, and then—faster than he'd have thought possible—he was in, all the way in, the black water closing over his head.

He had never been so cold. The water, when he went in, gave a new definition to what cold might be. He couldn't breathe. He couldn't see. He panicked instantly.

And then he was out again.

Gas-a-ho pulled him out with one mighty heave on his blanket roll, which was buoyant and high on his shoulders. Gas-a-ho had run to him, thrown himself full length on the snow, and grabbed the pack. Ta-se-ho had his feet.

The ice on which he lay made noise, a low grumble like the rage of a living thing, and Ta-se-ho pulled them both back, and back again, and then they were all crunching through the swift-breaking ice over shallow water that did not immediately promise death.

Ashore and exposed to the wind, drowning seemed kinder. And now Ta-se-ho was like a madman, driving them on, making them run, walk, and run again, over and over, along the exposed shore. To their left, the inland sea went on, apparently forever, in an unbroken snowfield. To their right, atop bluffs that lowered over them, were snow-covered trees and naked black spruce that went on to the horizon, a wilderness of trees that seemed to cover all the earth.

When Nita Qwan thought he must be near death, the old man stopped them in a cove that offered some protection from the wind and pulled the cover off his own sled. He took the pot from his sled and carried it to an exposed rock at the base of the tall sand and stone bluffs and placed it gently there.

Almost instantly, it began to give more heat. Nita Qwan fell to his knees.

"Strip him," Ta-se-ho said gruffly.

"My hands are still warm!" said Gas-a-ho in wonder.

"The greatest gift the Lady could give." Ta-se-ho did not smile. "He's far gone. He went all the way in."

Nita Qwan heard them only from a distance.

He merely knelt and worshipped the warmth.

The wind rose, and icy rain began to fall. They stripped him and only then did the two Outwallers begin to collect materials for a shelter.

Unbelievably, as soon as Nita Qwan was naked, he was warmer—much warmer. He began to wake up.

Ta-se-ho was tying gut to a stake. He looked over. "Did you see the spirit world?" he asked.

Nita Qwan was having trouble speaking. But he nodded.

Ta-se-ho shook his head. "I dreamed all this. You do not die."

Nita Qwan looked at the old man. "Do you?" he asked.

The old man looked away.

But by sunset, all three of them were warm enough, and dry. A roaring fire lit the edge of the coast and the bluffs behind them, and they made a chimney of hides and the fire came up through it, drying Nita Qwan's clothes and moccasins.

The next day they killed a deer. Ta-se-ho tracked the buck, and Nita Qwan put an arrow into him at a good distance, earning him much praise from the other two. The old hunter nodded.

"In this snow, I couldn't run down any of the deer's children," he said. He walked with a spear in his hand, but he never seemed to use it as anything but a walking staff. It was a fine spear, made far away by a skilled smith, and the old man had taken it as a war prize in his youth.

Like the spear, the deer was thin, but the meat was delicious, and they ate and ate and ate.

"How much farther to the People?" Gas-a-ho asked.

Ta-se-ho frowned. "Everything depends on the weather," he said. "If it is cold tonight, we will risk the inland sea again. We must. This is not just for us, brothers. Think of all the people coming back this way. Every day matters."

Morning saw them rise in full darkness. It was snowing, and coyotes bayed at the distant moon. Tapio had provided them with three beautiful crystal lights, and with the lights they were able to pack well and quickly, but even with light, there were numb fingers and badly tied knots. Each morning was a little worse—each morning, the damp and cold seeped into furs and blankets a little further. Nita Qwan's joints ached and he was hungry as soon as he rose.

He looked at Ta-se-ho, who bent over, touching his toes—and cursing.

"I am too old for this," he said with a bitter smile. Then his eyes went out to the hard surface of the inland sea. "Pray to Tar that the ice holds," he added.

Nita Qwan watched the ice while he ate some strips of dried venison and drank a cup of hot water laced with maple sugar.

"Let's go," muttered Gas-a-ho.

Ta-se-ho stood smoking his small stone pipe. He smoked slowly and carefully and watched the lake and the sky, letting the younger men collect the last camp items and pack the toboggan and tying down the hide cover.

"Ready," Gas-a-ho said, sounding tired already.

Ta-se-ho nodded. He threw tobacco to all four compass points, and the other two men sang wordlessly. Nita Qwan went onto the ice carefully.

But the ice held all day. The clouds were high and solid grey, and snow fell for most of the morning, and then the wind came in great gusts towards evening. They camped in the spruce hedge along the shore, a cold, miserable camp made habitable only by Tapio's pot. There wasn't enough wood to make a fire big enough to warm a man. But the pot warmed them, and warmed their water and their venison, and they slept.

They woke to fog. It was deep and bleak, and very cold. Despite the freezing fog, Ta-se-ho led them out onto the ice and again they walked, and walked, heads bowed, backs bent against the strain of towing the toboggans at the ends, walking as swiftly as the snow and ice under their feet would allow them. The fog was thick and somehow malevolent.

Twice that day, the ice cracked audibly, and Nita Qwan flinched, but in both cases Ta-se-ho seemed to commune with it and then led them on. He was aiming for a distant bluff that towered above the lake, visible when the wind shifted the fog, then lost again as the fog came back and covered the sun.

The old man made the other two men uneasy by taking the shortest route, which was across the great north bay of the inland sea. They walked almost thirty miles, the hardest day so far. With the intermittent fog and the flat surface of the inland sea, the day took on a mythical tinge, as though they were travelling across one of the frozen hells that most of the Outwallers feared. The presence of the lake under their feet, the groaning of the ice, the odd sounds in the fog...

From time to time the old man would stop, and turn around. Once he stopped and smoked.

To Nita Qwan, the day seemed endless and the fear increased all day—fear of drowning, fear of being lost. When the fog covered them they had no path and no landmarks, and yet the old man kept walking, barely visible a few yards in front.

Ta-se-ho stopped for the fifth or sixth time.

"Is this a break?" asked Gas-a-ho. He began to drop his pack.

"Silence," Ta-se-ho said.

They were perfectly still.

The ice groaned, a long, low crunching sound that came from everywhere and nowhere in the frozen, fog-bound hell into which they'd stumbled.

"Something is hunting us," Ta-se-ho said suddenly.

Gas-a-ho nodded sharply. His face became slack, like a person walking in sleep.

Nita Qwan took his bow from its deer hide case, took his best string from inside his shirt. It had been drying there for two days, and it was warm.

Carefully, trying not to display his near-panic and the trembling of his hands, Nita Qwan strung his bow. He rubbed it a little before he bent it, and he listened as he pressed it down.

It didn't crack. Either the bow was not so very cold, or he had prepared it well.

The string bit into the grooves in the horn tips, and he was armed.

Only then did he give voice to his fears. "What is it?" he said, watching the fog around him.

Ta-se-ho shook his head. "It is only a feeling," he said.

Gas-a-ho surfaced from inside his mind. "Flying!" he barked.

His right hand shot up, and a flash of lightning left his hand. It was an angry orange white and it left a dazzle on Nita Qwan's eyes.

There was a detonation that made them all flinch, following Gas-a-ho's lightning bolt by about one beat of a scared man's heart.

Just over Nita Qwan's head, something *screeched*.

The old man thrust with his spear—the spear moved faster than sight could fully perceive, and then everything happened at once—Gas-a-ho was down in the snow, blood flowering around him, and there were black feathers in the air around them, and Nita Qwan found himself fitting a broad-headed arrow of irkish steel to his bow. He was conscious that he had already drawn and loosed twice.

"Move!" Ta-se-ho said.

Nita Qwan got Gas-a-ho onto his own toboggan. The younger man was bleeding from a terrible wound right across his back where a talon had sliced through his backpack straps and into the meat of his shoulders. But even as he got the man onto his toboggan and began to pull, the blood flow slowed and then stopped.

Nita Qwan tried not to look up. He got the tumpline and brow band of Gas-a-ho's ruined pack over the younger man and tied the neatly sliced ends to the thongs that ran the length of the body of the sled.

Ta-se-ho put himself in the straps of the now heavily overloaded tobog-gan. "I'll pull," he said. "You watch the sky."

Nita Qwan took up his bow.

The old man leaned into the straps and began to run.

Above them, something gave vent to avian rage—a long, slow scream that froze the blood.

"Trees," Ta-se-ho panted. "We need to reach the trees."

"How far?" Nita Qwan asked.

The old man put his head down and ran.

It is very difficult to run on snow and ice with a bow in your hand and snow shoes on your feet. Harder to do so and watch the sky above you.

The wind came again—a gust, then a sudden wall of wind, so hard that it seeemed to lift them and move them along the surface of the inland sea. It came from behind them, pushing them forward.

In a hundred heartbeats, the fog began to break for the third time that day. The sun was setting in the west—already, the day had a red tinge.

The tree line of the shore was only half a mile away.

The great bluff towered over the lake, a pinnacle of stone that rose many,

many times the height of a man. Up close, even in a state of fear, Nita Qwan could see that the whole pinnacle of stone was carved—or perhaps moulded. It was fantastically complicated, even from this distance a terrifying, massive evocation of fractal geometry.

But more immediate was the pair of black avian shapes wheeling in the air above and behind them. They were half a mile away, too.

The two men ran on.

The two predators banked and came on again.

Nita Qwan turned, saw their intention, and planted three shafts in the snow beside him.

He loosed his first shaft when the range was too long. His second shaft vanished into the air, and he had no way of judging his aim. His third shaft went into one of the great black monsters.

The fourth shaft...

At this range, he could see that the nearer creature had a great deal of trouble remaining airborne, and had Ta-se-ho's spear deep in its side and a long burn mark.

The farther creature had a beak full of teeth—an unnatural sight that chilled the blood. It projected a wave-front of fear that caused Nita Qwan to lose the ability to breathe. But he got his fourth arrow on his bow, raised the shaft...

He loosed, the toboggan pulled by the old man seemed to explode, and Ta-se-ho leaped like a salmon.

His shaft vanished, black against black, into the mess of feathers on the farther monster's breast.

Orange lightning played over it.

Ta-se-ho caught his spear-shaft. He was dragged—he was flying for a hundred paces.

The barbed spearhead ripped free of the great black bird even as it turned its teeth on the old man.

He fell.

Blood vomited on the snow—the bright orange bird blood fell like rain.

The great black thing fell onto the ice.

The ice cracked and broke.

Nita Qwan could spare the old man no more attention. The mate of the fallen creature turned for another pass.

Nita Qwan undid his sash, dropping his heavy wool capote in the snow. Then he took four more arrows from his bark quiver and pushed them into the snow.

"I can't hold the wind," Gas-a-ho said, as clearly as if they'd been having a conversation.

Nita Qwan registered that without understanding.

His adversary levelled out, wing-tips flexing up and down in the cross-breeze.

As fast as he could, Nita Qwan loosed all four arrows into the oncoming monster's path.

The second one scored into a wing, and the giant bird seemed to lose fine control over its flight. It screamed, and the third arrow struck its breast—it paused, and the fourth arrow missed.

It passed well to the north of them, low, over the land, and kept flying.

The ice was breaking behind them.

"Save him," Gas-a-ho said. "I will hold the ice."

With one last glance at the sky, Nita Qwan threw his bow down atop his friend and took a hemp rope from his toboggan. He ran across the groaning ice towards the black water and the orange blood like fish roe on the snow. The setting sun threw a red pall over the whole ice field.

Ta-se-ho was alive. He wasn't swimming or floating.

He was walking.

They were deep in the bay, but the black water was only a hand-span deep here, and the old man was slopping along, and cursing.

Again, they built the biggest fire that they could. By luck, or the will of the spirits and gods, Nita Qwan found a whole downed birch tree nearly free of snow. While the wounded Gas-a-ho and the old man curled around Tapio's pot, Nita Qwan broke and stacked birch as fast as his frozen fingers and exhausted, post-combat muscles would allow. He stamped the snow flat, laid old rotted logs on it, and built a fire.

Ta-se-ho nodded. "That fire will tell every living thing on the inner sea we are here."

Nita Qwan paused, his tinder box in hand.

Ta-se-ho shrugged. "I'm wet through and he's lost a lot of blood. We can die right here, in a couple of hours, or risk the fire." He shrugged.

But even frozen and afraid, they did not lack cunning. Nita Qwan's hastily chosen campsite was close to the base of the spire of worked rock, in what was virtually a chamber cut into the living rock, closed on three sides. It took him four tries to get his tow to burst into flame, but he did—and he got a beeswax candle lit in the still air, and then put the flame to a scrap of birchbark.

In minutes, he had his companions stretched out under the canopy of a whole tree fire, the heat over their heads too much for a man to bear. The only way to be near it was lying flat, and the stone walls around them reflected the heat.

Nita Qwan bent over Gas-a-ho, but the younger man managed a weak smile. "I'm patching," he said.

Ta-se-ho nodded. "Leave him, Nita Qwan. He's deep in his art. Now that he's warm, he'll have more spirit."

"Will the fire bring more foes?" Nita Qwan asked.

Ta-se-ho made a face. "We are at the base of the *Tu-ro-seh*. We will have strange dreams tonight."

Nita Qwan shifted—his back was actually against the carved monolith. The carving was both bold and minute, and went in long whorls with no symmetry up the sides—but the closer that he focused on it, the more he saw. His eyes began to follow—

"Do not look too closely," Ta-se-ho said.

"Who made it?" Nita Qwan asked.

"The *Odine*," replied the hunter.

Nita Qwan shook his head. "I am new to the People, Old Hunter," he said. "Who are the Odine?"

"Better ask, who were they?" Ta-se-ho said. He got out his pipe and began the lengthy process of filling and lighting it. There was silence punctuated by the exuberant sounds of birch burning. The smell was delicious—the very smell of warmth and comfort.

In the firelight, the shapes on the monolith seemed to move. The illusion was greater than it should have been. The surface of the stone appeared to have a million snakes crawling over it, and each snake to be covered with worms, and each worm with centipedes, and each centipede with some tiny creature—on and on.

"Do not look too much," Ta-se-ho said again. He leaned back, fumbled for a burning stick, and found, like thousands of men before him, that a large fire is the worst place to light a pipe.

Finally he found a burning twig.

"Do you know how the *People* came here?" he asked.

Nita Qwan knew the legends of his own people. "My people—in Ifriquy'a—say that the black seas were parted and our people were led across the dry sea bed to our new home."

Ta-se-ho nodded. "Too short to make a good story. But a good idea for a story." He busied himself inhaling smoke.

"The earliest legends of the Sossag people are about the Odine. The Goddess Tar brought us here to defeat them. And we did. We destroyed them all—every tentacle and every worm." He nodded. "The north is studded with their monuments and their tunnels." He leaned back and exhaled smoke. "This is the tallest. The old women say that there is a city under our feet. Many who seek wisdom come here for the dreams of the old ones." He nodded. "I did."

"What did you dream about?" Nita Qwan asked.

The old man smoked quietly. "Awful things," he said eventually. "Nothing from which to take a name, or follow a path." He shrugged, and lay down. "But most of the Wild fears these places. Only men are too stupid, or too ill-attuned to stay near them. So perhaps the Odine are not dead, but merely sleep." He grinned.

Nita Qwan took a deep breath. "You are mocking me," he said.

Ta-se-ho shrugged. "Everything in this world is terror," the old man said. "If you care to see it that way. We should have died on the ice. We're not dead. Let that victory steady you. You worry too much."

"We should have died," Nita Qwan agreed. "What saved us?"

The old man tamped his pipe, and his eyes glittered across the fire. "Gas-a-ho, first and most. Even when he had his shoulders ripped open, he was casting. He brought the wind and took away the fog."

Nita Qwan had guessed as much.

"And sheer luck. Or the will of the spirits, if you believe in such things." The old man took a deep drag on his pipe.

"Do you believe in such things?" Nita Qwan asked.

"I think we shape our own luck," the old man said. "With work. And practice. And care. A chance for life to a trained man is just another death to an untrained man—yes? Good shooting today."

Nita Qwan all but blushed. The old man never praised.

"You could have died. Jumping for the spear—the salmon's leap." The words spilled out of Nita Qwan. "It was magnificent!"

The old man allowed a slow smile to cross his face. "It was stupid," he said. "I should have died." He laughed. "But instead, I flew like a bird!" His high-pitched laugh went out into the night. "I nearly shit myself when my feet left the ground."

"Why'd you do it?" Nita Qwan asked.

"The spear. I love that spear." The old man shook his head. "An old woman made a prophecy about it once, and look, she was right. She said one day the spear would fly away without me and I'd have to catch it. I thought she was talking about something deep and symbolic." He shook his head. "Want some pipe?"

Nita Qwan's dreams that night were more terrifying than anything he had actually experienced, and his only explanation later was that he had dreamt that he was being digested in the belly of a whale or a snake—his skin slowly flayed away by slime.

He was stunned, on waking, to find himself whole.

He had to pack for the other two, but there was still wood and he built up the fire in the late night darkness until it crackled again. Then he made breakfast. Gas-a-ho was alive, breathing deeply, the wound on his shoulders knitted and dry. Ta-se-ho was snoring, and from time to time he seemed to be fighting something.

Despite days of fatigue, Nita Qwan felt no temptation at all to return to sleep. So, as the light grew outside, he packed the toboggans.

Finally he woke his friends. Gas-a-ho stunned him by getting to his feet.

Ta-se-ho groaned. "Tomorrow will be worse," he muttered. "Oh, to be young again."

As the first orange rays of the new sun lit the landscape around them they were headed inland through what seemed like an endless alder thicket. It took them an hour to go a mile. The spire towered behind them.

"When did the People destroy the Odine?" Nita Qwan asked, as they emerged from the alder belt into an open woods of beech and spruce.

Gas-a-ho turned. "Ten thousand winters ago," he said. The words passed, and echoed among the trees.

Nita Qwan almost stopped in shock. "That is a very large number."

Gas-a-ho shrugged. "These are the things that the shamans know," he said. "We defeated the Odine at the behest of the Lady Tar. And now we keep them under their stones."

"Did you have bad dreams?" Nita Qwan asked.

The snub-nosed youngster gave him an impish smile. "No. For the sha-man born, the places of the Odine are places of rest and power. That is why we are taken to them as children."

Nita Qwan shook his head. "Why did the People kill the Odine?" he asked.

Gas-a-ho looked at Ta-se-ho. "I don't know. Do you?"

The old man was sniffing the wind like a coyote. He turned. "Why does anything in the Wild kill anything else? Mating, food, territory." He shrugged. "The way of the world. This world, anyway."

Nita Qwan laughed. "You have just reduced all the glorious legends of every people in this world to mere greed. And conquest. Like animals," he said.

Ta-se-ho grunted. "Ask me when my joints ache less and I'll tell a better story," he said. "Now let's go."

Forty hours later they stumbled into their own village. It now had a tall palisade, big saplings driven deep into the earth and briars and raspberry brambles woven about them to make a barrier impassable by men or most animals. The palisade was tall enough to tower above the snow.

Nita Qwan had feared that the village would be abandoned—that everyone would be dead, frozen corpses in the snow, surrounded by blood kept fresh by the cold. He'd dreamed of it since leaving the tall Odine spire. But they were met by flesh-and-blood men and women.

Nita Qwan's wife embraced him, her tummy so round that he had trou-ble reaching past it to kiss her. Kissing in public was seldom seen among the People, and she—once the purest of vixens—was scandalized.

But he was still the ambassador. He left her to go to Blue Knife, the paramount matron, and her circle. Together they went into a long house that smelled of juniper and birch and fifty people who didn't wash enough. Good winter smells, for the Sossag.

"Tell us," Blue Knife said without preamble.

"We have an alliance with Mogon," Nita Qwan said.

All six women smiled in immediate relief.

Nita Qwan held up his hand for silence. Ta-se-ho pushed into the long house with Gas-a-ho at his heels.

"We did not go to Mogon's caves. Instead, we went to N'gara." He tried to look impassive.

Blue Knife nodded. "Please explain," she said carefully.

Nita Qwan nodded. "Ta-se-ho found evidence that Mogon was ahead of us—that the great duchess herself was en route to N'gara. We followed her there."

Blue Knife exchanged a glance with Amij'ha and Small Hands. "Tapio Haltija is an ancient enemy of the Sossag people," she said.

"Yet you included him in the names, when I was sent," Nita Qwan said.

"We did," Blue Knife conceded.

"We wintered in his hold. There we found healing, and allies." Nita Qwan reached into the quilled bag made of the whole skin of a badger that he had worn slung around his body for months. From it, he withdrew the pipe he had been sent to take to Mogon, Duchess of the Western Swamps.

"I took this pipe to Mogon. And she has accepted it. I took this pipe to Tapio, our foe, and he has also accepted it." He reached into the badger skin pouch again, and withdrew a belt. It was as wide as a man's head, and as long as a man's arms spread wide—thirty-three rows of wampum beads, each bead the size of a pea. It glimmered like pearl and mother of pearl in the soft light of the long house.

The matrons all sighed softly.

"Tapio and Mogon and the Jack of Jacks and a witch-boglin creature from the west have all made this belt with us," he said. "And so have the Bear people of the Eastern Adnacrags."

For each people as he named them, there was a diamond in glittering white wampum set in the darkness of the purple, which seemed black in the long house.

"If you take this belt, we will be six nations of free peoples against Thorn," he said. "Tapio charged me to say the name."

Blue Knife nodded. "And you have not said the name until now?"

He shook his head.

"So now Tapio knows the belt has reached us. And indeed, we have also said *his* name three times." She looked at Nita Qwan. "My son, you have done well—whatever comes to pass, you have performed the charge that was laid on you. I take the pipe from you." She reached out and took it.

He bowed.

"Ta-se-ho, what think you?" she asked.

The old hunter grunted and sat crosslegged. "I think it is cold and wet out there, and I am too old for it," he said. "And I think he has done well. All three of us did well to get here alive. I saw Rukh sign in the snow."

"The Crannog people are moving against us already," Blue Knife acknowledged. "But the Horned One and Black Heron's warriors led two of them to their deaths in the snow just four nights ago."

Ta-se-ho nodded. "Mogon said, come to me. I have more trees and fields than my warriors need or want, and we are far from the sorcerer."

Nita Qwan nodded. "Tapio said we should travel now, because none of the sorcerer's monsters love the early spring."

Blue Knife paled. "Nor do the Sossag people love the early spring. I teach my babies to stay inside and wait for the sun and the dry ground."

Ta-se-ho nodded. "There are many wisdoms. But if we leave tonight—"

Every woman's head came up.

"—we can travel at least two days on the ice," he said. "And when the ice breaks up..." He shrugged. "The Rukh will never find us, much less catch us. Let the sorcerer chase us if he wishes. If his hate for the Sossag is that strong..." He moved his hand. His hand implied that they were already doomed, if this thing was the case.

"Tonight?" Blue Knife asked.

Ta-se-ho spoke with authority. "Tonight, or never," he said. "My left knee says we will have three cold nights. And then the thaw. Does anyone deny this?"

Blue Knife shook her head. She turned to the other matrons. "It is now," she said. "Take only what can be taken." She turned back to the old man. "Children and old people will die."

Ta-se-ho nodded. "I know. But otherwise, the People will die."

When the other matrons were gone, Blue Knife leaned to Nita Qwan. "There is something you are not telling me," she said.

Nita Qwan nodded. He looked into the air above him for moths.

Blue Knife understood. She sent a young girl with stark red hair—a new captive, or an escaped slave—for the Horned One, and he came.

"We are to leave tonight? Across the ice?" he asked.

"You foresaw it," Blue Knife said.

"That doesn't mean it doesn't piss me off," the shaman said. He grinned like a false-face mask at Nita Qwan. "My wife says you've done brilliantly. My apprentice seems to be stronger than I've ever been. Perhaps I should go and spend a summer ramming all the Dulwar girls at N'gara."

Blue Knife smiled. "I'm sure your wife will say yes if you put it that way," she said. "Nita Qwan is hesitant to tell me something. He looks for moths."

The shaman nodded. He pulled out a little drum and began to beat it a-rhythmically. Then he began to sing—tunelessly.

Even then, Nita Qwan bent over and whispered into Blue Knife's ear like a lover.

Three times he whispered. Each time she asked him a question. Finally, she sat back.

"He asks much, our people's most ancient enemy." She looked into the long house fire.

"But it is right at many levels," Nita Qwan said. "And now—tell me what of my brother, Ota Qwan?"

She met his eye. "He is dead."

Nita Qwan blinked. "The sorcerer killed him?"

She shook her head. "He calls himself Kevin Orley now. He has taken many towns in the south and east. He has sent us his command—that we give him men and food."

Nita Qwan sighed. He sighed for Ota Qwan—so many men in one skin. The name Kevin Orley meant nothing to him, but he thought that he understood. Ota Qwan had been lost to the sorcerer—as the matrons had intended.

"So," Nita Qwan said. "We must provide men. How many warriors?"

"Kevin Orley demanded one hundred from the eight towns of the People," Blue Knife said. "He demanded *you*."

Nita Qwan set his face. "It is as Tapio said," he admitted.

Blue Knife nodded. "So—we will send our best young men to the sorcerer while we run, naked, to the west. This could be a plan for Tapio to have his revenge on us."

Nita Qwan shrugged. "I speak with caution, as I am young and new to the Sossag people. But Tapio has no need of revenge, as my understanding is that he defeated us soundly and drove us from our homes. And much time has passed since then. And the Lady Mogon guarantees our survival."

"Yes," Blue Knife said. "Yes, I agree that all these things are likely. And yet—and yet, younger brother, what I would not give, right now, to have the hardest decision of my summer be the choice of day to pluck the corn." She sighed. "Go and pack. Be careful. Your wife will deliver in the snow if she is unlucky."

"I fear I have burned too much luck in the last week," Nita Qwan said. "You will send me with the warriors to the sorcerer?" he asked.

"When we reach the carrying place where the Great River flows into the inland sea—then I will send you away. You will lead the warriors who go. You will tell Kevin Orley of the terrible winter we have had, and the whole villages we lost to the Rukh." She smiled grimly. "I am sorry, Nita Qwan. But we will work hard to save your son's life."

His son—the matrons thought he would have a son!

And they would work hard to preserve the boy—

—because his father would be dead.

He rose. "I understand," he said.

"I'm sorry," Blue Knife said. "My only goal is to preserve the People."

Seven hours later, as the sun set in a spray of red fire in the west, the whole of the Sossag people, all six surviving villages, almost two thousand men and women and children, headed west into the setting sun. They had sledges and toboggans and a few had big travois, and they moved in a cha-otic way that belied great discipline, each family leaving a few minutes apart from the next, all taking slightly different routes out to the inner sea—some families travelled a whole day inland, and some went straight downstream to the ice.

The People fled. As they fled, they formed not a column but a wave front, because like animals migrating, they took courses that meant that despite any disaster they could imagine—the Rukh, a sudden thaw, the end of the ice—some of them would survive.

They moved as quickly as they could. And every warrior on every route but one stopped and cracked any ice sheet he could after he'd crossed it.

Ta-se-ho stood in what had been the town's central space with Nita Qwan and Gas-a-ho. They were the last to depart—Small Hands and her family were already well along to the west.

"Now you have power," Ta-se-ho said.

"Not for long," Nita Qwan said.

Gas-a-ho snorted.

Ta-se-ho shrugged. "You have it. The People have given it to you and you wear it well." He turned his face away. "Babies and old people will die."

Nita Qwan nodded. "I know."

Ta-se-ho grunted and lit his pipe. They passed it back and forth for a long time.

"Never forget," Ta-se-ho said. "And you will never become Kevin Orley." He put his pipe away. "I'm too old for this."

And then the three men began to walk west.

Ticondaga—Ghause Muriens

Ghause wriggled into her shift, her haunches cold from working naked in her casting chamber exposed to the chilly mountain air. Outside, snow was drifted six feet high or more against the fortress's impregnable walls and filled its ditches.

Her husband watched her. He was fully dressed, sitting comfortably in a low armchair that folded for easy stowage. Most of the castle's furniture was one form of camp furniture or another. The Muriens were a military family.

"I thank God on my knees every day," the Earl of Westwall said, "that my wife had the sense to sell her soul to Satan for beauty. Christ crucified, woman. How do you keep yourself so?"

"Flattery will get you everywhere," she said, but she didn't purr or wiggle her hips. It was too damned cold. "Do you know that when I rode south to Albinkirk, there were *flowers*?"

The earl shrugged. "It was one hell of a winter, and I use the term hell advisedly. Cold as a witch's tits."

He moved so fast, and he was so quiet, that despite the straight line, she was surprised to feel his warm hands on her breasts.

But the surprise was a pleasant one. She turned and raised her mouth to his, slid a hand down into his braes with the expertise that comes of knowing another person's body as intimately as you know your own.

Not that the earl's body was particularly challenging...

She made him work for her pleasure and then returned the favour—an hour that left her pleasantly tired and filled with unworked *potentia*. She drank hot wine and stared out into the first blue sky she'd seen in many weeks.

"Penny for your thoughts?" murmured her husband, his hand running over her stomach.

"Stop that," she said. "Be gentle or be firm."

He hated it when she told him how to touch her—had hated it for thirty years. He swung his bare feet off her bed and cursed the cold floor.

"I'm thinking of the King," she said pensively.

"Your brother," he said.

She shrugged. "Do you have any news?"

"Beyond that he's gone mad, let the fucking Galles into his court and attacked his own nobles?" The earl shook his head. "Galles in the south and this sorcerer as a neighbour. How bad is this summer going to be, wife?"

She stretched. "Bad," she said.

"This sorcerer..." he began.

She shook her head slightly.

"You think he'll come for us," the earl said. He was getting into his braes.

"I do. And Gabriel does."

"That milksop. I don't care what you claim he's done—he's hiding behind Gavin. He could no more lead an army than fight with a poleaxe."

She smiled. "You are seldom a fool, husband. But in this—I saw him fight with a poleaxe."

"Huh," he muttered. "He's late to it, then," the earl said.

She shrugged.

"Anyway, what does *he* know of the summer?"

Ghause sank back onto the goose feather bed. "I told you. All of them wanted him to be captain of the north."

The earl shook his head in ill-tempered wonder. "In place of me. In my God-damned place."

"Sweet, it is a *compliment* to have your firstborn appointed to a high command." She rolled to face him. Many fifty-year-old women might have hesitated to discuss high politics while naked. Ghause was not one of them. "Don't be a child."

He laughed. "Me? You want him as your captain because he'll do your bidding. But when the Wild comes over the border, I'll not be following the orders of your effeminate son."

She smiled. "Mine. Not yours?"

The earl shook his head. "My seed, perhaps, but none of my blood, I swear. That one is all eldritch potions and cobwebs."

"*Parthenogenesis*," she said quietly.

"What's that?" he asked.

"An Archaic word for a maiden making a child all by herself," Ghause said. "What do you think my brother is doing with his Queen?"

"Christ only knows," the earl said. He had his shirt on and his hose, and was buckling his garters. He didn't have access to her sorcerous arts and he was five years older than she, but he still carried himself like a king, had solid muscles front and back, and when he buckled the garters below his knees, his calves were as good as any young gallant's. "I had a messenger bird from a friend in Harndon who says he's going to try her for adultery."

Just for a moment, despite all her plans and all her vows and her desire for revenge, she felt for the Queen in Harndon. She felt something like kinship with her.

Not that her feeling of kinship would keep her from killing the Queen and her unborn child. Merely that she knew what he was, and that he was now, in a more elaborate way, doing to his young Queen what he had once done to his sister.

"Weak fool," she said. "Weak, stupid, vicious and indecisive."

The earl nodded. "But a damned fine jouster," he said. "You hate him. You always have." He narrowed his eyes for a moment. "We could have him killed."

Ghause leapt from the bed and kissed him. "Sometimes, I actually love you. But no. By all the dark powers, husband—do you know what would happen if he were to die now?"

The earl shrugged. "War? Chaos? Nothing to us. In fact, it would be a better environment to build our own kingdom. If Gabriel is to be trusted." His tone suggested that he was unlikely to trust the younger man with anything.

She frowned.

"Just because it doesn't fit with your fiendish plots doesn't mean that we can't use it," he said. "Listen, my lady. All our lives together, we've gone hand in hand—and kept our own secrets. I am content with that. In this instance, he's a fool, and he's threatening me with war. If he were dead—"

"The Galles would take his place. They'd use the girl-Queen as their pawn, and suddenly we'd be crawling with them." She pulled a heavy wool-velvet robe over her naked body and rang for more wine.

"The Galles, my spies tell me, have troubles of their own," he said. "Let's just kill him."

Ghause grew annoyed. "No," she said.

"Because you have some plot already in motion," her husband said.

"Yes!" she spat.

He laughed. "And all I get to do is fight the fucking sorcerer," he said.

She shrugged. "Not even that, I fear," she said. "His sorcery is too much for your army. And now he has an army of his own. Bide. Hold the castle and he will have other problems. He's made two great enemies, and his time is running out fast."

The earl sighed. "Woman, I am no more your tool than you are mine. 'Bide' is not a companionable word. Spring is coming—"

"And so is the sorcerer," she said. "He is coming, and we will need all our strength to hold here until our son comes."

The earl pursed his lips, rubbed his chin with the back of his hand. "Ah. Like that, eh? So we'll have the fight here?"

She smiled delicately.

"Christ, woman, I'm your husband and your partner in a hundred crimes. You might tell me what you have planned!"

She leaned over, her eyes fixed on his. She leaned closer and closer, and then her pointed tongue flicked out like a cat's and licked his lips.

"I might," she whispered. "But that would spoil the surprise."

Later, while forty knights pounded the pells in the courtyard and while the foot soldiers did their spear drill, she watched the Queen in a ball of rock crystal that was, to her certain knowledge, more than three thousand years old—perhaps as many as fifteen thousand. Some things were beyond her range of skills or belief. She suspected that it had been made by something truly alien, because when her concentration slipped, she could hear its makers haunting, a-rhythmic songs. And see them slipping like wraiths of slime through the caverns beneath the earth.

But she was many times the mistress of the stone, and she drove it south and east until she had the Queen, deep in her dungeon under the earth.

She missed her youngest son, Aneas. Without him she had no one with whom to discuss her plots. He was still near Albinkirk, serving with the field army. A knight on errantry. She'd watched him in the stone—fighting, flirting with a girl. The girl and her mother both looked familiar. She was pretty—

Ghause put a hand over the stone, and moved it and her will.

She watched the woman, whose hair was lank and whose lips moved constantly. Ghause watched her for a long time, trying to decide whether the woman had lost her wits or was acting. It was hard to know.

If her brother was going to kill his own wife, there was no need for Ghause to use the massive working on which she had laboured for eight months. The young Queen's hermetical defences were formidable—doubly so, as she had clearly been trained by Harmodius. Ghause knew that to kill her unborn baby, she would have to strike massively and accurately and all at once. There would be no second chance.

But it would be delicious if, instead, he killed her himself. Deluded by evil gossip into believing his wife untrue—what a fool.

She smiled at the purity of her revenge. And how it dovetailed into her other plans.

After all, what had the prophecy said?

"*The son of the King will rule all the spheres.*" She smiled, and her heart raced with anticipation. She would turn his actions against him, rob him of a legitimate son and make her own sacrifice worth . . . everything.

But she still felt something for his Queen. When she had been green and beautiful, she had felt nothing but jealousy and malice for her—but now, watching her hang her head and mumble, seeing her soiled kirtle and the weight of oppression and betrayal on her young shoulders . . .

"I'm sorry for your baby," Ghause said aloud. "But I'll avenge you, too."

Babies reminded her of how they were made, and she moved the stone's view—moved it back and forth over the fields, adding first one guiding spell and then another.

She saw things that surprised her. She saw the Queen's brother riding across the fields of the Albin. She thought it odd that he should be *north* of Harndon.

She followed her guiding spell north, and further north, and found her target. She glanced at her sons—Gavin was a handsome devil, and Gabriel looked like an archangel on a binge. She smiled.

And moved on to the nun. Sister Amicia.

Ghause had planted suggestions on the nun since the first time they'd met. She approved of the woman—liked her good sense and the width of her hips and her sense of humour. Gabriel needed a noble wife to bear him a son—to be, in time, Queen.

The little nun was not that woman.

But she would be the right ally, and the right mistress. And the right tool of control.

And she had power—deep, strong, well-trained power that grew and evolved almost before her eyes.

"You remind me of me," she said aloud. And knowing that link between them, she made a very subtle working—the sort of working, in fact, that she might cast on herself. She had done it once before, to render the distasteful more acceptable.

And now she passed her working carefully through the stone. She watched it strike home on its intended victim the way an archer watched a shaft shot high and far.

She smiled.

*

A hundred leagues north and west of Ticondaga, Thorn stood in his place of power, watching Ghause in the space between his raised hands. He was not wearing his human form, but a new stone form—a carefully evolved form of discs and whorls and stone coils that were laced together with cartilage and muscle taken from many sources. Thorn had all the bestiary of the earth at his disposal, now. He used it with brilliance and imagination and a certain dark elegance.

His new level of understanding the shifts of being that could be contained in his concept of reality—to put it loosely—included the knowledge that he could build into his power a subordinate working of enormous complexity that would continuously monitor and alter his form as circumstance required, even as he moved and shifted and had different requirements. So he could make his form of stone, and make the stone move. While this required a constant expenditure of *ops*, it also rendered him nearly invulnerable.

He had another form—he was already working on generations of them—in which he was almost entirely energy and smoke. But it was still too vulnerable to use except in special circumstances.

None of this crossed his conscious mind. Instead, he held his stone arms aloft effortlessly and watched Ghause practise her art. He watched her watch the Queen with growing frustration, having watched her prepare her spell for a hundred days and nights.

He had prepared his own working. Indeed, all his own plans now hinged on hers, an ironic twist that delighted him and annoyed his mentor immensely.

That, too, was good. Thorn was tiring of being Ash's tool. He had probed the black space in his head thoroughly. He had spent considerable time rebuilding what he felt might be missing of his own thoughts and perceptions. He made some slight experiments in hiding things from the black space.

He had re-discovered how much he detested moths. And he had *doubts*.

Irony was not something that the master sorcerer could share either with his tools or his allies. An inconvenient impasse had been reached.

Thorn's ally had gathered his army of unwilling slaves and his professional soldiers and the thin trickle of reinforcements he had received from Galle and moved them to the head of the lake above Ticondaga. Thorn's own servants—Kevin Orley not least among them—had joined the Black Knight's army.

Thorn took himself to them, his preparations complete. He crossed seventy leagues of virgin wilderness in the blink of an eye. He had learned to make the Wyrm's way—to make a hole in his reality, and to travel through it.

He had learned so many things that sometimes he feared that at the moment of truth, he would not be able to find all his powers and employ them.

Nonetheless, he appeared in the camp of the Gallish army on the day he had planned.

If Ser Hartmut was appalled to have a giant stone golem of interlocking helixes appear in front of his great black silk tent, he gave no sign. Instead, he nodded to a squire. "Wine," he said. "And a long spoon."

Thorn might once have laughed, but almost all of the human had been burned out of him, leaving little beyond ambition and a thirst for knowledge. "I am here," he said. His voice was deep, menacing, and alien, and his accent sounded curiously like the northern Huran.

Ser Hartmut nodded. "Then we can march on Ticondaga. It is only a matter of time before the earl's patrols find us."

Thorn did not move a pebble. "He will not find you."

Ser Hartmut looked around. He motioned for De La Marche to join them. He took wine from his squire, and waved the boy away. "Find Ser Kevin," he said.

Thorn might once have chuckled. "Ser Kevin."

Ser Hartmut did smile. "I took the liberty of knighting him," he said. "And providing him with some of the items of harness you had neglected to provide."

Thorn considered a variety of responses, and Ser Hartmut's desire to manipulate the Orley heir was transparent. But as he was finding more and more often, he didn't care enough to make a response.

Ser Hartmut didn't pretend to have a command council any more than Thorn himself. Having summoned the leaders, he now shrugged. "When do we march?" he asked.

"When I say," Thorn answered.

"I have reconnoitered Ticondaga twice," Ser Hartmut said. "Even with trebuchets and all the power of your *ops*, it will be a hard nut to crack. It will take all summer, unless I miss my guess." His outthrust jaw suggested an uneasiness that Ser Hartmut seldom displayed.

He fears the reports he hears from Galle, Thorn thought. *Well he might. But his power and his soldiers and his talent will all be here, serving me.* Irony piled on irony. Thorn had begun to see deeply into Ash's intricate plotting, and he had begun to be able to detect the malice—the deadly humour—of his vast mind.

Thorn thought that malice and humour might be his master's very weakness, too. But he tried never to let such a thought lie outermost in the many layers of his own thoughts, and when he could not help but think such, he whirled it away into a labyrinth of deceptive analysis.

"No," Thorn said over the multi-voiced conflict of his own divided mind. "No. The siege will not be that long."

Ser Hartmut bowed cordially to Kevin Orley, who bent his knee in return like a Galle. Thorn frowned inwardly to see his creature subservient to a mere man.

Ser Hartmut shook his head very slightly. He was in full harness, the rich black of his armour shining with oil and careful maintenance. Kevin Orley was his complement, in a plain harness of unmatched, very plain steel which had been carefully oiled.

Orley stood differently. Thorn watched him carefully. Time passed differently for a hermetical master than for a mere ephemeral, yet Thorn thought perhaps Kevin Orley had experienced more than he.

"You have learned something new," he said.

Orley met his eye. "I am beginning to learn discipline," he said.

Ser Hartmut permitted himself a smile.

"As a captain?" Thorn asked.

"I can only discipline others if I have discipline myself," Orley said.

"And you are a knight now," Thorn said.

"I have that honour," Kevin Orley said, his voice even.

"I was not asked," Thorn said.

Ser Hartmut frowned. "It is traditional, when launching a great endeavour, to make knights." He didn't move or touch his face or wriggle or blink like lesser men. Thorn found him fascinating—a man who had voluntarily expunged so much of his humanity, yet had no access to Power. An enigma. With a magical sword of incredible power.

Thorn turned his body, the stones protesting as his unconscious hermetical working powered the stone into shape after shape, a smooth transition in many dimensions. "And you, De La Marche?" he asked. "Are you now a knight?"

De La Marche had begun life as a sailor, and risen to command. He was a merchant, a ship-owner, and a trusted servant of his king. But not a knight.

The merchant-adventurer looked away.

"De La Marche has declined the honour of knighthood at my hand. He holds himself unworthy," Ser Hartmut said. Ser Hartmut's feelings were naked for a second, and Thorn could see the man's rage.

Even Thorn, at the apogee of his power and very close indeed to his goal, felt something closely akin to relief to see that Ser Hartmut was human enough to be enraged. And that De La Marche's refusal had hurt him.

Thorn would have expected De La Marche's refusal to cost the man everything—his life, reputation, honour, family. Ser Hartmut did not seem like the type to take a small revenge. But this sort of petty interaction was beneath Thorn now. He understood the great Powers better every day. As they evolved and developed, they lacked the time—or the *potentia*—to delve into petty matters. Great power required intense absorption. It left little time for revenge.

Petty revenge, anyway.

"Tell me when we will march," Ser Hartmut said again.

"In two days, we will have the whole of our strength," Thorn said. "Perhaps the Sossag will send their hundreds, or perhaps they will not. Either way, two days or perhaps three will see the last of our human soldiers. But I have other allies and other slaves—aye, and other avenues of attack."

"And other enemies," Ser Hartmut said.

Thorn swivelled back to face the Black Knight. "Other enemies?" he asked.

"The bears," Ser Hartmut said. "I am told by Ser Kevin that the bears will stand against you."

Thorn would have shrugged. "We will have twenty thousand boglins," he said. "And ten thousand men. And hundreds of other creatures." His black stone eyes swept over them. "We will crush the bears if they are foolish enough to fall under our claws. Otherwise, we will ignore them and take their vassalage later."

"You avoid the question," Ser Hartmut said.

Eventually, I will have to dispose of you. You, and Orley and the rest. All so greedy. Perhaps I should make De La Marche my ally.

"In two days, we will march. We will collect our allies from the north as we move—they will catch us up." Thorn nodded. "I will cover us in a cloud of unknowing, and we will move as close to Ticondaga as my powers will allow."

"And when will we strike?" Ser Hartmut insisted. "We're one day from Easter."

De La Marche spoke for the first time. "The ice isn't off the lakes yet, and the woods are still full of snow." He did not look fully at Thorn. "None of our men wish to march in this." His voice all but begged. "Let the men celebrate Easter in peace."

Ser Hartmut laughed. "I did not learn to win wars by doing what is easy."

"Men will die in those woods," De La Marche said.

Ser Hartmut shrugged. "None of them are any consequence to you or me or Master Thorn," he said.

"We don't have enough *raquettes* for all the sailors and the men-at-arms," De La Marche said.

Ser Hartmut nodded. "Only the scouts will need them," he said.

De La Marche looked at Thorn for a fraction of a heartbeat. "Our wizard will melt us a road?"

Ser Hartmut shook his head. "No," he said. "Our Huran captives— those ones who will not submit—will walk ahead of us." He waved one iron-clad hand. "They will tramp the snow flat. And cut the trees and make a road, all the way down the western shore of the lake."

De La Marche took in a great breath. "And where will they camp?" he asked. "With our men?"

Ser Hartmut shook his head. "Camp? They will work until they die.

And then we will send more ahead of us." He waved his hand. "They are not Christians. Not subjects of my King. They're not even really people. Let them die."

De La Marche sighed. "You will walk three thousand women and children to death to build a road for your army?" he asked.

Ser Hartmut nodded. "They defied me," he said. "Now they will pay. This is absolutely within the Rule of War."

De La Marche looked back and forth between Ser Hartmut and Thorn. "Of the two of you, I doubt that I can tell which is the worse," he said. "I will go and walk the snow with the poor savages you send to their deaths. I cannot live and watch you do this to them."

Ser Hartmut shook his head. "Do not, please, be a sentimental fool."

"I am a man," De La Marche said. His tone said what his words did not.

Even Thorn felt a tiny pinprick of anger in reponse. "We act on a stage so vast that you cannot perceive it," Thorn said. "Already my forces are south of Albinkirk, pinning our foes in place. A few Outwallers more or less—"

De La Marche nodded. "I thank God I do not *perceive* what you can," he said. He turned rudely and walked away.

Ser Hartmut turned to his squire. "Take him. Beat him unconscious and have him bound. Do not let his sailors see you do it." His squire walked away into the snow, and Ser Hartmut turned to Thorn. "He has become a fool. But if I allow this idiot martyrdom, his sailors will be wasted. They will not fight well, and they are my best troops, in a siege."

Thorn was weary of the whole matter and all the petty inversions that went with human interaction. "Two days," he said.

Ser Hartmut nodded. "Two days."

Ser John Crayford awoke in a strange place. It took him a long moment to identify where he was. The ceiling was white, and had a spider web of cracks around a marvellous old beam that had been carved in whorls like a hundred intertwined dragon's tails. His eye followed the whorls and the cracks.

There were two narrow windows with archery shutters—thick oak shutters that let in very little light. Each was pierced with a cross, so that either a longbow or a crossbow could be used on attackers.

As he looked at the windows, he knew where he was. Close by his right arm lay Helewise, naked. She was not asleep.

"Did I snore?" he asked.

She laughed. "Only when you were asleep," she answered.

"You were going to send me away when we finished." Ser John smiled.

She smiled back. "I'm an old woman," she said. "And yet I'm not sure that I am finished, even yet." She leaned over and threw a leg over his, and they kissed—the warmth, the foul to fair kiss of morning, a night shared.

Instantly aroused, Ser John laughed in his throat. "And last night you put out the candle," he said.

"Not every man is full aroused by sagging breasts and widening thighs," she whispered.

"Why are women so cruel to themselves?" he asked.

"Why, we learn it all from our lovers," she said. But she took the strength of his arousal as compliment enough.

They played the music again, as they had played the night before, although Ser John was more conscious of the noise the bed frame made this time—so conscious that he began to flag, and then to move softly. But he suited her so well that at last she made a sound somewhere between the contentment of a cat and the cough of a leopard—a surprising, unladylike sound.

And then she laughed.

"Imagine, a prisoner of the pleasures of lust at my age!" she said.

"Will you confess it to the little nun?" he asked.

"Would that embarrass you, bold knight?" she asked in return. She put a hand on his chest—and pushed. "Do you think any woman in this house doubts where you spent the night? There's no hiding anything in a house of twenty women."

Ser John looked abashed. "I thought—"

Helewise rose. She threw back a shutter. "Wilst marry me, Ser John?" she asked.

Ser John, looking at her in the stream of sunlight, thought he had never seen anyone so beautiful. "I would be most pleased to marry you, lass," he said.

"And all your other wives?" Helewise asked. Under the banter, he could hear a more sober note.

"Nay—I have no other lovers," he said. "Mayhap ten years gone, there was a head on my pillow some nights."

"Ten years?" she asked. She had a robe on now. "No wonder you find me beautiful."

She stepped out from behind her screen. "I mean it, John. I'm no light o' love and I have a daughter who'll know by evensong what her mother did this night. Plight your troth—or don't come into my bed again." She flung her hair and gave him an odd look. "My daughter is flirting with your Red Knight's youngest brother—you know that? If I play the fool with you..."

Ser John sat up. He shook his head. "I might say that I didn't push you here, my lady."

"Nor you did. I am a lustful mortal, as God made me." Helewise stretched. "But I'll not make a slut of my daughter through misjudgment."

Ser John rose, naked and more grey than brown, and kissed her. "Hush, lady. I don't need threats or admonitions." Naked, he knelt at her feet. "I beg you to marry me and be my love."

She smiled. "Oh, John." She bent to kiss him. Her robe fell open to the last button and her earthy smell hit him.

"Mercy," he said. "I'm an old man. I might die."

"The old plough runs the deepest furrow," she whispered.

"You made that up," he growled back.

Later, dressed and armed, he met his escort—knights and squires of far-off Jarsay—in the yard. The younger women of the manor all seemed busy with laundry—busy in a way that required their presence in the yard. He smiled beneficently as one does when all is right with the world, and he noticed with some amusement that many of the younger men in armour would not meet his eye.

His squire, Jamie the Hoek, had his great horse saddled and everything prepared just the way he liked it. From a gawky adolescent who knew little or arms and nothing of horses, Jamie had grown into a tall man of gentle manners who was welcome wherever he went—and was the best squire a knight could ever want. He was quiet, he worked very hard, and he had learned every skill of management, maintenance, repair and replacement that a squire might ever need to know. He could sew. He could even do a little embroidery. He could take the dent out of a helmet.

He could kill a boglin while covering his master's side.

He bowed. "Ser Captain, we understand congratulations are in order."

Ser John bowed back. "Gentles, you have the right of it. Lady Helewise and I will be wed at midsummer."

Now all the young men met his eye, and his hand was shaken, and he thought, *What a nice lot of boys these are. We were a rougher crowd in my day.* He'd taken a few days to warm to Ser Aneas—a cold young man—but the boy's infatuation for Heloise's daughter Philippa was—charming.

The youngest Muriens received a stirrup cup from his lady love.

"I think it's horrible," she said. "My mother—at her age!"

Aneas Muriens had a different kind of mother. "I think it—splendid," he said.

Philippa gazed at him a moment. "You do?" she asked.

They looked at each other so long that other knights chuckled, and Ser John had to clear his throat.

Long before the sun reached the apex of her travels across the sky, Ser John led his company out of the restored gates of the manor and past the new stone barn that the master masons were just completing. It had been warm enough for foundations to be dug, and new stone barns were rising across the whole of the area west and south of Albinkirk to replace the wooden barns burned the year before.

They rode north through the countryside, passed over two streams in roaring full spate by means of careful scouting and a willingness to get very wet. A dozen huntsmen—all professionals—rode well ahead, and they paused to look at every track on the road, or rather, the mud slide that passed at this time of year as a road.

Early afternoon. Birds sang, and the spring flowers were in full bloom, and Ser John, who had in truth missed a great deal of sleep the night before, began to feel its lack. He turned to say something about a nap to Jamie, when he saw one of the huntsmen coming along the verge of the road where the ground was harder. The man had his rouncy moving at a trot—when the ground was hard, he cantered.

Ser John had faced the Wild on too many patrols. "Gauntlets and helmets!" he called. "Lace up!"

Most of the southerners had learned to ride with their steel gauntlets on their hands, but very few men liked to ride about wearing their helmets.

The squires and pages handed out lances—fifteen-foot spears tipped in hard steel.

"Let's go!" Ser John said, fatigue temporarily forgotten. He led the column along the edge of the road, single file—an invitation to ambush except that he'd seen his own scouts work the apple orchard on the other side of the lane's wall.

He met the huntsman at the corner of the old wall.

"Boglins," the huntsman panted.

"Where away?" Ser John asked. "In broad daylight?"

The huntsman shrugged. "Saw 'em mysel'," he said. "Away over past the Granges."

Ser John looked under his hand.

"Big band—fifty or more. Running flat out—you know, so their wing-cases stand up."

"On me!" Ser John roared. He turned in the saddle and caught Lord Wimarc. "Take the squires and sweep the hillside," he said. "All the way down to the creek past the Grange. You know the ground?"

Lord Wimarc nodded. Since the death of his knight, he had withdrawn on himself, and his eyes were sunken and he had dark smudges under his eyes, but he was alert enough. "Aye, Captain," he said.

"If you catch them, dismount and hold them. Don't let them get at your horses." Ser John waved to the other squires. "Jamie, stay with me. The rest of you—follow Lord Wimarc."

As he turned his horse on the muddy ground, the scent of new grass and mud gave him a flash of Helewise, above him, her breast...

He flushed and focused on the reality of a warm day and a tired horse.

Off to his left he saw Lord Wimarc stand in his stirrups. The man's lance tip moved.

There was something on the hillside.

An explosion, like lightning—a ball of lightning...

Then the crack of a distant whip and one of the squires and his horse were a butcher's nightmare in an ugly instant.

"Blessed Saint George," muttered the knight behind him.

Ser John balanced on a sword's edge of indecision—he didn't know what he was going into, but he knew as sure as he was a sinful man that halting to figure it out would cost him men and horses.

He thought about his lady love, and laughed aloud as the thought stiffened his spine as if he was fifteen years old and had just seen breasts for the first time.

"Forward," he roared.

His ten lances, shorn of their squires, rode single file around the corner of the tall stone wall and the whole of the hillside came into view—a patchwork of green and brown fields stretching away for more than a mile, and a thick fringe of trees at the top of the next ridge, like hair on top of a balding man's head.

As soon as he took in the terrain, he knew that the enemy was beyond his own forces.

Almost at his feet, a mere bowshot away, was a pack of the new imps. Ser John had never seen them, but one of the Red Knight's squires—Adrian Goldsmith—had a talent for drawing, and had rendered the lithe creatures, like greyhounds from hell, in livid detail. All the company men said they were as fast as anything in the Wild, and that they went for horses.

Even as he watched, the dread creatures turned like a flock of birds and started across a newly turned field towards him. At his back were ten knights, ten archers and ten pages.

The field was muddy, the earth heavy with melted snow and spring rain, black and shiny.

There was a narrow ditch by the verge of the road. Behind them was the high stone wall of some farmer's apple orchard. It was too high for a mounted man to get over.

He gave the order before he knew what he'd committed to.

"Dismount!" he called, pulling up. "Horses to the rear—all the way back to the last farmyard, Rory!" he called to the oldest page, who was as white as a sheet.

He slid out of his saddle as the imps came on at the speed of an arrow from a heavy bow.

Even as his feet touched the ground and he seized his fighting hammer from his saddle bow, he wondered if he had made a poor decision. If they would be in among his horses before—

"On me!" he called. "On me! Archers in the second rank!"

It was all glacially slow.

But God was merciful. The imps—even the horrifying imps—were slowed in all that mud.

They seemed to flow over the field, though, and there were more of them—and more still flowing out of the far hedgerow.

"Let us ha' three arrows in front o' ye," said the archer at his back.

Rory had just taken Iskander's reins and was taking him to the rear, the war horse rolling his eyes and looking for something to kill. Ser John gave him a parting slap on the rump and stepped back.

"Three shafts!" roared the master archer—one of the company men.

The imps were a hundred yards away. They covered the earth like a pale green carpet of teeth and sinew. There had to be five hundred of them.

"Loose!" called the company man.

"Loose!" he said again.

"Loose!" he said again.

Three arrows in as many breaths. The imps were still far distant.

"Keep shooting," Ser John said. "Rory—get to the farmyard and send for help."

Rory, now mounted on Iskander, saluted.

Send someone to bury us.

Behind the wave of imps was a group of boglins, all pushing through and under the hedgerow. His tactic had worked beautifully—they had cut the enemy off.

He wanted to choke the huntsman. This wasn't a raiding force, but a small army. The sparkle of magic on the far hillside told him that the enemy had a sorcerer of some sort, too.

The company archers were a blur of speed, their arrows leaving their bows as fast as their arms could move, their grunts rhythmic and almost obscene, like the rhythm of the old bed the night before.

"Loose!" grunted the old bastard in front of him.

"Loose!" he said again.

"Exchange ranks!" Ser John roared.

The archers dived for the rear, putting a wall of flesh and steel between them and the imps.

"Over the wall!" called the old man.

Most of the archers had no harness beyond elbows and knees and basci-nets. The imps would flay them alive.

An incredible number of the imps were already down. Worse, the ones pinned to the ground by the heavy shafts were dragging themselves towards the fight.

Ser John set his weight without conscious thought, pole-hammer across his thighs, in the bastard guard.

The imps had to leap the ditch to reach them.

He killed two or three before one knocked him flat by momentum. But they were small and his faceplate and aventail kept him safe in the pan-icked seconds he was flat on his back. He drove his dagger into one—where had that come from?—got to his knees, and punched another with his steel fist. Something had his ankle, but that ankle was fully encased in steel.

He drew his sword, stabbed down into the thing on his ankle, cut roundhouse to clear a space.

An arrow clanged off his helmet. In the fall, his head had moved inside the padding and his vision was imperfect. He swung again, re-set his feet and got a hand up to push his helmet back on his head. There were two of them on his legs and one going for his balls, which had no armour. He shortened his grip, one hand on the hilt, one on the middle of the blade, and stabbed down, and down, and down, backing as he did, until he cut the creatures off his legs and killed them with blows to their spines.

The archers were now sitting atop the apple orchard wall, shooting light arrows straight down into the fight and killing many. Their arrows decimated the imps, but the dog-like reptiles still came on over their dead, like carrion crows on a corpse.

Ser John knew he had men down. There was too much room to swing his sword.

He cut—left, right, controlled swings into guards to clear the ground around him, but the monsters were not like human opponents who would give ground. They merely came on. The result of his swings was the three of them got under his guard, one hanging from his left wrist. He dropped the sword, broke the back of the one on his armoured wrist and then kicked his steel feet clear of them, thanking God for his sabatons.

His back grated on the stone wall. He had nowhere left to retreat to. A sword clicked into his right arm harness, and an imp fell away dead. He saw the familiar green and gold of the Muriens arms.

His dagger was dangling from the chain at his wrist and he got it back, buried it in an imp that was trying to bite him.

The arrows sliced down in front of him like a protective curtain. Out in the fields across the valley there was suddenly a light show—gold and green and purple and black.

A horn sounded. It was not a human sound. The horn blew over and over like a human hunting horn, but its tone was deep and booming and had the knell of doom to it.

Ser John got on with the business of killing. He pushed off the wall, accepted the price of friendly arrows slamming into his helmet, and he used his long dagger like a two-handed pick, his strikes accurate, his movements increasingly spare as he found the right way to fight the imps, using his armoured ankles and feet as a lure to draw them into the range of the dagger's bite, defending his groin carefully.

One of the Morean knights—Ser Giannis—had a spear with a long blade, and he was untouched in the centre of a whirl of death, his weapon passing back and forth, back and forth, stabbing and cutting. Farther along, one of the company knights, Ser Dagon la Forêt, used a poleaxe with equal artistry. Ser Aneas fought with a weapon in each hand, like a dancing master, except that he seemed to clear more space than most. One of the Jarsay knights was down and messily dead, and another had a dozen of the things on him like limpets because he wasn't wearing proper maille.

Ser John went and cleared the imps off him like a father getting leeches off a child. The imps were thinning.

Behind them were boglins. Despite eight knights and a dozen archers, the boglins kept coming. Ser John was so full of combat spirit, fear and elation at being alive that he didn't understand what was happening. He took a moment after the last imp was killed—Ser Dagon stepped on its head—to retrieve his pole-hammer.

Sixty boglins were no match for eight knights. But they still came on.

"Shoot them!" Ser John panted.

"No more arrows, Cap'n," said a voice above his head. "Sorry, boss."

Indeed, the whole area of the fight with the imps was like a field of stubble, except that the stubble was heavy war arrows shot almost straight down and standing in clumps where the fighting had been fiercest. A dozen men had loosed more than four hundred arrows in three minutes. Their entire load—almost forty a man.

The boglins were wallowing through the mud. Behind them, something bigger broke through the hedgerow. There was a flash of green fire, an explosion of mud, and a hole as long as a horse opened. Boglins poured through—as did daemons.

Ser John shook his helmeted head and tasted the sour air inside his bascinet. "Fuck," he said.

The boglins were so hampered by the mud that they'd have all been killed by the archers—had there been any arrows.

"Fuck it," the older man said and dropped over the wall. He began to pluck arrows from the ground—in a moment all the archers were there.

"Never get up the fuckin' wall again, mark my words," muttered the older archer.

The shorter Morean knight had a bottle of wine, of all things. He handed it to Ser John, who had a pull and then gave it to the old archer.

"Now that's right decent o' you, Ser John." He took a drink and handed it on.

He had a dozen muddy arrows in his belt.

The boglins were seventy yards away and looked exhausted, their wing cases half open and their vestigial wings hanging loose.

The archers began climbing back up the wall. Only one man could make it—their arms were tired—and he had to rig a rope.

The older archer loosed his dozen arrows into the boglins as they plodded on through the mud. So did the other archers as they waited their turn to climb.

The boglins lay down. Behind them, the mass of creatures—boglins and daemons—did not come forward. They began to move west, sliding along the hedgerow. At the burning hole, something big, like a cave troll, only darker, emerged. But its entire attention was focused down the hill, or across the valley.

Only then did Ser John understand.

"There's someone else behind them, harrying them!" he shouted. "Saint George and Alba! Christ and all his saints, lads! Ser Ricar must be behind them!"

Indeed, only now did he hear the roar—the waterfall-like rush of sound of combat. Ser John reckoned that the whole of the far hedgerow must be engulfed in fighting. He looked left and right.

The enemy force below him in the muddy field was now all moving west, many of the creatures crouching low to the ground. They were leaving a trail of stolen objects behind—a quilt, a blanket, shoes, a girl's doll and an apple basket. Somewhere they had struck a human settlement and left nothing but death behind, and now...

The shapeless black thing in the hedgerow gap whirled and cast. Ser John saw it—saw the casting—and then he was flat on his back again.

But he was mostly unharmed. He got up heavily, head throbbing and his neck feeling as if it would never be right again. The sigil he wore on his chest—the gift of Prior Wishart of the Order—burned as if heated on a stove. But he was alive.

He thought that the creatures—stripped of their imps—were near panic. But the hammer-like charge of his knights would slow to nothing in the same mud that had mired the imps.

He looked up. "What's your name, Master Archer?" he called.

"Wilful Murder. Sir." The man shrugged, as if acknowledging that it wasn't a typical name.

"Can you hit them from here?" he asked.

Wilful Murder grunted. As if against his better judgment, he jumped down from the wall—again.

"Long shot," he said. He drew to his ear, his right leg sinking as if under great weight, his whole body rocking as his heavy back muscles engaged. He loosed high, his body bent forward into the bow.

His arrow fell into the mob at the base of the field like a thunderbolt.

Heads turned.

"If you can reach out and touch yon then do!" Wilful called. "Otherwise, stay the fuck up on the wall."

Three men jumped down. They looked scared. A fourth man looked down the field for some heartbeats, shrugged, and dropped off the wall in turn. He began to prowl the ground for arrows.

"I need a lighter shaft," he said as he pushed past Ser John.

The handful of arrows had no obvious effect. The archers had to make too much effort to loose fast—each shaft took long seconds to pull and aim, and all of them flexed their right arms between pulls.

Then the heavy arrows were plunging, one every few heartbeats, into the mass of boglins at the base of the field.

Ser Giannis came over and opened his faceplate. "I have never faced this—this..." His face did an odd thing.

"The Wild," Ser John said as kindly as he could.

"Yes," Ser Giannis said. "Yes. But I think..."

Ser John was trying to get a sense of what was going on beyond the next hedge.

"I think that if the archers kill enough of them, the rest will charge us. Yes?" Ser Giannis pointed his elegant, ichor-caked spear down the field.

Ser Aneas laughed mirthlessly. "Many things my master-at-arms told me make sense now," he said.

A long bowshot away, one of Wilful Murder's arrows struck a daemon in the head, plummeting almost straight down. It went into the skull and struck the great creature to the mud, full length, like a blow from an angel.

The growling, roaring, crashing sound was closer.

The great horn spoke again—three long blasts.

"What the hell is that?" asked Ser Dagon.

A flash of metal in the gap in the hedge. Flash, flash.

Three long, deep blasts from the huge horn.

Again, there was an explosion of purple-red light, this time at the corner of the field. Fire licked at the hedgerow.

Three green balls of fire materialized in the air at half-heartbeat intervals and struck.

There was an explosion—another—then another. Like spring trees full of sap and struck by lightning, each sharp crack deafened the men at the top of the hill and blew new rings of blood and bone into the sunny sky.

Ser John found he was down on one knee, his ears ringing despite a fully enclosed helmet and heavy wool-stuffed helmet liner. There was a dazzle of spots in front of his eyes.

There were a lot of dead boglins at the base of the field. Even as he watched, the arm of a daemon, torn from its body, fell back to the earth.

The black thing now moved as if it was four legged and not two legged. It vanished through a new gap in the hedge.

Another flash of steel, and Ser John was fairly sure he was looking at Lord Wimarc, dismounted, about three hundred yards away. The boy had superb armour and something, even at that range, suggested him and his slim, upright posture.

Not for the last time, Ser John watched, wondering what in hell was happening.

"I think we're out of the fight," Ser Dagon muttered.

Ser John got back to his feet. His lower back burned with fatigue and he was soaked through with sweat—and cold.

"Master Archer!" he called.

"Which I'm right here, your honour," Wilful Murder muttered. "And not deaf, neither."

"Send an archer for the pages and the horses," Ser John said, unaware that he was shouting.

Jamie the Hoek coughed. "I'll go, Ser John," he said. "My horse is just around the wall—if Rory left it where he said he would."

"If the imps didn't get him," spat one of the knights. Ser Blaise was dead—and partly eaten. The young Jarsay knight, Ser Guy, had six wounds, all where the imps had gotten into his groin and armpits. He was fading fast.

The poor boy was weeping with pain. His arms were barely attached to his body. His legs—his entire lower torso was ruined. Shock could not do enough to protect him from what had happened to his body.

Ser John knelt by him and put a hand on his cheek.

The boy screamed. Something in him had changed, or the full realization of his fate had come to him, and his weeping sobs gave way to bitter screams.

Three hundred yards of mud away, Lord Wimarc waved. And began to trudge, not towards them but along the edge of the hedgerow. He was clearly following the defeated warband of enemy raiders.

"He's clean mad," muttered Ser Dagon, who was doing his best to ignore the young knight dying horribly at his feet.

The other squires began to appear—Tomas Craik and his brother Alan and all the rest of them, trudging wearily in good harness.

"Achilles and Hector together couldn't ha' driven all they off that land," said Ser Dagon.

The boy was shouting his screams now.

"I think our squires have the most honour in this fight," Ser John agreed. He wished he could get up. He wished the boy would die. He wished that there was something—anything—he could do.

He made himself pray, which was hard with the accusations of the boy's screams so close to his head.

There was another roar—the horn sounded again, one long wind, and suddenly the air was full of *ops*. Workings flew past, balls of fire of various colours flying back and forth.

"Christ and his phalanx of angels," muttered Ser Giannis.

"Haaaaarrrrhhhhh!" screamed the mass of pain and fear that had once been a knight of Jarsay.

Ser John picked him up, intending to crush him in an embrace. But Wilful Murder was there first. He leaned down as if tying his shoe and casually drew his ballock dagger across the young knight's throat.

"Go fast, boy," he said.

Ser John let the boy's blood flow down the front of his breastplate. He met the archer's eyes, and the man shrugged.

"Someone had to," Wilful Murder said.

And then Rory was back with the war horses.

Ser John looked around, wondering if he looked as tired and haggard as Ser Giannis or Ser Dagon did.

"I'm of a mind to find out what happened, and mayhap play a role before the sun sets," Ser John said. "But every man here has earned the right to say he has done enough."

The other seven knights looked at him—covered in their comrade's blood—and shook their heads.

"Let's go kill them," said Ser Dagon.

The road ran parallel to the fight for another half mile. Below them, as the spring sun began to set, they could see shapes moving across the cleared ground. Some of the hedged fields were quite small and Ser John didn't know the area well enough to guess which lane would get him a view of the fight—if any.

But as the sun's rays turned from gold to red, one of the huntsmen galloped up and pointed his crossbow south across the fields. "Past the farm gate," he said, and they rode. An hour of picking their way along the road and stopping frequently to watch or listen had allowed all the archers to catch them up, mounted on their smaller horses. The pages brought up the rear.

Ser John was the first through the gate. It was a fine farm with a good stone house like Helewise's, only smaller, and it had been spared by the last incursion of the Wild. Draper or Skinner—he knew the folk here.

Old Man Skinner stepped out of his door, a heavy arbalest cocked in his hand. "There's boglins in my lower orchard," he said. "I've been potting 'em for an hour. Took you lot long enough—Christ on the cross, you look rough, Ser John!" he said in sudden wonder. "Just my mouth a flappin'. I mean no harm. Water your horses—I'll get water in the trough."

And indeed, the horses needed water and a rest from men on their backs, and Goodwife Skinner, a big heavy woman with beautiful eyes and a no-nonsense face doled out sweet buns and tart cider. Men drank it without removing their blood-soaked gauntlets or gloves. Ser John looked about him, and they were all blue-red-black with ichor and blood and mud.

The horn—that horn would haunt his dreams—sounded very close.

"Get inside and bar your doors," Ser John snapped, pushing Goodwife Skinner into her kitchen door.

"An' don't we wish we could come in wi' you?" muttered Wilful Murder.

"To horse!" Ser John shouted.

His great war horse—the best he'd ever owned—seemed to give a human groan as he mounted. He trotted the horse past the barnyard and the farmer met him there at the corner, his heavy weapon spanned and ready. The farmer ran to the next gate and paused, looked around carefully and then opened the gate. He stepped through.

Ser John rode right by him. He wasn't sure why he did it, except perhaps the sense that it was his job to protect the farmer, not the farmer's job to protect him.

He felt the enemy through his horse before ever he saw them. They were in the *next* field, near the base of the valley. They'd come miles north and west, now—Lissen Carak would be only a dozen more miles that way. The edge of the woods was only a mile or two to the north, if that. That's where the raiders were headed.

Ser John went through the gate, past the farmer, and then trotted up the muddy field. He could see his enemy through the next gate.

The closed field in which he was riding was unploughed, or his horse would have sunk to the fetlocks. But there were only two gates—the one he'd passed through, and the one ahead.

He rode up to the gate. A gout of black fire struck it just as he reached it and it blew clean off its hinges and collapsed.

The four-footed black thing was loping towards him over an unploughed hayfield. Ser John didn't think. He just slammed down his visor and touched his spurs to Iskander, who responded with all the noble heart any knight could ask from a horse, exploding forward despite the soft, treacherous ground.

The huge black creature—it was almost amorphous, it moved so fast—reared up.

It *was* a troll.

It cast.

The sigil on his chest felt as if it was melting and running over his skin, and he shrieked, but he and his horse rode through a cloud of black-blue fire and he dropped his lance point a hand's breadth—

His lance caught it in the centre of the head. Even a ten-foot-high stone statue would be damaged by a war horse and rider powering a heavy lance. His strike was so sure, so exact, that his lance tip caught on its brow ridge and bent—and broke.

But the black troll went crashing down.

Ser John never had to give his horse a lead—he was turning as soon as it felt his weight change. He was naked, his back to his enemy—he saw a dozen daemons, streaked with mud and blood, running at him and, behind them, boglins and behind them, at the far edge of the field...

A flash of bright gold in the last of the sun.

He shook his head and drew his sword, prepared to sell his life dearly.

The great black stone troll was sitting, legs splayed, like a ten-foot child who had hurt itself.

It shook its head—paused, shook again...

Ser John smiled grimly. Iskander couldn't manage more than a stiff trot, but he powered by, put a fore-hoof into the troll with the ringing sound of iron-shod hooves on stone and then Ser John's war hammer fell with all the power of his shoulders on the thing's fractured head.

Instead of dying, it reached out, almost casually, and slammed Ser John out of the saddle, breaking his left arm and dropping him behind his horse. Ser John had time to see that his left vambrace was crushed.

He lay in the mud and waited to die. He couldn't raise his head.

Over his head, sorcery flew. He caught a piece of something and was showered in mud, then a wave of incredible heat passed over and he tried not to breathe.

Heavy arrows began to fall. He saw two come down, but he had trouble moving his head—some muscles in his back were damaged, or perhaps he was gutted and dying. It was hard to tell. There was no pain, even from his arm, so he knew that he had no way to tell.

And then, silence. He could hear very little inside his helmet. But he could feel the ground move as something big came up the field. His uninjured right hand went for his dagger.

It was heading for him.

Deep in Ser John's throat was a whimper, and he knew if he let that whimper out, it would be the way he died. So instead, he tried to see Helewise—see her wonderful naked body, see the cheerfulness of her, the fullness—

Helewise's breasts were a better thought with which to die than brother Christ, whatever the priests said.

The thing was coming. The ground shook.

He couldn't do it. His eyes opened.

Over him was a great furry creature covered in mud. It looked like a giant rat, but in a flicker of thought he knew it for a very dirty Golden Bear.

He exhaled.

The bear leaned over him. "You—again?" it asked, its voice deep and raspy and majestic.

Ser John thought he might laugh forever. "We've got to stop meeting like this," he said.

The day was not yet over, but it had ended for Ser John. The pages and archers had to fight off a pair of bargests that came—too late to turn the tide of the rout—out of the setting sun. They caught the pages on horseback and killed two, but their interest in feeding on the horses gave the archers time to drive them off.

Ser John lay in the roots of a great tree, his back against its old bole. They were just at the edge of the woods.

The old bear was as tall as the troll, and just as heavy. He wore a great bag dense with red and black porcupine quillwork, and had an axe—a heavy soldier's axe—from far-off Etrusca.

He sat—very like a man—back curved in fatigue, legs splayed. A very cautious Jamie the Hoek brought the bear water.

"I am called Flint," the old bear said.

Around them, in amongst the old maples at the edge of night, moved two dozen other bears. Even covered in mud—and they were caked in the stuff—they gave off the occasional gleam of gold.

Ser John extended his good hand. "I'm Ser John Crayford," he said. "The Captain of Albinkirk."

"You are the lord of the stinking houses," the bear said.

Ser John swallowed his pain. "I suppose. And you?"

"I lead the Crooked Tree clan," Flint said. "I have for fifty summers."

"You saved us," Ser John said.

"More than you know!" Flint nodded. "But in the winter, you and the Light that Shines came to the deep woods and saved *me*. And many of my people." He looked away—again, a very human head movement, but Ser John could not read the thing's face. "That was an army—going to raid all the way around your stinking houses."

Ser John bit his lip. When he could master the pain, he said, "Yes."

"The sorcerer is marching on Ticondaga with all his force," the old bear said. "We have refused to submit. But most of my people hate men—all men—more than they hate the sorcerer. Or at least as much."

Another bear came and squatted by the old bear. Ser John had the sense that the second bear was much younger—lithe, almost thin from winter.

"We awoke to find his spies in our dens. He had massacred a clan, merely to show that he could." Flint seemed to be talking to himself.

"How can I help?" Ser John asked.

The old bear looked at him, its muzzle weaving side to side. "Let us pass west," he said. "We have friends to the west."

"The Abbess?" asked the wounded knight.

"Is the Light that Shines not one of her mates?" asked the old bear.

Ser John groaned with a desire to laugh that conflicted with his obviously broken rib. Or ribs.

"The Abbess is a nun. Nuns are women who do not take mates." Ser John took a careful breath.

"Yes—some bears are the same, loving only their own, she-bear with she-bear," Flint said.

Ser John nodded. "Yes—but no. They take no mate at all."

"I have heard of this," said the old bear. "But assumed it was just one of those rumours of hate that young people concoct. You mean some humans choose not to mate at all? What do they do in spring? Hibernate?"

Ser John took another careful breath. "You speak the tongue of the west very well, for a bear."

"Some of us meet with men," the bear admitted. "At N'Pana, or even Ticondaga." The bear growled. "We do not work with fire, but a steel axe is a fearsome thing indeed."

"Then—if there is trade, you must know something about us?" the man asked.

The bear growled. "More than I'd like. Can you give us passage west? On the road, and safe from your people?"

Ser John sank back onto the bole. "Where are you going?" he asked. "Will you tell me what you know of the sorcerer?"

The bear got up on all fours. "I will tell you much. How badly hurt are you? Your outer shell is unbroken."

"I am hurt," Ser John admitted.

Jamie the Hoek came back out of the near darkness. "I thought you might like this," he said, handing the bear a pot.

The bear sat, much like a stuffed bear in a toy shop, legs again splayed. It put the pot between its paws and pulled off the top.

"Wild honey?" it said in a tone of pure greed.

Jamie, the perfect squire, smiled, and his teeth shone in the dark. "I thought you'd like that," he said again.

The bear lifted a sticky snout from an empty pot a little later, and growled.

Ser John was losing his ability to remain awake, but he tried to be courteous. "Lord Wimarc can escort you," he said. "We have an army on the road to Lissen Carak. Lord Wimarc will see you get safe passage. You may want to go through the woods though…"

The bear licked its obvious teeth and nodded at Jamie the Hoek. "I may have to change my opinion of men," it said.

Liviapolis—Morgon Mortirmir

Morgon Mortirmir had moved up in the world—far enough to be trusted with real research.

Unfortunately, he'd only exchanged one set of irritable magisters for another.

Still, life *was* better. He stroked his fashionable short beard, thinking of Tancreda Comnena, who still sometimes called him "plague."

Who was no longer planning to become a nun. They had an understanding, although her side of the understanding seemed mostly to have an unlimited licence to tease him.

Then he realized with annoyance that he was rubbing his short, pointed beard with the ink-stained fingers of his writing hand.

"Son of a bitch," he swore. He was tempted to drama—to hurl something—but his left hand was resting on a recently recovered thousand-year-old manuscript from somewhere east of Rhum and his right hand held an artifactualy-charged ivory pen, and he could spare neither.

He compromised by swearing. He was getting better at swearing. As long as he didn't blaspheme, the Master Grammarian, who still directed his studies, turned a blind eye.

He looked at the manuscript again. It was very old—probably far older than it appeared. On the surface, it was yet another re-hash of Aristotle. An astute Etruscan collector had noted some capitals—carefully illuminated—in an older hand, and had taken a magnifying glass to it.

It had been scraped clean somewhere in the east, a thousand years ago. Long before the Wild's hordes had swept across the Holy Land and destroyed every sign of man—back when Demetriopolis and Alexandria Fryggia were thriving cities and not horrifying necropoli where only the not-dead and the boldest or most desperate adventurer or scriptorium-collector dared go.

Morgon was determined that someday, when his powers were fully developed, he would assay Demetriopolis and Ptolemaica himself. The library had once been the world's greatest. The *Suda*, a collection of what appeared to be librarian's notes on the collection, even claimed to have had manuscripts—scrolls—from other spheres. *Other spheres!* His thoughts went off into a whirlwind of supposition, creation and destruction like an intellectual ouroboros.

But the reality of the manuscript under his elbow drew him back. Hidden under the ancient Aristotle was something far more wonderful. It was, in fact, an Archaic essay on farming. Embedded in it were six workings, none of which had been deciphered by the Grammarian. He'd handed the whole amazing relic to Morgon with the words "You're a genius—see if you can do anything with this."

Morgon had spent every hour of the last forty on one passage three paragraphs long.

He had every word of the Archaic deciphered.

He had all the traditional grammatical parts of a working—the opening, which was sometimes an invocation and sometimes an enhancement of memory; the *orologicum*, a modern term for the process by which any one working accessed the power available from *ops* and *potentia*; and the trigger, which had a variety of elegant names in Low Archaic and usually a single High Archaic word.

He had that.

He knew the purpose of the working, as well. Flavius Silva's Low Archaic was not on order with some of the other recently rediscovered ancients, but his words were easy enough to read, and Morgon had gone a step further by asking Tancreda to translate the whole passage, as she was a far better linguist than he.

"For the remedy of bad water for stock. Being that too often the farmer must use what water there is, whether that water be cool, flowing, and clean, or whether the farmer face a long summer and dry, and needeth to have his animals take even that which is green and full of filth."

Morgon could see it well enough.

And the trigger was *Purgo*.

So—a single word, usually very powerful. The underlying working was very complex. Complex, with a simple trigger—very powerful.

Yesterday, far more awake, Morgon had worked it, with Tancreda standing by (and her brother, too—Morean noblewomen did not spend time alone with male students for any reason) on a glass of hideous, dirty water, green with some sort of an algae bloom that was particulate in nature.

He mastered the working, powered it, and felt the *ops* inhabit the working and give it life.

And then—nothing. The water in the glass remained a lurid green, like an advertisement for the enmity of the Wild to the works of man.

He cast it three times, the third with Tancreda's brother, an apprentice of the first year, barely able to summon a candle flame, measuring the working's energy before and after *ops*.

Stefanos shrugged. "You cast a great deal of *ops*," he said.

Morgon had shaken his head.

Now, a day later, and so tired that he could barely write out his notes, he had an idea. The idea was foolish, but Tancreda told him he was a fool all the time.

She was close behind him, insisting that he stop and take a meal.

He shook his head. "In a moment," he said. He lifted the lurid glass of slime—and drank it.

Tancreda tried to dash it to the floor. "Oh, by the risen Christ, you will turn into something damned. At the least, you will never kiss me with that mouth again. Oh, my God. Stefanos, fetch a doctor—no, the Grammarian."

As if summoned, the Master Grammarian appeared at the door. "What has happened?" he demanded.

Mortirmir shrugged. *Were his guts churning? Did he imagine that?*

"He drank the water," Stefanos said. "Sir," he added a little too late.

"Water?" the Master Grammarian asked, but he was not a master magister for nothing, and he picked up the clawed-foot glass and examined it. "Algae—a form of plant—did you know that?"

"I thought it might be an animiculus," Mortirmir said.

"Why did you drink it?" demanded the Grammarian.

"I learned the working. It is supposed to purify water. Power goes in—quite a lot of power. But the water does not appear to change." Mortirmir shrugged.

"You can purify water by boiling it," the Grammarian noted.

Morgon stopped looking at his hands and *thought*. He looked at the Grammarian. "In which case, the water is purified, but the solids—mud, particulate matter, animaliculae—remain."

The Grammarian nodded. "Yes."

"And so with this working, but there is no warmth. I drank the water to ascertain the effect—whether it was, in fact, purified." He shook his head. "It certainly tastes like raw bile."

The Grammarian nodded. "Sensible, in an insane, over-tired way. Have me summoned if you fall sick." He walked out through the door.

Tancreda shook her head. "You will be sicker than all the sick dogs," she began.

Mortirmir shivered. But the process was on him—he ignored the lovely Despoina Comnena to pick up the magnifying glass he had used on the manuscript. Instead, he looked at the algae in the glass. Magnified, it was even more horrible.

But his idea bore no fruit. He looked and looked, but there were no malevolent darting shapes living in the weed—or the corpses thereof, which might have justified the expenditure of *ops*.

He was two hours into the creation of an enhancement working to create a lens of air when he realized that he knew nothing of lenses.

Tancreda rolled her eyes. "I will go to the library again," she said. "Why not just ask a glass grinder?"

Morgon slapped his knee. "Brilliant!" he said, and was out the door with neither purse nor cloak.

In the emptiness of his absence, Tancreda turned to her noble brother. "You see why I love him," she said.

He shrugged. "No. He's quite mad." He looked out into the street, where Morgon was running—long legs stretching as if in a sprint in the hippodrome.

Tancreda pulled on a cloak, found her talisman for the library, and pulled on a hood and a mask. "No. He doesn't always communicate well, but he's not mad."

"Why the sudden fascination with lenses? We were reading Old Archaic, and then—zip! That's all done." Stefanos laughed. "Like a small child."

"He can be hard to follow," Tancreda admitted. "But if I read him aright, he decided that the working does function, and that it is killing or removing or perhaps summoning something very small indeed. And now he needs to create the means to observe and prove his theory. Hence the lens."

Stefanos looked at her a moment. "You understood that from what—his grunting?"

Tancreda shrugged. "Give me twenty ducats. Yes—and the way his hand moved on the passage, and the way he picked up the glass. Yes."

"You're as mad as he," her brother said. "And don't imagine I don't know you've kissed him, you wanton."

The last was said with less venom than might be imagined.

"I still know where you keep your little Ifriquy'an," Tancreda said with equanimity. "So we'll have no holier than thou here."

"You can't marry him," her brother said. It was more a question than an answer. In fact, he whined it.

"I can, and I will," Tancreda said. "You'll see."

Stefanos had been seeing his sister get her way on all things since he was born. He didn't doubt her.

"Family dinners…" he moaned.

But the door slammed, and she was gone, leaving the young man alone with a fabulously ancient manuscript, a cat, and a glass of algae.

He patted the cat.

Two hundred leagues further west, an old man made a solitary camp where the mighty Cohocton met with the Dodock coming from the hills to the south. He moved stiffly, unpacking his mule and laying things out, then carefully feeding his fine riding horse and big mule. By the time the two animals were fed and calm, it was dark, and his fire of birch and dry maple was the only light—or warmth—for many miles.

He warmed his hands for a while and then fried some bacon in a small iron skillet with a folding handle.

The horse began to be restless.

The old man finished the bacon. Then he raised his head and looked into the darkness as if he could see into it.

After a while, he went to the bags that the patient mule had carried all day, opened one, and took out a bottle of red wine. It was an incongruous thing in such a rough camp—the old man had no tent, no bed, and no cups.

After a moment he produced a pair of horn cups.

He went back to his fire and built it up. He produced a folding brass candlestick—cunningly wrought—put a beeswax candle into it and lit it with a snap of his fingers.

A puff of wind blew it out.

He relit it. When he turned his back, it went out again.

He growled. Walking carefully in the darkness, he went over to the downed birch tree—the reason he'd chosen this site to camp—and stripped a long curl of bark.

He went back to his candle stick and made a wind shade from the bark, and then relit the candle with another snap of his fingers.

Then he sat on his rolled cloak and ate his bacon.

When he was done, he looked around carefully—again—and then took his small iron skillet down to the brook and washed it with sand and small pebbles. The horse snorted.

The old man went back to his fire, threw on a pair of small birch logs, and settled comfortably into a tree's roots to rest. He looked at the stars, and at the moon high above him.

He couldn't help but smile.

Carefully, he took a small pipe out of his purse, took tobacco from his hunting bag, and packed his pipe.

"A new vice," he said, the first words he'd said in days. "Well, well."

He was a handsome man, and not so very old, at that. He had heavy dark brows and salt and pepper hair tied back in a rough queue with deer hide thong. He wore a fine red caftan of wool lined in silk, and under that a good linen shirt, and he had Alban-style braes and hose and wore leather boots that would have reached his thighs if he had not rolled them down to his knees.

A long sword rested against the tree by his head.

He packed the pipe carefully, and then lit it from a coal at the outer edge of the fire. Sucked the smoke into his lungs and coughed.

Blew a tentative smoke ring.

"Come and have a cup of wine," he called suddenly.

Or maybe I'm just going mad, he thought.

There was a rustle by the stream. The babble of the brook covered many sounds but didn't cover them all.

His new body had wonderful hearing compared to his old body. And was particularly good at waking up without stiffness.

"Isss it good wine, I wonder?" asked a voice from beyond the fire.

"It is," the man said. He waved to the cups. "Would you pour?" He put the long-stemmed pipe to his lips and drew, then gradually blew the smoke out. It billowed in the light of the fire, seeming to flow and spread like water.

When a breeze blew it away, there was a man—or rather, a human-like figure—standing by the fire. He was dressed all in red; red hose, red pourpoint, laced in red and tipped in gold.

By the stream, a dozen faeries hovered, burning in their incandescent wonder.

The old man—not so old—drew in more smoke. "Good evening," he said.

"A merry meeting, and you a mossst pleasssant tressspassser," the figure said. "But the wine isss good."

"I am sorry for my tresspass," said the man with the pipe. He waved it. "I have done little damage except burn some downed wood. I have not hunted."

The other man tinkled slightly as he moved—his clothes had tiny golden bells attached, and when they rang, the faeries laughed. "You might be consssidered a good guessst in better timesss," the figure said. The firelight revealed the inhuman perfection of his face—he was an irk.

"Do I have the honour of addressing the Faery Knight?" asked the man.

"You do! The sssmell of your wine drew me asss sssurely asss an incantation and the calling of my true name!" The irk laughed.

"I don't know your true name, and I wouldn't say it aloud if I did," said the human. "But I was once told that you liked good wine. And Etruscan reds must be a trifle thin on the ground out here."

The irk laughed—and drank. "It isss very good. Perhapsss I will let you live—even let you hunt. The caribou will move in a few weeksss. I could sssspare a half million or ssso of them."

The man's eyes moved. "Caribou," he said aloud.

The Faery Knight nodded. "Ssso many all move at onssse that no forssse of man or the Wild can crosss their path. Millionsss and millionsss, all trekking north." He shrugged. "Almossst I could put a name on you. Who told you I liked wine?"

"The King of Alba," the man said.

"Ah. I pity him. A weak man and yet so ssstrong." The irk shrugged. "I liked hisss father better, but they come and go ssso ssswiftly."

The human was sucking on the foul smoke at the bottom of the pipe. He tapped it out on his boot sole.

"You do not fear me," said the irk.

"Should I?" asked the man.

"Do you want sssomething? The wine isss very good." He held out the horn cup. "May I have more?"

"Take the bottle if you like," said the man. "Though in truth, I'd be cheered by a cup myself. Will you go to war with Thorn?"

The irk did not betray startlement—but he did move. "I do not disss-cusss ssuch thingsss with chansse met ssstrangersss." Suddenly the irk was covered in a bubble of fire.

The man shook his head. "Truly, I mean no harm. Indeed, I've come to offer my fealty." He nodded. "For a time."

The red-clad irk let down his shield, poured wine into both cups and held one out to the man. "The lassst time I sssat with a man in thessse woodsss, Thorn attacked me." He frowned. "I did not come off bessst."

The man took a cup of wine from the irk's outstretched hand. "We must see to it that doesn't happen again," he said. "But Thorn is not the real enemy. Thorn is only another victim."

"You have sssaid hisss name often enough to invite him to your fire," the Faery Knight said.

The human nodded. "He will not come. He will not even attempt to contest my passage. In fact, he can neither see me, nor hear me, even when I say his name."

The irk nodded and knocked back his wine. "Then I know who you are. I congratulate you on being alive."

The man smiled. "It is rather delightful."

The Faery Knight laughed—all the færies laughed by the stream. "Per-hapsss that isss how we will pick up the sssidesss for this fight," he said. "Not good againssst evil, but merely thossse who find thisss world a delight againssst thossse who find it a burden. Thorn feelsss the world isss dark and grim."

"God knows he does his best to make it so. Very human of him," said the man.

"In the woodsss, it isss sssaid that you are on the dark path," the Faery Knight said.

The human shrugged. "The road to hell is paved with good intentions," he said. "Perhaps I'm on it. But I have a goal, and an enemy. I will fight until the fight is over, or I am beaten."

"Ssso," the irk said. He poured more wine. "You know the truth."

"I know a truth," said the man who had once been Harmodius.

They touched their cups.

"I will ask no vasssalage of one ssso puisssant asss you," said the irk. "We will be alliesss."

Harmodius touched the rim of his cup to the other. "Well met by fire-light, my lord. We will be...alliesss."

Bill Redmede was preparing for war. He and his Jacks—those who had survived the long march—had to make many things themselves that they'd always bought or stolen. Arrows first and foremost, but also clothes and quivers. Hard leather purses were replaced with softer Outwaller bags and wool hose with leather stockings of carefully tanned deerskin.

Most still had their white cotes, now stained and worn to a hundred earthy hues.

Bill watched them work—watched them loft shaft after shaft into the stumps he'd prepared for them, led them on runs through the woods with targets to the left and right. Winter had made them fat. But it had also made them steadier. Most of the men and not a few of the women had found mates among the Outwallers, almost as if a suggestion had been planted among them that they sink roots. Weddings—with no priests—had been celebrated. More than a few bellies were round, since Yule.

But since the snow began to retreat into the wood lines, and then to melt away altogether—since Nita Qwan's departure east, and then, ten days later, the sudden breakup of the ice—all the Dulwar and all the other Outwallers who lived around N'gara began to train their warriors, and Bill Redmede's people joined in with a will. And they learned from the Out-wallers, too—how to throw the small axes the Dulwars all carried, men and women, too, and how to make lighter arrows of the cane that grew around the inner sea and at this time of the year was standing, dried and ready to be harvested.

But Bill had agreed to the alliance. He knew what was coming, and what was expected.

Most of his men were going to war, and a few women, too. Bess was heavily pregnant, but grimly determined until the whole body of the Jacks voted together that no pregnant woman should come to the war.

"If'n we're all killed," Jamie Cartwright said, "you gels will keep our memory alive."

Bess cursed and didn't speak to anyone for a day.

Tapio—the Faery Knight—came and sat with her. She was always delighted to see him, as if he was an angel or a god.

He took one of her hands. "Besss," he said. "If we triumph you will have misssed nothing but violenssse." He shrugged. "But if we fail, I promissse you that our enemy will come here all too sssoon, and you and Tamsssin will have your belliesss full of fighting."

But even to the Faery Knight, she frowned. "I didn't become a Jack to get left behind because my body was full of a man's seed," she spat.

"I'm sssure there will be more war, asss sssure asss the sssun will ssshine," he said with a twisted smile. "All the creaturesss of thisss world make war. It isss what we have in common." He rose with an elegance no human frame could match, like a sinewy serpent.

So Bess straightened arrows and made the pine pitch resin that they used to help bind the heads to the shafts, and while the Outwallers did their war dances and Mogon's wardens came in from the north and Exrech's people swarmed in from the far west with tales of war and flood behind them, the Jacks completed their preparations, loaded their bags with food, and contemplated their allies.

Fitzalan had a new beard and a new, more mature manner. He didn't attack everything he saw anymore. He had an almond-eyed Outwaller woman named Liri from far to the west, where they said there was a river as broad as a lake. Her people were called Renerds, and their skin was a golden red, their eyes and hair much the same.

Or perhaps she had him. She seemed the more imperious of the two.

Two nights before the whole of the Faery Knight's army was due to march east, he held a great council in his hall. Harpers sang of wars from the past. No song was of glory, and most were of defeat and pain, the agony of loss, the despair of a bad wound. The music was haunting and beautiful.

Bill Redmede sat thinking of his distant brother. And of the Kingdom of Alba.

Of how little it all meant to him, now. He smiled grimly as he realized what Wat Tyler had known at midwinter.

To Redmede, this hall, N'gara, and its disparate inhabitants, had become home.

He twisted his mouth and glanced at Fitzalan, who was sharing a long stone pipe with Aun'shen, one of Mogon's lieutenants. Some of the great wardens smoked. Some also ate their meat raw.

Living at N'gara was predominantly a matter of not being offended by the alien behaviour of others.

"The comrades might get more spirit from happier songs," Redmede said.

Fitzalan shrugged. "They're true songs, those," he said.

Lady Tamsin appeared out of the air, or so it seemed. "The irks send warriors away with a reminder of where they go and what they leave behind," she said. "Perhaps for your kind, with the life so short, there is less to lose. Yet this seems to me odd—I would think that with the life so short, your people would be more careful of it."

Redmede found it hard to look at Tamsin for any length of time, so he tore his eyes away and looked at the harpers on the dais instead. Behind them, on the tapestry-that-lived, spear-armed warriors were cut down by humans in strange armour. Redmede had seen the armour somewhere before—on old statues outside Harndon. Archaic armour, helmets with crests, big rectangular shields. The legions.

Just when you thought you might understand the irks, or you thought they were just folks, they'd remind you that the older ones had been alive for a thousand years or so and remembered things that were long forgotten by most humans. Even in books.

Nor did they remember events the same way.

Redmede kept his eyes on the musicians. "Few of us are careful of life, my lady."

"For your own sweet Bess's sake, and all her kisses, mortal, the least you could do is bring yourself home." She smiled sweetly, like all the young women in all the passionate springs of the world rolled into one woman with pointed teeth. "Forget about glory. Go late, fight briefly, leave early and come home alive."

Bill Redmede laughed. "Lady, you incline me to desert."

Tamsin spread her hands. "War is a monster that eats the sentient races. I would counsel any friend to avoid him."

Bill Redmede nodded. "But who will stop the power of the sorcerer? Who will save the bears in the 'Dacks or the serfs in the fields?"

She nodded at the tapestry-that-lived. "Perhaps they should save themselves," she said. She raised a hand. "Peace, friend. You can make no argument that will reconcile Tamsin to the loss of her lord to war."

But in the council, the Faery Knight stood alone in the soft light on the dais, in his red clothes of leather and spidersilk. He spread his hands for silence, a gesture so evocative that all those in the hall fell silent, the boglins and the marsh trolls and the Golden Bears, the wardens and the irks and the men.

"Tomorrow we march to war," he said. The hall was silent. Not a fly buzzed, not a moth moved on silent wings.

"We do not march to conquer. We will fight only to protect our friends. Speed will be our armour, and silence our shield." He spread his arms wide and a glowing vision of the hills at the foot of the western Adnacrags appeared as if seen from a great height.

"West of Lissen Carak is the wall," he said. "It runs north to south here in the foothills." He pointed to the towers on the wall. "We will need to pass the wall here. There is a royal garrison, which we will destroy." He smiled, showing his fangs. "We have never believed that this land belonged to the so-called King of Alba anyway."

Some of the Jacks roared their approval. Others looked troubled.

"Once we pass the wall, we will have to move quickly. Several clanss of bears are moving toward us, and we must cover them and protect them."

"Where's Thorn?" bellowed a warden. She was Mogon's niece, Tremog. Her blue and white crest stood almost erect on her head.

Tapio nodded. "It is safe to call him by name here," he said, and he exchanged a glance with a tall, thin, dark-haired man who sat on a chair on the dais. "Although once we march, I ask that no member of our alliance mention his name. We wish to pass the outer wards of Alba undetected, and his spies are everywhere." He glanced again at the dark-haired man, who rose.

He spread his hands and spoke in a soft voice that nonetheless carried to every corner of the hall.

"Thorn is now marching to the siege of Ticondaga," he said. "Today he fought a battle on the road his slaves have made. The Earl of Westwall ambushed the sorcerer. Unfortunately, Thorn now has good professional military advice, and the earl's success was limited. Tomorrow, at the latest, he will invest the fortress."

"Will we fight him?" Tremog asked.

The dark-headed man looked to Tapio, who shrugged. "It is very difficult to see when too many Powers become entangled," he said with brutal honesty. "We lack the numbers or the hardihood or the sorcery to engage his main army in open battle, but if he chooses to fight us, we will be like coyotes at his heels."

Tremog's crest went down, and she seemed to tremble. Redmede knew that this was a warden sign of uncertainty, not rage.

"If we lack the force to meet him head to head, why send an army at all?" she asked.

Tapio nodded. "War is more than battle," he said. "War is food and drink and disease and patience and anger and hate and cold and stealth and terror as well as sweet silver and bitter iron and the glitter of arms in the sun or under the moon. We take as many blades as we can spare, and as many as we can feed, and as many as we can move quickly. Thorn has many times as many fighters. Can he feed them? Can he control them? Will other forces come into play?"

The man nodded. "At the very least, we will rescue the bears. Then, perhaps we will withdraw. Perhaps we will seek allies among Thorn's other enemies."

Tremog's tooth-lined maw spread wide and she gave a roar—what passed for laughter with the wardens. "You mean you do not trust us with your clever plan," she said. "Just say that and be done. What are we, the children of men, to lie to each other? You are our lord paramount. If you keep your own counsel, so be it. The worst we'll do is—wander off."

Many creatures laughed.

And Tapio laughed with them. "I have indeed been in too many councils of men," he confessed. "It is true that I have thoughts in my mind that I do not choose to share. But in the main, this is all of my counsel—that we pass the wall, collect the bears, and see what there is to be seen. Our retreat will be secure, and we have enough force to give Thorn real pause."

"You and this *man* speak as if you can see Thorn's forces and he cannot see ours!" said the bear. She took her great furry feet off the stone table and sat up. "Thorn is very powerful. How is it that he cannot see us?"

The dark-haired man smiled. "Suffice it to say that he is unlikely to look anywhere but here for Lord Tapio," he said.

"But when he does he will see us very quickly," Tapio insisted.

"Hence the secrecy," Redmede said. "Who is this gentleman?" he asked.

"I was dead," the dark-headed man said. "And since I desire not to be dead again soon, I won't reveal myself just now. But I will in time, and I promise you I won't betray you, any of you."

Tremog nodded. "The promises of men are very weak," she said. "But men learn wisdom in the Wild."

"And what of the west?" Many heads turned, and Liri, the beautiful Renard woman, stood. "I speak for no one by myself—but my people walk in the lakes, and I was sent here with a warning." She smiled at Fitzalan. "Pleasant as my winter has been—"

The Faery Knight inclined his head. "Lady of the Renardsss," he sang in his faery voice, "I have no easssy ansssswer to sssoothe you. The whole of the wessst isss moving. Beyond the great river, a hundred hivesss of boglinsss are ssspewing forth warriorsss—"

The wight, Exrech, rose from his alien crouch by the table and unfolded like a pocket knife to his full height. His white chiton armour and elongated, insectile head were the most alien things in a hall of aliens, and made Mogon's great saurians seem comforting and familiar.

When Exrech spoke, he did so by a mixture of exhalation, like a mammal, and the movement of his joints and wing cases that provided the hard consonants. They also provided popping and scratching noises that were—disconcerting.

He was unaware of the uneasiness he generated just by—being.

"I can speak of the west," he said in his flat, un-human delivery. "Our enemy—our true enemy—works his will on the Delta Hives and leaves our hives alone. Too often has he called on us for war. Our contract with him is expired. I cannot say more. But the west is moving—this war to which we go is only a tithe of what is coming."

The Faery Knight bowed. "Of all of us, it is possible that this wight and his people are the bravest, marching all the way east to our support when their own homes are at threat."

"Our contract with the sorcerer is at an end. He used a false scent and must be punished." Exrech seemed to shiver, and his body emitted a rustling sound like leaves.

"What will protect us here?" Tamsin asked.

"Sssmoke and misssdirection," Tapio sang. "And twenty million caribou."

Exrech raised his mandibles, a sign Bill Redmede had come to understand was agreement. "The river of hooves!" Exrech said. "No creature of the Wild—not even a thousand human knights—could cut a path across the river of hooves."

"Ssso for sssix weeksss, thisss peninsssula isss sssafe," the Faery Knight said.

That night, Thorn watched the heavens as Tapio Halij shielded his hold. It was a mighty working—almost as if he was moving his whole fortress into another sphere, the working was so deep and mighty.

It was a very odd choice, on the surface—a declaration of power that left Thorn in no doubt that the Faery Knight distrusted him and expected attack. But the more he contemplated the action, the more it appealed to his sense of his own power. Tapio was only confirming what Thorn knew—he was the mightier of the two, even if he lacked the power to destroy the old irk. So he drew into his shell like a turtle, secure that he could not easily be attacked.

"Fool," Thorn said. "After I take Ticondaga, I will be like a god." He tasted the moment at which he would subsume Ghause, and he shuddered as the excess of spirit passed down his animated limbs. In as much as the great sorcerer could feel pleasure, the notion of the absolute subjugation of Ghause—her extinction and his accession to her powers—gave him immense pleasure.

Inwardly, he frowned.

"When did I become so simple?" he asked the air around him.

"Be content," Ash said at his elbow. The entity was cloaked in flesh—he appeared as a man, a very old man, in a body taut with use and muscle. His skin was jet black—not the black of Ifriquy'a or Dar as Salaam, but a colour like lamp black. He wore the simple clothes of a peasant, but all in dirty grey. He had a scythe in his hand, and an hourglass.

Thorn watched the night. "You have a new guise," he said with distaste.

Ash snorted. "A very old guise."

"Are you like some rich girl of Harndon, with a different dress for every suitor?" Thorn asked.

Ash seemed to think for a moment. At least, his face did not move. The silence lengthened and Thorn began to feel he was not going to be answered. This had happened frequently—it was one of the ways Thorn had arrived at the realization that he was a tool and not an ally.

Ash hissed. "It might appear that way," he admitted.

An old teacher—back in the mists of time before Thorn, when he had been a boy and a human and a scholar—a teacher had told him never to ask a question to which he did not want to know the answer.

Where did that come from? Thorn asked himself.

But he asked anyway.

"Or is the way in which we perceive you shaped by our own—beings?" Thorn asked.

Ash laughed. It was not, for once, derisive or contemptuous. It was rich, and flavoured with humour and delight. "You are an apt pupil, sorcerer. In truth, to my eye, I am always the same. It is you—the sentients—who try to force me to the moulds of your minds."

Thorn was not afraid of the night or the abyss. He looked into Ash's eyes. "With people, and animals—if enough people call a dog cur, he'll learn to bite."

Ash inclined his head. The movement seemed genuine. "An eternity of striving, and I have one convert," Ash said. "Well...perhaps two or three. Yes—even I am manipulated by the beliefs of those around me. As are you and every other sentient."

Thorn looked at the stars. He pointed at them. "And those? Are they, as astrologers maintain, the pinpricks of light from other spheres—an infinity of spheres?"

Ash sighed. "Thorn, if I told you all I know, you would whip me with thongs of fire."

Thorn nodded. "You quote scripture."

Ash laughed—and this time it was derisive. "Everyone quotes scripture, Thorn. Or writes it to suit themselves."

"Will we take Ticondaga?" he asked.

Ash frowned. "Yes. Your plan—which is far too complex, too devious, and too bent on your ideas of vengeance—is a delight, and it will succeed. There is no mind in all this sphere—except mine—that can comprehend what you plan."

"You flatter me," Thorn said.

"Of course," Ash answered. "If you insist on treating me as a mentor, eventually I will behave like one."

"And after?" Thorn asked.

Ash might have shrugged. The old man's shoulders twitched. Perhaps he laughed. "We conquer this world, I break my bonds, and then we move through the portals to others, and take them, and eventually you gain enough in power to betray me, and we fight. And I destroy you utterly after we lay waste to the cosmos."

Thorn nodded, as if this was the most natural thing in the world. "And you are sure that it is you who destroys me?" he asked.

Ash laughed. "There is no sure, in all the multiverse," he said.

Thorn shook his great stone head. "Lord, all this badinage aside— Ghause kills the Queen. I kill Ghause. The King—"

"I have seen to the King." Ash nodded. "Ten times over."

"Ticondaga falls—surely they will all unite against me." Thorn was a better strategist than he had been. He saw the consequences clearly. War and strategy and the dealing of minds, one with another—he no longer disdained these as beneath him. Besides, the more time he spent on them, the more they seemed to have laws like the laws of the hermetical.

Ash nodded. His voice was easy, lulling, like a mother's speaking to a child. "Yes—it is good to see all the futures. But that is not a realistic one. I have sowed dissension for fifty years ready for this moment. Will the lamb lie down with the lion? Will the Galles ally with the Albans they have just tried to destroy? After Ticondaga, they will fall—Middleburg, Lissen Carak, Albinkirk, Liviapolis and Harndon and Arles in Occitan. And in the old world, as well, until we hold all the portals and all the points of power."

Thorn stood, transfixed by the note of falsity he had just heard. He blessed his face of stone and the magical enhancements on his body. He did not tremble, and he did not give away so much as a twitch of his fingers.

But he detected in that moment that Ash had a plan for the time after Ticondaga.

And it did not include Thorn.

Ash chuckled. "Why would I betray you? You are my chosen avatar in this sphere. I cannot win here without you. I've put a great deal of effort into you. You might say," Ash chuckled, "that I've put all my eggs in one basket."

Thorn's intellect struggled to understand what he might mean. Or what he might want. "You are blind to some things," he said, accusingly.

Ash turned and looked at him. Thorn had a momentary frisson of terror.

Then Ash said, "I admire your black moths. Very clever."

Thorn sighed like a winter breeze on desiccated leaves. "One of them cleared an entire village—and left no evidence of its passage."

"And another was killed by a squaw with a stick," Ash noted.

Thorn nodded. "My assassins will come out of the darkness after midnight. The generation I have sent to kill the Dark Sun—they should be almost immune to normal men. They exist more in the *aethereal* than the so-called real."

Ash pondered the stars. "You will waste your pets on this mortal you feel challenges you, but I tell you, he is nothing. He does not even enter into my calculations."

Thorn paused. "Really?" he asked.

Ash shook his black head. "He is nothing—a boy puffed with vanity and pride of birth. You react to him because he has all the things you did not have—wealth and power and good looks. If I am to be your mentor I must make you understand this. I can scarcely follow him in the *aethereal*, he is of so little account."

Thorn frowned. "That makes no sense. He burns in the *aethereal* like a sun."

Ash flicked his scythe. "You exaggerate."

Thorn was silent. Trying to make out what Ash might mean—or what he might have just given away.

"After Ticondaga, none will stand against you," Ash said.

Thorn thought, *So you keep saying.*

Liviapolis—Morgon Mortirmir

Deep in the university, at Liviapolis, Morgon woke to find that Tancreda had, after all, stayed with him. Her brother was snoring on a chair. She had brought him the manuscript he needed, and he'd begun to read—

More immediately, Tancreda was draped across Mortirmir, who was lying on a bench with a pair of Venike-made lenses in his right hand and a little known treatise by one of the magisters of the past called *Optika* in the other. He carefully dropped the book and the lenses to the floor.

Her hazel eyes opened.

"You are very beautiful," he said.

"Could I just once be very intelligent, or elegant, or perhaps stubborn or clever?" she asked sleepily. "Must it be beautiful? Always?" She narrowed her eyes. "Who found the manuscript on lenses? Mmmm? Was that beauty?"

Mortirmir glanced at the brother, and then, greatly daring, leaned over her and put his mouth on hers. He winked in his head at the absent shade of Harmodius.

Her lips remained tightly closed until the tip of his tongue licked them lightly, and then they sprang open—a delicious parting that left him giddy.

She moaned deep in her throat like an angry cat. But she was not angry, and she writhed across him until she'd shifted her weight and put an arm behind his head.

The hand on her neck probed a little and found even more luxuriant softness—she shifted again, her lips changing from left to right across his, and her tongue—

Suddenly she sat up. "You are not dead!" she said. "The working!"

For the first time since he was granted powers, Mortirmir cursed all of hermeticism.

Chapter Five

The Albin

Amicia spent their first day on the road reassuring herself and her sisters that she was not leading them to temptation, or even humiliation and death. Riding with the Red Knight and his household—who were, however she might wish to describe them, sell-swords and mercenaries and not knights errant—terrified her two companions.

Sister Mary was a tall, quiet girl with a brilliant mind and a straight back and a fine voice, both in the *aethereal* and in the real. She was young to be travelling, just seventeen, and her day-to-day struggles with the temptations of the world were palpable—sometimes amusing, and sometimes terrible. She was pretty, and afflicted with a need to be seen as pretty that conflicted with her quiet, and very genuine, piety. She was a poor rider, a peasant born, and she suffered from the youthful urge to refuse help. Her straight blond hair and ice-blue eyes were widely admired among the captain's men.

Sister Katherine was warmer, with curly red hair and a vicious sense of humor. She was the oldest of the three, a mature thirty, and she had born and lost a child as a young woman. She was noble born—and had worked away the pride of her birth on stone floors and a hundred forms of penance and laundry.

It hadn't been entirely successful.

In truth, both women had been handed to Sister Amicia as supports, but also as projects. Sister Katherine had a reputation for arrogance, and Sister Mary for wantonness.

It was, Sister Amicia thought, as if Sister Miriam was challenging her.

Despite which, the three had gotten off to a fine start. Healing knights and clearing boglins and hearing confessions had all been adventures, and the three had shared enough adventures in their first weeks together to create a bond that gossip and the stresses of castle or convent life might never have allowed. When Sister Mary paused by a pane of glass to look at her reflection, Amicia made no comment, and Sister Katherine's rosary of coral and gold drew no comment either.

The first day on the road had been difficult enough. Sister Mary usually walked or rode a donkey, but the column bound for the tournament was moving too fast for her, and she was mounted on one of the company's spare horses, and suffered cruelly from the first halt on. As a trained physiker and a hermeticist, she had an arsenal of cures she could deploy, but as a young woman, she bit her lip and endured and muttered darkly until Sister Amicia put a hand on her to steady her, and pushed *ops* into her thighs.

"Am I so obvious?" Sister Mary asked.

Amicia laughed. "Yes," she said.

Sister Katherine, on the other hand, was in her element—she was on a fine eastern mare, and she rode better than some of the soldiers.

"Tonight, if you'll allow it, I'll split my kirtle and ride astride," Sister Katherine said. "I can do yours and Mary's, too."

Sister Amicia sighed. Katherine was always at the edge of the allowed, looking for a way outside. "I'm not sure the world is ready for nuns who ride astride," Amicia said.

"By our lady, Sister—you say mass, they threaten you with heresy, and you are worried by riding astride?" Sister Katherine pouted.

The Red Knight, fully armed and wearing a scarlet surcoat of silk, shot with gold thread, trotted down the column with Toby, his squire, and Nell, his valet, at his golden-spurred heels. He was making his way down the column slowly—inspecting it. The three women had lots of warning.

The rain was sporadic. "Once your skirts are soaked, the thighs will hurt all the more," Katherine said. "And astride will be easier on Mary. This is no way to ride." She had to raise her voice to be heard. They were entering the great gorge of the Albin River.

Immediately behind the three nuns was the escort of Thrakian knights led by Ser Christos. He was smiling broadly when Amicia looked back. He had water dripping down his grey-black beard and he bowed his head. He called something in Archaic and his knights and stradiotes straightened up. A servant handed a linen rag forward, and all of them began wiping each other's metal dry.

A watery sun emerged from the clouds as they turned east, climbed a low ridge, and suddenly the world seemed to drop away before them. Around them, the Brogat rolled away in a series of hilly landscapes—to the west, the hills rose towards mountains currently hidden in rain. But the hillsides were already lush and green in early April, as if to belie the last days of Lent.

But to the east, the great river rolled in its deepest gorge before emerging into the plains of the Albin. The gorges of the great river were spectacular, and thousands of years of spring run-offs as strong or stronger than this year's had carved a mighty channel through the low hills of the central Brogat. Far below them on their left, the river charged along, muddy and green-brown with ice-cold snow melt and old leaves and new-swept loam all rolling along at the speed of a cavalry charge. The river was, in fact, so loud, and the walls of the great gorge echoed the river so well, that conversation was difficult.

It stunned the senses—the drop was two hundred feet and more to the channel below and the mad rush of the water and the wet grey rock and the white birches and the green of the leaves. Amicia found she had to remind herself to breathe, and when she turned her head from the drop, he was there.

He was smiling happily. He took a deep breath himself, looking out over the canyon and the river, and then he met her eyes. His smile didn't change. Before she could stop him, he took her bridle hand, kissed it, and passed her.

The path along the gorge was too narrow for Amicia to turn her horse easily, and she'd only bring chaos to the column. She rode on, turning in her saddle to look. But he was pointing out something on Sister Mary's saddle to his valet, and the young woman slid from her saddle and took Mary's horse's head.

He caught her eye again. His smile returned. He simply pointed and moved his hand—one of the company's signals that she knew from the siege. Move.

She saw no reason to disobey, so she turned to face forward, to the immense relief of her mount. They began to pick their way along the most spectacular view she had ever seen.

Under foot, birch and beech leaves sodden with rain made a brown-gold contrast to the green leaves above, and even as she raised her head from her noon prayers, the sun, brightening, kissed her with its warmth and she rode easily, thanking God from her very soul for the perfection of the day and the beauty of the view.

They rode along the gorge for three magnificent miles, and then the trail re-crested the ridge to their right and went a little west and down slope, leaving the roar of the water far enough east that normal conversation could commence.

There was an old wagon circle, well used and with twenty big firepots recently cleared at the base of the ridge, where a fine stream hurried to meet the great river to the east. A pair of stradiotes was there with most of the squires and valets. The wagons were already parked, and the captain's pavilion was already up.

It was only just after noon. But Amicia put a hand in the small of her back and was glad to stop. She found the captain's squire giving orders and approached on horseback.

"Eh, Sister?" he asked. "Cap'n says to offer you and your sisters a cup o' wine while the tents go up." He waved to the pavilion, where Nell was pouring wine for what appeared to be a large party. Two long tables had been constructed, and places set for twenty.

Amicia considered refusing, but one look at Sister Mary eliminated all thoughts of rebellion. She had chosen to travel with him, and she was going to have to see him every day.

The column had become quite strung out in the gorge. It took an hour for the last part of the rearguard to come up—more of Ser Christos and his stradiotes.

Sister Mary was already asleep in her folding chair. Sister Katherine went to make sure they had a tent of their own.

Amicia sipped her wine. After a little while, Ser Thomas Lachlan came and sat by her.

"Where are the herds?" she asked.

Ser Thomas laughed. "On the west road," he said. "Only the Red Knight would lead his party through the fewkin' gorge." He smiled. "There's a perfectly good road, just one more valley over west, like."

"Why the gorge, then?" Amicia asked.

Ser Thomas laughed. "You, I reckon," he said. "He's mad for ye—you know it, aye?"

Amicia found that despite her best intentions, she was blushing furiously.

He grinned at her. "I'm fer thinkin' you're not so agin' it as you seem."

Amicia drank a little more wine than she'd intended and coughed.

"Ah, well." Ser Thomas nodded. "I'm an old busybody." He leaned back, all six foot four of him. "Did ye like the gorge, lass?"

Amicia nodded. "I loved it. The rush of the water—the depth of the gorge. Magnificent."

Ser Thomas made room for Ser Gavin and Ser Michael as they entered. They bowed to her and talked in whispers because of the sleeping Sister Mary—all except Ser Thomas Lachlan, who didn't seem to have a whisper.

Outside the pavilion, a cultured voice laden with sarcasm asked, "What's our lord and master doing now? Finding minstrels to play for his lady love?"

She heard Toby say something softly.

The cultured voice said, "Oh, my God."

Chris Foliak, still in his arming clothes, stepped into the pavilion out of the spring evening. He was beet red, and when he saw how red Amicia was, he turned even redder.

Amicia got to her feet. "I think—" she began unsteadily.

Ser Thomas rose. "Don't go, lass. It's just Foliak's usual way of goin' about things—lead wi' his tongue. Eh, Kit?"

"Good sister, I apologize for my—" Even Chris Foliak wasn't sure what to say.

But luckily for everyone, Sister Mary chose that moment to moan, and awake.

"Oh—Amicia!" she said weakly.

Amicia took her by the hand and led her to their tent. There were only a hundred people in the whole party, and fifteen wagons—so their tent was not so hard to find. By it, Sister Katherine was leading a dozen young men and women in prayer. She flashed Sister Amicia a smile.

Sister Mary was so tired from riding that it was all she could do to get undressed to her shift. Amicia laid her down, covered her and watched her fall asleep unaided by any hermetical wisdom.

Katherine rose from her knees, coral prie-dieu in hand, and dusted herself off. "Blessed Virgin, Mary is going to *hate* horses tomorrow morning," she said. "This household has no chaplain since Father Arnaud died."

Amicia nodded.

"Well—you have a licence to say mass, Sister. I don't." Sister Katherine grinned. "Father Arnaud said mass every morning, I gather. They're not all impious rake-hells like their captain."

Amicia nodded, not sure whether she should defend the captain or join the attack. "You know I'm on this journey because my licence has been declared heretical," she said.

Sister Katherine nodded towards the large red pavilion. "I gather there's wine?" She smiled. "Listen, I'm related to half these men. I won't err or fall on my back for one, but I'd like to spend a week riding and talking about something other than laundry."

Amicia might have scolded her, but instead she laughed, too. "We can watch each other," she said.

The pavilion fell silent as the two nuns entered.

"Par Dieu, gentles," Ser Pierre said. "We'll have to watch our oaths and our manners."

"Good practice for a tourney before the King and Queen," Ser Michael said.

On the last line, the captain came in. Amicia noted that he smelled of sweat—male and horse—and of something metallic. As he entered, Nell appeared and put a cup of wine in his hand. Other men rose—not all together. No one bowed, but the deference was there. When he sat, they all sat.

He smiled at Amicia. "No need for guests to pay me so much courtesy," he said.

She returned his smile. "No one was ever hurt by too much courtesy." Other people had gone back to their conversations and she had his attention. "Would you like me to say mass for your people, while we are on the road?" she asked.

He looked around. "Yes. Yes, I suppose I would. If you're declared a heretic, will we all go straight to hell?"

She shook her head. "No, I imagine all the sin will fall on my shoulders."

He nodded. "Excellent, then. Any time you'd like to take on some more sin…" He paused. "No, that was asinine."

"Yes," she said, frankly. "I tell you what—you pass on all forms of double-entendre and I'll forbear easy religious comments about your life of violence."

He nodded. "Done. I'm not that good at double-entendre anyway."

He looked around. "Gentles," he said, and they were quiet. His easy exercise of power disturbed her. He did it too easily. He didn't wait for them to finish what they were saying, as Sister Miriam might have, or join another conversation and wait his turn. He paused, and they reacted.

He made a motion to Toby, and all the squires and pages left the tent.

"As I entered, Ser Michael mentioned that we would need our best behaviour to be at court with the King and Queen." He looked around. "What I have to say does not leave this table. It is not meant for the pages and squires, nor is it for the peasants who sell us food."

Now he had their attention.

"The King has arrested the Queen on charges of witchcraft. She is accused of murdering the Count D'Eu by sorcery." His voice was bland—he might have been discussing the weather.

Ser Michael turned pale. "Christ on the cross," he said. "Is he insane?"

The Red Knight shook his head. "Friends, I have been too slow. I should have recognized—never mind. But I no longer know what we're riding to—war or peace, a tournament or a darker contest." He looked around. "I think most of you have some idea where Ser Gelfred is. So you'll understand that we have news."

Ser Alcaeus smiled knowingly. Bad Tom shrugged.

The Red Knight leaned back and sipped his wine. "As we get closer to Harndon, we'll get better and more accurate reports. But if what I have today is accurate, and what Ser John Crayford had two days ago tallies with it, the Prince of Occitan is riding into southern Alba."

"And there's raids all along the frontiers," Bad Tom said.

"Master Smythe said: go to the tournament." The Red Knight shrugged. "Every bone in my body tells me to sit tight in Albinkirk and raise an army, but mayhap—with a great deal of luck—mayhap we can save something." He shrugged. "Any road, we'll be cautious, and move as if in a land at war."

The men all groaned.

Ser Michael shook his head. "I don't like it. Is the King...possessed?"

Since it was treason to propose such a thing, a certain hush fell.

Ser Gabriel leaned back and looked into his wine cup. "I thought I knew what was going on. The arrest of the Queen..." He shrugged. But Amicia noted that he merely sipped his wine. She had seen him drink more heavily. He was very carefully controlled.

Ser Michael looked over at Ser Thomas. "Send for the company," he suggested. His suggestion was stated in fairly imperious tones.

Ser Thomas wrinkled his nose.

Ser Gabriel managed a thin-lipped smile. "I'm tempted. But—if we take an army into the Albin, then we're the ones doing the provoking—and to all the people, all the merchants and yeomen and farmers, it will always seem that we provoked the King. The rightful King." He looked around—at Ser Christos and Ser Alcaeus. "We have a good force—enough knights to defeat any casual attempt to take us. And we have friends."

"And where exactly is Master Kronmir?" Ser Michael asked.

"Exactly where we need him to be, of course," Ser Gabriel said, with something of his old arrogance.

Two days of intermittent rain turned the roads to a froth of mud and leaves. The gorge road that ran along the ridge top had good rock under all the mud, and the wagons continued to move well enough. Twice, Amicia rode along a path so narrow that she looked down to the left and wished she had not, and once, she and Sister Mary, who was feeling a little more human, had to dismount and put their backs against a cart to keep it from taking a wagoner and two mules into the gorge. The second time they got covered in mud, they had to accept dry clothes from the pages.

Sister Katherine laughed. "I could wear hose and a jupon every day," she said. "If it weren't so infernally difficult to pee."

Nell smiled. "You get used to it," she said.

Sister Mary looked at Amicia, with her hair under a man's hood, and Katherine, with her curly red hair badly captured by an arming cap. "We will *all* be burned as heretics," she predicted.

Waking among the captain's household was as different from waking in the nunnery at Lissen Carak as could be imagined. It started with animals—the whole company was mounted, and a hundred men and women had three hundred animals—mules, horses, two pairs of oxen, a cow for milk; a pack of dogs led by a pair of mastiffs who belonged to Bad Tom but never seemed to be with him, and some cats who lived on the wagons, and the captain's falcons and Ser Michael's and a few terrified chickens. Morning came suddenly and almost violently, as the sun roused the animals to a chewing, barking, calling, biting, farting, neighing clamour.

Sister Katherine slept through it effortlessly. Sister Mary complained that she was getting no sleep at all.

"And all the men are looking at me. All the time." Sister Mary shuddered.

Sister Amicia forbore to comment and sat up. In the convent, they all went to careful lengths, as hospitallers, to be perfectly clean. They also dressed carefully so that as little flesh as possible showed at any given step. The Order had long experience of various passions and a very realistic view of what might happen to large communities of young men—or women— all working together.

The life of a military camp made most of these practices impossible. Men and women had to dress outside their tents, unless they wished to take so long that the captain's master of household might order the tent taken down around them, which had almost happened to Mary on their first morning on the road. Nicomedes was a Morean—tall, very thin, a scholar. And a hermeticist of some small talent, as Amicia quickly discovered. But he was the captain's major-domo, and he made sure that tents went up and down, fires were started and quenched, and food was cooked on time. He and Miss Sukey—Mag's daughter—ran almost every aspect of camp life, and if they ever quarrelled, Amicia never saw it.

So, on a damp morning with rain threatening, Amicia had to force herself out of her warm blankets—roll them tight against further damp, and put them in a sleeve of waxed linen to go behind her saddle—and then leave the tent in the light rain in her sleeping shift, which was also her second shift and bid fair to be her only shift if she tore out the shoulder in the better one.

From there, though, her convent training stood her in good stead. No matter how many pages and squires made time to watch her dress, she could get into her man's shirt and hose under the shift without showing her knees, much less anything more exotic. The boyish clothes didn't please her—the wool hose were prickly against her legs and the loose gowns of the Order offered a certain freedom—but the men's clothes were much easier on horseback. She and Katherine were dressed in heartbeats, and set about folding, brushing, and tying everything in their small camp. Katherine, by far the better horsewoman, went to fetch their mounts.

Nell came early with her boy. He was handsome, large-eyed and hard-muscled with something of the feral ferocity of all young men, but an edge of gentleness and care for Nell that Amicia liked. He held out three wooden bowls with sausage and eggs and two-day-old bread, toasted and buttered.

Amicia went into the tent where Mary was dressing carefully. "Don't forget to eat," she said.

That night, their fourth on the road, they had camped at a beautiful wagon circle right at the edge of a great bluff that looked south over the magnificent green and gold quilt of the well-farmed Albin highlands. She had found a little arbour a few paces to the west of the wagon circle, and she led her little congregation there, still munching her sausage, and as the sun swelled—red-gold and still threatening more rain from the east—she said mass with Mary as her only server from plain wooden dishes and the captain's silver cup. Ser Michael was there and Ser Christos and also a dozen drovers, ridden over from their own camp to the west, where the vast beef herds lowed like lost souls and the sheep baaa'd on and on, punctuating her sung benedictus and making her laugh—they all laughed as the sheep sounded so much like a choir of animals.

She was surprised to see Ser Christos—the Morean church had even firmer rules about mass than the Alban church, when it came to women. But it was a nice congregation, and she enjoyed it immensely.

Marcus, the Etruscan knight's squire, and Toby, the captain's, both came and gave her courtly bows. The archers all waved. Cully, the leader, and Cuddy, his boon companion, and Flarch, a dangerous man and a lecher, all paused to pay their respects.

"What's a handsome piece like you doing in a place like this, Sister?" Flarch asked with a leer.

"The work of God," Amicia said. "A pity it can't be said of all of us."

"That's you told," Cuddy hissed as the three archers walked off to their horses.

Through the trees, the captain's trumpeter polished his trumpet with a cloth. Everyone knew that was the last thing he did before blowing it, and Nicholas Ganfroy was no longer so young, or so poor at playing the trumpet. The company had other new recruits to haze.

Amicia emerged from the trees to find that Katherine had her horse saddled and in hand. Cupped in her own hand was the last shred of consecrated host, which she gave to Katherine with a blessing.

Katherine bowed, chewed, swallowed, and sung a prayer.

Nicholas Ganfroy, who now knew his business, looked them all over carefully before putting his trumpet to his lips. He blew the first note, and every page and groom led his charges—all the horses in his lance—to their places on the parade. The knights, men-at-arms, fighting pages and the handful of archers walked steadily out to their places in front of the line of horse holders.

Even while the company formed, there were already half a dozen outriders watching for them. Stavros's cousin Mikal, now a sort of under-officer, led two files of Thrakian light horsemen along the parallel ridges, linking up with Ser Thomas's Hillman scouts to the west.

Amicia, who enjoyed seeing things done well, enjoyed it all.

The captain came across the field even as Nicomedes and a dozen servants dropped his pavilion—the first tent up and the last tent down. He strolled across the parade ground and stopped at Ser Michael's lance to look at the new archer, Nell's friend.

The boy blushed. He stammered something.

The captain laughed and put a hand on his shoulder, and Ser Michael made a note on a wax tablet.

Then he walked straight across the soldiers to where all the women and non-combatants waited with their horses. There were not as many as usual. Sukey, Mag's daughter, now led the contingent. She'd ridden in—alone—a day before with no explanation on why she was late to the column. A year or two ago, Amicia would have assumed that all of the camp women were whores—and ministered to them anyway. But even four days on the road showed that they were the company's reserve of expert labour—they sewed. They seemed to sew from morning to night, when they weren't doing laundry, tending to the injured, or helping the pages with the horses. They also—mostly—had their own tents.

Amicia was a woman. Women's lives interested her more than men's.

The company had a great many women—in the ranks, and out of them.

Amicia assumed that the captain was coming to address Sukey on some matter of march discipline, but instead, after a bow to his head-woman, he walked up to the nuns. He smiled.

She smiled back.

"I think you have my cup, good Sister," he said.

She knew she blushed. But she held her smile. "It is the best in the camp," she said.

"I really don't mind loaning it to God," he said. "But He's got to give it back."

Sister Mary's harshly indrawn breath clashed with Sister Katherine's chuckle.

She handed him the cup. He raised it as if in a toast. "Just give it to Toby tomorrow," he said. Then he paused. "May I show you something beautiful this morning? Come ride with me."

If she had been prepared, Amicia would have found it easier to refuse. She didn't intend to be alone with him—then, or ever again.

But he was smiling . . .

She found that she had taken her rouncy from Sister Katherine—who gave her a lopsided smile—and walked over to join the captain, Toby, and the trumpeter.

Ganfroy raised his trumpet to his lips a second time, and the call to mount rang out.

The captain vaulted into his saddle while people cheered. Toby met her eye and shrugged.

"He's a terrible show-off," she said, loudly enough to be heard.

Ser Gabriel laughed. "I am, at that," he admitted.

Forty paces away, Nicomedes swung onto a tall wagon next to Sukey, who raised her riding whip and waved it.

Ser Gabriel waved to Ser Michael, who walked his horse over to them.

"The good sister and I are taking a little ride," the captain said.

Ser Michael nodded to Amicia. "You have a long spoon, Sister?" he asked.

She laughed and was surprised at how she sounded—a little wild. She clamped down.

Ser Michael took the staff of command from Ser Gabriel and held it aloft. He waved it at the Moreans—their ranks moved, anticipating the trumpet.

Then the trumpet crashed out, one more time, and the whole company rolled into motion.

"It's more like the convent than I would have believed," she said.

Down the column, each file moved smoothly into place except the last—Ser Michael's. Robin rode well, but the new archer was mooning and he was late moving forward. His horse caught his inattention and jumped—Sukey, in the lead wagon, had to rein in after her animals had done the work of getting the heavy wagon rolling.

"You useless sack of pig-shit. Someone tied your balls in a knot last night and now you can't find 'em?" Sukey's voice was mild—it was too early for anyone to manage real invective.

The boy flushed with anger and then swallowed it, and got his horse into the column. He was a poor rider.

"Just like the convent," Ser Gabriel said.

"Are you kidding?" Amicia laughed. "Miriam can manage all that in one half-raised eyebrow."

"Perhaps I could send her all my file-leaders." He wasn't paying her any attention at all. He was focused on his column.

During the siege, this had fascinated her. She had had her share of swains as a lass—and by and large, they mooned. Gabriel had his own ways of mooning, but he seldom took his attention off his work to do it and, as a woman, she preferred his focus to the puppy-dog behaviour of younger men.

Side by side they rode. The day was clearing from its early dampness to a good blue-and-white-skied April day.

"Any chance of fish for Friday?" she asked.

He looked at her.

She shrugged. "I'm easy in my conscience about a little dried sausage when breaking the fast of the night. But Friday is Good Friday and many of your people will not want to eat meat."

He nodded. "I think you'll find Nicomedes already has this on his plate—as it were." He nodded. "Fish are hard to come by until the Albin runs down to the salt. There's plenty of them there, but no one to fish for them, I think, except farm boys skipping out on work."

They rode east, towards the river, while the column rolled west.

"It may be that we'll all fast, on Friday," he said.

"Even you?" she asked. The river was getting louder as they climbed towards the height of the stony ridge.

"I am coming to terms with some of my views on God," he said. "New evidence has presented itself."

"You're going to let God off the hook, are you?" she asked, and even she was surprised at the acid tone she used.

"Perhaps," he said.

Then the wall of sound cut off any possibility of conversation.

Almost immediately, the trail went to the right, and down, winding and winding.

Very quickly, Amicia was reminded of how important sound was to balance and perception. The white noise of the water—out of sight, but obliterating all other sound—made her feel almost blind.

After some time, Gabriel dismounted and helped her dismount—without any display. Then he led his horse down the trail, which was narrower and softer, so that their horses and even their boots left tracks. A mist hung over the trees.

They seemed to walk in a world of their own. They didn't attempt to communicate, except that once he intruded into her memory palace to say, "It is very soft here—be careful," and she smiled and thanked him.

And then they emerged from the trees onto a broad, flat greensward. There were whole trees on the grass, washed up to show that at the full peak of the spring flood, the grass was awash. Nor was it a perfect lawn—legions of ducks and geese had ensured the future fertility of the spot.

The noise was still incredible.

He walked to the water's edge. A broad pool, the size of a small lake, rolled away into the fast flow of the river beyond. The banks were green, the water ice-cold and ocean deep. Out in the middle of the pool, a trout rose, red and gold and silver, the size of a big cat, took a fly neatly and rolled back under the cold black water.

But the pool didn't hold the gaze. The falls were the miracle. The falls fell three hundred feet from the bluff far above where they had camped. They fell in a single broad sheet, separated high above them by a spire that stuck straight up into the air like the tower of a small cathedral.

Her eye could not stop tracking the water as it fell and fell and fell—the pool devoured it and sent it away down the river.

Amicia fell to her knees and prayed. She prayed for herself, and for him, and for the place and to bless God for all of creation.

When she rose—her knees thoroughly damp—he had tied the horses. He beckoned to her, and she followed him willingly enough. She felt at ease. Confident. Happy.

He led her to the edge of the falls, so that the enormous rush of water was passing a hand-span from his face.

Then he stepped into the water.

Amicia had seen a waterfall before, if not one so mighty as this. She stepped into the waterfall, too. In fact, she was merely damp when she emerged into the cave behind the fall.

The cave was not silent, but the sound was merely noise here.

He was grinning. "You do trust me."

She shrugged. "I might say that I trust in God, and provoke you," she said. "But in truth, yes, my dear, I do trust you."

"Well, I thank you for your trust. I wanted you to come here." He shrugged. "I found it years ago. I always imagined bringing my lady love here."

She laughed. "Sadly—perhaps sadly for us both—I am a nun, and not your lady love."

He nodded. He fetched a stool—there were several. "I can build a fire to get you dry," he said.

She shrugged. "I'll get wet again going out," she said. "Nor would it be useful for me to strip for you."

"This place is very special," he said. He ignored her last comment. "Can you feel it, oh puissant Sister?"

She reached out into the *aethereal*.

She put her hand to her mouth.

"It is closed off. The earth on one side and the rush of flowing water on the other." He nodded. "I imagine something very powerful could make it in, or out, but this cave is virtually sealed in the *aethereal*." He sat on a stool and leaned back. "So here we can talk. About anything. No one is listening—not Harmodius, not Thorn, and not even Ash."

The name reverberated.

"Ash?" she asked.

"After Lissen Carak, I went and made an ally—I think—of a potent and ancient Power that men call the Wyrm of Ercch." He glanced at her and she nodded.

"I have learned a great deal talking to him. Mostly, I have learned that he opposes another Power, who he calls Ash, and who—" Gabriel smiled like a boy. "I know I sound like a fool, but who seems to be the Power moving the pieces on the chessboard—at Lissen Carak, and in Harndon. And perhaps elsewhere."

This was not the conversation for which she had prepared for the last hour while walking and riding and climbing. She took a deep breath.

"What do you guard, under the vaults and dungeons of Lissen Carak?" he asked her.

"That is not my secret," she said.

He nodded. "But you admit there is a secret there," he said. "What have you done that I cannot be killed?" he asked. "Even for you, this is a potent witchery."

She sat back on her stool. Leaned her head into the stone of the back wall, slanting upwards into the white blur of the water that made the front wall.

"Don't you think we'd be better with blatant seduction?" she asked.

He laughed. His laugh—the open honesty of it—made her laugh.

"Amicia, is your love of God so great, the feeling so wonderful, that you have no room in you for earthly love?" he asked.

She made a face. "What would you have me say? But yes." She shook her head. "I think there was a time—not so long ago—when I'd have fallen into your arms." She flushed. "But something has changed in me. There is a point, in prayer—in the ascent to God—when you must guard yourself carefully against sin. And then, I'm sorry, a point where sin seems a little foolish. When it no longer tempts. Where earthly love is but a pale companion."

"Ouch," he said. He wore a brave smile, but she saw she'd cut him too deeply.

"Oh, my dear—I only want everyone to be happy," she said.

He nodded. "What would you say if I said that's how I feel for you?"

She made the face again. "I'd say that you are twenty-three or -four and you'll feel differently in a year or two." She held up a hand. "I'd say that your preoccupation with war makes it impossible for you to love me—or God—very deeply."

He nodded. "Yes. I'd tell a squire with a new girl the same." He crossed his booted legs. "So—to hell with love. What did you do?"

She looked at him. So close. So much himself. So many things about him she *hated*. And loved. Not always as easy to let it go as she claimed, even now, when she could feel the—the simple reality of God's creation as firmly as she could feel the rock under her hip.

"I used..." She paused. She had a great deal to lose. And at another level, there were parts of this she had carefully avoided admitting, even to herself. "The Abbess was dead. The fortress almost fell. I had all that power Thorn released. I was failing—oh, Gabriel, how I was failing. The *potentia* was too much for me. The King—and the Queen—required healing."

She closed her eyes. "And then God put a hand on me and steadied me. And the *potentia* turned steadily to *ops*. And I cast and cast." She stared at the falls, but in her eyes were the results of a hundred healings, of men and women broken by battle and remade.

"I healed everything I touched," she said. She still wondered at the thought.

Gabriel nodded but said nothing.

She turned to him. "Whoever—steadied me. Spoke to me." She took a deep breath. "Then and later—but not since, which troubles Miriam. And me." She pursed her lips a moment and frowned. "Then—the night I was going to...I might have—" She paused.

"I don't want to do this," she said. "I'm sorry, Gabriel. I don't want to explain. I made a decision. Just as you do. The kind of decision that you make in battle—irrevocable, and binding. It is made. I have never hidden what I feel for you." She looked him in the eye. "But I will not act on it." She nodded crisply. "Ever."

"But—" he began.

She got up. "Don't ask. You love me? Don't ask. If you sent Michael to his death to save your company—would you?"

He pursed his lips. Had he known, for a moment his expression was the twin of what hers had been. "You're not an easy friend. Yes, I can see myself doing it."

She nodded. "Let's say it worked. Michael dead, the company saved. How often would you care to revisit that decision?"

He rose, too. "I think—I think I understand." He shook his head. "Oh, Amicia."

Impulsively, she put a hand behind his head and kissed him—quickly, on the lips, the way she might kiss Katherine or Father Arnaud. "I will teach your children," she said. "I just won't bear them."

He stood for a moment, as if stunned. Then he knelt at her feet, and kissed one of her hands.

From his knees, he smiled. "Am I really unkillable?" he asked.

She grinned. Breath flowed out of her, and her shoulders relaxed.

"Don't press your luck," she said.

After that, they spoke for almost an hour—easily, talking. Mostly, he told her what he had learned in Liviapolis, and from the Wyrm. She was reticent about the secrets of Lissen Carak, but she grunted at some of his theories.

"What did Father Arnaud think of your Wyrm?" she asked, when it was clearly time for them to go.

"The Wyrm restored his powers to heal," Gabriel said.

Instead of responding, she went and put a hand into the waterfall. She drank—the water chilled her hand almost instantly.

"Before we go back to the world," she said. "Tell me why you are coming to peace with God."

"Is this confession?" he asked. "Bless me, Mother, for it is roughly ten years since my last confession. Shall I start with the murders or the lechery?"

"Blasphemy comes so easily to you," she said.

"My mother has always seen herself as God's peer." He shrugged.

"I like your mother," Amicia said. "I think you need to stop hiding from her, and behind her. We all have mothers." She took his hands. "God?"

He nodded. "Oh, I think I have allowed myself to fall into the same trap that every highly-strung boy and girl since Adam and Eve has fallen into. That I was specially cursed by God."

"Rotten theology," she said.

"Mmm." His non-committal grunt was almost lost in the water sounds.

"I'm not yet entirely convinced. And then, instead of miraculous conversion, my dear Sister, you will find me merely a tiresome agnostic. Asking all the usual questions—why so there so much suffering? Why is the world run by a handful of malicious super-entities with special powers? Where is the proof of God's love?" He looked down at her hands. "I confess that when you hold my hands, I have a frisson of belief in God's love."

"Is there a better line of patter in all the spheres?" she said, eyes wide. "Love me, and I'll come to God?"

They laughed together. It was a good laugh.

"You will find another," she said.

"Never," he said.

"Yes, love. Now be easy." She reached out to touch him, and felt a frisson of power—merely an echo of power. But she knew the taste, and she smiled, because Ghause had put a love-spell on her, and it made her laugh. "Like to like," she murmured.

"What's that?" Gabriel said.

"Thanks," Amicia said. "This was—beautiful."

Gabriel bowed. "We should go back."

Two hours later, they re-joined the column south of the bluffs, and crossed Sixth Bridge at its head. Perhaps there were ribald comments, but Sister Amicia's demeanour laughed them to scorn. She rode with the captain, and her sisters, too, and by the time the column halted for a midday meal, their light-heartedness had spread down the column.

After lunch, Bad Tom joined them. The herds were now almost a full day behind. But he rode with Ser Gabriel and the nuns and Chris Foliak and Francis Atcourt, exchanged loud gests with Ser Danved, tried and failed to provoke Ser Bertran. They hawked for an hour, and secured some partridges for dinner, and they met Ser Gavin, who'd taken the advance guard well down the road.

While the two brothers were talking a bird appeared above them, and every hermetical practitioner in the column looked up, all together.

Ser Alcaeus, in the rear with the Moreans, spurred up the column in time to join the captain as he retrieved the enormous bird, an imperial messenger. He took the bird, smoothed its feathers and gentled it, and then deftly slipped off the two message tubes.

"Encrypted," he said. He handed them to the captain.

"How far to camp?" Ser Gabriel asked his brother.

Ser Gavin—a new man since seeing his affianced lady at Lissen Carak—pointed ahead. "Two leagues. Next ridge, and just beyond."

The captain pushed the two tubes up under his chin and looked at Ser Alcaeus. "If I stop here to read them," he said, "we won't have any supper."

Alcaeus made a moue. "It's Lent," he said. "Supper will be too dull for words."

266

Chris Foliak leaned over. "It's almost never Lent at my table," he said—but when he caught Amicia's eye, he had the good grace to look away.

The imperial messenger was the end of their day of Maying, as Amicia thought of it. They rode faster and with purpose—so fast that she dropped back with her sisters, afraid that Mary would have a mishap. So she missed the captain's arrival. But when she rode into the camp—with most of the tents already up, and no one behind her but the Moreans—she found Nell laying out their bedding.

"Many thanks, Nell!" she said. The beautiful day had dried the blankets, even on the rump of her horse, and she looked forward to sleep—dry sleep.

"Captain says for you to come when it's convenient," Nell said. "Which means as soon as you can, Sister."

She entered the red pavilion to the sound of silence. Ser Gavin was there, and Ser Michael, and Ser Thomas and Ser Christos, and Ser Alcaeus stood by the captain. He was writing on wax. Cully sat with his legs crossed, drinking wine.

Everyone looked serious. And they all looked at her—her heart missed a beat. They looked at her as if someone had died.

"What?" she asked.

Gabriel—she couldn't think of him as the captain, today—rose and came over to her.

"The King," he said gently. "The King has disestablished your order, with the consent of the archbishop. He has unmade the Order of Saint Thomas."

She sighed. "No king—not even the Patriarch—can unmake what God has made," she said.

Ser Michael rose. "On behalf of all the company, Sister," he said. "You and the Prior, and Father Arnaud—you are all an example to us every day."

Ser Gabriel nodded. "I agree," he said. "What will you do?"

"Have a cup of wine," Amicia said, sitting. She couldn't bring herself to laugh. "I need to think."

"You are welcome in our council, Sister," Ser Michael said, reminding her that she was, in fact, intruding on a council of war. It was obvious from the two maps on the table and the wax tablets at every hand.

"That can't have been the only news," Amicia said.

Ser Alcaeus looked as if he might protest, but Ser Gabriel smiled at her—a warmth to his smile which she bathed in for a moment. A guilty pleasure. "No. The Queen's trial is set for Tuesday next week—at the tournament. There's a long list of attainders, forfeitures and treasons."

"My father is to be executed," Ser Michael said with chilling equanimity.

"Half the nobility is to be taken and executed," Gabriel said. "Apparently by the other half, and a handful of Galles."

"Scarce a handful," Ser Thomas said. "Three hundred lances with that monster, Du Corse."

Ser Michael laughed. "Seldom is a man so aptly named."

"There's open faction and war in Harndon," Gabriel said. "The commons against the nobles, or so it appears. The King has managed to attaint Ser Gerald Random."

"The richest *and* the most loyal man in the kingdom," muttered Ser Gavin.

"There's refugees fleeing the city, the King is considering martial law, and it would appear that the Archbishop of Lorica is the prime mover of all this." Gabriel flung a small, almost transparent piece of parchment on the table.

Ser Michael frowned. "It's as if he *wants* civil war."

Gabriel nodded. "Someone wants civil war. Someone very clever."

Michael shook his head. "Send for the company."

Gabriel shook his head in turn. "Why? We're not under attack. Listen, my friends—we have a licence to ride armed to a tournament. We're going to the tournament, and we are within the law."

Suddenly, Amicia saw it. "You're going to fight for the Queen!" she said.

Ser Michael's head snapped around, and so did Ser Gavin's.

Gabriel had the look of insufferable triumphant pleasure that he wore when one of his little schemes went well. His lips pursed and his cheeks were stretched and he looked like a cat who had caught a mouse.

"I am, too," he said.

"May we all live to get you there," Ser Michael said. "You bastard. I want to fight for the Queen!"

Gabriel shook his head. "You're going to rescue your father. And some other people."

Bad Tom rubbed his hairy chin. "We're going to cut our way in and out?" he said with evident pleasure.

The Red Knight sighed. "No, Tom. No, we're going to make every effort to be reasonable, responsible knights who do not want to inflict public violence on people already at the verge of civil war."

Bad Tom grinned. "You're just saying that." He smiled. "You'll need to run courses every day."

Ser Gabriel nodded. "I will—but I don't want to be injured."

His brother laughed mirthlessly. "You are the original glory-thief. If you're injured, I'm sure one of us can find the time to take your place."

There was some forced laughter.

Bad Tom grinned ear to ear. "It's fewkin' de Vrailly?" he asked.

Ser Gabriel shrugged. "It won't be the King in person. De Vrailly is his champion."

Ser Gavin looked at his brother. "He's mine," he said. "As God is my witness. I want him."

The knights at the table looked at each other.

Ser Gavin leaned forward. "I'm the best jouster."

Ser Gabriel nodded. "Yes," he said slowly, and then smiled at his brother. "Some days." He sat back. "The Queen asked me, last fall. I don't think she knew what was at stake then—"

Tom Lachlan slapped his thigh. "At stake!" he said, laughing. "Damn me, that's good."

The next two days on the road were not like the first week. They moved faster, into the northern Albin, on better roads, crossing the great bridges over the river with each great bend, and paying tolls to local lords at every bridge. The King's officers maintained the bridges and the roads, and local men collected the tolls and passed them to Harndon. Trade on the Royal Road was one of the major sources of northern revenue.

"Why doesn't the Royal Road run all the way to Albinkirk?" Sister Katherine asked one evening.

Ser Gavin, who had just sung evensong with the nuns, made a face. "Mostly, because of my da," he said. "In the dark times before Chevin, the creatures of the Wild ruined every road they could find—they tried to cut Albinkirk off from Harndon altogether." He shook his head. "The great lords of the north used to maintain the northern stretches of the road. My da doesn't see any need to be connected to Harndon or to pay taxes there."

"So—" Amicia could see it as if on a map in her head—which it was, in a way, in her memory palace. "So north of Sixth Bridge..."

"North of Sixth Bridge is a network of little muddy trails rather than a single maintained road. Even under the old King, the gorge and the highlands made it hard to maintain a big road." Ser Gavin stared off into the evening. "If we had a good king, and time, and peace, we'd finish the road—and that would spur trade, and link the north more closely to the south."

"Ser Gerald showed that it could be done by boat. All the way to Lorica." Sister Amicia couldn't help but watch as Ser Thomas and Ser Gabriel came together on the plain to her right. Their armour glowed in the twilight, and their horses' hooves shook the earth.

Ser Gavin nodded. "I will go join them—I'm late getting armed. Random's boats made it, and will again this year. But it's four days getting around the falls, and in a wet spring, with the river high—a hard row above the falls in the gorge." He looked out over the rich fields. "But if the kingdom's ever to be united—the river and the road will both have to go all the way through."

South of Fifth Bridge, there was traffic on the roads. They passed a late convoy rolling north—a convoy that knew less than they did about events in Harndon. They were still three days from Lorica.

"Lorica on Good Friday," Amicia said to Sister Mary. "We can observe it in the Basilica!"

She made bright small talk with her nuns and tried to ignore the signs around her, but the soldiers looked grimmer and grimmer as they moved south. They had begun to see refugees on the roads—at first, they were mostly prosperous people with carts. But a day out from Lorica, they were seeing hundreds of people, families, and some had already been robbed. They looked like tinkers—dirty, carrying sacks of belongings with spare clothes and odd items attached any which way.

Neither the nuns nor the soldiers could ignore them. Many begged for food—many told harrowing tales.

Ser Gabriel found her towards afternoon on the tenth day on the road. "I'm not going to Lorica," he said.

"I saw you send Mikal off to the east," she replied.

"Good eye, then. There are small roads now, on both sides of the river. We'll turn east and make for the highlands and try to outflank the refugees."

"You're not telling me everything," she said.

For the first time, anger flashed across his face, and he was impatient. "I'm not lying. I can tell you what I guess, but what I know makes a very slim volume. I wish you were not here. Is that too frank? They want you. This is...orders of magnitude worse than what I expected. I feel like a fool—practising for a joust when the whole kingdom is coming apart like a doll crushed under a wagon wheel."

He looked away, as if he'd annoyed himself.

"You don't like to feel as if you are not in control," she said.

"That's facile. No one's in control in a war, but this is—insane. A king, ripping apart his own land and his own marriage?"

Amicia nodded. "Well, I shall miss Easter in the basilica of Lorica," she said. "But I'm not foolish enough to ride off on my own."

He nodded. "Good," he said.

That was it—no flirting and no discussion.

"I think we've become part of their company," she confided to Katherine, who laughed mirthlessly.

"One of the pages offered to marry me, if his knight would allow it," Katherine said. "I think I'm old enough to be his mother."

Sister Mary blushed.

They rode east, away from the setting sun.

That was a long night.

What the captain hadn't mentioned was that they wouldn't be stopping to camp. The turn east was accompanied by a further increase in speed, with veteran squires leading the files in alternating walking and trotting their horses. Even Katherine began to suffer, and by moonrise, Amicia was chewing her lower lip in mingled fatigue and pain. Sister Mary was moaning.

The column halted. The moon was three-quarters full; the narrow road was clear and fairly hard between darkened fields.

"Dismount," came down the column.

Ser Christos, very chivalrously, leapt from his riding horse and helped Sister Mary off her mount.

Sister Katherine slid from the saddle, tired but unbeaten. "Don't tell me that this is nothing next to Christ's Passion," she said. "I know it is nothing, but it is sufficient penance for everything I've ever thought about Miriam."

Pages came down the column, shadows shifting in the odd, moon-shot darkness. They had feedbags already prepared, and they helped the nuns put them on their horses' heads.

Nell appeared at Amicia's elbow. "Cap'n says you have about half an hour, and is everyone all right?" she asked, in his accent exactly.

Amicia waved a tired hand. "No one ever died of riding sores," she said. "I hope."

All too soon, they were off again, the whole column a quiet jingle of horse harness and mail and steel plate and leather. They passed through a small hamlet—dogs barked, but no one came to their doors.

Past the hamlet they turned suddenly south, and she realized they were riding along the crest of a tall, shallowly sloped ridge, and she could see the twinkling lights of a dozen distant villages—odd that they should have light so late.

South. She knew enough stars to know that they had turned south, towards Harndon, and that the smoke on the horizon to the west must be the breakfast fires of Lorica, the kingdom's second city.

They didn't stop or make camp.

By noon, Amicia was asleep in her saddle. She dozed away an hour or more, and woke sharply to find the column halted in deep forest. Behind her, Ser Christos was again helping Sister Mary to dismount—or rather, to collapse.

Pages appeared and gathered the horses. Amicia's was done—lathered all down his flanks and wild-eyed.

She didn't know the page who took her mount, but the boy smiled. "Never you mind, Sister, I'll have your little mare right as rain by tonight."

"So we're to sleep?" she asked. She was too tired for anger or complaint.

It was like the convent, after all.

The page shrugged. "No one told me. But if we're currying and feeding ta' horses, stands ta' reason we won't move for some time. Eh?" He winked.

Sister Amicia gathered the other two nuns and led them to the shade of a great oak tree. They lay down—Mary collapsed—and slept.

Amicia awoke with a tree root carving a hole in her side to realize that she had slept through Christ's Passion and she was instantly on her knees.

When most of the rest of the company was awake, she led them in prayers of contrition.

A valet brought her a bowl of oatmeal.

"Oatmeal?" she asked.

"Nicomedes says it's Good Friday," Bobert, the youngest valet, said. "No meat, no fish."

Ser Gabriel rode up, and Amicia was distantly pleased to see that his red jupon was rumpled and something had left a crease on his forehead. He smiled at her.

"This is your notion of Good Friday observance?" she asked.

"Fasting and travail?" He nodded. "Pretty much—ah, here's Tom."

Ser Thomas came up with a dozen heavily armed Hillmen at his tail, all mounted. "Well, Kenneth Dhu has the herd until we get this done," he said. "You made good time."

"Only the next week will see what 'good time' might have been," Ser Gabriel said.

Almost as soon as the column moved off they left the woods, which were not the deep forest Amicia had imagined but instead a small copse of carefully tended great oaks on a rich manor. As the sun set in the west, Amicia looked around her. She could see fields—and to the east, mountains, their tall, snow-capped summits catching sun.

"Wolf's Head, the Rabbit Ears, White Face and Hard Rede," Nell said, pointing to them. "My family's from these parts. Morea's another hundred leagues over that way."

Ser Christos smiled at the page. "Not my part of Morea, young maiden. This is the soft south, where men grow olives, not warriors."

Behind his back, Nell made a face. "Who'd want to grow warriors?" she asked.

They rode until the sky was dark and the stars twinkled overhead, and then dismounted and drank a cup of wine, every man and woman, their reins in their hands. Then most men changed horses, and the nuns were put up on three strange riding horses, and the next few miles passed swiftly as the three women learned to manage bigger, more dangerous animals. But no one was thrown, and they had another halt at a crossroad. There were four big wagons pulled into the other arm of the cross, blocking any traffic from the high hedges on either side.

Ser Christos grunted.

"What is it?" Amicia asked him.

"Food," Christos said. "I wondered. He's purchased food." He nodded, as if satisfied.

The captain himself materialized out of the darkness like an unclean spirit. "It's easy to get food now," he said. "Wait 'til we're running north. Then it will be exciting." But he smiled, and his smile suggested he was more comfortable with the situation than he had been the day before.

Morning found them in another grove—this one bigger, on the eastern slope of another great ridge. Amicia thought she glimpsed the Albin running down to the sea in the middle distance—twenty miles. That put them far east of Harndon.

Holy Saturday.

They made a small camp. The women cooked—a rare event in the company—and made beef soup with dumplings and new greens—something Amicia hadn't had before, but the nuns ate without complaint.

Ser Gavin and the other knights came for morning prayers. As they were singing, Sister Amicia saw one of the great imperial messengers circle and land on the captain's wrist, and suddenly her outdoor service was much smaller. But the captain must have brushed them off—most of the knights came back to sing.

They turned west. For some reason, Amicia's heart quickened. They moved at a trot for more than an hour and then turned south towards the river, rode into the outer wards of a small castle, dismounted, and collapsed into sleep.

When Amicia awoke, it was almost dark, and men were already mounting.

Ser Gabriel took her elbow. "We'll halt at the monastery at Bothey," he said. "Unless I miss my timing, you can all go hear Easter Vigil and greet the risen saviour."

"And you?" she asked.

"I'll spare you the details," he said. He didn't grin. He looked terrible, with straw on his clothes and deep circles under his eyes.

"Don't be a foolish martyr," she said. "You need rest, to fight. And Easter mass might help you in many ways."

Then, he smiled. "Perhaps," he said.

They rode into the late evening. The air was warm, fragrant with a later spring than they'd known ten days earlier in Albinkirk, where there was still snow under the trees. Here, it was the edge of summer, and in the last light of day, flowers bloomed in a riot of colour and scent along the road's edges, and all the hedgerows were thick walls of green guarding fields where the plantings were already a fist tall or taller.

Darkness fell. An owl hooted repeatedly ahead of the column, and then another, to their right—the north, she thought.

The whole column moved from a walk to a trot.

Sister Mary didn't even groan. She was a better rider every day, and she didn't complain at all. She hadn't moaned since they slept under the tree. Nor did Sister Katherine speak of the joys of riding anymore.

In fact, no one spoke at all. The saddles creaked, the armour clacked, and the company passed like shades of the past along the Harndon Road.

The moon climbed the sky.

She dozed, and then awoke to hear owls hooting to the front and to the right, again, and the column shuffled to a halt.

Amicia kept riding. She told herself that she wanted to be at mass if it could possibly be arranged, but she knew in her heart that she wanted to know what was happening. She could taste smoke—in the back of her throat, on the tip of her tongue. She saw the Moreans walling people—refugees—away from the column—at sword's point.

At the head of the column there were a dozen men standing on the road around two points of mage light.

There was a newcomer in the command group and she knew him immediately from the siege—and took his hand.

"Ser Gelfred!" she said.

He knelt in the road, and she blessed him—and in moments she and her sisters had work. Gelfred and his corporal, Daniel Favour, were both wounded—long slashes with much blood and little immediate danger beyond infection. The three nuns sang and healed.

"Ser Ranald's inside the palace with a dozen of the lads," Gelfred said. "I can't say more. You told us to keep our operations separate."

Ser Gabriel smiled without humour. "Don't do everything I tell you," he said. "So you have no idea what Ranald is up to?"

"Not no idea," Gelfred said. He smiled. "Sister, that's the first time in four days I haven't been in pain. God loves you."

She smiled.

Ser Gelfred was back to work. "Not no idea, Captain. We brought Lady Almspend away a week ago; and yester eve Ranald handed us Ser Gerald and one of the aldermen. Alderwomen." He shrugged. "And the paynim—no, I lie, he came from the knights."

"The knights?" Bad Tom asked.

"The Archbishop's disbanded the Order and declared all their lands and money forfeit. He tried to seize all of them." Gelfred shrugged. "They've too many friends—by all the Saints, even the Galles love the Order. They probably had warning before the King signed the writ. Prior Wishart took all his people—he's gone." Gelfred wrinkled his nose. "Not gone far. Waiting for you, I reckon." He jerked a thumb over his shoulder.

"Disbanded the Order," Sister Mary said.

"I told you, Sister," Amicia whispered.

"It's different, here," Mary said, sounding scared. "Disbanded? What of our vows?"

"Our vows are unchanged, as is the Order," Amicia said with far more confidence than she felt.

"And the smoke?" Ser Gavin asked.

"A good part of the south end of Harndon was afire yesterday," Gelfred said. "The commons burned the archbishop's palace." He didn't quite grin. "Someone took all the relics and—well—all the treasure from the cathedral."

Ser Gabriel was stone-faced. "Harndon is burning?" he asked.

Gelfred nodded.

"Someone's laughing," he said bitterly.

"There's more. The prince of Occitan is just south of the city. He's made a camp—not a fortified camp, but an open camp like a tournament." Gelfred coughed into his hand. "I—hmm—took the liberty of telling him that we had reason to believe the King would attack him." Gelfred raised both eyebrows. "I do not think he believed me," he added.

"How many men does he have?" Bad Tom asked, pragmatically.

"About what you have. A hundred lances—perhaps more." Gelfred shook his head. "The Galles have three hundred new lances, and all the King's Guard, and every sell-sword in the south." He didn't laugh, but again he allowed a smile of satisfaction to dent his mouth. "Including a fair number of my lads and Ranald's."

"Is the Prior at the monastery?" Ser Gabriel asked. He cocked an eyebrow.

Gelfred nodded. "Aye."

Gabriel nodded, too. "Well—Easter vigil for everyone, then," he said. "Mount."

An hour later, and the company rode under the two high towers of the famous Abbey of the South—the Abbey of Bothey. Bothey had long been a favourite Abbey of both the Kings of Alba and the Earls of Towbray. It had all the marks of riches and royal favour—gold and silver vessels, magnificent frescos, some very old indeed—carved choir stalls and an altar screen of two knights in ancient harness fighting a dragon.

For all their wealth, the monks were not decadent. The brothers of the Order tilled their own land, and the sisters from the "women's house" sowed grain and made the best fine linen in the Nova Terra.

The company were led silently into a dark chapel by cowled monks in black and brown habits. Even the captain was silent and respectful. The monks on the gates had included some with robes over full armour, and two stern-faced nuns had received Amicia and her sisters. The darkened chapel was the size of many a fair town church, with rafters sixty feet above a marble floor of interlocking hexagons. The chapel was so dark that Amicia could not see her hand in front of her face—literally, for she tried. She was led off to the right, where the nuns and novices of two orders stood in silent communion.

No bells rang.

It was the last moment of Lent.

There was a rustling in the dark, at the back of the church, a single candle was lit by a monk, and a priest of the Order of Saint Thomas began to pray.

The single candle illuminated the magnificent chapel of the Abbey of Bothey. Fifty years ago, one of the most gifted pargeters Harndon had ever nurtured had painted the whole chapel in one summer in the Etruscan manner; floor to ceiling paintings of the events of Christ's life and Passion. The gold leaf alone was staggering, swimming in burnished metallic light even with only a single lit candle—and the quality of the painting was superb. Saint James was martyred, Jesus healed a man made blind and the now-sighted man rebuked the military governor for unbelief, his armour a bronze-gold against the brilliant polished lemon-gold of the background.

And then monks and nuns began to sing, as did the knights of the Order, the brother sergeants and the sisters. There were twenty knights in their robes standing in the choir stalls, and a dozen sisters of the Order from the two houses in Southern Harndon. For Amicia and her sisters, it was a homecoming—a delight mixed with sadness. And the mass was one that Amicia would never forget, sung so well in a chapel so redolent with both splendour and meaning, surrounded by her own Order—and by the men and women of the company with whom she'd shared the road. As the first hour slipped away and the congregation sang the rolls of saints and martyrs, a taut expectancy filled the church, and as the bell outside tolled the middle of the night and the birth of a new day, Amicia lit her candle from a torch held by a knight of the Order, and the church sprang from darkness to bright light, and many of the monks and nuns produced hand bells from their robes and rang them joyously, so that the shrill riot of bells seemed to drive the darkness out and replace it with the throaty roar of gold and the coming dawn.

By the time the host was consecrated, every one of the company were on their knees on the hard stone floor—even the captain.

And after mass—as they celebrated their risen God—there was wine in the abbey's paved courtyard, and an air of festivity that many would not have associated with monks and nuns living a life of cloistered virtue. Monks in brown habits lay under the stars on the smooth grass of the cloister's central yard, discussing theology, and nuns sat in among the pillars of the double cloister, sipping strong red wine and laughing. Most of the knights of Saint Thomas were unarmed and unarmoured, the rest stood with their swords incongruous with their black monkish robes and academic caps, while the nuns of the Order—more worldly, and more given to the practice of medicine than to mystical contemplation—laughed louder and drank harder. For an hour or more, the threat of civil war was forgotten by most in the glory of God's resurrection.

Amicia found herself in a spirited conversation about the theological failings of the Patriarch of Rhum and the Archbishop of Lorica. The Minorites who held the abbey had more than a few hermetical practitioners among them—practical men and one woman who could make small fires, light candles, and the like. They were outraged—and deeply uneasy—at the sudden change in direction. They had thought themselves blessed, and were now told to believe themselves accursed. Many of the knights had some turn of talent—and having already had their Order declared anathema, they were in no mood to discuss the intellectual possibilities or the failings of the scholastics in Lucrece.

As a nun of the Abbey at Lissen Carak, Amicia was both welcome and something of an oddity—the northern sisters hardly ever left their fortress. Amicia discovered in a few minutes of conversation that she was notorious as both a powerful mage and as a woman licensed to preach.

Ser Tristan, an older Occitan knight of the Order, frowned and admitted that he might not have been in favour of any woman saying mass.

"But you are one of ours," he said. "And to hell with the archbishop."

Sister Amicia wasn't sure whether to be pleased or offended. She had been aware—at a distance—that there were factions in the church, but now she felt naive as she confronted their reality. Even in the midst of celebration, there were some to whom she was a hero, and others who clearly kept their distance.

She was reminded of her duty, and her place, over and over—a lesson in humility that she had the grace to accept.

After two cups of good wine and an hour of conversation, praise, censure, and a hundred introductions, she found that she was exhausted—almost too tired to sleep. While the knights who knew her from the siege carried her from group to group like a prize, introducing her to the monks, priests and nuns of both orders, Katherine and Mary had followed some of the other Thomasine sisters to the women's house, and Amicia was on the point of asking Ser Michael for directions—she could scarcely keep her eyes open—when a small girl came, curtsied, and said Prior Wishart had summoned her. She found him in the outer yard with two secular knights she didn't know and she put her hands in her sleeves and stood demurely, waiting. She was afraid she might fall asleep on her feet.

He glanced at her and smiled—a clear confirmation that she was to await him.

She allowed her eyelids to fall, and in the next few beats of her heart received a pulse of apprehension as great as she had ever known.

Something evil.

Her eyes snapped open and she looked around, but the low murmur of voices and the sound of celebration—from the town below them as much as from the yard—spoke only of the feast of Easter.

The prior came and took her hand. "I won't keep you long," he said.

He looked as tired as she felt.

"I need you to tell me anything you can," he said.

"About Ser Gabriel?" she asked, understanding all too well.

"Sister Amicia, we're teetering on the brink of civil war—or sliding past it." Prior Wishart took her arm and led her to the abbey walls and then up stone steps to the crenellations. In the distance, on the edge of the dark horizon, there was a glow. And the smell of smoke was no longer hidden by incense.

"Where is my duty now?" he asked.

She didn't think he was asking her.

"Can I trust him?" the Prior asked her.

She put her hands to her mouth. She almost giggled—a reaction of fatigue. "Yes," she said.

Prior Wishart peered at her from the darkness. "You have a—hmm—relationship with him," he said.

"I have not slept with him," she said a little too quickly.

"Sister, I have been a soldier and a priest for a long time." He looked out into the night. "If I thought you had then I would not curse you, but neither would I look to you for guidance. Some men—more men every day..." He paused. "They wonder if the man who is called the Red Knight—" He shrugged. "If he is the King's bastard son. I have heard it said many times now. And I have a report that his mother, the duchess, is suggesting the north should make its own king."

Amicia put her whole weight against one of the merlons. "Isn't our Order supposed to be above this sort of thing?" she asked.

"Never. No organization, no order, no group is above the manipulations of others. If we are strong, we can help shape the final outcomes, and if we are weak, we may become the tool of someone powerful—a tool that cannot make its own decisions." The Prior nodded. "One of my options is to take all of us across the sea, or into Morea. Another is to go into the north. To Lissen Carak. And await events there."

Amicia was too tired for all this. "All I know is that he and his people think they will rescue the Queen," she said.

"Ahh," the Prior said. He leaned down and kissed her on the forehead. "That is precisely what I wanted to hear." He put a hand on her head. "Will he fight for the Queen?"

Amicia felt she would betray a confidence by answering, but she shrugged inwardly. "I believe Ser Gabriel views himself as the Queen's Champion. Indeed, I believe she asked him—but before the role had quite such consequences."

"Against the King?" the Prior asked quickly.

Amicia pursed her lips and snapped, "I have never heard him say aught against the King, or the Queen. He bears no love for the Galles." She frowned. "I have attended a number of the meetings of his officers. They are open in their derision of the King's weakness. But then—" She looked hard at the prior. "But then, so am I."

"Bah," Prior Wishart said. "It's no treason at this point to think the King is mad or ensorcelled. Go sleep. Tomorrow will be very hard I suspect."

She curtsied. "I sense something...evil," she said.

Prior Wishart paused. "You are much stronger than I," he said. "Yet I do feel some—*malmaissance*. Where is it, though? Is it Harndon, burning?"

She took a deep breath, steadied herself, and searched with her *aethereal* eye.

"It's in the sky," she said quietly.

Wishart looked up. He looked for long enough that her eyelids began to sag.

"Happy Easter, Sister," he said. "I have to hope that it is a figment of our fatigue and our crisis. I cannot believe we are open here—on this night—to direct attack. Go and sleep."

She nodded, almost beyond speech, and went down from the wall. It was two or three hours after midnight—most of the abbey was asleep, and aside from the watch on the walls, most voices were stilled. The torches were out, and she took a wrong turn at the foot of the steps and found herself in the inner cloister, but aside from the monks lying on the grass, everyone was gone, and the only other men awake were some servants finishing the wine. She found the low tunnel, richly carved, that led from the inner cloister to the outer and, drawn by voices, she felt her way through the dark.

Halfway, in almost total darkness, she had another shock of apprehension. She thought for a moment it might be her fatigue as the Prior had said, but she closed her eyes and *entered her palace and made a very small working—an open net of woven* ops *to catch the workings of others. It was a working she had learned from Gabriel.*

She released it. And settled like a spider in a web to "see" what she might see in the aethereal.

She dropped out of her palace and felt her way forward, a portion of her awareness now tucked away in her palace.

Just at the end of the tunnel, four men were sitting in the shade of a grape arbor in the courtyard.

One of them was Gabriel—she'd know his voice anywhere. The big man was clearly Ser Thomas—a nose taller than any other man she'd ever met.

"Gabriel," she said sharply.

He rose.

"There's something—" she said, and extended her hand.

He reached out in the real.

The other two men were almost as big as Ser Thomas—a big red-headed knight of her own Order, who she knew by repute and by the sheer size of his nose. Ser Ricar Orcsbane.

And a black man the size of a small house, or so it seemed. The men rose as she approached and bowed—the black man very elegantly, by putting his hands together and bending at the waist.

"Sister Amicia, of the Order of Saint Thomas," Gabriel said, and repeated it in passable Etruscan. His smile was tired, but warmed her nonetheless.

In her heart, she thought, *I must get him to pay attention.*

"This magnificent gentleman is Ser Pavalo l-Walīd Muḥammad Payam." Ser Gabriel spoke the name cautiously—for once, it was a language he did not know. But the dark-skinned man bowed again and smiled at the sound of his name.

"You went to mass," Amicia said. "I saw you." She made herself smile, but she seized Gabriel's hand and tried to drag him by main force into her memory palace.

"He says he craves your blessing." Gabriel shrugged. "I have been to mass before and was not slain by lightning, nor do my infernal legions always make trouble."

"He took the host," Tom Lachlan said. "I expected the chapel to collapse."

Between one sentence and the next *he was there with her.*

"There's something out there—there. In that direction." She pointed at the simulacrum of her sensory net in the aethereal, *which was ripped asunder somewhere above her and to the north. Direction and distance were not the same in the* aethereal *as in the real.*

Gabriel looked at the screen of aethereal *force she had projected.*

In the real, Amicia put a hand on the dark-skinned man's hand and said a small prayer for his soul.

"I tried to get the infidel to come to mass," Tom said. He grinned. "I mean, if the captain was there, what would one more damned soul matter?"

Amicia had suddenly had enough. "Don't mock what you do not understand," she snapped.

Tom was seldom baulked. But like most very dangerous men, he was not a fool. He bowed his head. "Sister?" he asked quietly.

"Something is wrong," Ser Gabriel said. He was back in the real. He turned to look north. "Toby—my spear."

Toby detached himself from a wall and ran for the stables.

"Amicia, get behind us," Gabriel said. He still had her hand—and something about his instant willingness to believe her, to obey and react—

She turned to look.

Turned back to speak to him. She opened her mouth to say something neither of them would ever be able to forget, and she knew better—fatigue, religion, love, danger—it was a heady potion that transcended day-to-day and common sense, her usual guideposts all thrown down. The sense of *wrongness* now filled the air around her. Whatever it was, it was aimed for him, not her. She cast a protection, a mirror to confuse whatever the malevolence was; she borrowed his aura and put it on.

She raised a shield of glowing gold with a twitch of her be-ringed hand.

Something black fluttered out of the darkness onto her face, right through her shield.

At its touch, she screamed.

The Red Knight saw the change in her posture. He tossed the first working in his arsenal—

Fiat Lux.

Golden light leapt from a point fifty feet above them.

It revealed a beautiful horror—six magnificent, shimmering black moths, each the size of a great eagle, their wings the purest black satin shot with veins of blue-black that throbbed with *ops* and thick velvet-black bodies with elaborate black filigree and lace antennae—and probisci of obscene dimensions, long as baselards and swollen with a velvety hardness that made the skin crawl, tipped with adamant that shone like blued steel.

One of them fluttered against Amicia even as the light burgeoned.

Its probiscis throbbed with power and bit—and she screamed.

The Ifriquy'an's long, curved sword slipped from the scabbard and flowed out and up like liquid metal in the silver-gold of mixed moonlight and mage light. He was a pace behind Amicia and his sword struck at an angle from the scabbard—severed a great, rapidly beating wing *and the probiscis at its base* in one strike—the sword passed through its target and swept back, was reversed, and swept back up, almost the same line, cutting off a lock of her hair as her knees gave from the poison and opening the velvet body from base to eye-cases in a shower of *ops* and *potentia* and black acid blood.

Amicia fell in the loose-limbed sprawl of death.

The Red Knight's sword snapped from the scabbard and cut into another of the monsters—this one intended for him, wings spread and virulent poison already dripping. His sword slammed into it—and bounced off.

He'd had a clue that they were *aethereal* from the sparks. He rolled, a leather-soft wing clipped his thigh and something disgustingly velvety touched his hand—his arming sword reached out, striking a panicked blow. But as his point came on line he thrust—the blade tip snagged its material belly and because it was flying and had no anchor, it rebounded. The point, sharp as one of Mag's needles, had still failed to bite. But it was pushed, tumbling, through fifteen feet of darkness to slam into one of its mates.

Ser Gabriel realized then that they were *all* coming for him—but his attention was on Amicia. "They're magicked!" he shouted. "No mortal weapon will bite!"

He rolled under the table where the men had been sitting. One of them slipped past Ser Pavalo and landed awkwardly on the table—cups exploded out, and it flipped the table.

He saw Bad Tom, armed with the dragon's sword, split another one in half, the two sides lit in a white-veined horror for one beat of a frightened man's heart, the two wings each beating separately once, ripping the two halves apart and spraying black ichor. Ser Pavalo rolled, passing under a gout of the foul stuff, and rose to strike from beneath a moth with a rising cut—then whirled, and struck again as if gifted with eyes in the back of his head.

Gavin had no magic sword. He leapt onto the back of the one on the table. It was low and slow, and it didn't seem to have any weapons that could reach its back—Gavin got his arms *under* its wings as if putting a small man in a head lock, and pushed the body away from him with both hands and all the passion of abhorrence, and the wings seemed to shred.

It was all perfectly silent.

Gabriel saw two of the black velvet horrors unengaged—one attempting to rise over the melee, and the other settling on the prone figure of the dying nun.

"Amicia!" he screamed.

He threw himself towards her. In *the* aethereal, *he flooded her bridge with light—and, improvising heartbeat by heartbeat—tried forcing* ops *back down the bond—first through the ring, and then the strange working on his ankle.*

He refused to accept that the pale corpse on the bridge was hers.

He poured his power into their bond…

One of the moths had him. He was on his stomach, stretched over her body, and the moth was settling on him, the weight like that of a dog—he felt the…

In the moment that the thing's probisicis penetrated his back, he took his hate and terror and pushed it right up through the contact, into its body.

The moth exploded.

The poison *was lethal, but slower than hermetical counters—he set a construct to cleanse the wound with fire even as he reached for her—*

—and found her.

"Anything!" he shouted at the universe. "I will give *anything*."

Then, desperation winning over mastery, he pushed her aethereal *form off the bridge and into the torrent of green* potentia *that rushed under it.*

The power—the raw power that she channelled so often—washed the caked, burned flakes off her face and left new, fresh skin. Her green gown was gone and she was naked.

He knew his myths, and when he'd held her in the stream long enough, he hauled her by main force onto the bridge, rolled her over and held the leg by which he'd held her in the power.

He had his arms under her arms, his hands clasped under her breasts, when her eyes opened.

She took a breath.

And another.

He pulled her back onto the bridge.

In the real, she was fully clothed. But her eyes were open.

"I thought I was dead," she said aloud.

The last moth, struck repeatedly by two Fell Swords, tried to reach its prey once more and was spitted on the spear, wielded by Toby, who levered the corpse away from his captain and the nun.

"You're alive," Gabriel said. He backed away, his voice strange, his arms still clasped around her as if he was unwilling to let go, and he dragged her away from the corpses of the moths even as Prior Wishart and half the monks of the abbey came at a run, a forest of vengeful swords. There was a long scream from the direction of the cloister.

He was reluctant to let her go. Aware that he had just made a pact with—something—for her life. He could feel it.

He heard the screams. He hauled her into a chair and let her go—one hand lingering on her hair.

It was foolish—stupid—but he had not touched her in so long…

He snapped himself to attention and *fell into his own palace.*

"There are more of them," Prudentia said.

He nodded. Having immolated one at point blank range, he had their making in his head, and he knew how to unmake them. More, his rage was such—

"Take a breath," Prudentia said. "You are badly hurt yourself."

Instead, he reached out into the darkness, and located them—only three, and those without the ferocity of purpose that had so nearly defeated him.

One was in the town, having killed two women and a child and a cat.

One was in the cloister hunting monks.

One was high in the air overhead, watching. Or rather, monitoring.

Prudentia said, "by offering such a promise you have given something a back door into your soul."

Gabriel reached out into the night with the same working he had used at the Inn of Dorling. He layered it with a simple working of identity from his intimate contact with the one that had landed on him.

In a flash of golden fire, a low stone house in the town exploded.

To his left, in the cloister, the moth was suddenly outlined in an angry red—and then fell as ash over the rose garden.

High overhead, the largest of all the moths turned away for home.

But Gabriel was sometimes an impatient hunter, and he followed it across the sky with his thought, leaving his wounded body to collapse to the cobbles.

He had never tried this particular form of aethereal movement, and it was terrifying—like being at court while naked. He was bereft of many of his powers—a thing of wind and fancy.

But rage bore him up. Rage cancelled out rational thought and kept him to his mission. He followed the fleeing thing up into the light of the moon, and out, running north to its master.

It didn't get more than three miles. Gabriel took it in the air and subsumed it, and like a conjuror he caught the single strand of aethereal will by which it was bound to its distant master and he—kept it.

And then he had to find his way back to his body.

When he did, he found it bruised, and with a burn the size of his hand with an ashy black centre high on his back, from which emerged an ugly dark trickle of something that stank.

He touched the growing dampness on his back and his vision tunnelled.

He was in a bed in the infirmary of the abbey. He let his eyes flutter open, and there was the Prior.

"I got them all," he said grimly. "Is she alive?"

Prior Wishart allowed himself a tired smile. "She's alive. But your officers have decided that you are not going anywhere today. There are new events, and new reports—the busy world has gone on without you." He sat on the edge of Ser Gabriel's bed. "I am not a cruel man—she lives and thrives. Her power cleared the cursed venom from your back at sunrise. I think she is now asleep."

Ser Gabriel was pinned in the bed by the Prior. He wriggled, clearly reaching for his clothes.

"Give me a moment of your time, Prince Gabriel," the Prior said.

He handed his charge a cup of warm wine.

"Poppy?" Ser Gabriel asked.

"Only honey," the Prior said. "You will need all your wits today."

An hour later—almost noon—they all gathered at the Abbot's long table in his hall. Ser Gabriel sat with the Prior, and Ser Michael and Ser Alcaeus—with two imperial messenger birds supported on missal stands—sat opposite a swollen-faced Amicia and Ser Thomas, with Ser Gavin and Ser Ricar of the Order, the infidel, Ser Payam, and Ser Christos. There were two other knights of the Order and two lay knights. The Order had many secular members—knights who donated their time, especially to defend caravans or pilgrims.

But next to Ser Gelfred, at the head of the table, sat a young man in blue and yellow checky, whose curling beard and open-faced good looks were marred by youthful rage.

But he mastered himself and rose and bowed to all present.

Ser Gelfred rose with him. "Gentlemen and ladies, Prince Tancredo of Occitan."

"The Queen's brother," Amicia said quietly to Sister Katherine, who sat slightly behind her.

The prince smiled at her. It was like the rising of the sun. Amicia was woman enough to appreciate that, despite his flushed cheeks and the hard, vengeful look around his eyes, his tanned skin and ruddy blond hair and his sharp nose made him one of the handsomest men she'd ever seen. Next to Ser Gabriel's pale skin and dark hair—

They were a match in size and shape, as well.

The prince was still smiling at her.

"You are, *sans doute*, the most beautiful nun I have ever seen," he said with a bow.

Ser Gabriel's face made a funny twitch.

But he also bowed to her. "It is good to see you alive," he said.

She felt herself flush.

The other knights—Ser Payam and Ser Thomas and Ser Ricar, all of whom had been badly burned by the ichor in the moths—rose and praised her, and she looked out the window. "It is God, my friends, not me," she protested, but indeed, the praise of such men was sweet.

Ser Pavalo bowed to her again. He spoke in a language which sounded like Archaic.

"He says that he salutes your great power. He says, it is a gift from God." Gabriel nodded. "I think he is thanking you for the healing, but I confess my Etruscan's not as good as his and I'm not sure. Maybe he's saying you are the most beautiful nun he's ever seen, too."

She glared at Gabriel, and he mocked her with his smile.

Prior Wishart cleared his throat.

Gabriel had the good grace to look abashed. He bowed to the prince. "Your grace—it is a pleasure to have you among us."

Prior Wishart translated in liquid Occitan, which sounded to Albans like Gallish mixed half and half with Etruscan.

The prince nodded and frowned. He rolled out a long speech, sat back and crossed his arms on his chest.

"The prince says that his cousin Rohiri died this morning, covering his retreat—that he feels like a poltroon, and that he followed this man—this Gelfred—here expecting to save his sister and his own honour. And he says"—Prior Wishart frowned—"some other things which I decline to translate." He spoke sharply in Occitan to the prince.

Prince Tancredo's head snapped around. He glared at the Prior, flicked his glance to Amicia, and then flushed.

"I apologize," he said with a shrug. "I agree. I am not myself."

Ser Gabriel nodded. "She has that effect on all of us," he said.

"No, just you," Ser Michael said. "Well, and the prince."

Amicia gazed levelly at them, taking her high-carried head and careful diction from her former Abbess. "If you *gentlemen* are quite finished," she said. "I believe all of us are interested in rescuing the Queen."

Gelfred took the Red Knight's parchment chart of Alba, rolling it out on the table. All the knights present drew their daggers, rondels and base-lards, and placed them on the edges to pin the stiff hide in place.

He pointed at Harndon.

"The King—and de Vrailly—hold Harndon. They have five or six hundred lances and a strong infantry force."

"What of the guilds?" the Prior asked. "My own news is three days old."

Ser Alcaeus rose. "The guilds are scattered. The proscriptions have driven a great number of prominent city men into the countryside. Ser Gelfred has Ser Gerald—"

"Indeed, he will be in Lorica within the hour," Gelfred put in.

"But most of the armourers, smiths, and fishmongers, too—have fled the capital." Ser Alcaeus had a wax tablet he consulted.

"So—de Vrailly has the city," the Prior said.

Ser Gabriel nodded. "Yes. Win or lose, Ser Ricar and Master Pye made the call for the skilled trades to flee before it came to massacre."

Ser Ricar nodded.

"This morning," Ser Alcaeus went on, "de Vrailly led a royal army through the gates to assault the Prince of Occitan's camp."

Gelfred nodded. "I warned him."

"And here he is." Ser Gabriel nodded.

"De Vrailly and Du Corse, the best of their soldiers, defeated the Occitans after a few hours' fighting," Ser Alcaeus said, rather undiplomatically. The prince writhed in his seat. His Alban was clearly good enough to take offence. "My source says that some of the guilds served in the royal army, and that city crossbowmen shot down the last of the prince's knights."

The prince slammed his fist on the table.

The Red Knight put a hand on Ser Alcaeus's shoulder. "Enough!" he said. "The prince doesn't need to be reminded of his sacrifice. How many lances did he save?"

The prince nodded. "Sixty," he said. "Knights and squires, sixty of each." He turned to the Prior and said something.

Prior Wishart nodded. "Spearmen."

"Mais oui. Bien sur. We did not bring any pages or archers or, as you say, spear-men, as we thought that we were coming to a tourney—a *bohars.* And not a war."

Ser Michael leaned forward. He glanced at the captain, who met his eye—encouraging him to speak. "But it is not war yet," he said.

Bad Tom chuckled. "The barmy King has arrested his own wife an' your da and it's not war?" he asked.

Ser Michael managed a thin-lipped smile. "No, by God, it is not, Tom. My father had *not* paid his taxes, and his loyalty to the crown was…" He shrugged, and his steel pauldrons winked in the sunlight. "Not all it might have been. The arrest of the earl need not be cause for civil war. Nor, I think, is the arrest of the Queen."

All around the table, men nodded.

The Prior stroked his beard.

The prince looked away, lips pursed in annoyance.

"Killing the Queen, on the other hand," Ser Gabriel said quietly, "would probably break any remaining loyalties we all felt to the King. Is that not so?"

He looked around. "Gentlemen and ladies, I am a mercenary. I fight for money, and war is my business. In this instance, I find it ironic that I'm reminding you how disastrous war would be for this realm—internal civil war."

One of the Order's lay volunteers burst out. "It's not civil war, Ser Gabriel! It's all true-hearted Albans agin' the Galles."

But Prior Wishart shook his head—and so did Gelfred. Gelfred looked around slowly. "There were more Alban knights—and spearmen—fighting the Occitans than there were Galles," he said. "De Vrailly and de Rohan have many adherents. Some are greedy men, 'tis sure. But many are merely loyal Albans, fighting for their King."

Ser Gabriel nodded. "My lords, what we need to do is save the Queen. I think everyone here is aware that I am a warlock. I think many of you know how potent the good Sister Amicia is, as well." Again, he looked around. Outside, the sun was dimmed briefly by a racing cloud, and then brightened again to a summer-like golden intensity. Easter Monday was a beautiful day. "I suspect that the King is ensorcelled," he said.

Amicia nodded.

"This King has always been swayed by the nearest opinion, the last word." He shrugged. "Or so my lady mother, his sister, has always maintained. Such a man would be easy to control with sorcery, I believe." He looked around. "Whether he is drugged or ensorcelled, the immediate requirement is the rescue of the Queen. That is best done *inside* the rule of law, by one of us—me, unless you overrule me—fighting on her behalf tomorrow."

The Prince of Occitan looked startled. Then he spoke to Prior Wishart, and after two or three sentences, he sat back.

"Prince Tancredo asks if you really believe that the Galles will just let you ride into the tourney ground and fight tomorrow? Do you even think that they will *hold* the tournament? They've arrested or attainted most of the participants."

The Red Knight leaned back, and to Amicia he wore that insufferable look of pleasure he had when he felt he was smarter than everyone else. "They haven't attainted me," he said. "Or Michael, or Gavin, or Tom. In fact, no one at this table is attainted except the members of the Order— and the prince, against whom the King has ordered war. The rest of us can *legally* ride into the lists and fight." He looked at the Prince. "Prince Tancredo, even tyranny has rules. De Vrailly has to appear to follow the law. He cannot just kill the Queen."

Tom snorted. "O' course he can. Boyo, I love ye like a brother, but they can rope us all in an' kill us, every mother's son. An' tell the commons whatever story they please."

The Red Knight nodded. "I'm not as great a fool as that, Tom. I disagree—but we have several loaded dice in this."

Tom was cleaning his nails with a dirk as long as most men's swords. "Eh? Name 'em, y' loon." He grinned and waved the knife. "I mean, I'll come wi' ye regardless of what mad drivel of a plan you cook up, but I'd like to hear what we have on our side."

The Red Knight frowned. "I don't like to lay my plans out."

The table gave a collective sigh.

Amicia leaned forward. "I think that this time, Gabriel, you must share. We are all risking our lives. This is not one of your military pranks."

The Red Knight's face held a flash of annoyance—even anger. But then he met her eye and smiled.

"Yes. Well." He looked around. "I suppose that if we have a traitor at this point, we're fucked anyway."

The men and women of the Order flinched at his bad language. Amicia thought how like a small boy he sometimes was.

"First, we have Gelfred's men all across the countryside," he said slowly. "Because of them, and their chain of messengers, we have collected the men of the Order and Master Pye's convoy and all the Occitans who escaped from their camp. That will give us two hundred lances and a solid body of infantry. Not, I confess, enough to face the royal army in the field, if it comes to that. But a potent threat nonetheless, and all of them will converge on Lorica tomorrow morning to cover our retreat." He smiled at the Prior. "If you agree, of course, my lord, and you, Prince Tancredo."

"Well eno' but they won't cover the tourney field." Tom was flicking at some black skin where the acid had bitten into his forearms while fighting the moths, using his eating knife to flick the scabs off the already healed flesh beneath.

"No, but your cousin Ranald will," Ser Gabriel said.

All around the table men turned and commented, or grunted. "Ranald knows the palace and the King's Guard like the back of his hand, and he's had four weeks to build—and half of the red banda is with him."

Tom grinned. "I like that," he said. "Oh, aye. I like that."

Ser Gabriel bowed like a small boy at school accepting a prize. "Why thank you, Ser Thomas." He looked around. "I plan a few diversions as well."

Amicia thought, *He's still not telling us anything.* She leaned forward, greatly daring.

"And you have a plan," she said. "Let's hear it."

Ser Gabriel nodded at her. "I do have a plan. Our greatest ally will be surprise. With my knights, we ride in. I show the Queen's guerdon and offer to fight de Vrailly. We browbeat them into fighting—I think questioning de Vrailly's courage ought to get him moving faster than his councillors can stop him. I beat him—and we win." He smiled. "I think the Galles will be done as soon as de Vrailly's arse hits the dirt. If the Queen is proven guiltless—"

Prior Wishart shook his head. "I fear you are oversimplifying, my son. The archbishop—I know him, and his type. He will stop at nothing to make sure you are defeated. He will cheat."

The Red Knight grinned his smug grin. "That's just it," he said. "De Vrailly won't cheat. I don't think he can."

Amicia spoke up. "I want to try for the King," she said.

There was silence.

"I think I am the ablest healer in this gathering," she said. "If the King has an affliction—"

"Or a curse, or an ensorcelment—" Ser Gabriel said. He nodded at her like one conspirator to another.

"Sister Amicia is subject to arrest at any moment," Prior Wishart said. "And if caught, she can be burned."

Amicia shivered. But she squared her shoulders. "I'll dress as a maid," she said. "In a kirtle with flowers in my hair, I doubt anyone will take me for a nun." Her eyes bored into Gabriel's. "Please, gentles, no false gallantry."

"I wonder how close you can get to the King," Ser Gabriel said.

There was a silence, and Prior Wishart shook his head. "The guards would never let her close enough," he said. He turned to glare at the Red Knight, and noted that at some point Sister Amicia had left her chair.

In fact, she was standing at his elbow.

"You learned that from me!" Ser Gabriel spat.

"Yes," Amicia said.

Most of the people present laughed.

The Red Knight went on to lay out his plan in what detail he had. Neither the knights of the Order nor the Occitans were pleased to be relegated to forming the rearguard.

Ser Gabriel was adamant. "If you ride openly into the lists with us, we'll be law-breakers," he said.

Bad Tom grinned. "Laddie, we're all law-breakers. Eh? Not lambs. What if they just take us? A hundred crossbows and we're done—all our steel won't avail us aught."

Gabriel frowned, and his mouth twitched sideways, as it did when he felt he was being hounded. "We'll make something up," he said. "I agree with the Prior and Sister Amicia that the Galles have more hermetical power than they are showing—but enough to face me? And Amicia?" He smiled at her.

She frowned.

"And if they try to arrest you, *then* there's civil war," she said.

"We will fight our way out. And take the Queen with us," he said.

She nodded. "But I've heard that civil war is what the Galles *want*. So why not take you all the moment you show yourselves?"

Tom laughed. "She's got you there," he said.

Ser Gabriel's eyes narrowed. "De Vrailly can't allow it," he said.

"What if he's just a figurehead?" the Prior asked.

"No one has told him, if that's the case," Ser Gabriel said. "I maintain that if we move quickly, we can sweep them up into a duel."

Heads nodded.

Bad Tom sat back, sheathed his big dirk with a click, and put his booted feet out. He steepled his hands.

"Can you take de Vrailly?" he asked bluntly.

Ser Gabriel shrugged. "Yes," he said.

"You aren't sure," Tom said.

Gabriel met his eye. "No combat is that sure," he admitted.

"So, you are a loon. We're to ride into the lion's den at your back and watch you win or lose, and then, if'n you win, we snatch the Queen before the King changes his mind and we ride free to Lorica. Mind ye, if you lose or they decide to cheat or arrest ye, then we're all taken and die horribly on the rack, or being ripped apart by horses. Have I covered yer plan?" He flicked his chin in an offensive Hill gesture. "It's not yer best plan."

"Do you have a better?" Gabriel spat back. He did not like to be questioned. "Perhaps you can lead us in and out."

"When do I get to sell my beasties?" Tom asked.

"At Lorica," Gabriel said.

"Going to cover me for three days while I hold a market?" Tom asked.

"If I have to," Ser Gabriel said.

He and Bad Tom locked eyes. "It's over-bold even for me," Tom said.

Ser Gabriel looked around. "I agree. It's a crap plan. It is all I have, made with clay and straw. Because what we ought to do is retreat to Albinkirk, let the Galles kill the Queen, and raise our own army. We ought to, but that would play directly into the Galles' hands and my beloved mother's. If we pull this off instead, we can save a generation from war. And that, gentlemen, is our duty as knights."

"You are a pitiful excuse for a sell-sword," Bad Tom said. "I'll send to Donald Dhu to start selling now. We'll gain a day or two."

"You're in?" Ser Gabriel said.

"Oh, aye," Tom said. "I'd follow ye anywhere—if only to find out where y're goin'."

The knights pushed back their chairs. But the Red Knight's brother put a hand on the table by his brother.

"I'm the best lance," he said.

All conversation stopped.

"I've beaten you since we were boys, and I beat you at Christmas," Ser Gavin said.

Ser Gabriel turned and smiled at his brother. "It's true, brother," he said.

"I've sworn to kill him," Gavin said.

Ser Gabriel nodded. "The Queen asked me," he said.

Gavin's face grew red, and then white. "So you'll say me nay?" he hissed.

Ser Gabriel shook his head. "Gavin, we'll be *lucky* if we get to fight their champion. Anything that raises the odds of the fight helps us. I have the Queen's note and guerdon. They almost have to let me fight. Not you."

"Fine—then I'll wear your colours and keep my visor shut. You're being greedy, brother. It always has to be you. I say: let me do it. And I say: no power on earth will keep me from putting de Vrailly in the dirt."

"It's not a power on earth that I'm worried about," Ser Gabriel said. "I *have* to do this."

Gavin slammed his fist on the table, took Gabriel's silver cup, crushed it in his fist and hurled it across the room. Then he stalked out, his sabatons ringing on the stone floor.

Bad Tom watched him go, and then put a meaty hand on the Red Knight's armoured shoulder. "He's better than you," he said.

Ser Gabriel's face hardened.

Chapter Six

The Company

Amicia was awakened in the darkness by Sister Katherine. She dressed quickly, with the help of the sisters, in a plain yellow kirtle with a belt of green leaves. Sister Mary had plaited flowers from the monk's garden, and they put them in her hair, and then all the sisters prayed over her. She felt the adamant of their shared prayers close over her—a strong protection.

Outside, she mounted her horse more easily than she might have ten days before.

In the torchlight, she could see that the day was damp and foggy. The torches at the gates of the abbey were softly glowing specks like sparkle-bugs on a summer evening, and the knights—all of them in full harness—were already cursing the damp and the effect it would have on their armour. There were no stars visible.

The Red Knight sat alone, his armour brilliant. He looked slightly incongruous as he was on his riding horse in a riding saddle to preserve his war horse for the joust, and his feet went down rather too far towards the ground. He was staring into the fog. Ser Michael and Ser Thomas were doing all the work of gathering the column—a column stripped of anyone but knights and squires, a handful of veteran pages in harness, spare horses and lances.

The abbey courtyard heard more oaths and blasphemy in the next minutes than it had heard in fifty years. Amicia could hear the bravado and the fear, the heightened awareness. These men were afraid. Proud, but afraid.

Ser Michael came and bowed. "Ready on time *and* pretty as a picture," he said, with a hard smile.

She nodded. "May I speak to him?" she asked.

"Better not," Ser Michael said.

The Red Knight's brother emerged—late—from his lodging and fussed with his right knee until Toby came and re-buckled something while Nell stood close with a torch, and then Ser Gavin—the Green Knight, as they all called him now—mounted stiffly and turned his horse. He said something—thanks, probably—to Nell, and rode to his brother's side. That pleased Amicia, who hated to see people quarrel at the best of times.

The Green Knight handed the Red Knight a baton, which he flourished. He pointed silently at the gates, and monks swung them open.

Prior Wishart was there, fully armed, and the Prince of Occitan. The two brothers leaned down from their horses—beckoned to Ser Michael—and the five men had a brief conference. But before Amicia's horse could begin to fret, the baton waved again, and the column started out the gates, two by two, knights with their squires.

Prior Wishart appeared at her horse's head and took her bridle. "You are a brave young woman," he said. He smiled. "But we all knew that, I suspect. You are the only member of the Order to ride on this noble venture."

"I won't fail," she said.

Prior Wishart nodded. "You are the best for the mission," he said. "If they save the Queen—well and good. But if you can save the King..." He turned and spoke quietly. "Do not be afraid to take the King with you if you can, Amicia. Ser Ricar will be close to you at all times."

"Does Gabriel know?" she asked.

Prior Wishart sighed. "No, lass. This is our own gambit. The Prince of Occitan and the Muriens have little time for our King. I cannot trust his fate entirely to your Ser Gabriel."

She smiled. "I'll do what I can," she said.

He nodded, reached up and gave her a blessing.

"Where's the infidel knight?" she asked.

"Gone in the night," Prior Wishart answered. He shrugged. "He's no traitor, whatever his religion. I believe your Ser Gabriel sent him with a message."

Amicia nodded, eyes narrowed. "To Harmodius. That's who the black man is looking for—Harmodius. I don't know why, but he and Ser Gabriel have some...link."

Prior Wishart fingered his beard in the damp darkness. "Ahh," he said. "I had almost forgotten Harmodius. He is alive?"

Amicia's turn to ride out the gate had come. She found herself paired with Nell, who was looking at her impatiently. "It's complicated," she said. She waved, and then she and Nell were going side by side into the foggy darkness, black as pitch, beyond the gate. Her heart began to beat faster and faster.

She wished she might have spoken to Gabriel. She said a prayer for him, and for the fear he must feel.

The fog was still and cool, and they rode.

They rode for three hours. Every hour, the column halted for a few minutes—pages offered nose bags to horses, and water. At the third hour they came to an inn, and its gates were open and torches burned in the fog to guide them to water, a bite of fresh, warm bread and a cup of warm honey-mead in the dripping darkness. They halted for perhaps twenty minutes in the inn yard, and then rode out again—forty horses, twenty men and two women. She didn't know where they were, but she suspected they were very close to Harndon. The countryside around them was waking up, cocks were crowing, and from the sounds, the Albin River had to be to her left and the bells were probably Harndon bells ringing across the river.

The fog grew lighter, but no less dense. Somewhere over her head, the sun was rising, but not a ray of it penetrated the dense grey cloud that clung to all of them like wet smoke.

Then, to her confusion, they were among trees—big, old trees, oaks and maples and another tall, magnificent type she did not know from the Adna-crags that grew as wide around as a peasant's hut and so tall they vanished into the grey above.

"We're in the Royal Park at Haye," Nell whispered to her. The youngster seemed to know far more about the morning's plans than she did. "Ser Gelfred cleared all this an hour hence. Our people are at all the gates. This is where we wait."

"Wait?" Amicia asked.

Nell looked at her as she probably looked at new pages and archers. *Don't you know anything?* "We have to ride into the lists at just the right moment, Cap'n says." Nell spoke of the captain as a nun might speak of God. Her trust was absolute.

Most of the column dismounted. A young man—Daniel Favour, whom Amicia could remember as a boy in Hawkshead—rode out of the fog. He rode to the captain, exchanged a few words and then rode to Ser Gavin. The three men spoke perhaps three sentences, and then Favour mounted again. He paused his horse by Amicia and bowed. "Morning, Sister!" he said. "Funny thing, a couple of mountain brats meeting here, eh?"

Amicia laughed—her first unforced laugh of the morning. "You seem in high spirits, Daniel," she said.

Favour grinned. "Oh, we've put a rare jest over on the Galles, ain't we, Sister? I reckon they'll make a song o' us." He saluted her with his riding whip. He was in a light saddle such as the easterners used, on a tall, athletic horse. His breastplate shone, and she noticed that the day had brightened considerably.

Ser Michael came over and crouched by her, armour and all. "The Queen is being moved through the streets of Harndon even now," he said. He frowned. "The Galles have executed some prominent men already—Ailwin Darkwood, for one."

"And your father?" she asked. Even as she asked, she was praying for the soul of Ailwin Darkwood.

"On the list for execution," he said. Then he smiled. "But joining us at Lorica, or so I gather from the captain."

Amicia had come to a second-hand education in Alban politics, and she winced for her Order. "Michael," she said, using his first name on purpose. "Do your company purpose a civil war?"

"My da would," he admitted. "I like to think the captain has better notions."

"But you'll follow him either way?" she asked.

He gave her a strange look.

The day was brighter yet, and high overhead there was a hint that some-day the sky might be blue.

"Captain's worried the fog might break up too soon," Michael said.

"It is a miracle from God," Amicia said. "Perfectly suited to our needs."

"Well," said Gabriel's voice from behind her. "Not exactly from God, since I cast it myself. One of your Abbess's tricks, as I recall."

She turned and saw—Ser Gavin. His visor was down so that his voice was muffled, and he wore Gavin's green surcoat and gold pentagonal star.

He sat on her log, armour creaking, and popped his long, falcon-like visor. Inside Gavin's helmet was Gabriel's face.

He shrugged. "They're all against me," he said pleasantly. "Apparently Gavin's the better jouster and I'm needed to give orders." He waved a hand. "I raised the fog." He made a face. "I confess it is spectacular."

She nodded, delighted that he could admit even that much. "I think you do God too little credit," she said. "I'm glad Ser Gavin will hold the lance."

"I should be offended you think so little of my prowess," he said. "And me wearing your favour."

"You are a foolish boy," she said. "And when this adventure is over, Gabriel, I will have my favour back. I am no longer a maiden to be won."

"Yes, yes," he said heartily.

She could see it—a rather soiled square of plain linen—peeping out from under a pauldron.

"Yes, Bonne Soeur. We will part." He laughed.

"You don't believe me?" she asked, stung.

For answer, he bowed and flipped down his visor. Men were mounting. Something had changed while they were talking.

He vaulted into the saddle of his war horse. He was riding his own. Ser

Gavin came and knelt beside her. "I crave your blessing, Bonne Soeur," he said.

Amicia was tempted to tell Ser Gavin that Ser Gabriel would never crave anyone's blessing—but that was not her business. Her business was between men and God, and she put a hand on his helmet and blessed him.

He rose, and mounted his horse. She could see from his body language that he was afire with nerves, and although Nell was behind her, utterly impatient, she walked after the apparent Red Knight and took his bridle.

"You have nothing to fear," she said. "Go with God."

Ser Gavin's smile showed under his visor for a moment. "You are a good woman," he said. "And is my fear so visible?"

She shook her head, using her gentlest voice. "No, ser knight. But you would be a madman if you were not afraid, with the fate of two kingdoms on you." She reached up and put a gentle healing on him, and he breathed easier.

"Go with God," she said.

He saluted her.

"You're going to make us late!" Nell hissed at her.

But she mounted carefully, tried not to figure out which knight was actually Ser Ricar, and got her skirts displayed to best effect in time to join the column as it jogged through the gates. The fog was breaking up.

The tournament was waiting.

Chapter Seven

The Company

The sun was high and hot, but the last of the fog remained over the flat green fields south of First Bridge, creating an odd, sticky day. No breeze stirred the banners—and the commons, those that had taken the risk to attend, stood sullen in the damp heat, an unseasonable weather.

The broad jest began to circulate that the Galles would find it hard to find dry wood to burn the Queen.

The stands, and the long wooden barricades that marked the lists, were not empty. The stands were full of the gentry of the court, reinforced by the folk of the southern Albin—some hundreds of men and women dressed in their best. They were apprehensive—most had left home for the great day long before the King's arrest of the Queen was even a rumour.

And many of the commons had come, as well. The barricades were lined, three or four deep. Many of the refugees who had fled the burnings in the city had gone no further than relatives north of First Bridge or on the Lorica road, where the city's suburbs sprawled for three leagues, and unshaven chins and close bundled children spoke of many families who'd slept under the stars in order to see the King—or see the Queen burned.

But the mood of the commons was ugly enough. A squire was foolish enough to stop and make a great show of pissing on a fallen shield with the Queen's arms. He was an Alban, a southerner, and he did it for the entertainment of his friends. He was badly beaten by a dozen ploughmen who didn't see the world as he did.

Increasing numbers of peasants pressed in around the Queen until the

King, or his deputies, sent a strong detachment of the Royal Guard to watch over her. The Guardsmen, however, were careful not to offend the people, and did nothing to move the crowd itself, which grew denser.

It became so dense that Blanche had a hard time penetrating it. She couldn't have said when she went from being a laundry maid of some distinction to the Queen's last handmaid, but when she understood what Edmund and the apprentices planned, she had slipped out of Master Pye's house in her plainest clothes—her hair covered in an old wimple. She'd watched older women often enough to pass for one, although it hurt her pride. She bent her back a little, and waddled a little, and bound her breasts so that they were flat against her, wrapped her blaze of bright blond hair in a piece of clean old linen, and was transformed from the magnet of every male's attention into an old thing of no interest to anyone. It troubled her how quickly she could be ignored, as an old woman.

She spent Easter night in a shed next to the palace. She made it into the laundry without being questioned because most of the Guard was away fighting the Occitans, and it was from Goodwife Ross that she learned that some of the King's Guard seemed . . . different.

Twice now she'd visited the Queen—she'd become a poor creature who seemed broken into madness, except when you looked into her eyes.

So—at any rate—on Tuesday morning, Blanche was pushing through the press of the commons with a basket on her head. The press was so thick she might never have gotten to the ring around the Queen except that one of the King's Guard saw her and smiled.

"Let her through!" he called in a Hillman accent. "Here's a woman come to serve the Queen. Let her through, with God's good grace."

And the commons moved aside like the parting of the Dark Sea, and Blanche slipped past them to the barrier around the Queen's seat—ducked under it and came to the Queen.

She bobbed a deep curtsey. "Your grace?" she asked.

The Queen turned her head. Her eyes focused.

She smiled. "Blanche," she said.

Blanche hadn't been sure until then that the Queen even knew her name. She curtsied again. "Your grace, I've brought you soap, water and some food."

"She hasn't eaten in four days," one of the King's men muttered.

The Queen put a hand to her throat. "I might try . . . to eat," she said huskily. "The sun—has been so kind—"

The guardsmen muttered among themselves. She looked so . . . crazy, Blanche thought.

She looked even worse as she began to eat, seizing a loaf of bread and ripping pieces from it. Blanche had eight thick slices of bacon from a guardsman's fire and a slice of very questionable pie that had cost her a copper and a kiss. The kiss had been greasy, too.

The Queen tore through it with wolfish intensity, glancing up from time to time—like a dog, Blanche thought. Or something that feared a predator.

Blanche had a soldier's canteen over her shoulder—a heavy object of fired clay. She'd stolen it, in the first outright theft of her life. She handed it to the Queen, who drank off the entire contents without seeming to breathe.

She looked at Blanche and her eyes narrowed a fraction. "You should run," she said. "You've been seen."

Blanche curtsied. "Your grace, I am here for you. You should know that—"

"Run," said the Queen. "I will not have your blood on my head. *Now*."

Blanche ducked under the barrier, abandoning the basket and the canteen. The Queen's intensity communicated itself to her.

But the press was still thick—and there was shouting. Men were moving, and suddenly she had a lane, and like a flash—

She was caught. There were four of them, big men in the archbishop's purple livery. They knocked her down.

One said something, and the other three laughed, showing a mouth full of blackened stumps of teeth.

She expected help from the crowd, and when the men in purple reached for her, she screamed, but the peasants were cowed by the armour and the spears. Black Teeth slammed the top of his head into her forehead, so that the world spun. He laughed and pushed her again.

Her wimple came off, her glorious yellow-gold hair blowing in the wind.

There were fifty of them, the purple spearmen. They'd killed a man, and the crowd fled them, leaving them alone like an island of stone in a rising tide. A woman was screaming, and another man was trying to hold his guts in with his hands.

Her head hurt so much she wanted to throw up.

"It's the Queen's little bitch!" laughed a Gallish voice. "I'd know that hair anytime."

"It's been on every pillow in the Guard's hall, or so I hear," said another.

Hard hands closed on her arms.

She screamed again.

"Secure the person of the so-called Queen," ordered a new voice. "Who is this tall slut?"

"One of the Queen's women—"

"So-called Queen's women. A lady?" asked the voice. She got her eyes open. It was de Rohan—she knew him from the corridors. "I think not." He nodded. "Bring her."

"Why?" asked the archbishop. Blanche knew him, too. She'd never heard him speak, but there he was, young and fat as a capon, with short-cropped hair almost exactly the colour of her own. "What do we want with the slut?"

De Rohan sighed as if he was surrounded by fools. "Your excellency, in an hour or so, when we lead the so-called Queen to the stake..." He paused. "We may experience some difficulties with her, and with the canaille. I would love to have a lever with which to move the so-called Queen."

Blanche was pushed along. Hands fondled her—she was bruised by a vise-like grip on one of her breasts as a dozen soldiers pushed her to where de Rohan stood. They laughed.

He laughed.

He was standing at the gate to the barriers around the Queen. Two rather sorry-looking guardsmen stood there—not, she would have thought, the men who had been there a few minutes before. Both were slack-jawed and slack-eyed—possibly drunk.

The Queen, on the other hand, looked considerably better.

"Madame," de Rohan said. "Are you prepared to meet your fate?"

"Is it not rather the fate that you have made me, my lord?" she asked. "Nor is it yet noon—the hour appointed for my Champion."

"Any time from the first hour after matins until the middle of the day, madame." His arm suddenly shot out and he took Blanche by her ear—the pain was incredible. She screeched.

"Do you know this pretty slip, Desiderata?" he asked.

"Yes," said the Queen, sadly.

"Good. If you'd like her to live out the day—and not be the bedfellow of my servants for the next few weeks, until her spirit is a little less brazen—then you will obey me." He shrugged.

The Queen's eyes were gentle pools of brown looking at Blanche's. "This is low even for you, de Rohan," she said. "And I suspect that no matter what I promise you will inflict your child-like will on poor Blanche, who is guilty of no crime but loyalty to me." To Blanche she said, "You should have run, child."

Blanche found that she was crying. She wanted to be strong—as strong as she'd been for a week—but she felt helpless and abandoned and she knew what was to come. She knew it, as every woman feared it, and she couldn't keep her tears and despair at bay.

"How I hate you," she managed to say to de Rohan.

He didn't even turn his head. "I expect—" His warm hand found her jaw and his thumb was suddenly under her chin, probing deeply into the side of her neck until the pain made her rise on her toes and scream. "I expect you'll hate me more later," he said, dropping her. "To much the same effect, really." He looked at Desiderata. "Women are too weak for any purpose but to make babies," he added.

"And even when we do that, you kill us," the Queen said. "You might want to look, my lord. Your doom is nigh."

For the last half hour, the fog had been reduced to a blinding glare of haze. Now, with nonnes not far away, there was a sudden flash of metal and scarlet in the middle distance.

De Rohan looked a moment and gestured to the archbishop. "The so-called Queen is safe enough," he said.

"The canaille would save her, if only to spite me," the archbishop said. His chairmen grunted under him.

"We've dispersed them," de Rohan said. "And caught the go-between the Queen used with her lover. Let's go and tell the King." He motioned to his own black-and-yellow-clad retinue, and then he moved toward the King with something like unseemly haste.

"Hurry, de Rohan," Desiderata called, her voice fey. "Hurry to your end."

Twenty of the purple guardsmen remained. They used their spear points on anyone in the crowd who came closer than a spear's length to the barrier. Men cursed them, but none had the spine to resist them.

Amicia left the column as they rounded the last bend in the road. The lists were clear to see, even in the odd hazy light. The heat was stifling, the damp oppressive, so that in two layers of linen she felt she might wilt.

But she had Gelfred with her. He rode with her to an enclosure full of horses. There were two Royal Guardsmen there who seemed to think very little of his dismounting with a beautiful woman.

"You won't be leaving this way," he said. He smiled. "God be with you, my lady."

She handed him her reins, bobbed her head, and began to walk towards the back of the royal box above the stands. There were a dozen Royal Guards here at the back, and a small mob of other liveries—servants in almost every conceivable heraldry, with trays and bottles and linen towels over their arms, and a double dozen of various soldiers all eyeing each other with malice.

Amicia *entered her palace and began to work. It was a simple enough beguiling—few men wanted to stop a beautiful woman from going where she would, anyway, and those who would stop such a woman were even easier to dissuade, their lust a weapon with which to deceive them. Her beguiling was subtle and strong. She watched her body move over the grass, and saw them notice her and saw men smile, one to the other...*

She passed the guards. Behind them were two sets of wooden steps into the royal box, equidistant to right and left. But under the box was a small chamber—a retiring chamber that Amicia suspected had been placed there so that the King could be moved out of sight—if required.

She passed into the chamber as if it was hers by right.

"Bless you, Gelfred," she whispered.

She stood as close to directly beneath the King as she could manage.

She sighed. The wood was too dense, and blocked her aethereal *sight completely, or at least too much for such a delicate working.*

301

She passed back through the curtain, and past the guards. Men looked, and saw, or did not see, but now she passed among them, her will adamant, her face radiant.

One man sighed, and another groaned. But no one moved to stop her.

It was fifty paces to the end of the tall bleachers. She walked all the way, painfully aware that she had the eyes of a dozen men on her slim back. But no one shouted.

She passed the end of the bleachers. Out here, away from the pavilions and the enclosure for spare horses, the noise was greater. Above her in the stands, hundreds of ladies and gentlemen sat, eating morsels and drinking wine.

She turned and began to climb the steps. She climbed until she was parallel with the royal box. She could see a man in red who was probably the King, but long rows of people separated them, and his head bobbed back and forth.

The whole path from her position to the King was blocked with seated spectators.

She took a deep breath, and steadied her working. Then, to the first woman in the row, she said, "I'm sorry, I need to get to my father."

The woman stood to let her pass, frowning.

"There's someone coming," her husband said. The man was short, and wide, and wore too much gold. "By God—it's a whole team in red. Is it the King's men?"

Amicia couldn't help herself. She turned and looked.

Down at the entrance to the stands, fifty feet below her, there were ten knights and ten squires, all in brilliant steel armour—plate over maille, often edged in laten or bronze or brass.

She could see the Red Knight and the Green Knight, too. And Ser Tom.

The trumpeter was there as herald, dressed in the company scarlet with the lacs d'amour on his tabard.

Everyone in the stands was on their feet. Whether luck, fortune or God—she had her moment, and she scrambled along, no more interested in stealth, with the instinct of the pickpocket when a distraction is made available. She pushed and pressed almost recklessly.

The marshal strode across the lists. The crowd hushed.

Amicia pushed on.

The Red Knight's herald raised his trumpet from his hip, and it unfurled with the white dove on a sun-in-splendor of the Queen.

The crowd roared.

The sound was so loud that it startled Amicia and she almost let her working fall. Her heart was pounding—

She *wondered in the calm fastness of her palace what it was like to be in a closed helmet with nothing but the fear and all that sound, and all the hopes of thousands of people on your armour-burdened shoulders.*

She reached out in the aethereal *with her sight, and saw.*

First she saw the Queen. The Queen burned like a small sun—bright gold, un-alloyed, undimmed. She was in a sort of pen at the base of the stands, and the wood of the barriers surrounding held a working on it—a curious and not particularly stable working.

Nearer at hand, she saw a group of men moving quickly—a young fat man with no talent whatsoever, and by his side a grey man who flickered with potency.

"Ah, yes," she thought.

She glanced at the King, who was warded—ten times warded. He was covered in wardings, like a prisoner draped in chains. Amulets and sigils, runes and bindings were on him layer after layer. She had never seen anything like it, and suddenly—for the first time—she felt overmatched. For some reason she had expected a single, potent work—an internal mirror or a secret working that locked the target up as surely as a prison. Both Harmodius and the Abbess, in her head, remembered such working and had remedies.

But this tangle of cluttered thaumaturgy, with superstition, blind chance and careful science all mixed . . .

She looked again. It was like looking at the tangled remnants of a skein of linen after a kitten had attacked it.

Nor was she sure that the King's will was in any way affected by it all.

He was merely . . . warded.

Nicholas Ganfroy had practised for a year for this moment. His trumpet rang out, loud and clear, piercing the tumult of the crowd.

Into his split second of crowd-silence, he roared the Red Knight's challenge.

"He who styles himself the Red Knight bids defiance to any wight so craven as to pretend that the gracious Queen of Alba, high Desiderata, is other than the King's own wife; loyal, faithful, and true. And he offers to prove this assertion on the body of any so bold in his blood or wanting in brains that will maintain her unfaithfulness, or will offer to exchange blows. And the Red Knight maintains he offers battle for no pride in his own prowess, but only to see justice done. And if no knight will offer to uphold the charges against the gracious lady Queen, the Red Knight demands her instant release by the law of arms, the Rule of Law of Alba, and also the Rule of War of Galle."

Ganfroy's lungs were as brazen as his trumpet, and he'd practised, shouting into basements and wine cellars. His words carried clearly.

There was obvious consternation in the royal stands.

Amicia was no more than an arm's length from the Archbishop of Lorica, unnoticed in the press. The archbishop, and the Sieur de Rohan, had just returned, hurriedly climbing the steps to the royal box—Amicia was interested to note that the archbishop was already sweating. She had also marked the thin, threadbare man in the badly dyed scholar's scarlet as a hermeticist—his person carried two wards and a sigil.

Amicia was an observant woman, and she noticed that he wore a third device around his neck—a complex net of thin strands of dirty linen. It held no power, but the King wore a similar such amulet.

"Send the guard and have him taken," shouted the archbishop. His words were received with hoots and catcalls from all the gentry seated nearby.

De Vrailly was grinning as if he'd just won a prize. "It is the mercenary—the sell-sword. The Queen must have bought his services." He shook his head. "I understand him to be a good man of his arms, and his harness seems good." His handsome face split in a wide grin. "Ah, God is good! An answer to my prayers. God has sent him that we may have a fair trial."

De Rohan was trying to burrow through the close press towards the King. "Your grace—your grace!" he called.

Amicia was six feet from the King, below him, caught up amidst the press of Galles and Albans who followed the court.

Someone groped her.

She ignored her assailant and entered *into her bridge. There, she was interested to find, she wore the same kirtle in the* aethereal *that she wore in the world.*

She found the King in the aethereal. *She saw the welter and tangle of his protections and wards and curses and she bit her* aethereal *lip in frustration.*

She prayed. And curiously, as she prayed, she thought of her Abbess, that towering figure of wit and good sense, power and character—the old King's mistress, and a potent magister.

What would she have done?

Amicia moved her focus back, looking over the crowd around the King. She was looking for a link—a thread of gold or green that might connect any one of them to the King.

She didn't see any such.

It was possible, of course, that the King was acting of his own accord. The Prior didn't believe that though, and neither, apparently, did Gabriel.

She sighed, completing her prayer, and tried another tack. She looked at the King not as a hermetical practitioner, but as a hermetical healer. As her Order taught.

As quick as thought, she was praising God inside her head, and acting.

De Rohan clasped the King's hand. "I have ordered the arrest of the herald, and his knight," de Rohan said.

The King nodded heavily. "Yeess," he said slowly. His head barely raised off his chest.

"Sire!" De Vrailly pushed de Rohan roughly. "Sire—do not listen to him!"

The King made no movement.

"Stand down, de Vrailly. No one doubts your honour. But the King needs no champion in this." De Rohan gave his most placating smile.

The archbishop put a hand on de Vrailly's armoured elbow. "Do not presume—" he began.

The King's head shot up, as if he'd been stung by a hornet. For a moment he had a look of wild insanity.

Then his eyes focused.

De Vrailly was no longer looking at the King. "De Rohan, by all I hold sacred—I will strike you down with my own right hand if you impede the cause of this quarrel. The herald—presumptuous as his speech might be—has every turn of the right. We must fight, or be found to have lied. I am ready, armed in every point. *What possible exception can you make to the law of war, de Rohan?*"

The King stood.

A ring of silence spread out from his person, like the ripples of a pebble tossed in a pool of water.

His voice was low and rough, as if unused. "Do I understand that the Queen has a defender?" he asked slowly.

He took a step—an unsteady step. De Rohan clasped his elbow.

"Get the King a cup of his wine," he said to an attendant. "Your grace—"

But de Vrailly's face was mottled with anger, and he pushed de Rohan—quite roughly. They were both big men—de Rohan had, after all, been de Vrailly's standard bearer and was reckoned by some the best knight after de Vrailly himself. But de Vrailly's anger was like an angel's wrath, and he moved de Rohan as if he was made of paper.

"Your grace—the Red Knight, the sell-sword, has been paid by the Queen to defend her. And I am happy—indeed, delighted"—his face bore anything but delight—"to engage this wastrel on your behalf."

The King's eyes went back and forth. "The Red Knight?" he asked, his voice plaintive. "Oh, sweet Christ."

Inside the King's aura, Amicia felt the wave of pain pass over him.

Out in the lists, the Red Knight changed horses. He did nothing showy—he merely dismounted easily from his riding horse and remounted a huge roan war horse with nostrils so red that he appeared to breathe fire. Then he took a lance from his squire and raised it in the air.

The herald blew his trumpet again. "For the second time, the Red Knight challenges any child born of woman to meet him, steel to steel, in the lists. He maintains the right of the Queen, the chastity of her body, the purity of her heart. Let any who stand against her beware! My knight offers a contest of the weapons of war, until one shall be defeated, or dead."

The crowd *roared* in approval.

The Red Knight began to ride to the head of the lists, lance in hand.

The King was seen to bite his lip. His face writhed as if inhabited by snakes.

De Rohan glared at de Vrailly. "Your grace, this is mere foolish posturing. Let me press the order of arrest."

De Vrailly looked at his former standard bearer with utter contempt. "You are not only a caitiff but a fool," he said. "By God and Saint Denis, D'Eu was right about you. If you do not let me fight, these people will go to their graves believing their Queen was innocent."

De Rohan and de Vrailly locked gazes—Amicia could see that each thought the other a fool.

Amicia also noted—with shock—that de Vrailly burned like a second sun in her alternate, *aethereal* sight.

Out in the lists, a dozen Royal Guardsmen stood sullenly under the royal box. A man in de Rohan's livery was gesticulating at the Red Knight.

De Vrailly turned to the King. "You must let me fight—for your honour!"

The King's eyes went back and forth like those of a trapped animal.

At the base of the stands, the Queen sat on a stool in her plain grey kirtle, her golden-brown hair lank but her face at rest. She looked at her champion—and then up into the royal box.

"Even now, I pity him," the Queen said.

Blanche—over her first terror—cursed. "Pity who, your grace?" she asked. The coming of the Red Knight—Master Pye's friend, and Ser Gerald Random's and thus a good knight in her books—gave her hope, and Blanche had desperately needed some hope.

The Queen smiled. "The King, of course, my dear."

"Christ on the cross, your grace! Why spare the King any of your pity? He'll have no mercy for you." Blanche looked down the lists and clapped her hands. The Red Knight's near twin—the Green Knight—was cantering along the lists, entertaining the crowd, and shouting insults at the Galles.

The Queen was serene. "Those who have known pain should have mercy on others," she said. "There sits my husband—whom I swore to defend 'til death do us part." She frowned. "I find it hard to make room in my heart for him. But I would not wish his fate on any man."

Blanche sighed. "Beyond my likes and dislikes, I suppose, your grace," she said in obvious incomprehension.

The Queen raised a very sage eyebrow. "My gallant defender is the King's son," she said.

Blanche's white hand went to her throat. "Jesu Christe!" she said—a true prayer and no blasphemy. "The Red Knight is the King's by-blow?"

The Queen frowned.

Blanche cast her eyes down. "Apologies, your grace. I'm a laundress, not a courtesan—er—courtier."

The Queen flashed her a smile. "You are no courtesan," she said. "And you made me smile."

The Red Knight clasped gauntlets with the Green Knight and then rode down the lists towards the Queen. The whole of the crowd, gentle and common, was on their feet.

Amicia watched a servant bring a cup. She needed no potent workings to know that the cup held poison. Or some poppy or other sleeping stuff.

There was no one around her to help her, and she knew of no way to affect this in the *aethereal*, without giving away her working. So she pushed past a pair of purple-clad guardsmen. Her path was eased by a sudden movement of the archbishop, who was looking at the red-clad lawyer.

"Just see to it," the archbishop hissed.

His eyes went right past her, but his bulk opened a path until she was able to put her hip into the serving man. He didn't fall, but the cup of wine soaked Du Corse.

She stepped back—her heart beating overtime. Heads turned, but every head looked at the serving man.

He was red in the face, protesting his innocence.

De Rohan struck him with the back of his hand, his two rings cutting furrows in the servant's cheek. Amicia flinched.

The King shook his head vehemently.

De Vrailly stood his ground. "I am your Champion!" he said. "If I do not fight then you are *admitting the charges are false*." His accented Alban carried.

"*Free the Queen!*" shouted a bold onlooker.

The cry was taken up.

The archbishop leaned over and whispered in the King's ear.

The King turned. He was pale—but in control of his face.

The King stood straighter. "De Vrailly," he said. "For what it is worth, I believe my wife is innocent. Will you still fight?"

De Vrailly spat. "Bah!" he cried. "I'll prove her faithlessness and the murder of my friend D'Eu on this Red Knight."

The archbishop made a signal.

The King shook his head. "Very well," he said, with real regret.

De Vrailly began to walk down the steps to the lists.

The archbishop followed. As the King began to follow the archbishop to the lists, Amicia did her best to move along with him, an arm's length away.

The man in red looked at her—right at her.

He was in the midst of a working. Magicking a silver chalice—a chalice of water.

He went back to his working, the traces of his fingers and his symbols leaving marks in the *aethereal*. She lacked the kind of training that would tell her what he was doing—another poison?

Suddenly his eyes came back to her—now wide with realization.

She had no idea what gave her away.

The Red Knight walked his horse to the base of the steps as if he had nothing to fear from the Galles or the purple soldiers waiting there. The marshal of the lists had beckoned him, and now stood with a sword in one hand and a set of gospels in the other. All eyes were on him.

Amicia moved a few inches closer to the King and the archbishop, and readied her shields.

The archbishop took the chalice, held it aloft, and began to pray loudly.

Most people fell silent—many fell on their knees, and Amicia joined them because it took her out of the sight line of the man in the scarlet hood. In front of her, a Gallish squire brought out de Vrailly's magnificent war horse. The knight himself checked his girth and stirrups before turning and kneeling before the archbishop.

The Red Knight dismounted and knelt, too, a good sword's length between himself and the Gallish knight.

The prayer came to an end.

The marshal went to the Red Knight. "Do you swear on your honour, your arms and faith, to fight only in a cause that is just, and to abide by all the law of arms in the list?"

The Red Knight didn't open his visor, but his voice was loud. "I do," he said.

The marshal went to de Vrailly. "Do you swear on your honour, your arms and your faith, to fight only in a cause that is just, and to abide by all the law of arms in the list?"

"I do," de Vrailly said.

Both men rose.

"Stop!" roared the archbishop. He took the chalice. "The Red Knight is a notorious sorcerer. Have you any magical defence about you?" he shouted. "I accuse you! God has shown me!" And he flipped holy water from the chalice at the Red Knight.

It sparkled in the air—a brilliant lightshow of red and green and blue.

Amicia moved from her knees even as the crowd gasped.

The marshal frowned. "It is against the law of arms to bear anything worked with the arts into the lists," he roared.

The Red Knight started back. He was on his feet—

The marshal struck him lightly with his mace of office. "You are barred from the lists," he said.

Amicia heard the Red Knight grunt as if in pain, but she was already moving. She took the chalice from the archbishop's hands as smoothly as if he was cooperating with her in a dance, and upended the contents over the kneeling Gallish knight even as she placed her own working—a true working—to make the water show anything hermetical. The man in the red hood had merely faked the effect with an illusion.

In front of five thousand people, de Vrailly glowed. If the Red Knight had sparkled with faery light, de Vrailly burned like a torch of hermeticism.

The flame of the holy water hitting de Vrailly was so bright that a hundred paces away, Wat Tyler had to turn his head to keep the dazzle from his eyes. He cursed as he lost his target.

The other Galles were speechless. Amicia stepped back—but the man in red saw her. "She—" he began.

And then he pursed his lips, looked at the archbishop, and said nothing.

The crowd was clamouring.

The marshal had not been bought or paid for—he struck de Vrailly with his mace. "You, too, are barred from the lists," he said.

De Vrailly's visor was up—and his face worked like a baby's. He knelt there as if unable to move.

It was Du Corse who took charge. The crowd—both gentle and common—was restless. Commoners were beginning to challenge the lines of guards on the edge of the lists, and the twenty or so purple-liveried episcopal guards around the Queen were not looking either numerous or dangerous enough. He sent a page for his routiers and made a motion to his own standard bearer.

The archbishop was still stunned by the apparition of de Vrailly, the King's Champion, suffused with a sticky green fire that could only mean a deep hermetical protection—cast, of all things, by the Wild. Satan's snare.

In front of them, a line of knights appeared behind the Red Knight. A Green Knight put his hand on the Red Knight's shoulder, and behind him was a giant of a man in a plain steel harness and a surcoat of tweed, and then another giant, this one blond, bearing the differenced arms of the Earl of Towbray.

The Green Knight stood forth.

"I will stand for the Queen," he said. His voice carried.

At his back, Tom Lachlan raised his visor. "And I," he said.

Ser Michael didn't dismount, but he snapped his great helm off his head and let it hang from the buckle. "And I, your grace. My father is attainted, but I am not. There are many knights here to fight for your wife today, your grace. I am a peer of Alba. I demand justice."

The Green Knight did not raise his visor. He merely saluted the marshal. "Try your holy water on me," he said.

The marshal took the empty cup—and held it out to the archbishop.

The man in the red hood made his working—while the archbishop's own secretary frowned in disgust so plain that Amicia noted it.

Amicia did nothing to prevent his casting. The archbishop's hands moved with an ill grace.

The man in the red hood choked. The water flew, and did nothing but make the Green Knight's surcoat wet.

"Choose your champion!" he called, his voice mocking.

Amicia would have grinned, if she had not been so afraid.

Because, of course, Gabriel was a very creature of magick. And so, he had turned the working himself. His skill towered over Red Hood's the way an eagle towers over a squirrel.

The archbishop turned on his two secretaries.

Du Corse frowned and looked at de Rohan as the crowd roared its approval of the Green Knight. "Someone must fight him," he said.

De Rohan rolled his eyes. "Just take the lot," he hissed. "We have the men. Surround them and take them."

Du Corse shook his head. "Nay, cousin. Someone must fight." He looked at the commoners pushing against the guards. "Or we'll all be dead before nightfall."

"Very well," de Rohan said. "You."

Du Corse smiled a hard smile. "No," he said.

"L'Isle d'Adam, then."

Du Corse nodded. "But—" he said. "No. I recommend that you fight your own battle, de Rohan."

De Rohan's eyes narrowed.

Behind him, the King moved. Heads turned again.

"Yes," the King said. "You have been her loudest and most constant accuser, de Rohan. Take up your cousin's sword."

A chair had been brought for the King. He was sitting by the lists now—more alert than many of the Gallish knights had ever seen him.

Amicia began to edge away from the royal box.

One of de Rohan's yellow and black men-at-arms was pointing at her. She saw the man, and she *steadied her working, which had slipped as she had moved in the real.*

The man's gaze slid off her even as she sat suddenly between two Alban families in the lowest bench of the stands. There was no room for her, but men on either hand instinctively made space.

The black and yellow man-at-arms looked her way, and then his attention—and everyone else's—was on the lists.

Inside the Green Knight's helmet, Gabriel Muriens tried to distance himself from the heady brew of excitement and pure fear that rose to choke him.

His heart was beating like a hummingbird's wings, his chest felt tight and his arms weak.

"It is easier to face Thorn in desperate combat than to do this with five thousand people watching and everything on the line," he thought.

"I volunteered to do this," he thought.

"I don't know this knight," he thought.

All his thought had been bent on de Vrailly. And when he had admitted that Gavin was the better lance, he had freed himself from all of the anxiety of the moment, and settled for the petty stress of command.

And now it was all on him anyway. His mind multiplied his fears.

And he wondered how and why de Vrailly had been disqualified.

I should be relieved, he thought.

Instead, his lance felt like lead, and the points of his shoulder ached as if he'd jousted all day, and his great helm seemed to suffocate him.

But there was Toby, checking his stirrups, and Gavin, of all people, holding his shield.

"You bastard," Gavin said. He wasn't really smiling. He was mad as hell. "You always get your way."

"This was none of my doing," Gabriel said.

Gavin pulled the straps of his jousting shield tight over his arm harness with more emphasis than was necessary. "No, of course not," he said. His tone didn't give away whether he believed his brother or not.

"Gavin, I would not cede the lists to you and then take them away," he said.

"Really?" Gavin asked. "Then go with God and win. Even if you did, *brother,* I hope you win." Gavin slapped him on the shoulder. Gavin—on the ground—looked at Toby. "Who is riding for the King?"

"Marshal called him de Rohan." Toby shrugged.

"I don't know any of these Galles," Gavin admitted.

"Anyway," Gabriel said, a little pettishly through his great helm, "I'm not fighting de Vrailly."

Gavin nodded. "That's why I'm not pulling you off your horse and beating you with the butt of your own lance," he said. "You as nervous as you sound?"

Gabriel swallowed with some difficulty.

"Give him water," Gavin said. "Your man's in the saddle. You have a better horse. He's taller. He's got a very long lance. You know the trick we practised in Morea?"

Gabriel drank the water. He didn't quite feel like a new man, but he felt better. "You think?" he asked.

"His lance is five hand-spans longer than yours, and his arms are longer as well," Gavin said. "This is not sport—this is war. There are no tricks. If it were me, I'd lace my helm lightly so he could pluck it off without hurting my neck."

Deep in his helm, Gabriel laughed. "You made me laugh, Gavin. For that alone, I thank you."

"Marshal's telling us to lace up."

"Tell him I've been laced up an hour." Gabriel made his horse rear slightly, and the crowd shouted.

"Get him," Gavin said.

Bad Tom leaned in. "Just fewkin' kill him," he said. He smiled. "Be a right bastard and put your fewkin' iron in any way you can and don't show off or fewk around or act like yersel'." He grinned.

Gabriel looked at the marshal. He had his baton over his head, and was looking at the King.

"The moment I have him," Gabriel said, "go for the Queen."

"Even if he has you, boyo," Bad Tom said. "I can see Ranald fra' here."

The Green Knight flicked his lance at all of his friends.

He half reared—exactly as the baton dropped his horse's front hooves were touching the ground. Ataelus exploded forward.

Gabriel had the sensation that time, rather than stopping, was *sliding*. As his adversary accelerated, Gabriel lowered his lance point too far, seated the butt of his lance in his lance rest, and let his point drop below the level of his own waist like an utterly inept jouster.

Any strike at the opposing horse was a foul.

Everything was moving so fast, yet in the hoof beats before the crossing of the spears, Gabriel felt the *entanglement*. The world about him was like a lattice of ice crystals—an infinite connection, man to man, thought to thought, earth to horse to lance to plot to consequence.

He was in it.

De Rohan's lance was firm and solid, the steel tip all but invisible as they closed.

In practice, Gabriel had made this work once in three tries.

In the half a heartbeat that the spearheads passed one another, Gabriel used the cut-out corner of his shield as a fulcrum to lever his spear point *up*. His rising spear shaft crossed the oncoming might of the longer shaft, and struck it—hard.

His motion had been a trifle late, and the Gallish lance caught the bottom left of his great helm, slamming sideways into his head—he relaxed as much as his inner tension would allow, tried to be the jouster that his dead master-at-arms had wanted and that Ser Henri had derided, flowed with his adversary's blow and in the second half heartbeat his own point caught his adversary in the shield, just over his bridle hand—

His solid ash lance exploded in his hand—and he was past, the royal box a blur on his left as Ataelus hurtled down the lists. He was the best fighting horse Gabriel had ever had—he slowed without a touch of the rein.

There were no barriers down the middle, because this was a war joust.

And his adversary was already coming at him.

Of course—his lance had not broken. He was choosing to fight continuously, instead of allowing his opponent to re-arm.

Gabriel dropped the butt of his lance as Ataelus reared and pivoted on his rear legs, front legs kicking. Ataelus let out an equine battle cry, a great scream that filled the air, and then they were straight to a gallop.

Gabriel drew his long war-sword across his body. He still had his shield. There was something amiss about his adversary—but the man had his spear in its rest, and the point was coming, held across the charging horse's crupper in the proper way for fighting in the lists—

Five strides from contact, Gabriel gave Ataelus the slightest right knee and spur, and the horse turned—more of a gliding sidestep—

—and then another.

The lance tip now had to track a crossing target—

Gabriel caught the oncoming lance—off angle, if only slightly—on the forte of his long sword and flipped it aside with an enormous advantage in leverage and Ataelus took one more stride, *just* threading diagonally past the onrushing white charger so that the two knights passed, not left to left as de Rohan intended, but right to right.

De Rohan tried to raise the butt of his lance—

The Green Knight's pommel smashed into his visor. It did no damage beyond a spectacular flash of sparks—but the pommel slid to the shield side, crossing de Rohan's neck even as Ataelus turned on his *front* feet so that the two knights were crushed together for an instant.

The Green Knight's arm locked on de Rohan's head and he crashed to the dust as the Green Knight's sword arm swept him from his saddle like the closing of an iron gate, wrenching him over the seat of his high saddle and staggering his horse, too, so that it tottered and fell a few steps on.

Ataelus, fully in hand, finished his turn.

The Green Knight let Ataelus come to a halt. Twenty feet away, de Rohan clawed his jousting helm off his head and drew his sword. It was clear that his left hand was injured, and blood dripped from his gauntlet and arm.

De Rohan's sword went back. He spat. "Fuck it, then," he said.

Tom Lachlan and Ser Michael and ten other knights began to ride along the north side of the lists. No one was watching them. Only Ser Gavin stayed in his brother's box. He was watching the Green Knight with the intensity of a cat watching a mousehole.

"Do it," he whispered.

In the royal box, the King got to his feet. He towered over his courtiers, and he put his hands on the rail of the enclosure and leaned forward as if he would jump the rail.

Gabriel saw his knights move towards the Queen and he made a decision. He backed Ataelus a dozen steps.

Fifty paces away, Gavin said, "No. No, Gabriel."

The Green Knight unbuckled his great helm, pulled the lace under his chin, and dropped it in the sand. And then he dismounted.

Gavin shouted, "No! Just kill him!"

The Green Knight—now only in a steel cap over his aventail—walked carefully across the sand towards his opponent, who held his great sword over his head.

A hundred paces from the King, Wat Tyler drew his great yew bow all the way to his ear. He raised the head of his arrow four fingers' breadths above the head of his target. A dozen people saw him.

No one stopped him.

He loosed.

The Green Knight moved forward, passing one foot past the other like a dancer, his shoulders level.

He pressed straight in, not pausing for the usual circling.

Again, just as he pressed into de Rohan's measure, he felt the *entanglement*.

He almost flinched. As it was, he was a fraction late catching de Rohan's great blow—instead of rolling harmlessly off his rising *finestre* like rain off a good barn roof, the two swords crossed at the hilts, and he was weaker at the bind.

De Rohan *pushed*.

The Green Knight slammed his pommel, two-handed—into the exposed chainmail of the back of de Rohan's neck even as the Gallish knight snapped a rising cut into his torso, cutting his beautiful green silk surcoat and bruising him.

De Rohan staggered back.

Tom Lachlan was a horse-length in front. He had his horse well in hand and unlike Gavin, he trusted his captain to kill the Gallish knight and move on with the plan of the day.

Bad Tom had no need to wait around while the Galles and their rats came to their senses. Nor did he have any hesitation about killing Albans. Hillmen had been killing Albans for fifty generations.

He put his spurs to his horse when he was almost a lance length from the first episcopal guardsmen. His black beast seemed more to leap than to gallop, and his lance slew one guard, passing through his crushed breast-plate and destroying the hip of the man next to him before the horse was in among them, his hooves like four warhammers.

Had there not been nine more knights behind Tom Lachlan roaring his cry—"Lachlan for Aa!"—it might have been possible for the twenty or so guardsmen to rally and fight back. Or perhaps not.

Five of them were messily dead before Michael's mace crushed a helmet.

He set his horse at the barrier surrounding the Queen and, armoured knight and all, the gallant animal leaped. He landed and his mace licked out to kill the sergeant who, with more loyalty than might have been expected, had moved to put a spear in the Queen. Blanche had the other end of his spear. She was spattered with his death.

Chris Foliak's horse made the leap, too, and the dapper knight reached down a hand.

"A rescue, your grace," Foliak said. He didn't await her answer, but pulled her over his saddle.

Ser Alcaeus, a more prosaic man in every way, had lifted the gate to the barrier with his sword.

"Bring Blanche!" the Queen shouted, but the knights were all turning their horses, and Blanche had already slipped under the barrier—rescuing herself was her specialty, and the gore of a dozen dead guardsmen might haunt her memory later, but for now she was free, and running. She ran for the end of the lists. Something was happening in the middle—she'd lost track of the fight when the rescue started.

Thorn stood in the deep woods, a trebuchet's throw from the walls of Ticondaga, watching the castle and events therein through the lens of the awareness of fifty insects slaved to his will.

He had moved on from moths. And Ghause was far too busy working to defeat him to watch for his simpler intrusions.

Yet even as she shored up her castle's hermetical defences and turned his workings, her attention was elsewhere, and Thorn followed her as avidly as the moths followed a candle, waiting for her to make her great working. He had been ready for days—indeed, Ser Hartmut and Orley importuned him daily about his promises of breaking the castle's defences. The castle had sent out messengers through hidden passages.

Thorn cared nothing for any relief force. Ghause, his target, was focused on the Queen in far-off Harndon. He wished he knew why, the more easily to predict her actions. Six months, she had laid a working of such power and complexity that Thorn readily admitted he had underestimated her.

She was powerful.

But she had made an error. She had compounded that error. And now, as she watched the Queen's rescue in her crystal, he watched her.

Ser Hartmut and Kevin Orley were away to the south of the castle, storming Mount Hope, or so they claimed, intent on taking the one piece of ground that would overlook the castle walls.

Thorn felt Ash's imminence before it happened.

He *became* as two men—a pair of fools, dressed in faded, tattered motley.

Both men were juggling arrows.

And laughing—the sort of horrible, derisive laughter that bullies use to torment victims in the back alleys of the world.

Tyler's arrow slammed into the King.

The King fell.

Ash began to caper—both of him. "Beat that!" he said. "Do you not think that the silken girdle that binds the robe of Alba is ripped asunder?" His two bodies laughed, and their laughter was a cacophony and a polyphony of laughter. "She thought it was about the woman!" Ash roared in delight, and slapped all his thighs. "I lied to her, and she *believed me!*"

Thorn shuddered in distaste, wondering to what he had tied himself. "Tyler is more my creature than yours," he said.

Both heads turned. "There are no *creatures*. The wonder of the thing is that they do it to *themselves*." The laughter barked out, mad and high. "Oh, we shall have merry times. Look, Thorn. For all their work, we have just erased Alba as if it had never been—with one arrow."

One of him turned a somersault and the other began to juggle swords.

"But the Queen..." Thorn began—and then he saw it, too.

"The Queen has only a few hours to live," the Ashes chortled. "She'll be killed by her own!"

De Vrailly could not face humiliation, or people. He walked away—past the royal box, past the horse enclosure at the back, and then west to his own beautiful white pavilion.

There was no one there to disarm him—no wine, no water.

He knelt on his prie-dieu.

He raised his arms, and then, almost without volition, he screamed, "WHY?"

Amicia rose as she saw de Rohan knocked from his horse. No one would pay her any mind, whether she was be-spelled or not, and she slipped lightly along the bench, cursed by those who needed a better view.

She was still ten men away when the arrow struck the King. Instantly, she reached out *in the* aethereal.

She had healed him before, and had today wiped the drug from his body, so she bounded after him into the dimming darkness of his inner sanctum. He had no talent and so his sanctum had no form—

The arrow had struck below his heart. Even as she reached for the damage inside him, and tried to slow the tearing of his great heart, he was going.

Amicia knew what was at stake—the peace of Alba, the lives of innocents. She did what she would not otherwise have, what she had been taught never to do.

316

She followed the fleeting shadow that was leaving the sanctum, trying to hold it with one aethereal hand while her other hand bound the damaged vein that gushed blood into the cavity of his body and his lungs.

For a long breath, all seemed to be in balance. And then she realized that all her balance was a lie, and she was following him down into the darkness.

She had made a terrible error.

There was a near-riot around the Queen's barriers and men were running around the King's box—it was hard for Gabriel to assess what was happening twenty paces away while keeping his focus on de Rohan.

"The King is hit!" shouted a man.

A woman screamed.

Gabriel felt the ring on his finger burn and a great store of his *ops* torn away from him.

Amicia.

De Rohan read his body language aright, and attacked, a flurry of mighty two-handed strokes. That Gabriel guessed they were fuelled by desperation took nothing from their intensity.

De Rohan cut from his shoulder—right, left, right, like a strong boy practising at a pell. But de Rohan was the match for any knight. His blows were too hard to ignore, and fast—as fast as Mag's stitches in fine linen.

Gabriel gave a step. Then another—his second cover.

The third fast blow came with a deception, a reversal.

Part of it hit his skull cap, and he was stunned. But he'd trained to fight when stunned, and his body continued—his left hand grabbed the blade of his sword and he raised it, making any further smashing blows difficult to throw and pointless.

And now it was Gabriel who was desperate.

He could feel Amicia—slipping. Somewhere...

He lost de Rohan's sword and thrust desperately with his own, and hit something even as he took another blow in the side—this one under his arm. It drew blood, de Rohan's point pricking through his chain mail.

With terrifying clarity, he realized that whatever was happening to Amicia was severing her link to him. And his invulnerability.

De Rohan cut—a flashy lateral cut from the hip that snapped up to be almost vertical. Gabriel counter-cut.

He and de Rohan came together crossed at the hilts, and de Rohan tried to control his sword at the bind, pushing hard. He had an instant of initiative and he let his sword roll as he stepped, and he slammed his free left hand into de Rohan's face.

Blood flowed—

De Rohan's blade licked out—creased his cap and cut into his forehead—again. The flow of blood almost blinded him.

But his experience of near death at the hands of an assassin in Morea steadied him. The wounds to his forehead were not killing blows. His vision functioned.

De Rohan was very strong, even with his hand wounded. And he threw strong blows.

"I've given him too much time," Gabriel said in the calm of his palace. He took an instant—no time at all, in the real of the fight—to push all the ops he could easily find—straight down his link to Amicia.

Then he lowered his sword—all the way to *Coda Longa*.

Amicia was on her bridge and yet she was drowning, and there was neither calm nor focus, and her world was utterly black. She had let go of the King— he was gone into the grasp of death, and in her fear and anguish Amicia feared that she, too, was already dead and her disembodied soul was struggling futilely, as she could no longer make any contact with the real.

But something was keeping her anchored on her bridge. She could feel its aethereal planks under her feet.

It was utterly black around her, but as she struggled against the dark she saw a flash of pale light—the light of the sun, from the ring on her finger.

She found the strength to pray.

The bridge under her feet began to give way.

She was in the midst of death. She had gone too far—too far, too far.

For some reason she looked up.

Above her, in the contradictory way of the aethereal, there was light that never entered the depths where she was. Above her was God's light, and she was deep into death's darkness. The darkness seemed heavy and potent, and she imagined that she was past the point from which she could return to air and light, except—except—

Gabriel's sword snapped up, low to high, a rising head cut that turned slightly in its last hand's breadth.

De Rohan snapped a strong cover, throwing a hard blow at the flat of Gabriel's sword.

The Green Knight's sword snapped aside—driven hard to the outside.

Gabriel turned it, as he had always intended, the pommel rotating under his hand as the blade rotated on top of it, the point transcribing the base of a cone and the cross guard turning in place until the Green Knight's sword had changed sides of his adversary's blade in the beat of a faery's wing.

Gabriel reached in with his left hand, caught his own sword point and the middle of his opponent's blade in the same grip. Ruthlessly, he used his own left hand as a guide, his sharp blade cutting his glove and his hand as his point—neatly guided—slid through de Rohan's left eye and into his brain.

De Rohan was dead long before his knees hit the ground.

Before his head followed his knees, *Gabriel was in his own palace and his hands formed a pillar of fire—*

Amicia reached up towards heaven and grasped the rope of green fire that rolled down and took it. Only as her hands closed on it did she know what she had grasped—her working for Gabriel's invulnerability, which she held in her guard. She was voiding it.

She might have let go, but high in the light of the aethereal, *Gabriel pulled. And out of the shadow of death, she rose.*

She found her bridge—she perceived herself as under it, drowning in power, in potentia, *and she swam—she had never seen power like this—*

He was on her bridge. He grasped her by both hands and lifted, and she had her feet on solid ground. The aethereal *was more a dream state than a physical reality—she had, simultaneously, never left her bridge and now more fully occupied it.*

He looked at her. "Your bridge is a particularly complex metaphor," he said. "I don't think I could fall off my palace, but then, I can't see how I'd get back in, either."

She laughed—the sheer embrace of life. She reached out into the real. She wanted the real, and breath, and hope—

The King was still dead, two arms' lengths away, and the archbishop was bent over his body. Behind Amicia, out in the sandy length of the lists, the Green Knight stood over the body of his dead foe.

For a moment, everything was balanced.

Then the archbishop raised his head. "They killed the King!" he shouted, in passable Alban. His vaguely pointing hand was accusatory. And it pointed in the direction of the Green Knight, standing over his adversary.

Du Corse put a small horn to his lips and blew.

The man in the red hood raised a small shield. It was the first *open* display of hermetical talent of the day and people screamed. There was a stampede from the stands—above her, the men and women in the topmost rows began to fight to get out, and the stands moved—first resounding like a drum and then developing a motion—a swaying—

Amicia got off the lower rung of benches, hiked her kirtle, and ran. Ser Gelfred had told her to make for the western end of the lists, the red pavilion. It was hard to miss, and she was not afraid to stretch her legs. Hundreds of people—half the gentry of the home counties—were running.

But behind her, before she could go ten full strides, the stands began to collapse. Screams of fear changed to animal pain.

Amicia stopped. She looked back, into the cloud of dust. The length of a horse away, to her right, the archbishop was clear of the ruin of the royal box and the stands and was giving orders—his voice had a hint of hysteria, but men and women were obeying. Du Corse was using the spear in his hand to push men into line, making a box of foot soldiers around the archbishop.

A heavy arrow fell from the sky and struck a Gallish foot soldier to the ground. The arrow struck the top of his head and went through his helmet and through his skull.

Nor were the soldiers the only targets. Someone was dropping arrows into the screaming survivors of the collapse of the stands.

She smelled smoke.

Ser Gabriel stood alone in the middle of the lists. It took him too long to fully recover his senses, and he felt exhausted—the pain in his back from the moth, the sudden drain of *ops*—

It took him too long to register that the stands had collapsed, were afire, and someone was shooting into them. More than one man.

"Fuck," he said distinctly.

His plan was shredding away into chaos. He'd lost Amicia in the dust—and now, smoke—and he suspected that Bad Tom and Michael were doing exactly what they'd planned—riding like fury for Lorica.

His plan hadn't included being on foot without a horse in the middle of a disaster.

Habit made him wipe his blade clean. Only the last four inches had tasted blood, and he used de Rohan's surcoat.

Sheathed his sword. He did these simple tasks while his senses took in the chaos around him and he tried to make sense of it.

He could feel Amicia was casting. He felt her work almost directly, so closely were they linked.

She was healing.

"Son of a bitch," he muttered.

But he could sense where she was.

Amicia was a woman who believed things, and let her beliefs shape her actions.

She knew the possible consequences of lingering. But she was a healer, and hundreds of people were injured—maybe thousands. She made herself turn and go back to the stands. She found a middle-aged woman with a broken arm, and mended it, and helped the woman find her daughter, a child—neck broken but horrifyingly still alive.

This is why God made me, Amicia thought. She prayed, and as she prayed, she worked.

Wat Tyler continued to drop arrows. No one stopped him. In fact, people ran from him as if he'd attacked them, or merely averted their eyes.

When he'd dropped his last heavy arrow, he turned to find a dozen men and two young women watching—watching as if it were something entertaining.

"It's time we strike back," he said.

"Against the Galles?" one of the women asked him.

"Against them all, honey." Tyler wished he had more arrows. He'd never really thought he'd get the King—the fucking King. And he'd always imagined a hundred enraged men-at-arms coming at him like dogs on a wounded hart. Not this—a half-empty field and no foes. A hundred yards away, the collapse of the stands had shattered any organization, and he had done his part.

He turned to leave. His handful of new recruits were still loosing arrows—he could see one, even now, skidding in the air because Luke had plucked his string. He looked back. "I'm a Jack," he said. "We mean to pull all the nobles down and have a government without them. Any of you want to come—it's a hard, thankless life. And when they recover from today, they'll hunt us like wolves." He grinned. "Except that we bite back."

One man muttered that he'd just killed innocent men and women.

"No one is innocent," Tyler spat. "They take our land and our silver and years off our lives. Kill them all, comrade. The babes and the mothers, too."

The prettier girl—the one with almond eyes and red-blond hair and a fine wool overgown—started kirtling up her skirts. "I'll come with you," she said. "I can use a bow, too." She didn't smile—she looked grim as death. "I'm Lessa," she said.

"You're too fine to make a Jack," he said.

"Try me," she said. She didn't toss her head or flirt. Out on the sand, the archbishop's men were becoming visible as the dust settled and Tyler wished he had a dozen more arrows.

"I live with beggars and I move fast and if you slow me, I'll leave you," he said to her.

She shrugged.

Two of the men nodded. They were more his usual recruits—thickset, stubby-fingered ploughmen in thick wool, who stank of unwashed bodies from a yard away. They had heavy staffs and big leather bags.

"Take us, too," one said. They looked like enough to be brothers.

"Sam," said one.

"Tom," said the other.

Tyler liked the looks of both of them. "It's a hard life," he said.

"Try pushing the master's plough," said Sam. "Let's kill 'em all."

Tom clearly liked the looks of the girl.

Tyler winded his horn. Some of the episcopal soldiers looked his way, but he had to give the signal or some new clod would die.

Then, without another word, he ran north, into the clear air. There was a tree line past the black smithery, about two hundred paces. His rendezvous point.

He was a little surprised when he looked back to see *five* of them follow him.

The stands were well-ablaze. At the north end of the stands, a crowd had gathered—as best he could tell, they were pulling survivors from the smoke and broken timbers.

"Where's the Queen?" the archbishop demanded. "Get her, and put her to death."

What Du Corse might have hesitated to do an hour before now seemed to make better sense. He blew his horn three more times, and more and more of his men-at-arms began to rally. His standard bearer appeared, and his squire, and he mounted. The smoke troubled his war horse—he got a dozen lances behind him.

"Follow me," he said.

They only had to ride a hundred paces for him to see they were far too late. The Queen was gone—her guard massacred.

Du Corse's men-at-arms—Etruscans and Galles and a few Iberians—crossed themselves and muttered.

At his elbow, l'Isle d'Adam was standing in his stirrups. "Where did the arrows come from? The arrows that killed the King?"

A desire to protect the archbishop—the kingdom's chancellor, after all—had kept Du Corse from acting. Now, though, he realized that no one had gone for the King's killer.

"North," he said. "My impression is that the arrows came from the north." He caught l'Isle d'Adam's bridle. "No—time for that later. They have the Queen."

"Who has the Queen?" l'Isle d'Adam asked.

Du Corse wrinkled his nose. "This Red Knight, I assume."

L'Isle d'Adam tugged his beard. "And where is de Vrailly?"

Du Corse shook his helmeted head. "I haven't seen him since the marshal dismissed him," he said.

Jean de Vrailly knelt in his pavilion, before his triptych of the Virgin flanked by Saint George and Saint Eustachios.

"You lied," he shouted. "You are no angel of God!"

And then he hung his head and wept.

Blanche wasn't lost, but the collapse of the stands took her by surprise, and she was so close that a splinter went into her thigh—she shrieked, and then she was down—in a long moment of clarity she realized that it was not as bad as it felt; more the shock of the appearance of a dagger-like piece of wood in her leg than real pain. Carefully, she pulled the wicked splinter out.

Blood soaked her grey kirtle instantly.

The sight of the blood made her vision tunnel, and she tasted salt and bile.

I will not throw up.

Rough hands caught her under her shoulders.

"All right now, mistress. You'll be all right now," said a male voice.

She started to scream.

Another pair of hands caught her legs. "Quiet, now, mistress," said the other man. He was a priest, and seemed an unlikely assailant.

She protested, and they ignored her, grunting as they carried her. They took her past the fire, around the eastern end of the wreckage where the smoke was clear.

There was a woman—a very pretty woman—there in a stained yellow kirtle. She had flowers in her hair. There were a dozen men and women on the ground around her, and the two men carried Blanche closer and put her down gently on the packed dirt.

The priest bowed. "Another for you, lady," he said.

The woman in yellow knelt by Blanche and said a prayer. She pulled Blanche's kirtle and her shift up to her thigh, put a hand on the bleeding hole ripped by the splinter, and closed it.

Blanche moaned, not in pain, but the expectation of pain. But there was none.

The woman in yellow smiled at her.

"You healed me!" Blanche said. Of course she'd heard of such things. The reality was—beautiful, somehow, despite the screams and the clawing of smoke at the back of her throat and the running feet.

"Two children, lady—under a beam," begged a smoke-blackened man.

The lady rose, made the sign of the cross, and followed the man into the fire.

The dust of the collapse of the stands was beginning to settle, but the smoke was now everywhere, and the mild breeze seemed to push all the smoke to their end of the lists but despite the smoke and his anguish, Gabriel made himself run. He had reserves, and he burned them, running for the place most likely to find his horse. And perhaps his brother.

And against all odds, Gavin was there, and so was Ataelus.

"You are a fucking idiot," Gavin said, and then wasted twenty heart-beats crushing him in an embrace. "What would you have done if I'd ridden away? Grown wings and flown?"

Gabriel felt like crying—he'd never been so glad to see Gavin in his life.

"Tom's long gone. Five minutes or more. We need to get clear before the archbishop gets his head together and has us taken. Their constable has gathered twenty men-at-arms and he'll have more, no doubt." Gavin was fussing with his mount's girth.

"Gavin, I have totally misplayed this." Gabriel found himself staring at Nell, who was handing him his reins.

"Tell me another time. In the name of God, get on the horse." Gavin suited action to word and got his armoured leg across. "Have I mentioned what an idiot you are?"

Nell grinned, and vaulted onto her own rouncy. "Toby rode with the knights," she said.

The box—barriers on three sides—protected them from view, at least for a moment.

"Come on!" shouted Gavin.

"Amicia's—"

Gavin put the spurs to his horse and rode out of the box, headed east into the smoke.

Gabriel turned to his page. "I'm going for Sister Amicia," he said.

She nodded—and drew her sword.

Gabriel smiled. "God bless you," he said. He didn't even think about it.

Nell followed him as he turned south, towards the stands. The archbishop was in the middle of a knot of armoured men, and being moved—quickly—to the north, out of the smoke. Thousands of men and women and children were running, but the space of the lists themselves, because of the barriers, was mostly clear, and Gabriel rode along the lists, over his fallen enemy's forgotten corpse, and towards where he could feel the pulse of Amicia's working.

There was shouting behind them. Armoured men on horseback had noticed them.

Nell pointed. "Black and yellow coat armour," she shouted.

Gabriel wished he was not in harness, or on a war horse. But Ataelus was the best big horse he'd ever known, and he put on a pretty burst of speed—a tremendous spurt for a heavy horse—and they rode around the end of the wreckage of the stands. There was a crowd—a thick crowd, perhaps a thousand people. Bodies lay on blankets, and there were men—and women and children—in blood-soaked bandages, a long line leading to a small circle—

"She went into the fire!" said an old woman. "She's a living saint, sent by God himself!"

A hundred people were on their knees. Others collected the injured—and the dead.

They were not just the dead of the collapse of the wooden stands, either. Here was a young boy with a heavy war arrow that had ripped his soft flesh, and there, a toddler trampled to death by panicked people. Her mother had her in her arms and raised her to Gabriel.

"I stepped on her—oh, Jesus save me, I stepped on her, and she's dead."
She had the misery in her voice of the inconsolable.

A man shouted, "Soldiers coming!"

A woman screamed.

"Hold the horses," Gabriel snapped and dismounted, cursing the deep pinprick in his left underarm and all the pain in his hand—and head.

He *went into his palace and determined that he had little more than his reserves of* ops *and that his wounds were nothing—and that Amicia was indeed deep in the burning wreckage.*

He set his feet and cast—a wind

water—

and a cloud of bees.

He wove gold and green into a net, and cast all three at once.

Then he followed Amicia into the smoke.

The two children were the two Amicia had slipped past when first she climbed the stands—days ago, it seemed. The beam was the structure's main supporting beam, and it pinned them across their broken legs—massive fractures.

The fire was an inferno, hell come to earth.

As a little girl, Amicia's village had a bonfire for All Hallows. She could remember it—the making of it, the anticipation, and her horror as she saw its power, not just in the real, but the *aethereal.* Fire. Fast, and ruthless and without intelligence.

The fire had all the fuel of the royal box—hangings, painted with oils, and tapestries and wood partitions, furniture and beams and bleachers. It had an *aethereal* component, too. Someone—some*thing* had *pushed* the fire.

The two children were heartbeats from death with the smoke and fire—and the girl could not stop screaming. Her brother had already fainted.

Amicia lacked the *potentia,* after healing, and a foolish struggle with death, to both lift the beam and hold the fire. But her trust in God was so absolute that she drained herself, holding the fire at bay, while four brave normal men—a father, and three of his servants—heaved with futile intensity at the beam. The father was weeping openly at his own impotence.

"Why?" he screamed.

Amicia pushed on the flames.

Something on the other side pushed back, and laughed.

"Got you," Gabriel said at her shoulder. He put his hands on the beam and it moved.

A sudden gust of wind, like the back of a storm god's hand, slapped the fire away from Amicia.

She was knocked to her knees—instantly soaked to the skin, and steam rose, scalding, and stopped on her shield.

The bigger servant pulled the girl clear.

Gabriel grunted.

The father, his fine clothes ruined by smoke, got his son by the shoulders and pulled, and the boy screamed, denied the mercy of oblivion as his broken legs were wrenched from under the heavy wood.

They retreated the length of a house, and Amicia knelt. "Give me—" she demanded.

Gabriel put a hand on her shoulder.

"I'm out," he said. "Now get on my horse."

"You saved us all," the man said. "I'm—oh, my God—"

"Get on my horse—Nell!" he shouted.

The crowd had thinned—men-at-arms could be seen on the other side of the smoke.

Nell came through the crowd. She had no choice, and men cursed and women screamed at the two horses.

"I can save them," Amicia said.

"Get on my horse," Gabriel said. "Don't be a fool. There's no more you can do today. Other people can bandage them, and we're about to be taken. *Taken! Amicia!*"

He got up on Ataelus, and extended his hand—his good right hand.

Behind him, his bees set upon the soldiers and the crowd somewhat indiscriminately.

"You're the Green Knight?" asked a pretty blonde woman. She was so pretty, that with his life at stake and Amicia hesitating, he still saw her.

"Sometimes," he answered.

She became bolder, and caught his stirrup. "Are you going to the Queen?" she asked. "I'm one of her women. A laundress."

He could see no evil in her. "Nell!" he shouted.

Nell reached down and without a shade of his hesitation, grabbed Amicia's hand and dragged her across her saddle.

Gabriel might have laughed, except he was too tired and too angry. He reached for the blonde woman as he turned his horse, got his good hand under her armpit a little more roughly than he had intended, and put his spurs into poor Ataelus, who deserved nothing of the kind.

The blonde woman squawked, and then he had her. She got a leg over the saddle even as Ataelus exploded into one of his bursts of speed.

A knot of men-at-arms and mounted soldiers burst out of the smoke, the crowd, with the bees at their heels.

Gabriel looked back. They were riding through the camp Ser Gerald Random had built for the visiting knights. Half the pavilions were empty, and some held squatters. But there were streets of wedge tents and streets of round pavilions, and double-ended pavilions for the richer lords, with cross streets so retinues could move about. It was like a clean, neat, festive military camp, and the tents stretched away for a third of a mile. The ropes—guy ropes and pegged wind-ropes—often came well out into the streets making it, in fact, a riding nightmare, even without twenty armed pursuers.

He locked his left arm across the young woman in front of him. "If I have to fight," he shouted, "just fall off. Don't stay."

She didn't answer.

Ataelus was a fine horse—the best, really—but he was not fast. His pursuers hadn't made multiple passes in the lists, or been awake since dark morning.

They began to gain rapidly.

Nell, despite her smaller horse, had no such troubles—she was small, Amicia was thin, and they were drawing away from Ataelus and from the pursuit.

I'm going to be captured, Gabriel thought angrily.

He had a thought—*glanced into his palace and was saddened to see that the golden thread was gone from his ankle.*

Not so much gone, as a mere slip, a spider web filament.

So much for invulnerability.

He leaned into the ear of the woman in front of him. "I need you off," he said.

"I'm ready," she said.

He reined Ataelus in, turning to the right. Ataelus understood immediately, and when a little of his heavy speed was shed, he pivoted on his hind legs, almost fully stopped—and the woman slid to the ground with real agility, catching her skirts and rolling.

Nice legs...

Gabriel had his sword in his right hand and his reins in the left. There were at least a dozen men coming at him. But they were spread out over a furlong, and none of the leaders were knights.

They were on the main street of the northern knights' camp—where the Red Knight and his company would have been in other circumstances. Gabriel could see the red pavilion that was his rally point—he was south and west of it, too far away to do any good.

He had no curses left. He went through the first six men without taking a bad blow—his own actions had been a blur of covers and short, vicious counter-cuts—and the seventh man was all alone and Gabriel reached out with his injured left hand, caught his bridle, and pulled as he back cut with his sword from a high left guard, parrying the man's boar spear.

The pain was briefly intense as he pulled the horse's head over—until the horse rolled, crushing its rider.

"That was stupid," Gabriel said aloud, aware he'd just maimed his own hand.

In that moment, a red thunderbolt struck the rear of the men coming at him. Gavin—in his coat armour—had it all—the red surcoat, the panache, and the magnificent horse barding of red silk—and he looked like an ancient god of war as he struck the pursuers with a war hammer, killing and dismounting men with every swing.

Gabriel sat and watched his brother rout a small army. It was a brilliant feat of arms, and all Gabriel could manage was some desperate panting.

Gabriel backed Ataelus, looking to see if any of the men he'd dismounted were coming at him from behind. He turned his horse, and the blonde woman was astride one of the armoured pages, with a dagger at his throat.

He didn't take her threat seriously, and he struck her in the side with his armoured fist.

She killed him. One push from her slim hands and he was dead.

She turned her head away and rolled off him.

"The rendezvous is *this way*," Gavin said with some brotherly sarcasm. "Unless you've found more maidens to rescue? Christ, you have."

Gavin saluted with a shockingly bloody war hammer. "Your servant, fair maid."

The blonde woman put a hand to her mouth.

Gabriel put his own hand on hers. "Let's see if we can manage the mounting better on a second try," he said.

"You fair pulled my arm out of the socket last time," the woman said reproachfully.

"I promise to do better," Gabriel said.

"Who's he?" the woman asked, pointing at the gore-besmattered knight. The pursuers had baulked—facing Toby and Michael and Ser Bertran.

They made the mistake of charging while he got the blonde woman back onto his horse. Ser Danved appeared from a maze of tent ropes like a trick rider and unhorsed a knight—knocking man and horse to the ground from side-on. Ser Danved was a big man, and he and his horse cut the whole column of pursuers—the men who'd passed his one-man ambush were at even odds with Ser Michael and Ser Bertran and young Toby, and were quickly unhorsed. Gavin charged into the midst of the fight, and panicked horses burst into the tent lines and men went down in all directions as their horses crashed through standing tents, and the melee became general.

"I'm Blanche," the woman said. "In the pictures, the girl's always *behind* the knight."

Gabriel had to laugh.

It took another sharp fight to get clear of the camp; the whole of the *casa*, pages and archers included, proved a match for the disorganized Gallés, and cut their way free.

"We could just cut our way in and get de Vrailly," Gavin said. He was in high spirits.

"What, and just leave the Queen where we found her?" Gabriel cocked an eyebrow.

The Queen was on a good palfrey. She was as pale as milk.

They'd taken every horse of every man they'd unhorsed, so that they were like a moving livestock show—Ser Danved's joke. Nell and the other pages were driving a herd of war horses, all still saddled.

"In a day or two, someone is going to raise an army," Gabriel said. "Gelfred says this Du Corse has three hundred lances, and de Vrailly had the same last year."

"More," said Gavin.

Ser Michael swore. "And Albans who should know better—I saw men who were my father's knights. I put Kit Crowbeard on his arse not fifteen minutes ago—the traitor."

"Kit Crowbeard?" Gabriel asked.

"One of my father's retinue knights. His professionals." Michael frowned. "Did Ranald's people save my da?"

"Ask me when we link up with Ranald," Gabriel said. "I told him to keep his men away from the lists unless...well, he must have." Gabriel looked south. "I hope he did. Otherwise, they're all taken."

Bad Tom nodded. "Aye, I didn't linger to watch, but they were disarming the Royal Guard as soon as they could."

Gabriel signalled a halt.

"Everyone change horses," he ordered. He dismounted and held out his good hand to help Blanche, who ignored him and slid to the ground with neat athleticism.

"I must go to my lady," she said. She ran off along the road.

Gabriel stretched his back and watched the distant camp. "Where's Gelfred?" he asked Tom.

Tom Lachlan just shook his head. "No one came to the rendezvous," he said. "Mind ye, we had to go find you!"

Gabriel winced. "Not my finest hour."

"You found yersel' a nice piece. You should keep her," Tom said, in his friendly way.

"Or," Chris Foliak put in, "if'n you don't want her—"

"Gentlemen," the captain snapped, "if you are quite through—"

"He's just like himself," Ser Danved said loudly to Ser Bertran.

"I need a rouncy or two for the ladies. Unless Nell plans to take the good sister all the way to Lorica." He managed a smile at Amicia. "What happened?" he asked.

"The King?" she replied. "Oh, Gabriel..."

Blanche ran back to them. She curtsied in the dust of the road with a fine straight back.

"Look here, Captain," she said. "Sir."

Gabriel managed a bow which made his back burn as if a fire had been lit under it.

"My lady—the Queen—she can't go much further," Blanche said. "She's too proud to say, but she could birth at any moment." Blanche looked around. "You're all a fine lot—any of you fathers? Blood and fighting brings on the birth, so they say."

Gabriel was still watching the camp.

There was movement. They had the fire out, and he saw the glint of armour.

"Eight hours of light left," he said. Nell brought him Abraham, his oldest and calmest riding horse. He swung into the saddle. "Nell, you're a peach," he said.

Nell blushed.

He rode along the column to the Queen, sitting with her back against a small tree. She looked serene—and deathly pale.

Gabriel dismounted on willpower alone and managed a creaky bow. "Your grace—I can't stop here any longer or we will all be taken or killed."

Her marvellous brown-gold eyes met his. "I know," she said. "Blanche loves me, but she's trying to mother me." The Queen extended a hand and Gabriel got her to her feet. "I can keep him in for another few hours—days, if I must."

"You are a woman of power," he said.

"Of course," she said.

"I healed you last year, when the arrow struck you," he said. "That's how I know. I wonder if you could share some of your *ops* with us—with me and with Sister Amicia."

The Queen nodded. "Of course—whatever I can do."

Gabriel reached out and *touched her and entered into her palace—a veritable fortress. He'd never seen a palace so well guarded. In the middle of it rose walls of solid, shining gold—pure gold, so well fitted that he could scarcely see where each gold stone fitted to the last.*

She led him—slim and lovely—through a doubly barred gate and into the citadel.

"Is it true—that my love is dead?" she asked.

Gabriel nodded. "Killed by an arrow," he said.

She took a deep breath—even in the aethereal, *and pursed her lips. "Later, I will see if I will mourn," she said.*

In the midst of her citadel—a storybook citadel with trellises of fruit and birds on trees—there was a well, and she dipped clear water—pure ops— *from the well and gave it to him, and he drank.*

"This is never a good idea in the romances," he said.

"I would like to laugh," she said. "I would like to run amidst flowers and feel love again."

Gabriel finished the dipper. Then he reached out a hand and found Amicia and beckoned to her, and she came, stepping through the walls as if they were not there—because she had been invited—and the Queen gave her the dipper to drink.

And Amicia took the potentia *and worked it, and healed the wounds in his side and armpit. She rubbed her thumb across the back of his left hand and frowned.*

"Perhaps tomorrow," she said.

And then Sister Amicia walked along the column, healing small hurts of men—and horses.

Tom shook his head. "She's—" He looked around and hung his head.

Gabriel sighed. "Yes," he admitted. "Now, let's get out of here, before something goes wrong."

Chapter Eight

The Company

At Second Bridge they went east again—much the same route they'd used in the morning. It was possible that someone very quick might have sent a force by the west road on the other side of First Bridge and cut them off and, healing or no, Gabriel didn't fancy another combat.

But as they climbed the low hills of the southern Albin, so that they could see all the way along the main ridges back to Harndon, Gabriel was sure he saw a column on the main road and *another* moving on the far bank—there were dust clouds there.

"We should have killed 'em all while we had the chance," Ser Michael said. "I wish I knew where Da was."

"I am not even sure you're wrong," Gabriel said.

But Gavin came to his rescue. "No," he said. "We did what we set out to do. It's all the plan we could make. If we'd had two hundred men-at-arms..."

"Anyway," Tom said. "That stream's gone past, eh? It was na' a bad fight, as such things go. We didn't lose a man."

"Or a woman," said Blanche, who was riding with the Queen. She was doing well.

At the Freeford crossroads, where the Harndon Road and the Eastern Road crossed the Meylan Stream, Gabriel gave them an hour. Toby led the squires off in search of food and came back with a laden mule and links of sausages flung casually over his shoulder. They all ate, even the Queen. In fact, she was ravenous, and Blanche accosted the captain again.

"She needs to eat. She's not one of your mercenaries." Blanche put her hands on her hips. "You can't make her ride all night."

Most of the *casa* looked away in various directions. But Ser Michael bowed and said, "The captain is doing his best—"

"I'm helping him make the right choice," Blanche said.

Tom was looking back under his hand. "I think there's men on the road," he said.

It was early evening, and darkness was not so far.

"Get over the ford," Gabriel ordered. "Now."

Ser Michael reached down, plucked Blanche off the ground, and rode across the ford with her. The *casa* was mounted in moments, and Ser Francis and Chris Foliak got the Queen across—still eating.

Gabriel and his brother sat and chewed sausage.

"Local men," Gavin said after a time. There were fifty or sixty men coming—a handful mounted.

The two of them were still in all of their tournament finery. Gavin tossed the last knot of his sausage into the river behind him and missed the swirl and snap as a pike took it. He and Gabriel rode forward, side by side, their right hands in the air.

One of the mounted men pressed forward to meet them. He took off his right gauntlet and held it up, too. "Ser Stephan Griswald," he said. He was over fifty, and running to fat, and his coat of plates didn't fit well—but the sword at his side spoke of some use.

"Ser Gabriel Muriens," Gabriel said.

"That's they!" shouted a spearman.

In fact, there were three or four dozen spearmen—with gambesons and good helmets, most of them with a chain aventail.

Ser Stephan nodded heavily. "Those your men?" he asked, pointing at the knights across the stream.

"Yes," Gabriel said. In fact, his men were readying lances. "Are you the sheriff?"

"I am, my lord. And it is my duty to arrest you, in the name of the King." The sheriff reached out with his truncheon, like a mace.

Gabriel backed his horse. "The King is dead," he said. "And has been since this morning."

That brought the sheriff up short. "My writ has just come from the King," he said

"It is no legal writ, but a forgery by the archbishop," Gabriel said. "Did he order out the militia?" he asked.

The sheriff shook his head. "Every county. By the saints, my lord—the King is dead? What mischief is this?"

"He took an arrow in the chest." Gabriel nodded. "But you see the woman sitting under yon tree? That's the Queen. The Galles want her, my lord sheriff. And I will not give her up. So you and your brave lads will have to fight us."

Tom Lachlan was recrossing the ford with all the men-at-arms at his back. He and Ser Michael looked like the left and right hands of God in the setting sun.

"I think you'd need a legion of angels to arrest this lot," said another old man in armour. "Leave it go, Stephan."

The newcomer rode forward. Under the trees that lined the road it was almost night. He emerged—a straight-backed old man in fitted steel.

"Lord Corcy," Gavin said.

"Ah—Hard Hands himself. And that's young Michael, Towbray's scapegrace older son." He smiled and offered his hand. "Would you gentlemen send my duty to the Queen? And will you give your word not to attack us? You have more men and are far better armed—but we are"—he didn't chuckle, but he sounded amused—"the arm of the law."

Corcy was an old man, one of the old King's military barons.

Gabriel took his hand. "I give you my word. Just let us go, and that's the end." Then he dared. "Unless you'd hide us?"

Lord Corcy thought for a moment, and his face became hard. "No," he said.

Bad Tom came up on his bridle hand side. "If we kill them, they can't tell aught where we went," he said.

Lord Corcy's hand went to his sword hilt.

"Damn it, Tom!" Gabriel spat. "Lord Corcy, we will offer you no violence unless you attack us."

Corcy backed his horse. "My sons are at court," he said.

Ser Gavin nodded. "We understand."

Corcy's eyes were lost in the darkness under the visor of his light bascinet, but he shook his head. "I'll keep the news from court as long as I can. Who killed the King?" he asked suddenly.

"Honestly? I have no idea," Gabriel said. "If I had to guess, I'd say the Jacks killed him. Or the Galles." He shook his head. He was tired—too damned tired. He couldn't see the shape of the plots. He'd lost the threads.

Lord Corcy spoke out of the darkness of his helmet. "It will be war. Civil war. With wolves on every border."

Gabriel took his own hand off his sword hilt. "Not if I can help it," he said.

Corcy leaned forward, and just for a moment, his eyes glittered. "Think the Queen's brat is the King's?" he asked.

Gabriel was too tired for this. But it occurred to him, in that moment, that he had the Queen. In his possession.

Possibilities unrolled like carpets. No—like a spider rapidly spinning out silk, the plots unwound. Structure after structure, faster than speech. It was, in every way, the opposite of the feeling of *entanglement*.

The civil war starts right here, he thought. *I'm a side. And Corcy could be won over.*

Is the baby in her womb the King's?

Does it matter? As plots and plans and counter plans exploded in all directions in his head, he realized that it was not whether the Queen's baby was legitimate that mattered.

It was what he decided.

This is Mater's doing. But the sense of power was heady—like the moment in which he'd first really worked in the *aethereal*, and made fire.

If her child's a bastard.

Stillborn.

Dead.

Then I'm the King. Or at least, it's mine for the taking.

If the child is the King's . . .

. . . and I have the Queen—

He allowed himself a brief smile, and all the realities and futures rattled around the hermetical multiverse for the time it took for a pretty girl to flash her eyes.

"My lord, I believe the Queen's child is the rightful King of this realm," the captain said.

He heard Gavin's intake of breath. Tom wouldn't know, yet, what that pronouncement meant. Michael would.

Amicia would.

Sometimes, the "right" thing is the Right thing. It's beautiful when it works that way.

Ah, Mater. You are about to be cruelly disappointed.

I think.

Michael had it immediately. "My Lord Corcy, Ser Gabriel today upheld the Queen's right in the lists against the King's Champion, and slew him."

"Christ, boy, you killed de Vrailly?" Corcy asked.

"Only the Sieur de Rohan, I fear," Gabriel said.

The sheriff, silent until then, spoke up. "Trial by combat is barbaric," he said. "And not recognized by law."

Gabriel had to laugh, and did. "I agree," he said, and slapped his thigh a little too hard, so that he yelped in pain as his left hand reminded him that it was not healed.

But he had Corcy's eye.

"I would bend my knee to the Queen," Corcy said. "And though I am loath to offer you poor hospitality, I have a barn—a storage barn. It would hide you all." He let his horse take another step forward, so that he and the captain were shoulder to shoulder—inside each other's guards. "I will cover you for one night. God help me."

Gabriel's smile was genuine. He reached out, right hand to right. "I'll take you to the Queen. Immediately. How far to your barn?"

"Less than a league." Corcy looked at the sheriff.

The sheriff reached out his hand. "I'm for the Queen," he said impulsively.

Gabriel backed his horse in the near darkness. "How about it, gentles?" he called to the spearmen. "Who among you will bow to the Queen like loyal Albans?"

He turned to Corcy. "Which way?"

"This side of the river—up the Morea Road." Corcy nodded. "I'll ride with you and be my own guide—and hostage."

Michael knew the game. His father had played it all his life. "I'll just fetch the Queen back across, shall I?" he asked. "Gabriel? This is it? We're now...?" He shook his head.

Gabriel twitched his reins, and his eyes went from Bad Tom to Michael to Gavin. "For good or ill, we're about to become the Queen's men."

The Queen came back across the stream at a trot, and her pretty palfrey threw spray high into the red sunset air. She had knights all around her, and Amicia and Blanche attended her. Despite nine months of pregnancy and ten days of hell, her carriage was upright, her face was both beautiful and dignified, and her horsemanship, as always, was perfect.

Every knight on the road dismounted.

Gabriel joined them.

All the spearmen pushed to be in front.

Chris Foliak held the Queen's horse and she dismounted.

Then all the company knights were dismounting, and the squires and pages. By happenstance, she dismounted in front of a pair of wild rose bushes that bowed in early fulfilment of their blossom. Nell took the reins of her horse and knelt behind her.

"Ah," she said. Her voice held unconcealed delight.

"Your grace." Gabriel spoke loudly. "Your grace, these loyal gentlemen seek only to bend their knees to you and offer their loyal service to you—and to your house."

She walked among them, putting her right hand on their heads—on the sheriff, and on Lord Corcy, and on Bob Twill the ploughman. Her smile was like the last light of the sun.

"I honour every one of you for your daring and your loyalty," she said. "I swear to you by my honour and by the Virgin and my immortal soul that the child in my womb—seeking to get out!—is my husband's child and the rightful heir of Alba." She walked back to her horse.

"Lord Corcy has offered us lodging for the night," Gabriel whispered.

She dazzled him with her smile. "I accept," she said.

And then she folded in half and gave a great cry.

"Birth pangs," Blanche said. She caught the Queen and wrapped her in her arms, supporting her.

The Queen caught herself and straightened. She looked at Ser Gabriel. "I'm sorry, my lord," she said. "It is now."

Ghause had spent too much of her day watching her ancient crystal for news of the south. It was very difficult to hold the thing on one place for any length of time—the effort of will drained her, not of *ops,* but of the strength to manipulate it.

But she had to know, and so she went back like a child picking a scab, even when her enemy's infernal legions stormed the Saint George bastion's gatehouse and she had to strengthen her barriers and throw fire on them until her bold husband could rally his knights and drive them out.

Ser Henri died retaking the Saint George bastion. So did a dozen of her husband's best knights, and the earl, who had gone unwounded in twenty fights, took a blow that robbed him forever of his left eye. But they drove the Gallish knights and their Outwaller allies back off the walls.

And then Ghause had to heal the survivors. Another time, she would mourn Henri—the best chivalric lover any woman would ever want— brave, clever, handsome and hard and utterly silent.

The earl woke under her healing and that of the other *talents* attending— the four witches, men called them. His good right eye opened.

"One of the fuckers is wearing the Orley arms," he spat. "I almost had him—I—" He closed his eye. "Oh, sweet. I lost Henri."

Suddenly, and for all too many reasons, Ghause felt her eyes fill with tears. Not just for Henri. But for him. For all of them. She motioned the other witches away.

"We can hold this castle forever," Ghause said.

Her husband clasped her hand. "Just get me up and fighting," he said. "Their Black Knight is—something." He shook his head. "I couldn't get past him."

"He's thirty years younger than you, you old lecher." Ghause hid her feeling behind her usual asperity.

"I've killed a lot of men younger than me," he said, a hint of anger in his good eye. "Christ, you're hurting me."

She was trying to work on the eye, but its structures were too damned complicated, and she had to settle for killing infection and stopping any further damage. "I can't save your eye," she admitted.

He sighed. "I can still see what you look like naked," he said. "I may just be slower to catch you."

She smiled. "I'm no faster than you are, you old goat. It's the maids that will breathe a sigh of relief."

She gave his hand a squeeze and then went and found Aneas. He was unmarked, although he had fought almost without pause for two days. He had arrived with a dozen lances from Albinkirk just before the siege began and he'd become a pillar of defense—subtle, magical, and deadly.

"I need you to prepare the sortie. Your father's down for a day or two." Ghause spoke with absolute command. She didn't need the men trying to take control now. Even as she spoke, Thorn—or his dark master—tried her defences.

And what was happening at Harndon?

Aneas—ever the dutiful son—gave a tired salute. "Mother—"

"Yes, my plum?" she asked.

"Is anyone coming to rescue us? Where are Gavin and Gabriel?" He met her eye. "Mother—we can have the best hermetical defences in the known world and the highest walls, but we're already running out of *men*."

"You're not spreading this poison, my plum?" she asked lightly.

Aneas gave her a lopsided grin—a grin that his brothers also had. "I am the soul of cheerful confidence," he said. "Is anyone coming?"

She nodded. "Ser John Crayford is bringing the northern army," she said.

Aneas paused a moment. Then he collected his gauntlets. "You're lying, Mother," he said quietly.

He had never contradicted her before.

She shrugged. "We'll hold," she said.

Aneas pursed his lips and nodded. "Have you given thought to escape?" he asked. "The man who claims to be Kevin Orley has promised us all some spectacular tortures and humiliations."

"The Orleys were never worth a tinker's curse," she said, snapping her fingers. "And if I leave this rock, it will fall. You know that."

He frowned. "We have a bolt hole," he reminded her.

"I won't be captured," she said. "But I'm not going anywhere. Hold the walls, my last son. I'll hold the sorcerer."

And when Aneas was gone back to his men, she all but flew up the steps to her solar. She gazed into the ball—

Waved her hand, moving the scene this way and that, her whole intent concentrated on the crystal artifact.

"Mary Magdelene," Ghause swore. "He's dead!"

For too long—time she could not spare—she watched the catastrophe play out in the south. She had no idea how the tournament had played out, but the King—her brother—was dead, his corpse wrapped in linen. She was bonded with her brother in a very special way, and she found him easily, even in death. She watched the corpse, and the Galles and the Albans gather around it like the flies.

The new archbishop was giving a speech. Over her brother's corpse.

She bit her lip.

"Henri and you, in one day?" she asked the crystal. "Goodbye, *brother*."

Then she moved her hand and sent the scene spinning northward. After an agonized minute of scrolling she faced her fears. She unlaced the side of her kirtle with hurried fingers, and pulled both it and her shift over her head.

Naked, she summoned her power, and cast.

Thorn was in the midst of a complex summoning to support the siege—the parsing of two energies to augment a trebuchet. Covered by a nasty, rainy spring night, Ser Hartmut was moving his machines forward.

But an alarm went off, and he dropped all the summoned power, so suddenly a trebuchet arm suddenly whipped back, killing two sailors.

Thorn cared not, and in the twinkling of an insect's multifaceted eye, he was *gone*.

Instantly, Ghause had Gabriel in the stone. The summoning did her bidding. It was dangerous, given Thorn's proximity, but she had to know.

He was alive. Wounded—and tired.

There was his little nun. Such a useless lover, that boy—he still hadn't straddled the little twig, although she pined for it and Ghause had tried to put a geas on her.

And the nun and a tall blonde woman were supporting...

The so-called Queen.

Ghause spat.

"I didn't want to have to do this," she said to God and anyone else listening. "But—an eye for an eye."

In the fastness of her palace, she looked at the great working she'd designed and built for months.

Desiderata was one of the best defended entities that Ghause had ever worked against. She'd watched the Queen struggle directly with Thorn's dark master. She knew the woman's calibre now.

She knew a moment's pity. If she knew how to kill the babe without killing the mother, she'd have done it. She honoured any woman as strong as Desiderata. And she knew Desiderata to be a true daughter of Tar.

As Ghause was herself.

Just for the space of a few heartbeats, Ghause considered relinquishing her revenge. Her brother was dead.

But when she killed the babe, her son by her brother would be King. She didn't pause to consider the obstacles, because she herself had never let obstacles like bastardy and incest stop her from anything.

And besides—a small, ignoble portion of her just wanted to see if her great working was capable. Capable of breaching all that the dark master himself had failed to breach.

She stared into the crystal, reached through—

The moon had not risen a finger's breadth before they rode into the yard of the great stone barn that towered like a cathedral of farming—wood and stone sixty feet high and a hundred feet long.

Lord Corcy dismounted. Two young men ran out of the barn with spears—and halted, as the whole *casa* drew weapons.

"They're mine," he said. "Haver—put that spear down and tell your brother to do the same before these gentlemen mistrust us all." He turned to Gabriel. "My barn watch. Let me show you around."

Blanche pressed up close on her horse—his horse, in fact. "We need linen and hot water," she said. "Please," she added.

Lord Corcy nodded. "There's an office with a bed. And a fireplace." He pointed. To the two young men, he said, "Torches and lights. These folk need to be put up inside." He turned back to Gabriel. "Sometimes we have militia musters here—I've bedding for fifty."

"No more servants," Gabriel said. "I'm sorry, my lord, but I can't let you send to your castle."

"There won't be much for linens here," Corcy said.

Gabriel snapped his fingers and pointed and Toby appeared. "Clean linen. Get every clean shirt in the *casa* if you must."

Toby bowed and vanished like a conjuror's trick.

"You are well served, my lord," Corcy said.

"We've been through a fair amount." Gabriel bowed and followed Blanche. He got an arm under the Queen's shoulder and together with the strong blonde woman they got the Queen up the ramp of the barn and onto the threshing floor, and then through a big door to the right. There was a small panelled room.

Lord Corcy displaced Blanche and helped carry the Queen, whose legs suddenly stopped working altogether.

"Bed," Corcy said. He pointed with his chin. Up against the end stalls, where two very curious donkeys enjoyed the warmth of the barn's one warm room, there was a bed.

Blanche got the Queen's feet. Amicia had one of her hands and was singing a prayer.

Blanche's eyes met Gabriel's for a moment. "A stable?" she asked.

"There wasn't any room at the inn," Gabriel snapped.

Amicia's eye met his in intense disapproval, but Blanche laughed.

"You're a card," she said. "My lord."

Ghause felt the birth pangs as if they were her own.

If the babe was born, her spell was lost. In the *aethereal*, mother and child were one bond until birth. The *aethereal* cared nothing for nature and everything for association. Separate was separate. Together was the bond.

Outside, thunder rolled. The heavens protested her decision—lightning flashed, and she regretted nothing.

"Brother," she called. "I will make it as if you *had never been.*"

Thorn materialized hard by Ser Hartmut. They were so close to Ticonda-ga's walls that the run-off of the rain falling on the castle's roofs hundreds of feet above them fell on their heads.

Hartmut was leading his own mining team. He never seemed to tire, or relent.

He started—the only sign of surprise Thorn had ever seen—and half drew the hermetical artifact he called a sword. Thorn had learned by his arts that it was much more than a sword. It was more like a gate.

"You would do well not to surprise me," Ser Hartmut growled.

Kevin Orley flipped his visor open.

Thorn ignored him. "It is now. Prepare the assault."

Hartmut glared. "Now? In darkness, in the rain?" He was not afraid of Thorn, and he shrugged. "Eight days of your empty promises and our blood—"

"Rain will not stop us," Thorn said.

"Soldiers like to be warm and to eat," Hartmut said. "Mastery of this simple concept has won many battles, and forgetting it lost more."

Thorn simply turned. "Now," he said.

Ser Hartmut growled. Then he turned and, loaded with armour as he was, began to run back from the exposed post to which he'd crawled, towards his camp, where despite the rain, fires flickered.

Gabriel watched Amicia comfort the Queen. Most of her grave dignity was gone with the birth pangs—her face was furrowed in pain.

Blanche smiled at him. "Best be gone, my lord. Men have no stomach for this sort o' thing, being the weaker sex, as it were."

Gabriel had to return her smile—mostly because she had humour, and that was what he needed, just then.

"You might find out where yer squire has got to with all the linens," she added.

Lord Corcy himself was heating water in the fireplace. But before Gabriel could even pretend to be useful, Toby entered with an armload of linen sheets, shifts, and shirts. Nell came in behind him with a pair of pretty satin pillows, a woman's gown in brown velvet, and a nested set of copper kettles.

"Which," Nell said, with a curtsey to all present, "Ser Christopher says as he happens to have this gown and these pillows—"

"Only Foliak goes on campaign with a dress to put on his conquests," Gavin said from the huge doorway.

Blanche put her hands on her hips. "Men—out."

Ser Michael came in with more linen. "Sorry, lass. That's not some friend of your ma's having a baby. That's the rightful Queen of Alba. If I could, I'd pack every peer of the realm into the room."

Gabriel nodded at Michael. "I'd forgotten that," he said.

"Somewhere, Kaitlin isn't far from giving birth," Michael said. "Mayhap I've just given it all more thought."

"Christ and all the saints," swore Blanche. "The poor Queen!"

Amicia turned—with more venom than Gabriel had ever seen. Amicia looked *old*. She had lines on her face that she'd never had, and even the torchlight was unkind. Gabriel, who had two bad cuts on his head, a blinding headache and a left hand so sore as to penetrate all that, assumed he looked as bad.

He turned to Toby. "Get my harness off," he said. "I don't think we'll be attacked while the Queen gives birth. And I'm about to drop."

As if on cue, Bad Tom appeared at the far door, by the donkeys. He had a long sword in his hand.

"Barn's all ours," he said. He nodded to Lord Corcy.

Corcy had been replaced at the water kettle by Nell, and he stood with a hand to the small of his back. "Weren't you for killing us all, an hour back?"

Tom Lachlan laughed. "Nothing personal," he said. "Better this way."

Corcy nodded.

It was a big room, a third of the barn, and the squires and pages moved in among the knights, disarming them. The metal falling on the stone floor made a racket.

"Quiet!" demanded Amicia. "Can you so-called gentlemen not manage to let this poor woman have a little peace?"

The squires began to move about more quietly. Somehow, the scrape of metal on the floor seemed even louder.

The Queen screamed.

Ghause stood in her citadel, amidst the dark trees and the bright cascade of flowers.

The whole vastness of her working was all one brilliant plant with deep roots and a carefully cultivated single yellow rose that was as big and lush a blossom as the real had ever seen. It was perhaps more perfect for never having known real weather or real bees.

Ghause did not pray, as she did not think it fitting to pray when she was about to kill. But she did reach out to her lady.

"You promised me revenge," she reminded her patron.

And she thought—I hope Thorn is watching. Perhaps he'll slink home.

One slim hand reached out, and plucked the rose.

The world screamed.

Thorn could not smile in triumph, but the triumph was there. "I knew she would have to do it," he said to the rain and the darkness.

But Ash was elsewhere.

Thorn raised his own net of cobweb and deceit and false guidance—camouflage and deception such as nature practised on herself—as long prepared as her working. Into her magnificent black cathedral of a curse he launched his own working so that it nested inside, like the resident mice and bats and moths in a castle.

"Goodbye, Ghause," he said.

At the Queen's scream, Amicia stood.

Gabriel suddenly understood that this was not a matter of the birth.

Blanche caught the Queen's hand.

Gabriel stepped *straight into his palace. There, Prudentia stood on her plinth. She frowned.*

"It's your mother," she said. "Oh, Gabriel—"

Gabriel pushed open the door to the aethereal. *He loosed workings that he kept ready, a careful barrage—his own shield first, as he had learned from bitter experience, and then his glittering tapestry working.*

He spat names at his statues and his signs as his room whirled about him.

In the real, his heart had beaten once.

Then, having done what he could, he stepped to the door.

Prudentia moved to stop him. "Master," she cried. "This is death, come for the Queen, from your mother."

Gabriel nodded. "I've made all my decisions," he said.

"I'm no fan of your mother, boy. She killed me. But this—you would give your life to baulk her?"

Gabriel set his jaw in a way that those who knew him often dreaded. "Yes."

Prudentia stepped out of the way. "Goodbye."

"I'll be back, Pru," he said. Then he stepped out of his palace.

In the real, Toby saw the captain pause, and his face did—that thing.

Toby had the spear to hand—he'd just put it by the fire, having oiled the shaft. Nell saw him, and without more thought he snatched it and threw it to her, and she pressed it into the captain's unmoving hands.

In the aethereal, *the curse was like a thick black curtain of felt—if an entire quadrant of the sky could be made of black felt that extended for an infinite distance.*

Gabriel found himself on the infinite plain of the true aethereal. *He was not alone. He and Amicia stood side by side, and Desiderata stood a pace behind them.*

The curse was so remarkable that Gabriel wasted a non-breath in awe.

"I will not surrender," Desiderata said. Gabriel watched it rush at them.

There was something in it—something riding it. He had the senses—thanks mostly to Harmodius—to see the fine details in the aethereal.

He had the time to curse his bad fortune. And his mother.

And the delightful irony that if he could reach her to tell her that he was about to offer his life to defend her target, she would relinquish the working. That and other ironies. It was all—absurd.

He had nothing to lose, and the aethereal offered the illusion of time.

"What did you promise God for my life?" he asked Amicia.

Amicia didn't look at him. "Everything, of course," she said.

"All I did was cast a little love charm," he said.

She turned. Desiderata laughed aloud, for all that her existence was about to be blotted out. "She is not charmed," Desiderata said. "By my powers I tell you."

Gabriel wanted to grin like a boy with his first kiss. "Take power from me, Amicia. All you can. Spend, and save not."

The three of them joined hands.

"No," Desiderata said. "Let me."

Amicia turned her head away from Gabriel, and began, "In nomine patri…"

She began to walk forward into the black, and they went with her, arms raised.

And then, in the way of the aethereal, he held the spear.

Too much time, and no time.

He thought that the idea of felt was itself interesting. Usually, the manifestation of the working had something to do with the caster—and everything to do with the context.

Gabriel thought—how do you defeat a mountain of felt?

And then it filled their aethereal horizon like a sudden summer storm.

Gabriel cut with the spear.

But at the moment that they met the curse, it overcame everything.

Thorn's working was the flight of a butterfly passing a spider's web.

But Ghause was an old, powerful spider, and in that moment her foolishness was revealed, and she saw her adversary's working.

Discovered, but deep inside her defences, Thorn had no choice but to strike. He enveloped her power, the better to subsume her—to take every iota of her essence. Her soul. Her power.

Ghause laughed. "Richard Plangere—is that all you want of me?" she asked, and her voice dripped with the seductive contempt of an experienced woman.

She raised no shield in her instant to act. Instead, she cut him with an image—an erotic image, powered by her rich imagination and all her phantasms, full of the smells and tastes of sex.

Thorn roared. The sound shook the walls—soldiers hid their heads or trembled.

Cracks appeared in the stone of his skin, and moisture poured forth.

Damaged, he lashed back with hate.

Her laughter was extinguished as he killed her in one mighty blow, the working like a stone fist of *ops* carefully tended for the moment—

But not for this moment. *Thorn stood in the fastness of his dark palace. His frustration was immeasurable. He collected his stored* ops, *the power he had saved to battle her, and cast it at the great gates of Ticondaga. The gates exploded in a hail of stone and concrete and lethal wood splinters. Heedless of his own Wild infantry or the Galles and Outwallers who thought him an ally, he began to call down the stars themselves from the heavens and hurl them at the fortress, and his aim had only grown more accurate since the taking of Albinkirk.*

Like a fist of God, the first rock struck the high tower from which Ghause had cast, and blew it to atoms, leaving only a glow of incredible heat and glass-like slag where her corpse had been cooling in the high tower.

Aneas had enough talent to know the breath when his mother died—and to know what it meant.

He was in the inner yard, by the doors of the great hall, and he had a dozen veteran men-at-arms to hand.

"Follow me," he said.

Muriens men-at-arms didn't ask questions.

The Earl of Westwall had trouble with his eye—double vision, rather than no vision. But he armed as soon as his men told him of the size of the assault, and he was waiting in person when the gates were blown in by sorcery.

He was knocked from his feet. And as he struggled to rise to his knees, he knew she was dead. Nothing but her death would have allowed the spells on the gates to give way.

He would have cried. But there was no time. Stone trolls were coming up the ramp of rubble that had once been the gatehouse.

"You old bitch," he said with enormous fondness. And went at the trolls, and his death, with a high heart.

Gabriel had never been in this kind of sorcerous duel before. Neither, he suspected, had Harmodius—no help was coming from that quarter.

The spear cut the curse the way a heavy, sharp knife would cut a tapestry—with immense difficulty. The curse seemed to rip more than cut. The felt analogy was shredded into tougher filaments that tried to bind the spear in place. Further, tendrils of the curse gathered to him—his aethereal legs were matted with the stuff.

He cut back on a new line, amazed that the feeling of powering the cut with his waist and shoulders was exactly like using the weapon in the real and then such thoughts were lost in the heart-breaking futility of the third, weakest cut.

The curse was clearly winning.

It didn't seem to do him any harm.

So he stopped fighting, pointed the spear at the heart of it, and spoke one word in High Archaic.

"Fume."

If Amicia preferred God's power to his, he'd use it himself.

The curse burned. It burned best where he had cut it with the spear.

A tendril of the curse drifted across his eyes and another across his mouth even as he poured power into the fire. He tried to move the spear, but it was locked in place, a thousand black ribbons criss-crossing on the haft.

He brought his first casting—the shield—to his face, and the energy forced the tendrils away. He took a breath and cast, imagining his memory palace to find a piece of Mag's superb ice bridge working and throw it into the curse.

Water, fire and ice.

It was one way to unmake felt.

Amicia felt Gabriel leave her, and then she was with Desiderata in a castle of golden bricks with walls as tall as ten men and lofty towers.

"Why didn't he come with us?" Desiderata asked. "I could use his strong arms on my battlements."

"He always has to do things himself," Amicia said.

The wave of black water crashed against the stone palace. It was clever, the water—it went over the battlements and the towers, filling the courtyards and the spaces between.

But it could not enter the citadel, and it could not seem to undermine the walls.

Amicia raised a shield of brilliant gold, and another of sparkling green—no mean feat in the aethereal *itself.*

The magnificent golden outer wall collapsed.

"Oh, my God," Desiderata said. "Oh, blessed Virgin—this is not the dark lord of the dungeon."

The aethereal *ground on which the golden walls rested began to erode away, disintegrating like the dream it was.*

Amicia was beyond anything of her experience of the hermetical—or anything else. She could only bow her head and pray.

And continue to flood her shields with all the power that she possessed.

The citadel walls began to collapse from the bottom.

"My baby!" screamed Desiderata. She reached out, and put her hands on the walls of her palace and held them with her own will, commanding their obedience, and she began to build a flood of gold to link them.

The black water leached through the widening cracks and puddled on the new golden floor—and began to rise.

Outside was a gale of laughter.

Desiderata raised her head and her eyes met Amicia's with no fear. Only pride.

"There he is, come to see my fall," she said.

Between sleeping and waking...

Gabriel moved the spear easily, back and forth, and hunks of the curse like dead goat-hair fell away.

It was a waste of will, however, as the curse was suddenly dead, unpowered. Impotent.

Or complete.

Gabriel retreated like a beaten army—but one with its rearguard intact. Or that was his analogy, and analogies matter in the aethereal. *He chose to retreat through the door of his palace, because he could see nothing but the tattered remnants of the curse around him—no Amicia, and no Queen.*

The door was shut. He had a moment of panic before he realized that, almost by definition, he had the key. He opened it, and there was Pru.

He slammed the door shut, and leaned against it, spear in hand. "Told you I'd be back," he said.

Prudentia, who always rose to his arrogance, said nothing. Only, when he'd breathed a few times, she said, "You should know. Your mother is dead."

Of course she was dead.

The curse was unpowered.

A host of thoughts came into his head, and filled it.

The back of her hand struck him. "Are you an idiot?" she screamed.

Her hands folded across his back in a warm embrace.

Crouching over Prudentia's body.

His hand on her latch, and her head next to Ser Henri's on a pillow.

His first casting in her solar—a housefly subsumed, its tiny spirit in him.

Her voice in his ear the day—the day—

He mastered himself. It was what he did.

"And Amicia and the Queen?" he asked Prudentia.

"Ticondaga is falling even now," Prudentia said. "Can you not feel it?"

He could. Oh, now that he let himself, he could feel it. The stones of the ancient castle were in his soul, and they were being pounded with fire and rock and hate. Only the struggle with the curse would have covered this much terror.

For the first time in his life, Gabriel fled the aethereal, *because it was more terrible than the real.*

Nell pushed the spear into the captain's hands—and instantly he began to use it. She only just rolled free, and she had a scar on her right ankle for the rest of her life.

And in the next heartbeat or two, the Queen screamed again, and then said, quite clearly, "My baby!"

Tom pushed Toby out of the way and drew his sword. "By Tar," he roared. "Let me at it, whatever it is!"

But denied access to the *aethereal*, he was only a spectator to the captain's one-sided fight. The spear shone like a bolt of lightning, and blue-red fire crackled around the room.

All the candles went out, then the fire.

"Jesus Christ!" someone said.

Nell found herself by Lord Corcy. He was saying "pater noster" over and over again.

The darkness was absolute, and then sound went, too, and there was only the beat of her heart and the feel of the floor and the mantelpiece under her arm. The fear was itself like a heavy, wet piece of damp felt, and threatened to suffocate her—she couldn't breathe, couldn't breathe, couldn't see or hear—

And then a baby cried.

Blanche, at the Queen's side, had never quit her task, despite horror and terror and blindness. Her arms were between the Queen's legs, and when she had the head, she did what her mother had said to her fifty times—ran a hand back, and pulled gently.

Pulled the puling thing clear, and gave it a slap.

In that moment, the curse shattered.

No light returned, because the candles and torches and fire were truly extinguished. But the quality of darkness changed, and sound returned.

Nell struggled with her belt pouch to find her tinder kit.

Blanche clutched the baby, wiping all the birthing away with one of Bad Tom's best ruffled shirts. She dared not assay the darkened room, so she sat, the baby crushed to her.

She heard the other woman—the living saint—say, "*Fiat Lux.*"

A candle *popped* into flame. The light seemed as bright as daylight.

"God be praised," said the sheriff, on his knees. Then—a set look on his face—the man rose and approached the bed.

"Your grace," he said. "It is said that a woman in the moment of birth cannot lie. Whose child is this?"

Desiderata groaned. But her eyes opened in her sweat-slick face. "The King my husband's, and no other," she said.

Then the sheriff went back to his knees, and as Nell lit more candles, the other men bent their knees.

Ser Gabriel was crying.

No one present could remember seeing him cry, and Sauce, who might have had something to say, was two hundred leagues away.

But he reached out with the spear.

It pointed straight at the babe.

Before Blanche could think to protest, the spear moved, and cut the cord.

"God save the King," Ser Gabriel said. He knelt.

For a moment, that's how they all were—the Queen on the bed, where Blanche put her babe in her arms and knelt in her turn, and Amicia standing at the Queen's shoulder, her face seeming to emit light, and all the knights and pages and squires on their knees, bareheaded, in a barn on a late spring night.

There was Bad Tom, who had no notion of kneeling to any man, and there was Nell, whose eyes had filled with tears, and there was Ser Michael, who wore a grin as wide as a cheese, and Ser Gavin, who looked as if he'd been kicked, and there were two boys who watched the barn and Ser Bertran, silent as usual, and Ser Danved, silent for once, and Cully and Ricard Lantorn and Cat Evil—all on their knees, and Francis Atcourt and Chris Foliak and Lord Corcy and the sheriff and Toby and Jean and a dozen others in the candle-lit dark, all on their knees on the dirty stone flags.

"God save the King," they said.

Then Amicia began to sing. She raised her voice in her Order's Te Deum, softly at first. But Ricar Orcsbane knew it, and Lord Corcy, and Gabriel—they sang, and other voices took up the hymn until the barn was full of the sound.

And Gavin went to his brother.

"What?" he asked, before the amen had sounded. "What has happened?"

Gabriel held himself together long enough to stumble out into the night, his brother at his heels. He found a milking shed, turned, and took Gavin by the shoulders.

"What?" Gavin said. "You look like you lost your best friend." He paused. "We won, didn't we? We saved the baby." He looked at Gabriel's rare, open tears. "Christ, you're scaring me. Why do I feel this way?" he demanded.

Gabriel simply collapsed like a marionette with cut strings, and began to shiver; he said, "Nooooooo," for a while, and sobbed.

To Gavin, it was more terrifying than fighting a hasternoch or a wyvern. He was tempted to walk away into the comforting darkness, and he told himself that his brother would rather be alone.

But he also told himself that he had a lot of atoning left to do for being the cruel brother, and so finally he pushed himself into his brother's personal space with the same kind of effort that he'd have used to close for a grapple in a fight to the death. It was—embarrassing.

Gabriel threw his arms around his brother. "They are all dead," he said clearly. And then he let go of any attempt at self-control.

Eventually, embarrassed and more than a little angry, Gabriel pulled himself out of his brother's arms. "I hate that," he sputtered. "Fuck, fuck, fuck."

"What, being human?" Gavin nodded. "Who's all dead?"

"Mater. Pater. Ticondaga. They're all dead." He lost it again, moaning. He wept.

Gavin, puzzled, looked at him. "I'm sorry even to ask this—but are you sure?"

"Unngh—I'm—sure." He paused. "Ohhh. Ohh, God." He had trouble speaking, and his mouth opened and closed, opened and closed.

Gavin fidgeted. He couldn't take this seriously. His mother was *literally* a force of nature—not something that could even become dead.

"I killed them," Gabriel said. "Fuck. Fuck. I . . . got it so wrong."

Gavin began to fear that his brother couldn't be lying. But he walled off the horror—father and mother and brothers all dead. He simply willed it away. "How in God's name can *you* have killed them?" he asked.

Gabriel's tear-filled eyes glittered like something malevolent in the dark. They had a faint red sheen to them. "I was deceived. Thorn is stronger— aagh. Stronger than Mater thought, and stronger than I thought." He paused, caught his breath—lost it again, and sobbed anew.

Gavin cleared his throat. "And that's your fault?" he asked. "Isn't that a little selfish, even for you, brother?"

Gabriel raised his head. He didn't chuckle, or smile, but something in his eyes said that Gavin's shot had gone home.

"How can you know they're lost?" Gavin said reasonably.

Gabriel coughed and cleared his throat and rubbed his nose on the wool sleeve of his pourpoint. He cleared his throat again. "Like it or not, I've always been able to tell where Mater was—to some degree. Unless she hid herself." He choked a moment on some memory, and then sat suddenly on a bench. A milking bench.

"Oh, fuck, I have screwed this up," he said, and put his head in his hands.

The reality of the death of his mother and father was just starting to strike Gavin. He cared for his brother, and he'd been more interested in supporting him—he, who seldom if ever needed support. But things began to seep in around the edges . . .

"Pater, too?" he asked.

Gabriel raised his head. His eyes were oddly swollen, and Gavin had a flash of the last time he'd seen Gabriel like this—when he and Aneas and Agrain had ambushed Gabriel and beaten him to a pulp. A long time ago.

Then, he'd spat defiance through his tears.

Now, he shook his head. "I don't *know*." He met Gavin's eyes. "Damn it, Gavin, you have no sight in the *aethereal*. You have no idea. It's like a dream. Nothing is clear unless you make it clear, and if you exert your will to make it clear, you may be changing it."

He paused. "Oh, *merde*." He was recovering—Gavin could see the wheels turning. He was just comprehending, himself. He loved his father—a tough, crafty man who—

As if he'd been punched, Gavin went down on one knee.

Gabriel put his arms around his brother. "Turn about is fair play," he said into his brother's hair. But then he was crying again.

"Damn you," he muttered, struggling visibly for his self-control. But he failed.

Then they both cried together.

For no apparent reason, Nell found herself being a woman, not a military page. Well—there was a reason—there was a baby.

He had healthy lungs and a determined air of survival, and wanted everyone to know it. Big, tough men quailed at his cries.

Small, tough women did not. So Nell joined Petite Mouline, Ser Bertran's page, and a handful of other women tending the baby, while some of the company's best, and hardest-working men—Toby, for example, and Robin—cowered in corners and made extravagant excuses and furiously polished armour. Bad Tom busied himself setting a watch.

Blanche led the women. She clearly knew more about babies than the others, and they had no matrons or mothers to guide them.

Blanche had something of the captain's gift. As the hours wore on, Nell began to suspect that Blanche knew little more about babies than she did herself, but she had solid notions of cleanliness and a determined, confident air.

When the bells of the parish church rang twelve, the baby went to sleep like the extinguishing of a candle.

Throughout the barn, men muttered, sighed, and fell instantly asleep themselves.

Just after the bell rang for one o'clock, Blanche finished tidying up the birthing room and smiled gratefully at Nell, who had stayed with her when all the others had gone to sleep. The nun—everyone said she was a nun, despite her clothes—sat by the Queen, but she did not speak or move—she was eerily like a statue of the Virgin, and Blanche knew, in some instinctive way, that she was guarding the Queen, or the baby, or both.

She was, however, useless for the normal work, and there was an unholy amount of blood, mucus, and a thick black sludge emitted by the baby that was more disgusting than anything she'd faced in five solid years as a palace laundress.

Blanche piled all the foul linen in one horrible pack, and wrapped it in burlap, and was saddened to note the state of her own kirtle—a grey, shapeless beggar's garment to start with, it was now quite foul. Blanche, who always prided herself on her clean, neat prettiness, was a little surprised at her own state.

Nell, who seemed a sensible, smart lass even if she did dress like a man, was now falling asleep every time she stopped moving.

"Go sleep," Blanche said in her laundry command voice. "You've been a hero."

Nell grinned. "You don't know the half of it," she said. "I did some fighting today."

Blanche hadn't noticed that the other girl was wounded, but she had a nasty gash on her left forearm and another, already closed but black as pitch, on her ankle.

"The other bastard's hilt," Nell said.

Blanche sighed and tore the cleanest strip from her shift—one of her own shifts worn under the beggar's kirtle. She regretted it, but Nell was the closest thing she had to a friend in the lunatic asylum into which she felt she'd fallen. And Nell—another competent, hard-working girl—had the big cauldron boiling, having fed it a succession of small branches brought by guilty-looking young men. Including one tall fellow who kept smiling at Nell even through the chaos of the evening.

Blanche scooped some boiling water and made a quick, hot poultice as her mother had taught her and started to clean the wound. "Saints, sweetie, that's open. It'll go red and sick." Blanche took a deep breath to steady herself. "I should stitch it closed," she said.

Nell looked at her. "You know how?" she asked.

Blanche frowned. "I've seen it done," she said. "And I'm a fine sewer by trade—none better."

"Boil the thread and fire the needle," Nell said. "I seen that part in Morea."

Three minutes later, it was done. Nell looked at the neat, even stitches with something like reverence.

Blanche also looked pleased. "Never sewn flesh afore," she said. "Yech. What a day. That boy—your husband?" she asked.

Nell laughed. "Lover," she said. "I want to be a knight, like Sauce, not a baby maker."

Blanche gave a little cough. Her shock must have shown. Nell shrugged. "In the company, you do what you like as long as you don't make waves. I never been treated like I am here. Almost like I was a man."

Blanche grinned. "I don't want to be treated like a man," she said, and giggled despite her fatigue.

Nell managed a giggle, too. "Not like that, silly," she said. Then shrugged, no doubt thinking of Oak Pew. "Unless that's what suits you. All the captain cares about is work and fighting. There really ain't no other rules."

"Aren't any other rules," Blanche said. She smiled in apology. "Sorry, my ma was a daemon for words. Don't you have any women—no offence—in this company?"

Nell shrugged. "There's some. You meet Sukey?"

Blanche nodded. "Dark hair—brought all the sheets."

"She couldn't stay because she's in charge of everyone's billets. Like an officer. Her mother's the head woman of the whole company. Course, her mother's a sorceress, too. And a seamstress." Nell sat back. "Mag does near everything. She knows all the songs, too." She looked down at her arm, which Blanche was patting with a hot, wet rag.

Blanche took a strip of clean, dry linen, looked at it critically, and put it down to wash her hands.

"You have a boy?" Nell asked.

"No," Blanche admitted.

"No boy?" Nell asked. It seemed terrible to her.

Blanche smiled. "I'm no better than I ought to be, as my mother would say with a sniff. I've had a few boys. But at the palace, it makes trouble if you do aught more than flirt with staff, and out in the streets—" She pursed her lips. "There's a host of apprentices would like to have me. But I'm not ready to be caught." She laughed.

She wrapped Nell's arm quickly, and a little too tight.

"Where are you going to sleep?" Nell asked.

"Right here, on the floor," Blanche said. She began putting the filthy linen into the nice clean boiling water, as if she was the lowest laundry girl back at the palace.

Nell shook her head. "We have straw pallets and blankets and all proper—"

Blanche laughed at the idea that a straw pallet and a blanket was proper.

"Come sleep wi' my lance. I'll see you right. In the morning, Sukey will assign you somewhere."

Blanche nodded. "I'm the Queen's laundress," she said. "I don't really need to be assigned."

Nell looked as if she might say more, but Diccon chose that moment to poke his head in.

Blanche was appalled at how casually these people dealt with the Queen. But she saw her new friend's face light up.

"Run along and have a chat wi' your lad," she said in her best grown-up voice. "I'll finish this little pile of things and hang 'em. But come back and show me where to sleep, eh, my sweet?"

Nell nodded and gripped her hand like a man. "I'll be back," she said. "Diccon's never long," she said with a sly smile.

Diccon's head vanished.

"You know how babies is made?" Blanche asked.

"Oh, aye. I even practise, from time to time. You?" Nell shot back.

Both girls laughed, and then Nell went off into the dark stone barn, and Blanche kept boiling her linens, though her eyes would scarcely stay open.

She did a haphazard job, by her own standards. Really, what she needed was more clean water, and she was, just for a moment, too tired to fetch it and a little defeated by not knowing where it had come from.

The inner door opened, and she turned, hoping for Nell.

Instead, it was the dark-haired lord. The Red Knight, except he'd worn green all day.

She was seated, and tired, but she managed to get to her feet.

He waved a hand and looked at the Queen and the babe asleep on her breast. The Queen's eyes were open—Blanche had a moment of unease at what she might have heard, but she smiled.

"I'm alive," she said, in her normal voice. "Is that Blanche?"

Blanche curtsied.

"What are you doing here, Blanche?" she asked. "Never mind, my dear. May I have a cup of water?"

"Oh, your grace, I'm out of water," Blanche said. Both of them were whispering. The baby stayed asleep.

"I'll fetch water," the Red Knight said. He looked odd. Like he'd been crying. Blanche thought he was the handsomest man, but his eyes were red and puffy like a little boy caught stealing a cake.

"Just show me," Blanche said.

"I can fetch water," he insisted. He took the big bucket from where it sat by the fire. In the flickering light, it was easy to misjudge distance, and he bumped into her hard.

"A thousand apologies, Mistress," he said.

He went out.

Blanche was considering following him, but then the Queen would be alone, except for Sister Amicia who was, somehow, not quite human. Not directly with them. Blanche lacked a vocabulary to describe her, but she shone softly golden in the darkness.

The Queen called out. "I'm sorry to be so helpless, Blanche, but I am so hungry..."

Blanche had no idea where to get food, and she didn't want to interrupt Nell.

The Red Knight came back and managed to set the full bucket down by the fire without spilling a drop.

"My lord, can you—fetch some food for her grace?" Blanche hesitated. It was always dangerous, giving any kind of a demand to a lord. "I'm sorry, my lord, but it's for the Queen."

"Ser Gabriel will do," he said. "We did share a saddle all day. Your grace," he said, bowing in the Queen's direction, "what do you fancy that I can find for you? I wouldn't wake my worst enemy right now for service."

The Queen stretched out a hand and took his. "You saved us," she said.

Ser Gabriel knelt.

"Ghause..." the Queen said.

Gabriel cleared his throat. Blanche thought he might have sobbed. "She tried to kill you and the babe," he said.

"And now?" the Queen asked.

"I fear she is dead—though not through our efforts." Gabriel's smile was shaky in the firelight, and Blanche turned away, unwilling to watch. "I hope it is not treason to want my mother not on my conscience."

"Your *mother* is *dead*?" the Queen asked. "Oh, ser knight, I'm so sorry."

"If you are so sorry immediately after she tried to kill you and your baby," he said savagely, "then you are a saint."

Desiderata smiled. "A hungry saint," she said with a glance at Sister Amicia. "She is watching in the *aethereal*."

Ser Gabriel put a hand on her forehead with great tenderness. "In the Wild—when a Power reaches a certain—level—"

Desiderata nodded. "I know. Apotheosis."

Gabriel looked at Amicia. "I think she's close." He shrugged, trying to make light of it. "What happens to Christians? Sainthood?"

Desiderata smiled. "She will not leave us just yet, ser knight," she said with serene confidence, as if...

...as if someone else were speaking through her. Blanche shivered. She knew the Queen intimately—and the Queen was somehow *different*.

But Ser Gabriel merely bowed. "Can I help you with a hale winter apple, some sausage and a nice hard cheese?" he asked.

Blanche busied herself with the water. She served the Queen two cups and put a third at her elbow. Then she put the rest on to heat in a big, often-patched copper cauldron that seemed to have more rivets than a porcupine had quills. It held water well enough, though.

She stirred her first laundry load and skimmed the foulest crud off the top.

Ser Gabriel came back with food. At the first scent of the sausage, Blanche realized that she, too, was famished.

He knelt by the Queen and fed her.

While she was chewing, he asked, "Can you ride tomorrow, your grace?"

Blanche put a hand to her throat, but the Queen managed a chuckle.

"I guess I'll have to, won't I?" she asked. "De Vrailly won't give me a day to rest."

Ser Gabriel was cutting sausage with his eating knife. "I fancy it is the archbishop at the root of this, and not poor de Vrailly."

"Poor de Vrailly?" Desiderata asked, and the open malice in her voice was the Queen that Blanche knew. Human. And angry.

"He's a pawn," Ser Gabriel said. "We are all pawns."

"Now you sound like de Rohan," she said. "Yes, I can ride tomorrow. Or right now, if you let me have more cheese first. Promise me you'll feed Blanche, too. She's done nothing but ride and work all day."

Ser Gabriel nodded. He put the last piece of cheese in her mouth as if she was an infant. "I can give you about eight more hours," he said. "Unless the news is bad."

"Worse than the death of your mother?" Desiderata asked. "I'm sorry, that was pert."

Ser Gabriel managed a smile. "Yes. Many things could be worse. Mater and I seldom saw eye to eye."

"You saved me," Desiderata said again. "I will never forget it."

Ser Gabriel chuckled. It was a dark sound with no pleasure in it. "Can I tell you something?" he asked. He was cutting the apple into slices.

Blanche suspected that they'd forgotten she was there, but as a servant to royals, she was used enough to the feeling. But the Red Knight's manner scared her.

The knife paused on the apple.

"Yes, if you will," Desiderata said.

"My mother wanted me to be King," he said.

Desiderata's breath was loud.

The small eating knife rested against the apple's skin. And cut.

"It is the deepest irony," the Red Knight said, "that on the very night of her death, I have you and your babe under my hand."

He reached out, a piece of apple pressed to the knife blade by the pressure of his thumb. The knife blade passed within a fraction of an inch of the Queen's mouth and all but rested on her cheek as he pressed the apple slice between her lips.

The Queen's eyes were locked on his.

Sweet Christ, he seemed so nice.

Blanche was moving, but she was too far away.

"You never wanted to be King," Desiderata said. If the knife troubled her, she didn't give a sign. Blanche's lunge was checked by the pail of water, over which she tripped.

Both heads turned. The Red Knight rose, cut the last piece of apple in half, gave the Queen one part and ate the other himself. He shook his head. "The world is an odd place, your grace," he said. "Nothing is what it seems, and few things worth having are easy to have. I suppose there is a man who, finding the power of Alba under his horse's hooves on the road, would abandon everything he's ever done to make himself King." He bowed, but somehow his glance collected Blanche. He gave her a hand and helped her up. "The Queen is in no danger from me, Lady Blanche. I am not my mother."

Desiderata smiled—and it was like her old smile, full of a woman's provocative wisdom. "But you wanted me to know," she said.

The Red Knight shrugged. "I suppose. There's no one else to share the jest save Blanche. Lady Blanche, I'll fetch you some food."

"I'm not a lady," she hissed at his back. Her heart was beating very fast.

She had really thought he was about to kill the Queen.

When he was gone, the Queen's face sagged. "Oh, blessed Virgin, give me strength," she said. She managed a tired smile at Blanche. "Oh, he scared me, too, Blanche." She looked around. "We need a Royal Standard, Blanche."

Blanche laughed. "Your grace, I'm a fine hand with a needle, but even I couldn't run up a gold dragon tonight."

She held a cup of water for her mistress to drink, and used a cleanish spot on her kirtle to wipe the Queen's lips. "Sleep, your grace. I don't think he'd actually... but I'll still attend you."

"Nonsense, my dear. Go sleep. He's not as dangerous as he—"

Ser Gabriel came in. He had a tray this time—a tray which proved to be an archer's leather and steel buckler full of bread and cheese and apples.

He motioned to Blanche.

She looked at the Queen, but her eyes were already closed. Her babe lay on her breast with his eyes tightly shut and mouth slightly open.

Blanche glanced back at the Red Knight, who beckoned her. She shut the door to the Queen's chamber behind her. There was a small stall—probably the abode of a favoured riding horse—just off the passage. He had a camp stool and an upturned barrel there and he set the food down.

"May I join you?" he asked.

"I'm not gentry," she said. "You don't have to waste your fine manners on me."

"Alas, once started they're very hard to turn off." He sat on a leather trousseau rather suddenly, as if his knees had given way.

"Does all your chivalry extend to terrifying my mistress, then?" she asked.

He looked at her. His eyes were queer in the darkness—almost like a cat's. He took out a knife—the same knife—and began to cut another apple into slices. He held one out to her and she took it without thinking and ate it. The apple was tart and hard despite a winter in a cold cellar, and she could not stop herself from seizing the next two slices he offered, greedily.

His mouth made a strange shape—neither smile nor frown. "Sometimes, things need to be said, between people of power," he said. "Even between lovers, or parents. Things that show intent, or honesty. Or simply draw a line, for everyone's peace." He sat back, so his face was hidden, except his odd eyes.

It occurred to Blanche that he was giving her a real answer. It was like when her mother had first spoken to her as a woman. Heady stuff. She was alone with him. She suspected his motives. But he was interesting.

"You had to tell her that you could kill her and be King?" she asked. She was into the cheese.

So was he. "Do you think she'd rather go to sleep wondering what was on my mind?" he asked. "Or knowing?"

Blanche chewed. "Depends," she said.

"Too true," he said. "The bread's stale."

"I've had stale bread before," she said, and took a slice. It was good bread, if a day or two old. "We lived in Cheapside."

He poured wine into a somewhat crumpled silver cup. "We'll have to share," he said. "I tried to find Wilful's cup, or Michael's, but I couldn't in the dark."

She murmured a prayer and drank. The wine was dark red and had a lovely taste, almost as if it had cinnamon in it, with a little sweetness.

"Does your company always eat and drink this well?" she asked.

His teeth flashed. "Good food and good wine recruit more men—and women—than silver and gold," he said. "When Jehan and Sauce and I started the company, we agreed we'd always have good food." He said, "My father always fed his men..." And stopped, his face working. He put his face in his hands for a moment, and she wondered if he was laughing, but she thought perhaps—not.

She rose to her knees and handed him the wine cup. He took it carefully— so carefully that he didn't touch her. Blanche was used to a more forward kind of boy and dismissed her earlier suspicions of his intentions.

She wondered what it would be like to be his mistress. Was he rich? He was likely to be the Queen's captain for some time. He had nice manners— nicer than the court gallants she'd known.

She almost giggled aloud at such an absurd fantasy. Blanche, the laundry mistress, was more like her speed.

"You drank all the wine!" he said in mock annoyance. He had cried, then. Odd man. And now, like all men, sought to pretend he hadn't.

"I didn't mean to," she said.

"You tell that to all your boys," he said.

She blushed, but it was dark. "I'm so sorry, my lord," she said. "I should go look at the Queen. The wine was very good."

"Your servant, Lady Blanche," he said.

He rose—for a moment she thought he might...

Then he was past her, holding the door. "Since you tumbled the last bucket," he said wryly, "I'll draw another before I rest."

He came back with the bucket, and with Nell, who had a straw palliasse over her arms and her boy in tow. The two of them made her a bed at the foot of the Queen's. Nell looked well pleased—Blanche, in passing, plucked a straw out of her hair. Diccon, her young man, was diligent in avoiding his captain's glance.

The Red Knight nodded, and went out the door.

Blanche fell onto her pallet and was asleep before she could think.

Gabriel fell into the straw next to his brother. Gavin muttered something. He'd been kind enough to leave room and two blankets. Gabriel refused to think about Ticondaga or all the errors he'd made—because if he stayed awake mourning, the morrow would be worse.

He closed his eyes. Smiled at a thought instead of weeping, and *went into his palace of power. There—in the cold, clear world of the* aethereal—*he could work his own sleep.*

"You need to sleep," Pru said.

"That's what I'm here for," he said.

He cast a simple working, using only two symbols and one statue. Pru's hands moved, and he was asleep.

"Gabriel—they want you. Gabriel—get up!"

Gabriel surfaced slowly. His self-imposed working was strong enough to keep him down unless he made an effort of will. The effort of will broke the working, but it also brought him a flood of images.

"Ohh," he said. He moaned. "Oh, noooooo."

Mater, dead. Ticondaga—destroyed. Thorn, triumphant. The Queen. Amicia.

"Fuck," he said.

"Sorry." Gavin was shaking him. "It is Dan Favour, from Gelfred, and he says it has to be you."

"Fuck," he said again. He sat up. His eyes filled with tears and he banished them as best he could.

He rose from his blankets in shirt and hose and climbed over the rest of his lance and his *casa* sleeping in a small loft. Nell cursed him. Gavin had a taper lit and handed it to him.

"I'm going back to sleep," he said.

Gabriel wished he had that power. Instead he went down a ladder and then out to the main area of the barn, where long lines of men and women lay in rows on straw bundles or pallets. The barn was a cacophony of snores and heavy breathing.

The outside air was sharp and cold. He saw Ser Danved in full harness, standing watch with his lance by the road. Cully was dressed. He was buckling his sword belt while he talked to young Favour, who was head to toe in a dark green that looked mostly black in the fitful torchlight.

Cully gave a sketchy salute. "Sorry, Cap'n," he said. "But you ha' to hear this your own sel'."

Favour knelt on one knee. "My lord," he said. "Ser Gelfred ordered me to find you—he sent ten of us out. We have the main column formed as you ordered, south of Lorica." He looked at Cully. "But there's already an army on the roads—Galles and Albans and much of what's left of the Royal Guard. More'n a thousand lances, my lord."

Cully had the captain's case, and he unrolled a map. It was not very accurate, because it had been designed merely to give a traveller distances from various towns to Harndon.

"At last light, de Vrailly was at Second Bridge," Favour said.

"Get to the bad part," Cully said.

Favour cleared his throat. "There's banners with de Vrailly," he said. "Towbray's banners."

Gabriel struggled to be awake. "Towbray? He's in the dungeons—"

"Ser Gelfred picked up a couple of royal archers yester e'en," Favour said, his eyes on Cully. "Looking for new employment, they said, as the Earl of Towbray had sworn fealty to de Vrailly."

Gabriel nodded. "That could be," he said. "Wake Ser Michael." He frowned.

Lord Corcy appeared out of the darkness. "Towbray—that snake," he said.

Gabriel would, in that moment, have preferred almost any other man awake rather than the old Alban lord, who was possibly an ally but not yet proven. But there was no crying over spilled milk. "Towbray has a passion for changing sides, I agree," he said.

"His presence will cement the loyalty of many of the southern barons," Corcy said.

Gabriel stared into the darkness, and then down at his map. He measured a distance—Second Bridge to Lorica.

"How long for you to reach Gelfred?" he asked.

Favour bowed. "Before daylight. I swear it."

Ser Michael appeared from the barn. He looked the way Gabriel felt.

"Your pater's with de Vrailly," he said bluntly.

Michael froze.

Gabriel watched him carefully.

"Idiot," Michael swore.

Gabriel found that he'd stopped breathing for a moment, and now he breathed again. He put his arms around Michael. "I'm sorry," he said. "I've gotten knocked around the last few hours—it's as if the pillars of the earth have been knocked over."

Michael spat. "I came here to rescue him," he said.

"He refused to go with Ser Ranald, two days back," Favour said. "I'm that sorry, Ser Michael, but we was—not best pleased. He was the only royal prisoner to turn us down."

"That idiot," Ser Michael said. He looked at his captain and shrugged. "So?"

"Officers," the captain said.

Blanche was awakened to find Nell leaning over her.

"Wake up, girl!" Nell said. "Get the Queen up!"

The babe awoke and, finding the world changed, challenged it with a yell.

Outside, a brazen trumpet rang out a long call.

The barn seemed to explode into motion. Once, as a child, Blanche had seen her mother find a nest of mice in a chest in their garret. As soon as she touched it, mice ran in every direction, making her mother scream.

This was like that, except that the mice were unkempt men and women.

At the door, an archer stopped Nell.

"We attacked?" he asked.

"Not yet," Nell spat, and pushed past him, looking for horses.

Nothing had been packed well in the exhausted darkness. The cursing from beyond the door was fluent and very descriptive. Blanche might have admired it, but she had all her damp laundry to pile into a basket thrown through the door by Nell's boy.

The babe was louder than the trumpet.

Sister Amicia awoke—if she had been asleep. She picked the baby off her mother's lap as soon as it finished feeding and began to bounce it. She grinned a very un-saintlike grin at Blanche.

Blanche got the Queen bathed—just a sponge and lukewarm water—and into a shift that hung on her like a sack. Then she put the Queen in the same gown she'd worn the day before—the white gown of a bride or a penitent sinner. The gown in which the Queen would have been burned.

"Don't fuss," Desiderata said, taking her baby back from Amicia. "Don't fuss. If we're moving now, there's a reason. Be quick, Blanche. Leave anything you cannot carry."

Blanche frowned, thinking that it wouldn't be the Queen's problem if Blanche had no clothes and no clean swaddling for the baby.

But again, Nell appeared to save her. She had Blanche's palfrey of the day before in the small stall just outside the door, and she had a donkey. Cully, the master archer, stood by the donkey.

"Just gi' me your baskets," he said kindly. "I'll see 'em onto the animal."

Blanche favoured him with a smile. She knew she must look a fright, but there was nothing she could do—no bath, no clothes, no nothing.

The saddle on her palfrey was worth more than her whole wardrobe had ever been worth, and she wondered whose it had been.

Cully tightened a belt and set the tine of the buckle, and gave a tug at the laundry basket. It didn't move.

"You ha' any trouble with this animal, call me, my lady," he said.

"I'm no lady," Blanche said.

Cully grinned. But he said nothing, and then he was through the great double door of the barn.

"Archers—on me! Fall into the left with your horse to hand." He took his bascinet—as fine as many a knight's—off the pommel of his saddle and pulled the aventail over his head.

An archer brushed past her and his hands tried most of her body as he went past. The man leered back at her.

Blanche's right hand caught him just above his eyebrow and slammed him against the doorpost.

Another archer laughed. "She's a quick 'un, Cat!" he said. He grinned at Blanche, who glared.

Then the trumpet rang again, and armoured figures poured into the great barn's yard. Pages scurried by with horses—chargers and riding horses, sometimes as many as three horses to a page. The men-at-arms began to mount.

She got the Queen up on another palfrey brought by a page she didn't know. That page was also a woman, a pleasant, dark-haired woman old enough to be Nell's mother.

"They call me Petite Mouline," she said in an Alban deeply accented with Occitan. "The cap'n says that this 'orse is for the lady Queen, yes?"

Petite Mouline had a fine breastplate and her maille was dark and well oiled over a bright red arming coat. Her smile was warmer than the horse. "Oh, the *petit bébé*!"

The Queen emerged from her birthing room with the sister at her elbow, and she put a dainty foot into her stirrup and leaped into the saddle with a vitality that belied the last few hours.

Amicia mounted her own horse more carefully.

In the stone-flagged yard, Bad Tom's voice—as loud as Archangel Gabriel's trumpet—put the company—or rather, the fragment of the company with them—into order.

The Red Knight was in full harness. Outside, the moon was small and bright—bright enough to cast shadows on the ground and to light his shoulder armour in a dazzle of complex reflections.

He bowed to the Queen. "Your grace, I cry you pardon me. De Vrailly has moved faster than I expected."

"We must run—I understand."

He smiled. "Well, your grace, as to that—" He turned as Lord Corcy came up.

"I'm with you, my lord," Corcy said. "I must get home, collect my harness and the men I can trust. I hope you'll agree to let the sheriff and his men disperse."

"I'm afraid I must ask you all to come with us for a few leagues," the captain said.

Corcy nodded. "I was afraid you'd see it that way. I beg you to reconsider. These men won't betray you until pressed. I will swear any oath you name."

The Queen reached out and took Lord Corcy's hand. "I accept your word, my lord. Go, and return."

"We'll just keep your son as our guest," the captain said.

He and Corcy exchanged a long look, and Blanche thought there might be blood, but Corcy bowed. "Very well, my lord. Adam, remain here with these gentlemen. Where will I find you, sir?"

The Red Knight—in his proper colour, visible even in moonlight—nodded. "North of Lorica, and moving quickly," he said. "We'll have de Vrailly at our heels."

"I'll come as fast as I may," Lord Corcy said.

The sheriff was more openly angry. "Christ on the cross, gentles! I swore my oath! Let me be!"

The spearmen who'd accompanied him the day before muttered angrily.

Bad Tom came out of the yard. "We don't have horses for this lot," he said. "They'll only slow us down."

Blanche put a hand to her throat, convinced she was about to see these poor men butchered.

A tight ring of pages and archers surrounded them, and suddenly they had swords in their hands.

The captain put his hands on his hips. His golden belt glowed in the moonlight.

He winked. It seemed improbable, but she was sure he had winked.

"We'll be long gone to Lorica," he said. "Let them go."

The archers and pages sheathed their swords.

The sheriff and his men were even handed their weapons. They took no more damage than some taunts.

Most of them fled.

Blanche was interested to see that two men—both big, capable-looking peasants—remained. They had a brief conversation with Cully and were put up on wagons.

The Queen smiled at her. "Oh, it is good to be alive! The sun is coming. It is just across the rim of the world. There's a fox in yon hedgerow looking for a meal, and a family of mice in the foundation just here—by the blessed Virgin, it is the world." She looked at the worthy sister. "I did not expect to see this morn at all," she said.

Amicia nodded. "The fox will eat the mice," she said.

Desiderata's clear, delighted laugh rang out. "Only some, Amicia. That is the way of the world, too."

The column began to move.

Chapter Nine

The Company

They moved very quickly—back over some of the same ground they'd followed the day before. Blanche saw a pair of men meet the captain—he rode by the Queen—and both men were new to her, clad in green. The day began to break after they'd been on the road an hour.

Another pair of men in green met them and led them around a village whose cocks were crowing and where early morning fires filled the air with the homey smells of cooking and smoke—Freeford, she thought.

"Quiet!" Nell hissed behind her, and the whole column passed the town like ghosts. A shepherd coming out of the town with a small flock of goats was grabbed at sword's point and his goats were left bleating behind them.

They came to more open country at the foot of the great ridge and suddenly they were trotting—and then cantering. Blanche was not confident at this speed, and she couldn't do anything but keep her seat.

"Relax," the Queen said at her side. "Let your hips go with the animal. It's lovely. Stop making the horse do quite so much work."

"I'm sorry, your grace!" Blanche said.

"Ah, my dear, I never knew what a treasure you were until this adventure. He calls you 'Lady Blanche' and he has the right of it! You're a treasure. But you must learn to ride better." The Queen laughed.

Her laugh seemed to lift the spirits of the whole column.

A league on, and they passed a pair of farm gates and the column slowed to a walk again.

Bad Tom raised his voice. "Halt!" he roared. "Change horses!"

Nell put a fresh horse's reins into Blanche's hand. "That means you have five minutes to rest," she said.

Blanche dismounted, and her legs almost folded under her. Instead of helping the Queen, the Queen helped her.

Amicia rubbed her hips like a much older woman.

The Red Knight reappeared and handed around his silver cup full of wine. "Ladies, your pardon," he said. "We're racing time."

"We're not going north," the Queen snapped.

"No, your grace," he admitted.

"I'm not likely to tell anyone," she said. "Come, whose treason do you fear—Sister Amicia? Lady Blanche?"

He smiled. "If some of my men can reach a certain point—in time. If we can get there, too—" He shrugged. "Well there may be a fight." He bowed. "Some of my household knights will take you north on the road, to Lorica and safety. I'm sending Sukey and all the baggage."

"Nonsense," the Queen said. She handed her baby to Amicia. "If there's a battle, I want to see it."

Again, Blanche thought this sounded far more like her Queen.

"Your grace—" Ser Gabriel began.

"Spare me the poor weak woman speech," Desiderata snapped back.

The Red Knight's face clouded. "If you are captured, your grace, you are a dead woman. And your cause is dead. And so is your son."

"I think I know my plight well enough, ser knight." Desiderata's smile was cool.

Her son gave a great cry.

She clutched him to her again. "I know the risk. But if you lose—"

"Madame, this is not a set piece battle like a tournament. I hope to catch de Vrailly napping on the road or just breaking his camp. If I fail, he'll be on us like a dog on a rabbit and we'll be outnumbered twenty to one. Would you please ride north to Lorica, *Madame*?"

Desiderata smiled and put a hand on his steel arm. "Ser Knight—I would be with my army. If you lose—so be it. But if you triumph, I would have men say that my son was in battle the day he was birthed, and that his mother was no coward. Too few saw my trial by combat. My husband is dead. I would that men saw me, and knew me."

Ser Gabriel sat a moment on his great war horse. The sky was lightening behind him. He looked like the war incarnate, the avatar of knighthood.

He took a deep breath, and then shrugged. "Very well, your grace. You are the Queen." He nodded. "Amicia? Will you at least ride for Lorica?"

The nun shook her head. "No," she said. "You will need me."

The Red Knight smiled. "Blanche? I don't suppose you'd like to take a nice ride with two handsome knights...?"

Blanche laughed. "I would not leave my lady." Greatly daring, she said, "I've had offers of dawn rides from knights afore now. My mother told me never to go."

The Queen tilted back her head and roared. She reached out and caught Blanche's hand and squeezed it.

The Red Knight bowed in his saddle to the ladies and turned his war horse. But when he was out of earshot, he turned to Michael and said, quite savagely, "I may yet be King of Alba. Through no fault of my own."

Michael stared.

"If she falls..." Ser Gabriel shook his head. He rode to where Ser Francis Atcourt and Chris Foliak sat on their destriers.

He put a hand on Atcourt's shoulder. "If you two bring the Queen through this alive," he said, "I will give you whatever I can that you desire. A nice fief in Thrake? And I'll knight Chris on the spot, or see to it she does. If she goes down—" He shrugged. "Have the good manners to die with her."

Ser Francis Atcourt was not a young man. "I've never asked for aught," he said.

Ser Michael laughed. "It's better than fighting, holding land," he said.

Atcourt smiled his beatific smile. "I don't see you at home on your farms, my lord," he said.

He was always surprised at how seriously the professionals took knighthood.

Chris Foliak shook out the back cloak of his magnificent silk surcoat. "I rather fancy being a knight," he said. "And I always fight my best for a lady."

"Especially a rich, beautiful lady," Atcourt said. "But aye, Captain. So— she's staying with us?"

The captain nodded. "For our sins. Or perhaps because of them. Enough prattle, gentlemen." He took a war hammer from his saddle bow and waved it at Bad Tom, who vaulted into his saddle and bellowed.

Before a nun could say an Ave Maria, they were all mounted, and the jingle of horse harness mixed with the rattle of plate armour. In the west, the sun was rising.

Gavin rode beside his brother. He knew most of the men who came out of the dawn and guided them—members of Gelfred's green banda, the woodsmen and the prickers and scouts. They seldom stayed in sight long enough for more than a recognition signal and a waving hand to show the new line of movement, and then the green-clad figure would ride into the dust or vanish into a wood-edge. He saw Amy's Hob canter along a thicket with a crossbow out and cocked, and then ride around the edge—gone.

His brother waved to Bad Tom and as they trotted, called, "No shouts, no horns or trumpets now."

Tom's laugh was startlingly loud in the clear morning air.

They crested a shallow ridge, and found the whole valley of the great river at their feet. Distant bluffs marked the Harndon side of the Second Bridge.

Gelfred rode up a path as if the meeting had been planned for weeks. He wasn't smiling.

"De Vrailly's up and almost ready to march," he said. "You're late." Then Gelfred saw the Queen. In a moment he was off his horse in the road, and kneeling.

He kissed her offered hand. Then he reached into his plain green cote and pulled out a small, red banner. It had the pennon of a captain, and on it was a magnificent golden dragon.

"I brought it for the King," Gelfred said. "Ranald sent it. He said he couldn't bear the bastards to have the Royal Guard's pennon."

The captain rolled his eyes.

"It's his by right," Gelfred said. He reached out as if afraid of being bitten, and touched the baby. The baby made a fist, grabbing Gelfred's hand.

"What a fine crop of royalists I've grown," the captain said. "Chris, put it on your lance." He gazed out over the valley. "We're going to be visible on the crestline unless we move," the captain snapped. He smiled at Long Paw—now Ser Robert Caffel. Long Paw was not dressed as a knight, and he had a heavy bow over his shoulder, a mail shirt almost black with oil and a green hood that went almost to his waist.

Long Paw took his horse from Short Tooth, another green banda man. "All right where you said, Captain," he noted.

The captain waved his war hammer. "If only de Vrailly may follow our plan."

They rode down into the valley's long morning shadows.

An hour later, and the waiting was killing them all.

Mosquitoes—the first crop of the year—settled on the *casa* like a biblical plague. Cully looked reproachfully at Long Paw, six trees away. Long Paw merely shrugged.

Gavin felt the scales on his shoulders writhe and prickle.

He watched his brother, who was watching the road with a fixed intensity. It was the hour of the day when peasants went to their fields, when men yoked oxen or horses to ploughs if they had them, when the cocks ceased to crow and work began. As the weather was fine after days of rain, there should have been peasants on the road and in the fields to their front.

They were a mile or more from Second Bridge, where the road bent sharply to the east, following the contours of a hill. On the east side of the road—the inside of the curve—a round hill rose, covered in farm fields. At the top of the hill, almost hidden behind a high hedge that could be defended, stood the small village of Picton with chimneys smoking.

No one was moving in Picton's fields, either.

On the west side of the road the ground was flat for a few furlongs until it dropped sharply towards the river. It was heavily forested in big, old oak trees with some maples and, in the centre, a stand of ancient fir trees like the masts of heavy ships.

If the road circumventing Picton Hill was a bow, Cully, Gavin, Long Paw and the captain stood where the archer would grip it, in the dark patch of firs at the centre of the bow. Gavin could see the road for a bow-shot in each direction—almost to Second Bridge. And he could see up the Picton village road, a narrow lane between two hedges that ran up the hill like the arrow on the bow.

He hated waiting in ambush. He could see on his brother's face that he didn't like waiting either—he snorted quietly in frustration a little too often.

The mosquitoes were devastating. Ganfroy, the trumpeter, was fighting a losing battle with his self-control, trying to stay calm. He'd been bitten often enough that one side of his face was beginning to swell.

The captain snorted again. "I give up," he said. "Nicholas, when I raise my arm, sound the—"

Up in the Picton hedge at the top of the long hill, a mirror flashed—one, two, three times.

"Son of a bitch," the captain said.

The first riders were visible a few hundred heartbeats later. They were light horse—Alban prickers, young men in light armour on fast horses. They were in the Towbray livery, and they were moving fast.

They passed the captain's position in the open fir wood so close that their conversation was clearly audible.

"...fooling playing soldier," one young voice said with all the self-importance he could muster. "There's not a soldier in fifty leagues."

"Certes there's none near me," barked an older voice. "Now shut up and ride."

The prickers passed.

The mirror flashed again. This time, it flashed just once.

The captain shook his head. "Ready," he called softly.

Gavin didn't know any of the banners that rounded the bend a bowshot to their right, coming from the south. But the enemy vanguard was well closed up, and very professional—three hundred lances in crisp array, all in full armour. Behind them marched a dense column of infantry.

The mirror flashed again. This was a longer signal.

"Better than I deserve," the captain said, but his demeanour had changed. The anxiety was gone. He was smiling.

The enemy van was moving at the speed of a swiftly marching man. A babble of Gallish came floating on the morning air.

Gavin had time to think that just the vanguard outnumbered them enormously. And he cursed inwardly, as nowhere did he see de Vrailly's banner.

Ganfroy quivered with excitement. The captain put a hand on the younger man's arm.

"Nothing for us to do," he said. "Gelfred will open the dance."

The enemy vanguard began to pass them. They were so close that Gavin could see individual faces—some dark and heavy, some boorish, but many men were laughing and some—too many—looked like good men, good companions for an evening's drinking or a joust.

He'd never fought this way before. He didn't like seeing his enemies as cheerful, open-faced fellows.

Off to the south, there were screams. A cheer. More screams.

"Stand up!" the captain called.

All through the woods, men stood. They weren't in neat lines, and here and there, despite the bugs, a man had fallen asleep.

The captain stood with his back to the enemy, as if oblivious of them, watching the woods on either side of him. Then he raised a horn to his lips.

The men on the road were just reacting.

They still weren't sure what they were seeing.

Gavin loosened his sword in its sheath and gripped his spear. What he really wanted to do was scratch the new bites on his groin.

And perhaps hide.

The horn went to his brother's lips.

"Now and in the hour of our deaths," said a voice.

The horn sounded. As soon as it rang out, a hundred other horns were raised and blown, so that the woods rang with them, over and over, as if every hunting pack in Alba was coursing in the woods.

Archers with a clear lane of trees began to loose shafts.

Those without moved forward.

The horns went on and on.

Gavin still had his visor open. He saw Cully loose a shaft almost flat, and then take a few steps forward. Gavin moved with him. Gabriel had his spear in hand by then, and moved with them, and Long Paw had begun to loose—the range was suddenly very close, the road was right *there*.

A bolt or an arrow slammed into Gavin's bascinet, half-turning it on his head. He got his right hand up and pulled his visor down and his thumb moved of its own volition, latching the visor.

On the road in front of them were the Gallish infantry—the routiers. They were well-armoured and most of them had heavy pole weapons or long spears, and big, heavy shields.

But their shields had been on their backs when the first arrows struck, and there were a lot of dead and screaming men on the road.

Cully took three more steps forward. In a moment, he and Long Paw both drew, their hands coming all the way back to the edges of their mouths like they were matched automatons. They—and the Gallish routiers—were framed by two vast old trees against the brilliant sunlight of the fields beyond.

There were screams, and grunts. The company archers were loosing from so close that the shafts sometimes penetrated a shield. When they struck armoured flesh, the needle points went home with a horrible meaty sound, like a butcher making tough meat tender.

The routiers broke. They turned and ran into the field on the far side of the road. Most of them fell into the deep ditch at the road side and some few never rose again.

Ahead of them, Du Corse's three hundred lances—six hundred armoured horsemen—took a few arrows, lost some horses, and charged the woods like the professionals they were.

By that time, most of the rest of the company was at the road edge or on it.

"Whose is the banner?" the captain asked. "Is that Du Corse?"

Away to the south, brazen trumpets were roaring.

Gavin stood in his stirrups to look.

"Gelfred's killed all the baggage animals, and now their wagons are blocking the road," Gabriel said. "The problem is: we don't have the lances to finish off Du Corse."

The Gallish routiers had discovered that there were archers in the hedge-rows of the town. They were caught in the open fields, in spring, with no cover. The archers began to flay them. There were fewer than a hundred archers all told, but their arrows were fearfully accurate.

"Sound recall," Gabriel said crisply.

"Du Corse is in the woods," Gavin said.

His brother shook his head. "Let's go. It'll take de Vrailly a day to unfuck this."

Ganfroy sounded the call. Immediately archers to the west of the road came out of their cover. Many of them had horses to hand. Others simply ran—across the road, over the ditch, and up the hill.

A few terrified routiers ran around the end of the line of archers and went south to safety. More of them died as they were run down by mounted archers.

To Gavin's left, a dozen Galles re-emerged onto the road. And then suddenly there were fifty lances—more, perhaps.

"Oh well," the captain said as he closed his visor. Nell put his horse's reins in his hand and took his *ghiavarina*.

He swung a leg over Ataelus. Gavin got up on his Bohemund. A dozen more knights closed in around them, coming from the south.

"Up the lane," Gabriel ordered through his visor.

The Gallish men-at-arms were forming for a charge. They were being hit with occasional arrows—a torment of shafts, but not a torrent, and not an immediate danger. Here, a shaft found a horse—there, a man whose mail didn't fit under his arm.

The company knights—some of them, anyway—rode into the village lane and a short distance up the hill, and then turned to face their pursuers.

The Galles halted when they began to pack into the lane.

"Come on," muttered the Red Knight.

But the Galles hung back.

"They're moving into the field beyond the hedge," Ser Danved shouted.

"Back," the Red Knight called. Ganfroy sounded the retreat again. They had twenty lances by then—all the picked jousters in the company, the men who had intended to fight at the tournament.

Except Michael and Bad Tom.

They reached a point almost halfway up the hedge-lined lane.

Finally, the Galles at the foot of the hill followed them. There were no more arrows flying. The horns from the direction of Second Bridge were closer.

"Let's break a lance," the captain said. "For the Queen."

"The Queen!" his knights called.

Gabriel opened his visor and smiled at his brother. "This is the way war is supposed to work, isn't it?" he said. "We're hideously outnumbered, and we charge them. Two at a time. Care to join me?"

Gavin laughed. "You're mad," he said. "Of course."

"See the little bend?" Gabriel said. "See the path into the field?"

Even as he spoke, the lead Galles passed it.

But Gavin was an old hand at jousting, if not at this kind of war. "See you in the fields," he said, and pulled his visor down again.

He put spurs to his horse before Gabriel had his visor shut, and he was alone, flying down the narrow, cool lane. His war horse's hooves struck sparks off the white gravel of the road.

The men at the front of the Gallish column should have been ready, but they were far more concerned with the arrows that came through the hedge from time to time and had killed a valuable war horse.

He got his spear in the rest in good time, and he caught his first man almost at a stand. The blow from his lance snapped his neck inside his helmet and he fell like a man who had been hanged, his head lolling horribly.

The impact didn't break Gavin's lance, so he went on, unhorsing the second man on the right, and then Bohemund was savaging another horse and it was all a tangle, a swirling dog fight. The Galles were all as big as Gavin and as well-armoured. But Bohemund took him past the third and fourth man—

He knew from the sound that his brother had struck behind him. Something hit his helmet so hard his ears rang—he lost his sword, plucked out his dagger and rammed it into a man's armpit under his raised arm and then—no thanks to any planning—Bohemund plunged through the narrow gap in the hedge and out into the newly planted cornfield. The young maize was already tall enough to carpet the ground, and not yet tall enough to give any cover.

An arrow slammed into his back plate and he cursed. But he pointed his horse up the slope and crouched low on his saddle, hoping that the archers would see his arms on his surcoat.

Gabriel went through the Galles like a threaded needle where an awl has already passed. He unhorsed men on either side as if it was a tilting game—rings—and not a blow landed on him. He watched Gavin pass the gap in the hedge and he touched his spurs to Ataelus and they were through—he just managed to get his lance tip up and not unhorse himself on the hedge, which would have been embarrassing. As he passed the hedge, he had a flash of Ser Danved and Angelo di Laternum running their courses.

The open field was like a different world. They had emerged on the south side of the hedge, so none of Du Corse's men-at-arms were there. But new banners were flooding into the field from the south. The leading banner was the Earl of Towbray's.

Ser Bertran, Le Shakle and di Laternum all emerged from the hedge with Ser Danved at their heels, a heavy mace in his hand. He was roaring his war cry.

There was nowhere to rally in the patchwork of planted fields. Nor did Gabriel want another go. He pointed uphill with his lance. "Go!" he shouted. "Follow Gavin!"

In the fields below him, the Earl of Towbray's knights hooted and began to cross the first ditch. Gabriel watched them. On the road, a man took aim with a crossbow and loosed, and Gabriel had a moment's deep fear, and then the bolt sailed into the ground well short.

A heavy rider burst out of the hedge. He saluted as he rode past. "I'm the last, Monsieur!" called Jean, Ser Bertran's squire.

The Earl of Towbray's knights—fifty lances or more—crossed the ditch in good order and started up the hill. There were more men behind them—Albans and Galles, most not as well armoured as Towbray's professionals.

The Red Knight turned Ataelus and rode up the hill. The ploughed earth was hard going, and Ataelus was having a hard day—three fights in two days. He was impatient to get to the top—but he did *not* want to kill this horse.

Towbray's men were having a hard time, too.

He passed a point where the hill steepened, and suddenly, by turning in the saddle, he could see Du Corse's lances on the far side of the lane—over to the north, where, if he didn't move quickly, they could cut him off from his retreat.

Ataelus was snorting with furious effort, cresting the last and steepest bit of the muddy field.

"Come on, lad," he said. "Come on, Ataelus. Don't die on me here—never had a horse like you."

Ataelus's ears moved, and he gave a little more—and they were up.

Now he had a view of the whole battlefield. Gelfred's men were forming along the village hedges. His own pages and archers were now mixed in, and the knights—the jousters—were slapping each other in exhilaration.

Gabriel took a cup of water from Nell and drank it off. The Queen was there, and Amicia, already healing a man—a Gallish prisoner, apparently.

"Bravely done, ser knight!" the Queen called.

"Not bravely enough," he said. "Du Corse is a very good captain. He's slipped my ambush and now he's flooding the fields with men."

Gelfred came up on a palfrey. "They found another lane, my lord," he said. "I'm sorry—I must have missed it in the dark."

Gabriel could see that Towbray's men—and other Albans and Galles who must be under his banner—were pouring into the southern fields at the base of the hill like water through a leaky dyke. They weren't coming around the jam of baggage wagons. They were coming up another road to the south and east that almost outflanked the hill.

Gabriel looked out over the hillside at the wreck of his clever plan.

He just didn't have enough men.

Despite the various flaws in his battle, though, he had lost almost no men and Towbray's knights were completely uncoordinated with Du Corse on the other side of the hedge.

The Queen smiled. "Is that my old friend the Earl of Towbray?" she said. She took her newborn son from Blanche. "Those are Albans. This is what I came for, Ser Gabriel."

The Red Knight nodded. "Few enough archers. It's worth a try, your grace." He turned to Daniel Favour. "Go fetch Ser Michael and Ser Thomas and tell them my little ambush has failed and I need them on the hilltop." He'd put them off to the north a little in the woods, to complete the rout of anyone who attacked up the—

"Stop!" he cried. "Never mind, young Daniel. Go to them—and tell them to see if they can take Du Corse in the flank when he comes for the village."

Gavin shook his head. "They'll be thinner than goose fat on a peasant's bread."

Gabriel grinned—not a happy grin. "Have I ever lost a battle?" he asked.

There was no one around to remind him that he had.

The Queen rode down the hill out of the town. For a woman who had, in the last day, survived an attempt to burn her to death and a ride cross-country only to birth a baby in a barn, she looked more like a goddess than a human woman. Her skin glowed in the sun, her rich blond-brown hair seemed to have invented its own colour between gold and bronze, and she rode like a centaur, her plain linen veil trailing behind her.

The white linen penitent's gown that de Rohan had forced her to wear now shouted her innocence. The babe on her chest proclaimed who she must be—and who the babe must be.

Gabriel Muriens grabbed the royal pennon from Chris Foliak's hand. "Stay here," he said, and followed the Queen and her babe.

Foliak sputtered. "That's my knighthood riding away!"

"Let him be," Ser Francis said.

Down near the foot of the hill, the earl sat his charger with Ser Christopher Crowbeard—Kit to his boon companions.

"I mislike the hedges and the ploughed fields," Crowbeard was saying. "Let de Vrailly throw his sell-swords at yon."

Towbray looked down at the young corn shoots under his horse's hooves. Ahead of him, fifty good lances—knights and squires—had dismounted to rest their horses. Off to the right, a solid body of Harndon militia in red and blue emerged from the woods—crossbows and spearmen with great tall pavises. He had none of his own foot—de Vrailly had cut them up last summer, and now they were far away, home in the Jarsays. So he had no archers and no peasants to clear the hillside and test the enemy's intentions. If the hedge was lightly defended . . .

But if it wasn't . . .

A rider came through a gap in the town hedge just a long bowshot away.

"Blessed saint Mary Magdalene," Crowbeard said. "It's the Queen."

Towbray watched her ride effortlessly down the steepest point of the ridge.

A second, armoured rider came through the gap in the hedge. He had a lance and was flying . . .

Towbray spat, contemplatively, on the ground. "The Royal Standard," he said.

"She has a babe on her breast." Crowbeard paused. "Sweet Jesu, my lord earl. She's foaled."

Towbray nodded. "Just sit and watch, Kit," he said.

The Queen rode down the hill until she was in easy bowshot of the Towbray men-at-arms, and then she rode along their front, attended by just one knight. She rode from near the village lane to well over by the Harndon militia.

While she made her ride, the Galles of the rearguard finally broke through the carts and the panicked routiers choking the main road and began to enter the field behind Towbray. Half a mile away, Towbray could see de Vrailly's banner.

Some of his men-at-arms were kneeling.

Towbray chuckled. He watched her pass back, headed up the hill to the town on the crest.

A rider dressed in Du Corse's livery reined in. "My lord earl?" he asked. "Monsieur Du Corse asks your support in assaulting the village. Peek-ton," he said, pointing up the hill. "He orders that you cover this side of the lane, and he'll go up his side."

At the word *orders,* the earl frowned. But he thought a moment and nodded. "I agree."

The courier bowed and rode away, picking his way as best he could along the ploughed ground.

"What orders, my lord?" Crowbeard asked.

Towbray made a little motion with his eyebrows, almost lost in his bascinet, but Crowbeard had known him his whole life. "*Monsieur* Du Corse *orders* me to—how was it phrased? Cover? This side of the lane." He nodded. "Alban—such a difficult language. Do you think we could *cover* our side from the little rise just here?"

"You mean to leave Du Corse to his own devices and let him swing in the wind?" Crowbeard said.

Towbray made a clucking sound with his tongue. "I mean that on the one hand, Kit, the newborn King of Alba rode along our ranks and I doubt there's five lads out there with any heart for this fight—eh? And on the other, that Gallish prick had the nerve to give me—*me* orders."

"Might ha' been any pretty wench wi' some base-born bastard," Crowbeard said, but his heart wasn't in it.

Towbray shrugged. "Let's go and *cover* the hill," he said. He sent a messenger to order the Harndon militia to go forward to the base of the first swell.

Their dogged slowness made his men look positively eager for a fight.

Gabriel handed the pennon back to Foliak and slapped his armoured back with his own gauntlet. "I'd never have believed it," he said. He looked at Ser Francis, who was watching the Harndon militia through the hedge.

"Some of them even cheered us," said the Queen.

The captain dismounted. "Every jack of you on this hedge," he shouted. "Get up and go to the other side of the lane. Move. *Move!*"

Archers like Three Legs grumbled at having to pick up all the arrows they'd stuck in the ground, but they moved. Pages shifted their horses. Dan Favour was back—one wave and a glance and the captain knew he'd passed the message.

He looked at Francis Atcourt. "You and your lances and the Queen—that's all I'm leaving on this side," he said.

Atcourt bowed.

"Right," Gabriel said. He ran, sabatons clicking and clanking, across to the lane. He peered down it, but there was no squadron of death-or-glory Gallish knights ready to crush his cat-and-clay plan.

He left one page—the new man, Bill something, recruited that morning in the barnyard—to watch the road.

"Call out if you see any men—mounted or on foot—in the lane. Do you understand me, Bill?"

Bill looked terrified, but whether that was at the coming battle or the mere fact of conversing with a lord, Gabriel didn't know.

"You have a weapon?" he asked.

"No, lord," Bill said stolidly. "I had a spear, but it's back wi' the wagons, wherever they is." He paused. "Awhich I'm Bob, not Bill. Bob Twill, that's me."

Gabriel breathed out, a long and steadying exhalation. He unbuckled his arming sword and tossed it to Bob. "Don't lose it, Bob," he said.

The former ploughman clutched it.

Gabriel turned and ran for the other side of the hedgerow.

He arrived at one of the many gaps to find that Du Corse had arrayed his men well—a solid line of horsemen, well spaced out to make worse targets, and behind them he'd dismounted two hundred men-at-arms in a body.

Gabriel couldn't wipe the grin off his face. His brother came and they knocked their armoured fists together.

"Why are you so happy?" Gavin asked.

Gabriel wanted to hug him. "Unless Towbray attacks this minute or Du Corse decides to be rash instead of professional," he said, "we're about to hand him his head."

"Suddenly you're cocky," Gavin said.

"It's the Queen," Gabriel said. "Never mind. It's everyone. But we're going to pull this off. *Listen up!*" he roared, raising his voice. "Du Corse is going to roll up the hill and we're going to beat him. The moment his men break—and trust me, lads and lasses, they're going to break—we mount and follow them. See the road down there to the north where it enters the woods? *Go to there. Rally there.* Do not mess about. Ten minutes' hard fighting, and we ride free. I promise. You all hear me?"

They shouted.

"You see the King?" he asked them.

He pointed down the hedge to where the Queen sat on her palfrey and the Royal Standard floated.

They roared.

Gavin laughed. "You are shameless, brother."

Gabriel smiled. "You know what?" he said. "We are going to rock de Vrailly back. And then we're going to ride north and collect the rest of our forces." He paused, watching Du Corse, who was giving a speech. "And then, by my powers, I'm going to show Master Thorn something."

The Galles gave a throaty roar.

The horsemen put their beasts to the trot and then the canter. They had charged once, and they weren't fresh, and they, too, were on their second or third fight in a few days. Many of their horses hadn't recovered from a sea voyage. Those didn't get past a trot.

And when they passed Cully's almost-invisible line of withies stuck into the ground, the arrows fell on them.

Gabriel took a riding horse from Nell and rode back along the hedge to the Queen.

Towbray's men had come a third of the way up the hill. The militia hadn't even come as far.

"About time to go, your grace," he said. He smiled at Amicia.

She frowned. "You love war," she said. She shook her head. "It's an odd thing to love."

The Queen made a face. "I'm ready to go wherever you lead," she said to her captain.

He nodded at Ser Francis. "When we charge, follow us down," he said. "We'll cut our way out and ride for Lorica."

Ser Francis nodded. "What are the odds on my fief in Thrake?" he asked.

"Not bad at all," Gabriel answered. He trotted back to the hedge. All the archers were working as hard as men can work, their bodies straining into the big bows, their back muscles and arms doing a day's work in a few minutes.

Cully pulled a shaft to his ear and let it go.

Flarch and Ricard Lantorn called out, almost together, "Twenty." Most of the archers only had a hand of shafts in the ground at their feet along the gaps in the hedge, and maybe three more in their belts.

It was not yet even noon.

He rode to Gavin, dismounted, and tossed his reins to Nell, who gave him back his spear.

Out in the fields below, everything had changed.

Du Corse's cavalry were dead or dismounted. Many of them were still coming, because they were insanely brave. Near at hand, a man in a fine segmented breastplate had six or seven arrows in him and still came forward. He was only a few yards away.

Cuddy put a four-ounce arrow into his groin from almost close enough to touch, and the man went down to die in agony. But there were others.

A short bowshot behind them, Du Corse's dismounted men came on unscathed. Du Corse led them in person, and they cheered as they came, trudging over the damp ploughed fields in their heavy armour.

The first of the original mounted men burst into the hedge—a knight on a dying horse came first, and Gavin put him down with a single blow of his axe. Then a trio of men whose horses were dead—they *ran* into one of the gaps.

It was Gabriel's gap, and then the battle was no longer an intellectual exercise or a sport. Terror and pain filled the three with rage.

The Red Knight cut with his heavy spear and the first knight's head leapt from his body. This time, Gabriel knew what to expect and his weapon passed through the low guard on the left side, point down, and rose again as fast as his arms could uncurl—it cut through the second man's sword and his breastplate, too—up through his aventail, cutting through hundreds of links of riveted chain and then up through the man's jaw and out the top of his helmet in an impossible cut, as if the man and his armour were made of butter.

And around in a reverso, crossing Gabriel's hands briefly, right over left and then the right shot out along the haft. His adversary's parry was useless, and he died, and fell in two pieces.

The men around Gabriel began to cheer.

It gave him no pleasure. It was like cheating on a test.

At his feet, the Gallish line had quickened its pace despite the steep hill and the near mud.

Just to the right of the enemy line—at the edge of the woods—a banner broke out of the trees, and horsemen began to enter the field.

Gabriel's heart stopped. It was not Bad Tom, or Michael.

It was three antlered heads in black on a golden chevron and a white field, and a voice like thunder roared, "A Corcy!"

Gabriel leaned on his heavy spear. He sighed.

"Lord Corcy will not betray us," said Desiderata. "You have too little faith in men, Ser Gabriel."

She pointed. "Look!" she called.

And then Ser Michael and Bad Tom came out of the wood line, a little north and east of Corcy. They had all the Thrakian knights and men-at-arms, and Tom Lachlan led them in his favourite wedge, his heavy lance held well over his head.

"Mount!" Gabriel called. "Sound 'mount' Ganfroy!"

He was ready to weep again, from sheer relief. Just for a moment.

Corcy and his retainers struck the end of Du Corse's line. The men on foot were caught in the flank at open shields, and many were simply knocked down as the local knights rode them over.

Bad Tom's wedge crashed obliquely into the line of dismounted men-at-arms. They hit it like a plane cutting wood, and the ranks seemed to peel asunder.

Already, at the south end of the Gallish line, men were forming orbs. Pages were bringing war horses forward. It was not a rout—

Not quite a rout. But in the centre of the line Du Corse's standard wavered.

The captain pointed with his war hammer at Du Corse's standard. "Follow me!" he roared, and charged.

Down through the hedge poured his household knights—the tournament champions who'd been with him all day. Behind them came all the pages and archers—and the Queen and Blanche, and anyone else with a horse. Even Bob Twill the ploughman, on Blanche's spare rouncy.

Du Corse's banner went down. Tom Lachlan's great axe went up and down, and then he swept out his dread sword, and men cheered. Ser Michael's lance was as steady as a fence pole, and every man he touched, he threw to the ground, broken.

The whole mass bunched in one melee, the line crumbling and bunching, like a thin snake trying to eat a very big meal. But the company men stayed together, and followed their orders. They knocked a hole the width of twenty lances in Du Corse's line and took his banner, and then swept through.

Tom Lachlan, having knocked his own hole in the line, dismounted by Du Corse.

Lord Corcy rode right past him and slammed a slim steel axe into the wounded Galle's helmet. He reined in and raised his visor. "I need him to trade for my sons," he said.

Du Corse's men did not break. Some died, but more were simply knocked into the ground. The rest clumped into the corner of the field by the lane and prepared to sell their lives dearly. Only as they rallied did they see how few their assailants were, but by then the Thrake stradiotes had swept into their pages, and were herding a fortune in Gallish war horses—even ill-fed and spoiled by sea voyage as they were—up the road to Lorica.

A half dozen archers—trapped in the woods west of the road since the original charge of the Galles—slipped out of the trees and joined the company and were double mounted. Will Starling grinned and Daud the Red and Wha'hae slapped their bared arses at the distant Galles.

And then, the Queen well-protected in their midst, with a handful of high-ranking prisoners and some rich ransoms, they mounted fresh horses where they could and rode north, towards Lorica.

De Vrailly rode up to the Earl of Towbray. The hilltop town lowered above them.

Towbray shrugged. "The militia won't advance, and Du Corse ordered me to cover the hill," he said. "What can I do?"

De Vrailly glared at him with unconcealed contempt.

He rallied Du Corse's veterans and made camp in the field below the town, which he had the survivors of the routiers clear, loot, and burn to the ground. But burning Picton couldn't get him back his army's morale, or the three hundred horses he'd lost.

The archbishop ordered Corcy's sons hanged. De Vrailly remanded the order. The archbishop sat and dictated a dispatch, claiming victory as that they held the battlefield, and denouncing the Queen as a whore and strumpet who was spreading a false rumour that she'd born an heir.

De Vrailly made himself as distant as he could. The routiers were happy enough to burn Picton, but the Gallish knights were drawing away, in body, from the archbishop.

When the archbishop slept, de Vrailly summoned a herald and sent him to the Red Knight, at Lorica.

Then he went to his pavilion, where his squires had already laid out his plain bed and his prie-dieu with the triptych of the Virgin, Saint Gabriel and Saint Michael. He poured a cup of water from a magnificently ornate gold and crystal bottle on a shelf in the prie-dieu, blessed himself, and placed the cup carefully behind the flange that covered the inside of his right knee.

He knelt for a long time, in his harness, without even a single candle. His knees ached, and he ignored them. He ignored the feeling that his greave tops and his knee articulation were cutting gradually through his padded hose.

Pain is penance.

Come, beautiful angel. I have things to ask and say.

The pain continued, and so did the darkness. From time to time his meditations were broken—outside, he heard Jehan, his squire, trying to explain to the Corcy boys that he had saved their lives and that they should be grateful for being alive.

The archbishop's tempers were infantile.

De Vrailly thought of the figure of the Queen, seen in the distance, riding across the hillside, the banner streaming behind her. It had moved him, at some point beyond simple decisions.

So easy to believe that she is a witch.

He thought of the King—his friend. In many ways, his closest friend. No man in Galle had ever been so close to him.

I failed to protect him.

I never even saw the arrow, because I was sulking in my tent—because I was ensorcelled.

His rage grew.

His hands began to shake, and an unaccustomed heaviness grew in his throat and chest.

And then the angel manifested.

He hovered above de Vrailly's head, his fair form shining almost perfectly gold, his robes a paler white gold and his armour paler yet. In his right hand was a heavy spear, and his left hand held a small round shield with the cross in stark black.

You called for me, my knight.

De Vrailly looked at the angel and struggled for his rage and his belief.

We were tricked by the vile sorceress, and thwarted. But all is well, my knight. All is as it should be. Today, you will defeat the Queen's army and her cause will collapse. You will kill her champion—

De Vrailly mastered himself. He raised his head and his eyes met the angel's. "I am told that the King of Galle has been defeated in a great battle in Arelat," he said.

That is of no moment now, the angel said. *You will be King, here.*

De Vrailly rose from his knees. His right hand picked up the small silver cup, and with a flick of his wrist, the holy water struck the angel.

Black fire rent the angel. With a shriek, the angel shook himself—and was whole and gold and beautiful, without expression on his serene and commanding face.

That was childish.

De Vrailly was standing with his hand on his sword hilt. "The archbishop tells me that I am a child," he said.

Come, my knight. I confess that we failed at the tournament. I was surprised at a number of developments—but the black sorceress who opposes me was before me in many ways. I pray your pardon, mortal—I, too, can be confused. And even hurt.

De Vrailly thought of what he had just seen.

"By the black sorceress, you mean the Queen?" de Vrailly asked carefully.

I do not think you will find this line of questioning to your comfort, my knight. But yes, I mean the Queen, and the malign presence that defends and abets her—a succubus of hell.

De Vrailly wanted very much to believe what the angel said. He balanced on an exquisite, torturous knife edge.

"I think that you killed the King. I think that you manipulate events. I think I have been your pawn." De Vrailly threw the words like blows in a fight to the death. Now his head flooded with all his doubts—now he could marshal his doubts like armies, whereas when the angel first manifested, he couldn't even breathe. The holy water had changed something.

And yet, the archangel looked like everything that de Vrailly wanted. From this world, and from his God.

I think it would be better for you to banish these doubts and do what you were created to do, my child. I wish you to see that all the world is a shadow, and that there are many truths and many realities. But for you, there must be just one reality. One world, one spirit. The Queen is a sorceress who arranged that you be taken from your rightful place as the King's champion and manipulated events to kill the King. I have worked tirelessly to defend you—

"Have you put magical protections on me and my armour?" de Vrailly asked.

The angel paused. The pause was so brief that it scarcely existed, yet to de Vrailly, used to the angel almost seeming to read his thoughts, it seemed long.

I would never do anything that would prevent men from giving you the glory which you deserve of your right. Stop this, my knight. Go forth and conquer your enemies. Tomorrow the Queen will send someone to offer you single combat. Defeat him, kill him, and you will be master here. These doubts will only confuse you. This is not the time to be confused. This is the time to get revenge.

De Vrailly returned to his knees.

Sometime in the night, all the Harndon militia marched away from the army.

Chapter Ten

The Company

B ad Tom and Ser Michael and Long Paw and Gelfred pushed the column like daemons from hell. The captain was everywhere—up and down the column—from the moment they passed the gap under an arch of trees and took the road north to Lorica.

He had a brief officers' call in the saddle. He was terse, dividing their small force into a vanguard under Lord Corcy with his powerful force of knights—local men who knew the road and the ground around it, a main body under Gavin, and a rearguard under Tom Lachlan.

Twice, Michael and Tom turned and laid an ambush in the greenwood, with archers and a dozen knights filling the road, but no pursuit threatened them. At three in the afternoon, Gelfred launched back down the road with five of his best foresters—Will Scarlet, Dan Favour, Amy's Hob, Short Tooth and Daud—to scout.

But for the rest of the column the afternoon passed in a haze of dust and sun and horse sweat.

Bad Tom would roar, "Halt! Change horses!" and they'd have five minutes.

Bob Twill learned to eat while holding his horse. He learned to piss while holding his horse.

Worst of all, he learned to ride.

The Queen seemed to grow with every mile they rode—louder, larger, and happier. She rode the dusty lane with her babe clutched to her, and sang him songs in Occitan and Gallish, songs of chivalry and love. Her singing was a tonic, and when she came to one the men around her knew, they'd sing the chorus—*Prendes i garde* or *C'est la fin quoi que nus die*, which made the woods ring.

Lady Blanche—they were all calling her that in the exuberance of victory—rode with all the skill of Bob Twill, and her pretty face could not hide her annoyance at the Queen's constant correction of her seat and her hands. But she cleaned the baby and changed his linen, and at some point during the third halt, in a moment of vexation, she balled up the child's filthy towels and threw them into the woods.

"Fie! And linen towelling so dear!" The captain was just behind her, at the edge of the trees.

She flushed. "I'm sorry, my lord."

"I'm not. It's the most human thing I've seen from you all day." He tossed her an apple. "Toby!" he shouted.

Toby appeared, carrying the captain's standard. He was still mounted, although the rest of them were on foot.

"Clean shirt," the captain said. "And my towel. Give them to Lady Blanche."

Toby didn't ask questions. He reached behind his war saddle, to a very small leather trousseau. He extracted a linen shirt that smelled of lavender, and a slightly soiled damp towel.

"I used the towel to shave this morning," the captain admitted.

Blanche caught the work on the shirt—mice teeth on the cuffs, embroidered coat of arms, beautiful fine stitching as good as her own or better. "What's this for, then?" she asked. "My lord?"

"Tear the shirt up for swaddling," he said. "The towel's so you can wipe your hands clean before you eat the apple." He smiled.

She did just that. Then she tossed it to him—as if they were peers. He caught it and threw it to Toby, who shied away.

"Afraid of a little baby poo?" the captain cried.

Toby blushed furiously. He rolled the towel very tightly and put it away behind his war saddle as if afraid of disease.

He smiled at her and rode off down the column.

By nightfall, Michael and Tom had begun to use the rougher sides of their tongues, and the captain was the calm, cheerful one. Bob Twill was found to have stayed on the ground at a halt. Bad Tom rode back, scared him almost to incontinence, and got him on his exhausted horse.

Cat Evil, never the best rider, complained of the pace and found himself docked a day's pay.

"Mew mew mew!" Tom roared. "I don't hear nowt from the babe but laughter, and you lot—old soldiers—cry like babies. A little fight an' a few hours in the saddle—" He laughed. "We'll shake the fat off you."

Cat Evil, who was as thin as a young girl and had the long hair to match and a very nasty disposition, put a hand on his knife.

Tom laughed again. "If you ha' the piss to face *me*," he said, "then ye're not e'en tired yet. Bottle it and keep riding."

Most of the older men expected they'd halt at last light. Even Cully, who, as an officer and a trusted man, was careful not to vent his irritation at the pace, muttered that with no pursuit and no danger, it was cruel hard.

Ser Michael reined in. "Think it's possible that the captain knows something you don't know, Cully?"

Cully looked resentful, like a good hunting dog accused falsely of stealing food. But he kept his mouth shut, and didn't rise to Cuddy's open mutiny when they kept riding into the moonlight.

"We're going all the way to Lorica, then?" Michael asked. Ser Gabriel was up and down the column, and where Tom and Michael used ridicule and open coercion to keep men moving, Ser Gabriel was everyone's friend.

So far. He grinned at Michael, his teeth white in the moonlight. "Look ahead of you," he said.

In the middle distance, the cathedral of Lorica rose above the town's walls, which gleamed like white Etruscan marble in the moonlight. Just short of the walls, fires burned.

He waved, and turned his horse—his fourth of the day—back down the column. "Less than an hour now, friends," he called.

Outriders greeted them well outside the silent town. Ser Ranald embraced his cousin, and then dismounted and bent his knee to the Queen and her son.

The Queen gave him a hand. "It was you—in the darkness," she said.

"Not just me, your grace," he said. "But yes, I was there."

She smiled in the moonlight, and for the first time that Gavin had seen her, she seemed older, with lines around her mouth and under her eyes. Not old—just not the vision of youth she had been that afternoon, riding in the shadow-spackled sunlight.

"Will you command my son's guard?" she asked.

Ranald grinned. "I have the better half of it right here," he said. He waved in the direction of the camp.

But Ser Gabriel forbade any kind of ceremony. "Unless your grace overrules me directly," he said, "I want everyone to bed."

But Lady Almspend—Becca, to the Queen—was at Ranald's side, and there were more hugs, and the Queen all but fell into her friend's arms.

The captain rode up almost between them. "I'm sorry, your grace, but there's two hundred men who have fought for you this day, and they want to be asleep."

The Queen sat back. "Of course—I'm thoughtless. Go!"

But despite this admonition, men and women were roused as the column entered camp. Blanche was surprised at how orderly was the apparent chaos. Sukey, who she had thought ere this to be a decorative camp follower or possibly the Red Knight's lover, stood by the palisaded gate with two pages at her shoulders with torches and read off tent assignments. When Tom Lachlan rode up, Blanche was close behind. Too close.

Sukey graced him with a pleasant smile.

"Not my tent, Ser Tom," she said.

He grimaced.

"You'll find Donald Dhu and all the beeves he has yet unsold just a long bowshot to the west, by the river," she said.

"And if I don't want to ride any further, woman?" he asked.

She tossed her hair. "There's space in the ditch outside," she said. "Next!"

She put the Queen in the captain's pavilion, on his feather bed, and she was waiting when the Queen's woman—the tall blonde—came out of the pavilion with an armload of smelly linen.

"I have a bed for ye, if you'll sleep. Give all that to one of my drudges. Come." Sukey walked off towards the cook fires.

The same men—and a few women—who had bitched about fighting and riding all day were now sitting at fires drinking wine and re-telling it all. A dozen knights of the Order were listening to Ser Michael's account of the ambush. Two nuns were brushing out Sister Amicia's hair.

Prior Wishart, who Sukey knew from two days in camp, was deep in conversation with the captain, who gave her the "not now" sign. So she pushed past, Blanche at her heels, and took her around the fire that had become the hub of conversation—and thus, no work could be done—to the main fire line. There, despite the hour, twenty women and a few men were heating water, cooking, washing...

"Anne Banks! Get your nose out of his business and come over here," Sukey yelled. A young woman who had been kissing a young man came, in a sulky, put-upon way.

"Annie's a scullery and she'll do as she's told most o' the time," Sukey said. "Annie, this is Blanche, the Queen's—friend. She has a mort of linen needs cleaning."

Anne was prone to be difficult. Blanche knew her kind well enough. She smiled and kissed the younger woman's cheek. "For the baby, Miss Anne. I don't expect you to do my things." She laughed. "Except I don't have any things."

Annie nodded. "For the baby?" She took the whole armload without demur. "For—the King?" she said.

"His shit is just as shitty as any other baby's," Sukey noted. "Anne Banks, if you lie down with that boy and get a baby in you, you'll end a common harlot."

"Which they gets paid a damn sight better than sculleries. An' the work is restful," Annie said in a tone aimed to infuriate her officer.

Sukey smacked the girl with her open hand. "Don't be a fool," she said. "You want to hear about being a whore, talk to Sauce. I'm sorry, Lady Blanche."

"I'm no lady," Blanche said. "They just call me that."

Sukey was now clutching Anne to her chest. "I'm sorry, Annie. But you ain't got a mama to teach you, so all you get is me."

"You hit me!" Anne wailed.

Sukey winked at Blanche. Over Anne's head, she said, "You and I are of a size. Want some clothes?"

Blanche contemplated refusal, but it seemed stupid. "Yes," she said. "I can't pay."

Sukey smiled. It was an odd smile, as if she knew something that Blanche didn't know. Which she probably did.

Back towards the gate, a voice called, "Sukey!" like the sounding of a great horn.

"Damn the man," Sukey said. "Anne, wash those linens and bring them to . . ." She looked at Blanche. "I guess you're *casa* 24-R2."

"What's that?" Blanche asked. Anne picked up the linens without another sniff and curtsied as if Blanche was indeed a lady. Blanche responded—it was a little like the laundry at home.

"24-R2 is the twenty-fourth tent of the second corporal of the red band," Sukey said, already underway. "Look, I'll show you."

"Sukey!" called the deep voice.

"I'll kill him. You know, he went off and lay with another girl at the Inn of Dorling, and now he thinks he can walk back in here—"

"Suuu-key!"

Blanche, always everyone's confidante, giggled. "That's Bad Tom?" she asked.

"Aye," Sukey said. "That's Bad Tom."

"He's very handsome." Blanche hadn't thought it aloud before that. But Tom's sheer size was—remarkable.

"Aye he is, and he knows it, the devil." Sukey was walking fast through a darkened camp. "See the captain's pavilion? No, there. See? Red flags."

"I see it," Blanche allowed.

"All the lances of his household camp in a line behind—knights at the head of the camp, then men-at-arms and pages and then servants. See? R2 is Ser Francis, and a nicer gentleman you'll never meet. Twenty-four is just a spare at the back of camp. I walked all the way around so you'd see the how and the why. See? And see the cook fires?"

Blanche swallowed heavily. "Yes," she admitted. "So many tents!"

Sukey laughed. "Honey, wait until you see whole company—that's nearly five hundred tents. An army! Christ and all his saints, you can get lost walking around looking for a spot to piss."

"Suuk-keeyy!"

"He'll make a fool o' himself," Sukey said. She seemed perfectly well pleased. "Come to my tent and I'll gi' you a gown and a couple of shifts."

"You'll want to get to sleep," Blanche said.

Sukey laughed and licked her lips. "I doubt Tom has sleep in mind. He's been fightin'." She grinned. "Fightin' makes him think o' just one thing. Come on—I don't mind makin' him wait."

Back, by some incomprehensible path through the endless rows of white wedges in the moonlight, like a monster's teeth, like headstones in a churchyard. Blanche was instantly lost as soon as she couldn't see the captain's two red tent banners.

Then they emerged into a cross street, as broad as half a bowshot.

"Officer's line," Sukey said. "See, there's the cap'n's tent again. Got your bearings?"

Blanche shook her head.

"Well, never mind. Here's my little home."

Sukey's home was a wagon with a tent on the wagon box. She lit a taper with magick, as easy as kissing her own thumb.

"I don't ha' my mother's talent, but I can do a thing or two," she said.

By candlelight, Blanche could see Sukey better. She was beautiful, with rich black hair, a pert nose and freckles and light eyes that were improbable in her face—large and full of humour, at odds with her nose and mouth. She wore a fine kirtle with the skirts pulled high enough to show a fair amount of leg, and the front cut low enough to advertise her figure, which was as good as Blanche's own.

The two women eyed each other.

"I think you'll fit me to a T," Sukey said. She opened a chest in the wagon box. "Red?"

"I daren't," Blanche said.

"Cap'n won't care. It's his favourite colour," Sukey said.

"I serve the Queen," Blanche said. "Red's the King's colour."

"Oh, aye," Sukey said, as if the notion had no interest for her. "A nice dark brown?"

She held up a kirtle with side lacing and a low neck.

Blanche whistled. "That's fine cloth."

"Aye, my mother made it for me in Morea," Sukey said. She put her hands around Blanche's waist. "Oh, you're as little as me in the tummy. Take the brown—I never wear it. It makes me look poor. You ha' the hair for it."

She took down two shifts from a basket. "I can spare you two. I've no stockings—I'm barefoot myself until we reach Albinkirk."

Blanche took the other woman and kissed her. "You're a true friend."

"Sister, women in this lot need to be friends." Sukey laughed. "Besides, soon eno' I'll need favours of you."

"Su-key!" came a roar, almost outside the wagon.

"Get a room!" came an angry call from the tent lines.

Blanche took her prize wardrobe and dropped off the wagon box to the ground. "Thanks!" she said.

"I'm right here, you great ox," Sukey said.

"I brought you something," Bad Tom said.

"A couple of your doxies to do my scut work?" Sukey shot back.

"Don't be like that, woman," he said.

Blanche covered her ears and giggled.

"Like what? Spiteful? Mad as a cat in water?" Sukey asked.

Tom laughed. "You're jus' play-acting."

"Try me, Tom," she said.

"You? Dare me?" Tom said, and roared his laugh.

Blanche lengthened her stride.

She ran far enough to escape the sounds, and stopped to catch her breath.

She'd come the wrong way—or perhaps not. As she spun, she gradually got her bearings—the captain's banners, the pavilion, the cook fires near at hand.

She was ravenous. She came to the fire where so many had been gathered a quarter of an hour before. Now there were only a handful of men. Sister Amicia and her nuns were gone.

Toby was with the captain. "I'd need help to bed them all down," Toby was saying.

Ser Gabriel shook his head. "I can't order men out of their straw," he said.

Blanche stepped up boldly. "There's pages awake at the cook fires," she said.

Toby shrugged. "They'll be all the lackwits and awkward sods—"

Ser Gabriel put a hand on his shoulder. "You need me?" he asked.

Toby backed away hurriedly. "No—no, my lord. Go to bed."

Ser Gabriel nodded to her.

"Can I help?" she asked.

"We captured horses at the tournament and more at the end of the fight today. They don't belong to anyone yet, so they're all just milling about at the end of the horse lines. Toby is too professional to leave them, and too tired to do anything about it." He looked at her. "What do you have there?" he asked. He handed her his cup, which was full of sweet wine.

She drank it off before she thought about it.

"Damn, you did it again," he said.

"I'm sorry, my lord. Sukey took care of me, and gave me a kirtle and some linen." She paused. "Women's prattle."

"I like women," he said. "I especially like Sukey, who gets more work out of fewer people than anyone I've ever known. Sukey has a list for every occasion." He smiled. "Did Tom find her?"

"When she was ready for him," Blanche said. Then she winced.

But Ser Gabriel laughed. His right hand found a bottle, and he re-filled his cup. "I'm going to be un-gallant," he said, "and have some of this before you get it."

Blanche smiled at him. "You should go to bed, my lord," she said.

He kicked his feet in front of him, sat with his back against his war saddle and handed her the cup. He indicated his cloak, a great red cloak she'd seen tied behind his saddle. "This is my bed," he said, a little sharply. "Sukey gave my tent to the Queen and her baby, and now she's off playing with Tom."

"I have a tent," Blanche said. She almost bit her lip in vexation.

The silence went on far too long—ten heartbeats or so.

"I'm not sure just how I want to answer that," he said. But then, without further hesitation, he was kissing her. She never got clear in her mind how she came to be kneeling by him to be kissed.

Blanche had been kissed before, and she didn't melt. But she was ashamed of all the things that went through her mind before she let it float away on the kiss. Some of them were very practical.

Then she had both of his hands and she was kissing *him*. It made her want to laugh.

A log popped in the fire, and Toby cleared his throat very softly.

"Gelfred, my lord," he whispered. In one motion, he flipped the captain's red cloak open and threw it over Blanche even as Ser Gabriel flowed to his feet.

Blanche lay smothered in red wool, her heart beating fast as the hooves of a galloping horse strummed the earth.

"Road's clear all the way back to Second Bridge," Ser Gelfred said. "We picked up a herald on the road, who claims he's been sent to you from de Vrailly. I blindfolded him."

"Nicely done. Send him to Lord Corcy in the morning, Gelfred. De Vrailly will want Du Corse." He laughed. "Do you think they're related? Du Corse, and Corcy?"

"Never gave it a thought," Gelfred said. "I saw Alcaeus out by the gate. He'll be wanting you, too."

Blanche writhed inwardly. Her mind was spinning. Drink? How much had he drunk? He couldn't really want her. He'd want the Queen—that's how these things played out. Like with like. Aristo with aristo.

But it had been a spectacular kiss.

Gabriel was acutely conscious of the young woman under his cloak ten feet away in the flickering firelight. He gave Toby a look.

Toby walked off.

What was I thinking? She's hardly a light o' love.

Is that what I want? Or is it just what Tom wants for me?

There was the unmistakable sound of horse's hooves. Gelfred put a hand on his long sword hilt.

Gabriel knew the man by his seat—shorter stirrups, the Morean style. "Alcaeus!" he called. "I haven't seen you in two days and it's like being blind."

The Morean knight—dressed in a simple cote and long boots, like any messenger—threw a leg over his light saddle and dropped to the ground. His little mare simply dropped her head and started eating. She was clearly done in.

Toby appeared with Nell, who looked as mad as a viper. Between them they were carrying a ghost—no, it was a stack of linen sheets.

"Make me fucking work in the middle of the night—" She was spitting when she saw her captain and stopped.

"You weren't exactly working," Toby shot back.

Alcaeus seized the proffered wine cup and drained it. "Some prefer a company of infantry, and some love the sight of ships, and some love a troops of horse," he said in Archaic. "But the thing I love is good intelligence."

"I don't think that's quite what Sappho had in mind," Gabriel said, and laughed.

"You ready?" Alcaeus said. "It's all gone to hell."

To the Morean knight's right, Toby and Nell put up a folding frame and began to drape it with sheets.

Alcaeus looked at them with interest. "Do they really do your laundry in the middle of the night?" he asked. "And how is the sweet lady laundress? What a beauty."

"What a mouth," Gabriel said, hoping to head him off.

Alcaeus laughed. "She has wit. I fancy her. Bah—at any rate. I have birds and birds—message on message. But first, from our dear friend in Harndon."

He handed Gabriel a folded scrap of parchment, and Gabriel flipped it open and held it to the flames for light. It was Kronmir's hand.

The city is ours when we wish it. The archbishop employs a potent sorcerer, Master Gilles. Say the word and I can dispose of him. I am now the chief of intelligence for his eminence. There is word that the Galles have suffered a terrible defeat against some Wild opponent in Arelat. The Etruscan and Hoek merchants are in panic.

I believe that his eminence is in contact with our other foe.

A factor here has told me that the Emperor is planning to take the field in person.

I await orders. A very sticky, but fascinating problem, is it not?

Gabriel sipped his wine. "You've read it," he said.

"Ten times," Alcaeus said. "You trust him?"

"Yes," Gabriel said.

Alcaeus made a motion of the lips that suggested that his captain was naive, and perhaps shouldn't be trusted out alone after dark.

Toby appeared. "It's getting chilly," he said, and laid the captain's red cloak over his shoulders.

Gabriel got the message. *Boy, you are the finest squire who has ever lived,* he thought.

He breathed in, hoping her scent would be on his cloak, but in truth, he smelled only horse sweat and wood smoke.

I want her.

Mother would be so proud. Damn her.

The pang—he still forgot that she was dead for whole minutes at a time—came back like a fist in the stomach.

"What's wrong?" Alcaeus asked.

Gabriel shrugged. "I trust him because I've given him scope to play a bigger game. The biggest."

Alcaeus nodded. "You read men well," he said.

"The Emperor?" Gabriel asked. He was very tired.

"The Emperor has left his daughter Irene at Liviapolis with a skeleton guard, and he and Ser Milus are marching past Middleburg." Alcaeus took the cup from Gabriel and drank.

Not long ago, it was Blanche drinking from that cup.

Oh, Amicia, am I so fickle?

But you said no. So often.

I know you don't mean it.

Or that you do.

"So—we can take Harndon behind de Vrailly."

"I don't think de Vrailly is in command," Alcaeus said. Toby opened a folding stool behind him, and he sat. The ground by his side was empty, the sheets gone. Nell put a second stool behind Gelfred.

"I think the archbishop is now in command. De Vrailly is—not himself." Alcaeus shrugged. "At any rate, the archbishop has summoned the levies of the whole of Jarsay, the Albin and the Brogat. He's sitting at Second Bridge and fortifying his camp."

Gelfred nodded. "That goes with what my people tell me. We picked up a deserter who says that he ordered Corcy's sons hanged, but de Vrailly cancelled it."

Gabriel's pulse quickened. "Would de Vrailly change sides?"

Alcaeus shook his head. "If Kronmir could do it in person—perhaps. It would take a delicate touch and a great deal of—how do Albans put it?—sugar. The man is a monster. But no. Not where we are now." He held up a hand. "It is the north to which we must see."

He and Gelfred held the corners of a map—more a sketch.

"Pardon me, that I must speak of hard things." Alcaeus put a hand—very tentatively—on his captain's arm.

Gabriel nodded.

"The sorcerer has taken Ticondaga. His forces increase every day—the northern Wild is flocking to him." He shrugged. "Ser John Crayford and Ser Ricar have the northern army at Broadalbin north of Albinkirk. They have some survivors from Ticondaga, including your brother Aneas. I am to tell you that the duchess and earl both died in the taking." Alcaeus paused. "I'm sorry."

"I already knew. But Gavin will have to be told in the morning. I told him—I felt it in the *aethereal*. He will be glad Aneas is alive." Gabriel tried to smile, but nothing came. "I will be glad, too, when I have some gladness in me."

"I have an imperial messenger from Ser John. He has four hundred lances and he's ordering out the shire troops, but he will not attempt to make a stand in the wilderness. He wants us to know he's been fighting every day."

Gabriel tried to see it. If Thorn was at Ticondaga and all the creatures of the Wild were with him . . .

"Where is Ser John?" he asked.

"Broadalbin, north of Albinkirk. His messenger bird reported that he fears for Dorling." Alcaeus paused. "I thought that we believed Dorling unassailable, because of our . . . friend."

Gabriel stroked his beard. "I've made a number of mistakes in the last few weeks, Alcaeus. The greatest of them was assuming that Thorn was less gifted than I am. He's not. He's as willing to take risks. Suddenly he's daring. He may risk Dorling. He may even be right to."

"There's more," Alcaeus said. "Harcourt on the west wall fell to the Faery Knight yesterday. I didn't hear—the message went to Albinkirk by bird and I only have it from Ser John. Another army crossed the Great River just east of N'pano over a week ago, from the north."

"Oh, sweet Christ," Gelfred said. The man who never swore.

Alcaeus nodded. "One must assume that the Faery Knight and the sorcerer have come to some accommodation. The Faery Knight has an army—or he wouldn't have taken Harcourt." Alcaeus hesitated. "I'm sorry to say that Harmodius was said to be with the Faery Knight."

Gabriel took a deep steadying breath. "Ahh," he said.

Gelfred spat. "First Towbray and now Harmodius," he said. "I knew the magus was black-hearted, but this—"

"Judge not rashly," Gabriel said. He drank another sip of wine. "Toby, are you there?"

Toby appeared at his side.

"All officers at first light." He nodded. "Another busy day."

"May I make a recommendation now, in private?" Alcaeus asked.

"Of course," Gabriel said. The Morean was solemn—he put a hand out and rested it on Gabriel's shoulder.

"If you think we can trust Kronmir, then I say—take Harndon. Now. Destroy this upstart archbishop, crush him against the city walls, finish the rebellion." Alcaeus waved his hands.

"I like that, as right now the archbishop thinks we're the rebels." Gabriel managed a wry smile.

"And then hold Harndon." Alcaeus shrugged.

"Against the Wild?" Gabriel asked.

Alcaeus nodded. "We have a saying—when the tide rises, climb a big rock. Harndon is the biggest rock. And my reading of the ancients is that this has happened before—all of it. The big invasions, the sudden welling forth of the Wild. Places like Liviapolis and Harndon are built to withstand—exactly this." He paused. "I have this, too. It is an imperial message. But then you are still, I hope, an imperial officer."

He handed over a thin piece of the nearly transparent paper that the messenger birds—the big imperial ones—carried.

The Venike ambassador in the city reports that the armies of Galle and Arelat were destroyed in a great battle south of Nunburg in Arelat. Venike has formally requested assistance from the Emperor.

Gabriel spread the map out and stuck his green-hilted dagger through one corner and his eating knife through the opposite.

"That's for another day," he said. *Oh, Mr. Smythe, for an hour of your time. I think we're losing.*

"We're five days from Albinkirk, moving fast," he said. He nodded to himself. "Dorling's about the same from Albinkirk—shorter as the crow flies, but the road is dreadful."

Gelfred and Alcaeus both agreed.

Gabriel thought a moment. "If we lose Dorling, we can't link up with the Emperor."

"And leave the Faery Knight unopposed in the west, and the archbishop free to sack Lorica?" Alcaeus shook his head.

Gabriel scratched under his chin—he had three mosquito bites that seemed to occupy as much of his mind as Blanche and the Faery Knight combined.

"Any force coming from the west has to pass Lissen Carak," he said. "A tough nut."

"Small garrison," Alcaeus said.

"Not if you think in the *aethereal*." He didn't see a solution. If there was one at all, it was going to involve some miracles of marching, and every hour counted, starting a day ago.

But he had the glimmer of a plan. It was not his former plan at all. That galled him—that a plan had completely failed.

So much subtlety, gone with the arrow that killed the King.

"Right," he said. "I assume Ser Gerald Random is in Lorica?"

"No, he and most of the men who came with him are camped between us and the beeves. The Hillmen." Alcaeus waved.

"I need Ser Gerald, Sukey, Tom, Ranald and—" He looked around. "That's a start."

"First light?" Toby said hopefully.

"Now," Gabriel said.

He was never going to get to kiss Blanche again. He tried not to let that influence his decisions, but he reckoned that if he could end the meetings and find her . . .

Too late for all of that. By tomorrow, the moment would be gone.

He shrugged. His shrug was a dismissal of all that. *Let love go hang,* he thought bitterly.

Toby murmured in his ear, "Ser Thomas is—er—with Sukey."

"Good, you can get them both at once," Gabriel said.

Let love go hang. "Get Sister Amicia, too."

The map was still pinned to the ground with daggers and eating implements.

The captain's bearing made it plain that this was business. There was almost no grumbling. Toby and Nell built up the fire and began to serve roast pork and dumplings left over from a dinner most of them had never received.

"You bid fair to ruin a beautiful night," Tom grumbled.

The captain shook his head. "The world," he said, "is going to shit all around us. This is for everything, friends. So drink some wine, stretch your wits and get with me."

Alcaeus and Gelfred reviewed the intelligence reports while the rest chewed pork, spat gristle, and wolfed down the dumplings.

When Gelfred was done explaining the archbishop's position and what he had in his army, the captain nodded sharply.

"Tom, will you sell me all your beef?" he asked.

Tom shrugged. "Market price?" he asked.

"On the nail," the captain said.

Tom nodded, and spat in his hand.

The captain turned to Ser Gerald. "Loan me the cost of the beeves?" he asked.

"Against what?" Gerald asked cautiously.

"Against that I'm now the Earl of Westwall, or Gavin is, and the Duke of Thrake, too. I own the whole northern trade from one end of the wall to the other, and if we win this war, we'll make money as if we are transmuting water into gold." He turned to his brother. "I'm sorry, brother. I'm not as crass as I sound, but . . ."

Gavin grunted. "I get it," he said. "They're dead, and we need money."

Random eyed Tom Lachlan. "Yes," he said.

The captain spat in his hand and clasped hands with Tom.

"Where do you want them?" Tom asked.

"I want them marched back north—fifty head at every stopping point in a six-day march, and I want the rest grazing in the fields south and west of Albinkirk in one week."

"Tar's tits," Tom croaked. "That's a mort of driving."

"You're the Drover," Gabriel said. "Then keep going north and get your levies out of the Hills and join Ser John at Dorling. Take whatever beasts you need to feed the Emperor and four thousand men there."

"And hold Dorling?" Tom asked.

The captain shook his head. They were perfectly silent.

"No. I'm sorry, Tom, but unless the Wyrm wants to fight for it, we're sacrificing Dorling."

"Why am I going there, then?" Lachlan asked.

"Because the levies will only rise for you or Ranald or Donald Dhu. And because I can trust you to follow orders—words, by the way, that no one else has ever said about you, Tom." He smiled across the fire, and Tom grinned back.

"Only if I like 'em, boyo."

"Raise your levies and hold the Inn until the Emperor comes. And then retreat to Albinkirk, making the road behind you a wilderness." Gabriel leaned forward.

Tom crossed his arms. "With my Hillmen and the Emperor, I can defeat fucking Thorn."

"No, Tom, you can't. Not without me and Amicia and all the angels in heaven, too." Gabriel shook his head vehemently. "Unless the Wyrm's willing to go in person. And I shouldn't even say that out loud. But if he is—then fight."

Bad Tom scratched under his nose. "Retreating is not my best way," he said.

"Tom, if you pull this off and get the Emperor and Ser John Crayford alive to Albinkirk, I promise you the greatest battle ever." Gabriel nodded. "One toss, one fight, for everything."

Tom raised a hand the size of most men's heads. "Six days with my herd to Albinkirk. Two days hard riding to the Inn if no one stops us." He frowned. "Eight days, at least. Where will you be?"

Gabriel scratched his bites. "Sukey, I need you to start north with the camp and the baggage tomorrow. Leave enough tents standing here for the Royal Guard and the company packed tight, and take the rest on the road. We'll catch you at Sixth Bridge."

Sukey nodded. "I can do that," she said. "How soon can I start them up and packing?"

"Give them another hour," the captain said.

He turned back to Tom while Sukey wrote on her wax tablets. "In eight days, I need to be two days south of Albinkirk," he said. "Because the rest of us are going to turn on the archbishop right now—today. Win or die, and no quarter." He looked around. "No quarter for the archbishop, that is. The rest of them can surrender as they need."

Random all but cried out. "You're going *south?*"

"All or nothing," Gabriel replied. "And you and your friends are going straight to Harndon if we win."

Ser Gerald shook his head. "Have you lost your wits, Gabriel?"

There were people present who'd never heard the captain's name used so familiarly.

"In ten days we can have Harndon without a bolt loosed or a man dead," Random insisted.

Ser Gabriel nodded. "In ten days, Thorn can have done a hundred years of damage to the north country. In fifteen days—the world could be over."

Alcaeus was shaking his head vehemently. "Ser Gerald is correct," he insisted. "The archbishop's cause is lost even now."

It was Gabriel's turn to shake his head. He looked past his brother at Ser Michael, awake and yawning.

"It's your father," he said. "The archbishop will crown him King, won't he?"

Michael nodded heavily. "We have the next claim—it's distant, but—yes." He sighed. "Of course, that's how they bought Pater. It's what Pater always wanted." He looked at the Red Knight. "Of course, your claim through your mother ain't bad."

Gabriel ignored him. "I need Gavin—I'm sorry, brother—I need you to go west—now. As soon as dawn breaks. Somewhere on the south Cohocton, Mountjoy is fighting. Or sitting watching the border. Either way, he has all the Royal Foresters and most of the western lords of the Brogat."

"Wasn't he attainted?" asked Ser Michael.

"Only the fool archbishop would attaint a man with an army already in the field," Gavin said. "I know Mountjoy. I'm going to marry his daughter. He wouldn't leave his post." He nodded. "You want him?"

"At Albinkirk," Gabriel said.

"I still think you should move north yourself," Gavin said. He rubbed the scales on his shoulder. "The sorcerer and his allies—they're the real threat."

"In ten days, the archbishop might be alone with two hundred Gallish lances," Gabriel said. "But he might be the Chancellor of Alba with a thousand lances and some reluctant Alban support. Listen, friends—this is all beyond my experience. I'm listening when you speak. But my spirit says that if we march north, we'll never regain Harndon, and if we march south, we'll never regain Albinkirk or Lissen Carak."

Unnoticed beyond the firelight, Sister Amicia sighed and spoke softly, but everyone strained to hear her.

"As Gabriel well knows, if we lose Lissen Carak, we lose a great deal." She shook her head. "I am not at liberty to say all I know."

"It is possible that if we lose Lissen Carak we lose everything," Gabriel said. "Amicia, I have to ask you to ride with Tom, and go to Lissen Carak with all the knights of the Order. It's all the garrison I can put in, but with the men we hired last year, it should prove enough."

Amicia shook her head. "You will need me tomorrow."

Gabriel shook his head back. "Sister, *everyone* needs you. Your healing powers are beyond anything—anything. But you—you yourself—are the most potent relief force I can send to your convent."

Very quietly, she said, "But you might die."

Gabriel met her on the bridge. "If I die, Michael and Tom and Sauce will pull it out," he said. "If Lissen Carak falls—then he *opens the gates, doesn't he, Amicia?"*

She bit her lip—no mean feat in the aethereal.

"I think that's what this is about," she said. "The Abbess never told me."

"I was in those tunnels," Gabriel said. "I guessed then."

Amicia met his eye. "There are other places. Lissen Carak is not the only one."

Gabriel shrugged. "It's the one I can prevent," he said. "I think that the Faery Knight is against Thorn. I do not think Harmodius has turned. But Alcaeus thinks I'm naive."

Amicia sighed. "I want to believe in Harmodius," she allowed. "I will go to Lissen Carak."

Gabriel said, "We can win this."

Amicia nodded. "I want to believe you. But is it not a basic tenant of war not to divide your forces? And are you not dividing yourself in every direction?"

He grinned. "Oh, dear Amicia. Yes. But I must divide you now to have a chance to combine you all later."

She shook her head, and he left her, however much his soul cried out for him to stay—

Gabriel looked around. "So—tomorrow. Daybreak—one hour. Three battles. Ser Michael with the company in the van. Ser Ranald with the Royal Guard in the main body with the Queen, the young King, and any men of Lorica who will accompany us. Ser Gerald with the rearguard, commanding all the Harndoners we can raise."

Ser Gerald narrowed his eyes. "If Gelfred is right—and I'm sure he is—he's got two days of entrenchments behind which to cower. How are you going to get a battle we can win?"

The Red Knight laughed. "De Vrailly sent us a herald. I'm going to challenge him to battle."

Chapter Eleven

Pennons flapped and flags waved. It was a beautiful late spring in the Brogat.

"I still think that we were better behind our stockades, and bastions," the archbishop said.

"He challenged us," Jean de Vrailly said. He was a figure of shining steel, towering over the archbishop who had chosen to wear his state robes of purple and ermine.

"Let him wear himself out against our walls," the archbishop said, with a certain whine.

"He challenged us," Jean de Vrailly said again.

"I don't think that—"

De Vrailly turned his helmeted head. His visor was open and his angelic face seemed to shine from within. "Eminence, you make me regret I ever invited you here to help me rule this realm. I am a knight. The order of knighthood is the only one to which I have ever aspired. The Red Knight has challenged us to battle."

"And I say—"

"Silence." De Vrailly spoke sharply, and the archbishop flinched. No one had ever told him to be silent in all his life.

"You think I am a fool who believes in an outdated code. You think that we should cower behind our trenches and build trebuchets, conduct mass killings in Harndon to silence the city and goad our enemies into throwing themselves at our bastions and earthworks. I tell you, Eminence, that *you* are the fool, and that if we do that, we will find ourselves starving in a ring, a sea, of enemies, none of them contemptible. We lack the manpower to cow Harndon even if we had no foe in the field against us. The Harndoners *saw* the Queen and the babe. The challenge is just—the Red Knight knows the law of war. But even if it were unjust, we would be fools to do as you suggest. Do you understand me?"

The archbishop was red in the face. He struggled to find words, and finally, he turned his horse, summoned his guard, and rode away.

Ser Eustace d'Aubrichecourt turned his helmeted head. "Well said, Ser Jean."

Other knights murmured, and while they were doing so, a herald appeared at the far wood line. He rode across the field with one man behind him, cantering easily. He held the traditional green flag that heralds bore in times of war.

He came over the low rise—really, no more than the height of a man—that stood at long bowshot from de Vrailly's lines. Behind him, horsemen appeared in the wood line.

De Vrailly's men began to loosen swords in their sheaths and tighten straps and girths.

De Vrailly watched the herald come with nothing in his heart. He had closed himself to his angel since the day after the tournament, and he felt as if he was already dead.

He had been used. Betrayed.

I only wish to die well, he thought. Not a thought to share.

The herald rode down, aiming for de Vrailly's banner. At this distance, it was plain that the man behind him was Du Corse, on a good riding horse, wearing his arming coat and hose and boots.

L'Isle d'Adam and d'Aubrichecourt came forward and joined de Vrailly.

Du Corse looked grim.

"Welcome back," de Vrailly said. "Is it too much to hope that you have escaped?"

Du Corse shook his head. "I come on oath—on my word. In exchange for Corcy's sons."

De Vrailly smiled a grim smile. "I have them to hand." He turned to his squire. "Fetch them immediately. I will not be outdone in courtesy by this sell-sword."

"Hardly a sell-sword," Du Corse said. "He's the Queen's captain-general and the Duke of Thrake. I spoke to him this morning."

Du Corse pointed across the fields at the approaching army—a small army. In fact, only slightly smaller than de Vrailly's own.

The herald opened his mouth, but Du Corse silenced him with a glance.

"Ser Gabriel wishes us to know that our King has been badly defeated in Arelat. He offers three choices. If we take ship immediately, he will let us go. If not, he will meet you in single combat, immediately. Or, if neither of these will suffice, he says he will come to you with fire and sword. But he says to us all that in the last case only the true enemy will triumph."

The enemy were not halting to dress their lines. On the far left, a solid mass of red and steel rode forward. In the centre, another—all in scarlet, with the Royal Standard flying. On the right, a little farther away, a solid body in the red and blue of Harndon, and the checked blue and gold of Occitan.

De Vrailly watched them for as long as his heart could beat ten times.

"This Red Knight is nobly born, then?" de Vrailly asked.

L'Isle d'Adam frowned. "There's a rumour he's the old King's by-blow. But that's probably someone's petty hate. He's the Earl of Westwall's son."

Du Corse said, "The Earl of Westwall is dead. The Wild has breached the whole of the north and west. He told me so himself, and I believe him."

De Vrailly shook his head. "The archbishop would have us believe that it is our duty to cut our way through to Ser Hartmut, and that the Wild is in this case our ally."

The enemy were not halting yet. They were very quick.

The herald—boldly—spoke up. "I'm to tell you that you have only until he's in bowshot to decide," he said.

D'Aubrichecourt spat. "The archbishop would have us believe that the Wild is a fable while also using them as allies," he said. "Even as they defeat our King in Arelat." He shook his head in disgust.

De Vrailly paused when his squire brought up the Corcy boys—two young blond squires, Alban through and through.

"Young gentlemen, your father has ransomed you," he said.

The older, Robert, bent his knee.

The younger, Hamish, stuck his hands in his belt. "You had no right taking us in the first place," he said.

"Be quiet, little brother." Robert put out a hand but his small brother, twelve years old, wriggled away.

"It's dishonourable," Hamish said quietly.

Out in the field, Long Paw roared an order and the whole line halted. Pages came forward and began to collect horses.

Jean de Vrailly dismounted, too.

"He doesn't know what he's saying," l'Isle d'Adam said.

De Vrailly walked to the boy who stood without flinching.

He knelt. His voice was not steady. He said, "Sometimes, men make mistakes, child. Terrible, terrible mistakes. All they can do is atone as best they can. I offer you my apologies as a knight and as a man."

Hamish Corcy bowed low. "Apologies accepted, ser knight! You do me too much honour."

De Vrailly nodded. Then he went to his horse, and mounted. "Tell the Red Knight I will meet him man to man and horse to horse," he said.

The herald turned his horse and rode for the enemy.

De Vrailly turned his own horse so that it faced his people. His squire was mounting the two boys on a rouncy.

"Gentlemen," de Vrailly said, and all badinage stopped. "Whether I win or lose, I propose that we leave the Albans to their own ways and troubles and go to Galle to save the King. And I suggest that you take Du Corse as your commander."

Du Corse bowed in the saddle. The archbishop made to protest and was silenced by a glance from Du Corse.

De Vrailly pointed to his squire, and armed himself with his favourite lance—a very heavy shaft. But when his squire made to mount with two spares, de Vrailly shook his head.

"No, no. We will run one course, and then—" He shrugged. "Someone will die. Please—stay here with these good gentlemen. In fact, young Jehan—I bid you kneel." De Vrailly dismounted himself once again.

"With this buffet, I make you a knight. Never accept another from any but the King. Know the law of war. Love your friends and be harsh to your enemies." He leaned down and kissed the young man on both cheeks.

Jehan—Ser Jehan—was stunned. He began to weep.

De Vrailly vaulted onto his horse.

The Galles gave a thunderous cheer.

Ser Gabriel sat silently watching the Galles. They had a few Alban banners among them, mostly Towbray's, and Towbray himself was on the far left—the Galles plainly didn't trust him. Perhaps the feeling was mutual.

He flicked a glance at his Occitan allies. It was not that he distrusted them, as that he feared their anger and the prince's rash judgment.

Behind him, Ser Michael spat. "I wouldn't have believed that my own father would come to this."

"You could be King," Gabriel said.

"That's not even funny," Michael commented.

"You know what's worst about civil war?" Gabriel asked. The Galles were talking about something, and someone was kneeling.

The company was already dismounting. Cuddy groused, loudly, "I want to see 'em fight. Better them than me. I don't get to be fuckin' King."

Gabriel laughed and gestured at Cuddy. "That's about it. In a civil war, everyone realizes that it's all a dream and *anyone* can be King. And then we're just animals fighting over the grain supply."

The herald, his pennon flapping bravely, was riding towards them.

"Aha," Gabriel said. "Here we go."

His heart began to beat very hard.

Ser Michael turned. "We can take them, Gabriel," he said.

Gabriel nodded. "We can, but some of us will die and some of them will die, and my adversary will win with every corpse. Let's make this as cheap as we can."

"If you lose?" Michael asked bluntly.

"Then I get to relax, and stop plotting. It's all on you and my brother and Tom and Sauce. And Mr. Smythe and Harmodius and the Queen. And Amicia, and the rest of the people. The biggest revelation of the last few weeks has been that it's not all about me, Michael. Muddle through." He laughed.

"What do I do about the Galles?" Michael said, ignoring the rest.

"Offer them ships home. If they refuse, crush them here, take the losses, and offer no quarter. Towbray will desert them the moment he knows it's you." The Red Knight shrugged. "Make yourself King for all I care. I'll be dead."

"I doubt it," Michael said. "Here, let me squire you one last time. Damn, that was ill-said."

Gabriel laughed.

While Michael dealt with the way his arms tied on and where they sat, the herald approached.

"Ser Jean de Vrailly will meet you man to man in single combat," he said.

The Red Knight took a lance from Toby. He thought of leaving a parting message for Amicia, or for Blanche, even.

That seemed like something Mater would have done.

"If I win," he said, "I want you ready to march north immediately."

He wanted to grin or smile, but his heart was pounding, and his cheeks didn't work.

So instead, he turned his horse, and began to ride easily over the hayfield towards the distant shining figure of Jean de Vrailly.

Inside de Vrailly's visor, the angelic face frowned as he rode across the sunlit summer field.

Usually he went to fight without a thought—beyond, perhaps, a prayer.

No prayer came to his lips.

Instead, unbidden, a host of images rose like midges and mosquitoes. Simultaneously, he considered how the Red Knight had dispatched de Rohan, who, for all his faults, he had trained with his own hands, and he considered the sparkling fall of holy water that had declared him forfeit—a flow of holy water that said that his person, or his harness, was ensorcelled. He thought of the black fire clawing at the angel's armour in his tent, and he thought—most of all—of how his angel—

I think your angel is a daemon, said the ghost of D'Eu in his ear.

De Rohan had accused the Queen of sorcery and infidelity. And died.

Why does my angel never name the Red Knight?

Why has he ceased to speak of God?

Why did he not give me any answers?

But the utmost thought in de Vrailly's mind was one of mingled shame and apprehension, two thoughts which he seldom entertained. Because he had willingly donned the armour that had been tainted with sorcery, this day. He had other choices.

His lance went down into the rest with the ease of ten thousand repetitions.

He saw his opponent's arms—the six-pointed stars on the brilliant scarlet ground.

I have other choices. I hate. I doubt.

Everything.

And then his lance was *just there.*

Gabriel sweated behind his visor. He watched de Vrailly with most of his attention. He tried to focus on the man's movements, on his horse.

De Vrailly had a superb horse.

But behind the simplicity of preparation for combat was fear—the fear of death over all, and under that a layer of other fears like folded steel, each fear interwrapped with minute flaws and other hesitations like the dragon's breath of a blade folded over and over again in the forge to try and hide the imperfections in the iron and the steel.

Fear for the Queen, and fear for Michael confronting his father, and fear for the world that he loved and fear that he had behaved badly, that he would die badly, that he would fail.

Gabriel Muriens usually entered combat, which he feared more than anything else in his life, borne along on the heady river of command. With no time to examine the reality of what he faced, he entered into combat like a black mirror—empty and yet full. His imagination rarely had time to inflate the bladder of his cowardice.

But today he had a long bowshot to cross on a horse he could not afford to tire early—a near eternity in which to think. To imagine. To wonder.

Gavin was the better jouster. But de Vrailly was now the commander of the army, and would not have accepted a lesser man or rank. And Gavin's already gone west. In a day or two, he'll find Mountjoy. I hope.

In his vivid and coloured fantasy, Gabriel saw himself unhorsed, saw de Vrailly's lance smash through his breastplate to rip his intestines from his back—saw his helmet shred under a blow, saw Ataelus stumble and fall in the grass, saw Ataelus crash to earth under the hammer of de Vrailly's deadly lance, saw the minute twist of his deadly hands as de Vrailly slapped his own lance to the ground and unhorsed him with delicate ease, saw the crashing mace blow that ended his life, saw de Vrailly chivalrously dismount to pound him to the earth with his sword—

Saw every man who'd ever unhorsed him. Relived every painful fall, every bruise, every humiliation as the quintain slapped him, as his lance missed its mark, as he caught a foot in the stirrup going down—a long, long, silly fall, and all his brothers laughing, his master-at-arms laughing, even Pru, her apron covering her face.

Ah, yes, he thought. They were not doubts, but the sordid realities of a hundred failures—some real, some fancied. As a magister, he knew that the line between them was very thin indeed.

Mater is dead. Odd—a piercing sorrow he never expected, and a vast tide of shameful relief. Whatever happened in the next ten heartbeats, neither the Earl of Westwall nor the duchess would ever mention it, being dead.

He dropped his lance from erect to the lance rest under his right arm without any sense of volition.

He refused to enter his palace. In the strange labyrinth that was his idea of chivalry, to calm himself artificially in his palace in this one fight would be to cheat.

And because all the flaws in the dragon's breath, when forged by a master, make a stronger blade. All the flaws.

I will go down clean. This is who I am.

Eye.

Lance point.

Target.

Michael was a bowshot away. He could not breathe.

Neither adversary saluted. There was no flourish. They went at each other with a simple intensity of purpose.

To a veteran jouster, the open field, lack of barriers, and slight unevenness of the ground offered an endless subject for doubt.

Both horses went straight forward, perfectly in hand, perfectly balanced, their riders like statues in their saddles, tall and strong.

As the two came together, it seemed to Michael, watching, that both horses stepped offline. His pulse pounded in his throat, his dry mouth— he was clutching his saddle—

The sound carried after the impact was visible.

Both lances shattered, and both men rocked back. De Vrailly's head seemed to snap back, and Gabriel's body twisted badly, the shards of their lances falling like red and blue hail. But both horses had done what they'd been trained to—an oblique step at the moment of contact—and because there was no barrier, the two great chargers collided, breast to breast.

They rose, front hooves flailing, rearing as if neither monster had two hundred pounds and more of steel-clad man on their backs. They rose like fighting cocks, and iron-shod hooves flew like arrows on a stricken field—so fast, so many blows struck, that no watcher could even follow the course of the horse-fight.

De Vrailly's horse came down first, and in that beat of a heart, Ataelus landed two great blows—left, right.

The sound of them carried across the field. One struck the armoured plate on the front of de Vrailly's destrier, and the other did not, and sounded like a butcher's hammer on raw meat. But de Vrailly's destrier— slightly larger—sank his teeth into Ataelus below the neck armour—both animals writhed like fighting wyverns—

And both riders were thrown. Neither had ever recollected his balance from the breaking of the spears, and the sudden rear, the curvet and the roll finished both.

The two armies were almost completely silent. Many men were not breathing.

The earth had had three days of sun. Even in a hayfield, there was dust, and now the fight was obscured by the rising of the Cloud of Mars.

Armour glinted in the dust and both armies roared.

De Vrailly's sword came to his hand like a falcon to its master and he was on one knee. The dust was all around him.

Something was wrong. Some part of his great helmet was loose—the helmet moved on his head as he swung, and his left thigh was a dull ache that could turn to real pain, but he couldn't see what was hurt and had no real picture of anything after the moment of impact.

The dust was choking. His horse, Tristan, was fighting the Red Knight's horse with all the savagery of two wild lions, and they raised dust.

He saw the glint of armour and stepped towards it and felt the pain in his left thigh again. He raised his left hand to his helmet and it moved—

Gabriel struck the ground hard, on his left side, his shield trapped under his body. He rolled off the shield and began to get to his feet just as the two fighting horses passed over him. He got a blow in his back plate that pitched him forward on his feet again, and the pain was intense.

Something was gone in his left arm. Or hand.

He saw de Vrailly, and the bastard was standing, almost relaxed, with his left hand on the visor of his great helm.

His own left hand was broken—possibly the wrist.

He stepped forward, his legs good, just as de Vrailly closed. He had to draw straight into a parry as de Vrailly's huge blow crashed down, but he made the cover one-handed, took a little of it on the shield on his left arm, and the pain—

De Vrailly saw immediately that his opponent was covering his left—he threw a second blow and a third, aware that his own balance was precarious because of whatever had happened in his left thigh. Despite which, he pressed. His adversary parried and parried.

His third blow struck home.

Gabriel took the blow over his sinking left arm and shield, which he could no longer keep up. It smashed down from a high guard and struck just where the left pauldron met the maille of the shoulder under the aventail, which by bad fortune was caught on a buckle.

The blow knocked him to one knee, and for a long, sickening moment the pain stunned him.

A second blow slammed into his helmet.

And then the two horses crashed through the knights—so rapt in their own rage that each horse injured its own master, Gabriel knocked flat by Ataelus and losing his sword and de Vrailly caught by one of Tristan's hooves in the back of a greave and also knocked to his knees—close enough to Gabriel that he could see the Gallish knight's halting efforts to rise on his left leg, and the split where his lance had apparently opened a gap between the great helm's visor and the frame—and deformed the whole outer helm. Like many knights, de Vrailly wore an outer helm and an inner, called a cervelleur.

So close. Gabriel could see that his lance tip must have come a finger's breadth from ending the fight at the first pass.

In his bascinet, Ser Gabriel smiled. *Not bad*, he thought. *I did that well enough.*

And with that, he shook the shattered shield off his broken hand and arm, rolled to his right to rise with his empty right hand, and beat de Vrailly to his feet.

De Vrailly was slower rising.

Gabriel had a moment when he might have gotten on de Vrailly before the other knight could get to his feet. It passed. Gabriel couldn't have said whether he was chivalrous or merely tired and wounded, but the moment passed.

He had a dagger, facing the best knight in the world with four feet of steel.

He began to bounce up and down on his toes.

De Vrailly had a moment of real fear when the horses hit, and then he was down, on his face in all the choking dust, and then back up—up with a missed attempt as his left leg almost refused its function. The second try he made it.

The Red Knight was already on his feet. He had a long baselard in his right hand, the tip of it held with his left, and he was bouncing on his toes like a boxer.

De Vrailly flicked a cut and the Red Knight parried on his heavy dagger blade.

De Vrailly stepped forward and threw two cuts—a rising cut at the Red Knight's dagger hand from the guard of the Boar and the consequent falling blow, but the latter was out of distance as the Red Knight skipped back.

De Vrailly's left leg failed, like a dull student. He didn't fall, but suddenly the Red Knight was on him, covering into a close play. De Vrailly raised his hands—

Gabriel bided his time, managed the distance between them, and made his covers—and when the Gallish knight moved, he faltered in his forward motion and his sword moved into empty air.

Gabriel closed, powering into the bigger man with an effort of will that emerged as a shout. He got his left hand on de Vrailly's hands—missed his pommel, and his left hand screamed at him.

But he had all the time in the world to slam the baselard overhand into de Vrailly's neck where the aventail met the shoulder.

Except that the blow bounced, skidding off the mail as if off plate armour.

Quick as a cat, Gabriel struck again and again, as even de Vrailly's strength was not enough to push down the desperation of his arm. Three times his point struck home and failed to bite. No link broke. No penetration.

The armour was *protected*.

Gabriel was losing his fight with pain and with de Vrailly's strength, and he slipped free and spun so that de Vrailly's counter blow merely clipped the point of his own bascinet.

Despite the hermetical working on the maille, a trickle of blood flowed down off de Vrailly's shoulder onto his surcoat. The needle point of the baselard didn't have to break a link to go a finger joint's length into a man's flesh.

De Vrailly felt the fight-ending blows.

And he *knew*.

Inside the helmet, he sobbed once.

But training powered his arms. His left shoulder had three shallow penetrations and the pain was immense but the muscle steady.

He stepped back, rolled his great sword through a deceptive flourish—cut down from a high left side guard, his blow falling onto the Red Knight's crossed hands, and then down and down, past the long tail with the weapon put behind him like a dragon's tail and then rolling his hands precisely, his point coming in line—

Gabriel saw the feint, covered the rising cut—and knew the sequence with the same imagination that could see a thousand dusty deaths and could read the angle of his opponent's hands.

Thrust with deception from the low line, said some distant part of his head to his strong right arm without communicating to any part of his brain that registered thoughts. His last cover had put him right leg forward, his dagger well back on the left side, point down.

All. Or nothing.

He rotated on his hips, the true *volte stabile*, and he caught the tip of his dagger between the index finger and thumb of his left hand. He didn't think about it, and they worked well enough.

Neither man was thinking. All that was fighting was training and will, muscle and steel. The men were lost in the fight. The fight was, in every way, the men.

The thrust came forward. It was almost perfect, but again, at the moment of timing required, de Vrailly's left leg was slow.

For all that, the tip struck—not in the Red Knight's exposed armpit, as intended, but on the very front of his breastplate of Morean steel. Then—an aching heartbeat late—the Red Knight's dagger caught it near the middle third of the end and pushed it aside, so that the blade engraved a furrow up the Red Knight's breastplate to the top ridge, hesitated—and passed off into empty air.

Gabriel knew he'd been hit—but he pushed the blade away, his point in line, guided by the minimal pressure of his maimed left hand. The target drifted across his sight and he turned his high cover into a thrust. He used his left hand to guide the thrust, and when de Vrailly's desperately rising hands slammed into his left arm, in front at the moment of contact, he had a galvanic shock like a hermetical attack, and his own dagger sliced effortlessly through the chamois glove inside the palm of his steel gauntlet and cut deeply into his left palm even as his point went forward between his fingers—

It caught on the bent metal of the damaged edge of de Vrailly's helmet. The outer helmet was not hardened steel, or had been softened by repeated blows, and the point caught—harmlessly.

Without any intention beyond desperation, the Red Knight slammed his right foot down on de Vrailly's left.

De Vrailly's left leg crumpled. Neither man could keep his balance, and they fell together.

Michael had long since begun to ride forward. The two horses had separated—de Vrailly's charger was hurt, but still snorted with fury. Gabriel's Ataelus reared once more—and de Vrailly's horse shied away.

The dust was so thick around the horses and men that Michael could no longer see even the glint of swords or armour. He opened his helmet and raised a hand—a sign of peace—and rode forward, even as Du Corse and another knight came forward with the herald.

Behind him, Ser Michael roared, "Stand your ground, or by God," and there were murmurs.

In the Gallish ranks, men pushed forward. The centre of their line seemed to swell—as if about to give birth to a battle.

Archers in the company began to nock shafts.

Du Corse raised a hand. As he wore only an arming coat and had no weapon, his gesture carried.

Michael tugged his sword from its scabbard and dropped it on the ground.

The herald began to wave his green pennant back and forth.

Michael was close enough now to see into the haze of dust.

Both men were down.

And as he cantered up, with Du Corse converging from another angle, Michael saw no movement at all. The two men lay in a huddle of limbs and arms.

Gabriel never lost consciousness.

He had time to panic about his position, and to realize that he was atop de Vrailly, and de Vrailly was not moving. Gabriel's chin strap was broken, his neck hurt savagely, and his bascinet was twisted enough on his head to make seeing difficult. And his head was ringing.

He realized that he was covered in blood. It was an odd, slow realization—the stickiness of his right hand, the sheet of pain from his left with its slickness, the taste of blood in his own mouth and nose all slowly added together into a universe of blood.

He couldn't use his left hand, trapped between them, at all.

He tried to pull at his dagger to get in another blow, all with aching slowness, and it came free with a slick, wet feeling that told him where it had been.

He used the dagger to push off the ground, and got to his knees. Shook his head to clear his vision, and ignored all the pains, and settled his visor so that he could see.

But no further blow was required. Somewhere in the fall, his dagger's point had slipped from its position on the outer helm, baulked of its prey. It had followed the path of least resistance, probably driven by their contact with the ground, sliding in between the helmets, through de Vrailly's left eye.

The great knight was dead.

Gabriel Muriens sat back on his knees, his weight on de Vrailly's breastplate. He heard hoof beats. He dropped his dagger, having to shake it from his sticky fingers, and scrabbled with the buckle of his chin strap until he could pull his own helmet off his head, and then he drank in the air. He drank it in, again and again, blind to the men gathering around him.

He finally raised his head, and there was the herald, and Du Corse. And Michael. He thought of Gavin, whose fight this ought to have been. Many, many thoughts came into him then, as if he'd been an empty vessel and now he was again filled.

He wept.

And Ser Michael put an arm under his and raised him to his feet. "Come, my captain," he said. "These worthy gentlemen want to take the body of their friend, and go."

The words passed over Gabriel, and left no mark. But other men shouted orders, and other men made plans and, in an hour, the Galles were headed south in a dejected company, with Jean de Vrailly borne on a litter between four horses.

Ser Gerald Random followed them at a discreet distance with a tithe of the Harndon militia.

The rest of the Red Knight's little army turned on their heels and marched north. The day was not so old, and the men had not fought a battle. There was a great deal of grumbling, and Michael halted them, lectured them in a voice reminiscent of the old captain, and then promised double pay for the next month.

All the company cheered, and even Master Pye's armourers set up three hearty huzzahs.

And two leagues further on, at their third halt, the Queen rode down the column with the Red Knight at her side, clad in an arming doublet, bare-headed, and with his left arm in a sling, but with his sword at his side. As they rode, the army cheered, so that the cheers welled up at the front and carried all the way to the back, rippling along, and then the militia marched faster, and the men changed horses with more will.

Back at the front of the column, the Red Knight reined in.

"I confess that I feared you dead," said the Queen.

"Me, too," Gabriel admitted. It was the first sign of the return of humour. As he said later to his brother, he had been somewhere else.

"You proved the better knight," the Queen said.

Gabriel looked at her, in all her earthly beauty. He frowned. "Really?" he asked. He shook his head.

Silence returned. The queen found she could not speak, because, as she later told Blanche, there was something greater than human in his face, and he was so clearly somewhere else.

He broke the spell. "Now that we have broken the—rebellion? Were they rebels?" He looked out over the fields of the Brogat, brown and green, like a counterpane of linen in squares and rectangles and occasional crazy rhomboids to the edge of the horizon. Nearer at hand, spring flowers glowed at the verge of the dusty road, white and brilliant red poppies.

"They won't rally. Du Corse is a professional. He wants to return to Galle and we want him to return to Galle. I think your grace should rest a few days in Lorica and then ride south to your capital. Ser Gerald will have all in hand."

"Yes, Ser Gerald is like to be my chancellor," the Queen said. She frowned in her turn. "You know, we are not yet a government. I cannot rule of my own right. There must be a regency council." She glanced back, where the Earl of Towbray rode silently next to his son, having elected to change sides once more. "I should include all of the great magnates of my realm."

"Yes," said Gabriel, who was not as interested in this as he might have been.

"You are the Earl of Westwall. You were my husband's only other child. Let us mince no words, Ser Gabriel. Will you be regent?" She smiled.

"Oh, Desiderata," he said, and she smiled at her name. "I cannot see being the Earl of Westwall. I think that must be for Gavin."

"You are a strange man," she said. "Why?"

The Red Knight frowned and made a face. "A long story. But if you know that the King was my father, you must know all you need to know. I will not pretend to be the Earl of Westwall. Gavin will be a better earl than I—he loves the people and the place and all the monsters there. I will be happy in Thrake." He smiled a wan smile. "I think—that it is a little premature to think of all this, when the battles we have just fought are merely the prelude. The musicians are only warming up, and the dancers stretch their legs."

Desiderata rocked her head from side to side. "Perhaps. But I think that ruling is always like this—it is always a terrible crisis of one sort or another. Bad rulers use these crises as excuses not to handle routine, and things decay. Under my hand, there will be no decay. I will build a rose garden that men will remember until the sun fails and the moon falls."

"Madame, sometimes I fear that you sound like my mother," he said. He winced, because in the change in his reins he'd just managed to hurt his hand. But then he smiled. "But in truth, she would have been a great queen—as you will be. I think you should be your own Regent, your grace."

This was, perhaps, too much truth for the Queen of Alba, and she narrowed her eyes until she saw the blood dripping from his bandages and remembered that he had just given her back her kingdom.

In fact, he had two broken fingers and a deep cut across his hand that would probably maim him to some extent for the rest of his life, unless Amicia could work her miracles.

I put Jean de Vrailly in the dust.

My mother is dead.

Gabriel rode into the sunset, towards Lorica.

They made camp, having ridden forty miles in two days and fought a battle and lined up for a second. At the news that the Galles had dispersed, and that Gerald Random was marching on Harndon, Lorica opened its gates to the Queen with many an embarrassed flourish.

Blanche had the Queen's new lodgings—the abbot's guest chambers in the magnificent abbey of Saint Katherine of Tartary—swept and clean. She had a cradle for the babe and coverlets from Lorica's many ladies and great bourgeois who were suddenly all too willing to play host to the Queen and her son, the King.

Blanche went about her duties with a correct deference and a somewhat distant manner, as if her thoughts were elsewhere, because they were. News of the Red Knight's victory came in the late evening, before sunset;

she had just two hours to move the Queen from the captain's pavilion into the city, and that left her little time to consider—anything.

He was alive, and victorious.

He probably wouldn't even remember that she was alive. A kiss in moonlight—he no doubt had one a day. And bad cess to him.

And yet...

I could be—someone. I think he would be easy to love. I could work with Sukey and help Nell.

Through the whole move, she was supported with ruthless efficiency by Lady Almspend. Blanche had always disliked the cold, scholarly woman more than a little; Lady Almspend could rattle off orders without a care for the chaos she caused below stairs. But in the midst of the fast-moving events of the evening, she was a rock of strength, and Blanche was shocked to find herself treated as an equal, a partner, consulted and debated with and never ordered.

Lady Almspend, knowing her lover safe, was a very kind, gentle, and considerate woman. And she had a superb memory for the locations of things, from hairbrushes to diaper cloth. Moreover, she seemed to know everyone, from her time as royal chancellor and, with the Queen triumphant, Lady Rebecca suddenly seemed to have many, many friends in Lorica.

She produced a wet nurse as if out of the air, a fine, large girl, newly married, with a baby just barely born within the sacred banns and a fine jolly manner and lots of milk. The young King took to her left breast immediately and with relish. Her name was Rowan, and her baby son's name was Diccon.

"An' what will we call the li'l King?" Rowan asked, settling into a chair with a babe on each breast.

Lady Almspend turned to Blanche and gave a theatrical shrug. "We haven't named him or baptized him," she admitted.

"Oh, they die like flies at this age, don't they just," Rowan said. "Oh, my pardon, ladies. But they do. But I have good milk, and I'll keep him alive, by the rood and all the saints."

Blanche was not, ordinarily, a political thinker. But just for a moment she froze and wondered what would happen if the little King were to die. Children died.

She fell to her knees, crossed herself, and prayed.

For the first time in her life, but not the last, she wished that she did not know so much. So much of what was at stake, of what people could do, would do, might do.

When she rose, the Queen was arriving at the gates. Blanche watched her reception from the tower balcony, with Lady Almspend.

"Will we go north, my lady?" Blanche asked.

"Call me Becca," Lady Almspend said.

Again, the breath was stolen out of Blanche's lungs. "I'm a laundress, my lady," she said.

Rebecca Almspend had always dressed very plainly—to the amusement of the maids and laundresses. She wore dark, shapeless woollen hose under ill-fitted kirtles and large, practical, warm gowns in winter.

All the palace knew when she fell in love first with Ranald of the Royal Guard, because her shoes grew more pointed, her hose began to fit and even be of silk, and her kirtles seemed to shrink to fit her slight figure. But even today, a day of triumph, she wore a simple, dark blue overgown over a matching kirtle of no great distinction and with plain buttons and not so very many of them, while Blanche wore the magnificent brown wool kirtle that Sukey had given her, which fit her so well as to turn men's heads wherever she walked. It was not quite indecorous, but the bust and the hips lay on the edge of *too tight* and the long line of buttons of fine gilt silver on the sleeves were worth her laundry wages for a year and more.

Becca looked at her, head to toe, brown slipper to coiffed head, and laughed. "Well, if anyone entered and wanted to know which of us was a great lady and which a laundress, I'll wager I'd be the laundress. Fie, girl—you saved the Queen's life and you've been her constant companion—you birthed her son. You can be anything you wish. You have only to ask. Desiderata is the most generous creature in the world, and wouldn't hesitate to raise you. Lady? Duchess? My sweet, if we survive this war, it will be a new world. I am *determined* that women will be born anew in this new world. So I say—be a lady."

"Who'll do the laundry?" Blanche asked. "The Queen is *that* particular." They both laughed.

"Becca?" Blanche asked very quietly, as if afraid to be caught out.

"Yes, my dear Blanche," Lady Almspend replied a little too brightly.

"Do you know the Red Knight?" she asked.

"Not at all," Almspend replied. They could both hear hooves in the flagged courtyard, and night was falling and the babe was blessedly asleep. "But Ranald loves him. He knighted Ranald and sent him back to me. I don't need to know much more." As she spoke, she bustled about the Queen's chamber, laying a few of the Queen's surviving possessions in their accustomed places. Ranald had rescued what he could from her rooms in the palace.

Blanche realized that she was blushing.

Lady Almspend was too well-bred to notice.

And then the Queen swept in, tired, nay, exhausted, and yet in tearing spirits, with another victory behind her.

"That Red Knight is the very paragon of chivalry," she said. "So—odd, considering. I knew he could beat de Vrailly. God willed it." Desiderata

413

paused. There was her old familiar hairbrush, and there was Rebecca Almspend to wield it.

She looked at her friend, and suddenly, without volition, tears filled her eyes and she sat rather suddenly. "Oh, Becca," she said.

Rebecca shot a glance at Blanche and went and cradled her friend's head on her chest. "Your grace—"

"They killed Diota," the Queen said suddenly. "They killed her. They killed all my friends but you and Mary—all the knights. Oh, Mary, Mother of God." She choked, almost gagged on her tears, and then wept.

They were her first tears in many days.

Becca held her head and rocked her.

Her eyes met Blanche's. Blanche was frozen, but Becca blinked, and Blanche understood. She came and took one of the Queen's hands, very hesitantly, and squeezed it.

"We're here, your grace," she said.

"I hate the dark," Desiderata cried. She clung to Blanche as if Blanche was a floating plank and she was drowning.

"Shush, your grace. It's all over now," Almspend said as if she were holding a baby.

The Queen raised her face, and it was ugly with tears, the muscles of it moving as if her face were full of worms, and she gave voice to a wordless cry of anguish.

"Annnnghhh," she cried. "I loved him, even if he— Even when he— Sweet Christ, they are all dead. All my friends, and my love. Dead, dead, dead. They cut her head from her body and put it on a spike—I saw it."

Blanche was chilled—horrified.

Lady Almspend merely held her friend. Blanche slipped out and went to the prince, her brother, who came immediately, dropping his cervelleur into the hands of a squire without a word.

He nodded to Blanche. "You are the Queen's tire-woman? Your hair is like the silk of the east and your eyes are like the sky of early evening." He smiled. It was a beautiful smile. "I have waited days to say that." He was still in his arming clothes, sweat-soaked and smelling strongly of man and horse.

Blanche had met Occitans before, and she moved briskly along the corridor.

"I know my suit is hopeless, fair maiden, but give me a lock of your hair and I'll—"

"Your sister the Queen is in a bad way, your grace," Blanche said stiffly.

He bowed to her—still moving. He was as graceful as an irk, and there were those that said that there was irkish blood in the south. "I stink—I know it. But I promise you, I am a prince, and well able to—"

Blanche blushed. "*Your grace*," she barked. She bowled him through the door into Desiderata's outer chamber.

He looked back. "I am a fool, of course. You do not want reward for your love, but only—"

Then he saw his sister. To his credit, his face transformed, and from a comic lover he was instantly a caring brother. "Oh, sweet Mother of God," he said.

Desiderata fell into his arms, and Rebecca backed away.

Rebecca took in the extreme discomfort writ large on Blanche's face and nodded, even as Desiderata calmed.

"Her grace's breviary is still, I fear, in her captain's pavilion," she said. "Blanche, would you be kind enough to fetch it?"

Blanche curtsied, even as the Queen protested.

"Let her rest, Becca. She has gone through everything I've been through but the birth." The Queen's sobs were slowing, and with much the same transformation as her brother had shown, the Queen's face seemed to change. Lines smoothed, tendons were erased, and her breathing slowed.

Her brother held her by both hands. In Occitan, he said, "I haven't seen you cry like that since you broke your arm as a girl."

She took a deep breath. "I don't know where it came from," she said, her voice lower and easier.

Blanche sighed, accepted Lady Almspend's smile and nod, and fled before the prince's eye fell on her again.

She was vexed, and fatigue made her vexation feel like something more serious. The pain was like a splinter in her finger—the more she worried it, the more painful it was.

The prince fancied her and offered her *reward*. It was plain enough— that's what men of his class did to offset things like pregnancy and shame. They offered lower-class women money.

But the night before, she'd—this was the splinter in her soul—imagined *rewards* herself. What did that make her?

Sweet Christ, what did Sukey think? She stopped in the darkness, halfway across the smooth field of grass that grew for a long crossbow shot outside the city walls and on which the company was camped—camped, if few fires and no tents make a camp. The captain's pavilion—travel stained and with a slightly sagging ridgepole between its two high points—was the only tent in the camp.

Sukey was gone, of course.

Suddenly Blanche had no interest in going to that pavilion, where he sat. She could see the candle-lit space within—there was Toby, his squire, fussing, and there was Nell. And, her mother's voice said, what would *they* think?

Men had fancied Blanche since her breasts began to bud. She'd always enjoyed it and never let it drive her, like some girls, whose heads were turned forever—not by love, but by the *power*. But in this case, she bit her lip in annoyance, turning on her heel.

She was close by the pavilion by then, and she missed a tent-rope in the dark. It tripped her, and she squealed.

In a moment, there was a hard arm across her throat.

A tall, thin man glared at her. His eyes were unfriendly, and his face was like a ferret's. She remembered him from the birthing.

"What you got there, mate?" barked a voice near at hand.

The thin man gave her a hand up. "Never mind, Cully," he said. "It's just the captain's piece."

Blanche flushed. Her ankle hurt, and so did her pride. She sputtered.

Cat—that was his name—was not unkind. "No need to sneak, Miss. We all know ya now."

Unbidden, the language of her childhood hissed out. "Sod off, Beanpole! I'm not your captain's doxy or any man's."

Cat laughed. Cully grinned. "Oh, aye. Our mistake," Cully said. Then, seriously, "He's not—his self. He's . . ." Cully shook his head and his helmet glinted in the darkness and she realized they must be guards.

"Who's there?" called Toby.

Blanche writhed.

"The Queen's lady," Cully said.

The captain—visible as a shape, a very Red-Knight-like shape, right to his profile, on the lantern show of the tent wall—sprang to his feet. In another mood she might have been pleased by his alacrity.

Cully guided her firmly around the tent-stakes as if she were a wayward infant, which made her mad.

"Lady Blanche," the Red Knight said.

"I'm no lady, and I've a-told you so before, my lord. My lady, her grace, has sent me to ask for her breviary, which she left in your tent." She gave a stiff-backed curtsey. "And I'd appreciate it if any other little thing her grace left might be returned, so that I don't have to make another trip."

She could see she'd wounded him. In another mood, she might have relented.

"Toby, I'd like to speak to Blanche, if I might, and then perhaps—"

"No, my lord, I will not be alone with any man, thank you," Blanche said. She spat it more than said it.

His back went up, she saw it, and liked him better for it, right through her anger.

With a coldness she admired he looked down his nose at her. "Very well. Fetch the Queen's things, Toby, I'm going out to have a look at our posts."

"Oh, Christ Jesus," muttered Cully. "Lady . . ."

He made a sign to Cat, hidden by the tent flap, and the younger archer ran off into the darkness just before the captain stalked out of the tent and vanished into the darkness.

Nell looked at her accusingly. "What was that for?" she asked.

Toby didn't meet her eye, but his disapproval was obvious. He had the Queen's prayerbook, as well as a small reliquary that Ser Ranald had rescued and a ring, and he put them all in a soft bag and handed it to her.

"Look for yourself," he said, in almost exactly his master's tone. "We wouldn't want you to have to come again."

Blanche sniffed. It was a sniff of dismissal, contempt, the most formidable of all the weapons her mother had given her, and she had used it to put apprentices and laundry maids in their places on many occasions. She took the bag and did indeed walk around the pavilion, giving everything a careful look.

She knew the great tent well from a day spent with the Queen; the inner hangings, the small chest of bound books, the absence of any kind of religious equipment. On the back was a small tapestry of a knight and a unicorn.

She loved the tapestry.

But she was too angry—and hurt—to enjoy it. So she turned, delivered another sniff, and started out.

"I'll take you back to the bishop's palace," said Nell. "I wouldn't want anyone to do you an injury."

"I can find my own way," Blanche shot back.

"Can you?" Nell asked. "Military camps can be dangerous for unarmed women. You don't want Cat Evil finding you alone. Or any of the others. They're only tame to some fists, like falcons. They ain't tame."

Blanche, who'd survived months of the Galles at court, snorted. "And you'll protect me?" she asked. Nell was tall and big-boned, but she was fifteen years old to Blanche's twenty, and Blanche suspected she could drop the younger woman with a single blow. Laundry gave a girl muscles.

They were out in the darkness. "What's eating *you?*" Nell asked. "Why'd you go and spit at the cap'n? He likes you."

"He wants me," Blanche said sullenly. "That doesn't mean he likes me."

"Is that the rub? Toby says the two of you..." Nell made a hand motion that was, blessedly, hidden in the darkness.

"Toby doesn't know shit," Blanche spat.

"Now you don't sound like a lady," Nell allowed, so very reasonably that suddenly Blanche stopped, crouched—and burst into tears.

She found herself crying on Nell's shoulder. Like the Queen, she shook it off. "You should give me your coat," Blanche said. She pushed a smile. "It stinks."

Nell nodded. "I'd be happy—" she said. "I thought we was friends. But then you were—"

Blanche put up a hand. "I'm tired and—" She shook her head. "Damn it," she said. She knew the fatigue and the worry had sapped her. Last night's lack of sleep was no help. "I'm not a whore," she said.

Nell laughed. "No one said you was!" she allowed.

"Cully thought so, and Cat," Blanche said. They were walking more quickly.

"Aye, well, Cat pretty much hates women and Cully doesn't think there's another kind." Nell shrugged. "I never get close to Cat." She looked out into the darkness. The gate was close.

"But the cap'n likes you," she went on. "And people are going to catch holy hell 'cause you spat on him. He's out there right now, looking at sentries. Hear it? He's caught someone asleep. Pay lost, and maybe a beating."

"Very nice," Blanche said stiffly. "Not my fault."

Nell's face, by the light of the torches burning at the city gate, showed a worldly cynicism that belied her years. "No?" she asked. "If'n you say."

"You love him yourself—you lie with him if it's so important to everyone." Blanche regretted the words as soon as she said them.

Nell frowned. "No," she said, as if considering the proposition. "No, that wouldn't work. Bad for discipline, I expect." She shook her head. "You need sleep," she said, as if she were the older one. She gave Blanche a brief hug.

Blanche didn't resist.

Released, she fled in past the town guards. She thought that if she met Prince Tancredo in the corridors she'd kill him, but everyone was asleep but a handful of servants. She put the Queen's treasures in her outer room, found that Lady Almspend had rather thoughtfully made her up a pallet with a sheet and blanket next to her own, and lay down on it.

She wanted to go to sleep. Instead she lay thinking about what a fool she was for a long time.

Chapter Twelve

The Company

Dawn found a surly company, sour from too much wine and too much marching. The horses were tired, and the oats were not enough to raise their spirits. Pages stumbled, half asleep, along the lines.

To add insult to injury, a light rain began to fall on men who'd slept with no tents and a single blanket.

Dropsy, one of the archers, was chained to the captain's wagon, the only wagon left in the camp. Before they marched, the captain sat in judgment on him, and invoked the lesser penalty for sleeping on duty; not death and not a flogging. Instead, when all the men were formed, Cully stripped Dropsy to the skin and made him run down the ranks, and all the archers took a slap at him with their bows, or with arrows or leather belts or whatever they fancied. Running the gauntlet was a punishment as old as armies, and Nell, who hadn't seen it done before, might have expected that the archers would go easy on one of their own.

She might have expected it, but she didn't. The average archer's capacity for cruel humour exceeded his kindness on the best of days—nice men stayed home and farmed. Nor was Oak Pew any different—her heavily studded belt slapped into Dropsy's buttocks with a sound that made men wince and miss their blows.

Dropsy wailed at the pain and wept for it, but he didn't fall down and he didn't protest, and he was fast enough, when awake. He made it to the end more injured in pride than body. Cully was waiting with his filthy hose and his braes and shoes and a surgeon's mate, who put a salve in the deeper welts.

The captain watched it all like an angry hawk watches rabbits.

"Mount," he said to his trumpeter.

The men and women of the company were in a better mood for having punished Dropsy, and while the man still sobbed, which was disconcerting in a grown man and a killer, the rest ignored him, made dark jokes about his name and habits, and got their horses.

Mounted, they formed quickly, aware of the captain's mood. The Occitans were slower off the mark, and the captain sent Ser Michael to move them.

Then he rode over in front of the company.

"We're going into the worst place we've ever been," he said. "If we're lucky, we'll only have to march two hundred leagues and then fight once. But my friends, the fun is over. I was gentle with Dropsy. In a day, a man asleep could be our deaths and the failure of our cause." He looked them over. "The sorcerer has taken Ticondaga. To the best of our knowledge, he's going for the Inn of Dorling—and after that, Albinkirk." He sat back. "We will endeavour to stop him. But for the next few days, we will move very fast through country that may already be hostile. The next man or woman asleep on duty will be flogged—even if it is a knight."

Silence.

"Good. Company will wheel to the right by subsections forming a column of fours. March." The company's many subsections made quarter wheels, so that the whole manoeuvred like Moreans from being a long line three horsemen deep to a column four wide facing off to the right, down the road.

"Halt," he called, and each section alligned itself.

He raised his hammer over his head and winced. Most of his body hurt this morning. He shook his head and lowered the hammer.

The captain rode to the head of his column, where Toby and Nell and the rest of the *casa* waited. To the east, the sun crested the mountains of Morea. Ser Michael cantered up.

"The prince hasn't even awakened yet," he said.

The captain nodded. "Then we leave him behind."

Ser Michael nodded. "That'll go over well," he said.

The captain frowned and raised his hammer again. "March!" he roared.

Chapter Thirteen

D e La Marche died in the storming of Ticondaga. He didn't die on the battlements, cutting his way in. He died in the sack, when children were being destroyed and eaten, when men who'd begged for quarter were fed to monsters by cheering sailors, when a hundred atrocities passed in a few beats of a terrified victim's heart.

De La Marche stood in the yard running slick with fresh blood and tried to stop it, and a stone troll made a pulp of his head. Boglins ate part of him as he lay there and, later, something with too many legs ripped one of his arms off his corpse and took it away into the darkness.

Thorn stood like a great stone tree in the courtyard, watching. He did not move much—a waste of energy. He merely observed. The storming and consequent workings had robbed him of a great deal of his power, at least temporarily, and he had not had the replenishment from Ghause that he had anticipated.

The sack went on around him.

He saw De La Marche protest—saw him stand between predator and prey, and saw him go down. And later he saw the trenoch—a swamp thing—feast on the corpse and take some away for its disgusting young.

Thorn was also digesting a feast, but his feast was one of the mind.

Ser Hartmut came and stood beneath Thorn's great form. He said nothing, but also watched as men behaved worse than beasts and predators fed.

The garrison of Ticondaga provided a great deal of sport.

And eventually, when the attackers were sated, when even Kevin Orley's warriors sank on their haunches in disgust or shock or merely fatigue, Ash came.

His presence seemed to fill the yard, and Thorn had the disconcerting notion that the entity was feeding there, too. But he again manifested as a pair of fools, in filthy motley, who spoke with one brass voice.

"Look at them," he said. He pointed a stick shaped like a snake at where two sailors, Etruscan mercenaries or Galles, were tormenting a man whose screams had almost been exhausted. "Look at them. Give them license, and they show what they really are."

Thorn didn't turn his head. "What are they, Master?"

"Worse than anything the Wild ever conjured," Ash said. "Men are the cruellest and most vile creatures that have ever come to this place. Servants only of their own corruption and wickedness."

Thorn did not disagree.

"One of my other plans has miscarried," Ash said. "So I must ask you to march sooner, on Dorling."

Thorn was still working on the things he'd learned in the moments during and after Ghause's death. The out-welling of power—the incandescent *ops*—

He had learned much. And he was still pulling at some of the twisted ends, even as he wove others into new barriers.

In fact, Thorn was busy knotting and splicing around the black hole that stood somewhere in his mind. The cascade of thoughts by which he'd reached certain conclusions was hard to reconstruct, but he knew he'd taken some of Ghause's memories in his unsuccessful attempt to subsume her. One of them had triggered something.

The black hole in his mind was the same size and shape as the black eggs he carried. It had been put there at the same time, by the same hand.

For the same reason.

He was, himself, incubating something. He had an excellent idea of exactly what that was.

He had begun to take the steps required to deceive his master, and perhaps— to survive.

And more.

"One of your plans miscarried?" Thorn asked gravely.

"I cannot be everywhere," Ash hissed. "And the bitch Queen and her servants were there before me." The jesters—shaped like misshapen children with fat bodies and long, thin limbs—both giggled. And spat.

"Can you not?" Thorn asked, trying to mask his interest. He was weaving a net of the insubstantial stuff in which the mind built the palace, and he was endeavouring to use it to build a deception, so that Ash would see only what he expected.

Ser Hartmut grunted. "To whom are you speaking, Sorcerer?" he asked.

Thorn pointed a stony finger. "Do you not see two capering children, dressed in motley?" he asked.

Ser Hartmut shook his head. "I see many terrible things," he said. "But no jesters."

Thorn considered this.

Ash said, "No, even I cannot be everywhere. And you must have learned by now how opaque everything becomes—like muddy water—when too many fingers stir it."

Thorn considered this statement, too. In his head, his will was madly building, throwing up beaver dams of obfuscation behind thickets of deception between his thinking space and the area around the blackness.

"It doesn't matter much," Ash said. "I've out-witted her anyway, and she's left with her concentration on the wrong moment and the wrong avatar. So the loss of a few pawns—even my favourites—is no great loss."

Thorn thought that if the mad jesting twins were, themselves, people, then in fact, Ash was betraying fury, humiliation and loss.

"Be that as it may," the darkness said. "It's time to reveal a little more of our hand and limit the damage. Have you seen this?" Ash asked, and disclosed a nested set of workings, a box within a box within a box.

The whole was so labyrinthine that Thorn's head reeled.

"I had no idea," he said. "That life was so small."

"Small, and wild, all the way down to the smallest," Ash cackled. "And sometimes the manipulation of the smallest is of the greatest moment. On to Dorling, Journeyman!"

Thorn listened to the benighted children cackle and thought, *He has, somewhere, lost a battle. And he means to betray me. He is not God, nor yet Satan.*

I can do this. Very well.

"We must march to Dorling," Thorn said to Ser Hartmut. "As soon as we can."

Ser Hartmut chuckled darkly. "Perhaps when all the women are dead and the fires are out, you'll get this—horde—to move again. My experience is that most creatures, and not just men, take what they can and return home. Most creatures do not see war as a means to an end. It is merely an end."

Indeed, over the next day, almost as many creatures of the Wild left his army as joined it. New creatures and bands of men came in every day—Outwallers, bandits, cave trolls, small tribes of boglins under their shamans and many of the bigger creatures, too—a whole flight of wyverns Thorn had never seen before, from far to the north, and a new, strong band of wardens, big, heavily built saurians from north of the Squash Country—hereditary enemies of Mogon's and her ilk.

Many of the northern Huran who had come as volunteers left; some in disgust, and some merely because they had good loot, or a captive to adopt or torment.

Despite the shifting, Thorn's host was immense, and the loot of Ticondaga could not hold them long. Nor feed them. Hartmut's men and the sailors made a camp and fortified it, ate from their own stores and refused to share with any but Orley's warband.

Orley's warband were now so well armed and armoured that they appeared a regiment of dark knights with scars and tattoos and deerskin surcoats. Most had heavy bills, or axes, and some carried crossbows as well. Kevin Orley was already a name. Men flocked to his banner now, and he called himself the Earl of Westwall. The armoured fist of the Orleys now floated over the smoking ruins of Ticondaga.

Ser Hartmut was a good teacher in the ways of war, and Thorn listened to him as he planned. Then he ordered his horde to break up—to feed off a larger swathe of the Adnacrags and to inflict more terror and more damage.

"Meet me under the Ings of the Wolf's Head in five days," he said, his voice like the growl and roar of summer thunder. "And we will take Dorling and feast again."

Ser Hartmut organized the men—Galles, sailors, Outwallers, Orley's warband and all their camp-followers. On their last day at Ticondaga, they were joined—late—by the expected reinforcement from Galle—another hundred lances and a strong company of the routiers with their own captains; Guerlain Capot led the brigans, men as hard and as rough as Orley's men, and Ser Cristan de Badefol led a hundred Etruscan lances under a black banner. On his armour was the motto *"Enemy of God, Mercy and Justice"* in gold. It was said he had once been a member of the Order of Saint Thomas.

As soon as he arrived, he approached Ser Hartmut. They embraced—carefully—and de Badefol examined the ruin of Ticondaga.

"I told d'Abblemont that you'd take it," the Etruscan said. "I brought what I could. There's a lot of shit going on."

Ser Hartmut wrinkled his nose fastidiously at de Badefol's coarseness.

"Oh, don't be a choirboy," de Badefol said. "Just before we left port we heard that the King of Galle had been badly beaten in southern Arelat. There's a rumour up in Three Rivers—since a pair of Etruscan merchants came in—that the Etruscans have asked the Emperor for help, it's so bad." De Badefol watched a wyvern taking flight off the water—its great, slow, laboured wings brushing the water at every stretch so that, as it lifted into the grey morning air of the mountains, its wings left a succession of perfectly round spreads of ripples. After sixteen great heaves of its wings it was airborne—just clearing the distant tree line across the lake, where Chimney Point came down from the Green Hills' side. "By God, Ser Hartmut, I rejoice to see that we are directly in league with the forces of Satan. I've always been a devotee."

"You speak much nonsense and little wisdom, my friend."

"Does d'Abblemont know we are supporting the very side that makes war on the King in Galle and Arelat?" de Badefol asked.

"I care nothing for that," Ser Hartmut growled. "I have orders, and I obey them, until they are complete."

De Badefol nodded. "How very simple," he said. "Well, my bravos will probably take a few days to— Black Angels of Hell, what is that?"

A few yards away, a pair of boglins emerged from the ground. They had bored through the earth, as they did when it was soft, and now appeared within the human encampment. In moments they'd caught a goat and begun to devour her.

Ser Hartmut drew his sword, which burst into flame. He killed both of the boglins, the sword slicing effortlessly through their carcasses and leaving them in the same unjointed state to which they had rendered the goat.

Within seconds, carrion birds began to descend.

"Where the fuck am I?" de Badefol asked.

"This is the Wild," Ser Hartmut said. "Best get used to it. Here, one is either predator, or food."

Sixty miles east of Dorling, the Emperor mounted his horse, took his helmet from the junior spatharios, Derkensun, and his sword from the senior, Guntar Grossbeak, and rode to his officers, gathered to review his magnificent army. Derkensun was still unsure of his rank, cautious in ceremonial. Grossbeak—tall and with fading copper hair and the biggest nose of any man Derkensun had ever met, was a lord, a Jarl. From home. He had no experience in the guard—but a great name as a killer.

Derkensun liked him, but he was a symptom of the imperial army's greatest problem—too many new men.

The Emperor's army broke camp and marched in a damp dawn. The Meander flowed on their right and to the south, the outposts of the Green Hills rolled away into long downs, some crowned with ancient hill forts, complex rings of earth, and some with standing cairns so ancient that no man remembered who had built them.

The Emperor watched the head of his army, guarded today by his Nordikaans, each carrying a great axe or a long-bladed two-handed sword, and wearing hauberks to their knees or below—some of steel, some of dull iron, some of bronze. Many of the Nordikaans now sported Etruscan or Alban breastplates over their maille, and some wore the new-style bascinets with maille aventails to pad the axed hafts on their shoulders. Almost every man had acquired full plate leg armour since last year's bloody victory in Thrake. But the magnificent cloaks on their shoulders were the same, and many helmets glinted gold in the rising sun.

Behind the Emperor's person, today, rode the Scholae, the elite cavalry of Morea, with horn bows scabbarded by their sides and coats of plates or steel scale over light maille, with gold brocade surcoats and billed helmets, new made in distant Venezia from hardened steel. Each troop of the Scholae rode matched horses; black in the first troop, bay in the second, and grey in the third. The scarlet-clad Vardariotes were already far ahead, moving across the hills in a nearly invisible skirmish line that covered the front and both flanks of the column.

Behind the Scholae rode two regiments of the Emperor's stradiotes—his semi-feudal cavalry; the men of southern Morea and the men of the city. The northern Morea and Thrake would need a generation to recover from treason, stasis, and battle. But already since last year the stradiotes had changed in armament, and more of them rode larger horses and had heavier armour—made available at very favourable prices by the Etruscan factors.

Behind the stradiotes came a banda of mountaineers from the slopes between Alba and the Empire—tall, strong men and women with heavy javelins and heavier bows. They wore no armour at all beyond skull caps of iron. Many carried small round targets, but none had a knife longer than his forearm. The mountaineers had their own officers, bearded men on small ponies, and they marched quickly enough to keep up with the horsemen.

Behind them came a banda of Outwallers from south Huran, around Orawa, the extreme northern outposts of the Empire. They had come south to Middleburg and many had already shadowed the hosts of the sorcerer. Janos Turkos rode at their head, smoking. They kept no sort of order and sometimes left the column altogether.

Last, in the rearguard, came Ser Milus, with the company's great banner of Saint Catherine, and with him rode Morgan Mortirmir and fully half of the company, and perhaps half again—Ser Milus had been busy recruiting.

All totalled, the Emperor had five thousand seasoned veterans to march to war in the north. If he was worried, his beautiful, bland face gave none of that away.

The army cheered him, and then turned, almost as one man, and moved off to the west.

Morgon Mortirmir had enjoyed a pleasant semester polishing his skills—really just a few weeks—before the Emperor's messenger and Ser Milus's had collided on his inn's stairs summoning him to war. But he'd learned some fascinating things, and he'd used the first ten days out of Liviapolis on the road to work them into practical designs.

One was a simple hermetical device the size of a tinderbox that allowed a scout, when he pressed a stud, to make a string vibrate on another box held by another scout up to a league or more away. It was imperfect still and Morgon was sure it could be "sensed" in the *aethereal*, but it put in the Emperor's hand the ability to see over the next ridge as surely as his scouts could travel there. Morgon had concocted a dozen other devices—most of them intended to protect the column against spies, as the captain had warned him.

Some of them even worked.

The only outward show was that insects had a very hard time indeed getting close to the column, in camp or out of it—a side effect that delighted the soldiers and made Morgon outstandingly popular with the company.

Morgon was musing on the possibilities of a code—something simple—perhaps easily changed—for his communication devices. He had only made six of them—each one took more than a day of work and more than a day of his *potentia*. Ser Milus and Proconsularis Vlad, the acting commander of the Vardariotes, both requested more devices each day.

The master board—really, an old lute hermetically re-worked to respond directly to impulses from the *aethereal*—began to emit the notes that meant "alarm."

"Some kind of attack coming in," he said tersely. The language of the impulses was still too limited.

Ser Milus gave an order, and the great red company standard was waved back and forth.

Immediately, the column began to deploy. Morgon was far towards the back, well located to see the mountaineers struggling to spread out to the south, looking for cover—the Outwallers running down the banks of the Meander to the north on the same errand, each block covering one of the column's flanks.

The wyverns came in from the south. They were wary—they flew very low. Given how close they all were to the Circle of the Wyrm, Morgon was surprised that they dared at all.

There were a dozen of them—sleek shapes that flew along the edge of the hills to the south and west of them. Without the warning they'd have caught the whole column in march order, but instead, every archer had an arrow to his string.

But the leader of the wyverns was old, canny, and had much experience of men. And his instructions had been admirably precise. He circled to the east, his own band riding the same drafts he did, well closed up against being located too fast. They circled the last hill and swung out across the valley of the Meander, and Morgon saw the company archers begin lofting arrows—some men loosed far too early, but most of the archers were veterans, not just of war but of this war, and held their shafts.

From the baggage near the rear of the army, crossbow bolts flew.

The great winged creatures banked, coming in along the axis of the column and manoeuvring in the still air to make themselves poorer targets.

The company—deployed to the right and left of the baggage—raised their bows almost together as Smoke chanted ranges—and loosed.

A brave and untried young wyvern crumpled under forty heavy impacts and crashed to earth, bouncing once and ploughing a furrow in the sandy soil until its corpse crashed into a wagon whose oxen were still harnessed.

The oxen rolled their eyes and bolted heavily, passing along and then through the archers' line on the left of the road.

Two more wyverns fell victim to their hate and their feeding desires, disobeyed their chieftain and attacked the disordered archers. In heartbeats, Jack Kaves was dead, and his partner Slacker, and a dozen more archers were wounded and down.

Ser George Brewes bellowed and lashed out with his long spear, and Ser Giovanni Gentile stood by him. One of the younger wyverns took a deep thrust under his neck and powered himself into the air, but the other stayed to fight, and armoured men and women struck it from every side until it crumpled. Tippit and Half-Arse put goose feathers in a third monster, and then the survivors were banking away.

The trailing, wounded beast had trouble getting altitude, and the Vardariotes killed her, riding at breakneck speed under the stricken thing and loosing arrows straight up into her guts until she fell.

The men and women of the company pulled the dead horrors off the baggage wagons, and noted that their talons were smeared in a sticky black mess. Master Mortirmir was summoned, and took samples. It was obviously hermetical, but Morgon couldn't see what it was for—it wasn't a poison.

Morgon thought the whole incident a display of the enemy's foolish vanity—four wyverns was a poor return for two baggage wagons and six dead archers, if considered coldly.

It was hard to consider coldly. They buried the men and the two women who'd died with the baggage, crossbows in hand, and then they drove on. The column marched until noon.

And then, suddenly, horses began to die.

There was no warning. Among the company, it was horses with the baggage that went down first. Almost a dozen in the first minute, black froth coming from their nostrils.

Men went down as their mounts collapsed. The collapses were horrible—well-beloved mounts seemed almost to melt, their skin crawled with some form of death, and then, down they went, never to rise, and as they lay they bloated with terrifying rapidity, their guts stinking as they corrupted.

Morgon was not the only magister with the column, but he was the closest to the first horses to fall. He had the presence of mind to order his own horse—a lithe stallion called Averoes—to run—indeed, he struck Averoes sharply with his scabbard to drive the young horse away. Then he ran towards the nearest rotting animal, already *entering into his palace— the palace Harmodius had built.*

The checkerboard floor was unchanged, as were many of the other features, but he had changed the chess pieces for statues—thirty-two statues of many of his favourite people from history and his own times, philosophers and rulers and mystics and even musicians.

Again he summoned the black paste that had been on the wyverns' talons. In the aethereal, *it appeared not black but a living purple, like a slime mould. The colour burgeoned with life and hermetical energy.*

He had seen this on his first look, but it hadn't seemed dangerous—Morgon bore down, looking more closely. He had learned many tricks at the university, and one was how to make a lens of air. Morgon adapted it and cast, and instantly found himself the victim of his own workings—the simulacrum of the sticky paste was too coarse-grained a reproduction to examine in the aethereal.

In the real, he emerged, lumbered to a stop from a sprint, and tried not to fall into the fizzing black sludge that had once been Hetty's second horse. He worked a sample into the air in front of him, cast the lens of air, and then moved it—

The black-purple stuff was *alive.*

Fifty yards away, Ser Milus was walling the company's dying horses off from the rest of the army. He had no idea what was killing his horses, but he'd seen enough war to fear infection and the rapid spread of something— some horrible equine plague. Or a curse, or a hermetical working.

The horses at the back of the column were dying, and his own sight told him those at the front were not.

But men were turning and riding back to see.

He ordered men on foot to run forward and order the rest of the army to ride on, and then he thought of Morgon's box. But by then it was too late, and his beautiful eastern riding horse retched black bile and fell, and Milus was on the ground.

The first horse to fall exploded. And the air filled with fine black spores.

Morgon was less impressed by the spores. Spores he knew how to handle. Morgon raised *potentia,* made *ops,* and cast, almost without access to the *aethereal* or his palace. He could work fire without conscious access to his powers.

The cloud of spores flared and was gone.

Another dead horse exploded, and another.

Mortirmir cast, and cast.

Somewhere between the sixth horse and the ninth, he saw a more elegant solution. He dug the tip of his dagger into the sticky black stuff and used a simple *like to like* equivocation, and then displaced the stuff with fire.

He had not thought through all the ramifications of his working, and he was shocked to see several horses burn—screaming—or explode into fire without ever seeming to have contracted the plague. He had thought far enough ahead to protect the original sample on the wyvern's talons.

The rest burned.

An hour later, Ser Milus looked over his rearguard—now fewer than one man in ten was mounted.

They'd lost horses but none of the oxen. They'd lost almost all the company's remounts and more than half of the war horses.

They were on foot on the rolling, gravelly fields at the foot of the Green Hills.

Milus did what he could, ordering the baggage wagons loaded with armour and weapons, to make his column march faster. The Emperor pressed ahead. Milus had all but ordered him to do so. They had the captain's schedule, after all.

It was the following morning before they received an imperial messenger, and they could send the word to the other columns. By then, it was too late.

North of Albinkirk, a deep V-formation of barghasts struck Ser John Crayford's powerful armoured column at last light, just as the camp was being prepared. The bird-like reptiles swept in over the ancient trees...and were met by a rising, steel-tipped sleet of arrows. Three died immediately, and six more of the great avians were badly wounded, and their captain turned away, shrieking his rage. The attack was inept and the humans well prepared.

It was sheer bad luck that the youngest barghast to die fell almost atop the horse lines.

Mag's response was more effective, but she came to the problem late, summoned in the falling darkness only after the horse herd was infected and the spores were flying. But she, too, solved the spores with a *like to like* working. She was a far better healer than Morgon, and managed to save more than a few horses already infected. But she had to treat them one by one, and they tended to die too fast for her to be truly effective.

She saved almost seventy-five war horses. They lost almost a thousand animals altogether, and when the sun rose the next day, Ser John was still forty miles south of Dorling, and his whole column was on foot.

"Why not simply set the plague-motes on the men?" Thorn asked—although he already knew the answer.

"Men are much stronger against such sorceries than animals," Ash said. "And I want the men all together. Their time will come, and they will experience my power. But I will not spring my trap too soon."

He desires a great battle on his own terms—a great battle in which many will die. And every death will enrich him and his infernal eggs, until they all hatch. Even the one in my head. Thorn considered this a moment.

And then he will manifest, I believe. Is it blood? Is it the fleeing of souls into the aether? What is the source of his power?

Why can he not see the Dark Sun?

If I were close enough to the Dark Sun...

Thorn passed the time, as he moved his army of the Wild south in the thick, wooded hills and swamps of the southern Adnacrags, in moving things and creatures on the so-called Wyrm's Way. On his fourth attempt, he stood holding a turtle egg in his hand, and when he arrived at the end of his displacement, his hand was empty. The turtle egg lay in a pool of yellow yolk where he had been standing. He had successfully left it behind.

A raven swept in and began to eat the egg.

A raptor fell from the sky and drove the raven off the egg and began to eat it.

A barghast fell silently on the red-tailed hawk, slew it and began to eat it. When the barghast was done, it ate the egg as a dessert.

Thorn nodded.

The risk was, on the one hand, incredible, and on the other, almost banal. Ash surely intended his demise—in fact, he suspected he was nothing but the edible outer parts of the egg.

Not far to the west, the dark-bearded magister rode to the gates of Lissen Carak, and tapped gently with his staff. Behind him, the plain by the river—burned flat by last year's battles and now choked with raspberry bushes and alder clumps—was trampled by the Faery Knight's chevauchée. Out on the plain were four hundred irkish knights, in magnificent harnesses of bronze and gold, some riding stags while others rode horses. Behind them came Bill Redmede and three hundred Jacks and, behind them, a veritable tide of boglins. The rear was brought up by magnificent, alien bands of Outwallers in war paint and more irks, these tall and thin as ash trees, carrying heavy axes on their bronze-byrnie'd shoulders.

When her door warden and her sergeants informed her, Miriam went to the gate in person. She went out on the hoardings alone, covered by a pair of crossbowmen in each of the gate towers.

She did not recognize the man below her outside the portcullis at all. He had black and grey hair and a heavy face with a long, aquiline nose. He rode a bony horse.

"I am the Magister Harmodius," called the man on the bony horse.

"You've changed, then," she said.

"Yes," Harmodius said, as if impatient. "I've changed bodies."

"And sides, I suspect," Miriam said.

Harmodius shook his head. "We have fifty prisoners we wish to release to you. They have not been harmed."

The garrison of the Westwall castle was marched up to the gate, bedraggled and terrified. They'd lived some days in an army composed of rebels and monsters, and they had, with some justice, expected to be eaten.

"And then you'll be on your way?" Miriam asked, hiding her fears.

Harmodius, if it was indeed the magister, shook his head. "We are for our own purposes," he said.

"You are not welcome," Miriam said. "We hold this fortress for the King. If you make war on the King, get you gone."

Harmodius raised his hand. "Hear me, Miriam. We are not in open conflict with any force. The Faery Knight has marched to save some of his own people. They must be nearby. Let us only find them and shelter them, and our thanks will be yours forever."

Miriam shook her head. "You have betrayed your King and your God," she said. "Even now, these dreadful things feast on the dead at Ticondaga. And you have the effrontery to suggest that we let you camp on our plain? I cannot stop you, but by the God I worship, traitor, when you come for this fortress I will make you and your dark master rue it."

"Wait!" Harmodius begged.

But Miriam was gone from the battlements. The dark stone echoed his words, and they were lost in the air.

"Damn," he muttered.

Just south of Albinkirk and Southford, three barghasts and a pair of wyverns circled endlessly like late-summer deer flies over the tree-shaded paths at the northward end of the Royal Road.

Amicia detected them after morning prayer, shortly after her first communion with the choir of her sisters at Lissen Carak in many days. By mid-morning she felt them as a presence—not particularly malign, to her new consciousness, but most definitely hostile. She enlightened Ser Thomas and her escort of knights of the Order.

To Prior Wishart, she said, "I would like it if you would allow me to try my own way on these creatures before you turn to violence." She reached through her many links to Sister Miriam, as well.

Prior Wishart bit his tongue on a retort. She saw him do it and wished she hadn't needed to be so short with him. It seemed to her that every day the men and women around her handled their swords and their workings too willingly—that this tendency to use force marked the human condition more clearly than all the other sins of her race.

In prayer, she had begun to consider if it was men—and women—who were the monsters.

The Prior—whose only experience of the Wild had mostly involved killing it—clenched his teeth but shrugged. "Sister, you have talents beyond most of ours. And without your warning, we'd have no time to make these decisions. Please—assay what you can."

Amicia smiled. "You must stay well back from me," she insisted. "When I release them, I guess that the sorcerer will strike at me."

Prior Wishart shook his head. "Then stay with us, and we'll fight or fall together."

Tom Lachlan laughed. "A wyvern and a pair o' 'ghasts?" he said. "Tell you what, lass. You stay here. I'll go kill them." He smiled at her. "I need a bit of a dust-up."

Amicia shook her head. "No. Please—more killing will not help our cause. And right now the sorcerer is having it all his own way. I know—better than most—what the captain intends. Let me try this."

"To distract him?" Prior Wishart asked.

"Because it is the right thing to do!" Amicia said, surprised at her own vehemence. "We are religious, not killers like—"

Bad Tom smiled and all his teeth gleamed. "You mean me, lassie? Aye. I'm a killer." He leaned forward. "I warrant you'll want me around before this day is older." He was annoyed, she could see.

She ignored him and his annoyance. Amicia dismounted and walked forward on the path alone. They were on the western road, and she was aware in some distant place in her mind that the gorge and the great falls were only a few miles to the east. But that was not her work, not today or any other day—memories of that Amicia were increasingly difficult to access. She shut them away, or merely forgot them. Something was happening inside her, some cascade of belief and realization.

She banished her doubts and new discoveries, reached out for her sisters at Lissen Carak and then reached into the sky.

She touched the wyvern. Wyverns were, she knew, strong, almost elemental folk—stubborn, and difficult to break to anyone's will.

This one had been broken—or at least bent. The binding was unsubtle and of immense power. Her answer was more subtle, but the result was never in doubt—no matter how thick a rope is, a knife will cut it. Amicia severed the binding.

The wyvern, six hundred feet above her, turned—and flew away, with a low, deep cry of anger.

The second wyvern she liberated more quickly.

Fifty leagues to the north, while pushing his forces across an Alder break so wide and so tortuous that Thorn feared his army would sink into the mud rather than cross, he felt the opposition.

Ash *became* next to him, an insubstantial black mist that coalesced into a young child with two heads. "Fuck her and her piety," Ash screamed in his harmonious chorus of voices. "I hate humans."

Thorn felt *ops* torn from him and from the world around them. Trees died. An irk shaman five hundred winters old was leached of his powers and then his soul.

Thorn, I am not yet of this world. Give me your power and I'll teach this child of men to play with one of my bindings.

Thorn had little choice. But—greatly daring—he attempted to hide *potentia* in the new place in his head.

Ash cast. It was like the sun setting—beautiful, remorseless, full of awe and wonder. Thorn had never seen a working so puissant and so close up—the calling of a star from the heavens was child's play by comparison. As he reached the climax, Ash said, "Is she the one, though? Is this the will that has defaced my will?"

Thorn had no idea what that might mean.

Ash said the word. Thorn heard it and for a moment, he looked on the abyss, the dark between the spheres where evil lived and no angel dared fly.

On freeing the third wyvern, Amicia knew her adversary had accepted her challenge. She felt his resistance stiffen through her reversal of the summoning.

She felt the chill, damp air of the counter building in the north.

But she was close to her home—close enough to feel the pull of Lissen Carak and to know the comfort of the choir of sisters who waited there. They were singing. She reached into the flowing stream of their powers and lifted her hands into the air. *On her bridge, she stood in the same posture, almost on tiptoe with her hands high above her head.*

And as the great summoning, a masterwork, descended on her, she did something new—something that she had never before attempted, or even, before that very moment, thought possible.

Instead of answering power with power, she instead pronounced on the underpinnings of his creation an act of annihilation. She did not shield—she denied. She did not resist—she refuted.

Tom Lachlan sat on his horse watching the chit. A beautiful woman, wasted on the fleshless life of the convent—he could see what Gabriel saw in her. And when she stretched herself to cast her witchery, he almost drooled.

The burst of light took them all by surprise. One moment, she stood quietly, perhaps twenty yards ahead of them, and in another, she burned like the brightest torch imaginable. Just on the edge between one beat of his great heart and another, he saw her—she seemed a second sun illuminating the world, and all the world around them reflected the light of her, so that he could see Wishart's wisdom and boldness, his own reckless courage, Kenneth Dhu's boundless generosity, as if they were mirrors of virtue reflecting her greatness.

Wishart said, "Oh, my God."

The world seemed to invert. For a fraction of a grain of sand of an instant of time, Tom Lachlan and all the knights by him felt as if they had no selves—as if they stood outward on the rim of the sphere, gazing in at the workings of tiny men and monsters, and the inversion was such that men fell to their knees and muttered that they had been one with God.

Even Tom Lachlan.

Amicia, pierced and burning, said, "Black is white."

Ash roared.

Thorn didn't cower—his form would not allow him to cower. But Ash's semblance had changed and he rose like a cloud of fury over Thorn's twisting stone form.

"Unfair!" he roared. "Thorn—we must move quickly."

Thorn stood stolidly in water to his stony knees. "In this?" he asked.

The voice of the shadowy dragon ate at him like acid.

"One of them is at the very edge of Being. And she—she Denied me." Ash's eyes held not rage but fascination. "I must unmake her before my enemy has a potent ally. Forget Dorling. We'll have sweeter meat."

Thorn felt that he was speaking to a mad thing.

But Ash's voice calmed. The roar of death and the vein of ice retreated and there was intellect and command. "No," Ash said. "I must consider. I cannot have a foe on my flank—and the Wyrm, contemptible as he is in his bookish indolence, could be a powerful foe. I must force his talons to open. But that woman—a curse on all humans and their endless striving. She will unbalance us all. She doesn't even know what the game is."

Thorn thought he knew. And he thought he might know of whom Ash spoke.

And Ash had not detected his hoarding of *potentia*.

Thorn thought many things, and he kept them to himself.

Amicia found herself on her knees.

For a long, long time—almost an eternity—she had experienced something she could only call the joy of creation.

In her mind, the choir sang on.

One voice was not a woman's voice, but a man's.

"Amicia," he said. "Come back. It is too soon."

Miriam reached out with the power of the choir at her back and found her allies—odd allies. The faery folk and the magister had formed their own choir—an earthy green chorus, like a well-toned tavern revel compared to her beautifully ordered schola. But effective, despite singing carefully and softly in the *aethereal*, merely shaping and supporting her own with immense subtlety.

Supporting her.

She reached out—mind to mind, image to image, and boldly she went into Harmodius's palace, where she was pleased to see he was still a handsome young man in velvet.

"It is a sin to seize another's body," Miriam said. *"That seems a rude way to begin, but that's who I am."*

Harmodius nodded. "Well, Madame Abbess, would you think better of me if I said he was dead when I took it? Of course, I would then have to confess that he was only dead because I stormed him from within and killed him in his own palace."

Miriam shuddered, even in her own place of power. "That's impossible."

But suddenly they were in her place of power, and he was seated on a kneeling bench in his crimson velvet. "No, quite easy, Miriam," he said. "Really, you must accept that I mean no harm because if I meant harm, I could effect it."

Miriam nodded. "May I ask you politely to leave?" she asked. "And then perhaps we might build trust towards a meeting."

Harmodius smiled. "I'd like to say we saved your girl," he said. "But whatever happened out there was none of our doing. She's on the edge of Becoming."

Miriam put a hand to her metaphysical throat. "What?"

Harmodius shrugged. "You'll see," he said.

Back in the real, Harmodius was sitting with a pipe, forgotten, across his lap. The Faery Knight sat on a stool made of antlers—not dispensing justice or even holding court, but instead sewing on his deerskin hose.

"He'll come for her," the Faery Knight said. "Ssshe will be too great a temptassshion for him, and too great a potential threat." He nodded in approval. "Ssshe isss very dangerousss."

Harmodius rubbed his thumb along the sticky black tar that had formed on his pipe. "She will change his plans. Whatever they are." Harmodius smiled—and just for a moment, it was the chilling smile of Aeskepiles. "And whatever else it means, it will hold him focused on *her*."

The Faery Knight winced as he put his needle into his nearly immortal thumb. But he met the magister's eye. "You intend to take him on?"

Harmodius frowned. "We'll see."

"He'll kill you," the Faery Knight said. "I have fought thisss foe before. Never direct confrontation. Alwaysss the indirect approach."

Harmodius rose to his feet. "I hear you."

"You would be a great losss, mortal." The Faery Knight put out a hand, a very human gesture.

Harmodius nodded. "We're going to take losses."

An hour later, the Abbess sent them a copy of an imperial message warning of a horse plague delivered from the sky. The warning was timely—and the intent friendly. When the barghasts struck, they found a roof of *ops* bound white-hot air that burned their feathers and frightened them—and the choir within Lissen Carak turned them as they rose away.

"Now he'sss ssseen usss," Tapio said bitterly.

"Not if my new friend Miriam stripped off his spies fast enough," Harmodius allowed. "But we can't chance it. Best assume we've been discovered."

That night, Abenaki scouts to the north of Lissen Carak—out beyond Hawkshead—found the Black Mountain Pond clan and a great rout of bearish refugees moving slowly. They were pressed—at their backs was a tide of other creatures, old and new.

"We'll have to fight," Tapio said. He looked at the human magister. "Jussst to cover them."

Harmodius nodded. "It is too soon, and in the wrong place," he said. "Perfect."

Hundreds of leagues to the south, in Harndon, the Archbishop of Lorica sat in a chair at the foot of the royal dais. Bohemund de Foi was in the full regalia of his office, despite recent defeat and the obvious defection of most of the Gallish knights, who were already negotiating with traitors to secure ships to carry them back to Galle.

The Archbishop was not yet ready to concede the game, and he was not without resources. He had a servant summon his secretary, Maître Gris, who came in his monkish robes.

"Eminence," he said with a bow.

The archbishop nodded. "I need Master Gilles. And, I think, it is time we made more use of your *friend*."

Maître Gris frowned. "I cannot summon him like a servant," he said.

The archbishop frowned. "But he is a servant. Fetch him for me. I want him to kill this Random."

Maître Gris bowed again. "As you command, eminence. But messages to this man sometimes take time."

"Then you should stop talking," the archbishop shot back. "I am impatient."

When Master Gilles arrived, he was covered in charms. The archbishop glanced at him and raised an eyebrow. "You appear ridiculous," he said.

Master Gilles was clearly terrified. "I am alive," he said. "We have very powerful enemies."

"And allies," the archbishop said. "I want you to dispose of several people, beginning with that treacherous sell-sword."

"The Red Knight?" Master Gilles shook his head. "He is beyond me."

"No, you fool. I will leave him for my ally. But I mean Du Corse." The archbishop snapped his fingers at a servant.

The liveried servants of the palace were all members of the Royal Household and all too aware that there might be a new king, that the queen was alive, and that de Vrailly was dead. The service was deteriorating. There was rebellion in the corridors, and the archbishop knew that only fear would keep them docile.

The archbishop glanced back at Amaury, his captain. "Take this one and whip him until his manners are better," he said.

Captain Amaury nodded, struck the boy to the floor with his armoured fist, and two purple and yellow halberdiers seized the boy and dragged him out.

"You want me to kill the Seigneur Du Corse," Master Gilles said quietly.

"Yes," the archbishop said.

Master Gilles bridled for a moment, and then shook his head and sighed. "Very well, eminence. I will need an item of his clothing."

"I anticipated your request. I have a cap he wore but two days back." The archbishop handed the cap, still stained with sweat, to the magister.

"May I ask why?" the older man asked.

"He has disobeyed me repeatedly. He has led the revolt of the good knights against the wishes of Mother Church and against me. He signed a craven compact with the rebels when our army was the larger and would have won a straight fight in the field, or at the very least held the bridges while we rebuilt. And now...now he will not even aid me in holding the royal palace. He believes he is in a state of peace with the rebels. I am not. I will hold this citadel until my last breath. And when Du Corse is dead, by the will of God, the other knights will return to their allegiance. When my spy kills Gerald Random, I will have the city back in my hand in an hour." He nodded sharply and considered what he might have to do to summon his secret ally. He looked up, and Gilles was still there.

"But mostly, Gilles, because I order it, and you will obey." The archbishop smiled. "Now scuttle away and execute my will."

It was clear that the magister was going to waste his time in protest. The man bowed. "But..." he began.

Whatever he was intending to say was lost when the servant's door opened, and in came Maître Gris. With him was a man in green and black, a nondescript man of middle height with a cloak on his left arm and a pointed cap like a falcon's beak on his head. He was arm in arm with the monk, a surprising bit of familiarity.

Maître Gris bowed. His bow was stiff.

"Not so difficult to find, after all," the archbishop said sharply.

The stranger smiled. The smile didn't reach his eyes. "I was already in the palace," he said. "I have business here, anyway."

The two of them crossed the floor to the middle of the room, where Master Gilles still stood. The new man bowed very slightly, the cloak fell from his arm, and he spun as he raised his right hand and Master Gilles staggered back, gave a short scream of despair, and fell, clutching his stomach.

Without pausing, the new man's leg shot out and he rolled Maître Gris, swept his legs and dropped him on his face, with his right arm already dislocated behind his back. The monk gave a tortured scream. The green and black man kicked him with precision.

Unhurried, the black and green stranger stepped over the thrashing monk and pointed his left hand unerringly at the archbishop. Something metal winked in his hand.

"I don't think we've been properly introduced, eminence. I am Jules Kronmir, and for some days now I have fed poisoned information to your people...mistaken estimates, foolish inflations and downright lies. It has been great fun, and I confess that I feel at this late date that I can claim almost complete credit for the collapse of your forces. Because of me, you halted at Second Bridge when a quick pursuit might have destroyed the Red Knight, and because of me, de Vrailly pushed forward later, when it was the wrong move, and because of me, the city rose behind you." Kronmir was very close to the archbishop. "Ah, and because of me, your captains hired my people and my friends as Royal Guards." He laughed.

His eyes flicked to the two purple and yellow guards as they moved. They were unsure of themselves, halberds leveled but still out of distance to confront or attack the intruder.

He winked at the nearest. "What you gentlemen need to ask yourself is what, if anything, this useless sack of flesh has ever done for you? I would suggest that the answer is *not enough*. Even now, the corridors of this palace are being taken by the guilds. I recommend that you both lay down your arms, and surrender, and perhaps I'll arrange for you to have a future."

Both men placed their halberds gently on the marble floor.

"Cowards!" the archbishop spat. "Gilles!"

Kronmir smiled. "Master Gilles has several inches of Witchbane in his gut. I suspect he will recover in time, but he will not be casting any time soon. As for you—" Kronmir's voice dropped to a croon, like a mother singing a lullaby. "I wanted you to hear how easily I defeated you. After that, you die, and, I suspect, burn forever in hell."

The archbishop began the invocation of his ally.

The small steel *ballestrina* coughed. A six-inch steel dart went straight through the archbishop's skull, killing him instantly. The range was four inches, and the poison on the dart was wasted.

The archbishop's body fell forward, and his mitre fell to the floor with a silken rustle. The two purple and yellow thugs were kneeling on the floor.

Kronmir looked around, admiring his effect. Then he stepped up to the great arched window, leaned out, and jumped for the moat, his precious *ballestrina* clutched close.

Before Maître Gris could drag in another sobbing breath, a dozen Guild crossbowmen burst in through the main doors and rushed the room. They were on edge, weapons cocked and their captain had a drawn and bloodied sword, but they were steady enough that they did not shoot the two dis-armed haberdiers.

"By the rood!" spat the captain, a heavy man from the Butcher's Guild. "The bloody archbishop is dead!" He touched the magister, who lay sobbing on the floor. "Christ!" he muttered. "Witchbane!"

But despite the blood and the misery, the captain sounded relieved, and so, ten minutes later, was Ser Gerald Random now in full possession of the palace. He looked down at the archbishop's rapidly cooling corpse.

"*Sic transit gloria mundi*," he said. "Take the others, and keep them under guard."

Less than fifty paces away, Jules Kronmir was climbing out of the moat in broad daylight, the least elegant part of his plan. But he made it over the low retaining wall into a cart where Lucca, his best blade, waited with dry clothes in a tinker's donkey cart.

"What now, boss?" Lucca asked.

Kronmir had on a dry shirt and hose. He leaned back against the wall. "I think we'd like a ship," he said. "To Venike. I am only guessing. But employers like it when you plan ahead."

Lucca looked around as if a horde of boglins had just appeared. "Venike? Is it that bad? Are they on to us?"

Kronmir laughed. "There is no longer a 'they' to be 'on to us,'" he said. "Our side is in possession. And all the dirty work is done." He took the flask of wine that Lucca offered him, drank some and smiled his approval.

"Possibly my best work," he added.

Chapter Fourteen

Sixty leagues south of South Ford, moving the so-called royal army had become an exercise in metaphysical logistics. They'd had two days of solid rain and everyone was soaked to the skin, ill-tempered and bug-bitten.

The sky was always full of an enemy and, according to the messages received, that enemy carried a pestilence deadly to every horse in the army. The captain, as the most powerful magister present, found himself awake all day and all night, and had three skirmishes with them before the cunning predators retired to higher altitudes.

But the captain's need for sleep—his own weakness—and a need to rid himself of the omnipresent enemy made for the delay. He ordered the column to halt in an easily defended wagon camp just west of the gorge while he waited for the Queen's party, a day behind, to catch up.

The lost day was welcomed by many—dry bowstrings and dry clothes cooked yellow at fires, as if nature, too, had decreed a day of rest. Out of a misty morning came a bright afternoon. Men wandered about—walking out into the pristine woodlands or along the gorge in chaotic patterns that hid—to those above—that more were leaving camp than returning. The sun dappled the glades around the camp and lit the bright green leaves and the last farmer's fields of the now distant Brogat, and the men and women, Alban, Occitan and Morean, settled in to a good meal with heavy guards. Sukey's girls carried mess kettles out to the mounted vedettes and Gelfred's partisans and tried not to giggle as they passed rows of hungry men in hastily dug trenches. The guard changed an hour before sunset, and heavy patrols suddenly launched from both ends of the camp.

They found nothing, but they made the captain feel better, and they put on a good show for the distant barghasts.

Just at the edge of night, the Queen's party came in, trailing the monstrous avians like picnickers trailing mosquitoes.

Gabriel was ready—indeed, ever since the Queen had come back into his range, he'd been in contact with her, and now, both used weak counters and cast reckless and inaccurate missiles until the barghasts grew bold. Swooping from the safety of their altitude, they dropped on the Queen's party as they rode, fully exposed, along the low path in the gorge's edge. They leaped like wolves upon sheep.

Sheep seldom have hundreds of professional soldiers guarding them. Nor was the animal cunning of the barghast any match for Gelfred's hunter mind. He had designed the ambush, complete to slaughtered sheep left in forest openings—and crossbowmen in trees with woven leaf screens who could loose their bolts *down* into the gorge where the overbold barghasts circled *below* the archers, trapped like trout against a beaver dam.

Every caster present, no matter how lowly, cast together on the first shrill of the horns, and twenty-one set to frame the words *Fiat Lux*. Every avian was surrounded in a nimbus of light that perfectly outlined them against the darkening sky—

Before Desiderata's golden light began to pluck them from the air, before the captain rose from his body, dangerously exposed, to chase the last two down—before that, the population of barghasts was culled in a sheet of forged iron tips and heavy bodkin points and quarter-pound arrows. An ancient wyvern—an important clan leader—died in a moment.

The sky was empty.

The mood in camp was festive as the Queen dismounted and Ser Ranald caught her down and then held her arm as she swayed. Behind her, Rowan, the new Lorican wet-nurse, fed the baby, who had slept through the attack and all the consequent archery and sorcery and now looked around with wide-eyed curiosity at the adult exaltation.

The Red Knight bent his knee and kissed the Queen's hand. "Another good victory for your grace," he said.

"Another good victory for my captain," she allowed. "Come, Ser Gabriel. I wish to read all the dispatches."

"Grim reading, your grace," he said, and motioned to Toby to start lighting candles in his pavilion. The Queen had acquired courtiers and new men—but he knew most of them and he also knew his sole power over her would not last long. Corcy was at her side, and that seemed well enough. There were two pretty younger men he didn't know at all. And Towbray. The earl looked like a tired old falcon—bedraggled and yet still dangerous.

There was Blanche. Their eyes crossed, and she flushed, looked away, and frowned.

Damn.

Nicomedes laid out glasses and Alcaeus opened a leather pouch and stacked the messages in the neat imperial order of times and dates. Becca Almspend put a hand gently on the Queen's arm and then pulled out her spectacles and began to read.

"You see? I'm not even allowed to read my own messages," the Queen said.

"Not your own, your grace, but my master the Emperor's," Ser Alcaeus said. "Loaned to you perhaps."

A frosty silence lay over the table.

"Alcaeus?" the captain said, in that particular voice.

A pause.

"My apologies, your grace. I felt a point needed to be made, but I have spoken ill." Alcaeus's voice was silky with twenty years of surviving various courts, but his brow sprung beads of sweat.

Lady Almspend looked up from the dispatches. "I'm sure we all know the debt of gratitude we owe the Emperor in these dark days," she said.

Michael cleared his throat. Francis Atcourt looked out the pavilion wall at the suddenly fascinating tail end of the sunset.

"Right," the Red Knight snapped. "We all love each other. And each other's intelligence services."

Ser Ranald laughed aloud. "I think you'll love this particular well, my lord," he said, and handed Ser Gabriel a small twist of parchment.

Gabriel laughed aloud. "Well, I for one am going to hell," he said. "Because I find this delightful. Someone has gifted the archbishop six inches of steel—some sort of small crossbow bolt. I wonder how that might have come about?"

"Dead?" Michael asked. His eyes were on his father.

"Very satisfactorily dead," Ser Gabriel said, with relish. "What good... luck." He looked up and his eyes met Towbray's. "Don't you think, my lord, that it is remarkable how these events occur? That those who most offend her grace—die."

Towbray shot to his feet. "Is that a threat?" he asked, hand on his dagger.

The Red Knight sat back. Both his hands were visible. "Yes," he said.

He and the Queen exchanged a glance.

Towbray glared at his son. "If that's how you view me, I'll take my knights and retire to my estates," he said.

Ser Gabriel shook his head. "A man can die very quickly on his estates. I think you should ride with us, and get to know your son again, and perhaps meet his excellent wife. I promise you, my lord, that as long as you are with us and serving her grace's interests, you are perfectly safe. Well— apart from the boglins and barghasts."

Now the Queen smiled. "My brave Towbray needs no further threats," she said, her voice as pure gold as her magick. "I will keep him by my side for his good company and good counsel, and we'll have no more of this."

Throughout, Lady Almspend kept reading, the Queen's son kept feeding, and Toby and Blanche continued to serve their master and mistress. The service went on—food was served, wine brought.

Out in the darkness, the moon rose, the watch changed, and suddenly Sukey's voice could be heard. "Grow up in a barn, you useless fuck?" and all the gentles at table laughed or giggled.

Almspend handed the dispatches back to Ser Alcaeus. Charts and maps were unrolled—now scarred with many plans and many daggers.

Gelfred appeared out of the night, dressed in black, and with him was Donald Dhu's son Kenneth, dressed in deerskin and mail. Both settled into seats that Toby unfolded for them, as if their coming was appointed and ended some preliminaries.

"So," the captain said. "We lost a day, and the red banda's lost all their horses. There's worse to come. We know we've already lost messenger birds."

"How?" the Queen asked with real interest.

"Every message is numbered and we often sent duplicates. And we resend digests with lists of messages by dispatch rider and sometimes by occult means." Alcaeus failed to keep the smug and civilized superiority from his voice.

"Your grace, the Moreans—the Emperor—have more than a thousand years of experience at this, since Livia herself and her Legio XVIII came here." The Red Knight smiled at his unnecessary display of historical knowledge and Alcaeus grinned at his erudition.

"So glad we all know which legion came with the Empress," Francis Atcourt muttered.

"May I continue?" Ser Gabriel went on, as if he had not provided his own digression. "We're missing birds. Every bird we lose slows our communications and limits our knowledge. It's only going to get worse." He looked around. "Second, the red banda's little disaster is going to slow them. It's not a catastrophic loss, except that the Emperor will not have Ser Milus on whom to rely in the event of a crisis."

Ser Michael shook his head. "Meaning he's dumb as two thick planks and now he has no minder."

Ser Gabriel shook his head. "I *hope* it's not so bad as that—there's some good heads there. But with all courtesy to Ser Alcaeus, the Moreans can become quite pliable when the Emperor is in the field. I fear for them and I wish Tom would get there."

"Sweet Christ, my lord, you're suggesting that Tom Lachlan will be the voice of reason?" Ser Michael laughed ruefully.

There was a brief silence.

"I really wish you hadn't put it that way," Ser Gabriel said. He looked around. "In the good news category, we're shot of the archbishop and all of his baggage. Anyone else have anything positive to offer?" he asked.

Gelfred nodded. "Dan Favour's ride north made contact with Count

Zac's southernmost patrol. We're that close. Will Starling says Ser Tom and Amicia are two days ahead of us at the top of the gorge."

Gabriel made a face. "That's slow. They must have had trouble."

Michael shook his head. "We've been fast," he said. "Ask anyone." He rubbed the seat of his pants, and Desiderata laughed.

The Red Knight took a bowl of filberts from Toby and passed them around after taking a handful. "So—here we are. South end of the gorge, three days from Albinkirk. Here's the beeves, off to the west. Yes?"

Kenneth Dhu leaned in. "Better 'an that, milord. We're already at the Nail." The Nail was a large rock carved with ancient and somewhat intestinal carvings. Men tended to avoid it, but Hillmen always paid it a visit and left it presents.

"Amicia will reach Albinkirk tomorrow. She might even press on to Lissen Carak. Tom will reach Ser John Crayford. We ought to be able to move fast—we *should* be free of barghasts for a day, at least." He looked around. "I'd give anything to know where Gavin and Montjoy are, or the Emperor was exactly. But I have to guess he's at the Inn of Dorling." He put a large filbert there.

Lady Almspend leaned in. "There's messages from the west—an army of the Wild in the highlands north of Lissen Carak and another coming down the Cohocton—"

"Please don't think I've forgotten them. I just can't fight them all right now." The Red Knight had had no sleep for two nights and his eyes were red-rimmed and angry, although his tone remained mild. "As far as I can see, right now everything depends on the Emperor making it past Dorling before the sorcerer cuts the road. Then he has to choose to come towards us so that the sorcerer is merely chewing on his rearguard. You all remember that road—the sink holes, the deep woods."

"The wyverns," Ser Michael said.

"Exactly. And the same fords where the Sossag beat Hector."

Kenneth Dhu bridled. "Hector Lachlan was no beaten!" he hissed.

Gabriel passed a hand over his eyes and rubbed his cheeks. "Fair enough. Where all the Hillmen were killed in a glorious stand."

"Ye're mockin' us!" said Kenneth Dhu.

The captain glared at him. "May I continue?" he asked.

The younger man subsided.

"We do not want to fight this battle on that road. If we fight at Dorling we might have another kind of ally. If we fight at Albinkirk..." He looked around. "Well, that's always been my plan and Ser John Crayford's. To bring the sorcerer to battle in the fields around Albinkirk. We do not want to go fight him in the Wild. But—if the Emperor gets caught up at Dorling, then that's where the fight will be, and those last forty leagues through the hills will be *very* difficult. The faster we move tomorrow and the next day, the more options we will have on Friday. That's all I can say. So—I'm for bed. I'd like to leave at first light."

They all groaned—even the Queen. But Desiderata rose and smiled radiantly at all of them.

"My captain's words are my own orders," she said. "Let us to bed."

They rose, and bowed. The captain kissed her hand, and then the tent was empty save for a few—Gelfred, who waited to speak to his captain; Sukey, who wanted orders about the morning; and Blanche, who slipped back after seeing to her mistress—to try to speak to Sukey and return her gown.

Gabriel caught sight of her pale face and called Toby to him. "Do not allow Lady Blanche to leave—I wish to speak to her."

Toby made a face.

The captain spent five minutes with Gelfred as they planned—minutely—the best route for the morrow.

"Weather?" the captain asked.

"With God's grace, it should be splendid, or so my weather signs tell me." Gelfred smiled.

"Good—we need some luck," the captain said.

"Fortune is not God. It is God's grace that maketh the sun to shine." Gelfred spoke low and very firmly.

The captain nodded heavily.

"Under *God's grace* perhaps we can move a little faster. I'd like you to ask God's grace to include thunderstorms over the southern Adnacrags, too." He smiled, trying to coax a smile out of Gelfred.

Gelfred just looked at him—a mild enough rebuke. "I can see the whole of the day," he allowed. "You are tired, my lord."

"I am that. Beautiful job on the ambush, Gelfred. You are a craftsman." He forced himself to smile through the fatigue, to work the magic that bound people to him in hard times.

Gelfred beamed. "They are, for the most part, merely animals," he said. "Except the wardens."

Gabriel nodded. Gelfred touched his elbow lightly and drifted off into the dark, his black clothing already invisible, and Gabriel had time to think that Gelfred was getting as little sleep as he and perhaps less, and never seemed to show temper.

Sukey came up. Toby gave him a tisane and he drank it.

"First light," he said.

"Might as well roust 'em now," she said. "They're that tired, Cap'n."

"Yes. Get your girls cooking now so they have a big meal. Then let the girls sleep on the wagons."

"Only got six wagons, Cap'n. Rest is ahead—"

"We'll catch them tomorrow—Gelfred knows where they are. Yes, Sukey, this is going to be hard as hell come to earth. Just keep moving."

"Always the girls get the short end, Cap'n." She shrugged.

"Five silver pennies per woman, paid at next pay parade." He looked up, his eyelids so heavy he couldn't really look at her. "Best I can do."

"Fair. Girls have missed sleep for less," Sukey said. "Best get some yersel'. Want someone to warm your bed?"

Gabriel had enough energy left to laugh. "No," he said. "Or yes, but no. I need *sleep*."

Sukey tittered. "I thought you had the Queen's girl all sewn up. Too prissy?"

The captain shook his head. "I did something wrong," he admitted. *I had a command meeting over her hidden body,* he thought sleepily.

Sukey came closer. "Tom says it helps him sleep," she said.

"I'm not proposing to share you with Tom," he said, and regretted it. Her face closed, and she exhaled.

"Sorry, Sukey, that was crude." He was off in his timing—another evening she'd have laughed, perhaps if Tom was there.

Too tired.

"Never you mind," she said. "We'll be ready at first light." She walked off into the darkness.

"Lady Blanche walked away a few minutes ago," Toby reported primly. "Nell tried to reason with her . . ."

"Never mind," the captain said. "I'm unfit for human company. I think . . ."

"He just fell asleep while talking," Toby said to Nell. They had to fetch Robin and Diccon and two other big men to pick the captain up and carry him to his camp bed, and when there he muttered once or twice, and said, "Amicia," out loud.

All of them looked at each other.

Robin, still senior squire after two battles and anxious for knighthood, shook his head. "Bed," he said.

In a minute, the camp was silent, except for the sigh of the wind and the movement of the rings of sentries.

North of Dorling—Ser Hartmut

The ground sucked at his horse and when he walked to rest the great beast, the ground sucked at his sabatons.

Ser Hartmut had never been anywhere that he hated quite so much as the Wild south of Ticondaga. And his anger grew with each day of chaotic movement, until on the third day after the fall of the great fortress, he forced his tired, wet horse back along the column—really, more like a storm front—to find the shambling stone-cut monster that was his ally.

Hartmut didn't have subtlety in him. "Is this really the shortest way to Dorling?" he asked.

Thorn was blessedly free of the presence of his dark master. Hartmut would have told anyone—or even fought to the death to prove—that he was afraid of no man and no creature, but he hated being in the presence of the mocking black sprite that was Thorn's tutor. The thing's habit of taking the shape of children seemed to mock the whole conduct of war. It was almost worse when he couldn't see the Satanic thing. Now that he knew, he could always sense . . .

Thorn stopped and leaned on the massive spear shaft that was his new staff.

"Ser Hartmut, I am as dismayed by our pace as you are. New events have driven us to different courses."

Hartmut chewed his words as carefully as he could. He missed De La Marche—for all the man's soft piety, he had been an excellent foil and a pleasant companion. He would have handled this better. He was seldom prone to anger.

The loss of De La Marche—and of both his good squires—had reduced the company of his peers—even near peers—to Kevin Orley, who was quite mad, Cristan de Badefol, who was coarse and vulgar and a braggart, and a dozen like them. Of his own knights, only Ser Louis Soutain was anything close to a gentleman.

But he chewed his words as well as he might. "I have not been informed of any different courses. I think that we would be better served by sharing our knowledge."

Thorn, who had never relished being any man's servant, balked. "My *master*," he said with unconcealed bitterness, "wants us to have *options*."

Hartmut shook his head. "That is very like wanting to be in a state of indecision, Lord Sorcerer. In this case, we cut the road at Dorling or we reap the consequence of facing a united foe."

Thorn's inscrutably stone face remained immobile.

"May I strongly suggest we turn back east and march as quickly as we may to Dorling?" he said. "And where in all the names of hell *is* your master?"

Thorn could not shrug, but the stone sticks of his limbs rattled and the helixes that powered his great arms and legs slipped and clicked. "He has other concerns besides us," he said.

Hartmut's eyes narrowed. "Pass this message on, Lord Sorcerer. I am here on a mission for my prince. For all the vast numbers of things that slither and hop and fly, I'll note that my knights and my sailors seem to bear the brunt of the actual fighting, and from this I deduce that my services remain vital. Unless you and your master wish to continue without us, I strongly recommend we have a council, choose an objective, march *east and defeat the Emperor before he joins with all the other forces gathering out there, according to your own intelligence, sir.*" Hartmut's voice rose as he went on—iron filled it. "Do I make myself clear?"

Thorn's eyes were not stone. They held no anger—only what appeared to be immense weariness. "I will pass your message when my master returns," he allowed. "As to your services—this is now the mightiest host of the Wild gathered in many years—indeed, in centuries, here, or so all my arts tell me. Perhaps my master will feel he can be rid of you. Perhaps he will choose to be rid of you himself."

Hartmut snorted. "Yes, all your creepers and slithers will hold up so well against a charge of knights. And which of you has the experience to make a plan of campaign—aye, or alter one?" He snorted again. He bowed sketchily, and walked back to his own camp, where two of his pages had slung a sort of hammock between two dry trees over the bog.

Gilles, one of the more senior sailors, bowed and handed him wine silently.

Hartmut sipped the wine. "I think our captains are fools," he said.

Gilles's shock showed in his face.

Hartmut laughed, a sour laugh. "I have to talk to someone, Gilles."

Later, in the rainy dark, Ash manifested very fitfully and agreed to allow Hartmut and Thorn to turn east against Dorling.

"I can't even find the bitch," Ash shouted into the darkness. "Who is she?" But then he seemed to make a full recovery and became an attractive young woman with a strange concavity—a horrible one—in her back.

"If we go to Dorling, perhaps I can force my recalcitrant kin into the light. If he fights to protect his own, I'm justified in eating him, and if he won't..." Ash made an odd sound.

Then the manifestation was over, leaving only a struggling knot of white maggots to show the great dragon's passage. Thorn played with the notion that his master was deliberately lowering their morale, or was perhaps quite mad. But he crossed a few hundred paces of beaver swamp effortlessly and the insects didn't trouble him, not even the new wyvernflies as big as hummingbirds.

He found Ser Hartmut and wakened him.

"I spoke to the master," he said, tasting the word *master* and hating it. "He agrees. Dorling."

Chapter Fifteen

North of Lissen Carak—Harmodius

The forces pursuing the Black Mountain Pond Bears were not really an army, but more of a wave front. The Faery Knight's army moved to engage them, and everything Harmodius knew of war was turned on its ear. War of the Wild was not like the war of men.

The Faery Knight didn't hold a command council, or issue orders. He merely informed Mogon and the other captains where the enemy could be found—and what he intended to do. Before the sun rose shining above the tree canopy, Lissen Carak's plains were empty, and the forces that had marched from N'gara had formed their own weather front, almost two miles long, the ends trailing away in ever thinner spreads of beings that might have stretched for two more miles into the trackless wilderness. In the centre, the boglin warriors moved with precision, holding to routes as though they were marked on the ground—but then suddenly dropping to all sixes to swarm around an obstacle in a way that made a human's stomach churn. On the left, Redmede's humans and their Outwaller allies moved together in a long, thin skirmish line—the Outwaller war parties kept reserves of tried warriors in their brightest paint hidden, but the Jacks put all their men and fighting women in a single line, two deep, two yards between files.

Harmodius chose to ride behind the Jacks. The boglins were too alien, and Harmodius found it difficult, almost painful, even to converse with Exrech. The irks, once they put on their war faces, became hideous creatures out of nightmare and with behaviours to match.

"You regret what we become," Tapio said from behind him.

"I do. You give up so much beauty to be monsters," Harmodius said.

"War hasss that effect on all the sssentient peoplesss," Tapio said. "We merely wear it openly."

"You do not," Harmodius said.

"My gift. Perhaps my curse." The Faery Knight was the very image of glory in bronze and red and bucksin and green.

In front, Fitzalan came trotting back from the direction of the enemy with a bear cub in his arms. He put the Golden Bear on the ground and suddenly the woods to their immediate front were full of bears—upright like men or on all fours, some with bags, or axes, or bits of armour. They were muddy, emaciated, and exhausted—but as they passed through the gap between the western boglins and Redmede's Jacks, they let out a growl that might have been a cheer. An old bear galumphed to Redmede's side and swatted him with a heavy paw—another, even older, with fur so grey he seemed to have come from snow, rose before Harmodius.

"By the Maker," he said. "There *is* good even in men."

Tapio made his stag rear. He waved to Bill Redmede, who nodded and raised his horn.

A dozen other men and women raised theirs, and, to the left, the Dulwar war chief raised his. To the right, Exrech was lost amid the sun-dappled leaves.

The Faery Knight raised his great green ivory oliphaunt horn and blew, and two hundred horns made their dreadful music.

The line sprang forward. But it did not move like a line of men. It moved with an organic fluidity that would have led to disintegration in an army of men, but an army of the Wild lived by a different code.

And so, too, when they sighted the enemy.

Horns blew. And then, suddenly, every creature seemed to leap at every other.

War in the Wild, Harmodius realized, was not about winning, but about being the most successful predator.

Redmede stood off the first rush—some doglike running thing that lost him three Jacks before Harmodius cleared the woods with fire and bought them the minutes they needed to find better ground, fleeing to the left until they put a muddy-ditched beaver meadow between them and their pursuers.

The northerners were overjoyed at their initial success and pushed forward. In the centre, where boglin legion slammed into boglin legion and the vicious tides of death ran together, the western boglins lost fifty yards in the first scrum and left a hundred corpses as food for their enemies. But though the northerners were bigger, heavier, and had eaten better, they also tired faster. Exrech was everywhere, and eldritch fire licked at his mandibles as he stemmed the first rout. He steadied his horde on the south bank of a small stream and the height advantage was, for a moment, enough to stop the northerners in the water below and turn it black with their blood and ichor.

There was a hole between Redmede's position and Exrech's—and the foe began to flood it, pushing more and more creatures, boglins and sprites and Rukh and some shambling things Harmodius had never before seen, and they began to push forward even as Redmede's longbows wreaked havoc across a carefully chosen beaver meadow on a larger force of shambling things and Rukh who tried—four times, with bloody persistence—to cross the sodden open ground until, led by a pair of red-crested wardens, they went *around* the meadow to the east—and into the Dulwar ambush.

There was suddenly no front and no rear.

Harmodius found himself alone facing a rush on the back of the Jacks, and he spared not, passing an ankle-high sheet of white lightning and following with five massive fire concoctions that exploded into incandescence and left only the smell of cooked meat.

The Dulwar, stung by something from their own left, crowded into a stand of ancient beech trees with the Jacks. The Dulwar war chief was old—his eyes were already haggard.

Redmede called, "Two bows behind every tree!" and the Jacks closed into a ring, covering the Dulwar and then sorting them into the circle.

Boglins struck them some time later, and they fought them off. A Dulwar warrior was carried out of the circle—and three Jacks rose, charged out, and stripped the monsters of their prey. Fitzalan had been first, and his act of reckless daring put heart into them all—the more as it had been done for an ally.

Redmede looked to Harmodius. "Never seen anything like yon," he said. "But my sense is—if'n we sit here, we ain't helpin'."

Harmodius considered that bit of wisdom. "Too true," he said. "Bill, push off to the right and find Exrech, if he's still in the fight."

"Where are you going?" Redmede asked.

"Hunting," Harmodius said. "I understand this better now. I need to go hunt my own kind. That's what predators do, in this war."

Harmodius dismounted, sat cross-legged, and reached out into the *aethereal. It only took him a moment to find everything he wanted—there was Exrech, still spraying ops like a damaged cask sprays water, and there was the Faery Knight, cold and closed, waiting for something. And there—north and east, but not very far—two twin suns of green optimism and potential, burning hot.*

They were his natural prey. There were other users of potentia and ops scattered for six miles through the woods in a riot of aethereal combat, but none of them were anywhere near his level of puissance except those two.

Harmodius rose to his feet in the real, and began to walk north very cautiously. He could hear the movement of large creatures ahead of him, and he climbed a tree with a little help from an enhancement, and then cursed *when in the* aethereal, *the ripples of his working rolled away towards his enemies.*

They froze—slick, green figures, outlined only in their use of the forces beyond natura. He guessed them to be a pair of shamans—linked by some dark ceremony, perhaps, or merely by birth.

Two would be very powerful.

He waited, silent.

Finally they moved. He felt them—felt the heat of their green presence, felt them searching—for him, for the Faery Knight.

To the west, horns sounded, and Exrech's desperate defence was rewarded when the Dulwar and the Jacks came out of the woods into the flank of the foe and began to kill them.

Nearly at his feet, the wardens froze—and then began to move. They were the centre of a broad line of their own kind, two deep, fully armoured—a battle-winning reserve right in the gap.

Except that Harmodius had learned that in the Wild there were no true lines, nor weak gaps, but merely the fight of the moment, the slash of the claw.

He found the link between them. As they passed him, he reached out in the aethereal—*and severed it.*

Two twin minds, together since birth, snapped back in agony and bereavement, and he entrapped one, casting a quick working that left the nearest trapped in a wall of its own dark imaginings while Harmodius turned on the other. Suggestion, binding, ward and thrust—he flung them all in carefully selected order, undermining his opponent with the false knowledge of his twin's humiliating death, binding his legs in a simple and confusing physik that caused the larger caster to collapse, warding the counter attack—powerful, over-slow and grandiose.

Harmodius stepped out of his ward of shadow and plunged a spear of lightning into his prone opponent, so close he could have used a dagger, and his prey spasmed and triggered a cascade of stored workings—

Harmodius turned them on a mirror and let them strike his horrified twin, just a horse-length away, and then stripped aside his working and his suggestion so that each could recognize the other in terror—flinch in horror—

Harmodius finished the nearer with a needle-tight bolt of ops.

The first victim slammed a heavy working that must have come from an artifact—like a fall of rock, it struck Harmodius's wards and blew through them.

He fell—and only the sheer and wasted rage of his adversary saved him.

It screamed, leapt forward to finish him—

Too slow. Harmodius triggered a fire ball the size of a man's head. Most of it caught in the creature's wards, but some went through, and then they were pounding each other with ops—some raw, flung like children will fling water. It was the deadliest kind of hermetical combat—too close to parry effectively—

Harmodius was aware, too, that the woods around him were hostile. But something was happening in the real—and he could only cast, work, drink ops, make potentia and loose again, parry what he could on ever smaller shields and wards as his own workings drew too much—

And then his adversary ran out. One moment, he was a growing tower of puissance, his shields arcing into the trees, and the next he was a burning corpse. He stood for a moment, as if surprised.

Harmodius leapt forward and subsumed his essence like the predator he had become, drinking the alien creature's soul and all his powers.

The charred corpse collapsed.

Harmodius came back into the real to find the wardens fleeing. In the direction from which he'd come, there were irkish knights on stags—but behind him there was a line of Outwallers, killing wardens and taking trophies. The wardens—daemons—were trapped.

The Outwallers began to shoot them down, calling out to them, mocking them.

Harmodius saw them flinch away and gather for a last charge, and then Mogon, her blue crest towering over their red ones, burst from the underbrush with twenty of her household at her back, and the forest floor shook.

The Outwallers fell back before the great duchess. She made an odd scent as she passed them, and Harmodius went forward with her, safe, or so he felt, at her tail. The red-crested daemons were in a cluster, perhaps as many as fifty—certainly the heart of the enemy force.

They were defiant, until Mogon addressed them. Harmodius had no idea what she said, but they flinched, and then let their weapons drop. One, a young female, said something in response.

Mogon nodded, and the young female came forward out of the knot of beaten wardens—one of her great taloned fists entwined with that of a young male, but at last he let her go. She went, her crest high, and raised her small, strong arms as she knelt to Mogon.

With one casual swipe of her razor-sharp bronze axe, Mogon swept her head off her body so that her inlaid beak bit into the leaf mould almost between Harmodius's feet. Mogon subsumed her, ripping her essence from her body.

All the red crests flinched.

Mogon turned away. "That is done," she said. Behind her, the red crests were picking up their weapons and slinking away into the bog.

Mogon made a sign. "Here is seed that has borne a fine fruit," she said, and waved to the Outwallers who had trapped the wardens. "My Sossag."

Nita Qwan stepped forward and bent his knee to the great duchess, whose axe still slowly dripped gore.

"I declare you and yours free of my holds forever, owing none but the duty of hearth and home and hospitality," Mogon intoned. "This is a great deed you have done."

Ta-se-ho spoke up boldly. "We'll take our reward in food, Duchess. Ten days we've lain cold and followed this band over every lake and mountain."

Mogon reached to her belt. "Here—eat mine own." She flung him a deerskin pouch of marvellous work, porcupine quill and gold beads together. Then she turned, and one of her people flung her great cloak of feathers—heron, and bluejay, and eagle—over her shoulders and she motioned to Harmodius.

"Today, we have won a petty victory. Now we see what we see."

And when they had joined the Faery Knight, his long lance of crystal all besmattered with gore, Harmodius asked, "Where is the enemy? Will we pursue?"

The Faery Knight frowned. "Mogon let a few of her own people live. The ressst," he said, "are dinner." Harmodius flinched, and the Faery Knight showed his fangs.

"Thisss isss the Wild," he said. "The losssersss don't walk away. They're food."

Chapter Sixteen

North of Dorling—Ser Hartmut

The army of the Wild came out of the woods behind the Ings of the Wolf like dark water pooling in low ground, and saw the Emperor's army drawn up on the high ground opposite them, above the Inn itself, covering their camp.

Ser Hartmut gathered a dozen of his best lances and Ser Kevin and rode out along the edge of the long grass to reconnoitre. Minutes later, they retreated into the shadows of the woods with two men and six horses dead, and the screams of the Emperor's Vardariotes pursued them like laughter.

Ser Hartmut had a brief conference with Thorn and then filled the grass with boglins and other creatures as they came up. The Vardariotes and their psiloi conceded the ground slowly at first, but when one end of the psiloi line was over-run by boglins and eaten, the whole line gave way and the lower fields were quickly cleared.

Ser Hartmut's sailors and Guerlain Capot's brigans began to dig a fortified camp on the first good rise, as close to the Emperor's lines as they dared.

Ser Louis came up, red in the face from a hard pursuit against the elusive Vardariotes. He'd lost no men, but caught no easterners.

"Your face would curdle milk, cousin," he said, as his squire took his great helm.

"The Emperor beat us here, for all that our dark allies promised us his horses would be dead and his men forced to walk," Ser Hartmut said. While he was talking a pair of his brigans dragged a Morean—swarthy, middle-aged, a tough man with a long beard—in. His hands were bound, and his legs ran with blood.

"Got him off the bugs," one man said. "Milord. That is, we killed the bugs and took him, because you said you wanted prisoners."

Ser Hartmut nodded. He snapped his fingers, and Cree-ah, his latest squire, a Huran boy, came at a run.

"Pay them—a silver soldus each." He nodded.

Cree-ah bowed, reached into his master's purse and paid both men. He was a northern Huran, and he seemed to feel it was a great honour to serve the famous knight.

Ser Hartmut looked at the bleeding Morean. "Tell me about your army," he said.

The man frowned.

"Find someone who speaks Archaic, have him question the man, and if that's not enough, torture him. Threaten to give him back to the bog-lins." Ser Hartmut laughed grimly. "That ought to be enough threat for any man."

He was brought a cup of water and he sat on his stool and watched the imperial army at the top of the ridge. "He beat us here," he said, to no one in particular. "But now he's waiting. Can he be fool enough to fight?"

There was a rapid displacement of air, and then Thorn was there.

Ser Hartmut made a moue of distaste. "Did you hear me, and come?"

Thorn grunted. "No. I cannot hear you from a mile away. Not yet. I came for my own reasons. Tell me what you propose."

Hartmut looked around. "Where is your master?"

Thorn grunted again. "Close. We are on the ground that is claimed by one of his peers. He is very tense."

Ser Hartmut pointed up the hill, where men were digging rapidly, deepening the ditch in front of ramparts already eight feet of packed earth and logs high.

"It will not get any better. Unless we wait here for the siege train, in which case this is our whole summer." Hartmut shrugged.

"I am, if needs be, a siege train," Thorn said. He gestured with his staff and spoke some slow, old, dark word.

Nothing happened.

Ser Hartmut raised an eyebrow. "Be that as it may," he said, "we may as well attack before they are reinforced. Right now we have heavy odds—four or five to one, at least."

"My skywatchers tell me that there is another force behind them on the road—all afoot. My master killed their horses." He bent slightly at the waist. "We could send your humans further east, moving quickly—cut off this force and destroy it."

Ser Hartmut shook his head. "No. Send something else. These are soldiers, Lord Sorcerer. If you leave them alone, they'll get you, one way or another. They are cunning and they have thousands of years of experience behind them. I am your only tool against them—your boglins won't even take up time dying."

"So you insist," Thorn said.

"I do. And so much for your vaunted siege train." Ser Hartmut finished his water and rose.

He was knocked flat by the concussion, and suddenly the world seemed to swim before his eyes.

Men boiled out of the enemy camp like bees from an overturned apiary, and smoke rose, and dust so thick that they could see nothing.

As the dust began to clear, it was obvious that the enemy had formed all his cavalry at the head of his camp and the infantry was busy—on something. There was fire.

"A small token of my efficacy," Thorn said. "Five hundred weight of rock hurled farther than a man can ride in fifty days." He shrugged.

"You threw a huge rock into their camp?" Ser Hartmut asked. "Well— look at them now. All formed for an attack. They know their business. Never fought imperials, but one hears things." He nodded. He motioned to his own men, and Capot appeared in an old arming jacket, smoking a Huran pipe.

"Double the guard. And keep a double watch at all times, with cranequins spanned and ready. Are my orders clear?" Ser Hartmut was warming to the situation. A dire challenge.

He looked up the hill again. "Tomorrow, I'd like to try their works," he said.

"With your soldiers?" Thorn asked.

"With your bugs," Ser Hartmut said.

In the morning, Ser Hartmut marshalled the northern army as best he could, in three thick lines that covered the first slope of the green grass of the hills. The first line, according to his notions, was composed of fodder—boglins and sprites and the little rat-like things with enormous teeth that seemed like lightning-fast dogs. In the second line he put all the men except his knights—willing or unwilling—the Huran and the tame Sossag and the other Outwallers who had come for loot, for fame, or for fear. In the third line, he placed all of Orley's warband, and the great black stone trolls. His own lances were nowhere to be seen.

Despite which, it was a truly fearsome host.

Thorn reached into the *aethereal* and produced not one, but two great stones that fell amongst the defenders' works, shattering two days' work and collapsing one whole front wall of the earthwork that held the right flank of the imperial army closest to the road.

Ser Hartmut released his first line and they went up the great ridge, flowing over the uneven ground like brown oil, the light of the first truly sunny day in a week reflecting from their rigid heads and wing cases.

Near the top, they were caught and flayed by archery and deadly small war machines—springals on carts and small mangonels throwing buckets of gravel. Closer in and sorcery began to play a part as the Empire's sorcerers loosed their powers point blank into the boglins.

As soon as they commenced, Thorn began to kill them. The first was a pretty second-year university student with a solid knowledge of fire— her fire wind laid waste to hundreds of boglins and no few irks before he reached out for her and subsumed her without even bothering to use his powers. She screamed as her soul was destroyed—the utter despair of the young choked off without hope.

Then he struck again, and again. And again. In the time it took a thousand boglins to die, a generation of imperial mages was swept away, and he took their powers and their knowledge for his own.

Too late, the survivors shielded themselves, having never experienced anything like Thorn. Too late they attempted to find him and isolate him.

He began to rain fire on the forward walls.

Ser Hartmut watched it—and for a moment he thought the boglins were going to carry the earthworks. But they could not—they had enough feeling to experience dread, and their losses were hideous.

At a nod from Thorn—a better ally than he'd expected—Ser Hartmut sent the second line into motion. The top of the hill was a smoking ruin— no grass grew, and eldritch fire had swept the summit of the earthworks and the grass in front of it, defining the killing ground so well that some of the Outwallers flinched on getting to the edge of the charred ground.

But Hartmut's sailors went forward, and the brigans. A sheet of black fire passed over the crest and into the earthworks, the only sign of its passing a slight disturbance in the ground—and the screams began. This time, few of the springals and the mangonels managed to get off a rock or a bucket of gravel—but most of their crews were messily dead, sliced in half by Thorn's latest effort.

Now the enemy released their cavalry, and there was a sudden sortie. The earthworks were cunningly built, with careful angles and many hidden passages, and armoured men came from the front even as light horse poured into the flanks at both ends, riding recklessly through the high grass and loosing arrows as they came. The Outwallers at the far left took the brunt of the charge of the Vardariotes, and they died, cut down like ripe wheat.

Hartmut smiled. He had put the least reliable there, the useless mouths, and they served to cushion the blow of the Emperor's finest light horse. They took time to run and die.

Out of the woods at their backs appeared the flash of metal, and then his own lances under de Badefol were forming and charging. And from the third line, Kevin Orley's men ran forward like the Outwallers they were, heedless of the archery in their superior armour.

The Vardariotes didn't hesitate, but turned, cut their way through the Outwaller line, and ran, but the desperate flight saved only half, and the rest were ground to bloody paste between Orley's armoured warband and the knights.

Ser Hartmut hadn't even begun to sweat inside his armour.

He saw a dozen sailors and a pair of brigans vanish over the top of the centre earthwork. And then he saw another man unfurl his personal banner—it flew atop the wall.

He turned to Thorn. "Now we go up the hill," he said. "I'll need your trolls for the Nordikaan guard."

Thorn was black, and no shadow fell from him or on him. "Let us go up the hill," he said.

But the Moreans had other ideas.

Out on his far right, a column of cavalry in bright silver and scarlet appeared. They had taken their time to work around his right flank, and now they charged—uphill into the unshielded flank of his long assault line of men and monsters.

Hartmut sent his squire to collect Orley and de Badefol and rode himself towards the fighting. Thorn threw a massive working into the front of the bold riders, killing forty of them in a single sweep of his stone talons and as many of his own Outwallers, but the Scholae—for so they were—came on. The right flank of Outwallers—reliable men, southern Huran with good armour and crossbows—was suddenly swept back sharply, and threatened to collapse.

As Ser Hartmut had expected, the Nordikaans, of whom he had so often heard, came over the top of the central redoubt.

With them came a tall man on a magnificent horse. Even a long bowshot away, Ser Hartmut could see the magnificence of his clothes and armour and the dignity of his posture.

The Nordikaans went into his brigans and collapsed them. They tried to stand—their armour was as good or better, but the blond, axe-bearing guard towered over them, and the axes were like scythes for reaping men.

And they had the weight of the hill behind them.

"Thorn!" Ser Hartmut bellowed.

The deadly magus motioned to the ranks of stone trolls—forty of them—who stood like statues at the base of the ridge. "Go," he said. "Kill them all."

The lead troll opened his grey basalt lips and roared his challenge, and then they were away, running as fast as a man might charge on a horse, the earth protesting their weight and their stride.

From the woods behind them burst two of the great *hastenoch* and an even rarer creature—a great brown thing as big as four war horses, with tusks stained by a hundred years of prey and a great transverse mouth with two rows of teeth the size of rondel daggers, and four great feet like those of an oliphaunt's. Between them, like a wall of horror, was a loose line of Rukh, towering against the afternoon sun.

They flung themselves into the Scholae.

Harald Derkensun watched disaster unfold slowly, as it usually did, and wrap itself around the imperial army like some sort of malign lover.

One of the problems of being in the guard was that you generally knew everything the Emperor knew. So all the sword bearers—the inner guard—knew the Emperor was not supposed to have waited for the sorcerer alone at Dorling, and they knew that repeated messenger birds had begged him not to engage directly without support.

And they knew that the army was weak on healing and magistry because the Emperor had sent all the strongest talents back to help the Immortals, as he insisted on calling them, to struggle over the last of the open passes into the Green Hills, because their horses were dead.

The Emperor sat, perfectly calm, his handsome face serene, his scarlet cloak and boots spotless. He over-rode each of his senior officers, and sent the Scholae to make a flank attack to relieve the pressure on his centre—an admirable tactic, but not one, Derkensun suspected, suited to the current day, terrain, or numbers.

The Scholae obeyed.

In fact, everyone obeyed. Regiment by regiment, the Emperor flung in his army.

Derkensun could do nothing but stand silently and prepare to die. It had become obvious by mid-afternoon that unless the whole army broke, they would be drowned in a sea of monsters.

The Emperor remained serene, showing his military erudition from time to time—commenting on how very like Varo's arrangements at Caesarae were the enemy's three lines, and how like Chaluns it was, especially as the enemy was trying to break his centre.

The acting Count of the Vardariotes was an easterner with insufficient command of the language to argue, and too much stubbornness to refuse an order. He led his people out.

Derkensun saw them defeated. The great axe twitched on his shoulder, and then he was still.

Behind the rump of the Emperor's horse, he chanced a glance no longer than a single heartbeat with Grossbeak. In that one glance, both men knew that there was nothing to be done. Save the arrival of Ser Milus, or the Red Knight, or some other man of authority.

The afternoon failed, the Scholae charged, and for a moment, the whole battle hung on them.

And then a line of monsters came out of the woods and crushed them.

The two regiments waiting to the right and left—good steady stradiotes from the countryside around the city—began to shift uneasily. Now the line of earthworks was going to be outflanked on both sides. On their right, the Inn itself stood like a fortress, its towers full of archers—big men with long yew bows that they would use to effect.

On the left, the grass ran down and down to a distant stream below, and back behind to a series of sheep and cattle folds for the drovers on a set of otherwise bare hillsides that ran into the east, and the road threaded in among them, heading south to Albinkirk.

As the Scholae died in the field before them, the men on the left of the line—the mountaineers—began to flinch away.

The Emperor rode his horse into one of the gaps in the earthworks, heedless of his foes, and gazed out on the field while two Nordikaans held their round aspides up to protect him from darts.

"Tisk, tisk," the Emperor said, his first words in half an hour. He was unmoved by the death of his personal guard, manned by the younger sons of his friends and closest supporters in the capital. But he was clearly concerned when the mountaineers began to shuffle back.

"Go and tell the mountaineers to hold their positions," he said, as if speaking to an unreasonable child.

"And then keep riding south," muttered a Nordikaan guard.

The Emperor looked around, his face mild. "Friends, I fear the only way to restore this day is through our own endeavours." He looked down into the chaos. "A stout blow now—and the day is ours."

Derkensun exchanged another look with Grossbeak.

But then they were moving. The Emperor never even favoured them with an order, but simply rode out of one of the sortie gates without a further word, leaving his sword bearers and his Nordikaans to follow as best they could.

"Oh, Christ," intoned Grossbeak, to his right. "We're all about to die. Let's kill a lot of them first. Amen."

"Amen," called the guard.

There were many men missing—men who'd fallen in the early spring, in the north, against the Traitor. But the Nordikaans still had two hundred axes, and when they went into the front of the Galles, the Galles staggered and gave way.

For a few glorious minutes, the Nordikaans and the Emperor's inner circle—his Hetaeroi—cleared the ridge in front of the entrenchments. The mountaineers returned to their duty. The line held.

And then the great stone trolls started up the ridge. They were fast—fast enough to catch the eye—and huge, each as big as two men.

"What the fuck is that?" asked Grossbeak.

No one answered. The great black stone things rolled up the hill and the earth shook under the pounding of their feet.

Grossbeak—the Emperor's spatharios and technically one of his senior officers—took the Emperor's bridle. "What the fuck are they, sire?" he demanded.

The ground shook.

The Emperor sagged slightly. "We must meet them—and hold."

"Don't you worry, Lord." Grossbeak was shouting. "If they can die, we'll kill them. You get out of here. Now."

The Emperor drew his sword. "I will not—" he began.

A slingstone, buzzing like a wasp, caught the Emperor in the side of the head. His head snapped back, and he gave a cry—lost his stirrups, and fell.

A moan went up from the imperial lines.

Grossbeak didn't even pause. "GUARD!" he roared. "BACKSTEP!"

The trolls struck.

No line of men, however gifted, however strong, armed with any weapons, could stop that charge.

Many of the Nordikaans were knocked flat, and some never rose again. Others were merely batted aside—Derkensun was smashed back, as if a boulder had struck his shield, but the runes on his helmet held and he swung his axe with both hands, letting go the shield boss, and the weapon bounced painfully off raw rock.

At his side, Erik Lodder swung and his axe broke off a sizeable chunk of the thing that then caved in his chest.

Derkensun reversed his axe in the air and swung it low, into the thing's heavy legs. It was exactly like cutting at rock, except that every blow did some little damage and the great stone things roared and screamed and their stone fists were like flails crushing men.

The guard began to die. Their beautiful cloaks could not save them, nor their rune-encrusted armour.

Derkensun took a piece of a blow. It knocked him flat and when he rose, he had no helmet.

He was dazed. He was almost under one of the things, and he raised his axe and cut—into the back of the knee as it took a long stride, bent on reaping Grossbeak.

To his shock, the blow went in—and stuck, more like an axe into wood than flesh, and black blood spurted. The thing whirled, the axe was torn from his grasp, and then its leg failed it and it fell.

"Backs of the knees!" Derkensun shrieked. Other men were calling other things—that their faces were weak, that their groins were like wood.

The guard was dying.

Now the stone trolls were dying, too.

The Emperor fought well. Good breeding and the best training were not wasted on him, and he used a spear with miraculous properties until it broke, and then he drew his sword and was knocked from his horse.

Grossbeak got his arms under the Emperor and pulled him away from the trolls, and backed away, step by step, and the survivors of the guard closed around him. They made a shield wall, as best they could, and fell back, step by step, every step paid for with another veteran dead.

In the sortie gate they made a stand. A pair of brave wagoners had crewed a springal, and they managed to put a great bolt into a troll, breaking him in half so his oily juices sprayed across the parapet, and then they dropped another, a bolt that took the head clean off a second. But by then there were fewer than a hundred guardsmen left.

Most of the Emperor's officers and friends were dead in the bloody gate or on the grass in front.

Grossbeak had the Emperor over his shoulder. He turned to Derkensun. "We need to get out of here."

"Is he alive?" Derkensun asked.

"Yes," Grossbeak said. "Go for the horses."

The Nordikaans wore too much armour to march, and they rode everywhere. The horses were just behind the Emperor's position, a hundred paces away.

"No," Derkensun said.

"Yes," Grossbeak said. "Go."

Derkensun turned and ran. He ran back over the packed earth where the working soldiers had dug the day before—back over the first trench line they'd thrown up when they'd arrived, a whole day early, to find that they'd won the race to the Inn of Dorling. Back to the horse lines.

The pages were standing, as if they, too, were guardsmen.

"Follow me," Derkensun said. "The Emperor is down. We must save him."

He ran back, his leg armour winding him, his maille too heavy, dragging him down to the dirt, his notched axe accusatory that he was not fighting and dying with his brothers.

He got back before they lost the gate to the monsters outside. He managed a look to the left—and saw that the mountaineers were running. The officers looked at him.

"Retreat!" he roared. "Get your horses!"

The horses were picketed all along the back of the earthworks, and the city regiments didn't need a second invitation.

Grossbeak grinned at him even as two more of their brothers died under the stone fists.

"Best day's work you've ever done," he said. He threw the Emperor over Derkensun's horse. "Go, boy. Go live. That's an order. My fucking last." Grossbeak took his axe, and flung himself on the troll who'd just burst through the gate.

For ten heartbeats of a terrified man, his axe was everywhere.

And then the grey troll fell.

He stood on its chest and roared his battle cry, and three of them went for him—the last of the guard in the gate, alone against them all. His axe went back.

"Save the Emperor," he cried.

Derkensun had his leg over his saddle, his weight already forward, and the Emperor's chest in front of him. He got his horse's head around to see the chaos of a rout—twelve hundred men of the city regiments running for their horses, or pulling pins from the loose soil or simply cutting their reins. All around him, men were fleeing, and suddenly there were boglins and other creatures among the horses.

At some point, Derkensun had determined he was not going to die there. He threw his axe at the trolls, backed his mount three steps and turned her.

"Follow me!" he roared. And ran for the road to Albinkirk.

As night fell, Ser Hartmut sat in his camp, on his stool, and listened to his army feed on the defeated. There were no prisoners. Even their single captive from the morning had been taken and stripped to his bones when the enemy broke and the battle collapsed.

He sat and wished he had wine. After a time, Thorn came.

"I wish you the joy of your victory," Ser Hartmut said.

"Your victory, surely," Thorn said in his deep, a-harmonic voice.

"Where is your master?" Hartmut asked.

"Away," Thorn answered.

Ser Hartmut cleared his throat. "Now what? The enemy is beaten. Was the Emperor killed?"

Thorn spread his stone claws. "I fear, given our army's propensities, that it is difficult to ever ascertain who was killed. I saw him fall before I could turn my workings upon him. It's as well—he must be mightily protected."

Ser Hartmut shook his head. "If he went down, we can have the whole thing," he said. "There's no one to hold it but a slip of a girl and their militia. Not a knight amongst them."

"That is your dream, not mine," Thorn said. "Yours and Ser Kevin's. I gather he won his spurs today?"

"Most men fight well, when the enemy has broken and shows his back," Ser Hartmut said.

"You mean he did not fight well?" Thorn asked.

Ser Hartmut shrugged. "He killed men as they ran. He had no opportunity to show his metal." He leaned back. "I ask again—now what?"

Thorn shook his great horned head. "We smash the Inn of Dorling into the earth as a message," he said. "And then we turn on Albinkirk."

"Albinkirk and not the Empire?" Ser Hartmut asked. "Must we? The Empire is ours for the plucking."

"Do you think your compatriot, de Vrailly, will face us?" Thorn shrugged again. "It matters not. Tomorrow, every beast and creature that hears the call of my power in the Hills—aye, and all the way north to the ice—will come to my bidding. The greatest victory won by the Wild in a century." Thorn straightened, and his stone fists shot up. "Now we will be masters in our own house."

As if conjured, Ash came. This time, he came like a tail of black cloud— the ash of his name—and he twined about them for a moment before manifesting. He came as a naked man.

Half of him was jet black, and the other half ivory white.

"Oh, the Wyrm will dance to my tune tonight," he said. "A mighty victory, as men reckon such things. Utterly unimportant in the great turning of the spheres, but what is? Eh? Is anything worth all this striving and dying?" He laughed. "It's worth it if you win. Not so worth it if you get digested while you're even a little alive." He laughed again. "I have waited in this pivot moment for almost an eternity, and never the Wyrm faces me! Storm the Inn and kill all his people."

"Then Albinkirk?" Thorn asked, gravely.

"Then Lissen Carak, boy. Then we see some real *fun*." Ash cackled. "Then I open the gates and let in my allies, and we feast for eternity!" Then, soberly, "You did very well. I like to win. It is so much nicer than losing. Thank you both."

He vanished.

Farther to the south and west, night was falling on the rout, and tired men gave way to despair, lagged, and were eaten.

Janos Turkos was not yet one of the victims. His Huran warriors had not fought at all, but simply watched the disaster unfold with wary eyes. When the stradiotes began to mount their horses, Big Pine trotted back to the slight rise where the imperial riding officer sat on his small horse and smoked.

"We go," he said. "You, too, unless you want to be food." The Imperial Standard had gone down, and there were boglins above them in the great earthworks.

Turkos sighed, barely resisting tears. He knocked the dottle out of his pipe. He hadn't even drawn his sword, but he knew his duty—to both his Emperor and to his people.

The Huran psiloi were in among the sheepfolds at the leftmost end of the imperial line. Despite hours of effort by boglins and stone trolls and now by the antlered *hasternoch*, not one Wild creature had flanked the Emperor's line to find the ambush he had laid for anyone foolish enough to believe that the flank was open.

Long experience of war in the woods had also caused him to secure his retreat. He raised a hunting horn and blew it once.

Two hundred Huran rose from their places—many had lain without moving all day—and ran. They did it with no fuss and no discussion.

Six miles to the south the Huran rallied. It was the place they had chosen, and they ran to it and lay down behind a long stone wall, flanked on one side by a marsh and on the other by a stand of trees—a reaching tendril of the Wild woods that were just in sight across the last miles of downs and green hills.

They had run the six miles in a little less than two hours, without stopping, and now they lay down, drank water, and ate pemmican.

Turkos climbed a tree. When he came down, Big Tree was waiting with crossed arms.

"Going the wrong way," Big Tree said.

"We are not done yet," Turkos said. "There's another army out there— the army our Lord Emperor was supposed to have waited for." The light was failing, but there were men coming over the green fields. Men, and other things.

"Why do we wait?" Big Tree asked.

"Now we gather survivors, if we can," he said.

Big Tree looked into the distance and spat on the ground. "Like a busted ambush?" he asked.

Turkos nodded.

The first men to reach them were cavalrymen. Most were survivors of the Scholae. There was a full troop in good order on exhausted horses.

Turkos met them in the field and their officer all but fell from his horse in surprise. "Christ is Risen!" he called. Closer to, Turkos could see the man was a rich aristocrat in a superb scale corselet and filthy silk breeches. The front of his horse was crusty with black blood.

"Dismount!" the man croaked, and his troopers—more than twenty of them—slipped from their saddles. Some slumped to the ground and sat until veterans pushed them and their tired mounts towards the stream.

"Ser Giorgos Comnenos," the man said. "Thank Christ you are here. I don't think we could have lasted another hour." The man was all but crying.

Turkos put his arms around the man, although a stranger. "And the Emperor?" he asked.

Comnenos shrugged. "I have no idea," he said. "We charged three times. Then the monsters came. I confess—we ran." He looked off across the hills. "We were lucky—we were in the second line, resting, when the centre broke."

Comnenos nodded politely to the painted warrior who appeared at his side and offered him a flask of very strong liquor. "You must be Turkos," he said.

The riding officer bowed. "My apologies—I am Janos Turkos, and I thought we might make a stand here, and see what we could collect."

Even as he spoke, a Huran gave a long call like a heron, and all the warriors took cover but, again, the men who appeared out of the hillside were imperials—first, some stradiotes from a city regiment, and then some of the moutaineers.

They were hollow-eyed men, who had seen the loss of the centre.

One man begged them to let him go back. "My wife is in the camp!" he cried.

Another, an older mountaineer, insisted that the Emperor was dead.

Big Tree shook his head. "These men are broken," he said. "We should run."

Eventually, morning came. Ser Hartmut had slept ill, and he armed in a sullen silence that his squire dared not disturb, mounted his spare horse and rode through the fortified camp his men had constructed, aware of how many men were missing.

He found them at the top of the hill, as he expected—in the wreck of the captured imperial camp. There, thousands of victorious Outwallers and their allies paraded their captives or abused them—three thousand new slaves who had, the day before, been wives or husbands or children and were now mere objects for lust or drudgery.

He watched with disgust as two of his brigans drew their hooked swords and cut at each other over a woman already so abject and destroyed that he wondered she could be the cause of even a moment's erotic urge, much less a murderous rage.

He reached down and, with a flick of his arming sword, killed her.

She sank forward over her knees, and her head rolled a foot or two before coming to rest, still jetting blood.

Slowly, her body relaxed into the earth in the final embrace of the dead, where every muscle surrenders to gravity.

The two soldiers paused, swords drawn, and looked at him.

"I've saved both your lives, you fools," he said. "Get back to camp."

An hour later, with a hundred lances at his back and all of Orley's men, he began to clear the enemy camp. He and his knights systematically killed the enemy's camp followers and terrified their own allies into quitting the ground. At some point, the routiers and the sailors joined the massacre. It didn't take as long as he'd expected.

He ordered the whole camp burned, and turned his back on it.

Still there were new faces in his camp—haunted women, mostly young, and a dozen boys. And hundreds—even thousands—of their north Huran allies took their booty, which was by Outwaller standards immense, and their slaves—the cannier warriors had saved them—loaded their horses or their travois, or even their new captives, and abandoned the army, going north.

He went to Thorn.

"You must stop this, or we will have no Outwallers at all," he said.

Thorn stood on the hillside, looking down at the column of Hurans and other northerners quitting the army. "You know that most of the captives they take will be adopted, and become Huran?" he said. "Unlike your people, who rape their captives to death."

Ser Hartmut shrugged. "Sure, war has little beauty to it. I believe the poet said it was only sweet to those who'd never had a taste. I propose we attack the head of the column at last light and kill enough of them that the rest get the message."

Thorn turned his great stony head to look at the Black Knight. "You would massacre our allies to force them back to their allegiance?" he asked. "Are you a complete fool?"

"It would work, given time and a firm hand," Ser Hartmut insisted.

Thorn's voice held an unaccustomed bitterness. "It wouldn't work on the dead ones. I think you still underestimate the stubbornness of the Outwallers. But the thing that surprises me most is that men think I'm evil. That the Wild is the enemy." His eyes bored into Ser Hartmut's. "You have just massacred three thousand innocents to make sure your schedule is kept."

"It is not my schedule, but yours," Hartmut snapped. "And I merely do the hard things that need doing. I do not enjoy killing children. But sometimes such things must be done. If you are finished with your lilly-white moralizing, perhaps we can get the army into motion—the army that took more losses from defection than from battle."

"We will gain that many again in new adherents," Thorn said wearily, as if the process bored him. "They are already coming in."

"We need to march, nonetheless." Ser Hartmut was adamant.

Thorn waved a hand. "Let us wait a day. The northern wardens are close—let us at least bring them in." He paused. "And my master will want to take the Inn."

Indeed, the Inn still stood, its out-walls untouched, and was still heavily garrisoned. It had taken in many fleeing Morean soldiers and their women.

"An inn? I'll have it in an hour. Not a full day," Hartmut spat. "There are other armies in the field. So you have said."

Thorn stirred. "My master says little."

Ser Hartmut struggled with his temper and instead said, "Perhaps it is time to collect information ourselves?"

Thorn looked at him a long time. A man screamed—two Galles held him while a dozen boglins began to eat him. Men began to wager.

People laughed.

"This is who people really are, you know," Hartmut said quietly.

Thorn grunted. "So *my master* says. The two of you must get along well." He watched the atrocity and tried to remember who he had once been. He sighed. "I will try and get the wyverns to fly. Their losses have been terrible.

All our flying creatures have been decimated." Thorn shook his head. "I love the wyverns."

Hartmut spat. "This is not a time for petty likes or dislikes. I'll speak plainly, Lord Sorcerer. Your master is either mad, or has a plan that does not—mesh—with the plans my own royal master has made—or worse. I suspect betrayal. I wonder at his disinterest in our battle, our victory, the Emperor—I'm not a fool, Lord Sorcerer. He has a different objective than mere military victory."

Thorn regarded him again for a long time. One of his great arms moved, and his spear-staff traced lines in the leaf mould.

"Beware of voicing such things," Thorn said. "For myself, I have no doubts." He looked around. "Put your energies into taking the Inn."

Thorn turned on his heel and walked away, leaving the Black Knight standing in the leaf mould. He turned to walk away, and a thought struck him, and he paused, looking back.

I am never alone.

There it was, scratched in the dirt.

Hartmut ran two fingers through his black beard.

"By Satan's crotch," he whispered. And then, smiled.

Gilson's Hole—Ser John Crayford

Two days' march south of the ruin of the imperial camp, Ser John Crayford was sitting, utterly indecisive, in the clearing that had once been the village of Gilson's Hole.

No one lived there. It was just three good cabins and the ruins of six others, and a common that had once been grass and was now mud and raspberries.

Ser Ricar and Ser Alison—Sauce—reined in by him.

"I mislike it," he said. He was tired and saddle sore. They'd had two fights in the woods and he'd had to come back to the road—the rain had turned the southern Adnacrags into the Adnabogs, as his archers were saying to each other at every step.

Sauce flipped her great helm back on her shoulders to hang from its strap. "Sun's a nice change," she said. "Where the fuck's the Emperor?"

Ser Ricar shook his head. "What do you intend, John?"

John Crayford shook his head. He unbuckled his chin strap and pulled his light bascinet over his head and gave it to his squire. His face was writ large with his indecision. He leaned forward in his heavy saddle as if he could see through twenty miles of heavy forest and discern what was ahead of him.

"I intend—" he began. He scratched his beard.

"Look," he said—mostly to Sauce, whose endless and accurate criticisms were a source of real pain. "If the Emperor fights and loses, we could run into the sorcerer—"

"Any fucking time now," Sauce spat. "I've been saying that for two days, and we're still strung out on a forest road with no front and no cover."

Passing archers looked away.

Ser John reined in his temper. "But if he's holding, he'll need us."

"Captain said Albinkirk. This ain't Albinkirk." Sauce didn't moderate her tone. "This is a fucking noose, my lord, and you have put our heads all the *fucking* way in."

Ser Ricar sighed. "Sauce," he said quietly.

Sauce took off a gauntlet. She'd hurt her thumb cutting wood—they'd all cut wood in the rain—and it had swelled. "Sorry, John. But what the fuck? I know it's on you—I know it ain't my command. But—no offence—fuck the Emperor, one way or t'other. He's got a third of the company and that's my business, but the captain said Albinkirk, and here we are, almost to the Inn. Captain's trying to get the armies to combine."

There were hoof beats—definite and audible and coming fast, from behind. Count Zac had both ends of the column covered with his superb men and women—Ser John never considered attack.

But he stiffened.

"Twenty men," he said. "All right, Sauce. We camp. And dig in."

"Not what I want!" Sauce all but shouted.

"It's the compromise you get from me. Let Zac make contact with the Emperor. Maybe one of those precious black and white birds will show up with all the answers—but for now, we'll dig in here with a big marsh covering our front and this nice fort already built and this village for pre-cut logs."

He turned to Wilful Murder.

"Strip the village. I want redoubts either side of the road on the lower ridge and a palisade." He waved to the men behind Wilful Murder. "Get all the women and all the wagoners. Cut every tree out to a long bowshot and clear them. Close in, weave me an abattis. Find every thorn-apple you can. Mag—can you get a lot of poison ivy?"

"By our lady, Ser John, you're a cruel bastard."

"Aye, madame. We'll see." He didn't grin. "Sauce, I mean to hold here until I *know* something."

Sauce saluted crisply. "I'll shut up and soldier," she said, but muttered, "Captain said Albinkirk."

As if she'd said a charm, the riders burst from the far tree line into the remains of the little village. She knew Bad Tom instantly, and so did Ser John.

Tom Lachlan rode into the command group on a horse so tired that it had foam flecks at the corners of its mouth. He dismounted as soon as he rode in among them.

"Sauce, you're a sight for sore eyes." He grinned, and she leaned down and kissed him.

He turned. "What news? Oh, aye, and the cap'n was rather expecting you to be closer to Albinkirk, like."

"So I'm told," Ser John said.

"Well, this is better for me," Tom said. "I've orders to go save the Emperor from his own wee daft heid, so to speak. And raise the Hills." He looked around.

"The Emperor made it to the Inn of Dorling. That's our last word," Ser John said. "He was supposed to march for Albinkirk."

Tom grinned. "Aye, well, that could be said o' others, too, eh, Ser John?"

Ser Ricar made a visible effort to stifle a laugh.

Tom took in the work around the clearing—the thud of axes, and the six men with chalk lines at work on the areas either side of the road on the low ridge that dominated the Hole.

"Digging in?" he asked.

Ser John nodded.

Tom looked at the sky. "When did you hear the Emperor was at Dorling?"

"Two days ago," Ser John said. "No imperial messengers since then."

Tom shrugged. "I know another way to Dorling," he said. "The high drove road—the way Hector took. Gi' my lads a change o' horseflesh and we're away."

Ser Ricar frowned. "Christ's wounds, Ser Thomas! We could use a sword as strong as yours."

Bad Tom laughed. "If you're lucky, you won't need me at all—but I'll need you. Where's Zac?" he asked Sauce.

"Out ahead—on the road to Dorling," she said.

Bad Tom made a grunting noise. "Aweel, aweel, my lads and lasses. I'll away then. I was going to ask for the loan of him, but I can't wait."

Sauce frowned. "Stay the night and listen for the news."

Tom shook his head. "I fear the worst. Woods is silent—not an irk, not a boglin. Eh? No Outwallers. Eh? I need to know now. My kin are at the Inn and above it, and I won't leave 'em. And the cap'n told me to raise the folk—and that the Wyrm might not be able to help." He turned to Ser John. "Want my advice?"

John looked at the big man. "Yes," he said, not sure what he wanted.

"Dig in, wait one day, and then get gone. If the Emperor's coming, he'll be here tomorrow noon at the latest. If he's not coming, he's been eaten. Captain's sometimes wrong, but he says the fight's at Albinkirk."

"You're going the wrong way, then," Sauce said.

"Hillmen sail the Wild like Outwallers," Tom said. "Look for me and my folk at Albinkirk."

Ser Ricar leaned over. "I'm sorry to hold you, Tom, but... messages said the King is dead? The Queen has borne an heir?" He was very hesitant.

A hush fell. They were all King's men, except the company people, and before Ser Ricar—the King's Lieutenant in the North—was done speaking, a crowd was forming.

Lord Wishart brought Tom a big stallion.

Sauce caught his hand. "These men need to know, Tom," she said.

He nodded and pursed his lips like a girl. He stood, lost in thought a moment.

The sound of axes stopped.

He mounted, a sudden explosion of movement.

"I was there," he roared, in his "Lachlan for Aye" voice. "I was there when the Queen bore her son. I was there when the King died, killed by an assassin. Both of these things, I saw with my own ee'en. The Queen has appointed ministers. There are writs. The law functions. The Galles are beaten by now—I hope. And the Queen lives and breathes and has the King's son by her side and at her breast, and any man who doubts, come and sing to my sword."

Three thousand collective sighs. And then a cheer.

"Three cheers for the Queen!" Ser Ricar roared. "And the new King!"

"I didn't know you could give a speech," Sauce said mockingly when the cheers had finished.

Tom flicked her an equally mocking salute. "See you at Albinkirk," he said.

At his back, Donald Dhu and all his tail roared, swallowed their last wine, and rode away—south. There wasn't even a trail.

"South?" Ser John asked.

Sauce shrugged. "Let's dig," she said.

An hour later, a red-eyed Count Zac came in. At his back were thirty shattered Nordikaan guards on foundering horses.

Harald Derkensun fell to his knees trying to pull the Emperor from his horse, and all the guard were weeping.

Sauce was there in an instant, with Mag right behind her, but they were far, far too late.

The Emperor was dead.

"Our army is destroyed, and the Inn of Dorling lost," Derkensun said. "All our camp. Our people. Gone." He made a terrible noise in his throat. "I'd rather be dead."

The Emperor's face was as serene in death as it had always been in life.

"How'd—?" Ser Ricar began, but Ser John put a hand on his arm.

He went and held the Nordikaan for a moment. "All safe now," he said. "We'll beat them. And have our revenge."

And the Nordikaans behind Derkensun nodded.

All night long, men came in. Some came in in detachments, like soldiers, riding tired horses but with their heads up—a full troop of city cavalry

473

under a dukas, and twenty Vardariotes under a woman they called Lyka. But most were beaten men without weapons, or hope—men who had, in running, abandoned their wives and children to a horrific fate, and now had to live with their failure. There were men with wounds, and men who had abandoned friends to die. They brought fear and terror and self-loathing.

Ser John was an old, hard soldier, and he had Count Zac separate them from his own people by a wide margin. He sent them food and blankets and hot coals to make fires.

When morning came, he ignored their pleas and made them cut trees, and dig. He pushed his scouts as far north as they dared go, so far that they were in constant contact with the boglins and worse creatures suddenly loose across the hills.

He sent a steady stream of mounted messengers back to Albinkirk.

Morning wore on, and still the Moreans came in—more than two thousand already.

"Time to go," Sauce said.

Ser John shook his head. His mind was made up, now. He knew what he was about. "Not as long as we can cover these poor bastards, Sauce. Two days or three, and we'll have saved enough to make an army." He pointed at a file of Morean women who'd stolen horses in the rout and ridden for two days. "That woman says they were saved by what they called 'the rear-guard.' So out there somewhere is a formed body, still fighting."

"An army of wretched men who ran away?" she asked with contempt. "And a handful dying..."

"Sooner or later, everyone runs, even you." Ser John made a face. "They lost everything. That makes them very dangerous. And every day that the sorcerer doesn't come down this road is a day we get more of them. And then..." He paused. "There's your Ser Milus. Where is he?"

Sauce chewed on the end of her hair. "That's a very good question," she said. "Two hundred lances, and they wasn't in the rout. Where are they?"

The second full day at the Hole, and the insects were the worst they'd ever been—clouds of mosquitoes and some black flies rising like an evil miasma off the swamp water. From the north, no news. More refugees, and a steady trickle of desperate routiers, looking for salvation beyond hope and finding it in Sauce's hard-eyed pickets.

At noon, a single rider came in from the west, moving at a dead gallop with three riderless horses behind him.

"Galahad D'Acon, as I live and breathe," Ser John said, offering the boy a glass of the diminishing store of red wine.

The young man took the wine, drank it straight off, and sat rather suddenly. "The Queen is one day short of Albinkirk. She'll reach it tonight," he said. "She's raised the Royal Standard at Sixth Bridge, and the Red

Knight's got five hundred lances. He says, he asks all your intelligence and all your guidance."

Sauce leaned in. "He didn't say, get your arse back to Albinkirk?"

Galahad managed not to smile. "He said that as a veteran captain, Ser John doubtless had his reasons, and would he be so kind as to communicate them. The Queen adds she has made you Count John of Albinkirk." D'Acon reached into his belt pouch and took forth a chain, which he deftly put over the older man's head.

Ser John was struck dumb. A life of the comparative indifference of princes had not prepared him for any kind of promotion.

"Go to bed, son," Ser Ricar said to the young man, "and we'll send a rider—"

"Saving your pardon, my lord, but I'm magicked, or hermeticized, with some working that makes me—unseelie the enemy. And I'm under orders to take your best reports and return." D'Acon shrugged. "Certes I was little troubled on my way here."

Ser John snapped his fingers. "If there's an army behind us," he said.

Even Sauce looked different. She grinned. "Now we've got something."

Strong in the knowledge that the company was behind him, Count John of Albinkirk threw his best knights forward in the early afternoon, and by the fortune of war they rescued the imperial rearguard—two hundred Hurans under a war chief and an imperial officer, and another hundred mixed imperial cavalrymen. It was a small victory, but they stung the pursuers, charging into an open rabble of boglins and enemy Outwallers on both sides of the road and sending them, in turn, running. But the woods behind them were alive with monsters, and Count John had no reserves to spare.

Fifteen minutes' fighting sufficed to break the rearguard, exhausted but suddenly full of the energy of hope, free from the enemy. It also sufficed to teach Count John that he lacked the power to fight in the woods without either a mage or a lot of archery.

He had his knights and squires each take up one of the imperial Hurans on his saddle, and they trotted back to safety.

"Anyone behind you?" Count John asked Ser Giorgos.

"Not still alive," the imperial officer said.

The Outwallers were useless for building anything. They expressed disinterest and wandered away. None of them—except Orley's warband—could be made to build ladders except by force, and even then, the ladders they built were useless.

"Animals," Ser Hartmut spat.

But the sailors had a more proper view of work, and they produced a dozen heavy siege ladders in short order—wood being in abundant supply.

The wreck of the Morean camp was stripped for lumber, and trees were felled—not without some anger on the part of the creatures of the Wild. It was a long day, and an exhausting one.

The men on the walls of the Inn mocked them. They were loud and Ser Hartmut was curiously tender to it.

As the light began to dim and it became clear that early morning would mark the first assault, he went to find the sorcerer.

"We could save a good deal of time if you'd drop a rock on the castle," he said.

Thorn stirred his great limbs. "It would," he admitted. "But it is protected beyond my ability to affect it. It would take less time to send for your siege train from Ticondaga."

Ser Hartmut's temper exploded.

"That will take *weeks*," he said. "Weeks we do not have."

"We have won a great victory," Thorn intoned.

"Most great victories aren't worth the sweat of a single dead man," Ser Hartmut said, "and this is like to be one of them. Do you mean that all your vaunted sorcery is useless against a stone-built inn?"

"You have no idea what you are talking about," Thorn said. "Beware. When you speak of making war, I have learned that your wisdom is deeper and better than mine. Accept my word on this. I have no sorcery that will breach the Inn."

"Summon your master," Ser Hartmut spat. "If the student cannot pass the test, let's have the master."

"Beware what you wish for," Thorn said. "My master is in the west. And all is not well. Storm the Inn with ladders—surely *you* care nothing for the losses."

Ser Hartmut growled in his throat. "You confuse the killing of useless mouths who lower the condition of my men with the waste of precious soldiers, without whom there is no victory," he said coldly.

Thorn nodded. "I suppose I do. They all look the same to me." In the dirt, he scrawled, *As we all appear the same to my master.*

At first light the assault went over the ridge. The assault was entirely conducted by men—none of the monsters could be made to carry ladders or even understand them, except the stone trolls, and no ladder would hold one of them. Given time, Ser Hartmut imagined he might use slaves to build a ramp of earth...

Then he was pounding forward, his sabatons ringing on the hard ground of the old road and the Inn's outer yard.

For this kind of thing, you had to lead from the front.

The brigans had been storming towns all their bloody-handed professional lives, and they were quick and efficient. The great ladders—six of them—went up almost silently in the first light of day, and not a single arrow came down to kill a man.

The garrison was asleep. Ser Hartmut had hoped for some such sorcery from his allies, and he led the way up the first ladder against the lowest wall, the gate wall at the front of the great Inn. Neither oil nor red-hot sand greeted him, and he *ran* up the ladder in his full harness, and his sword flamed in his hand.

At the top—the first man on the wall—he let loose his mighty roar of battle, a wordless cry, and the brigans and sailors and knights at his back echoed it with a cry so savage that the boglins in the valley below shuddered, and the irks looked away from the savagery of man.

But the defenders didn't answer his war cry. They didn't face him on the empty walls, and they were not huddled in the courtyard, and they were not waiting at the Inn's great doors or in the common room or upstairs, or down.

The Inn was empty. There were no people, and no animals—no cups, no plates, no glass in the cupboards. The whole of the great stone complex was so empty that it was as if it had been stripped by robbers, or emptied by a rapacious seller looking to cheat the buyers of his goods. It was uncanny, curiously malevolent, and it cheated two thousand men of their sack, their rape and their looting.

At the base of the hill, Thorn watched and, as he watched, Ash manifested—more swiftly than usual, and more fully, being almost solid to the touch.

"He's clever, my kin," Ash said, and spat. His saliva burned the grass. "As usual, he avoids conflict with his cunning and cheats me of a simple contest. He has taken his people elsewhere. The coward."

"Where?" Thorn asked.

"How would I know?" Ash shrieked.

Thorn tried not to show his unease. "There is a rumour in camp that…" Thorn hesitated.

"That those fools, Treskaine and Loloth, were defeated? They were. Massacred." Ash's round, black eyes were themselves uncanny, and they rested on Thorn. "And their Outwallers betrayed them, for which they will pay. But you know who defeated them? My old friend Tapio." Ash nodded, solemnly.

"I should have killed him," Thorn said.

"You should have, but you lacked the ability, then." Ash nodded again. "Not now."

Thorn considered what the Faery Knight's position implied. "He is on our flank."

Ash laughed. "In the Wild, there is only here and now. Flank is a human concept, and thus, worthless."

Thorn grunted. "Humans excel at war."

Ash shook his black mane of hair. "No. That is a lie. As well say beavers build great cities."

Thorn took a great breath, and let it out slowly. "What do you wish of us?"

Ash nodded, pleased. "Take this rabble and go to Albinkirk."

Twenty Miles East of Dorling—Morgon Mortirmir

The moonlight made it possible to move, and Ser Milus had made it clear that the white banda would not halt until they reached Albinkirk, five days away. At least.

They'd left the road the first day, and tried to pass south and west, skirting the enemy. Instead, they were almost lost in the endless long green hills and valleys, all identical, all laid out in every direction so that no valley ran in the direction you expected, and scouts would climb to the top of one hill to find that they were merely at the base of another.

Most of the men-at-arms were stripped to mail shirts and breastplates, helmets and gauntlets. The rest were with the baggage, or simply left—a fortune in leg armour and war saddles abandoned on the high moors of the eastern Green Hills, for nesting mice and snakes.

"Just the parts of your harness you want most, if you face a couple of dozen boglins on a dark night," muttered Ser George Brewes. His curses were reflected a hundred times—almost all the rouncys were gone and almost all the war horses, so that the archers and the men-at-arms alike were walking. Every surviving horse, including a dozen magnificent chargers, were harnessed to the baggage wagons without which they could not move at all.

Morgon Mortirmir walked on, working carefully on a couple of different invocations simultaneously. He knew that something had gone awry from the soul-screams of his fellow practitioners a day back. That haunted him. He knew those *aethereal* voices, and they were gone.

He thanked God, guiltily, that none of them were Tancreda Comnena, whose family would never have allowed their daughter out of the confines of the city. A wise choice.

In the security of his palace, he *could see Thorn as a nimbus of green power almost due west. He could feel the comings and goings of other powers, and he was aware that in the last hours there had been some mighty shift in the currents and breezes of Power—something had been done, some great invocation cast, some massive working engendered.*

As he walked in the real, he was building traps and fall-backs in the aethereal, *for whatever had killed his peers.*

The hilltops that flanked the road held life, but no thaumaturgy that he could detect—merely wandering flocks of sheep and goats, and some herdsmen who were chary of the armoured men in the defile.

When all the herdsmen vanished, Morgon sought Ser Milus.

"My lord, the herds are gone. They were there—above us, towards Mons Draconis, and now they are gone."

Ser Milus was one of the few men besides wagoners and scouts still mounted. He put a fist in the middle of his back to ease the pain. "Son of a bitch," he muttered. "What the hell?"

Mortirmir shook his head in the darkness. "I have no idea, my lord, but I think there are men moving on the ridges—perhaps worse than men. But my notion is that there are horsemen."

Milus was grey in the moonlight, but eventually he summoned a few of his scouts—his own archer, Smoke, and Tippit and No Head.

"I'll put it to you straight, boys," he said. "I need you to ride up slope and see what the hell is happening."

"Ambush?" No Head asked. He sounded interested.

Mortirmir shrugged, a useless motion in the darkness. "Men on horses, I believe."

"You coming, smart boy?" Tippit asked.

Mortirmir stiffened his spine. "I'd be delighted," he said.

Tippit spat. "Let's get it done."

The four men rode up the slope slowly, without speaking, fifteen paces between horses. They were hard to see even in the moonlight, and Mortirmir kept drifting, but always managed to find his way back into the line.

The slope was deceptive, both steeper and longer than it had seemed from the base.

The burst of a partridge from cover shattered the night.

A dog barked. Shapes moved suddenly at the crest of the stony ridge, which rose steeply above them—still higher than Morgon had imagined.

"Freeze!" hissed No Head.

A voice shouted far away, and a horn sounded.

Sheep gave voice at the sound of the horn.

"I know that voice," No Head said.

"Shut the fuck up before we're all made into someone's breakfast," spat Tippit.

"Sod yourself, ya whack." No Head stood in his stirrups. "Hullo!" he roared.

The shout rang, and echoed off two great hillsides. A dozen No Heads greeted each other.

"Ya daft weasil!" growled Tippit. "Fuckin' scout? Fuckin' dimwit is what you are. That's what comes of readin' books!" He was sidling away.

Another horn sounded, this one closer, and then there were horsemen— at least a hundred of them—pouring over the ridge.

"Fuck me!" Tippit shouted. "It's the Wild Hunt."

But No Head had been in the company since its earliest days, and he sat on his small mare and waited while Tippit started noisily down the slope. "Wager you ten silver, hard coin, it's friends," he said.

Tippit pulled in his horse. "Yer only saying that 'cause if ya lose we're all dead anyway."

"That's just stupid," No Head said. "Death against ten silver?"

Smoke was a man of few words. But he put out a hand. "Shut up," he said gently. "Shut up and listen."

Nonetheless, his hand went to his sword.

Three horns sounded, and one was already down slope of them.

"Hulloooooo!" No Head roared.

The horsemen were close enough to be more than movement and noise. They were big men on ponies, their feet incongruously close to the ground, but the leader rode a war horse that stood seventeen hands, black as the night.

"Bad Tom," No Head shouted.

"You're in the wrong valley, you loons!" Bad Tom roared back. "Tar's tits, we almost gave up on you!"

Chapter Seventeen

Albinkirk—The Company

The arrival of the Queen and the young King should have been a wonder in the streets of Albinkirk, but the threat of imminent war—war with the Wild—was distracting, and the distraction was personified by the soul-splitting shrieks that emanated from the citadel. The citizens should have grown used to them, after three weeks, but they couldn't—the sounds were always discordant and sudden, and there was neither rhyme nor reason to them—just the endless screams of an anguished soul in the fires of hell, or so many said to one another as they looked at their terrified children and their equally terrified cats and dogs, ears back, hissing or barking.

The Queen entered her city of Albinkirk on the second Wednesday after Easter. She rode easily with her babe on her lap, and the Red Knight rode by her side. She was attended by a dozen ladies, and at their backs came more than two hundred knights, led by the Red Knight's retinue, and then the Royal Guard, both in scarlet, and they were followed by the riot of armorial bearings that marked the lords of the northern Brogat—Lord Wayland with his knights and retainers, and the Squire of Snellgund and his men, and a dozen lesser lords. Behind them came the archers of the company, such as were present, and then companies of archers from throughout the north and east of the realm—twenty small companies that the Red Knight had gathered on the road, or that had already made camp in the fields around the chapel at South Ford.

Last of all—a post of honour—came two dozen knights of the Order of Saint Thomas, led by their Prior. They had already gone as far west as Lissen Carak and returned in the night, but whatever they had said to the Queen and her captain was known only to a few. Men marked that they looked grave.

Blanche Gold was one of the few. She rode close to the Queen, ready to take the babe if required, and carrying water and a cup in case the Queen had need. That morning, Toby had brought her a fine riding horse with a new saddle, and she had not spurned it.

"For the entrance," he said, and he grinned.

She accepted it. In the midst of war, and peril, her own troubles had sunk away to nothing. The Queen's insistence that she be treated, not as a servant, but one of her ladies, had met with no resistance. War changed many things. The Queen's court was a riding court, and by the time she passed under the archway that marked the stained old gates of Albinkirk, Blanche was Lady Blanche in every way that mattered.

She liked it. Come war and Wild, she was happy enough.

To Blanche, the town looked dirty and ill-used. It was hard to hide that it had been taken—brutally—by the Wild the year before. A few house fronts were new—the Etruscan merchants had frescoed the fronts of their houses, and rebuilt the fine porticos that had once lent the street distinction. But for every house repaired, five looked at the street with gaping empty windows and broken doors. The cobbles themselves were ill kept, and raw sewage ran down the middle of the High Street.

It was all rather provincial to a woman from Harndon, with deep cisterns, sewers that functioned most days, and where a stream of effluvium like this was only seen by the poor north of Cheapside.

But Blanche took her cues from the Queen, who beamed with apparent pleasure at everything, smiled at children however furtive, and raised her son to be cheered by even the thinnest, meanest crowds.

They were well up the High Street when the first scream echoed down from the citadel. Men flinched. Women hid their heads.

The Queen looked around as if she'd been struck.

The Red Knight made a face. Blanche found she spent far too much time looking at him, assumed everyone knew she did it, and cursed herself for it, but one result was that she'd learned he had a repertoire of facial expressions he used when he thought no one was looking, or perhaps he didn't care—at any rate, she knew that one, and it told her he knew what the noise was. Even that he was responsible for it. He didn't say anything, though, and it was not repeated.

In the main square—scorched and broken and marked by last year's battle—the Queen stopped before the gates of the citadel and met the city's sacred lord—the Bishop of Albinkirk. He escorted her to mass in the once great cathedral, which currently had a roof only over part of the nave.

The knights of the Order did a great deal to aid the singing, as did a dozen monks and nuns who'd followed the Queen from Lorica.

Blanche enjoyed mass—the first proper mass in a proper church that she'd seen since the Troubles, as she had privately christened them, had begun. She enjoyed the thing, well done, with proper responses and good singing, and she reminded herself to go to confession as soon as ever she could—and then mass was over and she was swept along with the household, the Queen's household, into the nooks and crannies of a fortress on the edge of war that had never, on its proudest day, expected to receive even a very small court.

The citadel had barracks space for two hundred soldiers and perhaps as many servants and support staff, and maybe—at full stretch, and sharing beds—maybe forty knights and noblemen.

The staff were overwhelmed immediately. The absence of their master—Ser John, the famous Captain of Albinkirk—was a disaster, and he had no master of household, no wife, no kin to oversee. He was his own steward.

As a result the Queen stood, almost forgotten, in the great hall—a great hall almost completely undecorated.

Blanche watched her temper rise. She had come to see that Desiderata was not unmarked by nights in a dungeon and a day waiting to be burned at the stake. Some of her light-heartedness was gone, perhaps forever. And she felt slights where none were intended, where before she had been immune, and sunny.

Blanche gave her wine from the glass flask in her basket. There was none for the other ladies.

Blanche waited as long as she could. It had only been moments—two hundred heartbeats—but the Red Knight was already sitting—he was reading a report and issuing orders at a great rate, and he appeared to have forgotten the Queen, and Blanche knew they were headed for trouble.

She made an attempt to work through the staff—but they had closed against outsiders, and a senior woman—a cook or a laundress—stood at the end of the hall and told Master Nicomedes that there were simply no rooms for the Queen or any of the great knights. Blanche caught a glance from Nicomedes—it made her bold.

She walked up behind the Red Knight as he sat on a camp stool surrounded by his own men. Ser Michael was clerking, writing quickly. Prior Wishart had a fine, five-fold ivory tablet, each tablet holding a sheet of fine beeswax, and on it he took rapid notes. A very handsome young man of her own age stood waiting, surrounded by other men congratulating him—his face beamed with the happiness of heroic accomplishment. He wore a mail shirt and thigh-high boots and no weapon but a dagger. Behind him was another such—almost as handsome, but she didn't know him.

Ser Michael saw him first and put a hand on his captain's hand. "Galahad D'Acon," he said.

The Red Knight stopped dictating orders. In fact, all conversation stopped.

"You made it," Ser Gabriel said. He rose to his feet even as D'Acon dropped to one knee.

Blanche gathered her courage and hissed, "The Queen."

The Red Knight's head snapped around. He saw her—smiled, she treasured that—and then nodded.

"Ser Michael, be so kind as to fetch the Queen to hear her messenger," he said. Then, suddenly realising where the Queen was standing, he spoke rapidly to Toby. Toby grabbed Blanche's arm and together with Nell and Lord Robin and a dozen squires, they swiftly stripped the hall of stools and chairs. A great chair was taken from under the very nose of the hall's senior servants, who protested that it was Ser John's chair...

Almost seamlessly, the Queen was brought to the work table, seated in a chair almost worthy of her, her cloak taken, and given wine by Toby on bended knee.

"You must have ridden like the very wind itself," she said.

Young Galahad stayed on one knee and made no answer.

Blanche watched Ser Gabriel. He did not fidget with impatience. His hands, however, were trembling slightly.

Under the table, one foot was grinding, grinding, as if it could cut a hole through the stone flags.

Somewhere high above them, the damned soul screamed its torment again.

"Damn," the captain said.

The Queen looked at him and raised an eyebrow.

He cleared his throat.

"We are all anxious to hear your messages," the Queen said.

Galahad D'Acon nodded. "Your grace, I found Ser John—that is, the Count of Albinkirk—in fine spirits, well dug in with almost five hundred lances at Gilson's Hole."

Blanche saw the captain pound a fist into his own left palm—he and Ser Michael shared a grin.

"He reports..." Galahad dropped his voice. "The defeat suffered by the Emperor on Monday at the Inn of Dorling. The Emperor is dead, and his army badly beaten up. He's mustered more than a thousand survivors at Gilson's Hole and intends to cover their retreat."

Blanche saw it on all their faces—all the men and women that she'd come to know on the road. She knew they'd served the Emperor. She knew that they had friends in that army.

She saw Ser Christos, who was always courtly and fine to her with his pretty accent and his funny manners, turn grey and age a year. She saw Michael wince. But most of all she saw Ser Gabriel.

His face did not change. He swallowed carefully, but she'd been watching him for more than a week. She saw the blow go home as surely as if he'd been punched in the jaw.

His voice was even. "And Ser Milus?" he asked.

Galahad knew he was delivering bad news. "No word, my lord, except that your company was not with the Emperor."

The Red Knight nodded. "Of course not. They lost all their horses. Where is the Emperor's body?"

Ser Christos looked at him. For the Moreans, it was the right question. She saw that, too.

"At Gilson's Hole, under the guard of the surviving Nordikaans. Ser John wished to send them here, but not until he feels the road is secure."

Ser Christos shot to his feet. "I would like to volunteer," he said thickly. All the Moreans in the hall were on their feet.

Ser Gabriel met the Morean's eye. He glanced at the Queen. She looked puzzled.

"Go and fetch the Emperor," he said. "Take fifty knights. Chris, it is all I can spare. You know I would send more."

Ser Christos bowed. He was crying. He paused to bend a knee to the barbarian Queen, and Ser Alcaeus stepped up behind him.

"Your grace, it is almost a thousand years since an Emperor has been lost in battle," he said.

Desiderata was not slow. "Please, gentlemen..." she said. She rose. "Please give these gentlemen every assistance. I know that the loss of my husband bade fair to cripple me—I cannot imagine what effect the loss of the Emperor has on his people."

Ser Gabriel walked with Ser Christos and Ser Alcaeus to the door of the great hall, talking softly. The only thing she heard was, "Don't let the Nordikaans suicide."

Then the Moreans were gone, and with them, most of the company knights who had gone to the joust—so long before.

The second messenger was from Lissen Carak—an Order volunteer.

"Diccon Twig, your grace," he said with a bow. "I bring news that the Faery Knight is at the fortress with an army of the Wild."

Before anyone could speak, the Queen raised her hand—the sharpest gesture Blanche had seen her use.

"And seeks alliance with you," he went on. "If your grace allows, he will come here with his captains for parley under safe conduct."

"Give him my sacred word," the Queen said solemnly. "Let him have this, my regal ring with my seal, that he knows we mean what we say."

Diccon bowed. "My other message is more private," he said.

He looked around. "Is the Earl of Towbray's son, Ser Michael, here?"

Ser Michael shot forward.

"Ah, my lord—your wife is delivered of a daughter, already christened at first light: Mary. And your lady wife and babe do well." Young Twig bowed.

Ser Michael hugged him and kissed both his cheeks, to the younger man's acute embarrassment.

"You must send her here to us, that we may play with our children together," the Queen said.

The thing in the tower screamed again, and the Queen, standing—everyone was standing—shook her head. "What is that?" she asked in her beautifully authoritative voice.

The Red Knight flushed. "If it please your grace," he said. "It's probably my griffon. It needs company, and food. Would you care to see it? And perhaps we can find all these ladies and gentlemen food and lodging."

Blanche gave him a nod.

Luck—and a little shoving—got her a second at the turning of a stair.

"She's more alone than she's ever been. She *needs you*." She got those words out before Ser Michael realized who was interrupting.

Gabriel nodded. "Got it," he said tersely, and continued up the stairs. Michael pressed her from behind, and she climbed.

There were rooms in both big towers. Blanche looked into several and they were empty—empty of all but heavy chests which probably held wall hangings. It was a start.

She paused on a landing, let Ser Michael pass, and waited until Nicomedes came.

"Can we get Sukey and put her in charge of the castle?" she asked.

Nicomedes shook his dark, ascetic head. "She is managing a great camp," he said. His voice was sober, and it struck her that he, too, was Morean.

"If I start issuing rooms?" Blanche said.

Nicomedes nodded sharply. "I'll back you," he said.

"I need a tablet," she said.

Prior Wishart, passing, stopped. "For what, daughter?" he asked.

"Father, I need to assign people rooms. I need to get everyone out of their travel clothes. There needs to be food and drink..."

The great Prior handed her his ivory tablets. "All my knights can share one room," he said, "or sleep with the soldiers in the barracks."

She took him at his word. Before the court had climbed to the top—she never got to see the monster that afternoon, although she wanted to something fierce—she was all the way down the other stair. She found the senior servant, a handsome woman in a good blue wool gown with two dozen silver buttons.

"I'm Lady Blanche Gold, and I'll be handling the Queen's arrangements," she said. She gave the woman a brief, professional smile.

The woman shook her head. "We can't, my lady. We just can't—all the men are out with the militia, and we've no one here but laundry staff and cooks."

Blanche took a deep breath. "We're not afraid of work," she said. "There's a war. I'm going to put people into rooms. Your staff can just take them bedding. Let them see to it themselves. Are there empty houses in the town? Looked like it to me. What's your name?"

"I'm Elizabeth Gelling. This is Cook—we call her Cook." The woman in blue nodded.

Cook sketched a curtsey. "Your ladyship."

It almost made Blanche shout: "I'm one of you."

Almost. But that moment of honesty would lose her the battle. Ladies could give orders that laundry maids could not.

"May I have two maids to run for me?" she asked.

Two maids—barely old enough to be away from leading strings—were pushed forward.

Blanche didn't look back. "Attend me," she said. She turned and moved swiftly back to the great hall.

As she'd hoped, she found Toby and Robin setting for a campaign dinner in a great hall.

"I need you two," she said. She carried them with looks and smile—she knew how.

She outlined her plan of campaign and had them fully in four sentences.

"Cook needs to know who she's feeding. My notion is that anyone below the rank of earl takes a house in the town." She looked at them.

Toby shook his head. "Close, but won't work. I'll write a list." He took her tablet and wrote—starting with Ser Ranald. "He's got to be here. My master—Robin's—the Prior. All the messengers—they can go to the barracks, but then there's..." He scribbled furiously.

Blanche turned to Robin. "My best guess is that the whole garrison is out in the field. Please go count the beds in the barracks, and find out how many can be fed?"

Robin—Lord Robin—was putty in her hands, like an apprentice boy in Harndon. She looked past him. "Nell? Get me two more pages."

Nell might have put her foot down, but she was a careful young woman and she knew when good work was being done.

"We got two hundred wet an' hungry horses, Blanche," she said. "You can ha' me for an hour."

Trailed by two very young maids, Blanche and Nell proceeded to pass through the rooms of the upper citadel like an avenging army. Blanche simply reeled off the rooms to the men on Toby's list. She did them in the order he'd written them.

Then she paused and, propped on a doorframe, wrote all the Queen's ladies and servants, as best she knew them.

"Nell, get me Becca Almspend," she said.

Nell ran.

There were voices—laughter. The beautiful young man—perhaps the handsomest she'd ever seen—was Galahad D'Acon. She knew him from the old court, one of the Queen's squires. The heartthrob of every laundry maid.

"North tower, blue room, first floor," she said. "You share with Diccon Twig and any other messengers. Tell the maids what to fetch—they're overwhelmed. Be nice, Messer D'Acon."

She realized in the middle of speaking that he could treat her as a laundress and it would all unravel. But he grinned.

"Yes, Lady Blanche," he said. He bowed. "Diccon!" he roared down the stairs. "We have a room!"

As the rest of the nobles came down, she took them aside and gave them room assignments—explaining to each the difficulties.

By the time she reached Prior Wishart, Cook had numbers for dinner, Lord Gregario Wayland had volunteered a town house that would sleep a dozen other gentlemen in comfort, and had even offered to send linens and feather beds to the citadel. Blanche accepted them all. The Grand Squire—Shawn LeFleur, a man of impeccable courtesy—was instantly understanding when she tried him in private and discreet as a mouse when the Queen asked him what the trouble was. The pages had already found him an empty house and had his own retinue scrubbing and stripping it. People were backing her. It felt heavenly.

The Grand Squire began to be flirtatious. Blanche smiled and moved firmly on to her next task.

"Blanche," Lady Almspend said. "You called?"

Blanche was aware that she'd just summoned the Queen's best friend but, on the other hand, Lady Almspend was the very perfection of practicality in all things.

"My lady," she began.

"Becca," the lady in question insisted. "We may all be eaten by boglins. We can use each other's first names."

"Becca, I'm sorting rooms and I don't know the new ladies." Blanche pointed at her list.

Becca put a hand to her mouth. A spurt of laughter escaped.

"Which I had to call them something," Blanche said weakly.

Becca took the list and gravely pressed the wax flat. "Lady Fashion is Natalia de Wayland—Lord Gregario's wife. She can sew, Blanche—she's not a useless pretty face. The 'talkative' one is Lady Emma. The 'Bean Pole' is Lady Briar, and she would not thank you for that description. 'White Wimple' must be her daughter—pretty?"

"Yes," said Blanche.

"Ella or Hella. One of those. They can all go in one room. Well, Natalia will no doubt go with Lord Gregario. And I expect we'll put Rowan the wet nurse with the Queen."

"And you, my lady?" Blanche asked with a straight face. On the road, Lady Becca had been with her Ranald every night, but the road had different rules.

Becca smiled. "Give me a very small closet and I'll pretend to stay in it," she said pleasantly. "Where are you staying?" she asked.

Blanche paused. She had entirely forgotten herself.

"Good, we'll share," Becca said. "North Tower, highest floor. There's only Ser Gabriel and the Queen, which is perfect for both of us."

Blanche searched her tone for a hint of innuendo and found none.

"It will only get worse, Blanche. The Count of the Borders is a three-day march away and with him will be the Jarsay nobles—who were in revolt before and are now loyal—and Gabriel's brother Gavin, who is, I gather, the new Earl of Westwall." She pulled her spectacles off her nose. "I'll help tomorrow. Sufficient unto the day are the evils thereto—and I smell dinner. You have been magnificent."

Blanche sagged.

"Oh, no, you don't," Becca said. "Dinner—with the lords and ladies, or the servants will be on you like leeches. Come!" She dragged Blanche down a flight of stairs.

Blanche had expected pot house stew for a hundred. Instead, she found that the soup course was a fine egg yolk soup with rosewater and candied orange peel—fit for her mistress, delicious and beautifully served by twenty squires under Lord Robin.

"Where's Toby?" she whispered.

"Making sure the pages are fed." Robin smiled. "Go and eat."

Pork pies rolled out next, and Blanche recognized that Cook must be serving prepared food—emptying the larder. She ate with gusto.

The turkey with raspberries was superb, and the Queen glowed and toasted her knights. The court ate voraciously, as men and women who have been in the saddle days on end will do, and drank to match.

"Cook wishes a word," whispered a voice in her ear and was gone, and she smiled at her neighbour—the Grand Squire, now so polite as to be near to flirtatious—rose and slipped away along the table, pausing to offer a good curtsey to the Queen.

The Queen had her hand on the Red Knight's hand.

A sliver of ice went down her back, and she cursed.

The Red Knight turned and met Blanche's eye across the table. He had candles behind him, which gave him an incongruous halo. He smiled—and went back to talking to the Queen.

Damn him.

Nicomedes intercepted her at the head of the stairs.

"We'll go together," he said.

She smiled, and they walked down the broad serving stairs—so like the stairs at the palace in Harndon, she thought. They went down one flight and turned into the kitchen, which was more than half the size of the great hall, with two great fires roaring. The heat was enormous, but not unwelcome in late spring.

Cook came up, wiping her hands.

"That's all my food, served," she said. "Now what do we do?"

"Buy more?" Master Nicomedes said patiently.

Cook eyed him suspiciously. "Who are you, any road?"

Blanche nodded. "He is the Queen's master of household. And the captain's."

"What captain?"

"The Duke of Thrake," said Master Nicomedes.

"Oh!" said Cook.

"Give me or any of my people a list by first light and we'll have it on your work tables by matins," Nicomedes said. "I have household stores of my own."

"Saffron? Sugar?" Cook asked. "I'm out."

Blanche decided to stay to her role and pushed away the image of the Queen's hand on the Red Knight's. "As you seem settled, I'll return to my dinner," she said.

Nicomedes, a gallant man, bowed. "My lady," he said.

But escape was not so easy, and Goodwife Elizabeth was waiting for her at the stairs.

"I'm out of linens and straw pallets and bed cases and towels—and everything else." She looked defiant, as if being out of things justified defiance.

It was professional anger that made Blanche bridle, not false gentility. The laundry in the palace of Harndon had never, ever run out of anything. "Get more," she snapped.

"But where!" asked the woman who must be the laundress or some such.

Blanche snapped her fingers. "There must be lords and ladies hereabouts who would be honoured to spare the Queen a bed sheet or two," she said. "Or summon your women and get sewing."

"There's no spare linen. Lady, we're poor. We don't have the resources of a palace." She bowed her head, humiliated, and Blanche felt terrible.

"I'm sorry, Goodwife. Listen—I'll ask among the squires. Many of these gentlemen go to war very well appointed." She put a hand on the woman's arm and was horrified to hear a sob.

She buttonholed Toby and sent the squires scurrying for more sheets—for any spare linen not made up. She passed the great hall only long enough to find a cup of wine pressed into her hand and a bit of apple tart. She drank the one, ate the other, and found one of Sukey's girls holding a great bolt of linen—forty yards at least.

"Miss Sukey says her best compliments an' will this help." The young woman was not dressed for a palace but for a tavern, and the squires proved suddenly unable to do any work. Blanche smiled, took the roll of linen, and said, "Please go straight back and tell her that, as always, I owe her. This goes on the Queen's account. Can you sew?"

The young woman—Blanche's age or maybe younger—shook her head and grinned. "I can make a shift if someone else cuts it," she said.

Blanche laughed. "Tell Sukey I'll take every woman who can sew that she can spare."

The next time Blanche passed the great hall it was to answer a call direct from the Queen.

She found the queen in her chambers. They were fully appointed—bedspread, hangings, two good mattresses and a feather bed, counterpane and two beautiful blankets.

She and Lady Almspend and Lady Briar undressed the Queen, re-swaddled the baby and got the Queen in and out of a hot bath. Blanche, without thinking, swept all the Queen's linens into a bundle, wrapped it with the *zone* that the queen wore under her breasts, and—

Becca Almspend stripped it out of her hands. "That will save the girl a mort of work," she said, laughing.

Lady Briar—older, but new to court—smiled. "You must teach me to do that. It will save time." She grinned. She had a large but very pleasant mouth and more teeth than many. "Papa said we'd be worked like servants—but I didn't realize how good you'd be at it. I feel like a third wheel."

Becca smiled at Blanche. "We've had lots of practice and we're happy to have you, Briar," she said.

It was all Blanche could manage not to carry the bundle down the stairs. But before she was all the way to the great hall—her third visit—she passed a pair of laundry maids going up. They curtsied and she felt a fraud.

The commanders were all in the great hall. One fireplace was roaring, and all her seamstresses were there—twenty women and one archer, all sewing like mad.

She was surprised—and pleased—when Lady Briar and her daughter came, got stools fetched by squires, and opened their sewing kits. Lady Natalia was already there, her needle moving as fast as a professional seamstress's.

"Not enough sheets?" the daughter asked. "Happened at home, too."

She giggled. She was perhaps a year younger than Blanche.

Blanche opened her own sewing kit—a two-fold wallet with a fortune in tools and needles—set it on her knee, took up a sheet and began to hem.

"Blessed Virgin you are fast!" young Ella proclaimed. "I've never seen a lady hem like you. Look at her stitches, Mama!"

Briar was recounting a tale of her youth—a youth that couldn't have been so very long before—and she paused, shrugged, and went back to her story.

Lady Natalia leaned over to Blanche. "You do stitch uncommon fine," she said.

"You, too, Lady," Blanche said. Indeed, she'd never seen a lady—an actual member of the nobility—who could sew as well as Lady Natalia.

The new sheets took shape at the speed of needlecraft.

At the other end of the hall, there was a commotion. It was near midnight—the Bishop of Albinkirk and Prior Wishart were sharing a table, and both writing furiously.

Toby came through the great hall doors. He was very well dressed for the middle of the night, in a fine jupon and a hood.

"He's coming," Toby said. "Right now."

The hall fell silent, as if something sacred had occurred. *Like the moment at which the host is raised at mass,* Blanche thought.

As if her thoughts had been said aloud, Gabriel turned and saw her. She rose like a servant and went to his side.

He rose for her. "You should fetch the Queen," he said. "We're about to receive a prince."

"Her brother?" Blanche asked—but she knew he was already in the field, covering the northern approach to the town with his knights and a small force of infantry.

She ran. There was urgency in it, and she ran up three long flights of twisting tower stairs and found Becca combing out the Queen's magnificent hair while Lady Natalia stared into a trunk of clothes.

"My lady," she said. "The Duke of Thrake sends that we are about to receive a foreign prince, and bids you come, if'n you would."

"Gown," snapped the Queen. "Yes—brown. Good. Both of you button it while I put my hair up."

In two minutes they were in the hall. The Queen was barefoot—unthinkable in Harndon, and merely practical here. Lady Natalia and Lady Almspend went back to the better light to sew.

The hush remained on the hall. At the far end, in the firelight, the company women stitched away on baby clothes. Nearer, the Red Knight stood between the Prior and the bishop. The other magnates were already abed.

Toby came back in and bowed to the Queen as Lord Robin and Lord Wimarc settled her onto the chair that could act as a throne—and put the other great chair in the hall opposite her.

"Who is it?" the Queen asked.

The Red Knight came and stood beside her. "The Faery Knight," he said. "And Harmodius."

Tapio entered with Harmodius at his side. A little behind them were two irks, a huge adversarius in a feather cloak, and the black man from Ifriquy'a who had saved Blanche in Harndon, as well as a second black man, this one in paint and feathers like an Outwaller. Behind the Outwaller were two great bears and a—she had trouble swallowing—a giant white stick figure, like an enormous praying mantis in white armour.

She overcame her fear and hurried to Pavalo's side and pressed his hand—he put his hands together and bowed, but his eyes were on Harmodius. She had missed an exchange, but then the Faery Knight strode forward in a swirl of elfin cloak and a ringing of tiny golden bells, and knelt. He inclined his head, kissed the Queen's hand, and smiled, showing a few too many teeth.

"Daughter of man, your beauty isss everything report hasss made it."

She blushed. "I saw you at Yule!" She paused, and leaned forward to kiss him on both cheeks. "You, too, are beautiful, Son of the Wild."

"There's the biter, bit," Harmodius grumbled.

"I would never have known you, old friend," she said. He came forward and knelt at her feet, and kissed her hand.

"I have taken another body," he said, without preamble or defence.

The Bishop of Albinkirk winced.

"For the moment, it is enough that you live, and have come back to me." Desiderata got to her feet, and threw her arms around the magister's spare frame—and the older man blushed.

"Oh, how I have missed you," Desiderata said.

"Your grace," Harmodius said, and found himself stroking her hair. He pulled his hand away.

"Have you returned to be my minister?" she asked. "Or merely to visit?"

Harmodius looked troubled. "I am my own..." He paused. "There is so much to say, and no easy answers. We have come this night to make an alliance. But that alliance must be based on hard truths. And when the truths are said, there will be no unsaying them."

Desiderata put her hand to her throat—as she had never used to do—and her eyes dropped. "I, too, have learned some hard truths already," she said.

The Faery Knight and the Red Knight looked each other over like two boys sizing each other up for a match on the town green. Blanche watched them, fascinated by their similarities which easily overwhelmed their differences—despite the Faery Knight's slanted eyes, bright gold hair, and long teeth, despite the captain's black hair and more commonplace eyes, there was something about them that shouted "kin."

Ser Gabriel bowed to the company. "Your grace, my lords, I propose we sit and talk. Let's have it done. Together, I believe we can win this war—and perhaps put war to bed for a long, long time."

Harmodius sighed. "No, my boy. That's not what will happen now." He met the Red Knight's eyes. "But it is a fine dream, and you should cling to it."

Ser Gabriel winced. "Then—I think I speak for all—tell us." He looked at the great warden, as big as a war horse. "A heavier bench," he said to Toby.

The Queen motioned to Lady Briar. "Bring my son, if you would," she said.

"First, my companions," Harmodius said. "The Faery Knight—lord of N'gara in the west. Mogon, Duchess of the North—one of the great Powers of the Wild, and our firmest ally. Nita Qwan, a sachem of the Sossag peoples. Krevak, Lord of the Many Waters, is my peer in the *ars magika*."

"You are too kind," the last named irk said in flawless Archaic.

"Flint, of the Long Dam Clan. Accounted among the Wild peoples as the elder and wisest of us. Then—" Harmodius frowned. "Exrech, Birthlord of the Fourth Hive of the Great River."

There were gasps as men recognized the knight in white armour as a great boglin, a wight.

The Queen rose. "This is my captain—the Red Knight, Gabriel Muriens." At the name Muriens, Mogon snarled and Krevak smiled and showed his teeth.

"Lord Gregario of Wayland and Prior Wishart of the Order of Saint Thomas."

If the name Muriens had a poor effect, the name of the Order of Saint Thomas made the bears growl and the white thing twitch.

"We can all be enemies very, very easily." Harmodius looked around. "But then, only our true enemies will celebrate."

Mogon, the great warden, made a snuffling sound. "So you keep saying," she intoned. Blanche thought her voice was beautiful.

But it was one of the monstrous bears who stepped forward. "Man is not on trial here," he said. "Our wrongs at the hands of man are not what we come to address. Let it only be said by the Matron that there will be justice when the fighting is done, and we will have good hearts."

Blanche took the Queen water—while she poured, she realized that by Matron he meant the Queen. The wet nurse had just brought her the baby.

The Queen looked at the bear—old, and his fur grey with age. "Will you sit with me and give justice?" she asked.

"That would be fair," the bear replied.

Even Mogon nodded.

Harmodius cleared his throat. "This cooperation—a little late in coming—is splendid. But we all know we must stand together."

"Tell your tale, old man," Ser Gabriel said. He said it with a smile, but Blanche could see there was something between them.

Harmodius bent his head. "First, we must do what we did at Lissen Carak—all of us who work with power."

He and Gabriel locked eyes.

"You put a high bar on trust, old man," Ser Gabriel said. "But you can come to my house anytime."

The Queen smiled. "I am willing," she said.

And then, one by one, they all fell perfectly silent. Blanche watched as their faces changed—not slack, but alert, like people in prayer. Harmodius, the Red Knight, the Faery Knight, the Queen, the Prior, the Bishop of Albinkirk, Mogon, the younger bear, Lord Krevak—one by one, they fell into contemplation.

A golden nimbus, almost like a rising fog, seemed to fill the hall. It covered the floor and then rose slowly to the rafters—slow, unobtrusive, like water filling a pan. Blanche played with a little of it.

Ser Pavalo drank water noisily and sat.

Lord Gregario—a famous swordsman—smiled at the tall warrior from Ifriquy'a. "That is a most marvellous sword, ser knight."

Ser Pavalo nodded. "I show it?"

In the midst of a conference to decide the fate of nations, Lord Gregario, the squire, and Ser Pavalo began to talk about swords.

Men, thought Blanche.

The old bear gave her a look as if he shared her thought exactly.

They gathered in Harmodius's palace.

"Here, I will say what I have to say. I will not say that our enemy cannot listen to this—only that if he can, after all my precautions, we never had a chance." Harmodius shrugged.

Gabriel found himself sitting in a comfortable chair immediately by the old man.

He smiled at Harmodius, who, in the aethereal, *still looked like a young Harmodius and not a modified Aeskipiles. The others took seats—Mogon occupied a great throne of ivory that contrived not to eclipse Desiderata's plain chair of gilt wood.*

Desiderata tossed her hair. "Now we are met, let mirth abound," she said.

Tapio sat crosslegged, and the white gwylch didn't seem able to sit at all.

Desiderata raised her voice. It was an old song—one of the festival songs.

"Now we are met, let mirth abound, now we are met, let mirth abound.
And let the catch! And let the catch! And let the catch and toast, go
  'round!"

She sang, and they joined her—even Mogon, even Exrech, so that, despite different languages, their polyphony rolled up into the aethereal. *A golden-green radiance suffused Harmodius's inner mansion, and a great shield snapped into place.*

"A potent working," Mogon said.

Harmodius smiled. "That bodes better than I might have hoped," he said. "Your grace, you have come far."

"I have been sore tested," Desiderata said. She shrugged, and a hint of her

former self raised the corner of her mouth in an impish smile. "Come—even here, time dogs us. Tell your tale, old master."

Harmodius sat back. "Very well. Some you all know, and some you know parts of, or have seen only through a glass darkly, and even now, I am not sure that part of what I say is not pure fabrication, justification, embroidery. Let me say first—because all of us work in this power—that all of us know that belief and being and becoming and power can be one thing, the same thing, and that renders the process of remembering and history almost impossible."

Gabriel found himself nodding.

"Very well. We all inhabit a sphere—a great bubble of..." Harmodius laughed. "Of reality, let's say. Existence... yes? Some of the Wise hold it to be one single bubble, and others say there are seven spheres, or eight, or nine, each inside another. Yes?"

"And outside, God's heaven," Desiderata said.

"No, your grace. Forgive me, but, outside, a sort of chaos of nothing. Very, very like our own aethereal. *That's for another time. For us, what matters is that beyond this chaos are other spheres. Like ours."*

Mogon nodded—Desiderata put her hand to her throat.

Gabriel rubbed his beard and considered.

"Of these spheres we know almost nothing," Harmodius said. "And what we know is tantalizing, irrational and contradictory." He shook his head. "I digress. What makes our sphere unique—I hesitate even to say this much—is that it is some sort of nexus for all the others, or some others, and perhaps merely a large number. And therein lies our story and our fate. We are the crossroads."

Gabriel found Harmodius looking at him. "You are unsurprised."

"We shared the same head during all your research in Liviapolis," Gabriel said.

Mogon shifted her bulk. "This is no news at all to the Qwethnethogs." She nodded as her crest, inflated when tense, subsided like a fashionable beret. "We came here from somewhere else. Every birthling knows it."

Harmodius nodded. "There are two major pieces to my story. One—we are a crossroads. The other—we are pieces in a chess game." He waved his hand. "The two fit together to explain everything we see around us. We have sixty races that compete for resources. We know of peoples exterminated—we have the rubble of their works, and in Liviapolis, even records of some of their science."

Mogon nodded. "The Odine."

Harmodius sighed. "The Odine are but one, and I would not count them destroyed. But they are perhaps the most obvious. Let me make this quick. Powers—great Powers—vie to take and hold our crossroads. They bring the races bound to them to do the heavy fighting. To hold the ground, as Gabriel would say."

"Why?" Gabriel asked. "I mean, what's the prize? More slaves?"

Mogon sat slowly back. "Yes," she said. It was not an answer to Gabriel, but a comment. "Yes, this is shockingly simple. Of course."

Harmodius nodded. "Another of my order, a great man, far, far away in Dar as Salaam, has more access to the oldest of man's records than I." He looked around. "And older records still, not made by men. This is his life's work," he said, and produced, in the aethereal, *a scrap of memory parchment.*

"Five names. Five of perhaps seventeen creatures whose powers are like gods. Little, petty, scrapping gods." He held the list out.

Gabriel read them all at once, as one did in the aethereal.

Tar

Ash

Lot

Oak

Rot

"These are not true names," Desiderata said. The names shook her—it was written on her face.

Harmodius shook his head. "I think we know them all," he said.

Gabriel sighed. "Do they divide up into good and evil?" he asked. His tone was sarcastic, and the Faery Knight laughed and slapped his thigh.

"They all use the same tactics of manipulation and gross coercion," Harmodius said. "Draw your own conclusions."

Gabriel thought of Master Smythe. "I would merely emphasize that my side has a smaller body count and tends to minimize—negative outcomes."

"One of them is more honest than the others," he said.

Harmodius shrugged. "My order has made a choice: to fight them all."

Gabriel narrowed his eyes. "How's that going for you?" he asked. "That sounds like a typical un-pragmatic solution—something from a classroom. Noble, and doomed. I grant you their power. If they are divided among themselves—surely the classical solution is to use them against each other?"

The Faery Knight stretched his immortally long legs and shook his head. "This is either brilliant or rampant madness. Ser Gabriel, what makes you think these great powers, who are to us like gods, can be manipulated?"

Gabriel looked not at Harmodius, but at the Queen. "Are they all great dragons, do you think? The four, or the seventeen?"

Harmodius nodded. "We think they are all dragons."

Gabriel sat back. "This is the fascinating cutting edge of hermetical philosophy, no doubt, but—when we fight—" He looked around. "We're fighting Ash. Ash, making a bid to manifest directly into our sphere, and control the gates directly, one of which—perhaps the single most important one—is under Lissen Carak." He frowned. "Ash is a dragon?"

"Lissen Carak was the home and sacred ground of my people," Mogon said.

"And before that the Odine, and before them the Kraal, and so on and so on." Harmodius raised a hand. "If we do nothing, the cycle continues forever."

"Fascinating," Gabriel allowed. "But not immediately affecting my dispositions." He made a face. "Except that it's clear that he wants to fight at Albinkirk—he or Thorn or whoever controls that horde. And because he wants to fight here, I'm tempted to fight somewhere else." Gabriel leaned forward. "Does your Ifriquy'an know more gates? I would give a great deal to understand the geographia of this aethereal battlefield. If I'm understanding this at all."

Harmodius nodded. He withdrew a second sheet of the memory parchment. "Lissen Carak, as we all knew or at least guessed. In the Citadel of Arles, in Arelat." He nodded to the Queen.

Gabriel flinched as if he'd been bitten. "Of course!" he said. "I was there. The King of Galle tried to take Arles by treachery—a long tale. But I was there. I knew something felt—hollow."

"Hollow?" the Queen said. "I, too, know a place that feels hollow in my soul."

"I believe there's a lost gate under the palace in Harndon." Harmodius exchanged a long look with the Queen.

The Queen leaned back and let go a breath. "There is something there. An emptiness."

Harmodius nodded. "Let us say Harndon. Assuredly there is one in Dar as Salaam. I have felt it myself. In fact, it set Al Rashidi on his investigations, almost a hundred years ago. And of course, once you understand the game and the pieces, the whole of the Umbroth Wars make sense. The not-dead are just someone else's tools to take the gate."

Gabriel began to rock back and forth like a small child.

"Arles. In Arelat. Where the King of Galle has just, according to the Etruscans, been badly beaten by a mighty army of the Wild." Gabriel steadied himself.

Prior Wishart's face grew still, though even in the aethereal his fear showed.

The Queen looked from one to another.

"Umbroth Wars, gentles?" she asked.

"Almost a hundred years of attacks by the not-dead and the one we call Necromancer on the people of Dar as Salaam, the Abode of Peace," Harmodius said. "Before the attacks started, there were green fields. Now there is desert." He looked at Gabriel. "Rashidi says there are seven gates in this sphere. Or, to be complete, he says there are at least seven gates. And to that I must add that the terrain of today need not be the terrain on which the gates were set. This contest is so old that there might be gates under glaciers, inside volcanoes, or under the sea for all I know."

Prior Wishart drew a deep breath. "How long ago were the gates built?" he asked.

Harmodius didn't answer at first. He looked from one to another to another, around the circle. None flinched. The Faery Knight grinned and showed his teeth.

"You might have been a mountebank," the Faery Knight said. "Jussst tell them!"

"At least thirty thousand years," Harmodius said.

The bishop sighed. "My scripture tells me that the earth is between six and seven thousand years old," he said.

Harmodius shrugged. "It might simply be wrong."

The bishop acknowledged this with a nod.

"It might refer to somewhere else," Gabriel said. "We are no more from here than the Duchess Mogon."

"Thirty thousand years is a long time," the bishop said.

Lord Krevak nodded. "Even to my people, that is too long." He shrugged. "Too long to take seriously."

Desiderata glanced at her captain and then leaned towards Harmodius. "I see how this could forever alter everything. But I do not see how it alters the next few days. Is there a weapon? A way to prevent this manifestation?"

Mogon now spoke. "No—I see it. Manifestation is power and weakness."

Harmodius nodded. "If Ash is here," he said, "he is not anywhere else, and when he is entirely here—" He paused. "Then I think he can be destroyed. Only when they distribute themselves are they immortal. And less powerful."

Gabriel nodded. "Now I am not yawning. You want to kill a god."

"It will be very difficult," Harmodius said.

Gabriel winced. "We're going to be pinched hard to win a simple field battle to protect our crops against heavy numbers and better levels of ops."

"That part I leave to you," Harmodius said. "Our battle will be fought here, in the aethereal, and it will all be about misdirection."

"Mine, too," Gabriel said. "I feel I need to remind you all of something."

"Speak, man," the Faery Knight said.

Gabriel looked around. "As a knight it is my duty to protect the weak. My first duty. You may be right, but please, old man, admit that you may have all this backwards. My duty is to protect the peasants in the fields, the merchants, the women bearing babies." He looked around. "I agree that the game of gods should stop. I hate it. But men play it and wardens play it and dragons play it and wyverns and bears. It is not nearly as simple as killing a god. So let us focus, your grace and my lady and lords—on beating Thorn."

The Faery Knight nodded agreement. "We may not even be on the right side," he said. "We may be too puny to even understand the sides."

Gabriel smiled at him. "I can tell a good company by riding through the streets of their camp—once. Let me meet one whore, one servant, and I know their captain." His eyes narrowed. "I will not debate theology with you, my lords. But I know Ash by his works. I know two of these others—and whatever they may intend…" He shrugged.

"They run better companies?" the Faery Knight suggested.

"Just so," the Red Knight agreed, and they shared a brief smile. "I only mean this, Harmodius. You want to destroy a race of gods so that we can be free. I say—a pox on it. I serve the Queen and the Emperor and my own interest—everyone serves someone. Let our lords be just and generous, and we prosper."

Harmodius growled. "There speaks an aristocrat who has never known the lash."

Gabriel spat. "You lie."

"You—you, of all creatures, will forfeit your freedom?" Harmodius shook his head. "I think it is you who lies."

"I say, fight one battle at a time and do not rule out any ally." Gabriel put a hand to his head—a familiar headache.

"I say, they are false allies and will enslave us, generation after generation and you mortgage the future to win a battle today." Harmodius was adamant. "They are all equally our enemies."

Desiderata sat wrapped in thought. Gabriel could guess what had cut her. The others considered, each in their own way.

Gabriel took a deep aethereal breath. A meaningless symbol of a breath—a conversational habit.

"There must be other Powers," he said.

Harmodius nodded. "The Necromancer is one. The being Rashidi identifies as Rot is another. Who I suspect is leading the assault in Galle. Or managing it."

"Dragons?" Krevak asked.

"Not all Powers are dragons," Exrech said. "At least one Kraal still bloats the earth."

"Thorn seeks to become a Power." Gabriel raised an eyebrow.

Harmodius nodded heavily. "And Sister Amicia is on the very verge of becoming one."

"Like the dragons?" Gabriel asked.

"I don't actually know," Harmodius admitted slowly. "Al Rashidi doesn't know either."

Desiderata raised her head. "This is too deep for me," she said. She looked at the Bishop of Albinkirk.

He smiled. "That God's will and love extends to every level of the cosmos comes as no surprise to me," he said. "Beyond that, I would not comment, except to say that to plot the death of a creature, however powerful, who has done you no harm is awfully like murder, however you may see the consequences for future generations. But then, I am but a priest, and I fear that even violence in the defence of the weak is—sin. Murder."

The Faery Knight looked at him in wonder. "Are there other children of men who think as you do?" he asked.

The bishop nodded. "A few. We call ourselves Christians."

The Faery Knight laughed.

Even Gabriel had to laugh.

Harmodius nodded like a man waking from sleep. "Your grace—I know this will be painful. But my sense—from stories I have heard, and your very presence—is that you have already faced our foe. Directly. In the aethereal."

Desiderata appeared as she always had in the aethereal, *as a beautiful* young woman in a kirtle of gold, barefoot, with a ring of daisies in her hair and a belt of them around her waist. In the aethereal, she seemed both wanton and matronly, the very embodiment of woman's power.

Now Gabriel, who had healed her and knew her aethereal and outward self, looked at her and saw how clearly her ordeal in Harndon had marked her. In the aethereal, she still wore the form that she had had a year ago in the real. But pregnancy and torment had put crow's feet at the edges of her eyes and a different colour in her face. She had more gravity—more presence—than she had a year ago. But he would never have noticed the difference until he saw her golden form in the aethereal.

She did not smile. But nor did she wince, or stumble.

"I have faced Ash," she said quietly.

The aethereal was still.

"It was not a straight contest of powers. In which I would have been bested instantly. And I think—if I may pre-empt Master Harmodius—that he dwells in the aethereal and that our 'real' is very difficult for him. But for the battle of will—will, with ops as a weapon, to use your university terms—I built this."

Memories can be very difficult in the aethereal—the memory palace lives only in the user's mind, and the weakness of memory can make anything fluctuate. Living memory—actual events—can be subject to an infinite number of seductions and degradations, as every hermeticist knows—delusions of success or defeat, failures of will, troubles of image.

But for most casters, memories of direct manipulations of hermetical power have themselves a glow of solid experience, and the Queen's memory of the climaxes of Ash's assault on her wall were vivid, complex, and so fraught with emotion that Mogon groaned and Gabriel found himself weeping.

But when she was done, each of them built, under her instruction, one of the golden bricks—Mogon's were a magnificent, lurid green.

"I made no attempt to strike him. I wished only to protect my unborn child." She smiled. "Now, I wonder what was Ash and what was Ghause."

Harmodius had seen the shadow of another in her memory. "And what was Tar," he said.

"The Virgin would only protect me," the Queen said quickly.

Harmodius frowned. "They only see us as slaves and soldiers," he said. He looked pointedly at Gabriel.

Gabriel shook his head. "Harmodius—I would not be your foe. But I need my ally in order to win this battle—the more especially if your dark dragon manifests." He looked around. "I have no idea of what it would be like to fight a dragon. Militarily, I'm not even sure it can be done. Based on two observations of my own ally in his draconic form—" He paused. "I'm not sure I can plan for that."

Harmodius took a deep breath as if to make a passionate rejoinder. But he paused.

"We must win this fight," he said.

"We know," Desiderata said.

"Very well," Harmodius said. "I will limit myself to Ash."

Gabriel smiled at the Faery Knight. "You are content I should command?" he asked.

"No," the Faery Knight said. "I am content we can aid each other. Command is too imperious for me, Gabriel. Let us merely be friends, and the rest will follow."

"That's me told, as my archer would say," Gabriel said. He extended his hand. "I intend to fight in the woods, at Gilson's Hole."

"In the woods?" Desiderata asked. Her surprise leached into the aethereal.

"The army marches tonight, under cover of darkness," Gabriel said. "Much of it, anyway. Not your knights. We've summoned a mass levy of farmers and peasants to dig, and cut trees. What we have that our opponents lack is organization. I'm trying to win with it."

The Faery Knight put a hand to his forehead in mock salute—or perhaps genuine. "I am shocked. Perhaps he will be surprised."

"Let's find out," the captain said.

One by one, the others left the old man's palace.

Like a bad guest, Gabriel chose to stay. When they were all gone, he said, "Odd to be in your head, instead of you in mine."

Harmodius smiled. "Are we at odds?" he asked.

"Please do nothing against Master Smythe," Gabriel said.

"You mean Lot? You have my word. For now." Harmodius looked at something that Gabriel knew he couldn't see—but he'd been in the old man's rooms in his own mind, and he knew what was there—the mirror.

"I've lost my protection," he said.

"You think so?" Harmodius said. "Hmm."

"How will this Ash manifest?" Gabriel asked. "And how will you strike?"

"I think he will use death—each death is a major event in the aethereal," the old magister began.

"Really? I had no idea," Gabriel said.

"I missed your sarcasm," Harmodius said.

"And I, yours," Gabriel shot back.

They both glared—and both laughed.

"I think he uses death to power his essence." Harmodius shrugged. "I really know nothing—I guess everything. I will not tell you what I will do."

"And Amicia? Lissen Carak?" Gabriel asked. His pulse raced even in the aethereal.

"Defended. Amicia wishes to come with the army. I think she should not—but we need every scrap of hermetical talent." Harmodius set his jaw.

Gabriel nodded. "In as much as I am captain—you are magister. I believe I can defeat Thorn's material army. In fact, I'll go so far as to say I can defeat him with minimal losses."

"You've learned a great deal of humility," Harmodius said dryly. "But I will *add this. If you die and I die, and Ash manifests, and Thorn triumphs, and Lissen Carak does not fall—then we have not wholly lost."*

"I probably lost Ticondaga and all my folk by hubris," Gabriel said. "I have learned in just a few years making war that to dwell on errors is to make more." He shrugged. "I am afraid of a battle with so many imponderables. But I will do my best."

Harmodius nodded. "I will spare you the statement that you should not blame yourself."

Gabriel shrugged.

"What happens if we win on the ground and lose here?" Gabriel asked.

"We all die," Harmodius said.

"The converse is also true," Gabriel said. "You would have me die, so that untold numbers of beings I have never met are protected from Ash holding a gate." Gabriel shook his head. "I'm not that noble. Let's just beat him here." He managed a grin. "And live to tell about it."

Harmodius shook his head. "At best, our losses will be staggering."

Gabriel sighed. "I'll try and prevent that." But there was doubt in his voice.

In the real, Gabriel was the last but Harmodius to return. He looked around, feeling—rested. He tried to empty his wine cup, but that had apparently already happened, and the fire was down and most of the candles out.

Harmodius grunted. "I'm too old for all this," he said. "Good night."

"Where are you sleeping?" Gabriel asked.

"In this chair." Harmodius stretched. "Which even this body isn't young enough for."

"You can share my room," Gabriel volunteered. "Come, old man. Three flights of stairs and there's a feather bed."

"Lead on," Harmodius said.

They made it to the top with minimal grunting. Gabriel got the old man into his camp bed—the castle seemed to have no beds of its own, or perhaps other guests had them.

Toby didn't awake any of the times they stepped over him, and he looked exhausted. Gabriel let him sleep. He found the leather case where his wine was stored, and found both bottles empty.

"Damn," he said.

Harmodius, the most puissant magister in all of the Nova Terra, was already snoring.

Gabriel looked at him for a moment. The cased window was open and moonlight fell on the old man's outthrust arm, and the night was chilly, and Gabriel got his red cloak off the clothes piled on his chair and spread it over the old man. It smelled of wood smoke. That sparked a few memories.

He smiled again. Then he went out past his solar, where Nell was sleeping with a young man spooned against her. Gabriel nodded thoughtfully and took his page's canteen and pulled the stopper. There was water in it. He drank it.

It wasn't what he wanted, and he went into the hall, his cup still in his hand.

The Queen's door opened, and Blanche backed through it with a taper in her hand.

A variety of thoughts crossed Gabriel's mind all at once, and when she turned, they both flinched.

"I'm sorry," he said, although he had no idea for what he was apologizing.

She paused. "May I help you?" she asked. "The babe's asleep and so is her grace."

Gabriel waved his cup. *I'm the captain, damn it. I can be in the hall at midnight.* There was something in her air that damned him for being in the wrong place at the wrong time. "I was only looking for a cup of wine."

A loud snore ripped out of Harmodius's throat and echoed down the stone steps.

"He sounds as if he's choking," she said, and almost giggled.

They were looking into each other's eyes. It went on too long.

"I'll..." he began, cursing himself for ten types of a fool.

"I have wine," she said. Her voice was husky. "In my room." Her eyes never left his.

He reached out his hand.

She took it. "I want to see your—griffon," she whispered.

He laughed. She had no idea why. But he took her to the door and produced a key made of wrought steel.

"Will he scream?" she asked. Suddenly she was appalled—that she'd offered him wine, that she'd been so bold about the monster.

He shook his head. "Perhaps when we leave. Let me go first."

He opened the door and she was shocked—immediately—to find that the room revealed, which had once been a fine solar, was now roofless to the open night, and a canopy of stars rose above her. There were two chairs, and a heavy iron chain, and a— a—

A monster.

Gabriel went forward, crooning, and it— It was huge. It seemed to fill the very large tower room, as big as the whole home she'd grown up in with her mother. It put its head on the ground.

And rolled on its back like an enormous cat.

"Come on," Ser Gabriel said.

She breathed out and moved forward. And then, almost without thinking, she went straight up to the great thing. She reached out a hand and touched it. "How big will he get?" she asked.

"He's only half grown, aren't you, laddy?" Gabriel crooned. "He'll be big enough to ride in a month or two."

It had feathers on its head and an enormous, vicious beak, downward and backward curved like a scimitar of horn, and wickedly sharp, and two great black eyes that seemed fathomless. The feathers of its wings marched in endless organic rows, green and black and white and gold—true gold, as if all the gilders in the world had united to work on its feathers. But just behind the mighty muscles of its wings there was a line where downy, almost misshapen feathers marched along with hair, and then, from that line back, it looked to have a coat more like that of a horse or cow—except for the barbaric talons.

It should have seemed ungainly and ugly. Instead, it was—queerly beautiful, like a much-scarred tomcat or a favourite old shoe. She scratched the place on the great belly where the fur and the feathers met, and the great monster made a noise somewhere between a purr and a screech.

"Oh, he likes you," Ser Gabriel said.

With the purr came some other emanation. Blanche had little experience of matters *aethereal*—none, really. So for the first time, she felt the tickle of something unseelie in her head.

Ser Gabriel gave the beast a slap on the side of his beak. "None of that," he said.

Blanche suddenly felt a terrible, wonderful upwelling of love.

Inside her head, Gabriel's voice said, "Stop that."

Just for a moment she saw him, in a red doublet and hose, standing on a parquetry floor in some sort of cathedral, with statues and numbers all about him, and a beautiful woman on a pedestal behind him, dressed like the statues in churches.

"I'll do my own courting," the voice in her head said. "Down, Ariosto!"

The great creature raised his head and both her eyes met both of its eyes. Its impossibly rough tongue brushed her face. She laughed, although she trembled, and although she suddenly had the most intimate—erotic— picture of Ser Gabriel, and she blushed.

She started to turn away and her shoulder met Gabriel's.

His lips came down on hers. She didn't feel as if she was controlling her body, but she fit herself against him from her knee to her head. She had never done this with any boy. She felt wanton, deliciously so.

The griffon watched them, unblinking. Gabriel took his lips away from hers and brushed them against her neck, and then his hand tightened and he pulled her—gently—towards the door.

The great monster made a sound very like a sigh.

Blanche turned back, and Gabriel, lightly but firmly, stiff-armed her out the door.

He shut it firmly. Turned away from her, and locked it.

"If you kiss me," he said, his voice husky, "I'd rather it was of your own free will." He turned back. "Ariosto is— A creature of the Wild." He shrugged.

Blanche realized that she was breathing very hard, that her skin was flushed, and her hands unsteady. She was all too aware that the Queen's solar was the next door, that they were virtually in public.

She turned to her own door, suddenly quite sure what she wanted.

Utterly unsure how to express it.

"He's beautiful," she said.

Gabriel followed her, remaining just a step away.

"Come," she said simply. She couldn't imagine a speech that would express her thoughts and feelings. So she went to her door, and opened it.

They walked through the low, iron-bound oak door, and she shut it carefully. She put the small taper in her hand into a travelling stick on a low trunk. Time seemed to pass very slowly. Each of her movements seemed very precious. Graceful. Beautiful. She rose on her toes to fetch something.

I should be asleep, he thought, along with a thousand other thoughts.

She took the dented silver cup from his hand and poured him a cup of wine. She put something in her mouth.

She looked up at him, and took a sip—more than a sip. Boldly. And then put it in his hands and closed her own around his. "If—" Her voice shook. "If you make a baby on me, swear you'll rear it as one of your own."

"Blanche—"

"Swear. Or take your wine and go." She was shaking.

"Blanche—"

"Don't cozen me!" she said.

He took the wine, drank a fair amount without taking his eyes off her and frowned. He kissed her. It was effortless—they flowed together and were one, for so long that he almost spilled the rest of the wine.

And then she placed her hand firmly on his breastbone. She was not weak.

"Swear," she said. "I won't make you pretend you'll marry me. Just that you won't do what some noble bastard did to my mother."

Gabriel sat on the chest. His mind was going around and around, and half of it seemed to be chasing Amicia. And the other half was utterly captivated.

"It is not that I won't swear," he said. "It's that I don't like what I see in the mirror if I do."

Blanche's breath caught. "I know you'll marry the Queen," she said suddenly. "I know what I am, and what you are."

Gabriel didn't catch himself. He laughed.

"No," he said. "I can imagine many outcomes, but those pips are not on the dice." He smiled at her. "And I'm at least as much a bastard as you."

She leaned back, as if to look at him more closely. "Really?"

He got up. He was overcome with her—the palpable reality of her, her smell, her unwashed hair and the taste of her mouth and the clove she'd just chewed and what that said.

"State secret," he whispered.

She licked her lips. "I know who your parents are," she said.

He froze. She felt the tension in his muscles, and he took a step for the door, but it was as if he was in the *aethereal*. He *meant* to step to the door, but instead he was holding her. Her warmth went through his hands. Without a conscious thought, he pulled the veil off her hair and put a hand behind her head. Her kirtle opened at the side, and fit like a glove, but he managed to find the skin where her shoulder met her neck.

"Swear, damn you!" she said. She pushed him hard enough that he fell back across the chest. "Or leave," she said.

"That hurt," he said, and meant it. "I swear on my sword that any baby we make will be reared as my own." He caught his breath. "I'm only promising so that you won't hurt me again."

She laughed.

The taper gave up—a last flare of light that showed her laughing at his discomfiture, and then darkness. The moon was on the other side of the tower, and her window was closed and shuttered. There was some rustling.

"I feel I should tell you—" he said to the darkness.

"Stop talking," she said, very close.

Her lips found his.

After a pause, she said, "It's side opening, I've already unlaced it."

His hand finally found bare skin...

Chapter Eighteen

Gilson's Hole—Sauce

The first wave of boglins hit their new defences just after first light. It wasn't really an attack or even a probe—the boglins had a hard time with the marsh and the ditch at the base of the ridge was worse, already filled with swamp water. They milled about and threw sling stones—a new trick—and made skittering noises.

Then they began to move off into the newly forested land west of the Hole.

By then, the camp—well back from the barriers, between the old village and the old fort—was awake.

Sauce took a pair of lances to the top of the first wall of earth and Mag came up behind her.

Without any drama, she pointed a finger at the ground to the north and there was a flare of heat—the sort of shimmer that warm rock can give on a hot summer day.

Mag smiled. "I have sewing to finish," she said. She went back to camp.

Young Phillip—one of her Morean knights—looked a little pale.

Sauce made a face. "I used to think Tom was the scariest of the bunch," she said.

She walked off to look at her pickets.

She had to walk a long way. Given two full days and some farm labour, Ser John had managed a small miracle of construction. The low ridge—not so low in places, either—that hemmed in the Hole on the south and west was now crowned with a long, winding earthworks well-reinforced with lumber, and in front of it the trees were cleared to stumps for almost a hundred paces—right down to the marsh—and then piled beyond in a tangle of spruce and maple.

Closed redoubts watched the ends, with trenches. On the west side, the ridge ran to the very edge of the creek that helped define the position. On the east side, the ridge petered out into a deep, wide bog. Behind her there was the higher ground with the old fort. They didn't have the manpower to hold it—but it would take a determined assault willing to take heavy losses to get round the east end and past the redoubt—and the covered, secret surprise.

She knew the smell of roast boglin and it was heavy in the air. She wrinkled her nose and exchanged salutes with the armoured men in the south redoubt. They'd clearly stood to arms, and now looked sheepish and bored.

"Plenty of fighting later," she said. "Christ, only a fool looks forward to it."

She peered out over the wall. Someone out there was alive—a very accurate sling stone buzzed past her head.

"Fuck me," she muttered. But she was on display, and she enjoyed the salutes. They never got old. She grinned. "Don't get hit," she said. "That's an order."

A generation of very young Jarsay knights grinned back at her. She'd been, to all intents, the *primus pilus* for three weeks. Everyone knew her.

"Don't stand there like gowps," she snapped. "Get a couple of archers behind a mantlet and scour the killing ground. You know the drill."

The second attack had more meat in it. There was a directing intelligence behind it—at least, they heard horns and bellows—and a boiling mass of boglins threw surprising amounts of wood and grass and ferns and other organic matter—including charred boglins—into the ditch. They'd crossed the marsh silently, mostly the new imps and more boglins.

A heavy crossbow coughed from a covered position well up the ridge. On one of the few small mounds of dry in the swamp, a daemon was struck right through his body. His screams went on until one of his mates finished him. The boglins crossed, climbed up the revetment, and died.

Some of the farmers from the valley and the Brogat, working away at clearing trees and digging dirt, were appalled by the wave of boglins. Some ran. A few deserted.

A few started killing boglins with shovels.

"Sign 'em up," Sauce said. Both men proved to be farm labourers—men who owned nothing and were almost slaves.

"How'd we get all this farm labour?" she asked Ser John.

Ser John was watching the sky. They had four towers going up, all holding new-built torsion machines. He was wondering where the wyverns were. "The Captain of Albinkirk offered a year's remission of all taxes for ten days' digging," he said.

Sauce grinned. "That Captain of Albinkirk, he's one smart man."

A little after two in the afternoon, and the mess kettles were on for dinner. A convoy rolled in from Albinkirk—forty wagons full of food and munitions. Sheaves of new arrows, already on spacers in linen bags, and new tinned-iron kettles. Some new brass kettles made in Genua.

"Miss me?" the captain said, and Sauce threw her arms around him and kissed him. Some of the newer members of the company and some of the knights with Ser Ricar were appalled. Others cheered.

She leaned back to look at him. "You look like you got the cream."

He laughed. "We'll see," he said. "The cream may yet get me. In the meantime..."

He spent two hours with them, outlining the new alliance, quelling their fears of having a Wild ally, and riding along the two ridges south and west of the Hole and one high beech-tree-covered ridge north and west of the little stream.

When he was done, he bowed in the saddle to Ser John. "You've done it. It's beautiful."

Ser John was hesitant. "I was only going to be here until today— tomorrow at the outside."

The captain nodded, his eyes on the distant Green Hills. "I expect we'll fight tomorrow, but the real fight will be the day after." He kept watching the hills. "I may have this all wrong. The sorcerer can still just go north into the woods and come at us on the old Ticondaga road or across West Kanata."

Sauce raised an eyebrow. "But?"

"But he has much greater supply problems than we do," the captain said with his breezy confidence.

"A million monsters..."

"They still have to eat. And no supply train, no wagons, nothing." The captain was watching the woods. "He can go around—but will he have an army at the end?"

Ser John whistled. "You give me joy," he said.

The captain shook his head. "He could still decide to march into Morea. Then—" He sighed. "Then it's all for nothing, and we start making stuff up." He looked down at the first ridge, below them. "Every attack by boglins makes me happy. Bad Tom ought to reach you at sunset."

Sauce started. Ser John raised *both* eyebrows.

"Messengers. All the white banda will come in—here. Tom's Hillmen will stay out—off our right flank, in the ravines to the east, on the other bank of the Albin." He looked back at both of them. "I'm not going to repeat Chevin. I can only hope that Thorn *is*."

Ser John chewed the end of his moustache. Sauce chewed her hair.

Sauce said, "Why not hit one end of our line or another and roll us up?"

The captain shrugged. "Then we have a battle. I'm trying to *be* the sorcerer. He can't have much control over his minions beyond 'stop' and 'go.' I don't think the stone trolls can form fours and march to the flank. But we've had time to prepare and we've used it. It *should* prove a decisive advantage."

Sauce said, "But you have doubts."

The Red Knight nodded. "I always have doubts."

Sauce glanced at him.

"My military tutor had an interesting definition for this situation," the captain went on. "He said that a battle was a situation where two commanders each thought they had a decisive superiority and one was wrong." He was still watching the distant hills. "I keep putting myself in the shoes—or what-have-you—of the sorcerer. Why's he even here? He should go home and declare victory." He frowned. "I'm missing something."

"He killed your mother, and you think he should just go home?" Sauce said. "Don't you want to fight?"

He looked at her as if she had something hideous springing from her forehead. "That's amateur talk, Sauce. You taught me better than that. This is strictly business."

Sauce laughed. "I never said any such thing." She shrugged. "Maybe I did."

"You did. You were talking about johns, and sex. But it's the same lesson. No room here for hate. Strictly business. War is about mess kettles and latrines and having the last set of warm, dry fighters in reserve." He nodded. "I think the sorcerer hates us. That would be excellent."

"He killed your ma," Sauce said.

"Drop it, Sauce." His eyes were suddenly on her, and there at the edges was the red she'd expected all day.

"You've got to be human," she said.

"I've been very human recently. Right now, I'm the captain." He played with a glove.

She looked out over the wilderness that stretched away—everywhere—for miles.

"Why are we fighting here? You said Albinkirk." Sauce found that she was angry. He was up to something. She thought of all her conversations with Mag.

He had that look she hated, where he, in fact, had all the answers and all his talk was just bullshit.

"I thought we'd fight at Albinkirk, but things changed. I changed my mind. The Faery Knight, Bad Tom—the Emperor." He shrugged. "What *is* eating you?"

"We're going to fight the Wild with Wild things inside our own ranks, and on *their* ground." Sauce looked at him. "Everything I know about war, I learned from you, Jehan, Cully and Tom, and *everything* tells me this is the wrong place. In a swamp? In the woods?"

He looked at her and nodded.

"Yes," he said.

She frowned. "Suddenly, you are the Queen's Captain," she said. "I thought we were a free company. On adventure. Making our fortunes. Not making you King."

"King?" He laughed. "Oh, Sauce, I promise you I do not want to be King of Alba."

That relieved her. "Or King of the North?" she asked.

"Nor that." He smiled.

She still thought the smile was too charming and too false.

"What are you after, then?" she asked.

"After the battle," he said. "There's so many angles now, I can't remember them all. Let's win the battle. Then—we'll have a command meeting."

This made her smile. "Unless we're dead."

"Right, in which case the meeting is off." He smiled back, and for a moment, they were who they had once been.

Before he left, the captain spent another hour closeted with Mag. Neither of them shared what had been discussed.

At sunset, the white banda marched into camp from the east, along the same set of low ridges over which Bad Tom and his Hillmen had disappeared. They were on foot and all their wagons were gone—left on the other side of the river to the east.

The celebration was muted, and nearly ruined by the last-light assault of a mixed force of creatures of the Wild. But darkness did not help them negotiate the traps; superior night vision was of little use in seeing stakes dug in days before, and a pair of torsion engines dropped baskets of rocks on the beaten zone.

No Head watched it all from the westernmost tower with a bottle in one hand and a stylus in the other.

Half an hour later he reported to Sauce and Ser John, on the forward wall overlooking the Hole.

"Gelfred says they're well around us, and working up to an attack on the back of the camp." No Head opened his wax slate. "I have a whole forest of suggestions and additions to the current scheme."

Sauce looked smug.

Within ten minutes the whole camp was standing to arms. The farmers were drawn up well back from the walls, with improvised weapons to hand. There were archers in the towers and men-at-arms lining all four sides of the camp wall.

Just at moonrise there was a cacophony of horns. Mag was sewing away, making mess kettle bags for the new kettles at a great rate.

On the wall, Ser Bescanon sounded a horn.

Mag bit off her thread, took up a small piece of char and snapped her fingers. The char burnt to ash.

Sixty yards from the ditch of the camp's back wall, there was a deep hollow, almost a long bowshot from end to end, fully covered from the firing positions on the camp wall. All along that hollow, there were clay jars buried deep in the soft earth, each sealed with wax and with a piece of the very same char cloth—linen woven on the same bolt—in the midst of the jar.

And bits of rusty metal and old nails and the like.

And several pounds of Master Smythe's powder.

Mag's tiny working produced six prodigious explosions.

Immediately, the back gate of the camp opened and a mounted sortie went out—first a dozen Vardariots under Zac who spread like a magick curtain in front of the knights, and then forty knights armed cap-à-pied. Behind them came another forty men-at-arms who shook out into a loose line with two paces between armoured men.

The mounted men cleared the road by torchlight, and the dismounted men-at-arms did most of the killing. In the dark, a man in armour was very hard to injure, and anything without armour—especially stunned, wounded cave bears and irks—were easily dispatched.

The smell of hell come to earth—sulphur and saltpeter—hung in the damp night air.

In the night, Mag exchanged workings with something out in the darkness. She left two great golden shields over the whole of the camp when she went to her blanket roll. The golden shields caused as much lost sleep and consternation among the newer men and women as irks and boglins might have done.

Mag awoke to find the young Mortirmir was releasing fireballs from a tower—one working that loosed one small ball from each fingertip, where they hurried out into the darkness like malignant glow flies. By the time she climbed the tower to him, he was showing off, casting complex arcs of light and tiny focused beams of red.

"You could save some of that for when it matters," Mag said.

With a dramatic *swoosh*, Morgon produced a magnificent, gurgling bundle of focused *ops* like a tiny sun, complete to straying arms of white-hot gas. He flung it so far that it simply vanished.

"What was that for?" Mag asked. There was a precision to the way he used *ops* and the way he focused that she admired—more as a seamstress than as a magicker.

He turned and smiled his ingenuous smile. "Just because I can," he said. "Ser Milus says by now the woods are full a mile or more deep around us."

Off to the north and east, there was a sudden glow—then a deep, pulsing red burning, and then a hollow *thum* followed by a sharp *crack*.

"I wanted to see how far I could throw something really powerful. Bet someone's surprised."

Mag sighed. "I'm going back to bed. Please don't be such a small boy."

Chastened, Morgon climbed down off the tower.

In the morning, the survivors of the imperial army were paraded and re-armed. They received a curious collection of weapons—trade swords and crossbows stripped from the two Etruscan warehouses in Albinkirk, every spare sword, shield, or dented cap in the arsenal in the citadel; hunting bows, and even some stone throws used for hunting squirrels, crossbows that threw a clay pellet instead of a bolt.

All the spare horses—including every destrier the company captured in the south—went to re-horse the white banda and to fill out a full squadron of Morean cavalry.

The captain came with his household, and then the Queen came with hers, and behind them were another fifteen hundred peasants with shovels. But they never came into the company camp—instead, they halted almost a mile to the rear and began building a second camp on the ridge with the old fort.

The captain addressed the Moreans in Archaic. They didn't cheer, but neither did they grumble. Ser Christos stood on a barrel and told all the phylarchs that he had personally seen the Emperor's body prepared, and that they would take it back to the city together—when they had been victorious.

Then Ser Christos took all the Moreans except a handful and marched them away to the new camp.

Sauce watched them go. "What's he doing?" she asked Michael, who was already clerking in a tent—not his own.

Michael shook his head. "No idea. Except that he doesn't think the battle will be here."

Sauce groaned. "He said here! Now where?"

Michael was writing out orders—all in numbered sequences.

Sauce frowned at him. "This is too fucking complicated. Tom and I are gone and he's off the leash and making up dangerous plans that won't work."

Michael paused. "I think this will work," he said in a neutral tone.

"Why's he so talkative and chipper?" Sauce asked.

Michael cleared his throat.

"Tell!" Sauce said. "Michael, how often have I stood by you?"

"He's got a girl," Michael said.

"Not Amicia?" Sauce asked.

"Word is Amicia told him to sod off. And he's found someone a little more willing." Michael raised his pen. "Sauce, this could all be nonsense."

"The Queen?" Sauce barked. It was almost a screech.

"No," Michael said. "It's a long story. One of the Queen's ladies. A laundress."

That stopped Sauce in full anti-aristocratic spate. "A laundress?" she asked.

"Sauce, I *don't know*. Now may I finish writing out his orders?" He met her eye. In the captain's very voice he said, "Don't you have something you ought to be doing?"

Sauce laughed.

In the streets of the camp, Wilful Murder sat with Tippit and Cuddy and Cully.

"Where's No Head?" Long Paw asked. It was an old tradition, and even now that Long Paw was a knight he liked to see it done.

They were whetting their points. Each good arrow was taken out and its steel point sharpened. Bodkins that would pass between the links of mail and horse-droppers that would rip the guts out of a wyvern and the new arrows, big stonebreakers on half-inch shafts for cave trolls with blunt heads like the ones used for birds but filled with lead.

"No Head's too important for the like o' us," Wilful muttered. "Telling the diggers where to dig. Waste o' time, if you ask me."

Long Paw laughed. "Why? I like the odds—us behind twenty feet of rampart."

"We ain't fightin' here," Wilful Murder said in his hangdog voice.

"Like fuck!" Cully said. "Of course we're fightin' here."

Wilful Murder wore a straw hat on his arming cap, and he pushed it back off his forehead. "Oh, is that so?"

Cuddy sighed. "I'm sure you're going to tell us."

"The cap'n brought up horses for every one o' you what lost yer horses." Wilful Murder shrugged. "Stands to reason."

"Knights need horses," Cully said.

Tippit smiled.

"And all the archers?" Wilful said, in exactly the voice he'd use when he rolled the pips he needed to win a game. "Why the fuck we all suddenly got horses, if'n we ain't leaving?"

There was a pause.

Tippit cursed—one of his original, florid, somewhat terrifying curses—this one to do with seals and sex. Then he sighed. "I hate it when you make sense."

There was no trumpet. Just after midnight, Ganfroy went from tent line to tent line and woke the knights, and the rest went the way it should have—with a lot of forgotten equipment, men missing, Oak Pew unaccountably drunk, and a great deal of cursing. The chaos was made worse by the silent intrusion of new men—militia and local knights. Lord Wayland's retinue.

The Grand Squire. They were good knights but not professional soldiers. They were moving into the places vacated by the company.

"Up past their bed times," Wilful Murder muttered.

But it was done, and in under an hour, including the rapid serving out of rations—salt pork, bacon, peas and butter and good bread in big four-pound loaves.

Wilful Murder was unbelievably smug as they trotted into the first morning light, six miles almost due south of Gilson's Hole.

The whole company—green in front, then the household, then the red and then the white—jogged along at a fast walk by fours down the road in the first grey light.

"Fuck, I hate rain," muttered Tippit.

Then something changed, and the rhythm of movement changed. Birds were waking up, and the colour of the sky was lightening.

They turned. They were suddenly moving north, on a narrow road in deep woods. Some of the veterans of the spring march knew it as the West Road to Ticondaga.

"Gonna rain for sure," Tom Lantorn said at his side. "Look—woods is full o' men."

It was true. There were men with axes and shovels all along the road's edge.

By the time the sun was well up, they halted in a clearing that had firepits already dug. The Ticondaga road continued off to the north, towards Big Rock Lake. But a new road was opening, headed back north and east.

There was firewood stacked by each pit—good hardwood twigs and branches, carefully broken up and neatly piled. Men swung down, pages collected the horses, and women appeared out of the forest.

Sukey was there with twenty baggage wagons. "Don't get fresh," she said to Cuddy. "They ain't our girls, they're farm girls. Got me?"

The farm girls cooked—an enormous breakfast of fatback and eggs and spiced tea, a company favourite since Morea.

Cuddy paused at Wilful's fire. "We're fightin' today," he said.

Wilful ate the excellent eggs and nodded. "Guess so." Good food was a traditional sign of a dust-up ahead.

Cuddy nodded. "Don't forget to duck," he said. He moved on down the line, checking fires.

A little behind him came the captain and Sauce and Ser Bescanon.

"Just a little trick to save some time," he said at every fire. "I thought you'd all be pleased if we could just win, and be done."

Men would laugh, and women, too.

"I thought we all needed out of the swamp," he said at one fire.

"I needed a morning ride," he laughed at another.

"I brought my falcon—didn't you bring yours?" he said to Wilful Murder.

"I'm looking for the Loathly Lady," he cracked to Tippit, who shook his head.

All the while, they could hear the axes sounding in the woods.

North and East of Gilson's Hole
Thorn and Ser Hartmut

Hartmut had made a model. He'd crawled through muck once and sent other men during each of the attacks and he had a fair idea of the full extent of the entrenchments covering the maze of pathways around and through the Hole.

"This is the centre of their defence," Hartmut said. His audience included two daemon-mothers, as he'd called them, and all his own captains, and Thorn. One old wyvern—Sylch, the leader of one of the wings of wyverns—attended, but paid no attention, instead picking constantly at something between the spread talons of its right foot. The two useful warlords of the Huran were present, Black Blanket and Shag-an-ho, both keen men who he could almost like.

And Orley.

Orley held too much *ops*. It was clear that something had been done to him, and it made men shy of him. He now had black antlers growing from his head. He didn't even seem to know.

Hartmut tried to ignore whatever was wrong with Orley. He spoke directly to Thorn.

"They've cleared all this—hundreds of paces of woods and bog, knocked flat. This entire ridge is one fortified line." He shrugged. "Behind it, the camp is itself a fortress, with walls fifteen feet thick and ten feet high." He couldn't keep the tone from his voice. "We gave them a week, and they used what they had. Farmers, and wood, and earth."

Thorn swayed.

"None of my warlocks has had any effect on the old witch's defence," he said. "I must deal with her myself."

His hesitation showed. The mighty sorcerer lord hesitated . . .

Hartmut shrugged despite the weight of his armour and the overwhelming clouds of black flies.

"It is impregnable, unless we bring up trebuchets or build them new. Or unless you can simply unleash the hounds of hell to smash the earthworks."

Thorn nodded. "This is not the battle my master wanted," he said. "What other choices have we?"

Hartmut looked around at the captains. "We can fall back on Ticondaga and make it a base. We can fill the frontiers with blood all summer, keep these peasants from their fields, and strike where we wish until every cabin is burned and this captain has no reserve of manpower to fell his trees.

We can keep his forces in the field until the cost breaks his King. We can butcher the little people with our monsters until they know their King cannot protect them."

"Their King is dead."

Hartmut nodded. "They do not seem to miss him."

Thorn swayed. "This strategy of yours—it is not what my master wants."

Hartmut, who had served several princes, nodded. "It never is. But I always offer it."

"Give me another choice," Thorn said.

"You can always fling your army recklessly at this rock of earth and wood," Hartmut said. His contempt was obvious. "Unless your unseelie powers give you some absolute dominance, your army will die here."

Thorn nodded. "I *understand*. Give me another *choice*."

Hartmut frowned. "We could move north, around the position. On a wide front, so that we could overwhelm any opposition, surround and crush it in the mountains. Bypass any other strong points." He shrugged. "Try to cut the road off further along. Then our problem becomes their problem: supply."

"We can feast on the dead, and they cannot." Thorn's voice was hollow.

"They can bake and eat bread," Hartmut said. "Of the two, I'd rather eat bread."

"What of the east?" Thorn asked.

"He has another force in the east, but it's on the other side of the river and too small to affect us." Hartmut shrugged yet again. "I think he wants us to go east. Instead, with our latest ascension of your little monsters, I'd put three or four legions of them here and around the Hole, and fling them into the entrenchments all day. They can die slowly, and we'll win along the road and push the battle back to here."

"You are reckless in expending them," Thorn said.

"That's what they are for, surely?" Hartmut shrugged. "They are fodder. But in mass waves, they will tie down any force left here—while we turn his flank."

"His flank," Thorn said. "The Dark Sun."

Unnecessarily, Hartmut said, "He beat you before."

Thorn rustled, stone on stone. "I am aware."

Hartmut shook his head. "I need a private word, my Lord Sorcerer."

The Outwallers and the others drew back.

"Retreat, and fight another day," Hartmut said. "That is my advice."

"No," said Thorn.

"Then north, around them. As soon as we can." Hartmut took a breath. "Into the woods. Leave most of the boglins—they will only slow us. And in a mass—we have what, fifteen, twenty *thousand* of them? Let them go forward against the ridge."

Thorn seemed relieved. "And will there be a great battle?" he asked.

Hartmut paused. "We have odds of four or even five to one or better," he said. "If we are very lucky and we move fast, there will be no great battle. They'll simply fold away and be massacred as we turn their positions—or stand and starve. If the boglins break through—then we win a massive victory and the whole enemy force is massacred."

Thorn seemed for a moment to whisper to someone else.

"Massacre will do. It is essential that as many of them be together as can be arranged." Thorn swayed again. "And if we are not lucky?"

"It will be a terrible battle in the wilderness." Hartmut pursed his lips. "A fight unlike any I have ever seen. No possible way to predict the result."

"Perfect," Thorn said.

Hartmut nodded. "As you command," he said.

Chapter Nineteen

The Battle of Gilson's Hole

The skies opened just after breakfast. Old archers put their bowstrings in waxed linen bags and then put the bags under their hats. Young ones copied them.

The sound of axes never stopped.

A little after nine, the order came to mount.

Cully mounted slowly, all the aches in all his joints fuelled by tension and pure fear.

They rode east through beech trees, forest giants widely spaced with almost no underbrush—here and there, a wicked patch of hobblebush, and occasional openings, sometimes of grass but more often a thicket of raspberry and bramble. Cully rode at the captain's elbow, and they moved at an astounding speed through the woods, on a road just wide enough for two fully armoured men on big horses to pass—quickly. The road went on and on; one mile, and then another.

In the second mile, they came to the woodcutters—terrified men from the valleys to the south and east. And their guardians.

Golden Bears.

The column flinched, almost to a man and woman. And beyond the bears were irks—hundreds of them, tall and lanky and evil-looking, with mouths full of teeth and hands full of weapons.

Cully made himself ride on. The great Golden Bear to his left—whose yellow eyes were level with his own—on horseback—grinned. It said something that almost sounded like Alban.

Cully grinned back.

Behind him, Flarch grunted. "Fuck me," he said. "Did you hear the bear?"

Cully shook his head, still shaken.

"It said, 'Get some.'"

Cully's nerves got the better of him and he laughed, a little too high and loud. Men looked at him.

Off further to the left, a white stag broke cover. On its back was the most beautifully equipped knight Cully had ever seen.

"The Faery Knight!" men called. Some of the company men cheered—and many of the farmers.

The Faery Knight—who looked more poised and magnificent than the captain had ever managed—trotted his enormous stag to where Ser Gabriel waited on his riding horse. They clasped hands.

"Well met," said Ser Tapio. "Now what do we do?"

"Push east as fast as we can until we can see the Unicorn," the captain said. The Unicorn was a towering spire of white rock that rose alongside Buck Pond Mountain. "Then, if all goes well..."

Ser Tapio smiled a knowing smile, and they rode on together, their households staying as separate bodies for the first mile of broken ground, and then gradually intermingling. The faery knights were irks—most of them were slighter than men, and their armour far more old-fashioned. Most had bronze byrnies instead of steel habergeons and many wore leather defences where the men had steel plate, more cunningly formed. But the irks had their own breed of horses and a few stags and massive caribou that seemed to take the woods in easier strides, and they were festooned in charms and runes that few of the men and women could emulate.

They passed along the south shore of Big Rock Lake. From time to time the captain checked a wax tablet, and Cully saw, at a brief halt, that writing appeared in the wax, and he shook his head.

"They have started to attack the fort line," the captain admitted to the Faery Knight.

"Ahh," Ser Tapio replied. "Better than I feared. I worried we were hunters beating for a stag long since run away."

The captain shrugged. "Every mile we do this, our forces will be better at cooperating."

Indeed, along the front of the long, long column, bears and irks shared the skirmish line with Gelfred's men. To the north and west of the road, once the lake was passed, the column was paralleled by the movement of a long line of boglins who crossed the Wild the way ants cross a difficult area of pebbles, all touching. It was chilling and inhuman to watch, and most of the company stopped watching. But it did make them feel protected.

The woodcutters extending the road shuddered, and some had to control trembling and actual terror as the boglins passed, or when a pair of fell *hastenoch* clomped by, their squid-like mouths writhing horribly.

Many flinched when a troop of Outwallers ran along the new road for a few hundred yards—all moving in their endless war-lope, a near-silent flash of red paint and jingle of silver hawk's bells in the light rain.

Noon came. The scouts of all races pushed out, and the men dismounted, and the pages took the horses.

Nell held a hand for the Faery Knight's stag. It didn't even have reins.

"Go with the nissse young woman," Ser Tapio said. He smiled at her, showing his fangs. He rolled neatly off his saddle, a stunning display of acrobatics.

"Show-off," Ser Gabriel said. He dismounted with an ordinary turn and slide on his breastplate.

Morgon Mortirmir appeared from the white banda, and Toby passed him forward. Toby was the captain's field chamberlain—he decided who got into the inner circle and who could wait. Mortirmir looked excited.

"My lord," he said. He grinned, and stared openly at the Faery Knight, and the beautiful—horrifying—irk woman in brazen armour who stood at his shoulder.

"Oh!" she said. She put a brass hand to Morgon's cheek. "The power!"

"Handsss off, Lilith!" Ser Tapio said. There was some laughter from the irks.

"Yes?" the captain asked. He had a garlic sausage in his mouth and another in his hand.

"My lord." Morgon shrugged. "It's difficult to know where to begin... I've solved the horse plague."

Toby's face suggested he was regretting allowing the young man to interrupt the captain's lunch.

"Really?" Ser Gabriel asked.

"Yes. It was under my nose all along. Brutally simple." He shrugged. "In fact, I was right from the first—all a problem of magnification. You see—"

"Morgon." The captain's eyes were kind. "I'm about to face a major battle. I need to prepare. You have the ability to stop the horse plague?"

"Instantly."

"Bravo. Share it with me and every other hermeticist." He smiled softly. "Then leave me alone, please."

Morgon looked shame-faced. Nonetheless, both men's faces became slack for a few seconds.

The captain returned first. "You really do learn something every day," he said. "Tapio?"

Again he vanished into his palace, and Toby fetched water—the captain always returned from the *aethereal* hungry and thirsty.

The Faery Knight shook his head.

"Interesssting," he said. "Leave it to men to make sssomething of nothing. Sssomething horrible."

"I don't really see men as to blame for all the ills of the world." Ser Gabriel shook his head. "But come—let's right them, e'er we quarrel about them."

Ser Tapio smiled. "You are a wight after my own heart," he said.

The rain fell steadily—not a heavy storm, but a long, soaking spring day. The air was cold enough the men's breath could be seen and that of horses, and bears, and other things. When they started again, they soon passed the last of the road, a hundred men all cutting together.

A young, bearded man loped from the woodcutters and stood in the captain's way.

"Sorry—my lord, but my da and a whole lot of our folk—they went south, like, and we've lost 'em." The young man shook his head. "Da said somewhat of cutting the path back to we. An' I said—"

"Gelfred?" the captain said. "Lad, we'll do our best to find your da. You and yours are the furthest forward. Keep cutting! The Prince of Occitan is somewhere behind us. I need this path to be his signpost. What's your name?"

"Will, my lord."

"Will, keep your people together and keep cutting." He glanced up—he and the Faery Knight exchanged a look.

"The Unicorn is almost due north," the Faery Knight said. "I don't need to see it, to see it." He smiled and showed his fangs.

The captain turned back to young Will. "Turn the path south now, Will. You'll be safe enough behind us, then."

"Aye, my lord. But find me da?" the young man asked.

Will Starling, tall and stark in forester green, clapped the man on the shoulder. "We'll find him," he said.

As soon as the column turned south, the way became much more difficult. It took them an hour to pass south of a single overgrown beaver meadow, and only when they emerged back into a country of big trees and open spaces did Cully realize they were now riding south. The rain was lighter.

There was a long peal of thunder in the south. Then another.

Then Gelfred burst out of cover to the front. He waved both arms to the east and south.

The captain reined in, pulled out his ivory slate and wrote quickly.

Horns blew to the front.

Ser Tapio paused his stag.

Gelfred cantered up. "Just past the edge of the ridge—thousands of them."

"How far—exactly?" the captain snapped.

"Long bowshot," Gelfred said. He was spanning his crossbow as he turned his horse.

The captain sat back in his saddle. His eyes went three places—to Ser Michael, by his side; to Gelfred; and then, for a longer time, to Ser Tapio.

"Ganfroy!" he said, without further consultation. "Sound 'form your front.'" He paused and listened to the flawless call. "Sound 'change horses.'"

Ser Michael turned and began to pick his way rapidly to the north. Ser Milus was doing the same to the south, after he'd mounted his new charger.

"I want to attack," the captain said. His face said he was in agony. It was all taking too long. "We need the ridge top, or we should retire to the last ridge." Indeed, they were going downhill—the terrain descended in a series of gentle and steep ridges like ocean waves, all the way to the Albin River six miles away. "But we can do this, right here."

"This, too, we share," Ser Tapio said. "I agree."

The woods were open. The rear of the long column was badly hampered by the marsh and bog around the old beaver ponds, but thousands of animals crashing through the woods make their own road, and it was not as hard at the back as at the front.

"Your people are already on the flanks?"

"Mostly to the west. I will go there. Send me a hundred knights when I wind my horn three times." Ser Tapio smiled. "You have far more knights than I."

"Done," Ser Gabriel said, and they clasped hands. The Faery Knight waved one arm, and bells seemed to ring, and all his knights simply rode away. They were as fast as swallows changing directions—and then they were gone.

"Ser Bescanon—take thirty lances and hold them in reserve for Ser Tapio." Ser Gabriel's eyes registered his acceptance of the order and moved on.

The ridge to their front was full of horns. Around them their small army poured from column into line. The company troops did it well, despite the trees—they simply flowed into place. New men were slapped on the back or pushed. There were enough veterans—just—to get the line formed. Ser Milus's white banda was almost half newcomers, and the red banda not much better. Only Gelfred's green banda was all veterans.

Cully saw the captain still scribbling. There was fighting off to the left— well away to the left. Horns.

"I think we've found their whole force," the captain said. "I'm sending Sauce for our reserves."

He was smiling.

Cully hated that smile. "Reserves?" he asked.

The captain smiled that nasty smile. "Haven't you wondered where my brother's been, all this time?" he asked.

Cully began to cheer up.

They heard the hollow axe sounds all morning, from the west and south. Hartmut flinched every time the sound came clear. All he could imagine was a long line of forts running all the way across his path—

Before noon, the Dead Tree Qwethnethogs and the scouts of the Huran caught a band of axemen and destroyed them.

After that, there was no holding the army, and it flooded forward into the low hills, up each ridge on its steep face, and then a shallower descent. Hartmut didn't know the country, but he knew the general lay of the land.

He was concerned at how quickly a few miles of wilderness swallowed their whole force. By how open the woods proved to be.

It was more alien than anything he'd seen.

But Thorn seemed content with their route, and they pressed forward. It was terrible walking for the men—the sailors and the brigans—but Hartmut put them deep in the column so that the great daemons, the stone trolls and the other forest folk could make a trail for them. At last they broke out of the lowlands and into the higher ground with bigger trees, and every step they climbed seemed to rid them of the clinging hobblebush and the terrible alders.

Cunxis, one of the warlords of the Dead Trees, appeared out of the light rain, his feather cloak making him almost invisible until he chose to be seen.

"Thorn—they are right here! A whole army!"

Cunxis was intolerably excited; his red crest stood up, engorged with blood, and his teeth all but glowed white.

"Where?" Thorn demanded. There was a very faint sound of horns— above them on the next ridge. Further north.

Ears of many shapes pricked.

Without any order being given, the whole host began to flood up the ridge, led by the daemons of the Dead Tree Clan, followed—and sometimes outrun—by a thousand Outwaller warriors. The column had only been moving on a path ten or so creatures wide, crushing the underbrush as they moved, and now it gathered speed—but there were bands and bands, stretching away down the last three ridges...

Hartmut spat. "Halt," he roared at his own human auxiliaries. They halted—and creatures flowed around them.

The enemy—Outwallers and daemons—got to the top of the ridge first.

The captain swore—palpably.

"Don't halt!" the captain roared, when the line faltered. Even in the rain, the feather cloaks and the slick skin—and sheer size—showed the fearsome enemy. Everyone had nightmares of the daemons at Lissen Carak.

The ground was actually becoming more broken as they climbed the ridge, and on the narrow front where the daemons emerged from the rain, there was naked rock and a steep slope.

"Household—dismount," the captain called. Cursing—no knight likes to fight on foot—the veteran knights swung off their war horses and handed them back to pages—and in some cases lost only a few strides.

"Stay open," the captain ordered. He was on foot, and they were going up the slope—the steepest.

Heavy rocks came down on them. A daemon lobbed a rock as big as a man's head, and Chris Foliak died, his head crushed.

His squire pushed forward into his space and they continued up. Lord Wimarc slammed his face-plate closed as a smaller stone broke his nose.

Stones were not their only weapons. The daemons had heavy axes. They had halted, and stood waiting near the crest—and Outwaller warriors started to leak around their edges.

The household went up the last few yards with their archers loosing at very close range—most of them already at or behind trees as big as the columns that supported a church roof.

The daemons stopped the captain's household cold, and didn't give a foot's breadth. Nell fell there, cut almost in two by a daemon's axe, and Toby saw the captain go down—struck in the chest by a rock—he rolled, and got to his feet before Toby could take any action. Then Toby missed his guard and caught most of a blow—his helmet did not fail, but his head moved too far, he screamed and fell, and the captain's *ghiavarina* was everywhere for a few seconds. A daemon fell—another rolled forward, tripping on its own tangled guts.

"Back!" roared the captain.

Toby had never seen the company stopped. He could not, at first, believe it, and Cully, safe behind a tree at the base of the slope, had to pull the stunned boy out of the line of rocks now falling as the daemons taunted the beaten company.

The household retreated slowly, dragging their wounded. The rest of the company was not retreating—in some cases, like Ser Michael's lance, they had won the race to the crest.

"Was that Nell?" the captain asked Toby.

"Yes," Toby spat.

The archers continued, working through their livery arrows at a stunning rate. The thrown rocks were not enough answer, and their shafts began to tell. The daemons were suffering. One of their shamans tossed a working.

The captain unravelled it.

"Listen," the captain said to Toby. "Listen to the horns." He smiled.

Toby heard only the sound of desperate combat: horns, and horns, steel and shouting, and screams. Nell—Chris Foliak...He had never felt so tired. So beaten.

"Ready everyone?" the captain called. "Fast as you can to the top. Everyone kill one. This is it."

Toby looked around. *What did he hear? They were going again?*

The captain stepped out from behind his great tree and a stone hit his left arm. He raised his right and blew a long call on his horn.

The beaten household got up, or came out from behind their trees.

The captain was already a third of the way up the slope. He was flying over the rocks like a faery horse. Toby decided to try not watching his footing and jumping—in full plate armour—from rock to rock.

It was insanely foolish.

He fell, and his breastplate took the force of his fall on a sharp rock—rose, and jumped.

He could no longer see the captain, but suddenly, above him, there was a great beaked face.

Sometimes, you have to go up the hill first.

The irony was that he was fairly certain that this part of the battle was already won. He could hear the red banda's horns, and even Michael's shouts—from the ridge crest. He'd guessed the enemy would be on a narrow frontage—at first.

That didn't change the tactical reality that he had to hold the whole ridge crest to win. It was bad luck that the enemy had led their force with their very best assault troops.

The logic was unassailable.

But he'd blown their first chance, and now he had to lead from in front, and very possibly die.

He thought—in no order, and all at once—of Harmodius, of Amicia, of Blanche, of his mother, and, of all people, of Ser Tapio.

Win or lose—he could die here, and that was fine.

He began to run.

He had a plan—he had a plan for everything, and if he hadn't been labouring to breathe inside a pig-faced bascinet while climbing a cliff in armour, he might even have assayed a laugh, because he hadn't made any plan at all for Blanche, and she was a new world of delight and happiness that he didn't think he could ever grow used to.

Planning. Over-rated.

But he had planned not to use his powers until he met Thorn, and he found, here, on a naked rock slope with a hundred giant daemons ravening for his blood, that he really didn't want to lose another friend.

He leapt to the left—landed well, on a big spike of glacial scree—and flicked with his left gauntlet, opening his first of seven sequenced attacks. He'd layered days' worth of *ops* and stored the results in Pru's ever-faithful mind. He didn't have to enter his palace or speak a trigger.

Daemons died. Some simply lost their feet at the ankle. Their shaman revealed himself to cast—first a strong shield to prevent a repetition, and then a concussive hammer spell, very simple, very hard to shield.

Gabriel turned to working with the *ghiavarina,* and reached out through the dangerous terrain of the *aethereal,* found him, and took him. He subsumed the daemon even as the creature shrieked, begged mercy, and collapsed.

We are the monsters, Gabriel thought. *At least, I am. Kill my page, you fucks?*

Up he went, and the scythe of his thought reaped them.

In the *aether,* he roared.

Come, Thorn. Let's be done with it. Come, Thorn, and die.

It was all death.

To Ash, all deaths were of equal value. It was, in fact, going much as he had envisioned, and he rode the success, smiling at the little stumbling blocks. The boglins died, storming the first wall—very satisfying. Men died, and cave trolls died, and the sweet, honey taste of the Golden Bears—they died.

The vanguard held for one assault and then melted under the onslaught of a truly talented mage, and even Ash registered dimly that he ought to be aware of this one, and then the thought slid off the hardened surface of his mind, and he was waiting, lurking, his empowerment and achievement nearing completion, the *ant apotheosis* he'd scryed as the key to his next victory—to a cascade of endless victory. A way around the *others.* The path, at least, to freedom, and perhaps even—victory.

Death. Another and another five and two more and ten.

He felt the limit pass, and he, for whom joy was beyond the void, felt a flash of something very close...

Thorn felt his dark lord's rising elation and he rode it, even as he felt the cry for help from Cunxis and even as the flanks of his still-moving force began to lose the crest line and fall back. Almost none of his vast army was yet engaged. They poured up the third ridge like water running uphill, their once narrow front broadening organically as every creature strove with every other to reach the front.

But Ash was already there, like a lover on the edge of climax and demanding completion, his ravings pouring undiminished into the wilderness Thorn had created around the egg in his mind.

Come, Thorn, came the voice of the Dark Sun.

It was now, or never.

I come, he said. He translated—he let go the thing he'd held so long, changed his innermost process, abandoned the armoured body he'd created for the one of will and essence he preferred—there was a burst of black light...

Toby slammed his war hammer on the thing's taloned foot. There was nothing else to do, and he had to trust to luck and good armour.

His hammer struck, and the daemon, hampered by fear of whatever was killing his mates, missed, and Toby was up—he swung again and missed wildly, and the daemon was down on one great saurian knee and flicked his axe one-handed. The blow caught Toby at the edge of a cover, and turned him—now he was bleeding under his arm.

Both cut, almost together.

Toby's steel hammer, now powered by two hands, cut the more vertical line, covering his own head and delivering a powerful blow to his adversary—just as the captain taught. The blow struck, almost untouched—the daemon took it over the left eye.

And fell.

Toby paused for too long, incredulous. But above him on the slope, the great wardens were turning their backs and fleeing. To Toby's left there were new movements, but they flashed in the watery sunlight—men in armour, already at the crest—some on horses.

Ser Michael had taken the crest.

Toby saw the captain, then. He stood in a guard, facing empty air. He was just a few yards short of the crest, his great spear held low.

He was alone.

And then, he was not.

Thunder cracked—everywhere, as if a thousand bolts of lightning had struck simultaneously. And a tower of black smoke, as tall as the spire of a village church and lit from within by a dark red fire that also spread like angel's wings on either side, and rose to form a crown, or a halo.

Thorn towered over the Red Knight.

His staff came down, a direct blow in the real, and the Red Knight parried, a rising cover with the haft of the *ghiavarina* even as he stepped hard to the right.

To Toby's eyes, the heads of the two weapons, entangled in the interaction, burst into white-hot flame.

In Gabriel's consciousness, Thorn only threw the physical blow to cover his hermetical assault. It was not contemptuous, this time, and there were no theatrics. Six nested workings collapsed like an avalanche of brilliantly woven *ops* on his armoured form.

He played them all. In one virtuoso employment of every tool, he *stood with Prudentia and unloosed every protection, amulet, and prepared defence save one, and they unrolled—sword of light to parry a bolt of darkness, the timing perfect, the counter already flowing—the net, burned, the assault on will undermined, the flood almost damned, the envelopment counterenveloped and a second counter initiated, and the pure, white fog of* ops *batted away—mostly—*

Absorbed.

He was hit in three places—not every counter had been perfect, but armour

529

and runes kept it from being mortal, and he was on his feet, the spear still in his hand.

There was no thought. He cut with the spear—

Thorn covered with his staff, *took a hit from the slightly delayed counter to the bolt of darkness working, and* staggered, wounded.

He drew something from his waist as Gabriel's elemental counter-envelopment engorged itself on Thorn's first working and blew back into him. The sorcerer lost the thread of his casting and—

The Red Knight's first formed working in the aethereal *was just too slow— everything, every defence, had been pre-deployed, and now he was on his own. He was too slow—Thorn, twice wounded, managed to cast again and Gabriel's elation was punctured as he was staggered by Thorn's brilliant eclipse working—something gave in his side—*

Thorn's staff slammed into his arm. Armour crumpled like tin, and the bones of his forearm snapped—

Prudentia continued to spin, rolling the next working into completion awaiting only the trigger.

Pain rose like the roar of the rain and the rolling drums of thunder in the Red Knight's side and arm, but he was above it.

In a moment—*Blanche, her hand, the darkness*—he abandoned his plan. His right hand twirled the spear in a long feint, reversing his grip.

"*Fiat Lux,*" he cried, unleashing the working that had taken too long—

Thorn turned his massive working with a healthy respect and a massive shield—

But this time, the working had been the feint. The spear completed its turn, the grip reversed, and the Red Knight cast—with all his might—the Wyrm's spear into Thorn's unprotected groin.

On the other side of the ridge, Hartmut saw the intense strobes of light through the rain. To the right and behind him, the whole of Thorn's horde was rolling, flowing, in one continuous carpet up the slope of the last ridge.

The battle—if it was indeed a battle—was less than fifteen minutes old. Even his knights flinched from the massive detonations that marked the centre point of the conflict, and the steady flow of wounded daemons did nothing to encourage him.

"Thorn!" Hartmut bellowed.

He had no answer but rain, and a triple detonation of lightning—three fast flashes that imprinted on Hartmut forever the hideous ripple that was the rising beat of a single, impossibly large wing. And around the wing— the wing as big as the centre of an army—were bones. Bones stripped in one single instant of sorcerous domination of their flesh. Daemons and Outwallers, men and beasts, knights and horses—stripped to bones in one heartbeat.

And from it rose—

One wing. It was long, and a deep blue-black, shot with veins of softly glowing purple black, and it moved.

It moved with an elegant lethality.

Ser Hartmut was still having trouble with the scale, and doubted his eyes.

The rising wing's passage knocked him and his horse to the ground.

Mag rose to her feet.

"Here he comes," she said aloud. Which was interesting, as she was alone. There was not another soul—damned, blessed, or otherwise—in the first line of forts.

Just as she had arranged. Lord Wayland and the Grand Squire and their troops had withstood two assaults from an almost unimaginable horde of unsupported boglins. The northern Brogat levy had fought—with her hermetical support—until they had filled the marsh to the front and all the ditches with dead monsters.

Now the enemy was massing on the far side of the marsh—readying another assault. And Lord Wayland's men were delighted to obey the order to march for the rear, the higher, safer ground.

Mag stayed. Mag had her own plan.

"Here I come, John," she said, as if her love were right there, with her.

Like the whisper of rain coming on a summer's day, he came—a black cloud, a coalescing.

Mag rose on her tiptoes and poured fire into the formation of the monster miles to the north. She loosed her working in the *aethereal* in the moment that the thing was moving to the real and had a presence in both. It was taking shape—not, as she had hoped, being born, but leaping, fully -fledged, into the world.

Mag stood alone at the centre of an empty fortress of earth and wood, and let slip all the bonds that bound her power. She knew no university laws, and had no memory palace, and her access was direct and uncompromising.

Blue fire leapt into the sky.

Across the swamp, an entire nest's worth of boglins—an uncountable, crawling mass—prepared the last assault across the low ground. They had rafts and ladders and great hoardings of wild bramble and ropes of vine and grass, and among them were two years of the full crop of the Wild. They had been left with their Exrech to watch the Hillmen—and eat them. And then, when the army's flank was secure, and their cousins had made a path with their bodies, to storm the forts.

No Hillmen had come.

Almost five miles to the south, the Hillmen had forded the Upper Albin at first light, slipping and cursing on the wet stones and watching the distant tree line for the ambush that they would, themselves, have launched. Late in the crossing, a handful of irks opposed them, and Kenneth Dhu died with an irk's arrow in his throat. But the big men in their long byrnies got across and scoured the bank, and then they started moving, not west towards their allies, but almost due east and a little north, as if marching to Morea, ever deeper into the marshy low ground. Behind them, the surviving animals of the drove moved with them, parallel but on the eastern side of the river, where there was an old drove road. The horse-boys and a handful of old borderers moved the cattle herd.

When they came opposite the best ford for twenty miles, the Hillmen had already cleared it, striking into the ambush from the flank. Tom Lachlan never shouted his war cry, for his people did their work so suddenly that he never bloodied his sword.

"Now for it, lads," he said. "Bring the beasties across. Now we avenge Hector."

And indeed, now they were in the very country where great Hector had fallen, the same streams, and a cloud of faeries came with the morning rain and followed them, flitting about among the long horns of the cattle.

Donald Dhu was stony faced, but he kept running his thumb along the edge of his great blade, and Tom knew a man who'd marked himself for death.

"He was a fine boy," Tom said.

"This is a daft plan," Donald Dhu said. "You're as madcap as your cousin."

Tom Lachlan frowned. "Tell me that at sunset," he said.

"It's that Red Knight of yours," Donald Dhu said.

"I can thole him," Tom said.

"Ca' ye, just? E'en if he's killing off your own folk to save his?" Donald Dhu glared, eyes red-rimmed.

Tom didn't snarl. He might have, once. Now he simply looked. "Donald, darlin', you've lost yer fine boy and that's a cryin' shame. But if you go on like this, I'll split yer round head, myself." He nodded sharply, and drove his horse forward, giving the other man his back.

No man laughed—but Red Rowan and Daud the Cow shouldered their axes and followed Bad Tom, and soon enough the whole force of the Hillmen was pushing as fast as could be managed through the tangled edge of the marsh and swamp.

Two hours later, the beasts pushed out of the swamp. They were, in fact, at the very edge of the grassy meadows where Hector had left his herd a year before. Tom sent two of the younger warriors to have a look, and dismounted, settled his back to a tree, and had a nap. There was a big storm higher in the mountains, and they could hear the snap of lightning, the roll of thunder.

Tom awoke to the feeling he'd slept too long. But his men, almost a thousand of them, were well rested and had eaten a meal, and now he got them mounted and moved the herd back west—now along the line of the old road, through the open woods on either side.

The storm in the hills began to rise to an epic intensity, and it became clear—suddenly, in one single and titanic triple detonation—that this was not nature's hand, but the power of sentience.

"Tar's tits," Donald Dhu swore.

"Move them along," Tom yelled, and gave a shout. A hundred men took it up—a high-pitched noise between a keen and a yell—and the cattle began to move faster. Here and there, a younger animal, pushed by a stronger, fell, and the herd began to fan out over more forest.

Tom wished for wings, so he could fix a location for himself—but then, as if granted a dream by a god, he saw a giant maple tree with a vast bole and a huge bulging projection—a tree he knew well, that his people all called the Forest God. The tree was ancient and the bole a landmark well-known, and he grinned.

Something fell gave voice. It was shrill, and high, and utterly without pity for man. It shrieked of the dark when there were no stars, of aeons of time before the hand of man came to mar the earth—and even the Hillmen were afraid.

Most of them.

Although that shriek was a mile away or more, Tom Lachlan drew his great sword.

Then he turned to the horse-boys in the drag, raised his horn, and blew.

They answered with shouts, horns, and whips.

In twenty beats of a man's heart, the herd went from swiftly trotting individual beasts to a live thing of great mass, and a single will. It was panicked.

It ran.

More than a long bowshot wide, filling the woods from side to side, the herd ran west up the line of the road.

Ash rose, delighting in the rush of damp air beneath his wings, free for the first time in an aeon—embodied, and full of power and vitality—and cast a working almost contemptuously into the mortals to his front as he cleared the ridge, and destroyed half a thousand years' worth of N'gara irks. The red of his fire and the footprint of his destruction rooted the company and terrified even his own army.

He remembered breath, and he *breathed*.

He turned, almost lazily, and Mag's blue fire struck him in the side, under his right wing as it rose for more altitude—

His scream killed. His rage was palpable—red fire swept along the ridge. Men died—Cuddy and Tom Lantorn and Dagon La Forêt and Tancred di Piast, boiled to death in their armour, killed almost instantly as a hundred company lances died. Then his wound turned him south and east and his rage-fire passed over the red-crested daemons and into a cohort of trolls and down the helpless ranks of Outwallers preparing to retake the heights, eliminating them in four heartbeats the way a forge eats coal.

But Mag's fire still burned him. It did not stop—it was not a simple missile of elemental fire, but a master craft of cold anger and human subtlety by a woman who could plan and execute every stitch in an embroidered coverlet. She had not forgotten *anything*.

Shaken, Ash banked, and went for her. *In the* aethereal*, he reached for her and found—another golden wall. He roared, and threw pure ops at her—great uncontrolled balls of the stuff, and she stood his assault undiminished, and then struck him again.*

This time, he had her measure, and turned all but the slightest singe of her strike.

Four miles were nothing to his great wings—less than a minute. But for a minute she stood the whole force of his will, the whole of his wrath, the overwhelming and yet impotent force of his unchanelled might.

For that minute, Mag's fire burned in his side, and she struck back six more times, at an increasing tempo.

Almost, he was afraid.

*But in time—seventy beats of his great wings—*he was above her, and in a single hiss of his bright breath she was burned to ash, her shields overcome, her will extinguished.

He had come far down in the air, from the heights above, and now that he was almost at the level of the river he could see the rout of his rearguard—something had smashed his boglins flat.

But there were always more of them. The woods were still full, despite the triumph of some maggot lordling and his cattle, and he turned on one wingtip and roared his destruction into the upper camp, and Lord Wayland was burned, and the Grand Squire was badly scorched, and two hundred knights and half a generation of Brogat farmers died, breathing fire into their lungs.

He winged back over the battlefield west of the Hole and breathed again, and a generation of Hillmen cattle died, roasted. And then he turned to find the men. In his rage, he turned, and burned, losing altitude with every strike, until his vast wings blotted out the sun and he seemed to skim the very tops of the trees.

Tom Lachlan raised his sword over his head as the dragon appeared like a dark storm over the treetops, and suddenly there were faeries all about him.

The dragon was bigger than a castle. It was longer than the biggest building in Liviapolis—and it flew, like a great warship in the air, and it pushed before it a prow of invisible terror consequent to its size. Red Rowan and Willie Hutton, hard-faced killers, fell on their faces, Daud the Cow's great axe fell from his nerveless fingers, and Donald Dhu cursed God, but Tom Lachlan raised his head.

"By the oath we swore to you, Wyrm! Now I demand ye! Avenge my kin! We stand inside the Circle!" he roared.

His voice was unheard in the wind of Ash's passage—unheard, but not unfelt. He stood his ground, almost alone, against a creature a thousand times his size. But all around him came the faeries—a rush of them, like a coloured wind—and they suddenly flared like fire in new birch bark—exploding in all directions.

Hector's voice said, *Avenge me.*

It was merest chance—or the will of God—that the dragon had just spent its breath, and was inhaling—and looking for a far more fearsome foe than the single, puny man. His great wings beat, he raised his head, and he flinched, unwitting, from the burst of colour and potent souls that the faeries mimicked—and his armoured belly almost touched the ground along the road as he tried to rise.

Bad Tom leapt from the back of his horse as high as he could reach, and his great sword, given him by the Wyrm, struck. The winged faeries bore him up for five beats of his great heart. The wound should have been no more than a flea bite to a man, but Tom's arm was strong and his eye sure, and the great blade went deep and cut forty feet of belly flesh as the dragon swept on.

Tom fell to earth and rolled. Then he was back on his feet, sword over his head as great gouts of black blood fell to earth. He roared, "I hit the thing!" and then, "Lachlan for Aye!"

But the dragon had a new prey in his mind, and swept away. Because in answer to Tom Lachlan's call, another great dragon was rising over the battlefield.

There was nowhere on the battlefield of Gilson's Hole that men like Nita Qwan, moving carefully from tree to tree on the ever expanding envelopment of Thorn's column—or boglins, like Sleck, now trying to keep his feet in the push to save the ridge top, or irks like Tilowindle, trying to make sense of the death of everyone about him, or bears like Flint, paw to claw with a stone troll at the very crest of the great ridge—nowhere that they could not see the two dragons rolling in massive aerial combat over the battle below and around them. Ash glowed black, and a blue fire still burned, undimmed by Mag's death, and the smaller, sleeker Wyrm of Ercch, steel grey and brilliant scarlet, turned inside Ash's bulk.

Both vast behemoths breathed, and the sky caught fire.

Thorn grunted as the Red Knight's spearhead penetrated deep into his fiery shadow form, and he stumbled.

Then, with a twist, as the Red Knight prepared his last working, Thorn tore the spear from his cloak of shadow, dripping fluid, and cast it aside.

"My heart is not there, either," he said, but his voice was ruined, and he stumbled forward.

"Simple lightning," Gabriel said to Prudentia.

She obeyed. The statues whirled and the astrological signs lined up.

"Watch," he said.

Catching up the thread he'd saved for weeks—the connection that had tethered Thorn to his great moth—Gabriel passed his simple working down it, like water down an aqueduct to a thirsty town.

"Like to like," he said.

Thorn shuddered as the damage ripped through him under his shields, and fell, and his great wings of fire smote the earth, and the leaf mould caught—smoke rose from his ruin, and there was a scream like that of a woman giving birth and when Gabriel pushed forward Thorn's form had *vanished.* But his staff fell with a sharp clatter, and his fiery wings burned a moment longer and then went out.

Gabriel put a hesitant foot on the staff—unsure of his victory—in the very moment that Ash struck the Faery Knight's end of the line. The great serpent's fire fell to earth and all but blinded him, and then he'd raised his shields—three of them—and covered the household and part of the red banda as the monster's fire swept the ridge, killing a fifth of the company in four beats of his heart and then sweeping unchecked into the south. Gabriel was knocked to one knee by the sheer power of the bombardment of *ops.* But then the dragon turned away south, and he pushed his tired legs to lever his armoured body up. He could feel the sweat of fear like a cold, slimy hand on his back and guts. Something was wrong.

He was a few strides from the top of the ridge, and he ran forward, scooping his spear off the ground and discovering—to his shock—that his left hand was—gone. Along with much of his forearm. Simply—gone.

He fought the shock. It was all shock—the size of the dragon, his hand…

At the top, he could see.

At his feet writhed the vast bulk of an army still many times bigger than his own—already beaten to the ridge top, it had just been flayed by the dragon, who had cut a wider swathe through his own unprotected ranks than he had done to the company. His army had islands of hermetical defence—the Faery Knight, Duchess Mogon, Harmodius, Lord Krevak, Morgon Mortirmir and the Red Knight himself had all covered portions of their line.

"Oh, my God," Gabriel said aloud. Even as he spoke, the dragon was struck—burned blue, and turned away, flying down the ridges and south.

To Mag. Gabriel knew what she had done—what the inevitable out-
come must be—and he stood, transfixed, for most of the minute in which
she held her own against a god. He watched the dragon dwindle, the fire
burn, and saw each beat of the thing's mighty wings as a sign it had failed
to take her.

And then he awoke—he must use the time she gave, or it was for
nothing.

"On me!" he roared. "Ganfroy!"

Ganfroy was a broken doll cast down on the rocks, never to rise again.
His trumpet was bent under him.

Gabriel raised his own ivory horn and blew.

And they came.

Danved came, his sword broken in his hands, and he stooped and
plucked a stone-headed war hammer from the corpse of a red-crested daemon. Bertran came with the standard and Francis Atcourt and Phillipe de
Beause followed him. Cully came and Toby pushed himself off a rock and
Cat Evil and hollow-eyed Diccon who had loved Nell and knew where her
corpse lay, and Ricard Lantorn, painfully aware his brother had burned
to death almost at his side, and Flarch, and Adrian Goldsmith and even
Nicomedes—they all came and forced themselves into ranks, even as the
pages brought forward the horses.

On the left, he could see Ser Michael, pointing down the hill. On the
right, Ser Milus had lost half his lances in a single, devastating moment,
and the white banda on the right had halted—shocked.

Milus went into the charred corpses of his men, and took up the pole on
which the company's old Saint Catherine had hung. And by some virtue—
some working, some ancient rune—it still hung, so that when he raised it,
grey ash flew, and the silk banner licked out like a tongue of flame.

There was a thin cheer. It was not much of a cheer, but in the
circumstances—

Gabriel ran forward, ignoring the loss of his left hand. There was no
pain, and very little blood. So far.

He turned, and raised his spear—and pointed it, one-handed, into the
enemy below.

"Now!" he said. "Thorn didn't beat you and the dragon couldn't kill
you, so now we are going to WIN."

And instead of waiting for the enemy to come up the ridge, or even to
see the result of the aerial combat, the company and their allies went down
into the maelstrom of battle under the shadow of death and, when they
struck, the monsters flinched.

Hartmut couldn't take his eyes from the two dragons.

The rise of their great monster should, surely, have been the end of the
conflict. But now—now, as their enemy came down the ridge to his waiting

spearmen—he saw how much devastation the black dragon had wreaked. In stealing flesh, he had all but destroyed the vanguard that should have formed the left of the line, and his fire had blasted the daemons on his right and a thousand other creatures.

Thousands of boglins were locked in a vicious, chitinous battle at the crest of the ridge to his far right, and there—at the ridge's steepest, stoniest top—great bears and stone trolls were locked in the static agony of melee.

To his own left, the enemy's irks had begun to crest the ridge, and from beyond them an Outwaller arrow fell harmlessly among his men.

Despite *everything*, it was still in the balance. His men were well ordered, and fresh enough.

"Up the hill!" he called. "Straight into them."

The brigans levelled their spear points, and began a slow march up the hill. The sailors loosed a volley of bolts.

He was facing men. He could see them—good plate armour, and good swords, and he grinned. Nothing about men ever made him afraid, and he drew his sword. As it burst into flame, his people cheered. Ser Cristan pointed at the burning sword and roared a challenge. Ser Louis began to move his mounted knights to fill the open ground to the left—to clear the enemy Outwallers.

Hartmut thought—*I have them.*

To his left, the enemy Outwallers began to sprint *forward*. They were bypassing him, which gave him an instant of puzzlement, and they were moments from being overrun by Ser Louis and the cavalry. But even as the sailors poured another withering volley into the armoured men on the slopes above, they paid a terrible price as the longbow arrows fell amongst them...

Hartmut's face furrowed as he frowned.

It was too late to avoid the combat.

But there was a banner behind the savages—blue and yellow check. Occitan. And another he didn't know, and another—a line of *mounted knights* coming on his side of the slope, moving easily through the open woods behind the line of Outwallers, led by the *Prince of Occitan*.

He cursed God, and led his men into the company.

In the captain's clever plan, the levy of the northern Brogat should have been enough, and the Royal Guard enough again, to hold the higher ridge and block the road. But the captain had never imagined the sheer horror of the dragon's breath, nor the packed legions of boglins. When the north wall was lost, the timbers charred and the men seared to meat standing to the last, Rebecca Almspend and Desiderata stood for three long minutes in the centre of the camp, back to back, and killed anything they could see, wielding power in ways neither had ever directly attempted. Almspend's power had been that of a scholar, and the Queen's that of a lover. Until today.

Desiderata hurled power, praying aloud for a gleam of sunshine and watching, horrified, as the embodied Ash darkened the sky above—but he was locked in a death grip with his rival, and she threw only one lingering golden bolt to penetrate his hide before returning to the rising tide at her feet. A behemoth, tusks red, crushed men and tents, and behind it a line of *hastenoch* trampled those who fled and those who stood their ground with equal vigour. The barghasts swooped on any prey that pleased them.

Blanche Gold watched the ruin of all their hopes, and stood with a short sword by the little King's bed. She had no great power with which to fight dragons, and she had no *ops* to loan her Queen. So she guarded the wet nurse and the babe, and when the north wall fell, and the *things* came, she killed them.

And again, Pavalo Payam saved her. Again, as before, he appeared before she was wholly done, when she had killed two boglins and had one fastened to her left thigh—he cut through the wall of the tent, and his sword moved with the easy, economical flow that she remembered—that it was almost worth the pain to see again—and the creatures died. He cleared the tent, ignored the shrieking wet nurse, nodded to her—and continued out the back wall.

Blanche stood and shook for a moment, and then realized she was bleeding on the Queen's bedding, and took action.

But as she pressed a spare shift to her thigh, there was a roar—so long it seemed as if it came from ten thousand men, and not just a thousand.

Ser John Crayford watched the north wall lost, and cursed. Mostly, he was cursing a certain arrogant young man who'd had all the answers the day before. But also his own instinct. The size of the dragon trumped any kind of preparation.

Ser John had his own knights—a handful. And the Morean cavalry, which had been beaten badly a few days before. Ser Giorgos Comnenos. Ser Christos.

He shook his head, and turned to Ser Christos. "I must try to save my Queen," he said.

Ser Christos saw the rout, the collapse, the chaos in the middle of the camp. A thousand peasants were being flayed alive in seconds. He glanced at Ser Alcaeus, who'd seen it all at Albinkirk. And Ser Giorgos, who'd seen it at the Inn.

Ser Alcaeus looked at Ser John, and the look shared their absolute knowledge.

One-way trip.

Ser John would have liked to say goodbye to his Helewise. He'd have preferred to catch more fish in a hundred brooks—to live forever, just stroking her back or hearing her say his name, to see the red-gold flash as the trout took a lure.

"Fuck it," he said. He smiled without mirth. "Wedge. Two wedges."

Ser Christos and the Moreans could form a wedge very fast.

The two men touched gauntlets. "Save the Queen," Ser John said. "I will try to clear the wall."

Ser Christos thought a moment. "Then let's make this worth our lives," he said. He shouted a series of orders at the Moreans—the virtually untrusted Moreans—who were standing, untested, on the southernmost walls.

The Moreans took their hodge-podge of weapons and began to form their *taxeis* in close order. There were Nordikaans and mountaineers and dismounted city cavalry. There were stradiotes and old, veteran infantry-men from Thrake, and young camp servants who'd scarcely ever touched a weapon.

"They will not run again," Ser Giorgos said. "Neither will we. Let's go."

Ser John was almost happy.

"Let's make a song," he said, like the northerner he was.

The two wedges had little space in which to gather momentum—and the camp was an utter shambles. But there was not enough cover for the boglins to stand a charge of heavy horsemen.

The wedges cracked open the front of their wave of terror, and the close-ordered Moreans crashed into the disorder they created. The big axes began to swing. The spears licked out, and the shields remained tight, and a thousand boglins died. And still, the Morean infantry line pressed forward—step by step.

Ser Christos led his men brilliantly, and his sword was like a living rod of lightning, and a great wight died on it, head opened to its mandibles in a single mighty blow. And his wedge drove deep into the centre of the camp, where the hooves of his horses dealt more death than any weapon of man. At the edges of the squadron, men fell from horses tripped by tent stakes and died horrible deaths, consumed still living by myriad enemies, but the wedge itself trampled the enemy to a sticky ruin and cut their way to the Queen, where Ser Ranald's dwindling Royal Guard opened ranks to let them in. Exhausted men all but fell to the ground in the respite the cavalry gave them—men who had swung an axe or halberd for ten solid minutes, and felt as if they'd aged two years.

Ser Alcaeus asked no permission, but grabbed the Queen and threw her over his saddle. Beside him, men did the same for her women—the three still alive—and the babe. Ser Giorgos pulled a tall woman with bright gold hair onto his crupper and found that she had the King of Alba in her arms.

The line of Morean infantry was inexorable and despite men lost, the phalanx appeared untouched—men fell, and were stepped on. The spears and axes rolled another pace forward.

Boglins are living creatures. They seek to live.

Many began to seek life through flight.

Ser John Crayford cut his way to the north wall. He led his men along the relatively open ground that had been the camp's parade—he cleared the west face of the Royal Guard's square, buying men time to drink a sip of water, or merely take a breath—and then he struck the full, packed mass of the enemy in the north-west corner.

He broke his lance, and drew his sword. The boglins were small—too small for a short weapon—and he had to reach *down* to kill them. His charger did it better than he.

On they plunged, and for the first time in many years, Ser John remembered the joy of combat. The pounding rhythm of the gallop, the surge of near perfect exhilaration to see the men on either side of him, the feeling of oneness with his horse.

The feeling of a living thing coming to pieces under your weapon.

He got his horse onto the ramp to the north wall. Behind him, his banner moved, and still he cut—his charger killed—and they were up on the earthen bank of the wall.

All the ground down to the burning first line seemed to be teeming with enemies. Like a termite's nest, kicked.

He wished for a mighty adversary—a wight, or a cave troll. But instead, he simply fought well—carefully, as was his wont—and cleared the wall a few steps at a time, minding his horse's safety, and killing.

And killing.

And killing.

In time, he could not really raise his arm. His horse was bleeding—and sluggish—and had boglins fixed to it like leeches. Ser John couldn't smile. But he might have, given time. In the centre of the camp, the Morean phalanx had cleared the Royal Guard. One glance told him the Queen was safe. His charger—game to the end—stumbled. And there were no more miracles.

"Goodbye, Helewise," he said out loud. Then he rolled off his saddle into the monsters, and killed until they finally dragged him down.

Miles to the north, Harmodius stood almost alone. The battle line had swept over the ridge in front. He had nothing to do with that, and in fact—such was his mood—would not willingly have killed any living thing except a dragon.

He watched the two vast predators duel. After an initial, vicious encounter with power and talon, they had taken to making long, bloody passes—each circling for altitude and speed, and then coming back together again. He could follow them in the *aethereal* as well—where the whole of the place was an increasing fog of falsehood and spent *ops*. Harmodius had never seen power used on such a scale, and for the first time in his long life he sensed that a locale might itself be drained of *potentia*. Certainly something was happening in the *aethereal* that was beyond his experience. He watched it.

To the south, he saw it—in the misty *aethereal*—as Mortirmir opened up. That was humbling.

More *potentia* drained. In the centre of the hermetical combat, in the real, trees—late spring trees—began to lose their leaves. And then to die.

And above them, the rainy day began to turn to storm. Harmodius saw it happen—as if nature abhorred the fighting and strove to extinguish it. More and blacker clouds were rushing in. The rain grew stronger.

The Queen still lived, a banner of gold to the south.

The Faery Knight still lived, to the west, and Mogon, to the east.

Harmodius watched, and waited.

Morgon Mortirmir had no reason to be cautious. And a great deal of youthful arrogance that was, on this day and in this place, well-earned.

He killed.

He pounded Thorn's horde with balls of fire and when a shaman or a fledgling hedge mage among them showed his talent, Morgon concentrated his efforts until that target was dead—and went back to flensing the unprotected.

Around him, the white banda—all but broken by the dragon and stricken by its losses—re-purposed themselves as his bodyguard. He was content with that. He moved when he had to—clearing away the last *schiltron* of irks covering the flank of the Galles—and then, because they were intermixed with the company, passing over them to grind cave trolls to sand.

Nothing could stand before him. He offered no mercy. He unleashed workings no practitioner had ever considered, because so few men of his power had ever been willing to walk in front of an infantry line. He broke shields and baffled visions. He mimicked darkness and light. He raised phantoms, and then, bored, dropped lines of fire that broke ranks.

Eventually—horrified—the Wild threw everything it had left at him— power and creatures alike. Instead of concentrating their efforts on flanking the company and winning the battle, the Wild responded instinctively to Power.

Ser Gavin rode easily by Prince Tancredo as they cleared the ridge, moving from west to east—crushing knots of resistance—and then Sauce came.

"We're in it!" she roared. "Come on!" When no one moved faster, she said, "We're dying! Get a fucking move on!"

Gavin ignored the prince's sputtering outrage. He raised his lance. "Lead us!" he called.

Sauce turned her horse. They rode side by side for long minutes, and behind them, the Occitan knights and farther down the ridge, Lord Montjoy's western knights formed a long, thick line.

Riding sideways on a hill always tempts a horse to descend, and over the next third of a mile they went too far down so that, when they came to the edge of the main battle, the banners of the Galles were high above them, almost due north. The company's Saint Catherine could just be seen, and a big, black banner and, farther along, a bubble of gold that seemed to move and cast fire.

Gavin turned to the prince. "Your grace, we must charge. That is my brother's standard."

The prince looked up the hill—scattered with rocks, and overhung with trees of every side.

"This is not the ground," he said slowly. And then shook his head.

"Yes," he said suddenly. "Form! Form on me!" he roared in Occitan, and a hundred knights rode to his side—men fell in the rush to join their prince.

To the west, some of the Count of the Border's better disciplined men were higher on the ridge side and better formed. Sauce rode at them, waving. To her shock, a crossbow bolt hit her breastplate—and *whanged* away into the trees. She rocked in her war saddle and turned her helmeted head to see a line of crossbowmen—she ducked, far too late.

Her horse died. She fell—one long fall and two bounces...

She rolled to her feet and drew her dagger, the only weapon to survive the fall, and turned to face the three men who came at her, all with swords.

"*C'est une pucelle!*" shouted one. He laughed.

They *all* laughed. And in that laughter, they became all the men she'd ever hated. Two moved to flank her, and her hip hurt, and the earth was rumbling and the rain suddenly felt so hard—

Sauce moved. She got her back against a downed tree and rolled over it, kicking high, and then she was between the two who'd tried to go around her. She rammed her dagger into the side of one's head—in, and out—and her knee crushed the second man's testicles as her gauntleted hand broke his nose and one finger penetrated his left eye. She let gravity take him, but kept his sword, and turned.

The crossbowmen were winding. The third man was two paces away—at a dead run, buckler raised.

Sauce rolled her right wrist and her borrowed sword's point came on line. It went between the man's buckler and his sword—he'd had poor teachers—and went into his neck almost to the hilt. Sauce used the dagger as a crowbar to scrape him off her blade, dumped his screaming near-corpse to the ground, and ducked behind the log as the crossbows came up.

She had the satisfaction of seeing Ser Gavin's knights sweep across the back of the line of crossbowmen, uncontested. The ambush had caught only her.

She heard Gareth Montjoy's war cry, and saw the border knights charge.

The crossbowmen were steady. They loosed, and immediately spanned, and a dozen knights' saddles were empty.

Sauce crawled under the log as the crossbowmen began to span again, and ran, bent double, in plate armour—no mean feat.

There were thirty—no, more than fifty of them.

Sauce ran, light-footed, through the hobblebush and gorse, and they finally noticed her.

Ten paces out, and one had his weapon reloaded.

He aimed it. It was enormous, and she had no tree to save her, so she rolled forward like the acrobat she had once been. The ground was soft— too soft—and she scissored her armoured legs to get over the roll—she was not dead, but up again.

She got in among them as they began to draw their swords. The more experienced of them simply ran—they could not face Sauce and a charge from a line of knights. But the sword killed one, and the dagger another, and then the ground rumbled, the earth shook, and suddenly, Sauce thought to fall flat.

A horse kicked her in the back plate.

And then the charge was past her.

She got up.

She looked slowly around, and then popped her visor.

And stood, and shook.

"That was stupid," she said to no one.

Then she started walking to where she could see Saint Catherine gleaming red in the rain. To her left, a beautiful horn played three ringing notes. Almost in front of her, a company of Gallish knights met the Occitans head-on.

A beautiful horn sounded three long, clear notes.

The brigans—big, well-drilled men in heavy armour—were giving ground one grudging step at a time. The company now had the hill behind them, and they scented victory. Neither force wanted to lose any more men. There was an endless, nightmare intensity—a spurt of violence, a single killing like a murder, and then sullen heavy breathing. Perhaps they all feared the dragons had taken the issue out of their hands. Perhaps they merely wished to live. But they—the island of professional soldiers of both sides in a vast battle of beasts and amateurs—had slowed to a desultory slaughter.

Toby became aware, at some point in the fighting, that his knight had just one hand, and was fighting with, of all things, a curved falchion. He had a moment to breathe—one of the captain's little workings had just killed a dozen men, and Toby—like every man-at-arms around him—chose to grab two breaths instead of pushing forward into the gap.

He burrowed to the left, to get back into the spot behind the captain. His spot had been taken by—of all people—Diccon, a virtually unarmoured boy who now wielded the captain's heavy spear.

"I'll kill 'em all," Diccon gasped.

He had two wounds, both bad, both showing white bone.

The brigans gave a few more steps.

Off to the right, there were war cries, and shouts—even through the rain. A red banner showed for a moment.

The captain turned back and flipped his visor open. "Ser Bescanon, bless his black heart," he said. He stared into the rain as if by will alone he could see through it.

"You should step out of the line," Toby heard himself say.

The captain smiled. "I should," he agreed. "But I won't." He flipped his visor down and crouched slightly, as he always did when he fought. "Come on, you bastards," he shouted through his visor.

Twenty lances heard him, and moved forward.

The Fairy Knight ordered Bescanon's charge, and it had the smallest effect. At first.

Bescanon trotted his thirty lances over the crest and looked down on the maelstrom. He looked left, where the Faery Knight, outlined in lurid green sorcery, sat a rearing stag like a horned centaur. His knights—the survivors of the dragon's breath—and all his people were locked in death grips with the very centre of the enemy line—a huge behemoth, tentacled *hastenoch*, too many imps and wolves and a wing storm of barghasts.

Bescanon pointed his wedge at the side of a swamp creature, couched his lance as if in the lists, and slapped down his visor.

"Charge," he called.

Sauce saw the company banner and the charge. Bescanon—she knew his coat armour—vanished into the titanic melee to the west of the armoured brigans. She kept moving, trying to reach the banner—the Saint Catherine—and she prayed as she walked. She had the oddest position—a spectator in the midst of an enormous battle. Both sides seemed to have spent their reserves. Even Morgon Mortirmir merely glowed with protective energy. No more missiles rained from his fingertips.

In the time it took to power a tired, armoured leg over a log, it began to change.

Bescanon's small force killed two *hastenoch*, gored by lances in their unarmoured flanks until they fell—and the war horses pounded the imps to red meat, although a few fell in turn.

Then, suddenly, something gave—and the Faery Knight shot out of the melee and into the churned and boggy grounds behind it. He turned his great stag, red to the fetlocks, and began to harry the behemoth. And then the edges of the melee began to collapse, and men—who had been fighting savagely, hand to hand—came out of the trees to the left, with painted Outwallers amongst them, shrieking war cries.

Arrows began to strike the behemoth, even in the pouring sheets of rain. And almost, the great monster might have been a victim—something from the art on the rocks at the edge of the inner sea, or perhaps some cave all in the south. Ringed by irks and men, it took blow after blow, and trumpeted its rage and sorrow—to die alone, far from kin, to be tormented by these tiny predators, to fall for so little gained—

Its tragic trumpet-call pierced the rain and sounded for every creature that died in the mud that day.

And then it fell, and the Faery Knight was free. Like the bursting of a dam, his Wild Hunt spilled over the ridge at last, and fell into the flank of the mounted melee where fully armoured Occitan hacked uselessly at fully armoured Galle. The Jacks—those that survived dragon's breath and behemoth's tusk and irk's spear—found themselves in the flank of the Gallish knights and poured arrows into their horses . . . wet arrows from damp strings.

The Galles began to die.

The Faery Knight rode—almost alone, a vision of scarlet and white—across the back of the fight—he rode hundreds of paces, almost at arm's length from his foes, along the back of their hordes, and his own household knights flitted at his side, faster than a breeze in the woods. The rain masked them, but Sauce thought she'd never seen anything so fine, and the Red Knight thought the same, and Ser Gavin, intent on his own fight, and Morgon Mortirmir, were awed even after everything they'd seen.

The Faery Knight's handful seemed to skim the ground—along the wide, shallow trough of the fight, and then suddenly, turning like a shoal of bright minnows, up and to the left—up, and into the rear of the cave trolls where they fought Flint's people for the highest projection of the ridge. Up, and there was a flare of sorcery—and eldritch fire that played on the hills like holly in yule, white and red and green, as he sprung his last surprise, Tamsin's fire stored against need.

And Morgon Mortirmir made one last effort, running clear of the back of the company line, raising his hand, and loosing two workings . . .

The cave trolls broke. Some fell broken to pieces, others ran, the earth collapsing under them, only to mire in the wet ground at the bottom of the valley and trap them to die there.

Flint's bears, and Mogon, still tall in her cloak of feathers, gathered their survivors. The Faery Knight and his remaining riders placed themselves between them, and together they crashed down into the valley, destroying the last hope Thorn's Wild levies might have had.

Everything else ran.

Leaving only Hartmut.

The brigans fought on, unshaken, and it seemed to Toby that they all must die—of broken hearts, burst lungs, and rain.

He was no longer fighting with skill. He hit men with the haft of the spear, or simply poked at them, and they at him.

The captain was still making parries and throwing blows. But even he was slowing, and his blows became more feeble. Finally Toby caught a glimpse when the captain's sword went into an aventail—and came back, having done no damage.

But the horns, and the roars, were different. Toby had the spear locked under another man's arm, and he couldn't reach his dagger, and his life was in peril—and there was cheering. The other man pushed him down, wrenching his arm—dislocating his shoulder—and Toby went down, face-first, into the mud. But the cheering went on and Toby was determined not to die, and in a paroxysm of exhausted muscles he rolled over, dagger in hand.

The captain had put his sword in the other man's eye. He pushed the corpse to the ground.

And then, the Black Knight was there, mounted on a tall black horse.

A space cleared. The brigans wanted no more fight, and yet were too proud to yield. But something had changed—the cheers were everywhere.

"I am Ser Hartmut Li Orguelleus," he said. "I challenge you—face me, or be thought craven."

Toby could only just see him—a huge figure in black armour. With a sword that burned like a torch, and made a faint sound, like running water.

Ser Gabriel coughed. But then he sighed and raised his visor. "Ser Hartmut," he said.

"No!" roared Ser Gavin, and Ser Gabriel was thrown roughly to the ground. Gabriel looked up, somewhat surprised.

Ser Gavin towered over them on a sweat-besmothered war horse. His small axe dripped blood.

"My fucking brother has defrauded me of every worthwhile fight I should have had this spring," he said. "I'm Ser Gavin Muriens, Ser Hartmut, and I insist on being the one to kill you."

Ser Hartmut growled. Behind him, his men were flinching away down the hill.

Hartmut didn't speak further. He reached up and pulled his heavy great helm off his back and over his head. Then, as his horse fretted, he took a heavy lance from his squire and sheathed his fiery sword.

He charged.

Ser Gavin had no lance.

He charged anyway.

Hartmut's lance tip swooped down, and Gavin caught it on the haft of his little axe—his hand went out *under* the lance as the two horses crossed noses, and he caught the outside of his opponent's bridle in his left hand.

The black horse twisted, attempting to right its head.

The reins snapped.

Gavin's axe shot out—and struck Hartmut in the helmet. The blow did not damage him, but the Black Knight fell straight off his horse.

Gavin brought his mount around. Hartmut got to his feet—favouring his right leg—and drew his sword, which burst, again, into fire.

"An attack on my horse?" he said. "What a cowardly act!"

Ser Gavin laughed. "It is always comforting to take cover behind the rules, isn't it?" he asked. "Especially if the rules always benefit *you*."

"Dismount and face me!" Hartmut called. "Or be branded a coward."

Gavin showed no sign of dismounting. "You mean, get off my war horse and face your magic sword?" he asked.

The brigans were throwing down their weapons.

"You make a mockery of knighthood!" Ser Hartmut said.

Ser Gavin laughed. "I think, Ser Hartmut, that you killed my parents. I think that you have hidden behind a shield of pretence for your whole life. And now, I think you're going to die, and no one is going to call me base, or coward, or knave—no one at all. In fact, I suspect only my version of this fight will ever be heard."

Gavin's smile was terrible.

Then, he dismounted.

"I hold you in contempt—as a knight, and a man." Ser Gavin tossed his reins to Jean, Bertran's squire.

The Black Knight raised his sword, and attacked.

He struck air.

Gavin was fresh, and he simply evaded the other man's blows. Hartmut had fought for hours. Gavin let him swing. He ran—he skipped. He mocked.

At some point, Gabriel turned his head away.

Hartmut cursed, and cursed in Gallish, and swung, and swung, and stumbled. Behind him, De La Marche's sailors surrendered, the last force still fighting in the whole of Thorn's host.

Someone—later, men said it was Cully—tripped the Black Knight. He fell heavily, and for a moment, he lost his sword.

His great helm had tilted across his eyes. He roared his frustration, pulled the lace with armoured fingers and threw his helmet at Ser Gavin, who casually struck it to the ground with his little steel axe. Then he stood—a big man in black armour, wearing a steel cap over an aventail.

"I thought of this fight a long time," Ser Gavin said, conversationally. "It wasn't you I wanted to fight. But you'll do to make my point."

"Shut up and fight!" Ser Hartmut barked.

"You want rules to protect you when you are weak, and no rules to slow you when you are strong." Ser Gavin took a gliding, sideways step—

Gabriel's heart was in his mouth.

The long sword licked out—a heavy feint, the false blow of a man who fears no riposte.

Like the flight of an arrow, Gavin stepped into distance, flicked his axe, and buried the spike in the middle of Hartmut's face.

The Black Knight fell.

Gavin turned to his brother. "It should have been de Vrailly," he said.

Harmodius felt the rain slowing with the tempo of the combat. He felt it when Mogon accepted the surrender of the survivors of the Dead Tree and Flint took the bended knees of the Big Nose irks. Down at Gilson's Hole, the Hillmen pushed into the rear of the boglins—already hesitant— and broke them, and the little creatures melted away into the marsh and ravines.

Harmodius was not searching for them. He was searching for why they were still fighting, and eventually, as Ash turned high in the air, so high that the *aethereal* was thin and the *emperyeum* began, and savaged the Wyrm of Ercch; as Hartmut fell dead; as Bad Tom stepped up onto the ruined north wall of the Royal Camp, and the last fighting tapered away...

Harmodius found Thorn.

Thorn was a small shadow—in the *aethereal*, he was merely the shadow of a shadow.

"I knew you must still live," Harmodius said. "Your bound creatures are still fighting."

The shade of Richard Plangere, once so powerful, merely whimpered.

Harmodius took him, and tenderly—almost—*entered into his palace. Thorn lacked the strength to prevent even that. Harmodius plundered his memories ruthlessly, in a single heartbeat.*

"Why?" Harmodius demanded.

"I tried to escape him," Plangere said. "Please—my boy—let me go. All I wanted was the Wild. And the freedom to study."

Harmodius studied the damage. "Yes, my teacher. What Ash did to you was terrible." He frowned, and then hardened his heart. "But because of you, half the women of Alba are widows tonight. Go to hell, or wherever traitors go, and be accursed."

"You know the truth!" Thorn screamed. "I betrayed no one!"

Harmodius shook his head in the real. *"You betrayed us all," he said. "And not just man. If it is any consolation: I will try and undo what you have done."*

"You will merely become me, you fool."

"I think not," Harmodius said. *And then, like a creature of the Wild, he subsumed his foe.*

High in the *aether*, Ash felt his puppet die. His foe was mortally wounded, but Ash had to turn and let him flutter to the ugly reaches of earth. He considered it all—the fire, the rain, the ruin, and the death.

He gazed upon Harmodius, who stood in the *aethereal*, untouched, and ready—deadly, powerful, and possessed of all Thorn's knowledge, newly learned. And he looked at the others—the golden aura of the despicable Queen, tool of the false Tar, and the fallen Wyrm's toys... He loathed them all.

But blue fire still burned, and the Wyrm had struck him twice to the bone. And that sword—some child of man had struck him with something—horrible. Even an insect bite may fester.

Ash had never been one for a reckless gamble.

So he pivoted, so high above the battlefield that only a few could detect him, and let out a long shriek of triumph and derision.

One of the two eggs, which Thorn had carried and nurtured for so long, burst open, and a cloud of black spores filled the muggy, damp air, and burst into leprous, malignant life. The other *hatched*.

Ash would have chuckled, but breathing was difficult and he was too high. He turned west, and began to glide. He could do so, without effort, for a thousand miles.

The Wyrm fluttered as hard as he could, with one wing mostly shredded and the other full of holes.

It was a long way down. After a while, he spun, and lost what little control he had—lost consciousness—and fell.

Harmodius watched the victor glide away into the shadows of the far west, even as the other fell. The fall was long—the heavens were very high.

Higher than I thought.

Gabriel was *at his door, and then in his head.*

"He covered us, for hours. Can you save him?"

Harmodius chuckled grimly. "Save him? I'll dance on his grave."

Gabriel paused. "Listen—you are the closest thing to a teacher I have had in a long time. I want you to think of something. Today we are still standing because bear and irk and man stood together. Some irks and many men are deeply evil. What of it? We—whoever we are—we choose to believe that we can stand together. The bishop is no fool, Harmodius. This is murder."

Harmodius watched the dragon fall. "I did not kill him," he said.

"Are we an alliance of all the peoples of this sphere?" Gabriel asked. "Or are we just another set of Powers?"

Harmodius grunted.

"Save him," Gabriel begged.

Harmodius cursed. But he reached out, into the real, and gave without stint. He gave until trees died—gave more when Gabriel gave him his reserve. He poured in his ops, *and then, daring, he used Amicia's as well.*

Master Smythe awoke with his head on a linen pillow. He opened his eyes.

And met the eyes of the beautiful nun. He had never met her in human form, but he knew her well.

"I am not dead," he said.

Amicia smiled. "No," she said. "We saved you." She pushed a lock of hair back inside her wimple. "Only fair, as you saved us."

Master Smythe lay still for a long time, savouring that. He understood—with terrible clarity—what had been done to him. He had no right arm.

Not in the real.

At the next bed, another beautiful human woman stood by the bed of a tired, dark-haired man. Master Smythe knew him perfectly well. And his brother, who stood with yet another beautiful woman—dark-haired, where the woman by the Red Knight was pale.

"Gabriel," he said. "You lived. You won." He sat up a bit—an odd motion, unsuited to human form—and then turned and smiled at Gabriel's brother Gavin. "Who are all these beautiful women and what do they see in you two?" he asked.

The blonde woman turned away, drawing a sharp breath.

Gabriel extended a hand and caught hers. "This is Blanche Gold, and I have no idea what she sees in me," he said. "Stay," he said to her. "I have no secrets from you."

Gavin laughed. "Steady on, Blanche. I've never heard him say that to anyone." He grinned. "Master Smythe, this is Lady Mary, once known as 'Heart Heart,' and now my betrothed."

Master Smythe managed a wriggle that might have been taken as a bow.

The women sat. Master Smythe thought that they both had remarkable dignity, and made a note to court them. Perhaps one at a time.

He smiled.

Gabriel sat up. "I think *won* is too strong a word," he said, ignoring his brother. "We are still standing."

Master Smythe took a deep breath and savoured the experience of being alive. "The first alliance of the Wild and men," he said. "That is a victory, is it not?" He paused. "Where is Ash?"

There was a tiny shudder in the fabric of the *aether.*

"Harmodius says he's to the west." Gabriel frowned. "That is what I mean. Nothing's finished. The north of this kingdom is wrecked. Ten thousand are dead—and what of the Wild's losses? Twice that."

Blanche put a hand over his mouth. "Stop saying such things," she said. *"We won."*

"I can't take any joy in it," Gabriel said. "I thought it would be over."

Master Smythe sighed at the ways of men. "Nothing is ever *over*." He smiled at the beautiful women, who ignored him. "We can do so much together," Master Smythe said. He meant it to sound portentous.

The other man raised the stump of his left arm. "We could buy gloves together," he said.

Master Smythe lay back, and laughed. "Humans are terrifying," he said quietly.

The next day, the Red Knight—the Duke of Thrake, and the Queen's Captain—was dressed, carefully, by his leman and his squire, and then put—somewhat ceremoniously—into those parts of his armour that were still presentable and were light enough for him to wear.

Armed, and armoured, he left the hospital tent raised by the Order of Saint Thomas, to where Ataelus, his war horse, untouched and unused through the great battle, waited for him with fondness and was rewarded with an apple.

Then, with some help from Bad Tom, Toby and Ser Michael, he managed to mount.

Tom rode by his side. He wore the full harness and surcoat of the *primus pilus* of the company.

Out there, on the ground in front of the tents, waited the army.

Gabriel didn't flinch from his duty. He accepted the cheers, and then he rode slowly along the ranks. He felt curiously detached. He knew the butcher's bill—but he still kept expecting to see men where they were not. Ser John Crayford, Count of Albinkirk, would never again lead the Albinkirk Independent Company. There was no company to lead, and the Captain of Albinkirk was dead. Nell was not by his side, and Kit Foliak would never buy another gold embroidered sword belt. The north Brogat levy was led by a man he'd never met, a northern knight. Lord Gregario was in one of Amicia's wards, with the Grand Squire in the next bed.

There were thousands gone, and the dead were all about him, and if he wasn't careful, he'd begin to think that Nicholas Ganfroy was just at his elbow. Or Cuddy, killed in the last of the fighting with the Galles, or Flarch.

Gelfred was so badly wounded that even Amicia despaired for him. It was Sauce who took his salute, and Long Paw who rode by his side as he inspected the green banda at the right of the line—Amy's Hob was dead, and Will Starling was lost and presumed dead. And more, and their losses were not the worst.

In the white banda the scars showed—a new generation, dead, in a single dragon's breath. But where Morgon had stood, the company lived—there was Milus, and there George Brewes. And Gonzago D'Avia and young Fitzsimmons. And many men Milus had recruited and he'd never met—Moreans and Occitans, and even some Galles.

And the red banda—luckier. Still decimated, but only just. Ser Michael sat like a rock on his war horse, Attila, and gave him a crisp salute. Men all along the line were cheering.

Some were also coughing.

Gabriel ignored them. He smiled as much as he could, and passed among the men he'd known for five years and more—the ones left alive. Parcival D'Entre Deux Monts. Gavin Hazzart. And there was Wilful Murder, and there, Robin Hasty, and there, still alive, No Head. And beyond, just barely sober, Oak Pew. She coughed hard and spat something in her hand. Daniel Favour. Ser Ranald. Smoke. Adrian Goldsmith. Ser Bescanon. Ser Danved, talking even now, and Ser Bertran, still silent. His squire, Jean, was grinning, and Petite Mouline in a new red arming coat was beaming, brimful of happiness.

He walked his horse to where Wilful Murder sat. "You, and Cully, Tippit, and No Head and Long Paw. And some knights and squires. I guess we still have a company."

Wilful looked at Tippit, a few files away, and a small smile creased his aging face. "We could use some fucking archers," he said. "Ones not like some awkward sods I could mention."

It shouldn't have mattered.

But they weren't *all* dead.

He finished his inspection of his own company, aiming for that polite level where every man feels his polishing was not in vain and no one feels he's dying on parade, and then he moved off to the left, to the Moreans, who were in many ways the heroes of the hour and were cheering like fools. There he saw Janos Turkos, soon to be knighted, and Ser Giorgos Comnenos, who had saved Blanche, with the help of the Ifriquy'an, Ser Pavalo. And Count Zac, back where he belonged at the head of his easterners. Beyond them stood the Royal Guard, which had never felt the breath of the dragon and yet looked as if they had, and all the Occitans and western levies under Prince Tancredo and Lord Gareth, none of whom seemed to have polished anything. The Royal Foresters were not on parade. The Redmede brothers had taken the Jacks and the Foresters into the woods together, pursuing the broken enemy, trying to make sure that the victory had consequence.

Gabriel began to inspect at a fast trot.

Just the survivors amounted to nine thousand men.

At his shoulder, Tom Lachlan waited until he came to the end of the line of men. There, on the other side of the camp, stood a motley horde of other things, led by a magnificent knight on a white stag. By him stood Pavalo Payam, the Ifriquy'an, and Harmodius. They looked bored.

"You won," Tom Lachlan said. "Just take it in and let go."

"I—"

"Let go," Bad Tom said. "Drink hard. Ha' a tumble wi' your lass. Make up some lies to paste over what you mislike. It's fewkin' war, whether there's great dragonish Wyrms or just a wee huddle o' stupid men, tryin' to steal yer purse. Let it go."

Gabriel turned and met Tom's eye.

The Faery Knight saluted with a flourish. "Thisss isss the mossst foolisssh of human traditionssssr," he said. "I have no glory in war. Let'sss go sssome-where, and sssit in the ssshade. And drink. And sssee all your pretty peoplesss."

Gabriel frowned. "It's all to be done again, like a lesson learned wrong."

The Faery Knight shrugged. "I have a few sssenturiesss on you, little captain. It isss alwaysss to be done again."

But he didn't leave then and there, and they all bowed to the great duchess, Mogon, who stood with the Queen.

The Queen was frowning, the rarest of expressions on her face.

"Your grace?" Gabriel called.

She nodded. "What are they all shouting?" she asked. "My Archaic is not that good."

Gabriel had been deaf to the cheers—they oppressed him. And there was Blanche, smiling at him, and he blew her a kiss, to the delight of a thousand farmers and camp followers. There was Lady Mary Montroy, and there was Lady Rebecca Almspend, and the Earl of Towbray whispering in the Queen's ear.

The cries—the cheers—grew more coordinated, and Ataelus showed his distaste for the noise, turning a curvet and nipping at Tom's horse.

Bad Tom looked back at Ser Gavin. By him, Ser Alcaeus was smug. The Morean grinned.

"They're shouting 'Ave, Imperator,'" Ser Alcaeus said with intense satisfaction.